When the Moon Has No More Silver

When the Moon has no more silver left,
And the Sun's at the end of his gold.
—W. H. Davies

PRAISE FOR DARK ENOUGH TO SEE THE STARS IN A JAMESTOWN SKY

"A tale of tested faith, courage, friendship, and the refusal of some hardy souls ever to capitulate."
The Virginia Gazette

"From the very first page, the reader is aware of Lapallo's personal investment in making the story both historically accurate and beautiful."
Tidewater Review

"The description of the tempest 'hurican' the fleet of ships encounters off Bermuda is itself alone worth the read."
Pleasant Living Magazine

"The mention of the Jamestown colony brings to mind the work and the history of its men. Yet, Lapallo is helping to change that."
Suffolk News-Herald

"Lapallo has given the women that settled this colony a voice, and it's a powerful one."
Sharon Baldacci, author of A Sundog Moment

"Rich characters appear against the brutal background of the Starving Time."
Northern Neck News

WHAT READERS ARE SAYING

"Amazing, suspenseful, insightful, and spiritual. Lapallo tells the women's story eloquently. An awesome tribute to their lives."
Alison Shay

"Delightful—one of the best books I've read in years. I couldn't put it down!"
James Mims, retired Naval Commander, 96 years old

"Extensive research brought historical accounts in Jamestown to life in an exciting and personal manner."
Dr. Billy Kornegay

"My dad and I had fun discussing your book. I'm glad you stuck to the facts, and didn't just make up most of it. That way, I could get it straight in my head, instead of thinking, 'Wait! I learned something completely different in school!'"
Letter from Christina Cox, 13 years old

When the Moon
Has No More Silver

Based on the True Story of the
Women & Children at Jamestown

Second Book in
the Jamestown Sky Trilogy
1610-1620

by
Connie Lapallo

To Nora.
Godspeed to you
in all your journeys.
Connie Lapallo
2014

greyfox
PRESS

Cover design and painting, and content design by Sarah A. Lapallo
Author Photo by Eric Dobbs

Requests for permission to make copies of any part of this
work should be mailed to Permissions Department, Greyfox
Press, 9290 Greywood Drive, Mechanicsville, VA 23116

ISBN: 0-983398-20-8   978-0-9833982-0-2

Printed in the United States of America by Greyfox Press

Library of Congress Control Number: 2011929208

DEDICATION

To my husband Chris,
and to my children
Sarah, Michael, Kerry, and Adam
For everything

And to the women and children of Jamestown—
including Cecily Bailey Jordan Farrar,
my 12th great-grandmother;
Cecily's daughter, Temperance Bailey Cocke,
my 11th great-grandmother;
and especially to Joan Peirce, for her courage and inspiration
and for patiently indulging her young visitor,
so that I could write it down.

ACKNOWLEDGEMENTS

First, I have to thank my husband Chris for enormous help—reading the manuscript numerous times, aiding in research of old maps and manuscripts, creating our maps and charts, accompanying me to explore old historic sites, and for believing in this book when I sometimes faltered.

My daughter Sarah has helped me with design of the books, covers, business cards, website, and sign; with cover paintings, and costume research, design and sewing; and even with editing. She's contributed hundreds of hours.

To my children Michael, Kerry, and Adam, who give help in all kinds of ways.

Thanks to early readers who did so much for the launch of *Dark Enough to See the Stars in a Jamestown Sky*: Beth Leney of Houston, Texas (of the Lady Washington Chapter of the National Society Daughters of the American Revolution), Kathleen Seward, William Young (who portrays Captain Gabriel Archer, www.historyinperson.com), Sieglinde Nix at Agecroft Hall, and Debra Conti of Henricus. Thanks also to Sharon Baldacci, author of *A Sundog Moment*, for her friendship and encouragement. Thanks to interpreters and staff at Historic Jamestowne, Jamestown Settlement, Shirley Plantation, and Henricus for kindly recommending *Dark Enough to See the Stars in a Jamestown Sky* to visitors.

Thanks to Elaine Feltrin Knight for help with Portuguese. For help with Spanish, thanks to Susan French Owens, Marisa Isabel Tenorio, Marisa's daughters, Isabella and Valentina Jaramillo, and Marisa's mother Nelly Tenorio.

I'm grateful for the advice and expertise of Ley Diller for sharing her research about Bermuda Hundred; Traci Fannin-Poole, at Historic Jamestowne, for sharing great tips with me when she finds them; Frances Honich, retired interpreter at Jamestown Settlement for her insights on Jamestown's women; Ann Reid, Site Manager of Scotchtown, for demonstrating spinning to me; Pat Roble, Chesterfield County Historical Society Museum Curator and Master Gardener for advice on Virginia's native flowers; and Rebecca Suerdick (who portrays Mistress Marye Bucke) for sharing ideas about the Buckes.

Thanks also to Nancy Blackburn, Sally Fraser, Julie Gigante, Adam Lapallo, and Therese Silberman for reading the manuscript and offering comments and suggestions.

Finally, if you have read *Dark Enough to See the Stars in a Jamestown Sky* and written an encouraging note, recommended the book to others or to your book club, given it as a gift, or invited me to be a speaker, then I thank you, too.

Mulberry Island, Virginia

August 1649

Marking My Fortieth Year in the Colony

The moonbeams over Arno's vale in silver flood were pouring,
When first I heard the nightingale a long-lost love deploring.
So passionate, so full of pain, it sounded strange and eerie;
I longed to hear a simpler strain,—the wood-notes of the veery.
—Henry Van Dyke

I see my life go drifting like a river
From change to change; I have been many things–
—William Butler Yeats

Dawn breaks the eastern sky, and I am there to greet it. It has been my habit to rise at first dawn these many years, and I suppose I am too old to cease it now—even if I chose to. Which I do not.

I see the stars of the Virginia sky splayed before me, just as they were last night when my young visitor and I retired inside for the evening. Now these same stars greet me in the final moments of darkness before the day begins.

Dark enough to see the stars.

Watching the heavens unfold in their splendor always reminds me of my father.

"Joanie, for a mariner to steer his ship, it must be dark enough to see the stars, yet light enough to see the horizon." He would tamp his pipe thoughtfully before adding, "Life is that way as well."

I remember this puzzling me, for I was never sure I took all his meaning. I did seem to be always perplexed, certain my father meant more than I was able to understand.

He continued. "When I navigate the waters, I must be able to see *Stella Maris*—the North Star, the Pole Star. You know the star to which I refer?"

I nodded. "The big one! The bright one about which all stars seem to hover. It points north." I had not grown up the daughter of a merchant sailor for naught.

"Yes. And when I can see that star, I know exactly where I am in the sea. What I cannot know without the horizon line is where I am to go from there. The horizon line steadies me and assures me of my path, as the star assures me that I am where I should be."

I considered this then said, "But your instruments tell you those things." I had seen them: the astrolabe, the quadrant, and the cross staff.

"Yes, my instruments point me in due direction, as long as *I* point *them* at the North Star and the horizon. The present and the future: one is the lamp unto my feet, the other a light unto my path." He hesitated, tamping his pipe once more, the fine sailor's lines in his face creasing into a smile.

He continued, "Do you know, the great Vespucci said the moon and Mars taken together could determine longitude? No one knows if that is so. But whenever I watch moonlight playing off the water from the bow of the *Seawynd*, I wonder at that. When the moonbeams light my way and I can see the North Star, I am comfortable. But suppose clouds darken the stars, and the moon has no more silver?"

The thought of being alone in a wide, dark ocean frightened me. And it frightened me that my father found himself that way sometimes.

"What do you do then?"

"I trust in my faith that I am on the right path until the winking stars return, lighting up the sky; until the moon comes and sits again upon her silver throne. Darkness never stays darkness forever. Remember that, Lovey."

"Yet sometimes it seems so."

He laughed. "A good mariner always keeps his faith. It is not for us to control the lighting of the heavens. We trust in the light to return." The blue brilliance of his eyes, the amused smile. I thought many years would pass before I ever understood all that he meant.

And many years it has been.

Winds rustling the oaks and pines of Mulberry Island bring me back to the present in Virginia, not those long ago days in England before the century turned. Could that have been nearly sixty years ago? My father's reassuring voice drifts from me, as if the passing of years were a river carrying his words away to a distant sea.

"When the moon has no more silver," I murmur, skipping a rock so that it breaks the moon's path on the river. "How dark the moon was for so many years."

As for the stars, I understand now what my child's mind could not. My father did refer to actual navigation, yet he also saw a deeper meaning in the stars moving through the heavens—as hope for the future in the blackness of a soul's night. A blackness such as we had experienced during our Starving Time, more than a dozen years after my father's death. The light upon the horizon brought faith that the black night had not all been in vain, just as he had said.

Daylight returned for us when the ships arrived over the James River's horizon, bringing the food that kept us alive and saving the settlement. I could hear the pealing of those jubilant bells as though it had been but a year, not the forty that had since passed.

And you were right, Father. Sometimes the moonlight just vanishes beneath you, so that you know not where you are going or where you have been.

As the rim of a fiery sun breaks upon the river this summer morning, I listen to the birds of the river singing their morning matins. The sparrows and robins are never doubtful of the future, as I have often been in my seventy years. Instead, these birds sing because God gave them song and because every sunrise is glorious. Whether or not the birds live to see the next, they are here for this one, and so they celebrate.

Darkness never stays darkness forever, my father had said. Something to ponder this summer sunrise.

Sometimes, as this morning, dawn at the river reminds me of my grief following Maggie's death. This was perhaps the greatest hole I ever felt in my heart. We called Maggie our nightingale because her unusual singing voice had lifted us during the worst of the starving. And without Maggie's insistence that we plan before starvation struck, Janey, Tempie, and I would have died with so many others during that first year at James Town. What would I have done if I had lost my little daughter Janey? And Tempie was a friend who knew my heart as no one else did.

Maggie said to plan and to harvest from the woods, and harvest we had done. The season of acorns brought us much acorn meal, which we stashed in secret and mixed with our corn rations. The acorns, we knew, had kept us alive. But acorns alone could not save Maggie when bloody flux struck her mid-winter.

Tempie and I carried on alone, relying upon one another to keep little Janey and ourselves alive. But even Tempie has been gone these—oh, I paused to reckon—could it be now more than twenty years?

My young visitor had me talking late into the evening about those early years at James Town, stirring up the old butterflies in my mind. The dancing memories of times both sweet and bitter.

I was unsure whether I truly wanted to recall those times, for today is the moment to hold. Like the birds, I know not whether I will see a sunrise each day. Perhaps too much time spent remembering the past is futile and impractical.

I kneel at a patch of huckleberries and pluck a few. Just sweet enough to enjoy, although a little green as well.

Soon the mulberries will ripen, so that the boys can come and shake the trees, raining mulberries upon the ground. Then the children will gather them up, a task they willingly do, so that I can make mulberry tarts. I smile at the thought of the late summer treat.

Huckleberries and mulberries and tarts, I think. *The joys of an old woman and a young child are not so far apart.*

And then an idea comes to me. Perhaps these memories are like the berries—bitter in places, yet mixed with the sweet. Worth savoring a second time? Worth the effort to recall.

My thoughts are all my own this August morning as I hear a door creaking from the house behind me. Footsteps crunch their way toward the river, and I turn to see my young visitor approaching once more.

"They have told me you often come here in the mornings. I hope I am not intruding, Mistress?" Her eyes are earnest, stirring a kindness within me, despite my preference for morning solitude.

I pause. No, I suppose not. I smile at her and extend my hand. "Good day, and God be with you. How slept you, then?"

She laughs. "I slept well, but for the starving and the hurricane and the voyage on ship."

I gaze at her curiously.

"Your stories, Mistress! I dreamt of them all the night long."

"Ah, I see. And how was your voyage?" I suspect I have a twinkle in my eyes.

"I know not."

Now I see that she is teasing me as I have done with her.

"What do you mean, you know not? 'Twas *your* dream." I am hiding a smile, as she seems to be.

"I know not, because you have left me on ship with Cecily's letter to you. Mistress, please, Ma'am, will you tell me of her voyage and arrival? Would it be too taxing on you?" Again, the earnest expression.

I shrug. "My daughter Cecily arrived, and that was that." I will not give my story up *too* easily. Does she truly want to hear more?

"Mistress, I pledge a willing ear."

I look at the young woman before me. She is younger than I was when I arrived in Virginia. She has lived in Virginia all her life and knows no other. She was not yet born when Sir Thomas Dale's Laws were in force, when James Town's free men were prisoners of the law. *How could we have lost our English rights? The Virginia Company pledged them to us in the charter.*

Neither was she born when we bolted our door against Spanish attack or when Pocahontas became a prisoner. Or when the governor finally granted land. When the first General Assembly met and restored our rights. As Englishmen and adventurers, we began making our own laws. A council and a king an ocean away could never know exactly what our needs were, for Virginia was exceedingly complicated and brutally simple, all at once. We were stockholders in the Virginia Company, and we were governing the enterprise ourselves. This was a time of hope following the lean, hard years.

My young visitor had not lived during any of these sweeping changes. She could not understand the horror of the—

My stomach tightens in revulsion at the memory, pushed far away these many years.

No! I cannot tell it. I cannot relive the horror of the massacre…not for anyone.

I feel defiance rise within me. I cross my arms and shake my head. I am about to tell her that she has judged correctly. It *is* too taxing on me.

A voice in my mind interrupts my thoughts.

How will she know if she does not hear? How can she remember what she has not seen? Unless you who have lived it cause them to remember, rest assured, they will forget.

My defiance melts into sadness, for I suppose one never gets over a day such as that, a day just before Easter that started with no hint of what it would bring.

I look across the river, and the years melt away. I notice that the sky is painted velvet blue, dappled in golden starlight. The moon a great, silvery orb—like the eye of God. A thin line of pink brushes the river's edge. Tears cause the colors to swirl into a gentle rainbow.

Dark enough to see the stars.

Light enough to see the horizon.

I feel a touch on my arm, and my young visitor says gently, "I am sorry, Mistress. 'Twas impertinent of me to ask, for some memories are personal to a soul. It's a great fault of mine, questioning everything."

Her inquisitiveness reminds me of no one more than myself, always asking questions in my youth. I admit to being unable to deny her, although I will not let her know that.

"Long years, child. Some aches of the heart never mend, I reckon."

"Yes, ma'am." She nods and turns toward the house, but I stop her. Softly, I say, "I think I should enjoy some company on my garden bench to watch the sunrise." Am I sounding sentimental? I catch myself. "Besides, you young folks have little to do but hear stories." I feign a sigh, but allow her to reach for my hand and squeeze it.

"So Cecily arrived in James Town with Governor Gates as she expected to?" my visitor begins, as we place ourselves upon a bench overlooking the river.

The sun peeks above the river, as the river flows back upon the sea. My mind journeys to the time when much was afoot that neither Cecily nor I could have known. How many things had transpired to get that little girl upon that ship!

"Well, it was not so simple as either Cecily or I thought it would be. Many things had to happen first, many things of which I knew not when I received Cecily's letter that long ago March of 1611."

On Gossamer Nights
Early September 1610 ~ James Town

On gossamer nights when the moon is low,
And the stars in the mist are hiding,
Over the hill where the foxgloves grow
You may see the fairies riding.
Kling! Klang! Kling!
—Mary C.G. Byron

Sir Thomas Gates had kindly offered to bring my daughter Cecily back to James Town with him when he returned to Virginia next. He had sailed from us in July 1610.

As the fall approached, I knew the governor must now, God willing, be in England. Had he spoken with Cecily? Was she strong? Was she still alive? These things I had no way of knowing. I would soon find out, but 'til then I prayed for my daughter every day. I had not seen her in fifteen months, an eternity for a mother. And she was now ten years old.

I also did not know when Gates would return, so patience was my only ally. Patience, and Tempie Yeardley, who had seen me through the Starving Time.

My younger daughter Janey was now five and seemed to have almost forgotten her sister Cecily. This was no wonder. So much had occurred since Janey had seen her last. And little Janey had been so ill during the worst of the starvation that I choose not to remind her of what was past. Instead, I only encouraged her to grow well now, now that we had better nourishment. Yet, Janey remained a small, frail child, a season of growing lost to the starving.

Steadily, the three of us grew stronger as we prepared to face the fall of 1610.

Four months had passed since the shipwrecked leaders of the *Sea Venture*, Governor Gates and Admiral Somers, had delivered our husbands to us.

Gates had immediately nailed the Laws Divine Morall and Martial to a tree. We had been under martial law since then.

Lord De La Warr had reached Virginia about the same time. With fresh leadership, and more food and livestock, life in James Town had resumed some routine for Tempie and me. Yet we still endured the brutal, ongoing Indian Wars, which called away our husbands Will and George so often.

The months passed.

Tempie and I swept our little home and tried to carry on with life in a military settlement as best we could. We pretended the corncakes were better today than yesterday and that there were more of them. We talked of when Cecily would arrive and of how she would look.

We reminisced about the friends we had met and the ones we had lost in the year we had been in Virginia.

"Remember how Sarah Rolfe fed us so tenderly after the Starving Time?" we would say, as if we had never said it before.

And the other would nod. "An angel, that one."

The *Sea Venture* had shipwrecked Sarah on Bermuda, and she had afterward died upon arrival in Virginia along with so many others.

"Sarah fell to the seasoning," we would say. The damp, marish air was hard on a body. Some survived seasoning; most didn't, particularly if they landed during spring or summer.

Sometimes I caressed the ring that cranky Elizabeth had given me before she died. Elizabeth Mayhew, so unhappy to be coming to Virginia, had left me with parting, prophetic words. "You're going to see the winter here, while I shall be in other pastures with the Shepherd. My lot is easier than yours will be." How right she had been, for to endure the Starving Time winter was many times worse than dying outright, I reckoned. As for Elizabeth, I suspected, somehow, she was happier where she was.

Then there was old Grace Fleetwood, who had been courageous to the end, with little left of her but a bony frame and flyaway silver hair. Her half-mad husband had accused her of being a witch. If Captain Tucker had believed him, a witch dunking might have taken her life before starvation did. Grace had a strangeness about her, 'twas true, but she was no witch.

"I'm glad we took her in, Tempie." I said one day, and Tempie looked up from her darning, knowing exactly whom I meant. "Grace? Oh, I am, too. Sweet old soul."

"You were right to insist we do so."

Tempie resumed her darning. "I'm *always* right. You know that, Mistress Peirce," and we both laughed.

"Still," I said, becoming serious once more, "I couldn't have lived with myself if she'd died alone that winter."

That winter was all we had to say. *That* winter—the previous winter when we had nearly starved. I suspected, no matter how many winters ticked by, I would always refer to it as *that* winter. And anyone who had survived it would know exactly which one I meant.

Our friend Maggie we spoke of surprisingly little, for it remained too painful, even now. We loved her, we lost her. I missed her and thought of her every day, and I felt sure Tempie did too. I liked to imagine that Maggie watched over us. Perhaps that was even why we had survived the rest of *that* winter.

Who knew? I smiled. *Well, why be it not so?* 'Twas better than thinking of her in a cold grave in a corner of the fort. No gabled coffin covering her, no pastor bending low and whispering prayers for her soul, not even the solace of a church service.

I sighed, yet acknowledged that we had done well to get her buried in anything besides the mass trench, the grave of the famished and abandoned of James Town's Starving Time. So many perishing, so few sick and feeble hands left to do the burying.

I owed Walter the soldier for helping us then, for agreeing to bury Maggie with some little more dignity than the long ditch afforded. I would owe him the rest of our lives. Walter's fellow soldier Edward had not made it through the Starving Time himself. I wondered if someone had buried him? I hoped so, for him I owed as well.

Yet, we were making new friends among the survivors, those who had lived through the Starving Time as well as the seasoned survivors from Somers's, Gates's, and La Warr's fleets.

A few of the women had made it and pressed on.

Annie Laydon was now living with her husband back in James Town, having been at Point Comfort during the Starving Time. Now, we had opportunity to see Annie and her little daughter Ginny. Tempie and I were especially fond of Annie, who had been but fifteen and expecting her first child when we'd landed in 1609.

Mistress Joan Wright, the midwife, was spirited but sometimes seemed a bit tetchy.

We didn't know Thomasine Causey that well, but hoped she might survive long enough for us to get better acquainted.

And we had a special fondness for Maria Bucke, the pastor's wife, who had been shipwrecked in Bermuda. Reverend Bucke's first wife had died not long before Maria had married him at Christmastime 1608. When the Buckes sailed for Virginia, the reverend had left his two older daughters behind, hoping to send for them some day.

We were harder women for the journey. Or, perhaps, we were merely more practiced in a hard way of living, but not necessarily harder ourselves.

Sometimes we tittered like young girls, and sometimes we wept like babies.

Sometimes we were weary of the journey, and sometimes hopeful of the coming day.

Always unsure where the road led on this pilgrimage we had taken to Virginia. Where did it end? And would we see it through, or would it finish us as it had so many others?

Always we tried not to think too much about tomorrow. For as the Bible said, sufficient unto the day was the evil thereof.

Each day brought challenges filled with plenty of evil, plenty of trials in everyday living without needing to borrow from days ahead.

We would face troubles when they came a-bangin' at our door and no sooner.

And we dropped into our beds at night, exhausted and glad of it—for the more tired we were, the less likely the nightmares could creep into our heads.

So often before bed, I sat by little Janey and told her sweet stories, some my mother had told me, some I created. I told her of fairies and foxgloves, how the foxes secretly put the little flowers on their paws at night. And the way the foxes raced round and round the flowers and hid beneath them.

In my charming land, fairies flitted over the meadows, bewitching the foxes and crouching beneath toadstools to keep warm and dry. When the moon was full and the foxes asleep, the fairies climbed up the foxgloves to see far across the meadows, only to play pranks upon the foxes another day.

A fairy world, and when the night was quiet save the frogs and crickets and wind blowing 'cross the river, even Tempie and I could almost believe it were so.

Other sounds were not so lulling. We could often hear the lingering cry of wolves and growls we could not identify, be they wolves or bears or wild cats? All of them prowled Virginia.

Janey awoke often during the night, crying out. And when I went to her to ask what the matter be, she could not remember. Just terrors of the night. The mournful sounds of owls or the rustling leaves might mean, in her mind, an Indian hiding in the brush.

"No Indians, little lovey," I would say. "Just the sounds of the forest all about the fort's palisade."

And I prayed to God that this was so, never letting on to Janey that greater forces than we controlled our ends. The lie was there. For well we knew there *could* be Indians making sounds in the night.

But one did not tell a five-year-old that. One simply rocked her and whispered that all was peaceful in her lullaby world. Knowing, too, that this five-year-old had seen so much of James Town's harshness that she probably did not truly believe us anyway. But Tempie and I told her she was safe, and she chose to trust that this was so.

Many nights, Tempie or I hummed to Janey as she was drifting off to sleep.

> *Golden slumbers kiss your eyes,*
> *Smiles awake you when you rise;*
> *Sleep, pretty wanton, do not cry,*
> *And I will sing a lullaby,*
> *Rock them, rock them, lullaby.*
> *Care is heavy, therefore sleep you,*
> *You are care, and care must keep you.*

In truth, care kept all of us at James Town.

We watched newer settlers like Sarah Rolfe consumed by diseases we had grown accustomed to—victims of the seasoning—and we heard reports of the war our husbands fought with the natives. Sometimes we heard news from Will and George themselves. But more often, we heard reports from around James Town while the soldiers were still afield. We cowed to De La Warr's plans and did, quite simply, as the leaders told us to do.

Our home was small and primitive, with its dirt floors and rustic furnishings. Our meals, humble: wheat too old to remember its own harvesting in England, our Virginia corn, and now and again, some fish. The barley did not prosper, but English peas and Indian beans did. We occasionally received milk and eggs from the cows and hens. Yet these and the swine were breeding stock, and the Virginia Company did not allow us to slaughter them. But when an animal should die of its old age, well, that was cause for celebration. And some of the settlers joked, saying they might help that old sow along to the Promised Land.

All these victuals, after our recent starving, we were still grateful to have. Aye, the settlements and forts of Virginia were tucked at the edge of an ocean, on a continent time seemed to have overlooked.

But if, indeed, time had forgotten her, other forces had not.

We had no way of knowing that we were but pawns in a large chess game that had drawn the attention of all the crowns of Europe. The prize game piece was little James Town, with her marshes and her dirt paths and her strange huts of half-English and half-Indian construction.

Whosoever controlled Virginia's heart, James Town, controlled Virginia.

And whosoever controlled Virginia controlled a large swath of the New World—for the lands called Virginia stretched from Newfoundland in the north to Roanoke in the South, and as far west as the South Sea. The Continent or Kingdom of Virginia, some maps called it.

Whoever controlled the New World wrested much European power and hence much world power. Especially since surely here lay the doorway to the Far East. This was the fabled Northwest Passage, a river somewhere which cut across the New World and led to the South Sea. And all the world knew Virginia was brimming with broad rivers which crept like muddy fingers deep into the forests and brush, far into lands unknown to us. One of these rivers, surely, led all the way across the continent.

Yes, the eyes of all the world were stealing in upon us. How unaware we were.

And we had little way of knowing that, at that very moment in London, Sir Thomas Gates was staring down a Virginia Company court, a court who cared little about us, who saw only our failure, and who planned to yank the purse away. Little did I know that Gates might not be bringing Cecily home, since Gates himself might not be returning if Sir Thomas Smythe and the court had its way.

These men of the court knew there were safer, easier ventures abroad than Virginia. Would they cast more money at us? For settlers who would die and commodities we could not provide? Or would they abandon us here?

Cares keeping us, indeed. We were in our own golden slumber.

A Hundred Closed Doors

Early September 1610 ~ Sir Thomas Smythe's home on Philpot Lane, London

Tomorrow it will be
The King's move, I suppose, and we shall have
One more magnificent waste of nameless pawns,
And of a few more knights.
—Edwin Arlington Robinson

A door opens to me. I go in and am faced with a hundred closed doors.
—Antonio Porchia

We talked of it many times in later years, once we understood it all. How enduring hurricane and starvation were not the final challenges. How the Company had discussed leaving us here to fend for ourselves—out of gunpowder and out of food—to face an Indian nation bent on destroying us. We talked of how the Spanish were our enemy, and how the Indians were our enemy, and how the Company was our enemy most times, too. We talked of how it must have happened, behind those closed doors where hungry little girls with nightmares mattered very little.

We imagined the fight, deep inside the offices of the Virginia Company in London....

* * *

That September afternoon, Sir Thomas Gates walked briskly, despite his fatigue from the tilt boat voyage. The choppy Thames, the crowded barge, and a drizzling rain had all conspired to make the trip from Gravesend to London miserable. But the Virginia Company had summoned Gates, and he, of course, obeyed.

Fortunately, the tilt boat had dropped him at Billingsgate, but a few blocks from the elegant home of his friend, Sir Thomas Smythe, Company Treasurer.

Gates was lost in thought as he crossed Eastcheap at the corner of Botolph Lane, his soldier's mind locked in strategy about this forthcoming meeting. Gates knew that some one thousand souls had entered Virginia by the fall of 1610 and only about three hundred remained, two-thirds of the whole perished of disease, starvation, or Indian arrow.

And with all the abundance of Virginia land and forests, no marketable commodity had yet surfaced to return money to the stockholders. Lumber was necessary for English shipbuilding, but the profits were not there yet. Sassafras, growing freely in the New World, had some hope for its medicinal properties. Glassblowing had so far been unsuccessful due to difficulties in harnessing the labor of the Dutchmen and Poles.

We were trying to find a commodity, but adapting to a strange land, setting up a sound defense system, and adjusting to the unimaginable amount of illness and death were prolonging the ability of the venture to profit.

"We are in debate about Virginia, about the next course of action, and require your opinion on the matter," Smythe's letter had said.

The councilors will look to me for my valuation of this venture. Gates knew that even if he urged the Company to continue its support, the men's cold purses would carry weight, too. And he knew that if he suggested that the Company abandon the settlement, if he even hinted at it, the hope of an English future in Virginia would be lost. The New World would topple, like so many chess pieces, right into the hands of the Spanish king.

It was a burdensome question, to be sure.

Suppose he assented, gave the venture his heartiest approbation, and then the colonization effort turned to complete disaster? *Well,* he reminded himself, *Virginia has teetered very nearly on that already. Fire, mutiny, starvation, siege, Indian wars, drought, hurricane, shipwreck, putrifying illness, death on a massive scale... By God,* he thought. *By God.*

But Gates had this reassurance: Virginia was a beauteous, vast land with many rivers snaking through it. These rivers met at the Chesapeake's Bay, the finest bay any had ever seen. Virginia held treasures of fruit and nuts; forests filled with fish and fowl, game and minerals. The colony also now possessed strong leadership, new forts, trained military men, martial law, and a strategy that should serve the colony well going forward. If the stockholders would just be patient, profits would come. And England would be the stronger for keeping this abundant New World as its own, not abandoning it to Spain prematurely.

Nearly a quarter century had passed since Gates had first seen the New World. He had been with Sir Francis Drake when they rescued the earliest

Virginia colonists at Roanoke in 1586. Gates's opinion of Virginia's potential, fueled by Drake's enthusiasm, remained steadfast even after all these many years. Gates had proudly been the *first* signer of the *first* Virginia Company charter in 1606.

So much to gain by staying, by persevering and not giving in just when the future was about to turn in England's favor. Gates could not help feeling that God's hand held this venture, but it was not a hand that gave lightly such a wondrous place as Virginia.

A commodity was bound to surface, given enough time, experimentation, and most importantly, funding.

For this, Gates would have to convince the keeper of the purse strings and one of England's wealthiest merchants, Sir Thomas Smythe.

Smythe was a grand supporter of all overseas mercantile operations. How many governorships did the man have? He was governor of the Company that sought trade with East India and was governor, too, of the Muscovy Company, working with the Russian tsar. Smythe had even traveled to Russia a decade or so before as English ambassador. Added to that, Smythe governed both the Northwest Passage Company and the Levant Company, which sought trade with Turkey. And finally, he was Treasurer of the Virginia Company and its top leader.

Smythe knew trade, understanding how to use lands across the sea to his advantage.

Yet in those other countries, English merchants were only looking to join the already robust trade. These trade routes had already enriched the Dutch, Spanish, and Portuguese. So the English brought fine broadcloths to East India and to the Spice Islands, hoping to return with such things as pepper, mace, nutmeg, and cloves.

And we in Virginia have no such commodity, Gates thought, as he approached Smythe's front door. *A grand difference between bartering for an established trade good and starting one from naught.*

Gates sighed. He knew that Smythe was a practical man, a gifted trader and merchant, a man who knew how to turn a profit, who would find a profit or let the venture go. Without adequate returns, how could the Company continue funding Virginia? There was a limit to the generosity of even the most patriotic Englishman.

Gates knew that if he could sell Smythe on Virginia's merits, Smythe could probably sway the other council members.

Those members of council, along with Smythe, would be the ones to persuade future investors through pamphlets touting Virginia's promise. For Virginia to recover from her disastrous first three years, she was going to need new money and new blood. Gates winced at the ironic double meaning of the last word.

No, this was not going to be an easy persuasion. Yet he reminded himself that if he had confronted a five-day hurricane at sea, he could handle the Virginia Company.

Patience, gentlemen, patience, Gates said to himself, as he arrived at Smythe's front door and reached for the bronze lion-head knocker.

Storms and Tempests

Early September 1610 ~ Sir Thomas Smythe's home on Philpot Lane, London

The greater the difficulty, the more glory in surmounting it.
Skillful pilots gain their reputation from storms and tempests.
—Epicurus

The faces around the grand oak table carried mixed emotions as Gates entered the room. Smythe's servant had brought Gates to the door of the first-story chamber where Smythe held Virginia Company meetings. Smythe had two large homes in London, and his Philpot house had a separate chamber for each business venture. The wealth of the man was staggering.

Not so, Gates. The time and resources he had invested in Virginia had cost him everything. Well, nearly everything. He still had his wife, his sons and daughters, and a modest home in Devon. Also, his knighthood and his reputation. But of worldly goods, most all had gone into the venture.

Smythe and the councilors stood, and a spontaneous round of applause went up for the man who had almost literally risen from the dead. At the men's backs, fantastically, stood stuffed creatures and exotic sculptures from around the world, remembrances of the places and companies Smythe presided over.

"Gates, Gates!" cried a few councilors. Not one of these men had ever expected to see their comrade again. Word of the *Sea Venture's* loss in the hurricane had devastated the Virginia Company. What? Gates and Admiral Somers both lost? The grand dame *Sea Venture,* with all her one hundred fifty passengers, gone down? All the solders, artisans, women, and children vanished at sea? Even these property-conscious men could not get beyond the loss of the valiant souls onboard.

Gates smiled and nodded to both sides of the table. He was going to need all the charm he could muster.

"Gentlemen."

Smythe stood and came eagerly to see Gates, grabbing both Gates's hands in his own and then clapping him on the back.

"Like seeing a ghost!" he cried, shaking his head.

"A ghost who brings you news from Virginia," Gates said. "Wonderful to see you again, Smythe. And I do appreciate your warm welcome."

"Certainly," said Smythe cordially, taking his seat once more.

Smythe was a man of business, and business was at hand. "We, of course, require that you give your solemn and sacred oath, Sir, before you begin your testimony."

Gates nodded. He had expected this, too.

The Sergeant-at-Arms carried a large Geneva Bible, holding it before Virginia's governor. Gates placed his left hand upon it, raising his right hand before God as his witness, and vowed that his words would be true.

"Thank you, Gates. And again, welcome," Smythe said, settling back into his ornate chair. "As you know, we had feared the loss of your ship and all hands. God has graced us with survival of both you and Admiral Somers and all your men. To God be the glory." Smythe spoke matter-of-factly, without emotion, before continuing. "A *hurricano* at sea and a shipwreck! A devastating blow. Yet redemption in the end. And old Somers. How is he?"

"He is well! He has traveled back to the Bermudas with his nephew Matthew to obtain more supplies for Virginia, for when we arrived..." Gates paused. How much did they know of the Starving Time? Before the governor could proceed, Smythe interrupted.

"Gates, we ask that you deal plainly with us, that you make a true relation of what we have, and may expect to have, in Virginia."

Sir Thomas Gates nodded. Of course.

Smythe continued, "Word comes that you found but sixty survivors when at last you did arrive at James Town?" Apparently, Smythe knew about the Starving Time from someone else who had just arrived from Virginia, perhaps Silvester Jourdain.

No matter. Smythe, at least, had already heard about the horror. But by the sound of the groans and table slapping that went up, the Starving Time had not yet become common knowledge.

Gates's expression was grim. "'Tis so. And even those sixty within days of death." They might as well hear the news directly from him. He could not—would not—disguise what had occurred. Besides, he was under oath. He only wanted to ensure that this lot understood what the *future* held. The past was already behind them.

"Sickening losses," Smythe muttered. "Unbelievable misfortune." He paused, glanced around the table at his councilors, and then retrieved his pipe. He studied Gates. "And now? All is well in the plantation, we trust, now that the severed head is back upon the body?" Smythe was tamping the tobacco and appeared nonchalant.

Gates knew he was anything *but* nonchalant.

"As of my departure, the future is promising," Gates said with emphasis.

Smythe leaned forward in his carved-oak chair, his expression hard. "You might as well know that many investors are giving up, selling out."

Sir George Coppin interrupted Smythe, "Gates, here in England, men profane the name of Virginia nearly as much as the name of God."

"Then we are in good company, sirs, are we not?" Gates said. The rueful nods and shrugs told Gates that the councilors had faced a rough time.

Smythe, himself giving a weary nod, continued, "Some vow they'll invest no more in Virginia ever, viewing their present investments as entirely lost." He gazed at a paper in front of him and said quietly, "And lost they well may be. Whether the investment be small or large, nothing yet returned, not even by these last ships to arrive."

He turned to meet Gates's eyes. "Why, I've been to court more times than I can count trying to collect unpaid subscriptions. And new subscribers are nearly impossible to recruit. This venture, I'm afraid, is no longer viable or sustainable. The losses are too high, commodities haven't surfaced as we'd planned, and not enough support remains to keep Virginia going. These last ships came in virtually devoid of commodity—the venture's final straw, in the opinion of many." Gone was Smythe's feigned look of nonchalance. Gates saw that, in Smythe, the patriot had deferred to the merchant.

Gates knew, too, of the hatred James Town's colonists had for Smythe, blaming Smythe's miserliness for not dispensing provisions they needed to survive. The story had even come to Gates of the time the Indians had killed a mare and boiled it up, and the settlers had cried how they wished Sir Thomas Smythe had been a-riding upon her back in the kettle.

Gates's heart fell within him. How to tell all those at James Town who had worked so hard, who had survived hurricane, siege, and starvation, that the Company was withdrawing its support? Had it all been for nothing? He thought of the men, of both high stations and low, bailing furiously for five days as the hurricane battered the *Sea Venture*. He would never forget the wave so steep that it had swept over the ship and even crashed below deck, knocking him and his men off their seats, causing them to grovel upon the deck. The sea and storm had seemed alive to Gates then as though reminding all onboard that nature had no master, only servants. For all the furious, churning sea was concerned, Gates might have been a cabin boy and not a knight, military captain, and governor of Virginia. Gates had felt humbled as he clambered on the deck beneath the swirling water.

And he remembered how, when all hope had vanished beneath the sea rising ever deeper within the ship's hold, Gates had drawn comfort from the faces of his men. The trusting looks they wore even in such a moment. How he had felt his throat tighten as he toasted them. He had waded through the flooded decks, crying out, "My only ambition is but to climb up above hatches, to die in *aperto coelo*—in open sky—and in the company of my old friends."

The ship had found its way between two rocks which held it upright, at the haunted Bermudas, so that all the men, women, and children could make it to shore. The very hand of God had seemed to steady the broken, sea-filled vessel. One entrance to the island, and the hurricane had blown them to it.

Rather than languishing on a deserted isle, his men had worked in the Bermudas for ten months building two ships from cedar. The crew had even managed to assemble the seaworthy *Patience* with only a single bolt. The hope of James Town had burned brightly all those months.

Gates recalled the weary and starved George Percy, the man's willingness to stay with the colony despite his own illness and the horrors he had endured as Virginia's leader during the Starving Time siege. And how some of Gates's own men had arrived at James Town from the Bermudas, filled with the idea of reuniting with their wives, only to discover them dead or nearly so.

And he recalled two emaciated women, the wives of Yeardley and Peirce, with one little girl, who pledged to move onward from the devastating Starving Time. One had even asked Gates to bring her little daughter back to James Town when he came.

Must they all learn it was for naught? Renewed grief rose within him. Would Virginia heartbreaks never end?

Hanging Breathless
Early September 1610 ~ Sir Thomas Smythe's home
on Philpot Lane, London

*Three main impediments are objected. First the dangerous
passage by sea, secondly the barrenness of the country, thirdly
the unwholesomeness of the climate: the storm that separated
the admiral from the fleet proving the first, the famine amongst
our men importing the second, the sickness of our men arguing
the third. All which discouragements do astonish our men with
fear, as though our expenses were unprofitable, when our ends
are impossible.*
—A True Declaration of the Estate in Virginia,
   the Virginia Company, 1610

Thou, too, sail on, O Ship of State!
Sail on, O Union, strong and great!
Humanity with all its fears,
With all the hopes of future years,
Is hanging breathless on thy fate!
—Henry Wadsworth Longfellow

A map of Virginia lay on the grand table. The council surrounded it in the
impressive oak-paneled room and studied Gates intensely. These members were most glad to see him. They had presumed Gates lost at sea during
the *Sea Venture's* shipwreck. But his survival was old news. What had he to
tell them now? What could he say to make them keep this tenuous investment
that had yet shown no profit, but only staggering losses?

Gates's task was formidable, given the huge losses of both settlers and
money. Yet he still needed to say to the council, "Keep this investment."

*How does one take the facts and convince the council—convince Smythe—
not to give up? How did one keep a great ship afloat when it filled with water
by the ton faster than all hands could bail it out? Perseverance. Never stopping,*

but pumping with all one's strength. One never gives up, never gives in. All great storms pass, Gates thought, *and all ships destined for port reach it, but every bucket of water counts. Every hand must stay at the pump. And one must never surrender.* He found that he was unconsciously setting his jaw with this last thought.

Silence filled the chamber. The eyes of the great explorers, in portraits adorning linen-fold walls, bored into Gates. Here the great Hakluyt, there Sir Francis Drake, Sir Humphrey Gilbert, and Christopher Carleill. At the end of the room, lest any forget who signed all papers granting this Company its charter, was a portrait of His Majesty, King James I. There, too, hung the portrait of Bartholomew Gosnold, prime mover of the plantation, who had given his life just after his own arrival in Virginia at the beginning of the venture.

Resolve filled the knight.

He drew a deep breath and prepared the words he knew would give James Town one more chance as an English plantation or condemn it forever to be the future domain of the Spanish. And he reminded himself that if Spain seized Virginia, Spain would become so powerful there would be no more England. King Philip would see to that.

The silence was becoming uncomfortable. Smythe clearly felt he had thrown the gauntlet.

Dramatically, Gates let his eyes rove from one man's face to the next, slowly, around the great table. He lingered at each just long enough for the councilors to feel Gates's glare penetrating their own gazes. The knight let his eyes speak for him as the anger rose within him.

I have saved a hundred fifty men, women, and children from death by hurricane. I have built two ships from island cedar to bring my men and myself to James Town. I have pledged my money and *my life. Have you?*

The question went unspoken. He saw a few gentlemen shift uneasily.

Then, still wordlessly, Gates reached into the pouch at his waist and drew a handful of coins. He let the councilors wonder what he was doing as he counted silently.

Without warning, Gates flung the coins to the table. The shillings and pence gleamed silver as they bounced and rolled. Startled, the men flinched.

"There's a return on your investment! I cannot give you all the twelve pounds, ten shillings, the cost of one share. I would if I had it to give. But take this, those of you who were only in this for the profit, who concern yourselves not with England's future and with what we are bringing to our great nation—its very survival against the bloody Spanish. Throw your lot to the Spanish now! *For, in time, you will be her handmaids.*" The disdain in his voice was palpable, and Gates felt a ripple of shame move through the room.

Good, he thought. *They* should *be ashamed.*

He had wanted their full attention, and he received it.

Gates began to speak once more, his voice firm, his gaze direct. He had never wavered in battle. He would not waver now.

"Are you in it for silver and gold, or are you in it for God? Do you recall the Protestant missionary work we are also bound to do? Does your purse not fatten quickly enough for you, gentlemen?" He pointed his finger around the table at the council. "Because I assure you Spain's shall fatten before our eyes once she claims Virginia. And she *will* claim Virginia. Make you no mistake. The Spanish appreciate what is before them. When the day occurs, gentlemen, that Spain once more calls our beloved Chesapeake Bay *la Bahia de la Madre de Dios,* as she did before, then England shall have no recourse. For the Spain that conquers all the New World conquers England. And your grandchildren shall bow to the authority of the pope and sing Spanish lullabies."

Gates lowered his voice on these last words.

A cry of protest went up around the table. Smythe's was the loudest, and the councilors deferentially allowed him to speak.

"Strong words, Gates, and you may throw all the silver you like about the room. It does not change facts. Virginia looks like a losing proposition and potential profits appear as empty to our investors as their purses. Do you think you might gather all present and future investors from towns around the South and West Country and toss coins at them to change their minds?" His voice softened on old friendships. "And, make no mistake. I like and respect you, Gates. I respect your opinion, your valor. When we sent you and Somers, we sent England's best. But we are talking about stockholders. This is an investment, one which must pay in their lifetime...." Smythe's voice slipped into desperation on the last word as though hoping Gates would understand that this was nothing personal. It was business.

Gates paused again. Once more, he let his gaze meet those of the other council members present. He saw that some had a humbled expression. Others looked angry at his accusations that they had chosen greed over England's future. Some had come around. He would never get all of them, but if he could get *enough* to swing the vote toward continued support of the colony...

Gates began, "I apologize for my rudeness, gentlemen. I am simply trying to get your attention." He was about to say, "And I suspected it would take clamoring, rolling silver to do it!"—but he caught himself. He meant no disrespect, nor did he intend to insult anyone.

"I am not one who has great sums to throw around," Gates said with a nod to the scattered coins on the table. He dropped his voice. "I myself have invested all the money I have in this Company."

The men nodded. They knew that Gates, unlike many of them, had come from a humble background in Devon, his father a wool merchant, Thomas the youngest son.

"I speak to you as friends and comrades because I have fought alongside some of you at Nieuwpoort in Flanders, battling the Spanish *tercios* on the beaches. And I have fought on your behalf and on behalf of this plantation and of this investment. Your support has taken us this far. *Withdraw it not now!* We have not turned a profit yet, 'tis true." Gates saw some of the men nod encouragingly. Emboldened, he went on, "We have in fact, suffered losses on an unimaginable scale, *but we shall yet prevail.*"

With a nod to the most successful East Indian product, Gates added, "Virginia is not pepper, gentlemen. Land is not a commodity we buy and sprinkle wantonly upon our suppers. In time, we will create and ship many goods from Virginia. All the things you have heard, I confirm to you are true. There are mulberries for silk, rivers filled with sturgeon, and fur-bearing animals of all kinds. Wood of every sort, and vines crawling across the land. We will find a way and expand our burgeoning population to Virginia, to create another England in Virginia to expand England's prestige and power."

He laughed, and he could scarcely keep the sarcasm out of his voice. "Virginia is not a little island like our own home. No, do you not understand that those who see Virginia believe in it with their whole hearts? Do you not see that we cannot translate what we sense about this land? Can you imagine, for instance, a flock of waterfowl a mile wide and seven miles long? This is Virginia—wild, exotic, abundant. Do you not see that Virginia has more, far more, than words can convey, gentlemen?"

Gates paused then continued, "No grand venture such as ours succeeds in its first months, yea, even in its first years. Did not Moses wander the wilderness forty years before finding his Canaan? Gentlemen, I say to you that it has not been forty years, it has not even been forty months. How long has it been, gentlemen? But one thousand days since the first ships left Plymouth for Virginia. God is testing us to find us worthy of this abundant Promised Land we call *Virginia*. Virginia, my friends, is one of the goodliest lands under the sun, and I long to return. See that I myself am not only keeping my investment in the Company, *I am increasing it* by bringing my wife and daughters with me when I depart this spring. And other planters are sending for their wives and their children. Gentlemen, these valiant men, who have seen Virginia and lived in it as I have, believe in it enough to invest their most precious commodities: their families. Would you not do the same with your cold silver pounds and shillings?"

Sensing the mood change in the room, Gates continued, "Invest, gentlemen, not only for the good of these adventurers who have staked their lives in Virginia, not only for the good of the Company and for the savages we shall convert, but for the very honor of His Majesty himself. For the honor of England. Will the land be *Virginia* after our beloved Virgin Queen? Or will it again be the Spanish land of *Ajacán?* I say to you today, with your backing, the Spanish *shall not* control the New World." He finished with a flourish, slapping his hand upon the map of Virginia for effect.

Silence filled the great chamber. Each councilor sat as still as if he feared his movement would draw attention to himself and force him to make a decision. As one, each councilor held his breath. And for an instant, Gates had the uncanny sensation that all England held its breath, that future generations held their breaths as well.

No man and no thing moved save a large clock at the end of the room. Its rhythmic motion seemed to echo the critical time involved. Each minute, someone in the colony needed food. Each minute, the Indians might attack. Babies were born. Babies died. Critical resources in England grew tighter, each minute, each minute. The Spanish fleet lay in wait to take those shores. To take England.

Each minute, each minute, said the clock without judgment, without relenting.

Virginia, that grand dream. She had teetered on a precipice so many times. Was she a vision of some great future for England? Or merely a puff of smoke in Smythe's pipe?

To Dig a Little Deeper
Early September 1610 ~ Sir Thomas Smythe's home on Philpot Lane, London

[Lord De La Warr], upon the...certainty of future blessings, hath protested in his Letters, that he will sacrifice himselfe for his Countrie in this service, if he may be seconded; and if the Company doe give it over, hee will yet lay all his fortunes upon the prosecution of the Plantation.
—Samuel Purchas

No man raiseth a faire building, that laith not a firme foundation. It will not be impertinent, to dig a little deeper, that we may build a great deale higher."
—The Virginia Company, November 1610

The negotiations at the Virginia Company went on for days. First, there was the primary issue: whether to stay or to abandon the effort? The council decided to proceed as though they would continue the colony while constructing a strategy to allay the faults that had harmed the effort so far if such a thing existed. If, after much study, they could not repair these faults, they would end the venture.

And had they been right to send so many planters at once with the Second Charter of 1609? The great expedition with nine ships and five hundred settlers at once?

Yes, they decided. Anchoring a colony required the efforts of many men and women working together. No man, no group, could accomplish this Herculean feat alone.

What had been the problem, then? Why hadn't the plan worked?

The sea. Sea travel was dangerous and unpredictable, a fact all knew and none could change.

However, the company could alter the odds of arriving at Virginia safely and in good health. Not a man sat about the table who was not uncomfortably aware of the extreme good fortune—nay, the Grace of God!—in the survival of the nine ships to Virginia through a *hurricano*. This was a miracle on par with the favorable gale that blew the mighty Spanish Armada onto the northern rocks, saving England in a David-and-Goliath sort of way and humiliating the Spanish. This should not have happened, but it did. The *Sea Venture* should not have survived, but it did. God's hand, evident for all to see, blessing Protestant England.

But how could the Company contend with the dangers of sea travel?

The men decided that splitting a large group into two parts was the only defense against the sea's mercurial nature, increasing the odds that at least one of the expeditions would make it to Virginia.

The men set dates. In March 1611, a mere six months away, the next fleet would sail. For this voyage, the Virginia Company would attempt to enlist three hundred men, women, and children while also restocking Virginia's cattle, goats, and poultry.

"We need a leader for the first group. Prince Henry has recommended Sir Thomas Dale to us," Smythe said, leaning back in his chair.

Only sixteen years old, Prince Henry was England's brightest hope. He was intelligent, well-read, beloved, and wise. The king was none of these, common folk whispered, so the prince must certainly take after his mother.

The prince had carried a deep love for Virginia since the age of ten when he had begun visiting Sir Walter Ralegh in his jail cell at the Tower of London. Ralegh's adventure tales of the colonies in Virginia and Ireland inspired the boy to believe that Virginia *must* survive. Baffled that his father would imprison such a great explorer, the prince had asked, "Who but my father would keep such a bird in a cage?"

The Company knew that when Prince Henry became king, Virginia would receive his full support. And Sir Thomas Dale was a favorite of the prince, for Dale had guarded the one-year-old prince at Stirling Castle in Scotland.

Gates and Dale would have to work closely together in Virginia, which Gates assured Smythe they could do. Gates and Dale had fought together in battle before. Why not in Virginia? This man Dale was organized, devout, disciplined, and a task master with an unsurpassed military mind.

Dale would lead the first expedition sailing in March. Gates, eager to return to Virginia, would lead a second large expedition in May. This strategy would secure a large presence in Virginia arriving in two groups rather than one.

Dale and Gates: these two soldiers made all the council breathe easier.

They were the men for the job. No doubt about it. And with Baron De La Warr present to lead them both, suddenly, the tasks ahead seemed possible.

The men next discussed the location. James Town was simply too swampy, unhealthy for all the colonists although newcomers fared worst. By comparison, all the *Sea Venture* castaways at Bermuda had survived the year. Gates had an idea, and to make his point, he placed a finger upon a little symbol on the Virginia map.

"James Town sits thirty-six miles upriver from the mouth of the Chesapeake Bay. We know that James Town is marish. However, I beg you, assume not that all of Virginia is unhealthful. Consider the fens in Kent. We do not condemn all of County Kent for these, do we? 'Tis much the same in Virginia. While a marsh covers much of James Town, many other locations are dry."

He traced the James River on the map. "See, we must go further upriver for two sound reasons: the first, of course, being the unhealthfulness of the climate at James Town. We are all acutely aware of *that* by now."

Nods and murmurs of agreement.

Gates continued, "The second reason being that the present town sits too close to the mouth of the bay. Should the Spanish attack, we shall not have the lead time we need, especially since our group still remains relatively small to the flotilla they could send upon us." He paused to look around the table. "Vulnerability to Spanish attack, gentlemen, remains our greatest weakness."

They all agreed then. Dale would scout a location further upriver. With well-placed forts along the way, the Company would then control the entire peninsula between the James and Pamunkey Rivers as far as the fall lines.

The time for moving the colony westward would be late autumn. They dare not risk disrupting planting and harvesting for the move, or starvation could be upon them once more.

Pray God, the Spanish would hold off that long.

The Company next called in Silvester Jourdain, who, at the request of Sir George Somers, had written a treatise explaining why the Virginia Company should colonize and settle Bermuda.

"The Bermudas are the fairest islands in God's kingdom," Jourdain said. "We are blessed by their rockiness, a natural fortress and defensible location. The Spanish and Portuguese have avoided these islands for so long, as have we, because all believed them to be haunted. But the screeches were simply birds encircling this Eden at night. The natural abundance of wildlife and fish will make this colony a natural supporter a sister of the Virginia effort."

Bermuda, after all, had no freshwater, but much abundance and no natives to fight. Virginia had far more land and vast stretches of fresh water. The two colonies together, Jourdain claimed, made an unconquerable combination.

Gates and Somers, along with Admiral Christopher Newport, had decided while on Bermuda that these islands should be English. The leaders had even stationed three men on the island when they left to hold it for His Majesty and the Virginia Company.

Bermuda also had one other major factor to recommend it. Everyone knew that Sir George Somers adored and respected these islands, and all of England adored and respected Sir George Somers. The councilors agreed to petition the king for a new charter, and this one would expand the boundaries of Virginia from Newfoundland to Bermuda, all the way across the continent to the South Sea.

The most crucial aspect of all was how to finance such a mammoth undertaking. What mistakes had the Company and colony leaders made previously?

"Virginia is a land of abundance," Gates said. "But she is not a land of easy profits. Tremendous initiation time is involved. Our mistake has been to think that we could send commodities home immediately. This will take time. I look to you, gentlemen, for ideas on how to secure that time."

A new fund-raising campaign was critical. New broadsides detailing the hope in Virginia, playing to her strengths. Subscribers should focus on what Virginia had to offer. They, the Virginia Company, would attempt to combat her weaknesses through a strategy. But there was no need to advertise these weaknesses, they agreed.

Further, if they could but gain the king's approval, they could offer a lottery wherein the Company would give prizes for those who might win with all the funds going to the Virginia Company.

Gradually, a plan emerged from around the table. A year and a half had elapsed since the Second Charter. Seven years out from that charter would be May 1616. During this remaining time, if Virginia could not make a profit, the Company would have to abandon her.

First, the company must double the incoming funds for each year. In 1609, adventurers had paid twelve pounds ten shillings for a single share. The new price would be a subscription of seventy-five pounds, paid over three years at twenty-five pounds per year.

"Five and a half years," Smythe said. "You *must* turn a profit in that time. We will procure a new charter from the king as soon as we may, and the two expeditions will depart immediately upon being organized. The first may go out as soon as January. It is imperative that we make the most of the planting season of 1611. You have until May 1616. No longer. *The colony must be an unqualified success by then.*"

Smythe wanted that point clear. He turned to Gates. "Either you, Lord

De La Warr, or Sir Thomas Dale must report back to us at the end of the seventh year with the results. Of course, we will expect updates along the way. If Virginia is a failure at that time, we can support you no longer than that."

Sir Thomas Gates nodded. "Of course." Smythe had set the mission before him. Gates, with De La Warr's blessing, had won a major victory for the continuance of the colony.

The Virginia Company had addressed having a healthier settlement site in Virginia, a stronghold in the Bermudas, a wiser strategy for ocean crossing, and a funding and recruitment plan that gave the settlers three years to turn around this venture. The Company would also ensure that large numbers of artisans and craftsmen went on this voyage because these men could forge commodities.

This meeting had begun with the idea that Virginia was not sustainable. But it had concluded with a strategy to correct defects in the former plan and to grow her strong. The Virginia Company would not give up on her: its land, Virginia. Not yet, anyway. It was exciting and strange and exhilarating to think of how grandly these men had now conceived of her.

Well, it was exciting to the English. But the Spanish, with a spy in the council chambers, were growing uncomfortable.

The Eyes of All Europe
September 30, 1610 ~ the Spanish Ambassador's home in the Barbican, London

The eyes of all Europe are looking upon our endeavors to spread the Gospell among the Heathen people of Virginia, to plant our English nation there, and settle at in those parts...
—Sir Walter Cope, 1610

Don Alonso de Velasco had his king's ear and his attention, that much was certain. Now the Spanish ambassador hunched over his desk in London, composing a letter to the king in Madrid.

Velasco had been closely following this distasteful business of the Virginia Company with help and advice from Sir William Monson, English admiral of the Narrow Seas. Spain had captured Monson several times during the war of 1591, and Monson had secretly accepted employ with Spain. Monson, a skilled and experienced navigator, was happy to provide information to the Spanish for a price. He also cheerily provided the same guidance to the English. The good knight was a hero to both sides, and he seemed little to care that his treachery might cost overseas colonists their lives.

Another of Velasco's allies was the former ambassador Don Pedro de Zúñiga. Zúñiga had been the first Spanish ambassador to the English court since the Spanish and English had declared peace in 1604. Peace with the French in 1602, peace with the English in 1604, and peace with the Dutch in 1609. The weary Spanish had finally concluded forty years of fighting across Europe.

In the spirit of *good friendship*—Velasco thought he might choke on the words—the English had invited a Spanish ambassador to London and had sent an English ambassador to Madrid.

So here sat Velasco, Spain's second ambassador, living amongst the English infidels. He could not deny that he hated them, hated them just as much as

Ambassador Zúñiga had hated the English before him.

Velasco hated English arrogance, their claim to knowing God's will for them, which defied the pope's authority. And he hated their exuberance and their foolhardiness in thinking that they could accomplish a New World settlement like Virginia.

And the English had diplomatically never quite acknowledged Spain's claim to the New World, *all* of the New World. Oh, the English had never denied that claim. They had just never agreed to it. And now the Virginia Company scurried at unheard-of speeds to gather men, ships, and supplies for Virginia.

As though the English had a chance.

Didn't they realize they settled Virginia *only* because Span had not yet decided to pursue its claim to the entire New World? The English settled there only by the good graces of His Majesty King Philip of Spain. That reason and that alone.

And did the English not recall how Spain had reclaimed its land from the French in Florida fifty years before? The French well remembered. It had cost them the lives of virtually every Frenchman there, not to mention all the women and children taken captive.

Velasco knew, as all Europe knew, that the Spanish fleet could annihilate that pathetic little English town in one assault.

Velasco knew as well that only one diplomatic problem held his king back.

War with these unlikeable and arrogant Protestants taxed the Spanish coffers and wearied its population. Oh, war wearied the Protestants as well. No one, truth be told, wanted to go back into another conflict.

So England tiptoed by the Spanish Canary Islands en route to Virginia, and Spain tiptoed into the chambers of the Virginia Company to see exactly what the Virginia Company had planned.

Such a trifling settlement as James Town seemed unworthy of a major war effort, particularly when it appeared the venture would fall upon itself by mere incompetence. The Spanish certainly hoped the Indians would finish off the disease-infested colony and save King Philip the trouble. *Swatted, like a gnat, and she is gone,* Velasco thought.

Both he and Zúñiga had laughed when they learned of the great *hurricano* that had struck the English fleet on St. James Day last year. St. James, blessed San Tiago, a disciple of Jesus, who had ministered to the Spanish people during his lifetime and whose body had been angelically spirited away to Spain upon his death. The ghost of San Tiago himself commanded Spanish armies in the New World. How many Spaniards had fallen to their knees at such a sight?

Was there any clearer indication that the forces of heaven were angry with the Protestants and with England for their role in fracturing the Holy Catholic Church?

It had seemed for a while that this little Virginia colony would implode upon itself. And Velasco had been waiting for that event hopefully, as had all the court of King Philip. But now the English were sending more men, more ships, more supplies. They were expanding their boundaries and now even spoke of colonizing the Bermudas as well. Their bluster sickened him.

Velasco's missive to his king was brief. After a few pleasantries and relaying what facts he knew, Velasco hammered his point. The English were not giving up on Virginia and were moving quickly.

"They have determined that, at the end of January of the coming year, three ships shall sail with men, women, and ministers of their religion and with a full supply of arms and ammunition for all." His king, he was sure, would see the implicit dangers here and would understand how easily he could halt this English plan. "If Your Majesty were pleased to command that a few ships should be sent to that part of the world which would drive out the few people that have remained there and are so threatened by the Indians that they dare not leave the fort they have erected," Velasco wrote.

He would send the letter in the shoe of a faithful messenger. Now if only his king would listen.

Velasco placed his pen back into its inkwell with such fury that he almost toppled it.

How he hated the English.

Hostages to Fortune
Mid-December 1610 ~ Sir Thomas Gates's home
in Devon, England

How like a winter hath my absence been
From Thee, the pleasure of the fleeting year!
What freezings have I felt, what dark days seen,
What old December's bareness everywhere!
—William Shakespeare

He that hath a wife and children hath given hostages to fortune.
—Francis Bacon

Lady Gates had presumed her husband drowned at sea. Now he was home—actually *home*—for Christmastime, and she and their young daughters were thrilled to be together in Devon once more. Their sons Anthony and Tom, away at school, would also return soon. This reunion was a miracle as far as the Gates family was concerned.

Within a few months, Lady Gates and her daughters would sail for Virginia with Sir Thomas. The boys would have to stay behind for now to complete their schooling since Virginia had no proper schools.

While delighted to see his family, Sir Thomas Gates had many matters before him. For one thing, he would have to sail to the Netherlands directly after Christmas.

Many Virginia Company soldiers had spent years fighting alongside the Dutch against Spain. Since Gates and Dale were still captains in the Dutch military, the Virginia Company must ask the Dutch to give the men a leave of absence.

As expected, The Hague had already granted Dale three years' leave and promised to hold his captain's position.

Sir Thomas Gates would make the same request and expected the same response. The Dutch, along with the rest of Europe, were eyeing the New World. The Dutch smoothed the way for their friends and allies, the English, hoping the English would uphold future Dutch settlements there.

Gates had heard also that the matter of Virginia had been brought to the Spanish Council of War, a very serious threat to the young colony.

All these things were on Gates's mind. He did not share these thoughts with his wife. Yet he had one request to make of her, one he thought she would enjoy. He asked her if she would take their two daughters, Margaret and Elizabeth, to the home of one Tom Phippen in Dorset.

"There you will find a young girl named Cecily, the daughter of one of my men. I have promised his wife in James Town that I will bring Cecily with us when we come, that you will tend to the child as if she were your own until we make Virginia. The mother, Mistress Peirce, survived the Starving Time," he said by way of explanation. "There is a younger daughter in James Town as well."

Gates handed his wife a letter. "From Mistress Peirce for her daughter, given me before my departure from James Town." The letter, he imagined, contained some little about the famine, about the the father's survival of the hurricane, and of the Peirces' desire that Cecily join them when Gates returned to Virginia.

"This child is just older than Margaret, and I believe the little sister is near the age of Elizabeth," he finished.

Lady Gates held the letter with due care. "A daughter without a mother is a sad thing," she said thoughtfully. "As well, two sisters separated. They should have the joyous reunion we've had. Aye, Cecily will be mine aboard ship as you wish, and our own daughters will be delighted. This mother in James Town need not worry for her little girl."

A second thought occurred to her. "I will encourage Cecily to write her mother to let her know she is well. At least, I pray she is well. And Dale's expedition can carry this ahead to Mistress Peirce." Lady Gates was growing excited at the prospect of seeing the sisters' happy meeting and being a part of a reunion between mother and daughter.

"The unpredictable hand of God," she murmured, still holding the letter. She considered her own two daughters, how she would never want to be apart from them, how glad she was to have her husband with her once more.

Gates was appreciative and kissed his wife. "I knew you wouldn't mind, and I promised Mistress Peirce that Cecily would be in loving care for such an arduous journey."

He took a moment to study his wife's serene face, and he realized his stake in the Virginia Company had just jumped ten thousand percent. He was truly putting his life on the line for this venture, for *she* was his life. She, his daughters, his sons.

"The stakes grow costly," he said under his breath.

"Hm?" she asked, still reading the carefully lettered paper.

"Oh," he said casually. "I am only thinking of…investments."

Pumpkins and Parsnips and Walnut Tree Chips

Late January 1611 ~ James Town

If fresh meat be wanting to fill up our dish,
We have carrots and turnips as much as we wish;
And is there a mind for a delicate dish
We repair to the clam-banks, and there we catch fish.
Instead of pottage and puddings, and custards and pies,
Our pumpkins and parsnips are common supplies;
We have pumpkins at morning, and pumpkins at noon,
If it was not for pumpkins we should be undone.
If barley be wanting to make into malt,
We must be contented, and think it no fault;
For we can make liquor to sweeten our lips,
Of pumpkins and parsnips and walnut tree chips.
—New England rhyme, c. 1630

The Virginia winter had settled in, snowy and cold. In fact, snow had lain on the ground for most of the month. Now it fell again even as the sun dropped low over the river, leaving the snow a bright grey-blue.

In a bowl before my little girl, I placed a steaming meal. The delight in Janey's face lifted me.

"What have we, mama?" she asked.

"Well, child, we have boiled turnips and parsnips, carrots and cabbage, for Lord La Warr has planted winter roots."

Tempie and I sat down at the table to join Janey. Our husbands Will and George were away at Fort Algernon at Point Comfort on the bay.

Tempie and I passed this, our second winter in Virginia, mostly alone. We thought of our husbands often, but we knew we could not bring them home. They were soldiers, and we were in a hostile land. The situation forced us to accept what we could not change.

Yet, days like this brought glimmers of happier days to come.

The snow on the ground could not make us appreciate this winter less. No, not after last winter when we had eaten anything we could scavenge off the ground: poison red berries, acorns, cedar greens, even a little frozen chick-adee that had died at our door. We had survived mostly off acorns, roots, herbs, and walnuts. The stockpiled corn had disappeared far too soon, all the livestock stripped and eaten well before the worst of the starvation had set in. Some of the settlers had eaten poison snakes and muskcats, rats and mice. *Anything.*

Last winter, James Town had been a dreadful place, a place of horrors.

Now the cattle Lord De La Warr had brought were calving. Calving! Laws forbade us from having any of their meat yet, but the milk was tasty when the soldiers dispensed it. To be able to give my little girl a warm plate of food and milk made my heart glad. The cows, as I heard, were thriving on grass they found beneath snowy ground. In England, farmers brought their cattle inside during the winter, but here the cows managed to find grass on their own. 'Twas fortunate that, for we had none to give them.

Through the fall, we had supplemented our corn, dried fish, and venison with Indian foods. We had learned to sow the native crops of beans, squash, and corn. The Indians called these crops the three sisters and planted them all in the same hole. And too, we had Indian pumpions, great orange gourds. To these staples, we added walnuts and *pokahichary* nuts. While not a feast, it kept us from starving even though we missed our English meats and custards. We were, in truth, eating much the same foods as the natives.

Occasionally, on an excellent day, we had opportunity to savor raccoon meat. This tasted much like lamb to us. And even more rarely, someone would shoot a bear near Kecoughtan, and we would have Virginia veal, as we called it.

Yet, here before us sat the aroma of home in these winter roots. And now, with February approaching, we could expect the cauliflower, leeks, chard, turnips, and carrots to be coming in.

Fortunate the roots, for the wheat, peas, and oatmeal the Virginia Company sent were so often fetid, foul to the taste and smell.

Janey scraped the bottom of her bowl, trying to get every bit. So I said to her, "More, lovey?"

And she said, "Yes, please."

We knew Lord La Warr was ill. We had heard of his hot and violent ague nigh upon arrival the previous June. The doctor he had brought, Dr. Bohun, used bloodletting to cure him of that.

After only three weeks of being well, more sicknesses struck Lord La Warr. The ague relapsed badly and stayed with the baron for a month. While battling that, the flux had surprised him. Many days of that. Good Dr. Bohun had fed the baron white clay that the Patawomecks said could cure such things.

Then the cramp assaulted La Warr's already weak body, followed by gout. At last, scurvy hit the poor baron while he was unable to stir.

We had not cared for Lord La Warr upon his arrival. He had sanctimoniously blamed the Starving Time survivors for their own famine, which angered and disheartened us.

However, over time, we were seeing a better side to him, as we understood his frustration at the colony's failure to thrive. The baron had given much of his own wealth to the Virginia venture. We all dreamed of better days to come, but was it just that—only a dream?

Even this ill, La Warr was doing such things as ensuring some settlers sowed winter roots and some manured the fields for the spring corn planting. And the livestock were flourishing.

Tempie lifted a spoonful to her mouth and had such a sweet satisfied expression that I could not help but remember her skeletal face of last winter. My hair had come back in, as hers had. Even beneath her coif I could see that. And our bodies fleshed out at least a bit more.

Last spring there had been only sixty Starving Time survivors, including Tempie, Janey, and me. To these numbers, we had added one hundred fifty *Sea Venture* castaways, and then Lord La Warr had brought two hundred fifty more.

Still, this winter had been harsh, especially for the new arrivals. Of the four hundred who had come since the Starving Time, perhaps half had perished. The summer seasoning had taken many of these new arrivals or made them so ill that they could not live through the winter.

We who had endured the Starving Time were regaining our health. The seasoning, which struck only new arrivals, made us, oddly, some of the healthiest of the lot. Last spring, we had been the weak and ill ones. Now our strange cross to bear was to nurse newcomers who fell sick, tending them with the few little we had. We had put them up in our homes until they died or could cobble together something resembling a home or shelter.

I jealously guarded the little patch of herbs by my house, collecting seeds and hiding them away to plant next spring. I used the herbs themselves as physick for my friends and family as my mother had long ago taught me.

Cecily would be arriving soon, I prayed, upon the fleet of Sir Thomas Gates. When, I did not know, but soon. Surely, soon. If she arrived in health and could survive the summer seasoning, then we would all be well and together in Virginia. Before she had waved goodbye to me at the dock, I had made her a promise that lay hidden within two halves of a scallop shell.

An adventurer goes to a faraway place to see what is out there. But a pilgrim goes to a faraway place to see what is in here, I had told her, patting my heart. Then I had taken a whole scallop, the pilgrim's shell, and broken the two shells apart. *And when we are together again in James Town, we will put our two halves together to form one shell.*

I had asked her to hold up her hand, fingers spread, and to put it up against my own hand. *See the scallop we have made?*

Now my little cockleshell awaited Cecily and her half of the shell. My half had not broken. Pray God, hers had not either.

The winter would soon be over, and the able hands of Lord La Warr had heartened us with warm roots and milk. I felt warm as the roots, believing that perhaps all was well and the worst behind us.

Within a short few months, however, I would learn that the worst was far from over, as the baron's illnesses forced him to retreat to an island with healing springs. Our new leader would test us heartily, pushing us to the brink of what we could bear.

Dale.

A Heart of Fire in an Iron Frame
May 17, 1611 ~ Fort Algernon at Point Comfort

We must alsoe noat heere, that Sir Thos. Dale, at his arivall finding himself deluded by the aforesaid protestations, pulled Capt. Newport by the beard, and threatninge to hange him, for that he affirmed Sir Thos. Smith's relation to be true, demandinge of him whether it weare meant that the people heere in Virginia shoulde feed uppon trees.
—Brief Declaration of the Ancient Planters, c. 1624

I was an English shell,
Cunningly made and well,
With a heart of fire in an iron frame,
Ready to break in fury and flame...
—Arthur Christopher Benson

Sir Thomas Dale arrived in May expecting to find well-supplied forts near the bay, ready for defense. He further expected that Lord La Warr had seen to the planting of corn for the coming winter. He expected to find housing, not only for those present but for at least some of the hundreds of souls he brought with him.

Dale, landing and taking stock, would find none of those.

My first impression of Sir Thomas Dale was that he blew in like a mighty wind. Yet I came to see that this man was not wind, but fire. *All* fire. He was slender and swarthy with a glowering flame lighting his dark eyes and betraying his inner fire.

A capable man with a temper that blasted like an iron furnace, Dale lived only to serve his heavenly and earthly masters: God, King James, Prince Henry, and now the Virginia Company. The opinion of no others mattered to Dale.

England's greatest mistake, Dale felt, was losing Brittany, in France, a century ago. Dale swore that England would not now lose the Kingdom of Virginia. Dale would honor Prince Henry, proving to the prince that he had placed his faith well in Dale. Virginia would succeed, just as the prince believed it could.

And immediately upon arrival, Dale blew across the face of Virginia, up and down the James, not as wind but as wildfire. Except, unlike fire, he left everything in his path built *up*. Expanded, repaired, and rebuilt. Everything he built was upon the backs of the settlers.

Dale intended to turn the venture around as no one had done before him, and unlike Captain John Smith, Dale had the full blessing of the Virginia Company to do so. Dale was military in bearing and training, a long veteran of Ireland and the Netherlands, pious and Puritan in convictions. He believed strong, well-run, and well-protected forts were the only way to keep Virginia safe from Spaniard and Indian. He believed, too, in citizens devoted to God's service. He could be kindly to those who followed command, deadly to those who did not.

The *Lawes Divine Morall and Martiall* were the code, and we were bound to follow the laws, every word, or risk brutal punishment or death. Dale did not exclude women from these, as we would come to find out.

In whatever way the fire that was Dale flamed, all understood quickly that they should not stand in this man's path lest his fire consume them.

As for Dale, he wasted not a minute, and this was apparent from his first landing at Point Comfort.

My husband Will saw the fleet approach. English flags. There had been no relief since La Warr's expedition nearly a year before. Will was curious as to what this fleet held.

He would know soon enough.

The soldiers readied themselves to let the fleet's commander approach. Captain Newport had returned, Will saw. Newport had been captain of the doomed *Sea Venture*, had been a castaway on Bermuda, and had returned to England for more settlers shortly after arriving in Virginia. He was, apparently, captain of this fleet.

Beside Newport strode a thin man with piercing eyes that Will vaguely recognized. And then he remembered: the Netherlands. This man and Gates had become acquainted in the fighting. Will could not remember the officer's name, but he clicked his heels and said, "Welcome to Virginia, sir."

Dale shot him a look, and Will's heart raced although Will was unsure why. Then the officer nodded and walked on.

"One-armed Newport is the admiral now," a man coming off ship said to Will. "Word is, Admiral Somers died in Bermuda on a mission to bring wild hog meat back to Virginia. And here's your new commander, Sir Thomas Dale."

Will watched as other soldiers escorted Newport and Dale to Captain Davis's house.

The hour was late.

Hot, exhausted, and hungry, with a guard leading the way, Sir Thomas Dale and Admiral Newport approached the strange little house with clapboard roof and Indian mat walls.

Davis came to the door, recognition showing on his face, and let the two men in.

"Fetch Captain Percy," Davis told the guard, who tipped his hat and obeyed.

The two officers stepped over the threshold, and then a few moments later, George Percy also entered. Captain Davis welcomed everyone into the main chamber of his home.

Dale learned that Captains Davis and Percy were readying the *Hercules* for departure. The small ship had come in a few months before with thirty settlers. Dale also noted the crowded condition of the fort.

"We presently house most of Sir Thomas Gates's men while Gates is in England. And several members of Council are also about," Davis said.

Dale hurled questions at the two. Davis and Percy had never seen someone fresh off ship demonstrate such energy.

Davis introduced himself as being in charge of the fort at Point Comfort, as he had been since before the Starving Time.

Percy, Dale learned, was now interim Governor of Virginia since De La Warr had grown so ill and departed two months before. This was Dale's first surprise: rather than being a second to De La Warr, Dale would in fact be in command as marshal and acting governor.

"Pardon me, gentlemen," Newport said. He excused himself, saying he would be back shortly. Dale's interrogation continued in Newport's absence.

"Well, why the devil are so many of Gates's men crowded into this small fort? What of the other forts guarding the sea? I can only assume they must also be thus crowded with men?" Dale demanded.

Davis and Percy exchanged glances. "Forts Charles and Henry have fallen into disrepair, sir," Davis said uneasily.

Dale stood and roared, *"Disrepair? We are at war, captains! I could send the both of you* to the gallows for such an offense in my Lord La Warr's absence."

Percy sucked in his breath, putting his hands up in a motion both defensive and, he hoped, placating. "Begging your pardon, sir. Lord La Warr ordered those forts closed so that the soldiers there could lead an expedition upriver to search for mines." Percy felt a sweat bead upon his forehead. Faldoe the Helvetian had promised he could find mines near the falls, but all hope of that was lost when the Appomattocks queen had struck and killed all the men skilled in mining.

"Captains, we are not building mines. We are building a colony! You should know," Dale said, his face red with fury, "that we have strong intelligence that the Spanish are coiled like a snake, waiting to strike us. Those forts are critical—*critical!*—to our survival as a first defense. Put those forts back into active use *immediately.*"

"Yes, sir," said Davis and Percy together, chastened.

Then George Percy drew himself up. If Dale decided to hang Percy and Davis, who could stop him? In his four years at James Town, George Percy had suffered many indignities. Being threatened with hanging was not one of them. A slight man, made even slighter by weight lost during the Starving Time, Percy was a veteran of Virginia's challenges. Being an earl's brother gave Percy little comfort during the worst that Virginia had dealt him. What meant titles here? But Percy was apprised of the Virginia situation in a way Dale was not.

Percy cleared his throat. "Able-bodied men, sir, are few. Supplies and munitions limited, although these are in sore need, seeing as we are at constant war with the natives. Sickness abounds. Even basic food, clothing, and shelter have we little."

Dale's eyes narrowed. Truly, this man was frightening, Percy thought. Dale's words erupted as barks. "Hungry men are weak men! Victuals short? How short?" He banged his fist upon the table.

Davis met Dale's glare. He spoke, his tone matter-of-fact. "Our provisions, sir, arrive most often rotten with spider webs and maggots. And little enough even of these putrid victuals."

Percy, watching Davis speak, turned himself to the new acting governor with his assent. "All portions now rationed, sir."

"You grow not your own? Is this not what Sir Thomas Smythe promised these settlers in his broadside? 'Gardens and orchards, food and clothing provided at the Company charge'! What of it?" Dale's face was flushed, his hand reflexively on his sword. These conditions were not what Smythe had promised. Not at all.

Percy, however, did not flinch this time. He had suffered worse during his own sickness and starvation. He supposed he could deal with a raging knight.

"All men's efforts ordered to be directed toward the search for commodities, sir. The Company will not allow us to use any great endeavors toward farming. My Lord La Warr ordered winter roots planted, 'tis true, and left the ground manured for corn. But now those who would plant the corn have summer sickness and die in great numbers. We spend more time burying men than seeds." Percy spoke the truth. If this man Dale sent him to the gallows, so be it.

Percy continued, "A few scattered herb and kitchen gardens, but nothing on a grand scale and no real acreage for any settler, just what each man can grow around his own home *if* he can find seeds. The livestock Baron De La Warr brought are thriving, so we do have cattle, goats, swine, and poultry. But otherwise we've been struggling since the *Sea Venture's* loss led to the Starving Time. Still, we carry on, doing the best we can with what little we have." Percy was perplexed. "Smythe didn't inform you of our true conditions...?"

Dale stomped his foot, every muscle exuding furor. "No, by God, he did not!" Dale's astonishment at the deterioration of the colony flashed across his face. He understood in a heartbeat that all he had heard from the Virginia Company about the flourishing colony were lies. A desperate attempt to keep stock selling in hopes that Virginia's fortune would soon improve and the Company would make a profit, and then all would be true. Lies that had influenced Dale's decision to come. Lies Dale himself would have to repair if the colony were to survive.

"Sickness and death, how great? Debilitating many men?" He looked from Percy to Davis.

Percy spoke. "Both the *Sea Venture* castaways and those from Lord La Warr's fleet, hundreds of people, fell mightily ill upon arrival, sir, with pestilent diseases, agues, and fluxes. Both groups arrived at nearly the same time, doubling our troubles." Percy paused. "We lost one hundred fifty of them within a few months—three of every five, perished! And that mainly because we had no means to comfort them, so the sick became the dying." Although he did not wish them to, George Percy's shoulders slumped. He sighed. "We are in great want."

To this, Davis put in, "And then, sir, sickness so disabled the rest of La Warr's people that they were nigh helpless. The *Sea Venture* castaways, together with the Starving Time survivors, such as Captain Percy and I, had to care for these." He added, in supreme understatement, "For you see, sir, the old planters who endured the Starving Time have had only hard living since their arrival. They are accustomed to it, I suppose."

Dale understood in an instant that he had undertaken a task far, far larger than the one Sir Thomas Smythe had sold him. Prince Henry would surely have had his father wrest control of the colony if he but knew. Which, obviously, was why neither prince nor king had any idea of the dire state of the colony.

Dale felt his rage bubbling like roiling pottage. Unfortunately for him, the man he most wanted to grab by the throat lived three thousand miles away, comfortably in a mansion on Philpot Lane in London. *Smythe!*

Admiral Newport chose this ill-fated moment to join the three men. Entering the house, Newport turned and pushed the door shut with the hook attached to the nub of one arm. For years ago when Newport had returned from the West Indies, his arm had remained behind, severed by a Spanish sword.

Now hook and man swung about, completely unprepared for what happened next.

Dale pounced upon him as a cat leaping upon prey.

"You!" Dale bellowed, marching toward Newport and grabbing him roughly by his beard with one hand while the other pointed a finger menacingly in the admiral's face.

Dale gave the beard a yank that jerked Newport's face close to his own clenched teeth as he roared. "You signed the broadside! You returned to England *knowing firsthand these conditions* and affirmed *in writing* that Smythe's version was true. Is it meant that people here in Virginia *should feed upon trees?*" Dale pulled the beard side to side as he screamed, "Why, I ought to hang you, Chris Newport!"

For an instant, the two most powerful Englishmen in Virginia stood, nose to nose, their eyes narrowed in anger.

Then the admiral lifted his hook threateningly, knocking Dale's finger away from his face. "Let go my beard, I pray thee, sir," he said coolly, pushing his hook against Dale's cheek. "For I should hate to leave thee with but one eye."

The Warrior Soul
May 17-19, 1611 ~ the Forts at the Bay, and James Town

Either find a way, or make one.
—Hannibal, Carthaginian general

*The secret of victory…lurks invisible in the vitalizing spark,
intangible, yet as evident as lightning—the warrior Soul.*
—General George S. Patton, Jr.

"You may still feel the gallows' breeze, Newport," Dale said in a growl, letting go the beard, but not without a final snap.

Next morning, the men unladed barrels of meal and peas from Dale's fleet. Perhaps, hoped Will, the quality—the edibility—might be better than that from previous ships.

But no, these victuals, too, were so rancid that even the hogs turned snouts upward and refused to eat of them.

Season by season, Will thought. *We have to grow our own. We cannot depend on those in mansions with fat bellies to take care of sending us food, no matter what they have promised us as we work for the common good.*

The fight between the governor and admiral was making its rounds through the barracks. Dale understood the need for adequate provisions to keep men's bodies strong, their spirits ready for the challenges of war.

Dale was frightening, but Dale was hope.

This day, Will's company was departing with Sir Thomas Dale because the marshal wished to see Forts Henry and Charles for himself. Dale not only brought along soldiers, but also workmen. The rebuilding was beginning before Dale had even reached James Town. The rest of the fleet came along as well, for from here they would sail on to James Town.

The two forts stood near the mouth of the James River upon a rivulet Lord De La Warr had called the Southampton River.

Fort Charles stood closest to Fort Algernon. The ship docked here first.

Dale noted that the palisades were still strong, but the housing consisted of but a thatched cabin or two, sites where the men had once pitched tents, and several abandoned Indian homes covered with peeling bark.

Nearby, on the oppose side of the river, stood Fort Henry. Its condition was identical to its sister fort.

"Dear God," mumbled the marshal.

Will understood his company orders. He would spend the next four or five days setting acres of new corn while carpenters built cabins for the forts. Dale had decided that he would plant corn, leaving no dependence on infested food from England. Although, and this thought enraged Dale more, it was now mid-May, late in the planting season.

Meanwhile, Davis would command the three forts with each fort having a captain newly arrived in Virginia.

Hoping to find conditions better at James Town, Dale set off upriver. His face upon disembarking showed passion and anger. Dale espied a few unfortunate men bowling in the streets. He regarded this as evidence of the indolence of the entire colony—men, women, and children—even though the laws allowed men to bowl on Sunday after Sabbath services.

Yet in a blind fury, Dale ordered his soldiers to shackle and whip the bowlers—but not before he told them that he *ought* to hang them.

Dale's philosophy was soon clear. The solution to every problem lay in church, labor, whipping, or the gallows.

And as the snaps and cries echoed across town in the sweltering heat of a Virginia May, I felt chilled. My foreboding grew with each crack and groan.

Dale had left some of the three hundred new adventurers at Point Comfort. Others streamed from the ships here at James Town. Tired, wan from days of seasickness and the darkness of the 'tween deck, the newcomers straggled blinking into the light.

Standing in the dust of James Town's dry streets, we watched, and we knew: with summer coming hard upon us, probably only half of these staggering souls would survive. I truly wished to know none of them until a year had passed. Strange faces dying were easier to witness than familiar ones.

We old planters found ourselves in a peculiar position. We were trying to aid the sick and dying, all the while knowing that if they lived they would be but competitors for our own food, or that we might grow ill ourselves from tending them. Yet, the spark of hope remained: might some amongst them add more to the colony's welfare than they stole from it and from us?

Soldiers instructed the new settlers where to place their few belongings and trunks. Some might receive homes the dead no longer needed or live with old residents. Others would dig crude cabins in the ground or use linen as makeshift tents for now. Only the deaths of so many gave even this much housing.

Dale reckoned that two hundred had died since last summer. Three hundred newcomers meant one hundred were homeless for the moment. Clearly, the dangers in getting word across an ocean were that multitudes arrived before anyone in the colony knew to prepare for them. And even if they had known to prepare, most were too sick to do so.

We were certainly happier to see the animals than the people. Here were horses, cattle, goats, coneys, pigeons, poultry, cats for ratting, mastiffs, and even a bloodhound or two. Dale had more livestock aboard than even La Warr had brought. We were closer to reaching a time when we might be able to eat the flesh of these cows and hens, not just devour their eggs and milk.

A glance at the tools coming off ships showed this group to be largely artisans: coopers and carpenters, shipwrights and smiths, fishermen and tanners, brickmen and gardeners, husbandmen and laborers of all sorts, and more women, more children.

My Cecily, however, was not onboard. Instead, a soldier later handed me a letter from Cecily, saying that she was well and had met Lady Gates. Cecily wrote that she might be at sea even now. My heart thrilled. This was the first time in two years that I had word that she was alive.

However, I had meager time to think on this, as soldiers were barking orders even now. The feeble newcomers would have no chance to recover, as Dale had a work list, and all our names were on it.

A Pint of Sweat
May 19 to Mid-June, 1611 ~ James Town

A pint of sweat will save a gallon of blood.
—General George S. Patton, Jr.

Let me tell you all at home this one thing, and I pray remember it; if you give over this country and loose it, you, with your wisdoms, will leap such a gudgeon as our state hath not done the like since they lost the Kingdom of France....The more I range the country the more I admire it. I have seen the best countries in Europe....Put them all together, this country will be equivalent unto them if it be inhabitant with good people.
—Sir Thomas Dale, admonishing Virginia Company
Treasurer Sir Thomas Smythe, June 1613

After Secretary William Strachey formally swore in Dale as acting governor in De La Warr's absence, the Reverend Powell preached a Sunday sermon. Next, Dale met with the council and presented his list of improvements for the colony.

James Town, in Dale's view, was a military operation. As such, food and shelter were priorities so that the men might fight well.

The next day, soldier-leaders distributed work orders to companies and individuals and within hours the construction began.

In every direction, crews of men worked. The first were sawyers, preparing the plank. Soon, following the sound of the two-man saws, were the bangs of hammering and the blast of the forge, a new smith's forge. Nearby, other men fired brick as fast as they could. The dust flew, and sweat ran down the men's blood-red faces.

The day sweltered as Virginia's summer approached. But there was little rest or shade, not even for the women and older children for our names, too, were on the work orders.

As days wore on, we women and children settled into our assigned chores.

Some milked cows, gathered eggs, and churned butter. Others stitched and darned apparel, laundered the soldiers' clothes, worked the new gardens, rendered suet into tallow for candles and soap, cleaned the barracks or church, or gathered plants for brewing experiments or whatever tasks Dale had assigned. There were no choices, no arguments. Our days were preordained.

Early morn, we wakened upon drums beating. This would be about the time the sun rose at five o' clock. I prepared a meal using the last remaining portion of the previous day's allotment of food. We must finish all dressing and eating by six o'clock, when another drum signaled the start of the work morning.

We toiled until ten o'clock when the church bell called us to the church for divine service. When we had finished with our prayers, we returned home and waited for a storehouse clerk to bring us the day's portion of food. This gave us just a short while to prepare a midday meal.

At two o'clock, the drummer commanded us back to work for two more hours. Then at four o'clock, the tolling bell called us to our second church service of the day. From there, home for our evening meals.

Drums and bells, bells and drums. The sounds of life, the sounds we lived by.

This was every day, Monday through Saturday, except on Wednesday when Reverend Bucke also preached after the first divine service. We heard two sermons a week amidst fourteen church services.

Sunday there was no work. We stayed close to home for prayers. At eleven in the morning, we walked to the church for divine service and preaching.

After the Sabbath midday meal, Reverend Bucke conducted yet another divine service. Then the children went to catechism while we adults returned home for more prayers.

In truth, we did not pray all day Sunday. More often than not, we slipped over to one another's homes for fellowship. For us, that secretly meant news and gossip with Dale not looking over our shoulders.

Dale placed the women who had been in Virginia longest as leaders of each task. Thomasine Causey, a Starving Time survivor, and I were in charge of rendering suet into tallow and later tallow into soap and candles. We had six women to help us, all from Dale's fleet.

"Thomasine, these women do not look in fit condition to work," I whispered. She nodded, eyeing the frail and the battered. But such was not our decision to make, and so we began with a certain amount of suet, an amount of tallow to be rendered at day's end. We would report numbers and quantities to an ensign. We were responsible for these women's work—and they looked hardly able to care for themselves, much less to stand over a large cauldron outside in the summer heat. Thomasine and I pleaded with the ensign for an old tarp we might hang above us.

"These women will die if they do not have shade," Thomasine said, her hands on her hips. She didn't seem afraid of a whipping. "We have those carrying babes. Do you want the life of a baby on your hands, sir?"

The ensign checked with his captain, and we received the tarp. It had holes, but it kept most of the sun from beating upon us. We considered this a victory.

One woman, Mistress Woodlief, tried to stir the pot as the water inside began to bubble. She seemed weak, and I heaved a sigh. "Let me," I said, somewhat impatiently. Would we receive a flogging because these women were likely to fall to seasoning?

Yet a glance over my shoulder told me that Mistress Woodlief was distressed. Her eyes welled with tears. She knew she could not be up to the task given her. And I suspected Mistress Fontaine was getting an ague. Her eyes were too sparkly, her cheeks too rosy on the sickly face. With a sinking feeling, I realized that we would not only be responsible for the work of eight women, we would likely do most of it ourselves or risk punishment.

Will had told me that by coming early after the signing of the Second Charter we would have advantages not given to those later. Yet this was not what I had expected. I did not mind candle making, or soap making, or any of the tasks assigned to the women. Any country housewife would expect to do these things to keep her household in good order. Were we to fail, we would have answered to our husbands.

But now we were working at one task each, monitoring other women as Dale monitored us. A poor turnout, Dale proclaimed, meant whipping. We would not have the satisfaction of seeing the fruits of our work filling the cellars in our own homes. All goods were to go instead to a common store, which gave us little enthusiasm for our work.

Gradually, the suet became liquid, the bits of meat left to be strained away. By later today, the suet would be tallow, and after that, soap and candles. It was a hot, smelly task, and I could not help but envy those working on the gardens. Thomasine, alongside me, concurred.

"Well, Joan, by my leave, we did get the worst of the lot, didn't we?"

I groaned, which would do for agreement. Typically, in England, we rendered tallow during autumn and winter, but candles and soap we desperately needed. Suet had come on Dale's fleet, and those dressing venison had collected deer suet. Candles would not wait until the days were short, barked Dale. And unlike England, we were not making these goods for our own homes. We ourselves might never have use of them.

"When, Thomasine, did we become soldiers because our husbands did?"

Tempie was in charge of a group beating soldiers' breeches, shirts, jerkins, and doublets. Annie Laydon and Joan Wright, the midwife, oversaw the sewing of shirts and the repairing of tattered clothing. Judith Perry, a newcomer, worked alongside them as best she could.

Maria Bucke sat at a churn. I noticed how hot and uncomfortable she looked, for she was five months along with her first baby. *Poor dear, to work so hard,* I thought. No one rested with Dale in charge.

Dale had another plan that women should attempt trials of brewing as country wives did at home. Water, here or in England, was a terrible choice for a beverage. It made a body ill, certainly. And here we were, drinking the water and staying sick.

After several days and the dipping of many candles, Thomasine and I began a new daily task. Dale's men assigned us to the forest to collect sassafras. The friendly little plant with leaves resembling mittens had so far proven to be one of our best commodities along with lumber.

Fifty years before, the Indians had taught the French at Fort Caroline, south of here, that sassafras could cure fever and other ills. One day, the Spanish had suddenly attacked the little colony, killing the men and capturing the women and children. When the Spaniards became sick, a captured Frenchwoman told them sassafras, the ague tree, could cure them. The soldiers recovered, returning to Spain to tell all of Europe the wonders of sassafras. The plant's value was growing as quickly as the sassafras itself sprang up in our forests. Sometimes we even saw sailors off ships gathering sassafras to sell back home.

The Spanish had devastated and ended the French settlement. *Well we know they can do the same to us,* I thought, looking at the sprig in my hand. Odd how a little mittened plant could remind us of our own lingering danger.

At six in the morning, our work began, the sun barely up and the woods filled with the chipper sound of Virginia birds.

A bright yellow bird with black hood and wings sang high above while below a tiny bird hummed past in a blur of bright greens and blues as it moved toward the sweet wildflowers. Yellow, black, green, azure, grey, white, and red—the colorful Virginia birds could almost make me forget the drudgery of digging sassafras for hours on end. Almost, but not quite.

Sassafras ran wild along the edges of the forest. We used spades to dig the low plants and broke off branches we could reach from the larger trees.

Once we had gathered enough sassafras, I felt sure Dale would order us to grind the bark and roots into powder. Ships would then carry the powder home as a possible commodity. The king himself had requested his own supply of sassafras. Surely we would keep some for our own medicinal use as well.

Without ripe berries or corn yet, we would use sassafras roots as our first trial at brewing beer. The crushed leaves we found could thicken a pottage, allowing us to avoid using the spoiled wheat.

"How full is your basket, Joan?" Margery Fairfax called to me. Margery had come in with Sir Thomas Gates, and I found I liked her very much.

"Well, many a plant to dig yet," I said. My basket was not nearly half full. I knelt and chipped at the ground with the spade, being sure to get the valuable roots as well.

"Beer, eh? Sassafras beer? I'll believe *that* when I taste it!" Thomasine spoke up.

"Ah, give me a hearty ale or beer, even a claret when the money's good." This was Isabella Pace, a new arrival from Dale's fleet.

"Don't dream of home and ale, dear." Thomasine heaved up a plant, dirt spraying around her. She held it up for Isabella to see. "You'll be drinking the likes of this or worse. Welcome to your new home!"

"And in the fall, pumpion beer, I'd reckon," I said, more or less to myself. What could an orange beer taste like?

Judith seemed to be feeling faint and said little, but I could tell she knew better than to sit. We must have filled baskets by the end of the day. Dale did not permit us to rest during the given work hours, and a whipping for a first offense awaited those who did not fulfill their tasks. The message was clear.

Labor along quickly or feel Dale's wrath.

In Tattered Kirtle Blue
Mid-June 1611 ~ James Town

We shall draw from the heart of suffering itself the means of inspiration and survival.
—Winston Churchill

Just a slip o' girl in tattered kirtle blue...
—Martha Haskell Clark

Elsewhere, women prepared kitchen gardens while men worked at common gardens as quickly as they possibly could. The time for sowing rapidly closed. One could sense Dale's agitation at having arrived so late to oversee planting when our need for food and clothing was dire.

"Ah, we'll be spinning by the end of the year," Thomasine said. "Not sure how I feel about that."

I nodded. Within a few days of arrival, Dale had gone to the mainland across from James Town. He had surveyed the old Paspahegh town, since deserted, seeking land to set hemp and flax. I could still see the Paspahegh queen's death march after we had killed her children, something I tried to force from my mind.

However, Dale had found other land for the sowing. Men were pitching seeds of hemp and flax in the common gardens as we ourselves planted carrots, turnips, onions, parsnips, radishes, and beets.

The hemp and flax would be up by the end of September. Dale would send laborers, perhaps boys and girls as well, to pull the yellowing plants up by their roots, not a bit of cordage wasted! Then came rippling to rake out the seeds, retting to rot away the outside, breaking the stalks, scutching to remove the woody stem, and heckling to comb the strands until the long, flaxen-blonde stricks were ready to spin.

The hemp and flax stricks would then be ours to spin into linen thread for ropes and clothing.

"Aye. Reckon we'll start with spindle and whorl until carpenters finish some spinning wheels," added Lydia, a Starving Time survivor from Point Comfort.

"*If* we get spinning wheels," Isabella said.

Thomasine paused to look at the women scooping seeds out with their hands. "Oh, Dale will have flax wheels made. Never you mind that. With all our need for it? For sails and rope first, I'll say."

"Clothing last." My voice sounded resigned. We were receiving little in the way of garments. Our future clothes were there in the far fields, in some farmer's hand, waiting to fall onto the soil.

"Aye, and the clothing of the dead don't help much."

'Twas true enough. After the clothes we brought from England wore out, it was all the same. We lived in rags and died in rags.

Spinning had been our task in England, and the task of our mothers and their mothers before them so far back into time that no one knew when the first woman began twisting strands of flax or wool to make clothing thread. We expected to spin. Almost every one of us had a spindle and whorl tucked away for handspinning. But 'til now we'd had no use for it. We'd no had flax or hemp or wool, so there was naught we could spin. But soon, under Dale's watchful eye, we would at least have the plants if not the sheep.

No, the trouble lay not in spinning but in the fact that we *hadn't been* spinning for two years, that we'd had nothing to spin, and we had no way to purchase linen. We had brought thread with us and had rationed it as best we could. Periodically, a ship coming in brought some new. But this wasn't nearly enough. No wonder we all sought the clothing of those who died. The dead had no need of raiment, and we, the living, did. Sorely, we did.

I studied my own kirtle, bodice, and petticoat, once cream and blue, now grey and brown and growing more tattered every hour. It seemed we were all in rags such that we scarcely noticed how impoverished we all looked. We had grown used to seeing one another and ourselves in tatters. The only time we brushed our hands across our dresses as if to straighten them and to give them, magically, new color, thread, and life was at the arrival of a new ship.

And some woman would always say to the rest of us, "Worry not, my ladies. Those rumpled sea-weary women will look as we do soon enough!"

Someone else would say, "If only we but looked as they! *Not* the other way around."

Finally would come the thought on every woman's mind. *But when the seasoning claims most of them, we'll claim the clothes, sure!*

We were the survivors. We would keep the clothes.

Buildings went up so quickly that I could scarcely recognize the town.

Here a new munitions house, there a house for powder. Some of the men were working on a sturgeon-dressing house while others made casks to hold the sturgeon.

Spades and hoes dug out chunks of James Town Island, seeking the water for a new well.

Captain Lawson and his men pounded at planks that would soon be a stable for the horses.

Another captain oversaw the building of a barn for cattle to lodge in winter; the rest of the year it would store hay. And then a new blockhouse at the north side of the Back River would protect the cattle from Indians.

While ornery Captain Brewster and his crew repaired the church and storehouse, Captain Newport and the mariners built a bridge for a dry, safe place to unlade goods.

Dale had at last allotted private gardens for each man as well as the common one for flax and hemp and other seeds brought from England. We had no ploughs yet, so we managed with what we had: the spade and the hoe. The very wee hours of the morning or the evenings would find us wearily pulling weeds from our own gardens or tidying our homes. Complaining was needless; it brought only the whip.

Those same hours would also find us teaching our children reading and reckoning, for we had no schools and no teachers who had survived. I sat with Janey, teaching her the alphabet and arithmetic on a slate. For reading, we used the Bible and, hoping the Lord wouldn't mind, I also sat her in front of Gerard's *Herball, or, Generall Historie of Plants.* We began at chapter one, Meadow Grass. She and I were both tired but worked as long as daylight allowed. Sometimes, I even lit a candle if we could go a bit longer.

This will be fine for girls, but will never do for a son, I thought.

The days were long and the afternoons oppressively hot. At the end of each day, Tempie and I stumbled into the second church service, dirt smeared across our sweaty faces, clothes never to come clean, not that they ever had been. Sore, aching, tired. Blisters on our feet and too much sun on our faces, straw hats and all. We tried not to fall asleep as Reverend Bucke read the services.

And the reward for all this? A rebuilt James Town, and Dale had not even been in Virginia three weeks.

His next plan, as soon as he had sufficiently set the corn, was to head upriver to locate a site for the new town he planned to build, one that would afford protection against the Spanish that James Town could not. We would not be another Fort Caroline, God willing, struck to the ground by angry Spaniards.

However, before that could happen, the Indians and Dale were about to have their first encounter—one neither would soon forget.

Great Witches Amonge Them
Late June 1611 ~ James Town

*And to him they had regard, because…he had bewitched
them with sorceries.*
—Acts 8:11

Theire bee great witches amonge them…
—Reverend Alexander Whitaker about the Indians, 1611

"Oh, I know not what to make of it." Will, home for a few days, held a
pipe in his good hand. "'Twas the devil's magic—had to be!" He took
a sip of newly brewed sassafras beer. "Hm, well, I suppose it will cure what
ails a body."

That was true enough. Yet it remained a poor man's brew.

"Tastes horrible, though." Sam Jordan, who had arrived with Will, made
a face. "Uh, I intend no offense, Joan."

I cocked an eyebrow at him. "I take none, cousin. It's not your Kings
Arms ale, I take it?"

He shuddered as he swallowed.

I grimaced. "Well, there's my answer."

I had wrapped rags about Will's other hand where the blood from battle
had dried and gone dark. Will had winced as I poured first sassafras tincture
then vinegar over the wound, hoping both would keep it from going green.
Now time would tell. Time, prayer, sassafras and vinegar. A green wound
could be deadly. The thought made me uneasy, but the hand seemed to be
healing.

Sam remained lively in spite of his weariness with war. "Never fought a
battle like that in the Lowlands, did we?" he said to Will. He pushed his hair
back, making the bruises on his face that much more obvious.

Now that I'd tended the wounds, I was curious about the way the men
had referred to this strange fight. "What kind of battle has devil's magic?" I
asked them, taking a seat at the table.

"Well," Sam began, his eyes lighting to the story. "Dale wanted to find the source of the Nansemond River, which meant sailing upriver past the hostile Nansemond towns."

Will nodded, content to let Sam tell the story.

"The Indians attacked as expected, and we skirmished on water and on land. There we were. Dale had us in full armor. *Full* armor, mind you.

I smiled. Sam was Sam—his battle stories of the Lowlands, his battle stories here.

"Into the old Indian town we came marching, a silvery clatter of metal and swords and matchlocks, no less than a hundred men. We were taking the town. The full armor, that was to intimidate." The Indians had seen morions and breastplates, but never a man whose whole body was made of metal.

"Well," Sam continued, "Dale wanted to frighten, and frighten he did! The sun glinted off us, a bright glare, making it hard even for us to see. Then, Joan, the native war cry! To make your blood chill. Some came running with *tomahawks*, their war hatchets. And suddenly from the brush a firestorm of arrows. One banged off my breastplate, its force knocking me backward. But I never fell. The rumbling of stone arrows hitting armor drummed like rain pounding on metal all around us."

Will put in, "Sword on tomahawk! We couldn't refire the matchlocks fast enough. Their arrows but glanced off us. You could see the Nansemond confusion. Why did we not fall as we had done before? Our body armor was magic to the Indians, but soon enough, they discovered our eyes," Will added, pointing with a knuckle to his own eyes.

"Our eyes, Joan," Sam explained. "They quickly realized our only vulnerable spot. So they began the tomahawk swing to the face and arrows aimed for the eye."

Will shrugged. "Most of us took a few hits to the morion."

"Did you?" I asked. I usually tried not to think of how dangerous battle could be, even in full armor.

He nodded. "They struck my morion, missed my eyes," Will said with characteristic simplicity. "But Dale, by St. George, there's a charmed one."

This fired Sam up once more. "Did you see it, Will? I did! Hit the brim—" He motioned to his brow. "And old Percy cried, 'One thought lower, and they'd have shot his brains!'"

"Heated battle, too," Sam went on. "Despite the armor, we took many a wound. An arrow pierced Captain West's thigh, and another bloodied Captain Martin's arm. Aye, and many a common soldier felt the arrow's stab."

These captains were some of our leading men. I suddenly understood we could have lost Dale, West, and Martin, all at once.

"The captains are recovering now?" I asked. Will and Sam nodded together.

Of course, it was the same with foot soldier or captain. A bloody wound could kill.

"Yet the Indians slew none of our men while we took many of them down. Still, a tough fight," Will said heavily, studying the red rag around his hand.

I was perplexed. "But what about the sorcery?"

"Ah, Joan, I'm getting to that," Sam said. By this time, Janey had come in and was sitting on the bench, rapt upon Sam's story.

"Sorcery? Is it sorcery you wish to hear of, young lady?" Sam said with a flourish.

"Yes, sir!" she said eagerly. Her words were a lisp since one front tooth had fallen out.

"Ah, well, you see, after several battles, we returned to our ships. And what do you know? We hear a great commotion of chantin' and howlin' from the shore. And one of their *quiyoughcosoughs* led a mighty procession." He paused to look a Janey. "You know what be a *qui-yough-co-sough*?"

"A priest?"

I was in awe. We were all becoming familiar with native words and customs, even Janey.

"That's so. An Indian priest. And he had great smoky things in either hand like censers blowing incense in our church, throwing fire to the heavens. The crowd of Indians danced and whooped. Most words we could not understand. Some of our soldiers said the jumping reminded them of our Morris dancers...."

"But why were they dancing?" Janey asked.

"Well, we might not have known, Janey, had Mechumps not been aboard."

Namontack, Kemps, and Mechumps were three of our close Indian allies. *Mawchick chamay,* they often said. *The best of friends!* All had lived at the fort at times. Kemps, a close friend of Captain Percy, had died recently. Namontack and young Mechumps had sailed to England before I had arrived, and both had been returning to Virginia aboard the *Sea Venture* when it wrecked on the Bermudas.

Yet, only one brave had come home to Virginia. Rumor had it that Mechumps had killed Namontack on the island there, but as yet Mechumps had not confessed.

Despite this cloud of suspicion, Mechumps had remained a loyal friend. Upon returning to Virginia, the brave had gone to Orapax to see his sister Winganuske and her husband, the great Chief Powhatan. A year had passed since then.

Occasionally, if Powhatan agreed, Mechumps came to visit the fort again. Powhatan, it seemed, could not decide whether Mechumps served as spy for the great chief or for us. As our ally, Mechumps had been steadfast.

Mechumps had been with the men when they went up to the falls the past winter when the Appomattocks had killed the miners. He had also been at the fort when the men departed for Nansemond, and so the brave offered to serve as guide. All things English seemed to intrigue him as if he considered it a grand adventure.

"So Mechumps offered an explanation for all the dancing?" I asked.

"Aye." Will drew from his pipe. "He said, 'Soon, you will see the black *arrahaquotuwhs*—rainclouds—and very much *kameyhan*. Rain.' Mechumps held his hands upward as if to catch it. 'Heavy rain. They try to put out your matches and to wet and soil your powder.'"

"And then?" I asked, fascinated.

Sam went on. "The soldiers within earshot hooted. 'Well, tell 'em to give us a good crack of thunder, too, Mechumps!' cried one. But a boom from the heavens interrupted the jester, mid-laugh. All the men looked upward, as the sky suddenly darkened, thunder crashed overhead, and lightning sprayed the sky. And the men were not laughing any more, but running for cover. Five miles in every direction, the rain poured, leaving us all in wonder. It did not destroy our powder, though."

"Well, that's a relief!" I said. I understood that the shortage of powder was already a problem for us.

Will put in, "Then Mechumps said almost sternly, 'It is not wise to laugh at the rain god, my friend.' And one soldier ventured, 'Do they...do they truly cast a magic spell with the dance, Mechumps?' to which Mechumps replied, 'It is prayer, not magic. The *quiyoughcosoughs* do not reveal their ways. But they know how to reach the gods. And if you call it magic, they will be glad of this.' And he said no more."

Sam leaned back in his chair. "Our next journey, Dale led us further up-river to the falls, the same Indian stronghold where both Captain West and Lord De La Warr had retreated," Sam continued. "Dale would not retreat. This we knew. We went upriver in spite of Chief Powhatan warning us not to go."

Will said, "When Dale and Powhatan had met beforehand, the chief ordered Dale to stay away from that territory. The land upriver joins land belonging to the Monacans, Powhatan's enemies. Perhaps the chief is afraid we might one day band with the Monacans against him."

Dale told the chief that indeed he would go. If there were mines up there, Dale intended to find them.

Then Powhatan had spoken in his own language, as interpreter Harry Spelman translated. Spelman told Dale, "Powhatan says, 'I will make you drunk in six or seven days, Thomas Dale.'"

At these words, Dale had smirked. "How shall you do this? I am a temperate man." Dale had laughed at the challenge.

Harry had then posed this question to Powhatan, who replied in his native tongue, gesturing with his hands as his dark eyes flashed.

Harry relayed the message to the marshal. "The chief is not happy. His reply is, 'I say not how. You do not believe me, then? Wait and see, Newcomer. Six or seven days, that is all.'"

Will continued, "And so we went up river. The sixth night, we were at evening prayers, the chief's threat long forgotten," Will said evenly. "Dale and Percy and some of the better sort were using an Indian house as a *Corps de Garde*."

Sam broke in. "Suddenly, one fellow jumped up and looked about anxiously. 'Hear that?' he cried. We were camping on the ground nearby and heard it, too. From the cornfields echoed ghostly chants, drifting toward us. '*Oho oho hup hup. Oho oho hup hup. Oho oho hup hup!*' And...this, I swear an oath. But every English soldier on the ground appeared Indian to me!"

I looked from one man to the other. "You, too, Will? You saw men change into Indians?"

Will, practical Will, said simply. "I was bewitched."

"We started fighting one another, hitting each other in the head with the butts of our muskets, brawling like sailors," Sam said. "Strangest thing I ever did see." He turned to Will. "You looked like you were in full war paint and deerskins."

Will seemed embarrassed. "We don't know what happened."

I was incredulous. "Dale, too? Dale was fighting his fellow captains as if they were braves?"

"Dale, too," both men said as one.

It's true that never had the Nansemonds seen silver soldiers impenetrable to arrows.

But then neither could our men understand how the *quiyoughcosoughs* used their sorcery to hammer rain down or to bewitch them. All this left us wondering, did the Indians call on gods or devils? And did these entities have any power over us?

However, we had little time to mull on this, for we were soon to face a greater threat, one from across the ocean.

Not Single Spies, But in Battalions
July 1611 ~ James Town

Within a month, 4 ships with 300 men, a few women and many arms and ammunition are to leave England for [Virginia]. They have orders to fortify themselves once more and to build ships....If they leave [Virginia]...they can reach [Cuba] within 6 days sail, and it would be...very serious...for my fleets....Send out and obtain...what this means about Virginia, what forces and what strength they have....Be learned and prepared in your parts, so that no injury be done, reporting to me...with great exactness...
   —King Philip III of Spain, ordering the Cuban governor
   to spy on Virginia, February 20, 1611

When sorrows come, they come not single spies, but in battalions!
—William Shakespeare

66 Spanish prisoners in the Big House!" Maria, now great with child, said in a low tone one morning. She had heard her husband talking with the marshal.

We were back to gathering sassafras. I sometimes thought if I should see one more little green mitten pushing up from the soil, I should hack it. And not to harvest it. Then Maria's words sunk in.

How had Spaniards gotten here? What had happened? Suddenly, I had a foreboding I could not explain. As women, we could only receive news from our husbands or soldiers like Walter we had befriended. Will and Sam provided much, but they had since departed back to the forts at the sea. However, Tempie's husband George Yeardley had not yet left.

"Do you know anything else, Maria?" I asked breathlessly.

She shrugged. "I heard some little parts. A Spanish caravel came to Point Comfort. The captain pretended to be searching for a lost ship, but Captain Davis knew he was lying. The men feel sure 'twas a spying expedition. The wretched Spanish are trying to determine what we have, how big we are, how many forts and fighting men. That is why the marshal and captains believe the Spanish have come."

'Twas rare for Maria to call anyone *wretched*. But her baby was due soon, and she was weary. And news such as this certainly wearied us all.

"And the capture?" My spade was poised. I had ceased digging and now stood up.

"I don't know. There was a scuffle of some type. In the process, we seized three Spaniards, one of whom we believe to be an English traitor! *Armada* traitor," she said soberly.

I gasped. "Good Lord, Maria. No!" How could an Englishman betray his nation in her time of greatest peril? The Spanish had fought to conquer our shores in 1588. I had been but eight years old, but I could remember the fear we'd felt. After all, my family did live on the southern coast quite close to Spain. The Spanish had crossed the Bay of Biscay and entered the Narrow Sea. God had been with England then when great winds and storms blew the Spanish fleet back. Had it not been so, we might now have a Spanish-Catholic monarch. A thought too awful to bear. Now, we had an Armada traitor in our midst?

"A traitor of the worst sort. Now, he's piloted a Spanish ship into the Chesapeake's Bay," Maria said.

I was trying to understand, and so I pressed for more details, but Maria held up her hand. "I know little more than that," she said.

During church service, Maria and I pleaded with Tempie to question George, who might know more. Midday meal would be Tempie's opportunity.

"This I will do," she promised.

Tempie returned after the two o'clock drum call with what she'd been able to gather from her husband.

"Ladies, come hither and listen." Maria, Thomasine, and I stood close.

"We've captured three Spanish. One, the traitor calling himself Lembri. Another, Don de Molina, is a Spanish nobleman. A third we know little about. The marshal is certain they are spies. This man Molina is furious at his capture. He's dangerous, that's what the men are saying."

This confirmed rumors Dale's fleet had brought—rumors that the Spanish king and his ambassadors were watching us. Tempie went on. "We believe this ship came from Cuba. But *that* is not the disturbing part."

Each of us held our breaths, for this was already quite disturbing.

"The Spanish have captured our own master pilot, John Clark. So these three Spaniards will be hostages until—if—we can secure Clark's release. But the great fear is thus: before any ransoming can take place, the Spanish shall force Clark to lead a fleet back to us, and he will guide the warships upriver to James Town and to us."

Up, Men, to Your Posts!
August 2, 1611 ~ James Town

Up, men, to your posts! Don't forget today that you are from old Virginia.
—General George Pickett at Gettysburg, 1863

All arms, all arms! Bells tolled, and drums beat. Something was amiss. Something big.

George, Will, and Sam were still at the Eastern forts down by the mouth of the bay. My hands were deep in a bucket of water as I rinsed trenchers from the midday meal.

With George and Will away, Tempie was staying at my home so that we could share chores. Tempie had gone out to the well for more water, and Janey, now six, was in the garden pulling weeds. The drummer would soon signal us to begin the two o'clock shift, but this was not the steady rhythm we heard to begin work. No, not at all. The drummer was urgent, pounding hard and fast.

I dried my hands as I ran to the door, and Janey met me there. The fear on her little face was palpable.

In James Town, such an alarm could mean anything. The Paspahegh Indians had massacred every man at the blockhouse just a few months before, and despite all our preparations and bluffing, we felt vulnerable to attack if all the natives should band together. As well, the fear of a Spanish attack lingered since we had captured the Spaniards a month before.

Now my heart thundered in my chest as I watched soldiers gathering arms and racing to defensive positions. Some soldiers took their posts at the ordnance. Others held great snarling mastiffs, pulling against their chains. Clouds of dust billowed in the torrid August heat, and I understood immediately that the leaders perceived a serious threat to the settlement.

"To your homes, latch doors and windows!" cried one soldier, and I yanked Janey's hand into the house and slammed the door behind me. What, I wondered, was I slamming the door against?

"Tempie!" I screamed in sudden panic. She was beyond the bounds of the palisade at the well.

"Go beneath the bed!" I said to Janey, who nodded with solemn eyes and looked as if she would rather be with me. "Go now!" I ordered. "'Tis not time to stand idle!"

Seeing that my raised voice had increased her terror, I touched her hair and forced calmness upon myself. In a low deliberate tone, I said, "Go now, and wait for me. I must flag a soldier."

"Yes, ma'am," she whispered and turned to crawl under the bedstead.

Without looking back, I unlatched the door and tried to hail a passing soldier. All were fully armed and wearing breastplates and morions. Their clattering swords, pikes, armor, and matchlocks created a racket as they took positions around the perimeter of the fort. The clamor was deafening.

"A woman is at..." I began, but their bustling noise and hurry drowned my words. None of them paid me any mind.

I spied Walter, my friend, and tried to get his attention.

Mercifully, he saw me and paused just a moment, always with a speck of compassion for me ever since the day he had supervised Maggie's secret burial.

"Walter, Tempie's at the well! What is the alarm? Can she get back? Is it Paspaheghs or..."

Uncharacteristically flustered, Walter shook his head. "She'll get back if she hurries! No Indians, mistress. A fleet o' nine caravels off the coast!"

My heart dropped on the word. *Caravels.* The Spanish warship.

We Shall Defend Our Island
August 2, 1611 ~ James Town

We shall defend our island, whatever the cost may be, we shall fight on the beaches, we shall fight on the landing grounds, we shall fight in the fields and in the streets, we shall fight in the hills; we shall never surrender.
—Sir Winston Churchill

Had the Spanish forced the pilot Clark to lead them upriver? Had they already attacked Point Comfort? What of Will, Sam, and George? Had the Spanish overrun Forts Henry and Charles near the mouth of the bay? The more questions raced through my mind, the harder my heart thundered, and I realized I was shaking very hard.

Dale's full military training in the Lowlands showed as he turned into a field commander. With a sword raised, he shouted commands at two men, Captain Brewster and Lieutenant Abbott, ordering them downriver to learn what they could. Dale screamed at them, "All haste to the Point! Report back with details!"

Apparently an alarm had come from Point Comfort. Nine ships spied on the horizon, at least three of them with the distinctive sails and high poop deck of Spanish caravels. Captain Davis had sent a ship up to James Town with this message: *Spanish caravels en route to the mouth of the Bay. All arms!*

Now Dale was sending his top captain to find out more about the situation. Brewster and Abbott quickly loaded themselves and some forty men onto a ship and loosed it from its moorings.

As Brewster and Abbot's ship fought a contrary wind downriver, the leaders disappeared into the *corps de garde*—Dale, Percy, Strachey, Newport.

Dale must have called an emergency council meeting, I realized. I looked worriedly past the gates. *Where was Tempie?* All about me, men were preparing for battle, serious battle. There was not a man or woman who did not understand the scope of the situation.

If the Spanish wanted to bring little James Town to the ground, they could do it.

Minutes later, the leaders emerged looking flustered and even frightened. To see fear on Governor Dale's face—he, always so stoic—made me know that we may have fought our last battle.

Through the din of clanking and rattling armor, shouted commands, and boots pounding dust, I saw that the men were preparing to load our three remaining ships: the *Star,* the *Prosperous,* and the Bermuda-made *Deliverance.* Nine Spanish ships to our three. I was not a soldier, but I could count.

Two men pushed the north gate of the *palisado* shut, dropping its bolt. I realized it was the closest entry for Tempie if she were still at the well.

Dale was urging his men to get munitions onboard. "Faster, faster!" he cried. The soldiers were scrambling at full speed.

I needed to know more. I had learned well from Maggie. An ally on the inside was the only way to survive.

Never be at the mercy of forces, Maggie's voice seemed to urge me. *Get your own news from someone who knows, and then make you a wise decision.* Yes, Maggie, yes. But it was not always so simple!

The blacksmith Dobbs was going house to house, telling the women and children to get inside their homes and stay. When he came to me, I did not race back inside.

"Why are they loading the ships?"

He gave me an impatient look, but I attempted to block his way though I was much smaller than he was. I hammered words at him before he could interrupt. "A woman has not returned from the well, and I need to know what is happening!" My voice was part demand, part plea, and my eyes rapidly filled with frustrated, frightened tears. I was so tired of being, as Maggie said, at the mercy of forces over which I had no control.

I wiped the tears away with the back of my hand and saw them nearly mud from the dust. 'Twas no use. I dropped my head, defeated, expecting Dobbs to pass on without answering me. I was, after all, but a woman.

Yet, a woman's tears have some value, and in this case, they worked. Dobbs spat on the ground and narrowed his eyes. His disgust seemed to be for the soldiers and not for me.

"Council had to decide whether to meet the Spanish dogs in the river or try to hold 'em from the fort. So ol' Percy, he says, 'How 'bout we meet 'em in the river, 'cause our men can't run away in ships!'" Dobbs gave a laugh, something of a cackle, and I saw that most of his teeth were blackened or gone. I was glad he found this amusing. However, my husband was a soldier, his life was in danger, I had a terrified little girl under the bed, and my dearest friend was somewhere outside the fort, probably locked out.

"Thank you kindly, sir," I said coldly and turned to walk into the house. I was finding it hard to be grateful to this man, however helpful he had just been. Perhaps I wanted to take all my fear out on him, just as he wanted to take his hatred of the colony out on the soldiers.

"Mistress!" he called firmly. I turned to look at him. His voice had softened. "Your friend will have plenty of time to return. She probably just can't get back yet, what with all the commotion and the forest gate being bolted." I nodded. The tears had not stopped, and all I could say was, "Pray God, you are right, sir."

Just then, drums caught my ears—a signal to the troops, who instantly silenced their activity. Dale was shouting again, waving his rapier menacingly. His eyes were wild.

"'Tis a fair westerly wind that shall carry the Spanish upriver before we can load all our munitions! If we can but lade and prepare ourselves, we *can* be victorious. Yet, if God hath ordained an end to our lives this day, we can do no better than to die in service to our God, our king, and our prince!" A slight cracking on the word *prince*. "God be with us! We shall light our ships afire and charge the caravels. We shall take down as many bloody Spaniards as we can!"

Fire ships. Dale was prepared to set the small James Town fleet afire as the English had done to fight the Spanish Armada. A frightening mix of fiery ships and explosions. Englishmen swimming away before the barks collided *if* they were fortunate enough to get overboard in the fray.

Now I knew all I needed to know. Dale intended to fight to the death.

A Ship in Harbor
August 2, 1611 ~ James Town

A ship in harbor is safe, but that is not what ships are built for.
—John A. Shedd

Once back in the house, I slammed and latched the shutters, banishing some of the sounds of soldiers preparing for battle. But I disobeyed the order to lock the door. Tempie was not home, and I would not lock her out.

Terrified, Janey whimpered beneath the bed.

"Come out, lovey. Come out," I said gently. She had been a good little soldier herself, all through our time at James Town. Now I felt compassion for the small one trembling alone beneath the bed.

She pulled herself out, and I saw that her tears had run in dirty rivulets down her face. She fell into my arms, and we both sobbed together. I did not try to hide my fear this time, for her embrace comforted me as mine comforted her. She pushed her face into my bodice as though a threat she could not see did not exist.

I thought about all she had endured so young. At her age, I was living comfortably in England's Melcombe Regis, racing safely between flower and herb gardens in my backyard. My mother had been there consoling, planting, reaping, teaching me about herbs. My father had been at sea a great deal, 'twas true, importing and exporting goods to ports in Ireland and England. Still, when he had come home, it had been cause for celebration. They were days I had hoped would never end.

Now I looked at my own daughter, who didn't even know *why* we were huddled, why the alarms had sounded. Only a few months had passed since the day we'd heard the Paspahegh war cries as their warriors had overrun the blockhouse. Then, we had waited, holding our breaths, fearing the Indians would come into our homes. But other soldiers had stopped them. Janey had heard the same sounds now as then, the brattling of the men's armor as they braced for attack nearby.

Terrifying then, and terrifying now with the Spanish at our door. I felt dizzy with fear, light-headed, weak.

Had I failed Janey? We could have been home in Melcombe this very minute, safe upon the harbor.

A thought intruded. *But were you truly safe?*

I considered that for a moment as the minutes ticked idly by. I had no idea how much time had passed. It was as well to distract myself with thoughts.

We had not been safe when I was eight years old, living in a southwest harbor town, when the Spanish Armada had attacked the harbor. We had expected to fall; all Europe had expected us to fall. The Spanish had been attacking us from the south, sailing up our Narrow Sea and planning to make landfall.

The Spanish had wanted England, wanted her to be Spanish property, to convert the English Protestant threat to their Catholicism, and to reunify the Catholic Church. The Spanish goal was to place a Catholic monarch upon our throne, thus ending our English identity forever.

We had held our ground then, but our resources were dwindling in England. That much was undeniable, and we had yet to recover from all the trees pulled down to build ships to fight the Armada.

No, we were not safe in harbor. We only *thought* we were safe, but the Spanish were a threat either way.

In Virginia, we were risking all for England, for a land greater than the Spanish could one day take from us. Because this truth remained: if we were not equal to the Spanish power, she would one day overrun our English borders.

As she might overrun our Virginia borders this day.

If this were to be our last day at James Town, then so be it. We had tried. I was too weary, too fearful, to resist. I felt so nauseous I thought I might need to run out behind the house to be sick. But this was illegal. Illegal to do one's business too near the house. *Where was the chamber pot?* I glanced around. There. Nearby. The wave passed, struck again. Passed once more.

Should it be a constant battle simply to stay alive?

The most comforting Psalm we knew was the one I had prayed during the hurricane at sea, the twenty-third Psalm. I began to hum it for my little girl, hoping it would quiet her shaking. Bless her, she was so afraid.

Dreamlike thoughts raced through my mind as though they were logical and ordinary.

I thought again of the sassafras and old Fort Caroline. I remembered how the Spanish had let the fort stand for some little time and then had suddenly attacked. With superior numbers and surprise on their side, the Spanish put all the Frenchmen to the sword, even those who had surrendered. My stomach knotted and twisted as I recalled that the Spanish had captured the women and children. Now the true reality of the situation was clear.

"Janey. Stay here." To the chamber pot. Once. Twice. Three times. I wiped my mouth and shook. *Dear God.*

I walked back to Janey, dropping beside her, holding her close. If she believed hiding her eyes meant there were no danger, then I chose to believe protecting her with my body meant she was safe. And as we sat, hunched and shivering, I felt the cramping deep within my stomach. I suddenly knew, as I had suspected for a few weeks, that I was not this day protecting two. I was protecting three.

Stay calm, stay calm, I whispered to myself.

Before I had left England, the Psalm that had comforted me most was, *"Lo, I am with you to the uttermost parts of the sea."* Now it took a new meaning for me as I understood in a racing heartbeat that Tempie and I might be widows by nightfall and upon a caravel bound for a prison in Cuba.

Them Which Hated Me
August 2, 1611 ~ James Town

*Then the channels of waters were seen, and the foundations
of the world were discovered at thy rebuke, O Lord, at the blast
of the breath of thy nostrils. He sent from above, he took me, he
drew me out of many waters. He delivered me from my strong
enemy, and from them which hated me: for they were too strong
for me.*
—Psalm 18:15-17

Once more unto the breach, dear friends, once more...
—William Shakespeare

I heard someone rattling the door. The commotion outside still raged, and I felt momentary panic. But when the door flung open, there stood Tempie, ashen and breathless. She and Joan Wright had both wandered past the well, looking to see how ripe the huckleberries were. From afar they had heard the warning and fled to the fort, pounding on the locked gate until someone noticed them. They had thought the furious alarms were for approaching Indians, and they were in the woods outside the fort! And then a soldier manning the gate told them the alarm was for the Spanish.

Once inside the cottage, Tempie latched the door and then dropped to the floor where Janey and I were huddled. Still breathing heavily and trembling, she hugged us both.

"And that is not all," she said, gasping air. "Maria Bucke has gone to laboring."

I looked at Tempie in alarm. How could we let her labor alone? What would happen to the baby?

"What can we do?" I knew how sickly and weak *I* felt. I didn't know if I could muster the courage and strength to work, even for Maria.

"Do?" Tempie's tone was almost sarcastic. "We can do nothing for her, Joan. But Mistress Wright has gone to her side. She'll be a-giving the herbs and charms to staunch the labor." She shrugged. Under ordinary circumstances, nothing would have kept us from helping. But we were thrust once more, as we had been in the Starving Time, into thinking only of ourselves.

I shook my head, still feeling for Maria. "'Twill be no one else helping…" Typically she would have had six or seven women at her bedside. Tempie and I were to be two of those Maria had already asked us. *The poor woman. How frightened she must be.*

"Mistress Wright seemed in control, even in such chaos. She can manage if need be, I suppose."

"Well, good," I said nonsensically, for there was nothing good about any of this.

And there we sat, the three of us, rocking slightly, parched throats, clammy palms, and stomachs jumping as if mice ran around inside us. We listened to the din outside and wondered what was next.

After a while, Janey drifted into an exhausted sleep. This gave Tempie and me an opportunity to speak freely without scaring the child further.

"If Maggie were here, she'd say, 'Prepare! What can we do to help ourselves?'" Tempie whispered.

I nodded. "Maggie was on my mind, too, as though she were urging me to get news. I learned the same as you. Nine caravels off the coast, Dale's plan to fight them on the river using fire ships if necessary. The thing is this.…" I hesitated. "If the Spanish have taken the time to attack, they will be sure they win because this move will throw them back into war with England. So Spain had better get the land—our land—they came for. Else it be a foolish move." This one thought had been on my mind all along.

Tempie agreed, calmly now. Strange the things one spoke calmly about at James Town because the everyday was always so extraordinary. "You mean, nine ships will easily overpower us, and there may be more on the way. They also have caught us by surprise. This is just how they destroyed that French colony."

I nodded. "That's what I was thinking too." A lump formed in my throat, but I forced myself to continue. "They killed the Frenchmen and took the women and children hostage. What will they do with us? They could keep us here. But then when—*if*—Gates's expedition arrives, the Spanish will risk losing us as captives as they fight to hold the island. I think 'tis more likely they will take us to Cuba. They'll hold us prisoner at La Havana or perhaps carry us on to Madrid."

Tempie's face was grave. "I think," she said slowly, "that our men will have to fight as best they can, and the women are at the mercy of the outcome. We could try to escape to the woods, to the natives…"

I considered that. "The Indians do hate the Spanish." The local tribes still remembered some forty years prior when the Spanish had captured a young Virginia Indian Prince they renamed Don Luis. Who was Don Luis? No one knew.

Because of Don Luis, the natives were aware of the Spanish brutalities occurring in other parts of the New World. They had a system of tribal messengers. They heard that the Spanish infamously slaughtered the tribes they encountered. Even before the English arrived, the Spanish had impressed the Indians with their arrogance and brutality. "It may be the natives hate the Spanish more than they hate us," I added.

Tempie went on. "We are at war with the natives, but we *will* be at war with the Spanish. If the worst occurs, where should we go? Allow ourselves onboard with the Spanish or try to escape the fort to the natives? The natives will probably not kill women and children. They might allow us to live with them although we would be slaves." We understood that when natives captured women and children in battle, they brought them into their own tribes, and the prisoners acted as slaves until slowly becoming one with the capturing tribe.

Then an image of the Paspahegh queen marching to her death crossed my mind like a bad dream. "But they also remember the killing of their queen a few months ago. Then, too, we might never get back to Europe. We would not be able to cross Spanish lines to reach English ships even if such ships arrived and were not themselves captured or killed."

Tempie's eyes met mine, our thoughts in unison.

Outside, the preparations for battle ensued. Inside our home, we looked at our choices—and found them all terrifying.

Hours for Months, and Days for Years
August 2, 1611~ James Town

*Love reckons hours for months, and days for years; and every
little absence is an age.*
—John Dryden

This was a day, amongst frightening Virginia days, that I knew I would never forget. Some three hours had passed, I guessed, since Brewster and Abbott set off for the Point. This was longer than it should have taken to survey the situation and return, and Dale was no doubt worried as were we.

I whispered, "It seems, uh, ominous that the scouts have not yet returned."

At that moment, a pounding at the door startled us both. Shaking profusely, Tempie arose and walked to it.

"Who's there?" she cried as forcefully as she could.

"Walter."

Janey was awake now, and I was trembling all over, the nausea returning.

"Walter?" I asked weakly.

"Yes, mistresses. It's I. Open up. It's safe."

Tempie heaved up the big latch and yanked the door open.

Walter stood with his morion in his hands, sweat pouring from him, his hair matted and dirty. "Bringin' news, mistresses. I come to you because I knowed how frightened you were."

I sighed. Maggie had been right. It was *good* to have friends who would remember you when times were most desperate.

He continued. "Brewster and Abbott come back. There were nine ships, all right, three of them caravels. But the fleet won't Spanish after all. 'Twas Sir Thomas Gates! Sir Thomas Gates." He shook his head as if in disbelief. "I do declare, mistresses. Seems the Virginia Company hired caravels as cattle ships. So rest you quietly, then. Gates expects his fleet to be here by day's end with hundreds of people and more supplies."

"No Spanish," Tempie whispered feebly. She dropped to the floor in relief, her hand against her head.

"Gates?" My head was spinning. Was Cecily onboard?

"Walter, is there any more news about the fleet? How they fared? Was there contagion? What did Brewster say? My daughter may be on one of those ships!"

"Oh." He eyed Janey as though he were thinking, *Why would you bring another daughter to this place?* "Well, they did say they got hit by the calenture." My heart dropped again. The terrible heat and the long voyage often brought fever, delirium, and death. "Seems they stopped to water at the islands. The heat was bringing some folks down. Governor Gates is in mourning, for one who died of the heat was his lady. They buried her in the West Indies."

My mind whirled with so much to absorb.

Lady Gates, who had been Cecily's guardian on voyage? That meant the illness had struck close to Cecily herself if she were indeed on the ship.

After Walter left, I was still trembling but I went to my trunk and found a shell wrapped in a blanket. My half of the scallop was intact. It had survived the voyage, the hurricane, unscathed. Through all that had happened since, the shell was yet perfect.

Had Cecily's half survived the journey as well?

"Her shell must be whole. It must be unbroken! It must be undamaged!" I said rapidly as though this were the most important thing in the world, and that made no sense, even to me. What did it matter about a shell? But Tempie understood what I could not say.

Cecily must be whole. Not shattered, not buried on an island with her caretaker, Lady Gates.

Tempie was firm. "After more than two years, you will put your halves together this day. I promise you, both halves will be perfect. I promise you."

Betwixt a Smile and a Tear
August 2, 1611 ~ James Town

I am a poor wayfaring stranger
A-trav'ling through this land of woe...
And there's no sickness, toil or danger
In that bright world to which I go.

I know dark clouds gather 'round me
I know my way is rough and steep
Beauteous fields lie there before me
Where all the saints their vigils keep.

I'm going there to see my mother.
She said she'd meet me when I come...
—Traditional folk hymn

Thou pendulum betwixt a smile and tear...
—Lord Byron

I raced for the chamber pot once more then collapsed, collapsed into a sack of kirtle, bodice, and petticoat onto the floor beside Tempie, tears flooded my eyes. My terror had turned to amazement then joy, my joy to hope, and then my hope back to fear again. It was too much, and I did not think I could bear it. All the frustrations came pouring forth from me as though the river was flowing from me all at once. I was sobbing and could not stop.

"We have waited too long! She must be well. She must be..." *Alive. She must be alive.* But I could not say that as if saying the word made dangling between life and death too real. Too much of a possibility.

Gathering her own composure, Tempie swept her arm around me. Janey was beside us, patting my back. The child was utterly confused, but she recognized tears—and she was trying to wipe mine away with her hand.

"Mama, don't cry. Sisley's coming. Sisley's coming," she said with conviction.

I smiled at her but could not stop the flow of water.

"Pray God. Pray God," was all I could say.

Tempie seemed to be wondering how to handle this best. It could be wonderful news. Or disappointing. What if Cecily were not even aboard? Or worse, the news could be tragic. What if the calenture had claimed her too? I might be able to bear up if she were not aboard. Beyond that... I was still crying.

Eventide rolled in and with it, the grand fleet of Sir Thomas Gates. The fair winds we had expected to bring the Spanish brought us relief ships instead.

Tempie gave me one quick squeeze and looked deeply at me. "I will go and see what I can find out. Stay here with Janey, and do not leave. Wait for me."

She wants to be the one to bring me the news in case it is the worst. She does not want me to hear it in the midst of a confused throng at riverside, I thought.

"Yes," I said. I needed to hear it gently. I knew that. I had left Cecily behind with my brother's family for two years. Yes, there were reasons, but I had still done it. From Cecily's letter a few months before, it seemed she had fared well. But since then, at the very least, she had endured the death of Lady Gates on ship, which must have been frightening for an eleven-year-old.

"May I go see Sisley?" Janey asked Tempie. She had some vague recollection of the sister she had not seen in so long.

"No, lovey." Tempie was gentle but firm. "You need to stay with your mama. Can you tend her while I'm gone?"

Janey nodded with regal solemnity as though Tempie had just asked her to guard the queen's jewels. She resumed patting my back with such great seriousness I thought I should laugh as I cried.

Dusk was gently falling. Virginia crickets and locusts hummed through my window. Now and again, a warm breeze carried these sounds to me. I heard the muffled voices of adventurers disembarking, greeting friends; hogsheads rolling down the bridge; cattle lowing, their shuffling hooves scraping the planks of the frightening caravels. *Cattle, after all.* We had expected Spanish dogs but had received English cows instead. I smiled in spite of myself. I pictured the goats and pigs and cattle and chicken emerging, two by two. *Gates's ark.*

The sounds of new life in the settlement had replaced the earlier sounds of soldiers preparing for battle. I was pacing. I got up and walked around. I sat down. I stood again for no particular reason. I sat on the stool. I sat on the bed. I tapped my feet.

This was the longest day ever I could remember.

And then the door opened, and there stood Tempie, her face like a pool of water reflecting the full moon. She had her arms draped around a young girl, a girl who was taller, who was thinner, who was exhausted, pale, and disheveled from a long voyage. But a girl who was alive and who was my very own.

I jumped up and ran over to her. "My Cecily, my Cecily!" I whispered, and she began to cry, and then so did I. Tempie and Janey did too.

"Mama," was all Cecily said, as she collapsed into my arms. After a moment, she pulled away, and her shining eyes met mine. Then, from behind her back, she brought out a carefully wrapped bundle. I knew what it was. I reached for my own scallop shell on the table as she unwrapped her package.

Before me she held, as perfect as mine, her half of the scallop shell, the one broken so ceremoniously on a garden bench two years before. I had snapped it in half with the words, "See? It was one, but now it is two, but it is still part of the same whole."

She remembered, for she held hers against mine and said simply, "See, across two years and a great ocean, twice! It was two, but now 'tis one." I swept her into my arms. How much we had to learn about the time between.

Yes, Cecily, 'tis one. Even as she said it, I knew she could not truly understand what a wondrous feat this was. And now, her own adventures at James Town would join ours. Pray God, He would continue to keep her, and all of us, safe.

"I prayed for you and Janey and Father every day. Even when they said Father's ship went down, I kept praying that it didn't." Truly, the faith of a child was a marvelous thing.

She looked at me and smiled a simple smile, and her eyes were bright with wonder. "And it didn't!"

I folded my arms around her while my thoughts drifted across the span of years. *Whole have I kept it. Whole will I keep thee and thy family,* God had promised me one overcast day on Melcombe Harbor as I held the scallop. How much had conspired to make that voice untrue. It had at times seemed impossible, yet forces greater than ourselves had not fractured us. We were indeed whole. *Praise God, praise God,* I murmured. *I cried out in my despair, and You heard me. Thank you, Lord.*

I glanced over my daughter's shoulder, up at the rafters and at the bark matting the ceiling. Soon, Will would be home from the Point, I hoped. Gates would want George Yeardley with him, and since Will was one of George's men...

Would we all truly be one family under one roof again? Three nearly perished in a hurricane at sea. One shipwrecked in Bermuda, two starving in Virginia, one behind in England awaiting news. *And one,* I thought, touching my belly, *that no one knows of just yet. Too soon. Too soon.*

I turned to Cecily, my little girl praying for the rest. Had God heard the prayers of a small child? Filled with faith, she had never stopped praying for her father, even when all England and Virginia believed him dead. Oh, I had prayed for him for a while, but had stopped when the improbable became the impossible. Yet a little girl had believed he could still come home. *That I had such faith,* I thought. *When I was a little girl, I had it too. Strange that when we are young, we can so readily believe. But when we get old, we trust our eyes more than we trust God.*

"It may be, Cecily, that you prayed him through. Maybe you prayed *us* through, too." I thought of Janey's weak and withering body during the Starving Time. Yet she had not succumbed. Could her sister's prayers, an ocean away, have helped? "May you always have such faith," I whispered. And in my heart, somehow, I knew she'd need it.

My mind wandered to Sir Thomas Gates, to the loss he and his girls had endured. Lady Gates must have been a courageous woman, I thought. She could have said no and stayed behind in a fine home, but instead she had risked all. *All.* All for her husband, for her family—and for Virginia.

It seemed the hand of God did indeed ordain our goings out and our comings in.

As for Sir Thomas, I suspected this would put an end to his dream of retiring with his family in Virginia, finished before it even began, and that he would probably send his girls home to England. I imagined he would follow when his tour of duty finished here.

Virginia was a land where dreams were made and dreams were broken, and one never quite knew on which end of the pendulum he swung.

The Star of Empire
August 3, 1611~ James Town

Westward the star of empire takes its way.
—John Quincy Adams

*It were pitty to overthrowe the enterprize: for I shall yet live
to see [Virginia] an Inglishe nation.*
—Sir Walter Ralegh, 1602

The next day, I walked my girls over to the church for the ten o'clock
service where Governor Gates would speak. Dale and Gates had delayed
work orders due to the panic and the arrival of the fleet. They also needed to
make all aware that Gates would now be governor.

Tempie had come to church from Maria's home. However, Mistress
Wright and several of the other women were still at Maria's where, I heard,
Maria was about to give birth. I loved Maria, but felt the need to be close
to Cecily once more. After service, however, I would go visit and hope that
Maria understood. The women at the birthing chamber were praying that
they would be exempt from church. I suspected they would be. How could
Dale flog a woman aiding a new mother?

I glanced around. 'Twas unfortunate that so many of the soldiers were at
other forts. I knew Will would have enjoyed watching this display and hearing the governor's words.

George Yeardley had received permission to attend, for George and Gates
were still very close as military superiors and subordinates go. George had
sailed up from Point Comfort with Governor Gates.

The church bells had signaled the opening ceremony. Now bugles announced that all was about to start.

Sir Thomas Dale would formally transfer the governorship back to Sir
Thomas Gates. Lord De La Warr, we learned, had appeared in England prior
to Sir Thomas Gates's departure, so the Virginia Company had transferred
the governorship to Gates while Dale would officially be Marshal.

Truly, the Company showed wisdom in divesting the power amongst these gentlemen because if one grew sick or died, other leaders could step in. *For if they fall, the one can pick up his fellow,* I thought, remembering the verse from Ecclesiastes. Tempie, Maggie, and I had certainly proven that.

My little girls sat giggling in the church pew. Cecily had her arm wrapped protectively about her sister. Having nearly lost her once, Cecily did not plan to lose her again. All of James Town was foreign to Cecily, so Janey would teach her what she knew about the woods, about the fort's buildings, about strange flowers and birds.

I predicted the day would come when Janey would say, "See the stinky muskcat?" next time the little black and white striped animal somehow made its way inside the fort. And just this morning, I had heard, "Them's chicka-dees, Sisley, 'cause they say *chicka-dee-chicka-dee-chicka-dee-dee-dee!*" and both girls had laughed.

As young Annie Laydon had taught the older women, so too, would Janey teach Cecily. In James Town, what counted was not your age, but your experience in Virginia. Being able to survive in this world, so different from England, was all that mattered. And, like us, Cecily would have to adapt to military rule, to the natives' nearby presence, to the primitive conditions. Even to sitting in this rustic church. We had come from beautiful country churches of stone and stained glass. This one was so unassuming that were it not for the communion set and cross at the chancel and the plain cedar pews, one should not have known it was a church at all.

Now the church hushed as Sir Thomas Dale ceremoniously relinquished his commission as governor-in-charge to Sir Thomas Gates. And Sir Thomas Gates in turn presented Dale with his new commission as marshal. If De La Warr ever returned, Gates would give over governorship to La Warr and become lieutenant governor; but for now, Gates was in command.

Gates turned to the throng in the church, who had crowded every pew and also stood in the back. Clearly, we would need a larger church, depending on how many of these newcomers survived.

"My friends."

An unusual opening, so different from the berating we had received when Lord La Warr had preached to us after the Starving Time. Gates, it was clear, knew how to speak to troops, how to inspire victory, and how to pull a crowd together for a common cause. Something moved through the church. I could feel it. For Gates, unlike his predecessor the baron, had been born a humble man and had raised himself to his heights by being an able soldier. We ourselves were not so different from the man before us.

Sir Thomas Gates surveyed the room. His gaze fell upon his two daughters, seated in a front pew.

"We have reached a crossroads in the colonization of Virginia. We will continue onward, or we will give up in defeat. I see a few faces of those onboard the *Sea Venture*. We did not give up then, and we shall not give up now. I see, too, some Starving Time survivors." His glance landed upon Tempie, seated with her husband. *Gates is happy George did not lose his wife,* I thought. Then a pain stabbed me. *As he has lost his.*

The new governor continued, as power came through his voice. "We have new settlers: three hundred with Dale, one hundred fifty with me. Pray God, our time of tribulation at James Town is behind us. All we have endured is for nothing if we do not press on."

A murmur went through the church. A murmur of agreement, I thought, but it was hard to tell.

"We *will* press on. We will build a new fort upriver, and you shall never again endure fear as you did yesterday, that the Spanish shall attack us unprepared. We will fortify this new settlement with a moat to surround it fully where the river does not.

"Marshal Dale informs me he has already found a location. The Virginia Company has chosen as its name Henricus, honoring Prince Henry, patron and benefactor of Virginia.

"We shall push you hard, 'tis true. In fact, you may count on it." Here he smiled before continuing. "But you shall also reap the rewards such hard work will bring."

His voice became suddenly solemn as he added. "Four and a half years, gentlemen. Four and a half years, ladies. We have but four and a half short years to turn a profit. That, and no more." He repeated it as if to ensure no one missed his meaning. "If we do not turn a profit in *four and a half years*, the Virginia Company shall withdraw support."

A murmur went through the church. Four years was little time at all. And then what? Would we receive any land or profit? Of course, we would not receive profits. There would be none! And land would be worthless if the settlement dried up. The impact of this news was startling.

We were, I thought, the Israelites. Making bricks without straw.

Then, forcing a smile, Gates said, "We have said that Virginia will be the home of future generations of Englishmen."

His voice softened as he looked at his two girls. "I am sure of it."

"You know that I had brought my own wife to live here. *That* is how much I believe in Virginia." He paused. "You know, too, that she died during the voyage." His voice cracked slightly upon the word *died.*

Another murmur, sympathetic. I realized again how the hand of God had favored me with the survival of my own family. Why did it support some and not others? Was it all blind chance?

And as I sat, an unusual thing happened. The walls of the church seemed to fall away, and Gates's words blurred in my ears. I saw that Gates would send his daughters home to England, and they would forever be an English family.

It appeared my own family would stay since we had all survived. *The tree will branch here,* I thought although I knew not why. *There will be a Virginia tree and an English tree. 'Tis the set of the future.*

Had Gates's wife survived, his daughters would stay, marry planters, perhaps raise a family in Virginia.... In that moment, I had the uncanny sense that our lives were bigger than our lives, our destiny grander than we had imagined. Could there one day be a land filled with English men and women here in Virginia? With villages spreading up to the Patawomeck's River and beyond, down to the Roanoke Island and across the continent. To the South Sea.

Henricus, I understood suddenly, was just the beginning. It was a moment beyond time, a moment of imagination, a moment when the church in which I sat seemed a small dot in a great land that would be.

My prayer book clattered to the floor. For a moment I had lost myself, and I had seen something. And as I saw it, I knew it.

Someday.

Sir Thomas Gates was still talking, and his words drifted out the window and into the western sky.

Baptized in Tears
August 3, 1611 ~ James Town

The child of misery, baptized in tears!
—John Langhorne

As Dale and Gates fought for the colony's survival, so too did Maria's newborn baby fight for her life.

Mistress Wright had done a fine job of delaying Maria's labor, but the baby still had come early. I felt torn between staying with Cecily and helping Maria. Yet I knew Cecily was very, very tired. She had fallen asleep early last night and would probably go to bed as soon as she was able.

After returning home from the service, I settled the children in. "Girls, I must help Mistress Bucke," I said as I left for the parson's home.

I felt guilty for not coming yesterday after we understood that we were safe. Yet I knew I had to recover my own before I could aid anyone else. And the Spanish threat had left me tired and cramped. I did not want to lose my baby although the thought of birthing a child here terrified me.

Now I came, contrite for not being here sooner. I had pulled together a few herbs for Maria but had brought no victuals, as I had none.

Maria's delivery brought to mind another fear. Maria was perhaps twenty-one years old, an appropriate age to have a baby.

But women here endured many more hardships than at home, and life at James Town forced them to mature much earlier. While it was legal for girls to marry at age twelve and boys at fourteen, few did in England.

Typically, there a girl became a bride in her twenties, and motherhood came soon after.

Annie had been the first to marry very young here. She had been but fourteen when she'd married Jack Laydon. And so, as other young girls reached this age, they, too, married.

The truth was that Annie had not changed a society alone. She had simply been the first to recognize the necessity of such. Her mistress had died, she was alone, and early marriage was the best situation for her.

James Town was a harsh and rugged life with not enough girls to be brides. Marrying young as the natives did seemed fitting. By the time a girl was thirteen, men were eyeing her. Could she be their future wife? Would her father, if he were still alive, agree?

Cecily, had she been in Dorset, might have had nine years or more before she concerned herself with marriage. But in Virginia, her maidenhood was nearly over.

I hiked my petticoat over the door jamb and pushed these thoughts away until another day. For now, a basket to Maria.

Greeting me at his open door, Reverend Bucke looked uncharacteristically flustered. He mopped his brow against the summer heat, the just-released fear of attack, the possible loss of his baby.

At the morning's service, the reverend had preached a melancholy sermon. His duties required he leave his wife to the care of the midwife and the women who brought their shaky bodies to Maria's aid. No matter, for the birthing chamber was the domain of women and women only.

This day, the reverend sighed and nodded good day to me. I stammered an apology for not being here sooner, but he seemed not to hear me. His distraction was obvious.

I studied his eyes for just a moment. For Bucke, James Town was no easy place to shepherd with its wild, uncontrolled side, its fear, hunger, and sickness. The obvious punishment God meted to those who sinned in the colony befalling all. God had doled to him a flock unlike any other. His shoulders actually hunched beneath the weight.

"Mistress Peirce, Mistress Peirce, welcome. Come in, please. Women in the bedchamber, of course." He nodded to the closed door.

Joan Wright was there, as were Annie, Thomasine, Margery Fairfax, and Tempie. The chaos of Maria's bedside was anything but how a typical birthing should be. All missing—the food and the celebration, the hymns and prayers, the circle of friends during a time when a woman hovered so close to the possibility of death.

Yet somehow the little girl with dark hair and dark eyes had arrived into this world anyway. She slept in a small cradle by the bed. Even swaddled in rags, she looked too small and had a red, pinched face.

"Oh, oh, she's precious." I knelt to see the little one. Then I turned my attention to Maria. I felt terrible. "I'm sorry, Maria. I...I was sick myself yesterday. I...my daughter came in upon the *Swan*. I did not feel I could leave her...."

Maria waved her hand, and the women moved aside to allow me closer.

The new mother opened her arms in a forgiving gesture, and I hugged her.

Then shaking her head, Maria said, "What kind of world have I brought this child into?"

I understood. Ironically, I had asked myself the same question about Cecily in her new arrival.

Maria's voice was feeble but deliberate. She began to weep. The women gave me a look of concern as if to say, *See how she has been?*

"You know the world I mean!" she continued. "*This* place where we live under cruel laws and have not enough food." Her eyes were on the tiny form. "If I loved her, I would not have birthed her."

This was not Maria. Maria was a sweet and God-fearing woman, a woman who believed that God only gave what one could bear. But now Maria's wan face and sunken eyes spoke for her.

The child let out a whimpering cry. She was trying to survive, like a young baby sparrow fallen too soon from its nest. Even the child seemed to know things were not right.

Annie reached to lift the baby. "There, there," she whispered into the little girl's ear as she handed her to Maria. "Mother will feed you."

Maria held the baby to her and pressed her own face against the baby's little one.

Annie, sitting on the bed, touched Maria's arm, but Maria pulled away. Instead, Maria turned and looked into the eyes of her newborn. The little girl drew ragged breaths which caused her small body to shudder.

"Thou comest just a wee thing, and too soon, into such a world as this! Thy birth on the heels of a near Spanish raid, no time for planning, no time for the lying in. Just throwing thee into the world, and little enough time we made for that."

The silence in the bedchamber was deafening, the only sounds the baby's uneven breathing and sniffling mother. Maria kissed the infant's forehead, tears streaming from her eyes, a hopeless look upon her face. Slowly, she spoke. "Remember the story of Naomi from the Book of Ruth?"

We nodded.

Maria continued. "Naomi's name meant *sweetness*, and indeed it did seem a sweet life when Naomi left for Moab with her husband and sons. But by the time Naomi returned, she had lost everything."

We sat in silence, no one knowing what to say.

Her eyes never leaving the infant, Maria began quoting a passage from Ruth.

"*And they said, Is not this Naomi? And she answered them, Call me not Naomi, but call me Mara: for the Almighty hath given me much bitterness. I went out full, and the Lord hath caused me to return empty.*"

Maria's voice broke, but she went on. *"Why call ye me Naomi, seeing the Lord hath humbled me, and the Almighty hath brought me unto adversity?* You, child, are Mara, for you are born into a bitter world. May it not always be so."

Maria then gazed around at us, gathered so helplessly 'round her bed. "Call her Mara," she said simply.

Thomasine turned to those of us assembled around Maria's bedside. "Ladies, have we not had enough? Birthing children into this world with nothing as promised us? The Virginia Company has betrayed us! Not enough food for our children? Mud huts? Working as slaves under company law? The constant risk of attack by Indian or Spaniard? Do our husbands not still have rights under English law? Dear ones, what would happen if we asked our husbands if we might return to England? Who would go home, given the chance?"

Thomasine had asked an honest, forthright question. She had spoken my thoughts, and it seemed, the thoughts of all present. This topic, verging on treason and promising a whipping, or worse, had now invaded the birthing chamber, the world of women.

Stillness filled the room. I glanced at Tempie and Annie. Annie was shaking her head. Was she signifying hopelessness or disagreeing with Thomasine? Tempie stared toward the shuttered window.

What *would* happen if we returned home? Why were we staying? Under Dale's regime, the future appeared harsher than ever. Yes, I knew I had seen a vision in church, but that had been but an idle daydream.

The women looked askance at one another, but as yet, no one spoke. Speaking up, agreeing with Thomasine, was tantamount to treason.

Or was it? Exactly what *were* our rights as the wives of free Englishmen?

"I would!" Margery's hand went up. "I would, indeed. Wouldn't we all?" The women began murmuring. They would go, they would go.

What about me? What was my answer?

I felt faint and weak. I could not stomach the bad food much longer. Hard enough to eat *good* food on a healthy belly since, unbeknownst to everyone but myself, I was expecting a child of my own.

The question of delivering a baby in Virginia was more pertinent to me than anyone here present could know.

Call her Mara. I supposed we were all *Mara.*

Strangers and Pilgrims
August 25, 1611 ~ James Town

*I brought home from [Virginia] this yeare myself, a falcon,
and a tassell, the one sent by Sir Thomas Dale to his highnes the
Prince, and the other was presented to the Earle of Salsburye,
faire ones.*
—William Strachey, 1611

*These all died in faith, not having received the promises, but
having seen them afar off, and were persuaded of them, and embraced them, and confessed that they were strangers and pilgrims
on the earth. For they that say such things declare plainly that
they seek a country.*
—Hebrews 11:13-14

I'd had little chance to talk with Cecily, just the two of us. I missed the days in Dorset, sitting with her on the bench in the garden. Was life truly simpler then, or did I imagine it? That had only been two years before but seemed a distant dream.

I had attempted a few conversations with her, asking, "How did you fare with Aunt Bettie?" to which she would reply, "Oh, fine."

"And your studies? You learned a-much?"

She would nod, "Aye, mother."

Now I felt as if we were nearly strangers after so long apart. How to break through? For Cecily was now eleven, and within a few years would be married. I had little time to rebuild.

For her part, Cecily had adapted well, or so it appeared. She had come to Virginia as an adult, 'twas true. She, too, had work to do in Sir Thomas Dale's town. She had been working the tallow.

Now I struggled under the strict regime of our daily schedule at different tasks to find time with her. I also wished to attempt schooling with her in the evenings as I had begun with Janey. Yet with both of us assigned to strenuous work, it remained difficult to be together when we were not both exhausted. We went from task to task, from work to church to meals to work to church to meals. Day in, day out. I needed a bridge to her, I sensed.

Those crucial years between nine and eleven I had missed. Cecily had always been independent, and two years apart from me had only made her more so. I supposed it was fortunate that I had not known that one year would become two. For if I had known it would be two, could I have left her? Of course, had I known about the shipwreck and Starving Time, I should never have departed Plymouth Hoe!

Well, I reminded myself, *'Tis as they say, the mill cannot grind with the water that is past.*

This particular afternoon, we were strolling past the ships where mariners were lading goods to travel home. Church was over; midday meal not yet begun. I had taken Cecily with me to the well to fetch water. Any time with her I could seize, I did.

Suddenly, two perches near the bridge at the river drew Cecily's attention. Upon them sat tethered male and female peregrines.

A smile lit Cecily's face as she went closer. "Falcons, mother!"

"Aye," I said, glad for any opportunity of a conversation with her. "The female is called a falcon, and the male is a tassel or a tiercel."

"What means a *tassel*?" she asked.

"Well, it comes from the word for third. The male of these great birds is only one-third the size of the female. Social rank determines who may own these birds. These falcons must be going to someone important in England," I told her. It would be illegal—a felony—for anyone presently in the colony to own either of these birds. Only the Baron De La Warr, if he were here, would have been able to own the tassel. And even *he* would not have been allowed the grand and splendid female peregrine.

One of the mariners was passing by, and I stopped him, saying, "Pardon me, sir, but do you know to whom these birds are going?"

He pushed his hat back upon his head. His duties in the sun were hot, and his face showed the lines of someone who spends much time outdoors.

"Aye, Mistress, I do. And I suppose you want to know, too?" he said kindly to Cecily, seeing her interest.

"Aye, sir."

"Well, missy, the smaller tassel is bound for the Earl of Salisbury." Cecily sucked in her breath. "But the great bird, the female, is to belong to Prince Henry himself! Sir Thomas Dale is sending them as gifts."

"Prince Henry shall see the same bird I am seeing! It will be his pet? From across the ocean?" Cecily was studying the large bird, which had vibrant black eyes encircled by white.

The mariner winked at Cecily. "Yes, ma'am, it will belong to him. 'Spect the prince will be right pleased since he's never been to the New World, himself." He walked away, whistling as he went.

Cecily paused for a moment then looked at me. "I have come to the New World, but the prince has not? Will he *ever* come?"

I shrugged. "His home must be in England where his kingdom is. He has an important role as the future king, one he cannot jeopardize by risking his life for an ocean voyage. Virginia is a dangerous place. Yet, the prince so loves the New World he learns all he can about it. They say he even dreams of Virginia at night. And 'tis he who encourages his father to sign the charters. The prince is but seventeen now, but one day when he becomes king, Virginia will never lack support." *Pray God.*

Cecily looked about her with new interest. "But I have *seen* the New World. I have *put my shoes* upon it. I know how Virginia smells, and how it looks, and how it tastes."

"You have seen with your own eyes," I agreed.

"The prince will see the peregrine and maps of the New World and wonder about it all...."

"Aye, lovey. We will never live in a prince's castle, but he will never see our land across the ocean."

"I am an adventurer and a pilgrim," she said suddenly with force.

She remembered!

"Aye. And now you are, also, a planter," I said, "for you have planted yourself here in Virginia."

I wrapped my arms around her. "My daughter, you were brave to wait behind two years. Do you know that? And I am so, so proud of you!"

Her eyes welled with tears. "'Twas very hard, mama. I missed you, and I feared for you, and then to hear Father was dead..." Her voice faded. "I did not think my cousins could understand. *Their* parents were safe with them, safe in Dorset. But you were far away with so many dangers. I could not see you, or write to you, or hear from you at all. What if you forgot me? All I had was God to confide in. I prayed, and I had faith we would be together again... because...because you said so."

Pray God, I had been right. Survival had seemed a distant hope many times through the worst of the hurricane and the starvation.

"I think, mama, that the scallop saw me through," she said, her face thoughtful.

"The scallop?" She was talking at last, and I wanted to hear everything she had to say.

"Aye, because I knew—I *knew*—you had the other half. And I could touch the ridge where they were joined and knew we would be together soon, too. I was afraid for Janey. She was so little, and I missed her, especially at night," she added quietly. The girls had once shared a bed at home in England.

"Janey was brave," I whispered, remembering the gaunt little body, the hollow eyes. "As were you. Courage, they say, is its own reward."

She nodded.

Then, feeling suddenly inspired, I pointed at the great birds, which studied us curiously. The eyes of the female, strikingly rimmed with white, held a mysterious light.

"Do you know what means her name *peregrine?*"

Cecily shook her head.

"It comes from *peregrinus,* a Latin word. Can you recall it from your studies?" I suddenly felt like my mother, always prompting for answers. My mother had been a born tutor, and for the first time I considered that I might be too.

Cecily paused and said, "I *think* it means... Oh, it means stranger or *pilgrim.*"

I put my arm around my little girl as we both admired the stunning bird. "Aye, that is so. These birds are pilgrims, just like you. They can fly far, far distances. They will travel upon a ship across the whole ocean from the home they know, but they will always remember the Virginia forests and Virginia rivers." I scanned the wide James in front of us. "Do they know where they are going?" I asked her.

The majestic birds were watching us. *Go on,* they seemed to say, *tell us.* Their eyes were intense, dark, intelligent.

Cecily laughed. "I think not! How could they know? They only know that a man collected them from their home in the trees. Do you suppose they're afraid?" she asked suddenly with concern.

I gazed into the peregrine's eyes. She gazed back. I imagined her speaking. *I might be afraid if I allowed myself to be,* I heard her say. *But I cannot escape my destiny, so I go willingly. Outside events never tarnish my nobility, my majesty. I set my wings to the wind, and I soar higher than any living creature because to that I was born. And when I catapult to earth, I drop fast as a sleek stone. But—* her look was sly—*I never fall all the way to the ground, do I?*

Joan, I chided myself with a smile. *You do go on.*

To Cecily, I said, "She does not allow herself to be afraid. A great prince who will love her awaits her on the other side of the ocean. She doesn't know where she is going, but she is trusting of her outcome, always majestic in manner. She will take each day as it comes and be...surprised. Maybe full of wonderment. At times, the rocking of the ship, perhaps a storm at sea, may agitate her. Cause her to be fearful. But the end of her journey is always the same: her prince awaits."

I paused. "She will journey far until one day this great bird will sit upon the arm of the prince, the future king of England himself! If she could talk, she would tell Prince Henry all about her home." I paused. "Pilgrims eventually find what they seek. This falcon does not know she will live in a castle with the future king. She only knows that her leg is bound, and she is no longer in her forest home. The mariners will place her on the ship, and she may be frightened. She may look for her mate, the tassel. He will be near, and both will wonder where they are going. What will it be like? But only upon completion of the journey will she sit upon the prince's arm."

"And she will think it was worth it all?" Cecily asked, giving me a sideways glance.

"I hope so, my little pilgrim," I said quietly. "The prince is very, very kind. He will love and treat this bird very well. She is a noble bird, and no one lower than a prince may have her. Journeys are oft unknown, for only at the end of a pilgrimage does one truly understand it."

"The birds are traveling one way across the ocean and I traveled the other," Cecily said.

"Yes. But your journey's end is the same. My father always told me that a King was waiting for him at the end of his journey, and so does the same Prince wait for you."

She looked at me quizzically. "A prince? For me?"

"The Prince of Peace, Lovey. You deserve no less."

"Oh..." She smiled, satisfied. "No matter how long and rough the journey, Jesus is waiting at the end. I see. We'll be good pilgrims, won't we, mama? And Janey, too."

"We'll do our best, lovey. We'll do our best." I squeezed her hand. Then Cecily pulled away, wandering closer to the birds to talk to them. "You're going across the ocean," she said with amazement. "To live with the prince!"

I studied the little girl with wide blue eyes, and remembered her father Tom, whom she had never met. I recalled the day I had gotten the news that he would not be coming home from the Dutch fighting. Cecily and I had little known what lay ahead of us! How little we still did know. Would Virginia be kind to her? Was Virginia kind to anyone? Where would she go? What would she see? What would life be like for her as a mother in the Virginia of tomorrow? Or would the colony even exist that long? Then I thought of the women at Maria's beside. *Or will she wish to go home as desperately as I sometimes do?*

When the four and a half years were up, she would be sixteen, probably already married or else returning to England if the Virginia Company collapsed.

I imagined one of my grandfather's clocks, somewhere in London, tolling the hour, reminding us that our time to make this work was dwindling. We would succeed here, or we wouldn't. If we did, Cecily would have children here. She would, God willing, receive the land due her. Her future was exceedingly bright, and terribly frightening, all at once. Like the dice men cast on ship to pass time, so were we casting dice. Every move seemed some immense wager.

But like those birds, we simply accepted each day and let events unfold. Some we could control and perhaps even alter. Some we could not. If things go well, if things go well...generations of our grandchildren might call Virginia home. The opportunities and abundance of Virginia stretched wide before them, as did the dangers. Perhaps, we were doing this for them. Or for ourselves? Or for England? Truly, why *were* we doing this?

My first husband Tom had died in the war before Cecily was even born, but sometimes he came back to my mind. How delighted he had been that he would become a father. "Take care of your daughter, Tom," I whispered under my breath. "And if you have any influence with the Prince of Peace, ask Him to watch over your little pilgrim Cecily, too."

Outbound, Your Bark Awaits You
August 27, 1611 ~ James Town

Outbound, your bark awaits you. Were I one
Whose prayer availeth much, my wish should be
Your favoring trade-wind and consenting sea…
God keep you both, make beautiful your way,
Comfort, console, and bless; and safely bring,
Ere yet I make upon a vaster sea
The unreturning voyage, my friends to me.
—John Greenleaf Whittier

Young Margaret and Elizabeth Gates were departing nearly as soon as they had arrived, returning to England without their mother. They stood to one side of the ship awaiting their father. They seemed very small next to the ship tied off to a pine.

In the brief span of the midday break, Cecily, Janey, and I went there to say goodbye. With us, we brought an herb satchel for Cecily's young friends. Cecily hugged the girls, and we thanked them for bringing her here.

Then I added, "Now, here are gum-dragon cakes with cinnamon, ginger and wormwood. These will settle your belly on the voyage. You can mix them with your beer. And stir the powdered sassafras root in as well."

The girls nodded and smiled, but with a pained expression on their faces. *They look so lost,* I thought. To see motherless children… I gave them each a quick hug and kiss, saying, "Godspeed, Godspeed." To myself, I said, *I will never have the chance to thank you, my Lady Gates. But I hope this helps your girls have a healthful voyage home.*

I think I should have liked Lady Gates, if I had been so fortunate as to have met her.

"What was she like, Cecily?" I had asked her that morning, as the three of us ground the herbs and placed them into little pieces of ragged linen.

"Oh, mother, she was lovely, just lovely. You *would* have liked her.

Elizabeth, Margaret, and I took the best care of her we could as she grew ill on the voyage. 'Oh, look at the green fields,' she'd say. 'Mama, you're at sea. There are no green fields!' Margaret had cried. 'No, no, the fields are green and ready. And I think I am ready, too,' Lady Gates murmured. Then she dropped into a restless sleep. I think it was the heat, the calenture, you know," Cecily had said, seeming lost in thought as she worked the mortar and pestle.

The poor woman. I felt my heart breaking anew for her loss.

When Cecily looked up, her eyes were wide. "We stopped at an island to water and to rest. The calenture was very bad. Sometimes I myself felt very dizzy. But being on the island made me feel better. We buried Lady Gates there beneath a palm tree." Cecily's voice drifted off. "Governor Gates wrapped his arms around his children while Margaret and Elizabeth held each other. 'What shall we do without our mama?' They wept. I wept, too. Lady Gates had been so kind to me. She knew you had starved. She said we would never starve here again."

Tears stung my eyes. Lady Gates had bold faith.

Cecily sounded as if she had handled herself well. I felt proud that perhaps she would grow up to be a strong woman. God knew, to survive in James Town, she would have to be. And both she and Janey were showing an interest in herbs. This could only aid them both in what promised to be a long and arduous life in Virginia.

Sir Thomas Gates had walked up as we were giving his daughters the herbs. For just a moment, his eyes met mine. He smiled, but it was a sad smile. I bowed my head deferentially.

He nodded. "Thank you again, sir," I said to him.

The Gates family walked toward the bridge, the girls looking downriver as though to see what awaited them. Then they looked backward seeming to be uncertain that they were doing the right thing by leaving.

Uncertain whether to stay or to go. A feeling I understood.

August was simmering on like pottage over a low fire. This month always promised the most severe heat that Virginia offered us. Sometimes the air even shimmered like the smoky air around a blacksmith's forge. The relentless heat and drought colored the mood of the town, as tempers burned in the August flame.

With the scorch of August came, too, a dual injustice: a reminder that fall was soon to come, and with its cooler days and nights loomed a greater, darker shadow behind it.

Winter.

I found that, as I approached my third winter in Virginia, I dreaded it equally each time despite the fact that I could reason myself out of another Starving Time. The food was poor, but it was something, 'twas true. Still, I was fretful, and other Starving Time survivors seemed agitated as well.

Would the winter feelings of fear pass in time? We had no way of knowing. But I found my uneasiness growing even as the small new life grew inside me as well.

I trembled to imagine a winter here, carrying a baby, and then birthing one under Dale's iron rule. These thoughts and fears, I kept to myself.

So when the ships carrying Margaret and Elizabeth Gates began boarding, I found myself casting an envious look at the two girls. I watched the girls crossing the bridge, studying their shoes, their final thoughts I could read from where I stood.

This is the last time my feet shall touch Virginia soil. Next time I set them down on dry land, we shall be in England once again!

How I wished I could say the same for the three of us, the girls and me. For Will, I knew, would not abandon the effort.

My doubts and misgivings had been growing, maybe because I felt more fragile in every way carrying the baby. Maybe because of winter. Maybe because the threatened Spanish attack had been just another terrifying episode in many long and unending ones.

Maybe because I just didn't want to be here or to do this anymore.

No. Truly, I didn't.

I kicked around a pebble and watched the dirt billow into clouds of Virginia dust, which settled back down again onto my shoes.

We had no hope of seeing English dust any time soon.

And there was a further, frightening thought: did Sir Thomas Gates know something we did not? Or was he simply sending his girls home because they had lost their mother?

My mind knew it to be the latter, but my heart feared just the same.

A mariner carried the pilgrim birds aboard ship in wooden slatted boxes. The birds looked uncomfortable and uncertain. All my bluster, my fine speeches to Cecily, left me as if they were the dust puffs around my feet.

I suspected, and I had no way of knowing why, that those birds didn't belong in England any more than we belonged here.

Sir Thomas Gates had warmly hugged and kissed his two daughters and sent written instruction that they were to be in the charge of his wife's family in Kent. He sent a letter to his friend Sir Thomas Smythe as well, asking that Smythe check on his children during his own absence.

That could have been my girls, I thought, but did not say this. What if I had died? Would Will have sent the girls home? Will seemed so certain the Company could right all the wrongs. Could it?

Maybe, I found myself thinking, *maybe we should all be on that ship! Would anyone give permission to leave if we asked?* Rumblings along the James Town streets said no. Those who had asked declared the governor declined them and threatened them with treason.

Treason because they asked to return home? Had we not all given enough?

A Michaelmas Rot

Michaelmas Day, September 29, 1611 ~ James Town

If you eat goose on Michaelmas Day, you will not lack money all the year round.
A Michaelmas rot comes ne'er in the pot.
—Traditional English proverbs

Many famished in holes and other poore cabbins in the grounde, not respected because sicknes had disabled them for labour, nor was their sufficient for them that were more able to worke, our best allowance beinge but nine ounces of corrupt and putrified meale and haife a pinte of oatmeale or pease (of like ill condition) for each person a daye. Those provisions were sent over...by the appointment (as we conceave) of Sir Thomas Smith.
—Brief Declaration of the Ancient Planters, c. 1624

Michaelmas, and no goose. 'Twas an irrational thought, born of irrational times. Of course, 'twould be no goose, as there had been none in '09 and '10. I wondered if I would ever have Michaelmas goose again. Would ever even have goose again. I drew a deep sigh.

In Dorset, 'round about now, folks would be planning celebrations. They would hoist upon the tables fat geese with apples, filling other platters and bowls with carrots and turnips, blackberry tarts, sweetmeats, and gingerbread with just a hint of licorice. Then, ballads and bonfires all the night long.

Mop Fairs. For a moment I smiled, picturing the craftsmen and tradesmen coming to town carrying symbols of their profession seeking yearly work, October to October. And those with no trade toting a mop head.

Happy and festive the days now in England, for harvest was nearly complete while autumn's witchy chill had not yet arrived. And the songs and dances and toasts to St. Michael, the most valiant of all heaven's angels, would echo joyfully for days and days and days.

No one was singing here. Rain had poured upon us four or five days straight. Now, just a clammy drizzle. I bowed my head, not in prayer, but against the damp cold. My coif and Cecily's biggin afforded our heads some little protection, but not nearly enough to keep us dry.

Mud covered our shoes, making a sucking sound as we lifted each foot forward. Our clothes were growing wetter, and the cold soaked us to our bones.

Food lines were long, and tempers flaring. Typically, clerks or soldiers carried food to our homes. They checked to see if all were still alive, counted out the portions. But the muddy roads made it difficult to pull the cart, and being out in the rain so long caused the moldy grain to grow moldier. So at church service, Reverend Bucke told us to form a line at the storehouse.

I'd brought Cecily with me as we waited to gather the meal allotments for our family. Each of us held a tin; mine for the larger portion of wheat, hers for the smaller amount of peas or oatmeal.

Mistress Wright behind me touched my sleeve, and an unhappy grin spread across her face. "They say, *a Michaelmas rot comes ne'er in the pot*. I don't believe a word of it, do you?"

I smiled wanly and shook my head. No, I didn't believe it either. Not here.

"Make thee no mistake. The meal's rotten as it always be. *A Michaelmas rot comes* e'er *in the pot* when Sir Thomas Smythe is a-stirring it,*"* she muttered.

With each shipment of people came provisions, no supplies any better than those before. The man in front of me stared into his newly filled tin, swore under his breath, and walked off with a backward glare at the soldier dispensing the food.

Seeming not to notice, the soldier simply said, "Next." I handed him the larger wheat tin first.

As the measured ladles dipped into the barrel, I counted silently. Heaven forbid they should short us! *Five, ten pounds of wheat. Yes.* The soldier then reached for a one-pound measure and scooped two more in. *Good! Twelve pounds.* I waited expectantly. Finally, he chose a much smaller measure and doled out four more ounces. *There, the meal. Now, would it be oatmeal or peas alongside for today?*

He handed me the filled tin, and I held it in both arms. If it should topple on the ground... I imagined those behind me rushing to scoop it up, dirt and all.

Take my muddy, moldy wheat, for I am having goose! Would that it were so.

Cecily passed her tin to the soldier, who held it in one hand while reaching into the second barrel with the other. I glimpsed grain, not peas. *Oatmeal it would be. One half pint for Will, one third pint for Cecily and me, one fourth pint for Janey, per day.* Scoop, scoop, scoop.

"Sir, if a woman were with child...?" I gave him a pleading look. It was worth a try.

He shook his head. "I'm sorry, mistress." And his eyes seemed genuinely sympathetic. "If we gave to one, every woman in the fort would suddenly 'remember' a babe on the way."

I had expected as much.

"Thank you," he said idly, as he placed the daily mark beside the Peirce household on his ledger.

My heart dropped low in my chest, for 'twas always the same. Seven ounces of putrefied meal for Cecily and me per day, five for Janey. Nine for Will the times he was in James Town, as he was this week. Then the small additional portion of oatmeal or peas.

I could not prepare this food and make it savory—no one could. Even dry in the tin, the meal didn't look right with its peculiarly sickening dark color, flecks of green, and fishy smell. *Fish ought to smell fishy, but wheat ought to smell like wheat,* I thought with revulsion.

The oatmeal, too, smelled not sweet or grassy, but rather bitter and acrid. Rotten, the both of them. When cooked, both meals would have spider webs, and nothing I could do to remedy that. I would remove whatever moths I found in it first. And at that, not enough to keep us well fed even on spoiled rations.

This was it. No meats, for we were growing our livestock herds—not slaughtering. Little corn of our own, for we had only the three allotted acres, few corn kernels to plant, and little time to till the field.

Yet, since Dale's arrival, we did at least have these gardens. But the plentiful food Smythe had promised departing adventurers was mysterious. No one had ever seen it. No one ever expected to.

"Smythe be cursed!" shouted a man behind us, and I caught myself flinching.

"Curse Smythe? Curse Winne the draper and Casell the baker who provide this hogs' food."

"Hogs won't eat of it. They're too wise. We ought to take a lesson from the swine in what to shove into our mouths!"

Sniggering broke out in the line around the first man. Cecily started to laugh herself, and I clapped my hand across her mouth. "No," I hissed, and she startled, giving me a half-frightened, half-quizzical look. *What did I do wrong?* her eyes seemed to ask.

My hand still over her mouth, I leaned to her ear and whispered. "Even children can go to the stocks, be whipped, or starved...or worse." I took my hand away and stroked her neck, pressing my cheek to hers. Her eyes filled with tears, and she whimpered.

A summer's day in Dorset, a little girl, a scallop shell. Like Sir Thomas Smythe, I had promised so much, just as the Company had promised me, and neither they, nor I, could deliver.

Now I stood here in a food line, waiting for rancid meal portions barely at survival level in either quality or quantity. What had I done? And we could not even complain, could not swear an oath onto the men who had done this to us—for a whip snapped readily, a threat of gallows hung ever in the September air.

I found myself thinking of home and of leaving more and more. Thomasine's outcry at the birth of little Mara echoed. "Who would go home, given the chance?" she'd asked. *Who would not?* These thoughts had gone from idle wanderings of the mind to truly considering the possibility. *What if...? What if we could go home again?*

Cecily was growing taller. I wrapped my arm around her shoulder, leaned in, and whispered, "I am sorry, Cecily. For so many things..."

O God, How Weary
September 29, 1611 ~ James Town

*So that therby our frendes were moved both to desist from
sendinge and to doubt the truth of our letters, most part of which
weare by [Sir Thomas Smythe] usually intercepted and kept
backe; farther giveinge order by his directions to the governor
heere, that all mens letters should be searched at the goinge away
of ships, and if in anye of them weare founde that the true estate
of the Collony was declared, they were presented to the governor
and the indighters of them severely punished...*
—Brief Declaration of the Old Planters, c. 1624

*O God, O God, how weary, stale, flat, and unprofitable
seem to me all the uses of this world!*
—William Shakespeare

I spooned the oatmeal onto Will's trencher. I had tried to disguise the
moldy wheat by adding it to corn to make a kind of bread. So much
for the victuals the Virginia Company provided. We continued to grow our
Indian crops—beans, squash, corn, and pumpions. We were making as good
use of the three acres as we might, given the lack of seeds we had from home
and the lack of time to tend the field. I looked at the aged oatmeal. *No,
thank you.*

"No goose." I looked at Will. "No celebrations, no festivities, and that I
can live with. But I miss being able to serve a traditional meal to celebrate St.
Michael. It is horrid to be a mother serving such as this. I serve it, Will, for I
hate to throw it out. We cannot yet replace the oats. And I miss the foods we
grew up with—those you and I thought we would always eat."

The Indian foods certainly helped. When trading times were better, we
could procure seeds for these, and we had some set aside, but not enough.
Sometimes we could go further up the bay to the friendlier Patawomecks
for such.

Will patted my hand. "We have our three acres now. I'll send a letter to my cousin Richard, asking—nay, begging!—for seeds. And we'll plant our own flax and hemp as well."

I understood. We had no coins, nothing to offer his cousin. If we could find that commodity, that thing that we could trade to England to make a living and to pay back the Virginia Company...

But right now, we relied on the mercy of our friends and family at home. I studied my proud husband in his ragged doublet. "You do look like a pauper, Will. As do I. And the children." My voice was wistful. Only Cecily looked less tattered. But soon enough, she would be in rags, too.

"It won't be long before the hemp and flax will be ready, and a few flax wheels are complete as well." Will tried to sound convincing, but he knew as I did the need for clothing was too great, the spinning, even with all women working, would take so long. This was like digging the ditch around a fort with a spoon.

Will leaned in. "Speaking of letters. I have been away, but I need to be sure you know about letters home."

I lifted my eyebrows, a trencher of Indian squash and oatmeal in my hands, as I prepared to set the food at my place.

"What do you mean?" His ominous tone frightened me. What of letters home? Such things were private. Weren't they?

"If you write your brothers, or anyone, say only positive things about the settlement and the Virginia Company."

This was too much! I dropped the trencher onto the table with an angry *bang* and placed my hands on my hips. "Will, we are Englishmen with Englishmen's rights! The Company promised that to us long ago before e'er we stepped foot on the ship. They have no authority—"

"Aye, dear, 'twas promised to us, it's true. But we do not now *have* rights." He lowered his voice lest anyone passing near the window hear. "As the extremity of Dale's laws prove. These laws punish more severely than any martial law in Europe. Right now, we are bound to these laws and to what the Company tells us we can do. We have to hope this changes soon. But we cannot leave, and we cannot argue. You know Dale and his infamous gallows. We have no true court, no manner of appeal. Gates exercises some moderation, but his fellow Dale does not. And most of the settlement shall be moving upriver with Dale, you and the girls as well. You will be under Dale most directly. While, ultimately, I shall be here at James Town, which we shall hold as a military post."

Alarm grew within me. "But I want to be with *you* under Gates, and not alone in the clutches of the merciless Sir Thomas Dale."

He nodded solemnly. "I understand. I would have you here if I could. But

I cannot. The plan is to move most all women and children upriver to greater safety. You all were a huge encumbrance when it appeared the Spanish were in the bay. You would impede the fighting and be a sore point of negotiation if they should capture any of you." He glanced at his daughters. "No, we can't risk that the Spanish shall yet come, and everything indicates that they are considering doing just that."

I pressed my hand against my eyes. I did not look at him when I asked, "And the letters? They read them, don't they? The Company will not even allow us this freedom of a free people, this freedom to write what we choose. To speak *the truth*." I said it with a face of stone. The true measure of control over us was far worse than any could have imagined it could be.

He nodded, seeming ashamed of the situation he had brought his family into. "If the letters speak of any death or sickness or…or…hardships here, they call it libel against the Virginia Company." He paused, looking downward at his stale oatmeal, moving it around with his spoon. "Libel Dale punishes with hands and feet tied together every night for a month. And the letter shall never reach its intended destination, anyway. Make the letter pleasant, and it shall pass through censure."

Amazingly, I had lost my appetite for the rancid oatmeal and pushed the trencher away. "Oh, God, Will. It never ends."

Pole to Pole of Poverty
September 29, 1611 ~ James Town

From pole to pole of Poverty
We stumble through the years...
—Bernard O'Dowd

To man, faith; to woman, doubt. She bears the heavier
burden. Does not woman invariably suffer for two?
—Honore de Balzac

Later that evening after the girls had gone to bed, Will sat close to me on the table bench. I was using old thread, darning the stockings of the household as best as I could. Winter was fast approaching.

"Joan, I know it's difficult. It's been difficult. But we do have hope. Henricus is our future right now. An important future." His tone was serious.

I set the needles down, feeling irritable. "Hope? How so? Do you suppose the Indians upriver shall be more mindful of trading with us? Friendlier? No, wait. That's closer to the falls where the natives previously ran us off. It's near the Arrohattocs's town. *They'll* surely be thrilled to have *us* as new neighbors. And we have no passes home, no way to write our sorrows to our friends at home or to beg for help, no way of leaving, no decent food, and only the slimmest hope of growing our own! We have another long winter ahead of us, and...and the winter *terrifies* me."

Will placed his fingers against my mouth. "I know. I understand. This is..." He hesitated, seeming a little overcome with emotion. "This is far worse than I ever imagined when I asked you—told you—to come here. The Virginia Company made promises it could not keep. Fortune and luck have gone against us at every turn. But frankly, Joan, we're here, and here is where we'll be until something changes. The most promising hope is the new settlement upriver. Dale has ambitious plans for it. Those plans include wide, broad cornfields. Corn not just for us, but for those who come each year. In other words, we feed them the first year while they muddle through the seasoning, and then they will plant their own. But no more will their food come from our already sparse rations."

"Fine, fine," I said, my tone sarcastic. "Housing? What of that, Will Peirce? How long in dirt huts with Indian mats covering them?"

"Better housing. Brick foundations. Plans for a brick church, even. More space, a little more, uh, refined." He looked upward, and I could almost read his thoughts. How far we were from the home we'd left behind in Melcombe. Refined? We had not yet even moved into the fifteenth century!

He put his arms around me and drew me to him, kissing my cheek. "The land is good, Joan. The land is good. We must prove ourselves worthy in God's eyes...."

I pushed him away.

"I have proven myself! God should not ask more than that."

That bordered on blasphemy. Will, seemingly taken aback, got up and walked over to get his pipe. He pulled a splinter of wood from the hearth, lit it, then set his tobacco afire. He said nothing while he drew a deep drink from his pipe. Then, almost as if speaking to himself, he said, "Hm, this Indian tobacco is so bitter, harsh. If only there were a way to make it sweeter. Until we can get this acridness from our tobacco, we can never compete with the hearty Spanish brand."

"I said I've proven myself. I...I want to go home, Will."

There. I had declared it.

His eyes met mine while I continued. "And I am not the only one. We discussed it at Maria's bedside. Maria wants to go home as do most of the other women. We've suffered enough, Will. Dale's inhumane laws are just too much. I would call it more than we can bear, but we've had more than we could bear since we arrived, as early as the Starving Time. Or, wait, was it before that—the hurricane? God does not want us here, this we fear. We have waited for things to improve, and our hopes have dwindled. We do not..." My voice broke. "We do not wish to birth or raise our children here."

He laid the pipe down. "You are truly asking to leave?" I saw comprehension strike him. "This is not a moment's anger or frustration over Michaelmas." His words were not a question, for the resolution in my own eyes and voice must have struck him.

I nodded. "I have turned it over in my mind since that night at Maria's. I have lain awake and thought of it. What would we be throwing away if the girls and I leave? What would we be risking if we stay?"

He said nothing, but he considered me seriously as I continued. "I have concluded we risk our lives if we stay. We lose only property and time invested if we go."

Realization dawned in Will's eyes. "So that's it, then? You want to go home? You all want to go home—the women?"

I nodded. "Annie had her babe during the Starving Time. Sarah Rolfe birthed, and buried, her daughter on the island of Bermuda. Lady Gates's death left her children bereft of their mother. Now Maria—a godly woman, Will—has been forced to labor and deliver while fearing Spanish banging on her birthing chamber door! No help, no celebration or prayer. Just her struggling with only Mistress Wright and several who left their bolted doors to aid her. And little Mara, 'twill be a surprise if that sickly child survives." I shook my head. "We are as ragged as the poorest on the streets of London. Church mice are poor, but they—even *they!*—have more security than we do. No, Will, it is too much. Much too much. Do you think there's any chance Governor Gates or Sir Thomas Dale would agree to a...to a pass home?"

Will's shoulders dropped as he stared at the walnut plank table. He did not meet my eyes. "No," he said, his voice a croak. "No, no passes. They will never allow it even if we husbands agreed. Even if we speak up on your behalves. And I don't want you to suffer, but I don't want you to leave, either."

"We are truly not together here, Will. I see you only when you are not out at the other forts on missions fighting the natives. We had plans, we had a dream, but that dream has turned to nightmare, inch by inch. All the women, the old planters, feel the same as I. If we could but get a pass..."

His voice was a cross between hard and defeated. "You will not get a pass. You might as well put the thought out of your mind, Joan. You are here. The other wives are here. The children are here as well."

"But the Gates girls..."

"...were a special allowance due to Gates's influence and to their mother's death," he finished for me.

"What if George Yeardley..."

Again he interrupted me. "Joan, George Yeardley is as stuck as the rest of us! Do you not understand that Company orders bind Gates and Dale? *The Company will not let us leave.* You might as well consider yourself a soldier on military assignment. I am sorry to be so blunt, but it's what we've got." He threw his hands up.

What we have, we have. Maggie's words from the Starving Time.

No, I don't want to make the best of it! I am a wife and a mother, not a soldier! I want to go home.

George had been our hope, that he might intervene on our behalf if Tempie asked him. Now Will had dashed that.

"You know that Maria named her baby Mara? For God has dealt with us bitterly, she said."

He nodded. I waited for him to speak. Nothing.

A dram of an odd brew, pumpion beer, sat on the table. I wanted to throw it, to hear it smash loudly against the wall. I wanted Will and Dale and Gates *and Sir Thomas Smythe* to hear me! "This is the most terrifying place e'er God created for a babe to be born!" I shouted. How rarely I raised my voice, but the shouted words pleaded, *Hear me.*

He dropped his head in his hands. "What would you have me do? I am as trapped as you are, Joan."

"Not quite." I was surprised at how cold my words were.

He looked up, a question in his eyes. I answered it, for 'twas time he knew.

"Unlike you, I eat spoiled food to feed two, myself and our baby. Unlike you, I will be delivering a child into this settlement, a place God has forsaken. And He has, Will. Forsaken it, I mean. I am not sure God is here at all. Aye, Will, you are going to be a father. The father of a baby born to wear rags and eat filth. *In this place.*"

Pilgrims in This Vale of Tears
September 29, 1611 ~ James Town

Gently, Lord, oh, gently lead us,
Pilgrims in this vale of tears,
—Thomas Hastings

When peace, like a river, attendeth my way,
When sorrows like sea billows roll;
Whatever my lot, Thou has taught me to say,
It is well, it is well, with my soul.
—Horatio Spafford

The island suddenly seemed very, very small.

All of Virginia, in fact, seemed small as if closing in upon me.

And the ocean—that seemed too wide and too endless. It had become, in my mind, a barrier, rather than what it should have been: a thoroughfare back to England.

Will had said no. He had said that I must think of myself as a soldier, that the Virginia Company was not giving passes home.

What was a pass? Why did I need one?

If I chose to leave, why could I not? Before I had departed England, had anyone told me I would be unable to go home if I so chose?

No, they had not.

The baby in me had given his first kick, and yet all I felt was a deep hopelessness, a fear of the impending winter, and a sense of ensnarement as if I could not breathe and the very air of James Town would suffocate me.

The air was not too bitter yet, but a few red leaves began to sprinkle my way. Just a few. The vast majority were still green, and the forest gave little sign of the desolate Virginia winter to come.

"You shall fall," I said to the leaves, as I walked the path to the Back River.

I had come to find the Back River a quiet place to be alone and away from the madness that was James Town. Dale's new blockhouse, built to keep the natives from stealing our cattle, made this place much safer than before. Soldiers patrolled in the watchtowers, keeping permanent guard. I paid them little mind, for I could think of only one thing.

Will said no. Will said no.

Why had I gotten my hopes up for what could not be? Why had I seen the Gates girls departing and allowed myself to believe that Governor Gates might afford my two girls and me the same privilege?

Now Will would be leaving again for what surely was a more dangerous location—the building of Henricus.

At some point, with its *palisados* up, Henricus would be a more secure site from the Spanish, but the natives were protective of their town sites and hunting grounds upriver. The Indians knew once a fort was up, it would likely stay up. So they fought the hardest during the building of forts.

Will was going there to this dangerous place, and later we would all go.

Hope of a better life here was like a Will with the wisp, a ghost fire one could chase but never reach.

God, you might have expected better from me, but this day I cannot give it. You said all would be well here, and it is not. I sat down in a crumple of tattered clothes and despair on the riverbank.

I did not say 'twould be an easy path.

"I thought I could go home!" I said aloud while looking up at the grey clouds that had gathered. "I did not know that saying aye meant trapping myself in this New World forever."

Because you cannot go home this day does not mean you may ne'er go home. A soft voice spoke to me. *Release it. Give it to me. That is always the right thing to do.*

Give what? Sadness? Fear? Rejection? Denial? Hopelessness? Moldy victuals? What part, Lord, what part? Anger burst within me.

All of it.

Footsteps behind me caused me to jump.

Picking her way toward me was not a native nor a soldier, but Tempie.

"Will said you wanted to take a walk after dinner, to be alone a while. I know this is where you come." She looked up and down the river. "It has a pretty color today, doesn't it? The river, I mean?"

"No." I refused to look at the river as anything but water I could not cross to get to where I wanted to go.

Suddenly the tears began to tumble onto my cheeks, and I felt the hopelessness rise within me. "I cannot go, Tempie. I cannot go. No one can."

She dropped down beside me and looked at me earnestly. "I know," she said. "I heard."

"I will be as Maria Bucke soon. Tempie, I am with child!"

Her smile was knowing. "Aye. That I have supposed."

I smiled back in spite of myself, as I wiped some of the wetness from my face. "How did you know? You're not surprised?"

She laughed. "No. I'm not surprised, Joan. You've had troubles of the belly. The victuals not going down so well." She glanced down. "Your waist a bit thicker, and no one fattens in Virginia from the food alone."

I laughed in spite of myself. "Well, that is so."

"But mostly," she continued more seriously, "is that you have given up. You have gotten yourself worked up in thoughts that cannot be. You seem to feel the only solution is to leave. You have set your mind upon it as if that were the only way out."

I let my eyes wander down the smaller river to where it met the James. From that distant blue line, the ships set out for the sea and away from here.

"Isn't it?" I said idly. "You do not have children to raise here—feeding them such horrible food. Birthing them here amidst the fear and suffering." Tempie's frailty from the Starving Time had caused her to fear she might never bear children. And here I was complaining. I dropped my head self-consciously. "I'm sorry. I...I do not mean to offend. 'Tis easy for no one."

"Least of all a mother," she said sympathetically. "I am not offended. I am here to listen."

I went on to unburden myself then. How I missed my home. How it seemed so beautiful and pleasant in England. The food, the vendors at the Michaelmas fairs. No Indians to fight... "And Michaelmas goose!" I said suddenly.

She turned her eyes to mine. "Goose? *Goose?*" And she began to laugh. "Lovey, I would sit here and cry over many a thing. But not goose."

I don't know why I started to laugh too, even as I felt tears still blurring my vision. Perhaps just the way she said it. *You're crying over goose?*

I gave her a playful shove. "'Twas you goin' on about it last summer! Pork and 'a nice fat goose,' you used to say."

"Ah, geese come, and geese go," she said as if that were a proverb from the Bible.

After that, we sat in silence for a while just listening to the shushing of the river upon the shore, the cry of seabirds as they passed over.

At last, I said, "Those peregrines in the cages. Did you see them?"

She looked at me curiously. "I did not see, but I heard."

"The female—she did not want to go, did not look comfortable in a slatted box, confined from the forest she knew so well. But she was accepting. If I could be but as accepting as she! What are we but falcons, trapped in a traveling cage? We know no more of the future than they. Life here is endless change, never stability. England, I understood. I do not understand this place any more than the peregrine understood the wooden bars. And we are no more free to escape our gaol than they are. We are ensnared, Tempie. Tethered and trapped."

After a moment, Tempie said simply, "Aye."

More silence, which neither of us felt a need to fill.

"Tempie, I miss Michaelmas the way it used to be," I said after a few moments. It felt childish to say, but there it was.

Tempie thought for a moment. "Michaelmas was a wondrous time of year," she said wistfully. "But consider this, Joan. Does St. Michael *require* a feast to bless and protect, or does he protect where'er we be? I mean, is the hearty meal for you or for him? I believe St. Michael has been with us from the beginning. Else, why did we not perish in the hurricane? How did we make it through the seasoning and the Starving Time? Why have the Spanish not taken us down yet? Look around and ask yourself if St. Michael the Protector has not been with us all along."

I drew in my breath sharply as the truth of what she said struck me. Tears blurred my view of the river, and I said at last, "Oh, he has been here. He has been here as you say. St. Michael the Archangel." My voice dropped to an awe-filled whisper as if I were summoning him, as if I might actually see him towering nearby, hand upon sword ready to fight for us.

And again we sat in silence. Why my fear then?

I knew.

"Tempie, I suppose my true fear is of winter's approach," I said at last as if even saying the words would bring some terrible tragedy to befall.

She nodded. "As am I," she said quietly. She patted my arm. "I suspect we always will be. Being in England, I should think, would not change that."

I turned to her because this thought had never occurred to me.

She continued with a shrug. "Fear is fear, Joan. Will you let it get the best of you, or will you carry on? When the door is closed before you, when you cannot knock it down? What's left? You may rage at the door all you like. When raging won't open it, then what?"

I said nothing. I did not like any of the answers I knew were true.

"Acceptance, Joan. Acceptance brings peace in its time, think you not? Take each day as it comes, enjoy your blessings...."

I moved to interrupt, and she stopped me.

"We *do* have blessings. Count them and see. How many can you name? Cecily is here, safe from a long journey. Janey is recovering and growing. Will and George survived the hurricane and shipwreck." She paused. "We have each other. We have both survived our fair share of tribulations."

I nodded. These things were real, things we could love and bless even if Virginia itself and the Company did not always bless us.

"The day must come when we are free to leave. Surely, that day will come. Knowing that brings a measure of peace, doesn't it? If not today, then someday. Next week, next month." She paused. "Next year? We will likely not have to stay here the rest of our lives if we live long enough. After all, we succeed by 1616, or we depart. Patience, dear friend, patience."

"Might they abandon us? 'No more silver thrown to you?' Do you think they would do that, Tempie?"

She paused and looked away. "I think they might. But somehow we would find a way home. I think every carpenter and shipwright here would be building away. The men would fell those trees so fast…. If the Company abandons us, then at least we can decide what our fates will be. If they do not abandon us, it will mean against the odds perhaps we have succeeded."

Yes.

I listened as, seeming to speak more to herself than to me, she went on. "I have fought this in my mind as well. Don't you think I wish I could sail home? We all wish that, of course. But once I stopped fighting the urge to leave, I am finally finding peace. Peace just to be."

A memory returned, one I would never choose to recall. But it came anyway.

I was in the 'tween deck of the *Blessing*. Sweet Harrison, our sailor friend, had brought Maggie and me a warning. *Ain't nothin' can save a ship from a hurricane if a hurricane wants her. But prayers might help, so say 'em. And if we don't get through, pray your drowning's quick.* The mighty tempest had thrown us about like rag dolls. The rain and winds beat upon us as the ocean came alive in great waves that towered over the ship. How insignificant the *Blessing* and souls upon her had seemed at that moment. And when the hurricane's fury had yanked Janey from my arms, all seemed lost.

But then a deep voice had filled my heart with words, distinct and forceful. *The* Blessing *shall hold. Hold your blessings.*

Hold your blessings.

Surely that was sound advice now as it had been then. How could Tempie have known? The truth was she couldn't have. She had simply brought me the same wisdom now that had come to me then.

"Tempie, you are my angel."

"And you are mine."

Silence once more, as we each sorted our own thoughts.

"And Maggie…she's an angel to us both, I should think." I liked to believe that.

"Just so." Tempie's eyes were distant upon the other shore of the river.

"Maggie stayed with us somehow. I just feel it."

The baby kicked, and the sun dipped just a little, dropping below the grey cloud. Its rays sprayed from beneath the cloud as if shining a light just for me. The sun had been hiding as if it were not there at all, as if it never had been and never would be. Yet with the passing of a little time, the sun found its way back, proving it was here all along. That it had never truly left.

We could just be. Be, like the river. Be, like the hidden sun. And be, like the leaves, even as they fell in a march toward winter.

Name Them One by One
September 29, 1611 ~ James Town

When upon life's billows you are tempest tossed,
When you are discouraged, thinking all is lost,
Count your many blessings, name them one by one,
And it will surprise you what the Lord hath done....
Count your many blessings, angels will attend,
Help and comfort give you to your journey's end.
—Johnson Oatman, Jr.

That night after Will and the children had gone to bed, I poured a bit of ink into the inkwell. The old feather from a wild turkey made a fine quill.

The candle burned down, and the fire was low. Fortunately, the nights were not yet as cold as they could be.

I reckoned it now to be at least half past nine. Typically, I would not sit up this late into the night. Morning, with its chores and Dale's tasks, would be here soon enough.

But this night, I craved the time alone in the darkness and alone with my thoughts.

Before me sat a daybook, one of several Will had managed to barter off an incoming ship.

I had held the book up to Will as he came from the bedchamber in his long shirt. "May I?"

He nodded. "Don't stay up too late, Joan."

And in the daybook, I wrote:
Ye 29ᵗʰ of September, 1611. James His Town. Blessings E'en Heere.

Beneath that, I wrote the numeral *1* and beside it: *Cecily arrived safely &*
in health, praise bee to God.

Two. *Will a fine father & a good souldier.*

Three. *Janey, Tempie & I survived Starving.*

Four. *Will survived the hurricane!*

And, of course. *Our new babe to come.*

I added, *A roofe over our heades.*

The list went down the page. How amazing to me that the words flowed to my mind faster than I could dip and blot the ink and put them down. So many blessings? *Even here?* Why had I not seen this before?

Cecily had not fallen to the calenture as Lady Gates had. Janey had mostly recovered from the starvation. Maggie had died, 'twas true. But having had Maggie, even for a short time, had blessed Tempie and me immeasurably.

I wrote simply, *Our Maggie.*

Then, *Maggie's musick & her poetry.*

The list continued. *Tempie's Booke of Psalms undamaged in hurricano.* How many times had those Psalms set to music sustained us?

And, of course, *Maggie's tambourine.*

Tempie makes mee laughe.

What of the soldier Walter? He was a blessing himself! I wrote, *Walter.*

As a separate item, *Walter burried Maggie.*

Harrison hee helped us in the hurricane.

Annie.

Sarah Rolfe shee tooke care of us.

Elizabeth her ring she left to mee. It spun about my scrawny finger, but I loved its dainty carved rose.

Old Grace, shee blessed Tempie & mee ere shee dyed.

The blessings grew. For each one I wrote, another came to mind, like a vine pruned so that two sprouts could grow.

Mistress Wright's midwiffery skills.

Mara Bucke shee still lives.

Ginny Laydon shee too survived the Starving Time.

The fire's happy crackling caused me to write, *Wee have a warm fier.*

We soon to have flaxe and hempe and wheeles to spin. The spinning might be endless, but at least it gave a hope of better garments.

I looked up to the little candle, gamely lighting my work. *Wee yet have tallow for candels.* I tried not to think of the sweat that had gone into making them. No, only blessings here.

I do so like pumpion, Indian squash & bean & Indian corne. Our Virginia victuals.

My herbes and medicks soe wonderfully prosper heere.

My mother's carefull instruction to mee about herbes. A warm memory flooded me. Spring in Melcombe Regis. My mother's sweet voice. Singing *Greensleeves* as we cleaned for Father.

Oh! *Father & his storries.*

And my father's dying gift to me, the ever-present weight about my neck. *My olde pilgrime's badge,* I wrote. The iron badge was hundreds of years old. My great-great-grandfather Phippen had brought it home from a pilgrimage to the tomb of St. James in Compostela, Spain.

The scallop-shaped badge reminded me of the scallop Cecily and I had split that long ago day on an old stone bench in Dorset. I wrote: *Our cockle-shelles did not breake!* They were whole.

Tom, Cecily's father, hee was a goode mann.

I kept writing. An owl hooted somewhere beyond the palisade. *Grim bird! Bring me not bad news tonight.* I pushed the omen out of my mind and turned my thoughts instead to Virginia's song birds.

The redd cardinal birde which cheered o'er Maggie's grave.

The chickadee which fedd us one daye wee most desperatte for meate and hope.

A laugh as I scrawled, *Acornes our Manna from Heaven.* They had fed us during the Starving Time.

Littel white flowers for Tempie & mee.

Our toaste to friendshippe while wee yet starved.

I love the Backe River & James His River.

No Spaniards came. I started to write "yet," but decided not to think that.

Before I knew it, I had listed fifty-eight blessings. The candle was burning lower, but my spirit was aflame.

Fifty-eight! Even at James Town.

I snuffed out the candle and took myself to the bedchamber where Will's slow breathing greeted me. Steady, as Will himself was.

I kissed his ear and shut my eyes.

By early spring, we would be at Henricus. I must remember to ask Will before he left: what exactly did Dale plan to *do* at Henricus? What could we expect? Gates had planned a meeting at the church where he would tell us more.

But for tonight, I knew that the answer was just as Tempie had said. *Once I stopped fighting the urge to leave, I finally found peace. Peace just to be.*

However, a new chapter in our lives was cresting the horizon. Finding peace there would not be easy.

The Western Star
October 1, 1611 ~ James Town

I will not sleep from mental fight
Nor shall my sword sleep in my hand
Till we have built Jerusalem
In England's green and pleasant land
—William Blake

Her blue eyes sought the west afar,
For lovers love the western star.
—Sir Walter Scott

I became determined to see the best in what we had. Else I should lose heart, as I had been rapidly doing before. Tempie was right. How did anger serve me? How did it serve the baby I carried? Perhaps life would be better at Henricus. At least, I tried to hope so.

Will was soon leaving to help build the new town. It seemed he came home again only to depart once more. I took hold of his arm. "Will, wait. I know this is a...foolish question, but *must you go?* You just arrived back from the forts at the river mouth."

He nodded. "Aye, I know, I know. I'm sorry. But yes, I must go. 'Tis an order," he said almost apologetically. I knew that he liked his absences no more than I did. But he often reminded me that he could have been fighting in the Lowlands, in Ireland, in Cartagena. From that perspective, being in the Virginia woods seemed much closer.

"Joan, I've been thinking about this. I had not told you before. I'd hoped to spare you worry. But I now feel that you must understand the scope of what we could face. Dale is driving us hard, but the Spanish threat is more potent than ever."

"What?" I covered my eyes as if that would block the news.

Some parts I knew. Dale had been fighting for Virginia's survival. Fighting to grow her settlements upriver into Indian territory more removed from threat of Spanish attack.

Love or hate Sir Thomas Dale—and we mostly hated him—his actions forced us to admit that Dale was a man who got things done. He was disciplined, organized, and a firm believer that one's will could accomplish any plan, particularly if God had ordained that plan.

Clearly, Dale believed that his plans and those of the Company were God-ordained because he had set to work as if he could not fail.

The fire that burnt within him during May, now, in September, raged as an inferno. Dale had seen our vulnerability when caravels appeared off the coast. He had tasted Spanish defeat, had seen a momentary vision of Spanish invaders overrunning and massacring our people. Dale's success or failure in that battle would have had long implications for all Englishmen, those in Virginia and those in England.

Perfection drove Dale as if it were a whip and he the horse. The marshal felt God had warned him that Virginia's weakness to the Spaniard could be her downfall. The Virginia Company had been right, but almost too slow, in ordering a remote, well fortified upriver settlement.

These things, I knew. But there was more, Will said. "Sir Thomas Gates brought news from Madrid. The English ambassador reported forty sail of ship were leaving Lisbon to attack Virginia. *Forty sail!* Gates assured Dale and the men—I was there—that even the ambassador thought this far-fetched. But the seed is there, Joan. Word from the ambassador is that, rumors aside, the Spanish are undoubtedly worried about our plantation. The captured spies in the bay were not here by chance, Gates said. Thus, Dale and Gates are determined to move us westward at a furious pace further beyond the reaches of Spanish raiders. And that, too, is one reason for the censored letters. It would not serve us for the Spanish to know how weak we truly are," Will finished.

I stood speechless.

A look of concern crossed his face. "We have to get to Henricus before the Spanish..." He stopped abruptly. "Well, word is that Molina, the spy—and he *is* a spy—has admitted to Dale that we should fear no threat *this* year, but says he cannot speak for next. And the leaders suspect Molina is somehow passing intelligence to his king through Spanish sympathizers here. But we have not discerned how."

"Speed, then," I said with a skipped heartbeat, remembering the fear Tempie and I had felt when we'd considered running away to the Indians.

"All speed. Before another attack and before planting season. We'll be leaving within a few days, hoping Henricus will be ready within a fortnight. Then we prepare for our crops, our animals, our hospital, and our church lands." Will looked thoughtful. "Dale is a harsh taskmaster, 'tis true, but his plan is ingenious." Will admired anyone who surveyed the angles of a situation. "The goal is this: in the months of April through August, we focus on planting and harvesting. Never to be hungry again. During the months of

September through March, we build towns and secure new lands as needed. Our immediate project is to dig a cut-through, river to river," he explained. "The plan is solid, Joan. Solid." He was attempting to reassure me, I saw.

Still, his confidence did give me some security. As much security as I could have, anyway. Even so, this new settlement was largely unknown to me. *But dear God, the Spanish!*

Will went on. "Dale has done fine work in preparing planks ahead of time. We can get straight to building."

As I began to understand the depth of Spanish power over us, I understood more the need for haste. "Do you truly believe Henricus is a way out for us?"

"I do. A wonderful strategic site fifty miles upriver. Besides being safer, Henricus is closer to the mines in the low hills. Did you know Strachey even found a lion's claw in a cave out there?"

I knew he was trying to distract me. And I was not above being distracted. "A lion's claw?"

So there would be lions prowling around Henricus. The Indians occasionally wore lion skins, and some of the English on westward excursions had seen these beasts. Around James Town Island, we had bear, grey wolves, red foxes, and eagles, and great sturgeon fifteen feet long in the river. There were frogs here that would equal full ten of our largest frogs in England. These frogs sounded like bulls to us, and so we had taken to calling them "bull frogs." In Virginia, some frogs even lived in trees and made a peculiar racket during the summer. And of course, there were the beautiful peregrines Cecily and I had seen. Virginia was a wild, exotic place. I had to admit the thought of moving west enticed and frightened me at the same time.

"How well do you think my herbs will grow there?"

"Marvelously. The land is much fertile, the best we've seen yet. And, Joan, it's healthful up there as well. Henricus will sit upon a high bluff on the river with wholesome air and less swampland. Henricus shall sit between the Appomattock and Arrohattoc towns."

I tried to understand the plan. "You said you were 'cutting from river to river'? Is there another river near the site?"

Will smiled, a gentle, calming smile, and I remembered how glad I was to have him home again if even for a short time. *I could add that to my list of blessings.* That realization caused me to listen to him and to be grateful for even a brief visit rather than to fret.

"My dear, we are cutting across the *same* river."

Had I missed something in my own musings? I wrinkled my brow. "The same river?"

He pulled a slate and chalk toward him.

"Let me show you. Here we are." He drew a wide James River and an island nearly connected to its Northern shore. Pointing with his pencil, he said, "There's James Town Island. Now, further west, the River of the Appomattocks splits from the James River." He drew a fork. "The James snakes off to the right. And, see, it even looks like a snake, the way it weaves like an *S*. These are the curls. The river just naturally wraps around parcels of land and protects them. That's what makes this area so valuable for defense."

He pointed to a smaller *S*. "This will be where Henricus sits. You see the river forms a natural moat around the land on three sides." The chalk made a *scritch scritch* sound as he filled in the lines. "On the fourth side, we'll dig a ditch, river to river, which will separate the piece of land and turn it into an island." Will paused and looked up at me. "We learned this in the Lowlands from the Prince of Orange. He conceived the Dutch Water Line to protect his towns. We shall use a similar idea to create a water fortress about Henricus. Dale will see that palisades encircle the fort, of course. A very promising location." He seemed glad to be able to give me something akin to hopeful news.

"You're going to actually dig a channel between the river coils?" I asked.

Will nodded. "That gives us a canal joining the two sides of the river."

"The rest of the island, outside the palisade, will be for the livestock and corn, then?"

He shook his head, then rethought it. "Well, there *will* be some cattle and fields there, but the main supplies of these will be elsewhere." Will had filled in the bottom part of the *S* as Henricus. Now, he pointed to the top. "He's going to call that Coxendale. We'll put a five-mile long palisade all the way around the land and river encompassing Henricus so that Coxendale alone will have twelve *miles* of land enclosed."

"Wow," I said, mimicking a word the Indians used when impressed. While the word sounded peculiar to our ears, it also seemed aptly to express surprise. It made us feel, somehow, a little more Virginian as native words began to mingle with our English ones. The natives, too, used some our words, a strange sort of brotherhood in a land where men were not at all brothers.

Will continued. "The Coxendale palisade will go around the river surrounding the island so that Coxendale will somewhat act as an outer defense for Henricus and also form a great pen for our hogs. And there will be glebe land there, for Reverend Whitaker. One hundred acres!"

Reverend Whitaker was an ardent young Cambridge scholar who had arrived with Dale. I was not surprised he would be the pastor at Dale's settlement. Whitaker felt the Lord had called him to missions work amongst the natives, and Dale himself was very mindful of converting the Indians. That meant Reverend Bucke, who had arrived with Gates, would stay with the governor at James Town. Which, sadly, meant Maria would likely stay behind in James Town when we all moved to Henricus.

Will was still talking. "And, Joan, you'll like this. We're going to build a retreat or guest house for the sick and for those just arriving who need time to acclimate. It shall have eighty beds."

"A hospital!" Perhaps we would no longer have to heal the sick in our own homes, especially those newly off ship.

"Yes. Dale plans to call it Mount Malady."

I chuckled at the name in spite of myself.

Will laughed, too. "The blockhouses will be Hope in Faith, Charity in Wisdom, Patience, and Elizabeth."

Dale had undoubtedly named Fort Elizabeth for King James's daughter. One was always wise to remember the king's children when christening sites.

Will was growing excited. "And across from Dale's Dutch Ditch, into the Main, we'll put another palisade..." He was still sketching. "That will be two miles from town with a palisade two miles across. Great cornfields there! Dale feels he can feed all the settlers now in Virginia and all who will come within three years from this great field alone.

"There will also be a huge circuit, twenty miles enclosed by river and four miles of palisades. This will be Rochdale for cattle, hogs, and other livestock. Joan, we'll have to work hard, but I believe we may be on our way to prosperity at long last."

Still, James Town was the known. What would a move mean? How deep into the heart of Virginia wilderness we'd be! And Dale would be the taskmaster there while Gates would keep a contingency of soldiers at James Town.

"When...when would we move?" I still felt uneasy.

"Three hundred men will soon be on their way upriver to construct the forts. The palisade around Henricus first, our primary defense against the Indians. Then we'll build the church and storehouse. Dale is sending a message. First, defense. Second, God. Then, storing up for future needs. Only then comes comfort, the houses we'll construct. The other forts and palisades will follow. We'll work through the days and even nights, building as fast as possible. Discipline and efficiency paramount. In March, if all goes well, most settlers will move to Henricus. There to plant, ourselves and our crops."

And our baby. I placed my hand on my belly. My little one was due just before that time.

Will, seeming not to notice, went on. "If those great fields across the river produce as well as we hope, we'll be much less dependent on moldy, shipped food. Dale with Gates—strong leadership at last."

Aye, all well and good. But the Company was still going bankrupt. And as yet, we had no commodity, nothing of value to sell.

The answer, as it were, came in a small package from Trinidad.

Which Seed Shall Prosper
January 12, 1611 ~ James Town

SIRE....Your Majesty commanded me to look into...two vessels that had sailed from here for the East Indies; but this was uncertain. For they have only gone to Virginia and/or to the Island of Trinidad...in search of tobacco.
—Don Alonzo de Velasco in London to King Philip of
    Spain, May 26, 1611

Who waits until the wind shall silent keep,
Will never find the ready hour to sow.
Who watcheth clouds will have no time to reap.
At daydawn plant thy seed, and be not slow
At night. God doth not slumber take nor sleep:
Which seed shall prosper thou shalt never know.
—Helen Hunt Jackson

John Rolfe came rapping at the door one bitter, cold evening. The hour was late, the girls already in the loft. So I was surprised to see him, especially since Will was away at Henricus. Still, I ushered him in.

Then I hesitated. At such a time, had I been in the West Country, I might I have offered him apple cider or apple wine. Some warm drink against the winter chill. But here we had no such thing as we had no apple or pear trees—although Governor Gates had planted a few orchard trees which were still young. The nearest fruit here might have been *maracocks* which the natives planted. We used their word, calling the fruit maypops. Nothing so good as a maypop on a hot day. The Indians made a drink of maypops and walnut milk. But I didn't even have that. No, nothing at all to offer John.

However, he seemed not to notice. Instead he smiled and was as excited as I have ever seen him. Will and John had become friends while marooned on the Bermudas. Will, I knew, respected John's blend of practicality and dreams.

"Good evening, Joan. Sorry to be by so late, but I was hoping you could help me."

I smiled. "Well, I can't cook you anything decent if that's what you're after."

He laughed. "No, no, it's your book, Gerard's *Herball*. You have one, don't you? I thought I recalled you did."

"I do." The *Herball* was one of the better items I had brought from home. It had been a help many times. It even included some New World plants, which was helpful as we attempted to learn more about them. "You're certainly welcome to look at it." I noticed that in one hand he carried a linen sack.

His smile was broad, and I gave him a curious look. He was obviously delighted about something.

"Would you mind lifting the book down?" My belly had grown bigger, and I felt unwieldy.

He did, setting it on the table.

"Now, what are you seeking, John?"

"Well, you'll know soon enough anyway. I have gotten some seeds! Precious as gold, they are."

I looked at him curiously, an eyebrow cocked. I had no idea what he meant.

His grin grew wider as he held up the grubby sack. "This is just a portion of them, of course. I left most back in my home. Can't take a chance, you know." He was speaking more to himself than to me.

"Uh, John?" Now my curiosity was getting the better of me. "*What* have you left back in your house?"

"Ah, Joan. It's tobacco! Seeds from Trinidad, no less," he said proudly.

My mouth formed a great gaping *O* of astonishment. "Trinidad? How did you get Spanish seed here?" I asked in a hushed whisper. "The Spanish forbid the sale of *any* tobacco seeds to foreign nations under penalty of death. The market is theirs. They claim every…every *puff* of it!"

John laughed before saying, "They also claimed the entire New World." He shrugged. "They claim many things."

Just before the first settlers had come to James Town, King Philip had made it clear: he would restrict the sowing of his sweet tobacco to the islands of Cuba, Puerto Rico, Venezuela and Santo Domingo. The Spanish knew that we could not profit from the bitter Powhatan tobacco. The king of Spain was enriching himself off his smoky weed.

I didn't care for the pipe myself, but John, Will, Sam, George—many of the men and some women—drank tobacco regularly.

Europeans had been befuddled when first they saw an Indian with a tube-like thing between his lips and smoke pouring from the native's mouth. That had been when Columbus first brought native tobacco to Europe. Once, a Spaniard had spent seven years in prison after coming to Spain blowing smoke from his mouth and nose. The poor man had emerged from prison only to find all of Spain smoking tobacco.

Tobacco finally became popular in England about the time my father had been born. In that short span, all of Europe now pulled on pipes. The best and *only* place to get tobacco was from the Spanish. We smoked what we had from the natives, but Indian tobacco was bitter.

John had apparently decided to experiment with growing Caribbean tobacco. I understood at once the genius of his plan.

"You hope to compete with the Spanish," I said excitedly.

"Well," John said tentatively. "I would rather this not go further than you and Will. Sam, George, and Tempie are 'safe ears,' too. Trustworthy ears. 'Tis a long shot since the Caribbean Isles have milder weather. I'll have to experiment—see how it works." We knew that tobacco didn't grow well in England's cold. Yet, could the Spanish weed flourish in Virginia…?

"But how did you… *Trinidad?*" I asked again. I was looking toward the bag with envy. I so much wanted to see Caribbean tobacco seeds.

John explained. "The Trinidadians are running a tobacco operation out of their island. These fine leafs they procure across the water in Venezuela, at the Orinoco River. The Spanish king has not yet discovered these tobacco sales going on there, or so I hear. Even though King Philip has forbidden all trading of tobacco seed, the Spanish rarely visit the island. As they say, *When the cat's away, the mouse may play!* And so the traders *do* play. The captain who sold me these counted fourteen English and Dutch ships docked in port there. King Philip will catch on soon, surely. But for now, I have been able to buy some seed. While the door still remains open."

I was thoughtful. "So you received the tobacco from the *John and Francis?*" The ship had only arrived the day before.

"Indeed. I knew the ship belonged to Sir Robert Mansell. Mansell is quite the trader. So I thought it worth asking, and sure enough, the ship had gone through Trinidad. I spoke covertly with the captain, having only a little silver I brought from home. For that, I received a portion of the seeds the captain had purchased. Trinidadian tobacco is the finest anywhere."

He was still clutching the little sack. "I don't suppose you want to see these?" His look was sly. "Herbalist that you are."

I blushed. "I am not sure I qualify as an 'herbalist,' but…" How I *did* want to see those seeds!

John beamed, cradling the sack. He was as proud as a new father.

I threw back my head and laughed. "Yes, John, show me your little Spanish babies, then."

He laughed too as he opened the sack. I peered inside. The seeds were very tiny and dark brown.

John grinned again. "Mistress Peirce, you *do* like planting things, don't you? Let's see what's in your big book."

I went to the index then flipped pages. "Tobacco...tobacco... Here it is! 'Of Yellow Henbane, or English Tobacco.' No, but close." I flipped the page. "Ah! 'Of Tobacco or Henbane of Peru,'" I read. "'There be two sorts or kinds of Tobacco, one great, the other lesser; the greater was brought into Europe out of the provinces of America, which we call the West Indies: the other from Trinidada...'" I looked up. "Trinidada! That's yours."

"Keep going, keep going!" John said excitedly. He always had such a calm demeanor. I was most surprised, and a little amused, by his enthusiasm.

I began skimming the page, running my finger across it. "Gerard says the English tobacco, yellow henbane, has yellow flowers and is a small plant."

"That's the bitter kind, the kind the natives here use for their ceremonies," John put in.

"Yes. Then, there are two Peruvian tobaccos. Tobacco of Peru has white flowers and is the larger of the two. Tobacco of Trinidad is smaller and has pale purple to bluish colored flowers."

John had sat down at the bench, his arms folded in front of him. "What's it say about growing it?"

"Well, it says it must be 'sown in the most fruitful ground that may be found, carelessly cast abroad in the sowing.' Gerard says not to rake it. He says he tried different ways, and broadcasting the seeds is best. He never plants all his seed at once 'lest some unkindly blast should happen after the sowing.' He says to sow some at the end of March, some in April, some the beginning of May. Lots of medicinal uses for it," I murmured, reading on. "Says it helps migraines, toothaches, gout, worms of the belly, scabs, poisons.... I *love* this book!" Gerard was always so helpful, not only listing how to grow the plants, but what they could cure and how to prepare the remedies.

"I *love* my tobacco! I can't wait to try this out come growing season at Henricus. Mechumps isn't at the fort, but perhaps he can offer some advice. And I think Gerard has something there. I don't dare plant it all at once. I'll have to experiment. Full sun would make sense, wouldn't it?"

I nodded. "I would think so. Trinidad's surely going to be hotter than it is here."

For a moment, a cloud crossed his face. "And that's the main question. Can it grow here? Is Virginia tropical enough?" The Indian tobacco were small plants, but Spanish tobacco was large and full with great leaves.

"John, that's the question we all have about all our endeavors. Will is enthusiastic about mulberry plants and silkworms. Can we do it? Will it work? Or wine making. How will the grapes fare? We're trying all manner of plants from the Bermudas. It will just take some experimenting, some time."

"Joan." His voice was suddenly serious. "Time is the one thing we *don't* have."

The Quietude of Earth
January 23, 1612 ~ James Town

Now the quietude of earth
Nestles deep my heart within
Friendships new and strange have birth
Since I left the city's din.
—A. E. Russell

January had blown in bitter, grey, and blustery. Virginia, I felt, had little beauty this time of year. But then at January's end came snow, softening the town, the fort, the forest beyond. As whiteness covered all beyond the window and muffled the sounds of settlement, I awaited the familiar pains.

With all this in mind, I sat at the table to make a list and write invitations for my upcoming lying in, that month during which I would be unable to leave the house.

Godparents? Will and I had discussed it prior to his leaving. We both agreed that Sam and Tempie were the obvious choices.

Now, I thought, which five friends, my god siblings, should I invite? I clambered unsteadily toward the sideboard where I kept my daybook, quill, and ink well. Then I plopped into Will's chair, for I thought I should never fit behind the bench. The ink I had newly made, so I dipped and scrawled. *Gossips: Tempie, Annie...*

I stopped. These two were certain. Who else should I choose? Not receiving an invitation could be a snub, but the birth only required five women. Else the bedchamber became too full. I thought of Maria, of course, and quickly jotted her name.

And which others? *Not Maggie.* How Maggie would have thrilled to the birth. For a moment, I envisioned the lullabies my nightingale would have sung to the baby. And then, as the image became too painful, I hurried my thoughts back to the present.

"Other gossips," I murmured. Cecily was a mite young, and my mother—how I would have loved her calming presence. The herbs, the potions, the delicious caudle she would have made.... And my eyes filled with tears. "Go on, go on," I said aloud. "The past is done, mind you. Move on, then." Still, 'twas true that no woman ever missed her own mother as much as the night she herself was in childbirth.

Sarah Rolfe would have been such a wonderful choice. I would never forget the gentle woman who nursed Tempie and me back to health after the Starving Time. But Sarah, too, was gone.

Margery Fairfax was due just a month after I was. I decided not to invite her lest it be too taxing on her.

I liked Thomasine. Her brusqueness was refreshing. And so I wrote her name down, too.

I counted. This made only four gossips, but I wasn't sure how many women I could pull away from their work. I would go with four, an amount I could justify if pressed.

No doubt existed as to who would be midwife. That would be Mistress Joan Wright, who had learned to midwife from her mother and her mother's mother. Mistress Wright had a peculiar but not unfriendly, way. She had sometimes mumbled of things to come, things that did indeed occur. She had told Mistress Starke a flux would take her and that she had better make plans for her children. Soon after, Mistress Starke had indeed succumbed to sudden flux. This caused the neighbors to cry, "Witch! Witch!" when the midwife walked past. Mistress Wright also had eyes of icy blue and wrote with the left hand—two other traits all witches shared.

All these things unnerved the other women, but our midwife assured us she was no witch. And in truth, she did not seem one. She knew her herbs, charms, and prayers and possessed her own birthing stool, a relic of her family. She had proved able in aiding Mistress Bucke's delivery of young Mara. Mara, in fact, was thriving as well as might be for an early birth.

Another question remained. How would I pay the midwife? We had nothing of value to offer her. *I'll pay with herbs,* I thought. No woman could have too many in a place such as this. Having no hard money, we relied on bartering amongst ourselves and from the arriving sailors.

I cut the paper into pieces. I could not afford to waste it. Then upon each one, I dipped the turkey quill and wrote the words for which I'd longed: *I aske thatt you bee my Gossip uponne my baby's byrth.*

James Town had stolen much tradition that had been our God-given right in England. Dale forced the sick to toil, and being infirm brought no relief to work duties.

But we women had endeavored to keep our childbirth rituals, even here. Did Sir Thomas Dale frown upon the work time lost to childbirth? We pleaded another woman summoning us to her bedside lest she lose the child.

We begged that we must be present at the birth to act as proper god-siblings, or gossips, as they say, to the mother. We reminded the soldiers that a baby born today would be working in a few years.

Dale, for all his obedience to rules, seemed unwilling to enter a birthing woman's bedchamber. We supposed he didn't wish to risk losing the life of a future adventurer or the child's mother. For God knew, there existed risk enough already for everyone. As yet, no soldier had snapped the whip at a new mother or gossip for time lost to work.

Fortunately for us, Dale was upriver at Henricus ensuring his men completed the new town by planting time. And Gates was much less likely to force a woman quickly through her birthing. We women whispered these things after church or while gathering turnips and peas from backyard gardens. We discussed it in low tones over tallow and the churn or while stitching soldiers' clothing with too little thread.

We as women had decided we would attend our traditional birthing ceremony until someone ordered us not to. In England, we knew a man never dared interfere with childbirth. Delivering babies was a time when women deeply bonded and kept their secrets amongst themselves—and if men wondered at the activities of the birthing chambers, they never asked. For during that month, and that month alone, a woman could abandon all wifely duties.

I folded each and wrote the friend's name on the outside, placing the invitations in the chest for the day the labor began. There were few things in this world that a woman, rather than a man, controlled. Childbirth was one.

The Midwife Said Unto Her, Fear Not
February 5, 1612 ~ James Town

And it came to pass, when she was in hard labor, that the midwife said unto her, Fear not; thou shalt have this son also.
—Genesis 35:17

The first labor pains struck on the Sabbath at church, which I viewed as a good sign.

Wouldn't it be nice to have a son? I remembered with a pang my little one who had died more than eight years before, just as he was learning to walk. The plague had taken him and, in fact, all the life from me until his sister Janey had been born. Now I found myself yearning for another son.

But the mysteries of birth were many. Whether the child would be a boy or girl was but the least of my worries. We had to hope that the baby would survive and that I would too. Tempie and I had discussed before that, should anything ever happen to me, she would act as mother until Will remarried. And even then, she vowed to keep an eye on the girls just in case the stepmother should be not to her liking. If the child survived and I did not, Tempie would take all three children into her fold. All women liked to make arrangements for their death before childbirth. This was never so important as in the wilds of Virginia.

Before I had left church, I asked Reverend Bucke to bless me and to send prayers around me to hold me for a month, the next time I would likely be at church. James Town's severe laws were far more drastic than any laws in England. If we missed our twice-a-day church service, the marshal might withhold our rations, whip us, even put us to death. Marshal Dale accepted virtually no reason for non-attendance. Childbirth, however, placed a woman in a completely different category. Or so we hoped.

Typically, a husband's one and only responsibility was to see the invitations safely delivered. But Will was not here, so I asked Janey to do it.

The chest creaked open as Janey retrieved the little notes. Then, she bundled as well as she might against the new-fallen snow. The February wind whisked through the door as she stepped through, followed by the sound of the door closing firmly behind her. She would go first to Tempie's home. From there, she would be making her way about the town to the homes of Annie, Maria, Thomasine, and Mistress Wright.

A second pain shot through me, so I climbed into bed.

Meanwhile, Cecily stoked the fire. "Can I help you, mother?" she asked with concern.

I hesitated. She would likely be a mother herself in just a few years, so perhaps she should stay. Then I thought the better of it. If things went badly... "No, lovey. You and Janey just go over to Mistress Fairfax's until the night is over. Someone will come get you."

Our home contained one great room, a loft, a cellar, and a bedchamber that was a concession to us having two daughters and a child on the way. The single bedchamber gave me a place for my lying-in even if it did not allow Will proper sleeping quarters during that month.

A mother with a new baby must have a chamber to herself. This was an important part of her healing. Before departing for Henricus, Will had hammered an old bedstead together in case he should be home at any time during my month. He would then sleep alone and in the main chamber. The girls slept in a loft room, so they could remain in the house after the birth.

"We're going to have nicer homes at Henricus," Will had assured me. The small waddle-and-daub cabins of James Town contained only the bare necessities. For now, that would have to do.

In less than an hour, all the women arrived carrying baskets, and the excited chirping began. Then I called my girls to me to give them a hug and a kiss. One never knew... "Be good," was all I could say. Then the two set off for Margery's home.

Tempie fluffed my pillow and made the chamber extra tidy. When done, she sat upon the bed and held my hand.

"I'm to be an auntie again!" she said. Then a bit lower added, "And someday, I...."

I squeezed her hand. "And someday, you."

The women set to work, first stuffing rags into the keyhole and covering the one window. A dark, warm place was best for mother and baby and symbolized the security of the womb. My gossips then placed candles around the chamber, making sure one cast light near me. The bedchamber instantly took on a warm glow. The brightness of the snow still reflected in, casting a white light amongst the orange flames. It was lovely, I thought.

Maria and Tempie gathered the ingredients for the caudle. Upon a table near the fire, they pulled from their baskets eggs, milk, sack, a wee bit of sugar, cornmeal, and nutmeg.

"I had to ask permission for the eggs, sugar, and milk," Maria explained, with a wink. "They were not going to turn an expectant mother away for her caudle. Who knows what would happen without it?"

'Twas true, our caudles at home would have used much sugar and oatmeal instead of cornmeal, but we made do. My heart warmed to my friends' generosities, giving much of the little they had.

Annie carried a cauldron into the room and hung it over the fire, and then the mixing began. The warm caudle, when cooked, would yield a healthful concoction—especially beneficial for me, but we would all toast and share a dram.

Tempie had brought the sack. The Yeardleys had one bottle, and Tempie had donated a portion of it to me. I felt fortunate to have it for the caudle. Each of the women had contributed a little nutmeg, as no one had much.

Thomasine and Annie brought in armloads of firewood and stoked the fire into a roar.

Yet there was no doubt at all who was in charge of this operation, for the gossips were but helpers. The midwife was the authority.

Mistress Wright set her birthing stool near the fire. She used an old rag to wipe the stool clean of dust and to let the fire warm it some. "Been in the cellar," she said by way of explanation. "Got snow on it during the walk here, so it's a little too chill for you!" Her voice was curt, but she smiled.

Another pain, this one sharper.

Mistress Wright came to my side and pushed here and there upon my belly "That'll be a boy. See how he lies down low?"

My heart jumped, even as I groaned with a labor pain. A boy! Did Mistress Wright truly know these things?

"Names, Joan? Have you a name picked out?" Maria asked. This would be important for them to know, in case the baby survived and I did not.

"If a boy..." I glanced at Mistress Wright, who glared slightly. "I mean, since it's a boy, his name shall be Thomas. Thomas is an old name in Will's family. The name will also honor Sir Thomas Gates and, um, Sir Thomas Dale." Will was loyal to Gates, but honoring Sir Thomas Dale was more a formality to him, a coincidence of both men having the same name as the old Peirce name.

Tempie clapped. "A boy, Joan! Think of it."

I sighed. I *had* thought of it. "In James Town, one concedes a son very early," I said.

The other women nodded. They knew what I meant. Reverend Bucke could tutor in religious education, Latin, and Greek. But to receive a proper education, a boy would have to return to England at the tender age of seven unless we set up a school before then.

"You have seven years, Joan! Much can happen in that time." Annie was stirring a cauldron over the fire, her back to me.

"Aye, much indeed."

To the Battle-Ground of Life
February 5-6, 1612 ~ James Town

Lo, to the battle-ground of Life,
Child, you have come, like a conquering shout,
Out of a struggle—into strife;
Out of a darkness—into doubt.

Girt with the fragile armor of youth,
Child, you must ride into endless wars,
With the sword of protest, the buckler of truth,
And a banner of love to sweep the stars.
—Louis Untermeyer

O lovely Sisters! well it shows
How wide and fair your bounty flows.
—Joanna Baillie

Now Mistress Wright came to my bed to start rituals. The other women sat quietly around her, looking on. I felt my heart patter unexpectedly.

"We begin by praying Psalm 117," the midwife said with authority none dared question.

A pain passed through me, and I moaned, breathing in, breathing out.

We all clasped hands and lowered our heads as Mistress Wright intoned the Psalm. "*O praise the Lord, all ye nations: praise him, all ye people. For his merciful kindness is great toward us: and the truth of the Lord endureth for ever. Praise ye the Lord. Amen.*"

She reached into a sack she'd brought and retrieved an eagle-stone pendant.

"Oh, let me see!" Annie cried, but Mistress Wright by her sharp look upbraided her. Stung, Annie withdrew her hand.

"Its magic is not for you!" said the midwife sternly.

I reached for Annie's arm and patted it. I did not like anyone to speak harshly to my Annie. Her eyes met mine, and I smiled slightly. *Mistress Wright is set in her ways.* Annie returned the smile cautiously, I noted. She did not want the midwife to chasten her once more.

"See the stone, symbol of two in one, of wholeness," Mistress Wright said, holding the purple stone, its chain dangling loose, for me to see. She shook the charm over my body, letting us hear its rattle. The exotic stone swung on its chain, round and round, and I thought vaguely that it had come from a beach in Cyprus or in Africa, or so the London street peddlers always said. Round and round, spinning and twirling. I felt myself grow dizzy as the room seemed to whirl with the stone.

Typically, Mistress Wright would have had me wear the stone tied to my arm to prevent early loss of child, but she could not. "I've only one," she had said firmly. She kept it with her, and she alone used it only during childbirth. There was, alas, no source of eagle-stones in Virginia.

Now, whispering words we could not understand, the midwife rubbed the stone across my belly and then reached around to tie the stone to my thigh. This stone, I knew, would pull the baby from my womb. Mistress Wright would carefully remove the eagle stone after my delivery, lest the attempt at birth continue on and on.

The smell of the simmering caudle filled the warm, candlelit room as the midwife next pulled a large old cross from her bag. "We must pray the baby safely into this world," she announced. The room hushed as she waved the cross over my belly. I cried in pain as another wave pierced me. *In time, little one.*

"*O infans, sive vivus, sive mortus, exi foras, quia Christus te vocat ad lucem,*" Mistress Wright chanted solemnly. She waved the cross over me once more and repeated the charm more forcefully. "*O infans, sive vivus, sive mortus, exi foras, quia Christus te vocat ad lucem!*" And then, a third time she said the prayer, this time almost in a shout. The women recoiled backwards from the power that seemed to flow from the midwife.

"Now you!" she cried to the women encircling my bed. The women dutifully intoned the words as she led them: "*O infans, sive vivus, sive mortus, exi foras, quia Christus te vocat ad lucem.*" The pains in my belly came and went, growing closer together, I thought. The chant was working. I stifled a cry.

"And again and again!" She led them twice more in the prayer, and the words hung in the smoky air as if by themselves.

"Thrice is most powerful," Mistress Wright said in a hushed tone.

Maria spoke first. "Your mother taught you this charm?"

The midwife nodded, "Aye, it has been in my family before my grandmother, before my great-grandmother. Every generation, the firstborn female is born to midwife, and each learns the birthing charm from her mother before her."

Mistress Wright then shut her eyes and dropped her head. "All pray," she instructed, and we bowed our heads, too.

She chanted, *"In the name of the Father and of the Son and of the Holy Ghost, come safe and go safe, what have we here?"* She repeated these words over and over, intensity building until at last a great pain caused me to scream. I felt myself growing too warm, nearly hot. Sweat poured from me as fierce pain stabbed my body, and I ventured, "Might we lower the fire?"

The midwife shook her head. "Nay, 'tis unsafe to birth in a chamber too cool." She smiled, but not at me. "The Spirit is in the room, and soon the baby shall be too," she said reverently.

Tempie shivered, but not from cold, I realized. She was to be mother to my children should anything happen to me this night. And the magic and the fear and the simmering caudle gave the room a sense of the mystical, a sense that anything might happen.

Next came the herbs, which the midwife sprinkled around my bed.

"What are they?" Thomasine asked. Everyone seemed afraid to ask questions after Annie's berating.

"They be cyclamen and sowbread, roses, lilies, and aquilegia. These sweet smells aid the travail."

Thomasine had returned to stirring the caudle. "'Tis done," she said. I hoped the midwife would allow me to have some. I felt I needed it. I was growing faint.

Mistress Wright nodded. "Serve it up, then." Maria held drams as Thomasine dipped it out.

Tempie brought mine to me and helped me hold the heavy dram. "Sip slowly." She held as I drank.

I never had moments such as these without my mind racing back to the lowest days of the Starving Time. I saw myself using a trembling hand to spoon broth into Tempie's mouth. What had been in that pottage? Cedar branches? I could not remember. But I smiled gratefully and said, "The world always swings back, doesn't it?" Tempie looked confused but said, "Oh, aye."

The warm, sweet, richness gave me renewed strength even as the pain rushed through me.

Herbs done, Mistress Wright passed the cross over me again and again, this time reading Psalms from her Bible.

The caudle simmered over the fire. The room felt warm and safe from the bitter cold and snow outside. Warm with light, warm with heat, warm with friendship. My heart soared even as I prayed that I would survive this childbirth, that my son would survive, too.

The afternoon gave way to evening, the evening to night. Then slowly the brightening room showed us that the sun must be rising over the snowdrifts of James Town although blankets still covered our windows. Drums called us to work, but we stayed as we were. The long night was over, and a baby's shrill cries cut the morning air.

"Well, 'tis a boy indeed!" Annie said, cradling the little one as Tempie cut the navel string. Mistress Wright cast Annie a sharp look as if to say, "Would it have been anything else?"

"Ah, a soldier he'll be, just like his father," Thomasine added, beaming at the precious bundle. My heart fell even as I knew she was right.

As was tradition, the midwife cleaned and swaddled the newborn. Afterward, every gossip rocked and cooed to the baby, passing the child to each in turn. Finally, the last of my god-siblings would hand him to me.

"What a wee rosy wrinkled face!" Maria cried. He yawned, and every woman in the room swooned as though they had never seen such a thing.

The candles flickered, the fire crackled. Annie held the baby, swaying and singing softly to the child in her arms. Maria leaned in over Annie's shoulder, both women's faces awash in candlelight as they gazed at the now sleeping infant. Annie led the comforting old tune, as the others added their voices:

> *My little sweet darling, my comfort and joy,*
> *Sing lullaby, lulla!*
> *In beauty surpassing the princes of Troy,*
> *Sing lullaby, lulla!*
> *Now suck, child, and sleep, child, thy mother's sweet boy,*
> *Sing lullaby, lulla!*
> *The gods bless and keep thee from cruel annoy.*
> *Sing lulla, lulla, sweet baby,*
> *Lullaby, lulla.*

The gentle holiness within the room soothed me as peace swept through me. It was over.

Mistress Wright began reading the childbirth Psalms in a low murmur. The long night was past, the sun up, and we had both survived. Praise God.

I felt myself drifting off to sleep, whispering, "Thank you, Lord, for my son Tommy. And for letting us both live to see the dawn."

Clouds and Sea-Shell Whisperings
February 7 to March 4, 1612 ~ James Town

Love for sweet and simple things,
Like clouds and sea-shell whisperings.
—Oliver Jenkins

Away we go—and what care we
For treasons, tumults, and for wars?
We are as calm in our delight
As is the crescent-moon so bright
Among the scattered stars.
—William Wordsworth

When the Henricus ship returned to James Town for supplies, Tempie slipped the captain a note. "Mistress Peirce has delivered a son. Might her husband and Master Jordan be able to return to baptize the baby as father and godfather?"

A few days later, Will and Sam were home. A plea to Dale for the spiritual well-being of the baby had done the trick, Will said. "Besides, Dale wants me stationed here with Gates, anyway."

Now, Will carried baby Tom to the church with our two girls, our godparents, and of course, all the gossips who had witnessed the birth. The Reverend Bucke stood ready to perform the baptism.

While the festivity occurred, I waited alone in bed to hear of it later. One of the great ironies of being a new mother was that after carrying a child for nine months, I was unable to leave the bed to see this, the most important moment of his life until his marriage.

Through the early days after my delivery, they came—my gossips. My friends took turns tending the baby, helping with household chores, preparing meals for Will, and sometimes just plopping upon my bed to catch me up on the latest goings on about town. Although they had their duties for Sir

Thomas Dale, still they could come during the early morning, afternoon, or evening breaks. James Town was such a peculiar place. All the women were tied to military work orders such that they struggled to find time to help during my recovery. Yet, somehow, they each managed to come as often as they could.

"You are fortunate to have had the baby now," Tempie told me one day, her feet dangling off the side of my bed.

"How so?"

"Well, it appears Margery Fairfax shall have to break her lying in time to travel to Henricus."

I gasped. "That could be dangerous to mother and babe." Being up? Being out? Traveling?

"Aye. She'll have to fare as best she can. She could stay in James Town and move the next month, but her gossips will all be upriver. Well, all except Maria, of course, who will stay back in James Town with her husband.

Dale and Gates planned the move for the middle of March. I would just have time to be out of bed and prepare our things for the new town.

As if reading my thoughts, Tempie added, "I know you won't have much time once you're up, but I'll help you pack. We'll all help." At that moment, from the cradle next to the bed, young Tom stirred and gave a squeaky wail. Tempie added, "But first things first. You've a hungry babe!"

By the middle of February, I had my first upsitting for as was traditional, I had lain in bed in recovery a full two weeks. Annie and Tempie arrived first, carrying fresh bedding. The smell of laundered linen, ragged though it was, cheered me, and the sight of my friends cheered me even more.

On my upsitting day, my gossips again returned, festive, bringing what little foods they had and mixing caudle. Laughter filling the birthing chamber, and love for them swelling my heart.

Providence had thrown us all together in the strange world of Virginia, but we who had survived had bonded tight. Some, like Maria, had endured a hurricane only to end up a castaway on a deserted island. One, Annie, had arrived all alone, finding herself a young girl married and expecting with not a single female to help *her* birthing until we had arrived. And some, like Tempie, Thomasine, and I, had survived the hurricane and Starving Time. We all had our stories to tell. And in such a moment, we celebrated our own lives as much as the new life in my arms, for we had buried many.

A week after the upsitting, I was wandering my entire house though still confined to it. For three weeks I had seen no men, barely even Will, and he had remained sleeping in his makeshift bed in the outer room. Sam had left directly after the baptism to return to Henricus.

The gossips had alternated coming to tend the baby for me during this time. Cecily had taken on managing many of the household chores with Janey's help.

By the first Sunday in March, my churching time had come. It was time for me to return to church for my ritual re-entrance to society. *How interesting*, I thought, *that today is March 4th, for today I do 'march forth' as a new mother again.* I always thought this date to be a hopeful one.

That morning my gossips returned, bringing again the foods they had and celebrating my return to health. Birthing was always the riskiest time in a woman's life each time she endured it. If two survivors emerged from childbirth, all was success.

Annie held the baby as Tempie adjusted my veil, for I must cover my face until I were clean once more. And together as we left the house in a clucking, laughing group, all the town would know that my lying-in time was over.

At the church, I went to the bench we had newly designated the upsitting pew, as there were now enough women entering childbirth at James Town to need one. There, Reverend Bucke removed my veil and said the requisite prayers. God bless him, all our good pastor's prayers were doleful, it seemed. And so the minister mournfully read Psalm 121, the mother's Psalm of deliverance and preservation.

> *A song of degrees. I will lift mine eyes unto the mountains, from whence mine help shall come.*
> *Mine help cometh from the Lord, which hath made the heaven and the earth.*
> *He will not suffer thy foot to slip: for he that keepeth thee, will not slumber.*
> *Behold, he that keepeth Israel, will neither slumber nor sleep.*
> *The Lord is thy keeper: the Lord is thy shadow at thy right hand.*
> *The sun shall not smite thee by day, nor the moon by night.*
> *The Lord shall preserve thee from all evil: he shall keep thy soul.*
> *The Lord shall preserve thy going out, and thy coming in from henceforth and forever.*

And I began to weep. Perhaps for relief. Perhaps for the enduring love of friends cherished. Or perhaps for fear of the days to come. Yet this much was certain. I would be glad in the days ahead that God did not slumber even if we did. And that neither sun nor moon would smite us in the end.

Or so I hoped.

In a Bend on a Rugged Peninsula
March 14, 1612 ~ Henricus

They have placed their hope on [Henricus]…which they have founded twenty leagues up the river in a bend on a rugged peninsula with a narrow entrance by land, and they are persuaded that there they can defend themselves against the whole world.…
—Don Diego de Molina, prisoner at James Town,
   in a letter smuggled to King Philip of Spain, 1613

God made the country and man made the town.
—17th century English proverb

My arms crossed protectively on my chest. I gazed about, feeling something like a waif as if I belonged nowhere. Tempie, my girls, and I stood in a line awaiting directions as to where our homes would be. This gave us time to study our surroundings.

Dale had apparently laid out the rapidly built town in an orderly manner. *Pray God, things to be better here than at James Town.* Still, I could not help but notice what happens when men raise a town as quickly as this. I let my eyes sweep around and saw that each frame house, each building of any sort, had a sloppy look to it. Brick church? No, not even a brick foundation. And no brick foundation of the homes either. Just wood, as we were growing used to. Posts deep in the ground provided the earthfast support.

"These will not last five years," I whispered to Tempie.

She nodded. "With continual repairs, *perhaps* five. No more."

Cecily swayed side to side with baby Tommy in her arms. Both girls stared wide-eyed at Henricus, their new home.

Farther downriver, James Town remained as little more than a military compound. Governor Sir Thomas Gates, in charge there, had lent Dale many men to forge Henricus. The rest had labored throughout the fall to repair James Town's many buildings.

The forts at the bay under Captain Davis would be our first protection. James Town would be yet another barrier before any plundering Spanish could reach the major stronghold at Henricus.

Here, the smell of freshly cut pine wafted through the early morning air. The stench of manure as well. The swamps and greenery had not yet reached their spring bloom. However, I saw one sign of winter's passing. A few chickadees with their little black caps flitted from tree to tree. This would be a lovely and healthful place, upriver and on high ground. Perhaps we would not continually fight disease as we had in marish James Town.

Henricus would include all facets of a thriving community, all that we could replicate in Virginia, of course. The fort's palisaded area was *huge*. I reckoned it to be twenty times larger than the one at James Town, seven acres here, to be exact.

"Where be the parsonage?" asked Mistress Turner, standing behind me.

"My husband said it would be across that side of the river," I told her over my shoulder.

"Aye, it's over yonder," said one grizzled, ragged man further back. "The parsonage Whitaker calls Rock Hall." The man spat. "'Twas supposed to be brick, but that ain't going to happen, not any time soon. I reckon he ought to call it 'Wood Hall.'"

"Don't taunt the pastor's house, Bart. That'll send you to the devil, it will," another man said.

"Ain't that where I'm at?"

My eyes met Tempie's, and the thought flew between us. *Healthful bodies, perhaps. But the disease of the mind would still be rampant here, that much was sure.*

Tempie and I had decided to live together at least for a while. Our husbands were rarely home, and it provided a measure of safety and comfort to have another adult in the house.

"Name?" asked a busy soldier, looking at a list in his hands. "And how many for the house?"

"Five for the house including one baby, sir. *And* I believe you know my name. How are you, Walter?"

The dusty, tired face looked up, warm brown eyes meeting mine. "Mistress Peirce! Mistress Yeardley. A pleasure to see ye again. Uh, I reckon," he added. "And the little ones! Ah, a new babe. And Janey and..." He glanced at Cecily. "This the one you were waitin' for?" He gave a half smile. His expression said, *So glad you were alive when she arrived.*

"You sound tentative about seeing us again," Tempie said, a wry grin playing at her mouth.

Walter raised his eyebrows. "'Tain't seeing ye again, Missus. It's seeing ye again *here*. I just, uh, well, ma'am. It's a rough place." He glanced around nervously. Speaking ill of the marshal, or any leader, was cause for three whippings on the first offense.

Walter pointed into the town. "Two streets over, four houses to the left. That one's yours." The line behind us was growing.

"Walter." I touched his doublet sleeve. A little familiar, but we were friends. "Can you come to our home on your break and allow us to prepare rations for you?" I had never fully gotten over my guilt at not sharing my acorn flour with him during the Starving Time.

He smiled. "Mistress Peirce, I may have to take you up on that. Besides—" He lowered his voice. "Want to talk w' you a bit." His look had quickly changed from pleased to serious.

I nodded and glanced at Tempie. Again I thought, *Oh, Maggie, how right you were. Well-placed friends who know what's going on have saved our skins more than once on this journey.*

The little home was similar to the one at James Town. Will had promised—hoped for—improvements, but I saw few. Yet, if my children stayed well, I did not care so much about the house itself, I supposed.

After the ten o'clock church service, Walter appeared at our door. We had not yet unpacked our trunks, and few of our furnishings were yet off ship. But two men had brought the table and bench and the cradle wherein the baby now slept.

I had made a poor man's Indian bread with the corn delivered us while Tempie retrieved a small stash of butter she'd brought from James Town. How did you thank someone who had risked punishment to bury your friend? With corn pone and butter; it was all we had.

Walter pulled off his hat at the door as I bade him inside.

"Ah, I smell the corn pone!" he said with a nod toward the bread oven, a niche tucked beside the fireplace. We sometimes called our bread *pone* as the natives did. Bread made with Indian maize, not wheat, was something we had never had in England. Here, it was a staple.

The cornbread did smell wonderful, such a change from the little we'd had during the Starving Time. Those like Walter, Tempie and I, who had endured famine still appreciated every morsel of warm food placed before us. I supposed we always would.

Walter took a seat at the table, and I placed a hearty chunk of bread on a trencher before him. The butter melted and dripped, and Walter's pleasure was obvious.

I took a seat across from him, as did Tempie. The girls sat down to have a piece of bread as well.

"How went the building of the town?" I asked, having heard little about it from Will during my lying in. Even if he could have, I knew Will would not have told me much. He would have feared worrying me in my weakened condition.

Walter spread more butter upon his bread and heaved a sigh. "The marshal worked us day and night. We slept 'pon the ground 'til we could get the palisade up. Dale's first concern, the Indians, don't you know." He took a bite. "Delicious, and I thank you, missus, I do."

I nodded. "You're so welcome. How fared ye with the natives?" The Indian wars were ongoing.

Walter sighed. "Well, Marshal Dale, he sailed up here on the ship." Dale had ordered hundreds of soldiers to help build Henricus. They would never have fit on one small ship, so the rest traveled by foot following the river for some fifty miles westward.

Walter continued, "I was amongst the poor fellows having to walk all that way, knowing we could expect an Indian attack." He gave us a smile that hoped for sympathy.

We obliged. "Pity you, Walter," Tempie murmured. Having buried our friend Maggie for us during the Starving Time, Walter was all but a ragged old saint, in our opinion. So mustering sympathy was not hard.

The girls were sitting at the table, their elbows bent upward, their hands tucked about their face. Their eager expressions seemed to fuel the tired soldier's story.

"Don't suppose you maids ever seen ol' Jack-of-the-Feather, have ye?"

Eyes widened, the girls shook their heads in unison. And then Cecily added, "But our father has told us about him."

Walter chuckled. "Reckon your father's seen him quite a few times, Jack being the Indians' chief captain." The English had nicknamed this warrior Jack-of-the-Feather because of the large bird wings affixed to his shoulders, but his true name was Nemattanew.

"Did he have his big wings on?" Janey asked.

The soldier stretched his arms wide. "Oh, sure he did. He never fights without them. This big they were, maybe bigger! The wings of a great swan."

Walter then gripped two imaginary balls on either side of his head, saying, "And ol' Jack wears great talons hanging from his ears. Why, he's blue and red, all covered in oil and blue birds' feathers, and red puccoon 'neath that. Of course, all their warriors do that. Why, most times Jack jumps out into the open field, all them bird parts as if he means to challenge us and then take off to the sky.

The girls laughed.

"Most times, the Indians fight from behind trees and bushes, but not Jack-of-the-Feather."

"How come?" Cecily asked.

"Well, because ol' Jack, he's not afeared of our matchlocks. He tells all his warriors that English weapons can't do him no harm."

The natives, we had learned, liked to wear animal parts that carried special meaning. What the great wings meant, we could only guess. But some said they symbolized Jack's ability to always escape, his immunity from English bullets. His immortality from any hurt we could do him.

"And did Jack's men attack you?" I asked. Will had probably been in yet another Indian battle, I realized.

Walter nodded. "He and his braves shot at us from beneath cover all the way to Henricus. And it didn't stop there no sir." He shook his head. "We arrived under Cap'n Brewster, and those Indians fought us the whole time we was puttin' up the *palisado*. Hindering the work the whole time, they were. Arrohattocs tribe *this* time. You see, Henricus is settin' right close to their town."

The further west we went, the more Indian towns we found. Surely, these towns sprinkled across this whole land, I thought.

"Is that what you wanted to speak with us about, Walter?" Tempie asked.

He glanced at the girls, who were happily taking bites from their bread, crumbs and butter leaving telltale signs around their lips. He then looked askance at me. *Not for their ears,* he seemed to be saying.

"Uh, girls, would you mind going to take a look around the town? I might need to know where things are, and then you can tell me!"

"Yes, ma'am," said Cecily. "Come on, Janey." She reached for her little sister's hand.

Once they had shut the door, Walter said, "Thank you, mistress. I felt I should warn you. Have your husbands told you how brutal this place is?"

"All of Virginia is brutal," I said. We were used to it—that "different kind of wild," Harrison had called it. Nothing new there.

Walter lowered his voice. "No, ma'am. You *think* you know brutal. But George Percy, Governor Gates, the Baron La Warr are incomparable to Marshal Dale in cruelty. You'll find that here, Dale administers the whip, the stockade, and even the wheel with much abandon. He has sentenced men to work in chains for years for petty thieving." His cheery storytelling tone had changed to bitterness. His eyes scowled.

"He has to keep order," I said weakly. I thought of the men in line earlier, how they'd carried a mixture of hatred and laziness. Yet, Dale at the helm without Gates's moderating influence? This was what Walter meant.

"Order!" Walter cried, then dropped his voice once more. "Order? A man so much as coughs at the wrong time, he's brought before the marshal. Oh,

I'm exaggeratin', of course. But I seen two men steal from the company store and get bound to a tree until they *starved* to death."

I felt a ghastly, sickness in my stomach. *Intentional* starving? For those who had endured it, this was a particularly harsh thought.

"Or how about the man who stole some cornmeal and had a bodkin thrust through his tongue? Tied him up to a tree 'til he starved to death, too. Dale caught some runnin' off to the Indians. Some of 'em he hanged, and some he shot. Some he staked, and some he burned. And a few he broke on the wheel. And that ain't all! Did your husbands hear about Lieutenant Abbott?"

I wasn't sure I wanted to hear more, but Tempie replied, "Abbott? The one who led the raid when the Paspaheghs attacked the blockhouse?" I remembered as well. Abbott's men had faced a force of unknown size that day and had prevented the Paspahegh from moving farther inland and attacking us in the fort. We had heard the Indians' cries of *"Paspahegh!"* even as we ate our breakfasts. I shuddered. Abbott, in our minds, was a hero.

"He was the one who went with Brewster to see if the caravels were Spanish attackers, too, isn't he?" I asked.

"One and the same on both counts. Able man. Good soldier," Walter continued. "But Dale pushed that man so hard that you know what Abbott done? He led a mutiny! And can you imagine what kind of punishment Dale inflicts on mutineers if he starves a thief to death?"

I flinched.

"The wheel, that's what. Tied his arms and legs up to it and broke all his bones with a club. Abbott's screaming carried all whole way across Henricus." Walter shook his head, grimacing. "What a waste. Lowlands veteran, too. Served all the way back in Virginia, even under Cap'n John Smith."

Tempie spoke up, a frightened look in her eyes. "Walter, why are you telling us all this?"

"Mistress," Walter said. "You need to watch *everything* you do. Do it right, follow the laws, and don't take no shortcuts or circumvent nothin'. Because I tell you this: Dale will get you if you do. The man has no mercy, not like Gates or Percy or even the baron. Man or woman, he won't care. Children neither, I'd reckon. Dale's mission—his *only* mission—is to keep us fed and safe from Indians and the Spanish. And if he has to kill us to do it, he will."

Spinning, Bearing Children, and Weeping
April 21, 1612 ~ Henricus

What is marriage, mother? Daughter, it is spinning, bearing children, and weeping.
—Portuguese proverb

I have heard the spinning woman of the sky,
Who sings as she spins,
No one knows where my web ends,
Or where it begins....

For the thin-spun, glistening, silver thread
Out of her breast is drawn,
And her white feet caught in the silver web,
Through dark and dawn.
—Alice Corbin Henderson

Spin, spin, spin. My foot upon the treadle. *Pump, pump, pump.* The flax wheel tumbled around with a gentle hum. I drafted the hemp into the wheel, which twisted it into yarn. Dipping my fingers in water, drafting and pumping the treadle as the wheel hummed.

Hum, hum. Round and round.

Only women received flax wheels although there weren't enough to go around to all. The carpenters crafted the wheels as quickly as they could. So many women and girls assigned to spinning, so few wheels.

Cecily and Janey sat on the bench, and each held a distaff covered with hemp stricks. The hemp spun onto the spindle below, round and round, spinning and spinning.

In a cradle next to Janey, Tommy slept. When he stirred, Janey would give the cradle a little push. If that didn't stop his fretting, she picked him up and rocked him or gave him to me to feed.

Some days we spun alone, sometimes in groups. Occasionally, Tempie and Margery, also spinners, brought their work to my house or I to theirs. Janey helped with Margery's baby Giles as she did with Tommy. Margery had been in labor on the trip to Henricus—a dreadful time for her, but somehow she'd survived. She had given birth to twins, but the little girl had come blue. Giles, however, was a lusty little baby, which comforted Margery greatly.

Today, a soft April breeze whispered through the open door. The work was hard, and when the day ended, I fell heavily into bed. In England, we spun to earn extra money or to create our own household thread. But here, spinning was not a choice, nor did it ever end. We spun, and we planted, and we mended—whatever Dale assigned us. We also cooked meals and tended our own plot of land. We asked no questions, raised no arguments. We were afraid of Dale; we were not free. We could not leave, could not choose, and could not cease toiling until work hours ended at which time we handed over whatever we had produced. In between, we attended church twice daily.

Spin, spin, spin.

I tried through my fatigue to be grateful. I listened to the sounds of spinning and humming and to the warm whispering breeze moving through the room, rustling the girls' hair. I smiled. It was work, but it was peaceful.

Until the screams from the whipping post caused the three of us to jump and the baby to stir.

Someone, several people, it sounded like, were feeling Dale's wrath. But who, and for what? I stopped the wheel and rushed to peer out the door. We couldn't see the post from where we were. Other heads poked out of houses as well.

The girls were beside me, too, and Janey looked at me with concern. "Who's getting a whippin', mama?"

I shook my head. "I don't know, child. It could be anyone for anything." The list seemed endless. Stealing, missing church, profaning the governor or Marshal, missing work detail, doing less than the law required...

The baby had begun to cry, so Janey went to him, picking him up and nuzzling his ear. "Don't cry, little Tommy," she whispered.

"Stop, stop!" I heard a man's pleading voice. "In God's name, stop!"

"God is the marshal as far as I'm concerned," came the retort. "I flail or I be flailed. Move away!"

The cracking and slashing of the horrible cat-o-nine tails pierced the air. The whooshing of its nine leather straps followed by the harsh *snap* as it cracked skin made me cringe. Someone, tied to this tree, would be unable to run, barely even to flinch. I thought soldiers were whipping several at once, as the snaps and screams muddled together. How many lashes? I tried to block the sounds, but I was sure I heard at least a dozen. More, I thought.

Something in these screams jolted me. They were familiar somehow.

Worse, at least one of those screaming *might* be a woman.

Tempie rushed in and slammed the door, and I could see she was crying. "Joan, Joan, bless her, Joan!"

Hardened as we were to the new world of Dale's work, Tempie or I rarely cried. We also rarely attended the everyday sounds of whipping, choosing instead to block them from our ears, pretend we weren't hearing them. But the screams cutting like a sword through the morning air, a man's desperate plea for the lashes to stop, and Tempie's dusty, tear-splattered face told me that something was terribly wrong.

"Tempie, who…?"

"Poor thing, poor thing." Tempie had her hands covering her face as steady sobs broke through, and at once I understood. The sound of too many whippings had finally taken its toll on her.

Who was it? Why was Tempie crying? "Tell me, Tempie. Who? We have seen many lashed…."

"Annie." Her voice was choked. "Annie and Mistress Wright to be next!"

The Injustice Which Is Done Us
April 21, 1612 ~ Henricus

And the taskmasters...spake to the people, saying, Thus saith Pharaoh, I will not give you straw. Go ye, get you straw where ye can find it: yet not ought of your work shall be diminished.... And the taskmasters hasted them, saying, Fulfil your works, your daily tasks, as when there was straw. And the officers of the children of Israel, which Pharaoh's taskmasters had set over them, were beaten...
—Exodus 5:10-14

So long as we do not take even the injustice which is done us, and which forces the burning tears from us; so long as we do not take even this for just and right, we are in the thickest darkness without dawn.
—Ibn Rahel

"Annie? *Our* Annie?" Now my voice cracked. "Mis...Mistress Wright?" Just a few months before, we had all been together, birthing young Tommy. I glanced at the child yawning in Janey's arms. I could not have delivered him without Annie and Mistress Wright, and Mistress Wright was the only midwife we had.

Tempie nodded quickly, her eyes streaming tears. "I saw. I saw Annie's arms tied to the post. She buckled, but did not fall.... Jack asked them to whip him instead, but the soldier refused. 'Her offense, her punishment. If I don't do as I'm told, 'tis *me* they'll have here next,' was all the soldier said." Tempie shook with fear and anger.

Slash, snap. Another scream. Only Annie's cries now. They must be done whipping the man.

"Oh, my God," I whispered. She was right. It *was* Annie. Except I had never heard Anne Laydon scream. Had never seen her waver. This young girl had shown such courage as the only woman in a settlement of men after her mistress died. She had been but fifteen when our group landed, having married Jack Laydon the winter before. She had delivered her little Ginny, born at Christmas of our Starving Time, 1609, James Town's first English baby. Annie's spirit and sureness and her friendship with the Indian princess Pocahontas before we arrived had provided a wealth of knowledge to us about the forests and woods. Without that knowledge we might well have died, all of us, all the women, that first winter.

Another scream, and I clenched my eyes and my back arched of its own as though I, too, felt the lash.

"Girls!" I shouted. *Get them away from here!* "Run now, run to Mistress Fairfax's house. Leave Tommy. Go, now!"

Their eyes wide in terror, the two did as I demanded. Annie, whipped, would surely come here, or I would go there. The little I could protect the children, I would do.

To Tempie, I said, "What's she done?" My voice was a whisper now. "What could that child *possibly* have done to draw the wrath of Dale? To break a *law*." I spit the last word out. I suddenly felt contempt for laws that would compel a young, hard-working girl to the post. I felt contempt for any man who would whip a woman such as Annie. Or any man who would order it. Anger ripped through me.

Now I understood. The man crying out must have been Jack.

"No!" Jack's voice echoed across the town. "No, please don't hurt her!" There was anguish in it, the sound of a man whose wife was in danger and who stood powerless.

"Two soldiers grabbed Jack and pulled him back." Tempie said, looking at me, her face streaked with tears. Her fear and sorrow mirrored the helplessness we all felt under the crushing laws of Sir Thomas Dale. "Jack was trying to break free...." Her voice trailed off.

I felt torn between wanting to run out and offer any comfort I could and being unable to face seeing the cat-o-nine tails lashing Annie. I wouldn't be able to get near, I knew, but she *might* see me. She might know I was with her, that I knew she could never deserve such a fate.

"How did she look?" My voice was tremulous, a whisper.

"Angry. As angry as I've ever seen her. And defiant. The soldiers pushed her to the post. She had..." Tempie stopped and swallowed hard. "Annie was screaming, 'No, no, please! Tell the governor. Mercy, mercy, for my baby. Mercy for my baby.'"

"Her baby? Was Ginny nearby? Was Annie afraid she'd see?"

How *would* a wee one, a little over two, feel seeing her mother that way?

"I...I don't know, Joan. I didn't see Ginny."

We were still trying to take this in when a rapping came upon the door.

I could hear a woman's sobs and a man's shaken voice. "Mistress Peirce knows herbs."

I flung the door open to see my Annie, doubled in pain, her knees buckling beneath her, rips in her clothing from the whip, blood trickling through. Her face muddy, tear-stained and swollen, the color of beets. Jack Laydon and Judith Perry supported her around her waist and helped her across the threshold. Annie's legs trembled beneath her.

"We brought her to you, Joan," Judith said helplessly. "Please, help this poor thing. Please. You have your herbs…" Judith had been with Annie when the soldiers had grabbed her; her stricken face said she had witnessed the entire beating.

At that moment, another snap, and no scream I could hear.

Mistress Wright. She's too proud to scream. Yet.

I thought of Mistress Wright's valuable knowledge of birthing. And there she stood, like a common criminal, a cat-o-nine tails ripping her back. I squeezed my eyes shut, drew a deep breath, then turned to the couple limping across the threshold.

Jack eased Annie toward the bed, and I walked beside her touching her arm, saying, "There, lovey, lie down. There, that's it." I made my voice calmer than I felt—fear and anger I must lay aside, for they would cloud my mind from the correct medicinal herbs. From the mist came a memory of my mother's illness when I had been too shaken to tend her properly. She had told *me* which herbs to give her as well as myself. "Chamomile for you," she had said, "to calm."

I was trying to think quickly. Chamomile, yes. That would help here, too. But what else? *Wounds and beatings, wood sage,* I thought, reaching for the jar.

Annie lay doubled over on her side, softly whimpering. Tempie and Judith sat beside her on the bed, soothing her. Then Tempie gently tugged at the torn bodice where the raw, bloody wounds emerged. I saw both Tempie and Judith flinch and recoil, as Annie jumped in pain.

My heart pounded as I began pulling down jars from the herb shelf. *Chamomile to calm.* "Why…why did they *do* this to her?" Tempie asked Jack, her hand resting upon Annie's shoulder. I paused and turned to hear the answer.

Jack's steely eyes met Tempie's, and I saw his eyes were rife with hatred.

"She and Mistress Wright were making shirts for the colony's servants. You know that?"

Snap, scream. The horrible sounds of Mistress Wright's beating echoed distantly.

We both nodded, and I felt sick. *Annie did not complete the task to Dale's satisfaction.*

"The governor allotted us only six needleful of thread for each shirt," Judith added.

"Not enough!" Tempie cried.

"No, not enough by far. Some of us had thread at home. Annie and Mistress Wright didn't have any, so they unraveled the bottoms to use the thread from there. Their shorts were shorter than the rest."

"*Of course* they do not have enough thread!" I threw my hand backward toward the still spinning wheel. "We have just received hemp! We cannot... cannot spin straw into gold, as the tale goes. It's not Annie's fault they haven't enough thread! Neither is it ours."

"You can't beat a woman who hasn't enough thread to complete the task." Tempie's voice was steely. "That's like old Pharaoh, telling the Israelites to make bricks without straw."

I felt disgust and revulsion well within me. A fine woman, a hard worker, an impossible task. Aye, straw into gold, bricks without straw, shirts without thread. Where was the difference?

Still unable to comprehend laws of such cruelty, I walked to Annie and knelt in front of her. She writhed with pain, and I was about to ask her whether it be in waves or like a knife thrust in or—

Annie's intense look of grief and despair stopped me, and she grabbed my wrist. Her eyes were pleading. *Help me!* they seemed to cry.

"Baby," she murmured. "Losing the baby."

Little Lamb, Who Made Thee?
April 21-22, 1612 ~ Henricus

Little lamb, who made thee?
Does thou know who made thee,
Gave thee life, and bid thee feed
By the stream and o'er the mead;
Gave thee clothing of delight,
Softest clothing, woolly, bright;
Gave thee such a tender voice,
Making all the vales rejoice?
Little lamb, who made thee?
Does thou know who made thee?
—William Blake

Gone —flitted away,
Taken the stars from the night and the sun
From the day!
—Alfred Tennyson

A baby! I had not known Annie was expecting. That only increased the horror of the flogging, but there was no time to consider that now.

Desperately, I made a tincture of chamomile, sassafras, wood sage, catnip and red raspberry leaves. I hoped that at least these last two would relax Annie and cause her to sleep. Beyond that, catnip and red raspberry were our best hopes for stalling the labor. In my heart, I knew it was futile, but for Annie's sake I had to try.

"If we only had the eagle-stone!" I cried. Tied to Annie's arm, it could perhaps forestall the labor. But Mistress Wright was in sore shape herself, surely. The last of her screams died away. Our midwife was in no condition to tend a woman losing a baby. I glanced at Tempie. We would have to do all we could on our own.

We gave her the tincture, prayed over her, and dressed her wounds. But in the end, it was to no avail. Ginny Laydon, two years old, would never know the younger brother that Annie was carrying that day. The baby was stillborn later that evening. A wee thing, no larger than a sparrow in my hand.

Annie rested as I mopped her face and gave her shepherd's purse, a remedy to staunch the bleeding. Tempie had made a caudle, but Annie refused to drink it.

"No, no, thank you," she mumbled, as she slipped into a restless sleep. She would stay with me for the night.

The evening's somberness was a distant cry from the festive birth of baby Tommy—toasting with caudle, working together, the warmth of friends, Mistress Wright's help. Furor roiled within me, and I felt I could have taken Marshal Dale down, mine own self.

When she awoke the next morning, Annie pushed herself up and groaned in pain from the lashing.

"Joan."

I went to her and sat on the edge of the bed, smoothing her hair. She touched my arm lightly, and her tear-stained face looked helplessly into mine. I remembered her merry eyes, the confidence and cheer she had given us when we first arrived. She had been but fifteen then, her spirit unbreakable, her desire to go on and to help the newly arriving women her first concern. My heart ached for her now, and though I was not much older than she was, I realized I felt motherly toward her. She was, after all, but seventeen.

How fast the young girls grow old in Virginia.

"My son." Her words were firm. "I want to bury my son. They took him from me."

I wrapped my arms around her and then held her face in my hands.

"Of course, of course, dear Annie. He is a child of God, and we will see that he has a proper Christian burial. Poor little lamb," I said softly, and I did not look at the tiny bundle, wrapped in linen in a basket on the table. "But Annie, you know that little lambs thrive in the Shepherd's arms. Your son is in good hands."

Annie nodded, her eyes sparkling blue with great, uncried tears. "Aye, Joan." And she lay back down and said no more.

This Child is Not Mine
April 22, 1612 ~ Henricus

This child is not mine as the first was,
I cannot sing it to rest,
I cannot lift it up fatherly
And bless it upon my breast;
Yet it lies in my little one's cradle...
—James Russell Lowell

Here a pretty Baby lies
Sung asleep with Lullabies:
Pray be silent, and not stirre
Th' easie earth that covers her.
—Robert Herrick

The day before, Jack Laydon had slipped quietly out so that I could tend to Annie. Babies, no matter the circumstance, were always the domain of women. The room had become an unwanted birthing chamber.

Thomasine had come by, holding little Ginny's hand. Tempie opened the door a crack and said, "Take her to your house, Thomasine." Thomasine nodded gravely. She understood. The whole town knew about the flogging. But Ginny had not seen the awful sight. She had been inside the Laydons' home. Surely the child had heard, but we could only hope she had not recognized her mother's voice in the screams.

Jack, meanwhile, had sat on a bench in front of our home, waiting, listening for word of his wife and infant. Tempie had come out and merely gave him a sad and searching look with a shake of her head.

"Do you know what it was?"

"A boy," Tempie had whispered.

Defeated, Jack had trudged back toward his own house alone so that I might watch Annie through the night.

Now, with the morning light, he returned. In his hands was something resembling a small chest with a gabled lid.

I knew what it was.

"For my son," he said with dignity. His eyes were full, but he did not cry. "I could do nothing for my wife." His voice was bitter. "Not to stop the whipping, not to protect the baby or to ease the pain of the lashes." Then his voice rose in defiance. "But this I do well. This I can do," he repeated, looking closely at the little coffin as though to ensure he had not missed a joint, that every seam was perfect and even.

"See the special lathework?" He was speaking more to himself than to me, but I nodded. "The only gift he shall ever receive from his father shall be the best I can do even if it is *this*."

And that, I thought, *sums up the kind of man you are.* But all I could do was nod as the words would not come out of my mouth.

This reminded me of another time and another place when Maggie had died. When we had offered our rings to the soldiers if they might—*might*— bury her.

Death, I thought, was always cruel, but it was particularly cruel in Virginia.

After the last church service of the day, Jack approached Pastor Whitaker while Annie rested at home. Would the preacher mind baptizing the baby and performing a ceremony at the grave? It was an unusual request with the baby being so small. Jack didn't know whether the pastor would deny him. But he gathered his courage to ask. He explained the situation, the flogging, the miscarriage.

Would the reverend consider his wife unworthy to baptize her child? Jack waited, his eyes fixed upon the preacher.

Whitaker patted Jack's arm. "It would be an honor, brother."

I decided at that moment I liked the new pastor at Henricus.

Reverend Whitaker accompanied Jack into the churchyard so that Jack could dig a hole. Tempie and I went back to my home and fetched Annie and the little coffin. Then we knocked on the doors of Judith, Thomasine, and Margery. Our somber faces said it all. They each came forward, understanding. We were the ones who would have likely been Annie's gossips. Now, we attended to a very different task.

Alongside, too, were Cecily and Janey. Janey had Ginny's little hand while Cecily cuddled Tommy. Margery had her infant Giles in her arms. Margery and I were painfully aware that the little coffin Annie carried could well have held our own babies.

Annie had asked that there be no one else present. We had tried to tell her she should remain in bed, but she had refused. Annie, weak and bruised, had determined she would nonetheless be here. Nothing, she said, no beating wounds, no lying in, would stop her.

The time was half five.

Quietly, with bowed heads, the gossips sang the Psalms over him, the same ones Tempie and I had sung over so many perished during the Starving Time. The Reverend Whitaker kindly read the burial service over the little grave, his words warm and mournful, like an elegy. Then, with great ceremony, we laid the precious wooden box in with the baby's head to the east.

This would be the only son that Jack Laydon ever had.

Afterward, Tempie and I stood alongside the grieving mother and father. Little Ginny, unable to understand, stood beside Janey. Janey had her arm wrapped around the younger girl's shoulder and once or twice bent to kiss her head. And then, too, Cecily had her arm about Janey, and so they formed a chain of little English girls in Virginia.

"Would that I had some daisies," Annie whispered to her husband, and again my mother's words, from a lifetime away, were in my ears. *Day's eyes, they greet the day. And we plant them to remember the children we have lost.*

For a moment, my own little boy, John, perished of plague nine years before, flashed through my mind. I would never, across an ocean, be able to plant the daisies over his grave or decorate it in flowers.

He was alone and far away, and I felt a stab of longing for him. Yet I still had my girls and infant son, and a swell of gratitude filled me somehow. Small miracles in terrible places and times.

A shadow in the setting sun, flitting from the trees, between and amongst them, reminded me of a young boy running. *All in my mind,* I thought, as I watched the shadow braiding in and through the trees. Then, a second thought. *Well, why not? Perhaps little brothers and sisters are never truly left behind in graveyards. They are too playful and refuse to stay.* Their souls eager for a higher journey, just as my father had said.

"Godspeed to you, in *all* your journeys, little ones," I whispered, as we all walked away.

One Stitch at a Time
April 28, 1612 ~ Henricus

With fingers weary and worn,
With eyelids heavy and red,
A woman sat, in unwomanly rags,
Plying her needle and thread...
Stitch! stitch! stitch!

"In poverty, hunger and dirt,
Sewing at once, with a double thread,
A Shroud as well as a Shirt....

"A little weeping would ease my heart,
But in their briny bed
My tears must stop, for every drop
Hinders needle and thread!"
—Thomas Hood

Take your needle, my child, and work at your pattern; it will
come out a rose by and by. Life is like that—one stitch at a time
taken patiently and the pattern will come out all right like the
embroidery.
—Oliver Wendell Holmes

"They can punish the mother, aye, but when they punish the unborn babe, that is filthy!" Tempie said in disgust.

The incident had been a week before, but Tempie and I were still furious at the treatment Annie had received. We had visited Mistress Wright after the burial of the baby. The midwife had said little, her shutters darkened and closed, and we had left with heavy hearts.

Now, George Yeardley had returned from James Town for an extended period, so he would be seeking a house for himself and Tempie today. So many were dying; a house was surely available.

Meanwhile, Tempie had awaited the noon break to vent her anger to her husband. Sometimes we all looked to him to use his influence with those in power. Influence, George said, that was weak at best.

"They did not know," George said quietly.

"They did not ask!" Tempie retorted loudly, her voice hot with anger. "Do not defend Dale and his...his...floggers! Would that *I* had been with child and lost it because of a whipping. Would you then simply say, 'They did not know'?"

George looked around uneasily as though afraid others might hear. It was unwise to criticize the marshal. It was also illegal.

"Tempie," he said evenly, "no one knew she was with child, and..." He hastened to add, seeing her raise her finger to interrupt him, "And, yes, you are quite right that no one asked. Dale applies the laws with a force and brutality that Gates will not like. But this settlement is under Dale's thumb, and the marshal feels that without strict enforcement we will all die at the hands of the Indians or Spanish. He feels that he is *saving* us."

"Thumbs, thumbs, Dale's thumbs," Tempie muttered. "Hang the man by his thumbs. See how he likes it!"

George nodded with a wry smile at his wife. "Could we keep that sentiment to ourselves in this house? I would rather not look out and see my wife dangling from some post by *her* thumbs."

It was nearly a joke, but not quite. These days, hanging by one's thumbs was far too common. So was the wheel, with men tied to the spokes, beaten with a club.

I poured some of the aged pumpion beer into their flagons, wiped the pewter pitcher off, and fussed around by the fire. I did not want to intrude on their conversation. Cecily and Janey were immersed in a game of marbles on the floor, and my mind wandered. Soon Cecily would be off upon her own. This was hardly the English world we had imagined for her.

"Do you still believe in the venture?" George was speaking again, more quietly now. His elbows rested upon the long table, his hands clasped upon one another and pressed against his chin. His eyes bored into Tempie.

Tempie looked startled. "Why, what do you mean? It is Dale I do not care for. Of course I still believe in the venture!"

"Then you will have to care for Dale," George said matter-of-factly, and Tempie cocked her head at him.

"Aye?"

He reached for her hand and said seriously, "Tempie, this settlement is going to require a tremendous heave. A push, not unlike the strain required to birth a child. Pardon me," he said quickly. "I do not mean to be insensitive to the loss of the Laydon child."

Tempie grimaced, but nodded.

"It will not be an easy birth, this new settlement upriver."

"Nothing in this place is *ever* easy," Tempie said, bitterness in her voice.

George nodded understandingly. "Well said. Yes, you have a right to feel that way. You have endured much, as has Joan, and even little Janey. All who have been here, in one manner or another, have been tested nearly beyond human limits."

Tempie said nothing, but softened a little. She needed only acknowledgement that she *understood* suffering for the sake of Virginia's survival and her own.

"I mean to say," George continued, "that Dale is a stern warrior, 'tis true. He is no one's favorite, not even in the Big House." The big house was what we often called the barracks, the largest building where lived the soldiers. "Yet he *does* seem to have Virginia's best interests at heart. If we do not get this settlement built and fortified quickly, we are at great risk. Spanish invaders could capture and kill us between a sunrise and sunset. The murmurs in England and even from our Spanish ambassador in Madrid say that the Spanish king grows increasingly impatient with this colony. Think you not that the threat of the caravels was a real one?"

Tempie very nearly rolled her eyes—I saw the motion begin—but she restrained herself. She did not like it when George spoke patronizingly. But her husband went on, seemingly oblivious that Tempie had perceived it this way.

"We now run a double risk. If we do not with all haste finish fortification on this new settlement Henricus, then we are still unable to defend ourselves from the Spanish and from the Indians, who do not want us this far upriver."

"And what has this to do with a too-short shirt?" Tempie asked impatiently. "Or causing the loss of a baby? Annie has been as good a 'soldier' as they come here. She was at Point Comfort during the Starving Time, 'tis true..."

"And that was fortunate, or little Ginny might not be here with us today," I interrupted. The crabs and mussels from the sea had saved many lives at Point Comfort while we had been starving at James Town when Ginny had been a newborn.

"Yes, exactly so," Tempie said. "Annie was carrying a child when *no other* women were even here to midwife her! Fortunate we arrived during her time, aye. She did not even have the promise of a native woman's help. She had lost her friend Pocahontas. And why? Because the men had made warfare in such a way that separated these two friends. And Pocahontas had been teaching Annie valuable lessons about this Virginia world."

"There was so much more we could have learned from Pocahontas," I put in, thinking back. Pocahontas had only begun to teach Annie about Virginia plants. I desperately wished to know more.

"Aye," Tempie was saying seriously. "But our Annie has persevered on. She has not complained. She has…" Tempie was on fire, but George broke in.

"She has been a valiant soldier for this cause," he said with solemnity. There was no touch of derision. He meant this seriously.

Silence filled the table for a moment in a world where men could honestly consider a woman *a soldier for the cause*. Then George spoke once more. "And so have you all. You have been the wives of soldiers, or in Annie's case, the wife of a carpenter but you have indeed been soldiers yourselves. None of us wishes to take that away from you." He paused to smile. "If I could give you a medal or make you a knight, I would."

"A medal for cooking and spinning? I don't think Dale would approve." Tempie had a wry smile upon her face. "And besides, perhaps I have scorched my pottage once too often and must be chained." She cast a sideways, very-Tempie look at me. "Scorch it, you get whipped. Set it afire, and you're on the wheel."

I bit back a smile despite myself.

George seemed amused then continued, "But you see that Dale *values* the service the women provide, which is why he insists it be held to standards."

Every time the topic circulated back to Annie's punishment, Tempie threatened to lose her temper once more. But she took a deep breath and composed herself.

"Standards? *Without thread?*"

"Tempie." George was quiet again. "We will make mistakes. The flogging of Mistress Laydon was a cruel mistake indeed. I am not excusing this. I like Master Laydon. I like Mistress Laydon, too. I would never have had their baby lost over, yes, short shirts. But recognize that Dale has to create the impossible. He has to tame a wilderness and protect every man, woman, and child within its boundaries from five forces: the Spanish without, the natives within, hunger, disease, and Company abandonment. Bankruptcy threatens to topple us at every turn as well. Every good soldier knows there will be losses along the way. This we cannot help. It is for the…"

He hesitated. "It is for the greater good. For the protection of England itself against future Spanish attack. Without a strong base in the New World, we will soon be at the mercy of Spain and the pope once more. Spain will become rich again as soon as it rebuilds its coffers, especially if it has this whole continent to explore and exploit." In an echo of words Will had said to me three long years before, George added, "This is our Canaan, our Eden." He paused and said with finality and emphasis, "There *will be* losses."

"I saw it," I broke in suddenly, taking a seat on the bench next to Tempie. "I saw what it will be." I had spoken without considering whether I should or not.

George looked at me curiously while Tempie said, "Saw it? Annie's lashing? But you weren't…"

I interrupted. "No, not the lashing." I shut my eyes. "Thank God."

I opened them again slowly, as Tempie said, "Then what did you see?" She looked perplexed.

"It," I said simply. "It. What it will be. What we will be one day. We will grow. We will get bigger and stretch very far…"

Tempie shook her head, and I knew she didn't understand.

I had piqued George's interest. "Stretching further up the James River, you say?"

"More," I said. "Further. And west of that, and north, and even south. At least as far as Roanoke Island, maybe further."

"Do you 'see' things often, Joan?" George asked. I could not tell if he was skeptical or not.

I plunged ahead. "No, not usually. I am not a witch or anything!" I said hastily. Tempie laughed, swinging an arm around my shoulder.

"Well, that I can vouch for. She certainly didn't bewitch any deer or raccons and send them our way during the Starving Time. You know, if you had that ability, you could have pulled a whole fleet of sturgeon up the river to us, couldn't you? I am disappointed in you…"

Our laughter broke the tension that had been in the room throughout.

"I don't think sturgeon travel in 'fleets,' Tempie," George said.

"Well, whatever they travel in even if it's by Spanish caravel. Joan could have gotten them to us. *If* she had the ability. Which I seriously doubt."

"Doubt on, for I do not," I said. "No, George, I just… Somehow while we were in the church at James Town when the governor was talking about moving us upriver. Something happened, and I saw a tree with two branches, English and Virginian. And I felt the power of movement, of time moving us into the future. A grander…something." I paused, the larger implications still left unsaid. "Though upon many a tragedy, I am sure."

"Hm, that's interesting," George said. I suspected he was just humoring me, but no matter. I knew what I had seen, what I had felt. But I *would* have to refrain from speaking of it idly. It took little to convince others that one was a witch or desired to be one.

"The picture is bigger than a thread and a baby," I said to neither of them in particular. "Much bigger."

At that, the two o'clock drummer signaled, calling us back to work, and George rose. "There's wisdom in those words, Tempie," he said with a nod toward me. "Hold the larger canvas in your mind. You'll need it in the days ahead. Soldier!" he added with a laugh as he placed his cap back upon his head and let himself out.

Tempie turned to me with a bemused expression.

"Traitor," was all she said.

Upon the Brink of the Wild Stream
September 1612 ~ James Town

Upon the brink of the wild stream
He stood, and dreamt a mighty dream.
—Alexander Pushkin

As it was his turn to take a shift, Will stood sentry at the door of the Big House in James Town. Through the door, Will could hear muted voices. Inside were Samuel Argall, Governor Gates, and Marshal Dale.

Samuel Argall had returned to Virginia bearing the new rank of admiral. The king had given Admiral Newport a position in his Navy, leaving Argall to take his place here.

Now, the admiral, the governor, and the marshal huddled inside, planning their next moves. Will pushed closer to the door. What he could hear, he could hear. He would take his information any way he could get it.

"The French?" Will heard Gates ask.

"As soon as possible. Orders from the Company," Argall replied.

Are we attacking the French? Will wondered. He knew the French were in Newfoundland, which the French called New France and the English called North Virginia. Herein, of course, the problem. The land could not belong to both.

Will had heard that a French ship had run afoul of winds and blown onto the coast in England. Gates had come to the colony with this knowledge.

"We're to make known our claim to the Dutch as well," Will heard.

The Dutch had a trading post on the island of Manhattas, further north and also within Virginia. This was not a permanent settlement as the French were trying to build. The English would survey the outpost, ensure that the Dutch knew on whose land they squatted.

The Indian and Spanish are watching us, and we are watching the French and Dutch. This great stretch of land, from La Florida to Newfoundland, seemed peaceful from a distance. But tensions were churning beneath the surface.

The irony of such a fight was not lost on Will. Here, the soldiers of the

James River could barely hold their small plot of land. Now they were traveling to Canada to tell the French to get out.

Argall had arrived just the day before on the *Treasurer,* a ship Argall and
Lord Rich owned together. Possessing his own ship in a Virginia virtually
devoid of fleet gave Argall much power. Will had an uneasy feeling about
that, too.

Yet, Argall had made a name for himself as a talented fisherman. He
seemed able to sense the best fishing spots, and he was the first to note that
the fish seemed to run at various seasons. Argall had been up the coasts to
Newfoundland and back. He knew the waters, he understood the Indian
tribes, and he had excellent instincts.

Now, listening intently, Will could only catch words and phrases.

"Charter for Bermuda…Somers Isles or Virginiola…" Argall went on.

Bermuda is now part of our charter! Will couldn't hear all, but he could
hear enough. *The Company must be naming the island after Somers.* The
elderly, revered naval hero had loved the islands. Somers had returned to the
Bermudas to butcher wild hogs and to bring them back to starving Virginia.
There, on his last mission, Admiral Somers had lain dying. The old Admiral
had asked his nephew to carry the pork, and his body, back to Virginia. *But
bury my heart in Bermuda,* he had told his nephew. The nephew had buried
his uncle's heart as requested, but he then pickled Somers's body and carried it
and himself back to England instead of Virginia.

The islands had a temperate climate. *Summers, Somers,* Will thought.
Obviously a play on the name.

"…*must* work…" Argall's voice had a tinge of desperation which Will
could hear through the door.

What must work?

"…last hope, truly."

What, what?

"…this lottery…."

*Ah. The subscribers are disheartened, not paying their fees, and so the Company
is using a lottery!* Will couldn't believe the fate of his new colony rested on
scraps of paper put into a hat.

The discussion continued. Will heard the words *Nansemonds, Appomattocks,*
and *saltworks.*

He could guess the rest. The English would seek retribution against the
Nansemonds for the attack when the English had last traveled there. *The
voyage of the magic rain.* Also revenge against the Appomattocks for trickery
against the English miners. Such retribution always occurred in the fall so
that the English could plunder the natives' corn as punishment. Will knew
his captain would likely send him to these skirmishes.

Will wondered if he would go to Canada to fight the French. *We are comfortable in our claim on Newfoundland,* Will mused. The Italian John Cabot had explored Newfoundland for England more than a century before. Cabot had come to Europe with tales of the codfish running so thick they could slow a boat, so thick the men caught them by hanging wicker baskets over the ship's side.

Cabot's early exploration had prompted England to defend its land claim vociferously, though we took no issue with seasonal fishermen from other European countries.

If Will were to go to Newfoundland, when would that be? Will reckoned Argall would wish to sail to Newfoundland in summer when the fishing was better. Catch fish, kill French.

Will was certain Argall would bring home as much salted cod as possible. All the better for the saltworks to be in place first. The saltworks were a pet project of Dale's and an important one at that. Creating a saltworks on the Eastern shore probably, would allow the settlement their own store of salt for curing meat and fish.

"Spring, I sail to the Patawomecks to trade for corn!" Will heard Argall announce. The Patawomeck were mostly allies. Argall had visited them before and considered himself to have friends among this tribe on the outskirts of the Powhatan confederacy.

Will knew he would be busy. Battles with the Nansemonds, the Appomattocks, and possibly the French and Dutch. Will probably wouldn't have to help with the saltworks, unless the Eastern Shore Indians fought the idea. Not likely. These were the most agreeable of all the Virginia tribes.

With all these great military initiatives at hand, how could Will have known that the simple trading voyage to the Patawomecks would be the most momentous? For there, the *Treasurer* would make a startling discovery—a discovery that would change the course of Virginia's history.

Transplanting an Old Tree
Early to Mid-November 1612 ~ Henricus

We never had a thought of exchanging our land for any other, as we think that we would not find a country that would suit us as well as this that we now occupy, it being the land of our forefathers, if you should exchange our lands for any other, fearing the consequences may be similar to transplanting an old tree, which would wither and die away, and we are fearful we would come to the same...
—Levi Colbert (Itawamba Minco), Chickasaw Chief, in a letter to U.S. Government Commissioners, 1826

Americans are always moving on.
It's an old Spanish custom gone astray.
A sort of English fever, I believe,
Or just a mere desire to take French leave,
I couldn't say. I couldn't really say.
But, when the whistle blows, they go away....
—Bird whistles, sleepy with Virginia night,
Veery and oriole,
Calling the morning from the Chesapeake...
—Stephen Vincent Benét

Will was correct that he would be among those battling the Appomattocks. He had put on his uniform with great seriousness that early November morn, yet he was grateful for an opportunity to visit the children and me at Henricus.

"Shouldn't I move to James Town with you?" I asked him as I set hot corn pone, dried fish, and pumpion before him. "Get you not lonely there?"

He smiled, but Will Peirce the soldier answered. A serious, thoughtful man.

He shook his head. "No." Then, he hastened to add, "Do not misunderstand. I *do* get lonesome! And I do miss you." He patted my arm. "Truly, I do. And indeed some wives are there. Not many, of course. Captain Sharpe, for one, has his wife at James Town. She lives not with us in the barracks, of course." He laughed self-consciously.

"Then why not me?" I felt irritable. We'd had only brief time together at James Town before being riven again.

"Safety," he said, and his eyes were dark. "Threat of Spanish attack remains strong, and we are antagonizing the French and Dutch as well. I want you here, a better fortress around you. Not where you and the children must quickly spirit upriver *if* we get sufficient warning. I am a patient man. I can wait to see you."

"Well, I am an impatient woman!" I began, then stopped. "But an impatient woman who would like to keep my children alive." A memory of Janey cowering under the bed last year and the terror we felt as Dale prepared to load his fire ships swept over me. I clasped his hand and nodded. "You're right. I know you're sacrificing, too."

My stomach dropped in fear. Today Will was marching to battle again. Always another battle, another war. Yet always he came home. Each time, a new threat, a new risk.

"Where are you off to this time?" I choked out the words. What if this day were the one? The one where another soldier passed word to me that...

"The land of the Appomattocks." He adjusted his buff coat, then reached for his bread. He looked at me quizzically. "Honey?"

"Aye?"

"No, I mean, is this honey? It's delicious!"

I laughed, forgetting for a moment my fretting. "Yes, yes. I had been saving it. It's the last of that you bartered for off that ship." He ate a spoonful of pumpion then reached for another piece of fish, which reminded me of something. "Mistress Toler said her husband's brother shipped him some new books of interest. One was called *Coryat's Crudities*. Well, Thomas Coryat's been walking across Europe, and now he believes we should all eat with forks as the Italians do."

"Ah, the effeminate Italians! Almost as bad as the French. Why the devil would one need to pitchfork victuals into his mouth if he has hands?" Will shook his head. "You'll never catch an Englishman using one of those things! And most never an English soldier." Will wiped his mouth. "Excellent, Joan. Excellent meal before battle. For today we take retribution for the trickery on De La Warr's miners when Queen Opossunoquonuske enticed our men to a dance and then murdered them all."

Dale made sure to punish every deed, even in this case where nearly two years had lapsed. The memories of the English governors were long as, I suspected, were the memories of the Powhatan chiefs.

With Will gone to war again there remained nothing for me to do but wait, work, and worry. His return a few weeks later allayed my fears.

In the end, Will said, this battle had been an easy victory. The English lost not a single life, and only a few natives died before Queen Opossunoquonuske, their queen, agreed to uproot to territories south. The queen had argued that her tribe were traders, as we were. That this land was Kennecock, part of the Great Path South where forest trails and rivers rambled to the land of the Occoneechee. The Occoneechee, the queen said, were the greatest Indian traders of all, who lived on central trading rivers snaking from distant corners of the New World.

Dale had been unmoved, for his plan had changed dramatically upon surveying the Appomattocks lands situated between two rivers. Here stretched broad fertile fields, terraced, with a vantage point and lower fields near the rivers. The James River was gracious enough to curl around behind the land as well as across its front, meaning rivers were well nigh on three sides. Retribution had turned to removal, Will said.

"Where will they go?" I asked. An image of a native woman's face came to mind, the last march of the Paspahegh queen. A moment that changed me, for I had seen then that an English mother and a native mother were not so different after all.

Will lit a pipe with some of John's trial of tobacco. It had grown a weak crop but not a dead one. "Still bitter," Will mumbled. John had distributed seeds amongst his friends Will, Ralph Hamor, Sam Jordan, and other men. Next season, they would all continue the experiment, and John pledged to send a sample home to England on the next ship out.

Will blew the smoke out slowly. "The move was peaceable, Joan," he said as if reading my thoughts. "We did give them trade goods for the land, and they agreed."

I understood the workings. The natives had not wanted to leave their expansive fields situated upon two rivers, the trading post for Powhatan's other tribes north and east. Yet, Dale's barter was an insistence, and the queen had seen the men in armor, the burning matchlocks outnumbering her arrows. She had taken what she could for the land and agreed to move from it. I recalled the Paspaheghs had put forth a great fight for their land, and in the end lost almost all including their king, queen, and the queen's children. The Appomattocks knew such a battle was futile.

"I believe," Will was saying, "that the tribe is headed upriver still on the trading route. Not as convenient to the James River, but yet upon the path to the Occoneechee tribe south of here."

And a chill went through me, as I wondered if all these submissive tribes were truly submitting or just waiting for another day.

Standing on the land after his victory, Dale had proclaimed the territory "the new Bermudas," for this land afforded natural protection just as rocky cliffs protected the Bermuda islands from invaders.

Studying the land, Dale's inspiration had struck as a lightning bolt, even as the Appomattocks fled before his men. Dale would offer these lands as a corporation. Surely, the Company would approve. Those agreeing to join this business would work for the Company for three years. At the end of that time, the men signing on would be forever free. These men would farm and build the new Bermuda so that it would become a strong adjunct to Henricus. Men, by their own enterprise, would cease relying on the Company store for food.

Soon after, Dale held a meeting at the church. Who would invest but three more years to be free at the end of that time? Dale had been forceful, powerful, eloquent. He had raised his right finger, pointing to the heavens and quoting Psalm One: *And he shall be like a tree planted by the rivers of water that bringeth forth his fruit in his season; his leaf also shall not wither; and whatsoever he doeth shall prosper.*

"This enterprise of Bermuda within the enterprise of Virginia shall be free, and each man's sweat shall yield its fruit in its season." Dale would erect a two-mile palisade river to river and would grant all signers leave to erect a four-room home. The settlement would encircle the river cusp. "Houses higher, fields below!"

Enthusiasm was rampant. The Bermuda signers, already stockholders in the Virginia Company, would now also own shares in the Bermuda Hundred Corporation. These signers would labor in Bermuda Hundred for three years for Company profit, then all profit would go to the individuals. Those who enlisted recognized that they had already been working almost as slaves for as many as five years. The offer seemed promising, the first pledge of any sort of freedom we'd been offered.

The coming year, 1613, all would sow crops at their present homes. Building of the new settlement, Dale said, would occur that summer until time to return home for harvest. Once the harvest was complete, the men would make final arrangements for moving to Bermuda Nether Hundred. By March 1614, we would have the new settlement planted with both corn and people.

The celebrations rose into the evening, the ringing bells, the fervor. "Aye, aye, where do I sign?" Flagons raised, toasts shouted. Mulberry, Sassafras and pumpion beer, be what it may, raised in toasts. Hope, at last, had returned to the English in Virginia. Could we at last be free in but three more years?

"Doesn't it remind you of signing to come here? Great enthusiasm. Can Bermuda Hundred save us?" Thomasine asked dubiously. We had all seen enough to be cynical.

Could it, indeed?

In the end, nearly every free man in the colony signed on including Admiral Argall, Marshal Dale, the Laydons, the Yeardleys, John Rolfe, Sam Jordan, and the Peirces.

Betrayed Like the Princess of Old
Mid-April 1613 ~ Henricus

The Earth seems a desolate mother,—
Betrayed like the princess of old,
The ermine stripped from her shoulders,
And her bosom all naked and cold.
—Charles Henry Webb

Brer Fox, he lay low.
—Joel Chandler Harris

We had been at Henricus a year. Dale's men were still frantically building the palisades enclosing the parcels around Henricus, palisades that stretched for miles across the Virginia forests. Come late summer, the palisade at Bermuda Hundred would go up as well.

That morning in April was one of the finest Virginia offered with a sweet breeze, blue birds, red birds, robins, and wrens darting from branch to branch, each bursting with its unique song. Another winter past.

After two weeks of dreaded tallow rendering, I had at last learned that I should spend the next week spinning. Tempie had been spinning for a week already, having received orders to cease clothes beating.

On this fair day, both in weather and in work, I had offered to pull my wheel to Tempie's home. Spinning together was enjoyable for both of us, and she and George were living just two doors away. On days such as this, we could almost forget that the marshal worked us so many hours, ordaining our hours from dawn until dusk, seven days each week.

Still, even with long work hours, I could abide spinning.

As we worked the stricks, we learned we could ably work both our feet and our mouths, and this we did.

We had not been at the task long before Annie came bursting through the door. Distraught, she cried, "She ain't a fox to be caught in a trap!"

Tempie and I stopped our work although we should not do so. Annie, too, should not have left her work.

Tempie said, almost sternly, "Annie, you risk whipping again!" Then, more curious, "Who's been caught in a trap?"

"Pocahontas!" Annie began to cry. "What's she done? She's always been a friend to the English folks here."

We listened as Annie explained that word had just reached the settlement. On Argall's trading voyage to the Patawomecks, the admiral had captured Princess Pocahontas, Powhatan's daughter.

"How could that rascal do it?" Annie's distress was evident. "What does he mean, stealing her?"

I knew not what to say. What *did* he mean, stealing her? What had happened?

Later, the story would emerge. Argall had been exploring far north and west up the Pembroke River until he reached waters no longer navigable by ship. He had then sailed a shallop all the way to the Pembroke's headwaters in the mountains. There he had found strange things, such as great wild cattle roaming, mines, peculiar white and red earth that the Indians ate for physick, and water springing from the ground. He had eaten the cattle, which he believed to be animal the Portuguese called *búfalo*. The meat was quite wholesome, and the beasts easy to kill as they lumbered along. Argall had taken note of all these discoveries as possible commodities.

The admiral had been preoccupied with such things, far from the homes of our tribes, when his Indian guides mentioned that they knew the whereabouts of Powhatan's daughter.

The braves then had sly Argall's full attention. The guides told him that Pocahontas was visiting the Patawomeck king, that she had been there some three months trading her father's goods.

Argall had reckoned he could play on old friendships with the Patawomeck king Japazaws and might be able to capture the princess. Then the English could use Pocahontas to barter for stolen tools and English soldiers the Powhatans were holding hostage. Pocahontas was, after all, the favorite of her father King Powhatan.

Argall had offered Japazaws and his wife a copper kettle for their niece. Whether for fear of not accepting or because her Uncle Japazaws genuinely desired the kettle was never clear, but the gambit worked. Argall said with the natives valuing copper so highly, the big copper kettle would give Japazaws great prestige, even wealth.

Annie's anger flared. "Pocahontas has been twice betrayed! The English, whom she called 'friend,' betrayed her. And so did her uncle. Her own family sold her for *copper*! I've got to go see her. Will you help me?" She looked at me pleadingly.

Before I could speak, Annie turned to Tempie. "Tempie, help me! Will you ask Captain Yeardley to let me see her?"

Tempie stammered. "Annie...I...George... I don't know. She's a captive princess. You know how Dale..." Tempie looked at me helplessly.

I jumped in, understanding Tempie's position, but feeling for Annie. "Let time do its work, Annie. We'll wait for our moment. Let us see what they plan to do with her. They'll use her kindly."

The English prided themselves on well treatment of prisoners. Even the Spanish spies still being held at James Town agreed that their English captors allowed them considerable freedom.

"Besides, they won't view her as a prisoner. They'll treat her highly as both a princess and a woman." I was talking fast, hoping what I said was true.

"They did not respect the Paspahegh queen." Annie looked at me, almost glaring.

My heart dropped as I recalled the scene. The meeting of the queen's eyes and mine, her death march to the woods. "'Tis so," I replied quietly. What could I say to that?

Tempie, obviously sympathetic to Annie as well, interceded. "The leaders will value Pocahontas higher than the Paspahegh queen. Pocahontas is the daughter of the high chief Powhatan, the king's favorite daughter, so they say. Dale and Gates will be loathe to treat her badly as due respect between two warring countries with her being the leader's daughter. And she has friends here, those from the first two years like you who remember her."

Annie was, in fact, the only English woman who ever met the fabled princess, for Annie had arrived before Powhatan moved his home far up the Chickahominy's River. With that move, the chief had forbidden his daughter from coming to us anymore. So the soldiers said.

Annie had her arms crossed. "I am going to Sir Thomas Dale and *demand*—" she began.

"Annie." My voice was low but firm. "We cannot make demands in Dale's Henricus."

Silently, Annie pushed the sleeve of her kirtle up where remained a scar of her flogging. "And what have I to lose if I do? I bore up under it once. I can bear up under it again." Then, with a disappointed backward glance at us, Annie marched out.

"Annie, wait, wait!" I called after her. But Annie strode away.

Tempie came up behind me in the doorway. "'Tis not the way to accomplish something here. It requires more...cunning than force."

I smiled. "Dale's men have the force..."

"And we women have the cunning."

I did agree with Annie. We owed Pocahontas for the help she had given us, for by tutoring Annie in herbs and animals, Pocahontas had inadvertently given us tools we needed to help survive the Starving Time.

I was thinking aloud, speaking slowly to Tempie as I considered what the leaders might do. "They'll try to teach Pocahontas about Christianity. That would be a feather in the Virginia Company's cap, proof that we can accomplish what we set out to do: convert heathens. The idea will be that she might convert others in her tribes and be influential with her father and all of his peoples."

Tempie nodded. "Aye, that makes sense. But who will be her mentor? Reverend Bucke or Alexander Whitaker?" If it were Bucke, still at James Town, we might be able to convince Maria to influence her husband on Annie's behalf. Suddenly, I knew the answer.

I snapped my fingers. "Whitaker!"

"How be you so sure?" Tempie looked puzzled.

"'Tis simple," I said. "Henricus is more remote and better protected than James Town. 'Tis more comfortable, and more women are here as well. And besides, Reverend Whitaker has a heart for converting the natives. He was a celebrated divine in England. They say his friends were astonished that he wanted to come to Virginia, but Whitaker told them 'twas God drew him here. Missionary work is a passion he and Dale share. Dale will want a hand in this, too." Dale was here with Whitaker.

"Remember poor old Reverend Glover?" Tempie asked. I did. Preacher Glover had come to Virginia, an elderly pastor who felt God could use him here. Remarkably, some of the leading religious men had made a true effort to come to Virginia. But Glover had perished the previous year after only a few months' stay. He had not survived the seasoning.

"Glover had a good heart. Whitaker, as near as I can tell, is also a kindly man. And he knows the Laydons. By God, he buried their little babe. And gracious he was," I added.

"We shouldn't do anything until after church services," Tempie said.

She was right. Bringing attention to ourselves for not working would help no one.

"Aye, Tempie. After church service and after midday meal, I will go to her house and speak with Annie. I believe we can get through to Whitaker. And if the pastor feels Pocahontas can benefit by seeing Annie, Dale will not disagree. We just have to wait until Pocahontas arrives."

The Wise, the Courtly, and the True
April 1613 ~ Henricus

Old friends to talk! —
Ay, bring those chosen few,
The wise, the courtly, and the true...
—Robert Hinckley Messinger

I had only a short time after the meal and before the drum sounded for afternoon work. I hurried to the Laydon cottage and knocked tentatively at the door.

Jack opened it and smiled warmly when he saw me. "Come in, Joan. Annie's here."

Annie raised her head. I could see that her face was tear-streaked. She looked away from me quickly.

"I thought I could count on you and Tempie!" she wailed.

I went to her and embraced her. "Annie, you *can* count on us. But we must be wise about this. Another flailing will do you no good, nor do any good for Pocahontas." I paused to let Annie take my meaning. "Tempie and I believe they'll bring the princess to Whitaker. For conversion."

Annie glanced up with interest as I continued. "Reverend Whitaker is a kind man. He was very good to you when the baby died. Surely he'll let us see Pocahontas. But we must not go making demands. We can ask the preacher if we might visit with her, talk to her. I truly think the leaders will bring her here."

"So you'll go with me?" Annie clapped her hands together.

"I will," I said firmly. "I think we owe it to Pocahontas. We cannot secure her release. You know Tempie has no power over what George does even if George *did* have enough sway to get her released. But with the reverend's permission, we can visit Pocahontas and let her know we care about her...and that we are sorry."

Annie reached over and clasped my hand. "Thank you, Joan. I appreciate it. She was a good friend to me when we were but young girls. I haven't seen her in four years." She looked over at little Ginny rocking a rag doll on the bed. "So much has changed. The whole siege and Starving Time have come between us."

"And Indian wars," I added in a low voice. We were in full warfare most of the time, now.

"That too."

Less than a week later, we heard that Pocahontas had come to Henricus, just as we had suspected she would. And our instincts had been correct that she would come under the tutelage of the Reverend Alexander Whitaker. At twenty-seven, the reverend was a pious and learned man. He had great belief that our English mission here in the New World was to teach the natives Christianity. Here, the old arguments fell into play: we descended from tribes in England who knew not the truth until Romans brought the Word to us. Should we not give the same to our brothers, the tribes here in Virginia?

But controversy reigned. Could the natives learn Christianity? Or could they not? Should they? Whitaker was one who knew his own heart, who desired to be a missionary to these peoples. The Protestant light shown for him, and he earnestly desired to shine it for others.

The pastor called his parsonage Rock Hall because it was a passage between Henricus and Rock Dale where the livestock ranged. A miles-long palisade joined the settlements. Rock Dale and Rock Hall were on the southern side of the river while Henricus was on the north. However, the river coiled in such snakelike fashion that at times the north side of the river was south of the south side of the river, an amusing play of geography.

Annie and I caught the parson after the Sunday service. A tall, willowy man with deeply set brown eyes and black hair, Reverend Whitaker reached out and took Annie's hand. While the darkness of his features might have appeared severe, his slow and gentle voice put us immediately at ease. "And how fared you since the loss of your child? I do pray for the baby's soul, mistress. For there were nary a chance to baptize him alive, the wee mite. But, never you fear, the Lord knows that."

He respects the Laydons for the dignity they accorded their small, lost baby, I thought. That could help Annie's cause, certainly.

Annie smiled gratefully. "Thank you, sir. I've been well. Sad, you know." She twisted the sleeve of her kirtle nervously. "Uh, reverend?" She hesitated.

He leaned in and nodded as if encouraging her.

"I was wondering, uh, that is, we—" She moved her hand between the two of us. "Mistress Peirce and myself, we were wondering if we could visit with Pocahontas."

He looked surprised by the request. "To pay a neighborly call?"

Pocahontas had been at the settlement just a few days. Perhaps the princess would one day attend services herself if she were interested in Christianity. But we knew not if that would happen or how long that would be. Annie felt a passion to let Pocahontas know as soon as possible, that she, too, was here. Pocahontas would be aware, surely, that the Starving Time had taken a great toll. She probably expected her friend had not survived this far.

"Aye, sir. You see, I knew her, sir. I knew her long before when she came to visit James Town as a girl. She might remember. Seeing me might be a…a comfort." She looked hopefully at the parson. The sincerity in Annie's eyes was tangible, and I felt Whitaker would agree.

The parson then turned his attention to me, reaching for my hand and covering it with both his own. "Fine, indeed. Mistress Peirce, Mistress Laydon. Sorrow fills our Pocahontas as she longs for her home and her own people. Come by after church and before the two o'clock drumbeat tomorrow, and I shall be expecting you."

A smile burst upon Annie's face. "Oh, thank you, sir! Thank you!"

And that was how, the next day, Annie and I found ourselves walking the several miles to the parsonage. We had crossed the river in a shallop which acted as ferry and now approached the reverend's house, feeling our nervousness growing.

The Spirit That Remembers
April 1613 ~ Henricus

Faithful, indeed, is the spirit that remembers
After such years of change and suffering!
—Emily Brontë

'Stay' is a charming word in a friend's vocabulary.
—Louisa May Alcott

Rock Hall was slightly larger than most of the homes at Henricus, still much smaller than a parsonage in England would be, but more generously surrounded with land.

I felt a flutter in my chest as I lifted the knocker, for neither Annie nor I had ever been to the parson's home before.

Whitaker's servant girl Martha pulled the door back with a smile and greeting, and we walked into the great room. Through that room, I could see another chamber with a small shelf of books, the parson's study, no doubt. He only had a few books, more than anyone here, but a scant collection for a scholar, I thought.

Two rooms to the right served as chambers for Martha and Pocahontas while to the left of the great room, I assumed, was the parson's own chamber and that of his servant boy.

"Come right this way, mistresses," Martha said politely.

At that moment, Reverend Whitaker emerged from his study. He smiled again, and I felt the room warm all around him. *Here,* I thought, *is a man who truly loves God. Strange how the light of the eyes gives it away.*

"I have told Pocahontas that you were coming. She is this way." And the pastor led us into a room with a bedstead, a chest, and a chair angled toward the window. In the chair sat the princess Pocahontas, her head turned away from us.

"Pocahontas? You have visitors," the pastor said gently.

Neither body nor head moved at all. We might have thought she was deaf had we not known better.

Reverend Whitaker shrugged. I could tell he did not expect much from this meeting. He then departed the room to give us privacy, I supposed. *He trusts us,* I thought. That was a good sign.

The room was fairly dark, but the light shone through the window in such a way that it fell upon this young woman elegantly.

There is something special about this one, too. I did not know why I felt that way, but her aspect said to me that someone had chosen her. But who? God? I was not sure. She did not believe in our God. And I couldn't imagine that God would put her on such a difficult path, anyway.

I remembered the journey that pilgrims took to the tomb of St. James. A voice in my head spoke quickly, affirmatively. *The road to Compostela is always rocky.* Was Pocahontas herself on a pilgrimage? Were all of us, every Englishman? Every native? Could a non-Christian be a pilgrim?

All these thoughts raced through my mind in an instant as I observed her serene but sad countenance. *How odd,* I thought, *that both Whitaker and Pocahontas have such a presence. One rarely encounters that. These two must have a destiny together that two such presences should come together like this from two countries, worlds apart.*

Whitaker had said that God had called him here despite his own reluctance to come to such a wild and unpredictable place.

Why? Somehow, I could never escape the feeling that what we did here was more than the simple day-to-day struggles, that it had a larger purpose. I only wished that I understood it better. *Perhaps someday.*

Pocahontas was still staring out the window and had not acknowledged our entrance.

Annie gathered her courage and spoke tentatively, almost nervously, to the young woman sitting in the chair. "Pocahontas? 'Tis I, Annie. Do you remember me?" Annie's voice shook somewhat. We could not be sure how much the Indian girl understood.

Pocahontas turned her head slowly in the direction of the voice. She stared at Annie for a moment, neither a smile nor frown upon her face, betraying no emotion. Silently, she nodded.

I studied her. Her hair was long, black, shiny. Her skin darker than ours, her face sculpted. Her eyes rich, brown, and almond. She was, I reckoned, about seventeen, just a few years younger than Annie.

Annie looked at me helplessly, obviously at a loss for words. Then she tried again.

"I'm sorry for what happened, Pocahontas. Truly, I am," Annie's voice was plaintive, sincere.

Again, Pocahontas nodded wordlessly. She understood the emotion if not all the words, of this I felt sure. The young woman then turned her head back to the window.

Annie's shoulders sagged in defeat and embarrassment. "I...I suppose I shouldn't have come. 'Twas a mistake. I only meant to say that I am still here, still alive, and at this settlement as you are. I wanted to be there for you. I remembered you. I remembered your friendship when I was all alone at James Town. I missed you all this time, and I...I never hoped that this was the way I would see you again." Annie's voice tumbled out, surely too quickly for the young woman to grasp, but she was unable to staunch the flood of words. Annie's sadness was palpable, and she threw her hands across her eyes as the tears began anew. Still no response from the young woman, who this time did not look toward us, but kept her eyes on the window.

Turning to me, Annie said with resignation, "Let's depart, Joan. We should not have come."

We moved toward the door, I with a hand on Annie's back. I felt so sorry for her.

Suddenly, a voice from the chair said simply but sincerely, "An-nie. Stay."

Annie turned toward her friend, and their eyes locked upon one another. Pocahontas stood, and Annie rushed to her and threw her arms around the Indian woman. "I missed you, I missed you," Annie said. Then in a whisper lest any punishing ears overhear, Annie drew back. "Pocahontas, I'm sorry. I'm so sorry they did this to you."

Pocahontas was weeping, too, and each pulled back to study one another's faces. Pocahontas nodded her assent but seemed unable to speak further. Suddenly, in a native gesture of friendship, Pocahontas reached out her hands. Entwining her fingers with Annie's, she murmured, *Mawchick chamay.* Pocahontas then pulled her hands away and with a serious expression, crossed the fingers of each hand as if her pointer embraced the next, repeating, *Mawchick chamay.*

Annie had grasped a few native words during her time in Virginia. "We *are* the best of friends," she whispered. Then, sound by sound, Annie added, *"Maw-chick cha-may."* She reached out her hand, letting her fingers mingle with the young Princess's, as Pocahontas had done. Annie then stood straight. She crossed the fingers on both her hands, imitating her friend. *"Mawchick chamay!"* she repeated once more, a determined expression upon her face.

As the two friends embraced once more, I turned away, fearing to intrude on their reunion.

His White and His Red Children
Late April to June 1613 ~ Henricus

One God created us: [Indians] have reasonable souls and intellectual faculties as well as we. We all have Adam for our common parent.
   —Reverend Alexander Whitaker, writing from Henricus, 1612

Brother, the Great Spirit has made us all, but He has made a great difference between His white and His red children. He has given us different complexions and different customs.... Since He has made so great a difference between us in other things, why may we not conclude that He has given us a different religion according to our understanding? The Great Spirit does right. He knows what is best for His children; we are satisfied.
   —Sogoyewapha or "Red Jacket," Seneca tribesman and War of 1812 veteran

After that, Annie and I made regular afternoon calls on Pocahontas. Although a deep sadness still pervaded the princess, she seemed to look forward to our visits. I found her to be warm, polite, and enchanting.

Sometimes, she and Annie reminisced about running through the woods when they were young girls. At times, they discussed the turns their lives had taken.

Her English was growing better as the days passed. And each visit, we tried to teach her more words. The Reverend Whitaker was also spending large amounts of time in teaching her as were Sir Thomas Dale and John Rolfe. John's first *Trinidado* tobacco crop had been weak, and he supposed that perhaps Pocahontas might advise him. It was the native women, after all, who were in charge of the tobacco.

Pocahontas's greatest sadness, it seemed, was that the soldiers had taken her from her husband Kocoum and her little son. She hoped to return to them soon. She wished her father had not stolen the guns and that he would meet the ransom demands. She wished our towns would not encroach too closely upon the Indians, causing frictions. She wished our people would not lie to hers about their true intentions. She hated the killing on both sides. Most of all, she wished our two peoples could live peacefully in the same land. All of this, she conveyed through a mixture of English and Powhatan language and hand gestures.

Her hopes and dreams were not so far afield from our own, and this brought kinship between us three women. Reverend Whitaker allowed us to speak without censure.

Her emotions were jumbled. Why had her father not met the demands yet? Or had he, and the English were being dishonest? She was aware of the Paspahegh queen's murder, but felt Dale would spare her life. The reverend had told her this, and she believed him. But would Sir Thomas Dale override the pastor? How were Kocoum and her son? Would anyone know? When would Dale allow her to return? Or would he?

As the weeks went by, April turning to May, the trust Pocahontas had for us grew. She seemed comfortable confiding in us. She sensed, somehow, that we were true, as much as she could believe any English person were true. Annie had such a forthright way about her as though her soul were clear and the sun shone right through it. And perhaps because I was with Annie, I was trustworthy as well.

One day, Annie took both of Pocahontas's hands in her own, telling her, "You were my only friend when I was a lone young girl at James Town." Annie had been but fourteen, and though the Indians did not count years as we did, we thought Pocahontas had been about twelve. Although some four and a half years had passed, Annie had not forgotten.

"Now I am here for you. 'Tis true I cannot free you. I have no such power, but if I could, I would. I can only come see you and let you know that you're not alone—as you let me know that *I* was not alone." At these words, the Indian girl smiled and squeezed her friend's hands in return.

Pocahontas wore the traditional English clothing that the parson had provided to her. In our world, native costume was far too revealing. It was customary that Indians and English traded boys, that each boy would wear the clothes of the other culture. The clothes of their own cultures were simply not available or practicable.

Pocahontas looked vaguely uncomfortable in the English clothes, and she would pull the kirtle this way, adjust the bodice that.

"Why do you wrap yourself round with...too much...*rahsawans?*"

Pocahontas asked one day while tugging awkwardly at the bodice laces.

Annie laughed. "*Laces.* Those *rahsawans* are called laces. It's just custom, I suppose. Why do *you* wear deer hide?"

Pocahontas smiled and shrugged. "The deer are happy in them, and so are we!" When she smiled, her face lit. But such smiles were rare, for the sadness still hung over her.

One day, she told us that she had requested that the English allow her sister Matachanna to visit her.

"Did Marshal Dale agree to that?" Annie asked. But before Pocahontas replied, I knew the answer. Of course he did. Matachanna was but another soul to win.

"Yes, they are sending a messenger to my father," Pocahontas was saying.

Whitaker had been teaching Pocahontas the ways of the Bible, about Jesus, about the history of the people across the ocean in a country called Israel. The Indian girl was, Whitaker said, an apt student, learning readily, listening intently, curious about faraway lands. Dale also spent time teaching Pocahontas at the parson's after evening sermons. Will had heard Dale say that if he won but this one soul, all his time and effort in Virginia would have been well spent.

One day, Pocahontas drew Annie and me near, saying in a confidential tone, "My father Wahunsonacock, whom you call the great Powhatan, has been to the land called *Espan-ya.*"

When she said it, a silence fell over us. Annie and I stared at each other.

Espan-ya? Was this an Indian town? But it certainly sounded like what the Spanish called their homeland, Spain.

"*España,* Pocahontas?" I said. "What do you mean?"

"The land of the *Es-pan-yo-les.* Your enemies," she said slowly as if this would help us believe.

The land of the Españoles? The Spaniards? We were at a loss.

Pocahontas gave us a hurt look. "You do not believe me? I tell you it is so!" She lowered her voice. "Many years ago, when my father was a boy, some He-su-eet-as priests came to Tsenacomoco," she said, using the Indian name for Virginia.

Annie had a quizzical look. "*He-su-eet-as?*"

"*He-su-eet-as. Hehsuettas,*" I said, trying to make sense of it. "Ah... 'Hesuitas' is the way the Spanish would say *Jesuits!*" I exclaimed in surprise. How would Pocahontas know about Jesuits unless Powhatan had actually encountered them? And if she'd heard the English mention Jesuits, why would she pronounce the word as the Spanish did?

"Fie, Joan! Do you reckon?" Annie said to me, her eyes wide.

I nodded. Then we both turned back to Pocahontas.

"Go on," we said, intrigued.

"The Spanish came to Tsenacomoco and captured my father. They took him across the ocean, and taught him Spanish. They gave him a new name, Don Luis. He was away for nine planting seasons. He became *Cat-ó-lica*."

We sat in stunned silence. *Powhatan himself was Don Luis?*

We tried to sort this out. It certainly sounded as if Pocahontas used the Spanish word for *Catholic*. Powhatan had been Catholic? Given a Spanish name?

Struggling to find the English words for so complex a concept, Pocahontas was able to make us understand. The Jesuits had brought Powhatan back to Virginia, expecting him to teach his people about Christianity. Powhatan's brother Opechancanough had been ruling in Powhatan's place.

"My father's brother Opechancanough said, 'See, this is rightfully yours. I have been waiting for your return.' So my father became *Werowance* of all Tsenacomoco. Then he attacked and killed the Spanish and returned to his own people. Did you not wonder why he knew so much about the ways of the land across the sea?"

Annie and I didn't answer. We couldn't.

"My father hates the Spanish even more than he hates the English! He hoped for...for..." She searched for a word. "*Mawchick chamay.* To be very much friends with English," she finished.

I felt I was reeling with knowledge of something that, as far as I was aware, no other Englishman knew. This was a powerful secret and meant she trusted us much. *A confidence we will keep,* I thought.

"So I know something about the ways of the Christians, but I do not like how they...they..." She made a motion with each hand as if yanking something toward herself, and looked at Annie questioningly. "*Commotoouh?*"

"Steal?" Annie asked in return. "To take from someone?"

Pocahontas nodded, recognizing the word. "I do not like how they *steal* away those they wish to teach," she said. "If I become a Christian, I will not be the first in my family," she finished, as she ate a piece of corn pone we had brought. "I like what I have known of this son of *Ahone*, Jesus, and the stories of *quiyoughcosoughs* Moses, Abraham and Noah, too. However, my father returned to the beliefs of his people, and given a chance, I would too."

Virginia Stands in Desperate Hazard
May 24, 1613 ~ Henricus

Here the rumour of a rupture between England and Spain over Virginia grows daily.
　　—Vicenzo Gussoni, Venetian Ambassador, writing from
　　　Turin, Italy, November 1612

[The Prince] was the great Captain of our Israel, the hope to have builded up this heavenly new Jerusalem he interred (I think) the whole frame of this business, fell into his grave: for most men's forward (at least seeming so) desires are quenched, and Virginia stands in desperate hazard.
　　—Sir Thomas Dale, expecting the prince's death to put
　　　an end to Virginia, June 1614

On May 24, the *Elizabeth* docked at Henricus.
New ships always brought forth the curious. Adventurers poured from their homes and milled about. Would they receive letters from England? What news did the ship bring? For one could never guess what an arriving ship might bear. The news had been too quiet; we'd had no incoming ships since Argall's *Treasurer* the previous fall.

Sometimes the news was happy and cheering, other times mixed. An entire European world was going on without us.

For Tempie, the *Elizabeth* brought a letter.

Tempie tore it open before even departing the dock. As she did, she said, "'Tis from my mother, Joan." She screwed up her face in concern. "I have written her and hoped to make some peace."

I took her meaning. Tempie's mother had not wished her daughter to come to Virginia even though her family had ties with many important men in England who supported the cause. Tempie's father, Anthony Flowerdieu, had died while Tempie was still a girl. Tempie's mother, Martha Stanley, had then married a Captain Garrett.

Tempie respected the captain, but she sorely missed her father. In Tempie's mind, she would always be a Flowerdieu first, and she was proud of both her Stanley and Flowerdieu heritage. Tempie felt her father would have been proud of her decision to come to Virginia. However, her mother disagreed, calling it a disgraceful place for a woman with noble roots. And so Tempie had left England against her mother's wishes.

Tempie read silently then lifted her head. "I can hear her. I can hear her saying these words. It's as if four years haven't passed, as if she's standing before me." She continued reading. "Oh! Oh, no... She's gone. Marie, my sister. She died last year." Tempie's lip began to quiver. "*Come home*, mother says. 'I fear I myself do not have many years. How I wish to see you, my daughter, that we may make matters right between us. Please, at your earliest leave, *come home*.'"

Tempie sighed. "Mother, I can't. They will not let us go." Tempie, staring at the scrawled words before her, spoke as if to her mother.

I understood. The letter was all that Tempie had left of her mother.

"Joan, it's like being a...a prisoner, isn't it? We cannot escape from here."

I said nothing. So many times I had endured these feelings myself.

"Did it work?" she added softly.

"Work?"

"Counting your blessings. Did it help?"

I patted her arm. "It did," I said as if not believing it myself. "Trouble and longing capture the eye so much more readily. The hard part is deciding the blessings even exist. But you helped me see they were there."

"I am going to think. To pray. Perhaps to list my own blessings," Tempie said, more to the sky than to me. "Maybe an answer shall come."

As she walked away, something caught my attention on ship. My heart leapt as I saw Captain Adams and Governor Gates striding briskly toward Dale's quarters. It was not Gates who sparked my interest, however, but Adams. Captain Adams had been the master of my ship, the *Blessing*. Perhaps my friend Harrison had returned to Virginia with his master!

I strode closer for a look at the mariners unlading barrels, rolling them down the plank, furling sails.

Harrison had been the mariner who had alerted Maggie and me to the hurricane before the other passengers were aware that we were approaching anything other than an ordinary tempest. In Virginia, Harrison had informed us of John Smith's injury, for the sailor had been on the expedition to the falls when the gunpowder exploded. He had alerted us that someone may have been attempting to murder Captain Smith. And he had given little Janey a Spanish coin, a good luck talisman, which I still kept safe for her until she was old enough to have it herself.

I remembered the grizzled old sailor fondly, for he had done his best to keep Maggie, Janey, and me in his care.

And then I saw him. He was still on deck, a mop in his hand as he scrubbed and cleaned. He glanced up, and I waved my arm.

"Master Harrison!" I cried, unable to restrain myself. Harrison's station in life was not such that one would have typically called him *master*. Maggie and I had used the term of respect to win his loyalty. However, now Harrison to me was truly deserving of the title.

A grin spread across his wizened mariner's face, and his eyes crinkled around the edges. What was it about the sea that always created such dark skin and map lines about men's faces just as it had done my father? Perhaps that familiarity was the source of comfort I felt upon seeing Harrison, a whisper of remembering my father's return visits home. Or perhaps it was just that I felt such affection for him.

"Ahoy, Mistress Peirce! How do?" he called, grabbing his hat and waving it, apparently unable to restrain himself either. I felt sure he was not supposed to cease his work.

"Fine, sir, fine!" I replied. Yet at that very instant my heart sank. He would ask about Maggie. She had enjoyed such a playful relationship with him, he saying we were a hen's ship, she telling him that he needed hens on his ship if for no other reason than to spare him from his own singing.

As if the same thought had seized Harrison at exactly that moment, he looked about. "And that other mistress, the ornery one. How she be?"

My eyes were suddenly solemn, and I shook my head.

He stopped scrubbing. His eyes grew solemn as well.

"Starving Time, mistress?"

"Starving Time, sir."

"I see." He looked down at his mop and idly ran it along the deck. "Sorry, mistress. So, so sorry," he mumbled, and I could barely hear him.

Then he lifted an eyebrow. "And your girl?" He tried to sound casual, yet his concern for Janey was obvious. It seemed she reminded him of his own daughter, who had died of plague while Harrison was at sea, years ago.

"My girl is fine!" I called out, delighted to share happier news. "Fine."

He smiled again. "I'm a-right glad to hear that, I am." He paused and bit his lip. "We didn't expect much."

I looked at him curiously. "What do you mean?"

He stopped his work again and looked squarely at me, his gaze deep. "I left you in a right bad way. If we'd a-knowed a Starving Time was coming, why, I'd-a brought you and Mistress Deale and your girl and stowed you right away!" He laughed, and I found him charming in a rough kind of way.

"And you would have, too!" I exclaimed, smiling before turning suddenly sober. "And we would have gone with you if we'd known." My voice trailed off. Of course, there was no leaving James Town that fall of 1609. We were bound to stay. But I knew what he meant. If any of us had known the true horror of what was to come, we probably would have overtaken the captain and rushed aboard. Dare anyone think ninety determined women couldn't overtake a crew?

"You said you didn't expect much, but you knew the Starving Time was over. What do you mean, sir?"

Now it was his turn to become somber. He considered a moment, then seemed to decide that the direct answer was best. He shrugged. "Why, over in England, they thinks you're all dead!"

"What!" Now it was my turn to be shocked. "Why…why would they think that?"

"'Tis the rumor going about. Word is ye all are dead. Beg pardon, mistress. Some say the Indians slaughtered all of ye. Some say, no, 'twas the Spanish, sure. No matter the cause, says the folks at home, for dead is dead. No ships home to England in a year or more. That just proved it, they say. 'Dead men can't sail ships.' Why, Cap'n Adams wasn't sure what we'd find here, and he told us so. Told us to be prepared for anything." His voice dropped off. "Maybe even a Spanish flag." His eyes had a helpless look. He clearly did not like relaying such news.

I felt suddenly faint. Why would such rumors be flooding through England? What had started them?

As if reading my mind, Harrison went on, "The Spanish. It was the Spanish what spread that idea, that's what I think. They saw you all here with the settlements growing." He swept his arm outward. "Henricus looks like a fine place compared to that James Town." He lifted his cap off again, wiped the sweat from his brow, and replaced the cap. "We watered at the Bermudas, Somers Isles, that is, on the way here, made a delivery of goods. It's a colony now, too. Did you hear that?"

I nodded. "We knew it had been approved in the new charter." I had a longing to see those islands where Will and Sam had spent nearly a year. But I doubted I ever would. "It's off to a good start?"

"Aye, she's a right smart-looking place as well. Beautiful, beautiful. To think how many years we avoided it as the haunted isle of devils!" He laughed, and so did I.

"And we brings you silk worms in seeds, mistress. Hundreds and hundreds of 'em down in the 'tween deck. They come from the king's own stock. The king is fond o' the idea of having his own colony to manufacture silk."

I smiled. New commodities always meant new hope. Will believed that silkworms were the most likely commodity we could make succeed. Mulberry leaves, the worms' favorite food, abounded in Virginia.

"But that ain't all the news, mistress."

"Oh, tell me! We feel so isolated here sometimes, Master Harrison."

"Well, it's sad news, mistress. The worst."

Now my heart fell again. It was *hard* to be so far away and then hear all the news this way!

"We've lost... We've lost..." He seemed overcome with emotion.

"Yes?" I encouraged him. *What* had we lost?

"We've lost the prince. Young Prince Henry died in March of a sudden sickness. England's bright star, snuffed out like *that!*" He snapped his fingers.

"Oh, Harrison." I was at a loss for words. The prince gone! Illogically, I thought of the peregrine. She had sat on her prince's arm, but only for a few months. Somehow it felt to me that, when the prince died, all my fine words about pilgrims' hope died with him. My heart sank.

"And that ain't all, mistress."

"Stop, Harrison. I don't know if I can bear more." But I could guess: without the prince, support for the Virginia venture would wane.

The old mariner continued, "The Company, so I hear, is encouraging Governor Gates to give up the settlement and to send everyone home. The ones in charge think the whole thing's finally reached a breaking point. We got us a letter here to Gates and Dale that says just that. That's what we crew are hearing, anyway." His woeful eyes made me want to cry.

I understood. Without the prince's urging, would the king continue to support Virginia? The Company itself had nothing of value to show investors. We had dreamed that one day, with Prince Henry on the throne, support for Virginia would come so much more readily. The younger prince Charles cared little enough about the colony. That dream, then, was as shattered as all the others.

"Oh, pounds were hard enough to come by, even before.... The Company started a lottery." Harrison squinted at me. "You know about that?"

I did.

"Well, that brought in some silver, I hear. Not enough. Then the prince died, and mistress, it was like the *heart* went right out of the desire for Virginia."

I felt weak. I had not expected news this dramatic. Gone, the prince who had said he'd fight the Spanish *himself* in the West Indies to keep Virginia safe, who had believed so much in Virginia as a pillar of England's future. Gone, England's bright star. Involuntarily, I covered my mouth with my hand. News this deep, this far reaching, I could not fathom, standing near the bridge this May day.

Harrison looked around cautiously. "One more thing, mistress, and I'm sorry to be the bearer of this."

My head swam. He had *more* to tell me?

"You see that Cap'n Adams went straight to find that Marshal Dale, and that we brought Gates with us up here?" I nodded.

"They're breaking the news to Dale about the prince. 'Spected he would take it right hard, him being the prince's guard when the prince were but a baby."

Sir Thomas Dale guarding a baby. Images flew through my mind. Dale, all military rules and discipline, caring for a baby, loving the baby even? Loving the prince? Well, of course, he did. Dale was building Virginia up for the prince's honor. Dale would be grief stricken, and I suddenly understood Dale more as a man than as a harsh soldier. Yet I had lost my voice and could only continue nodding foolishly.

"Gates and Adams, they also come to put their heads together because the Cap'n brings news that..." He hesitated.

"Go on." My voice was shaking. England thought we were all dead, the prince had died, and the Company wanted to abandon Virginia. What more could he tell me? This had already been far worse than I'd imagined.

He paused, removing his cap again. The hot Virginia sun was taking a toll on him as he worked. "Well, they've intercepted letters between the Spanish ambassador and his king. And rumors are coming out of Spain and Italy and France, all over Europe..."

"What kind of rumors?" I was no longer looking at him. My eyes were closed.

"Well, that matter o' Virginia.... Mistress, it's gone before the Spanish Council of War. Every day that goes by, the rumors get stronger all over Europe. Brace yourself, mistress, that's what my master come to tell you. Prepare for attack."

Blackest Night Between the Worlds
Late May to Early September 1613 ~ Henricus

I shall go out when the light comes in;
Would I might take one ray with me!
It is blackest night between the worlds,
And how is a soul to see?
—Anne Reeve Aldrich

Prepare for attack.

Will had been right to send me here to Henricus further away from danger. But what could I truly do to prepare?

The rest of the day, my stomach churned. I was becoming sick with worry. So many things out of our hands, beyond our ken. So many things, and I here alone with three children. Will would likely not even be in our settlement if the Spanish came again. What could I do?

Nothing, not a thing.

"I am making myself ill," I said aloud one sleepless night. All over something that may never happen. Were the Spanish here now? *No.* 'Twas true they could show up in a blaze of caravels and guns at any moment. But in this moment, they were not here. And they might never come. We had not yet abandoned the colony. If we did abandon it, I could go home. If we did not, then we would have something, some measure of success. Those in England saying such things might be no more than malicious gossipers.

The only way to survive this, I realized, was to treat this day and tomorrow as if they were perfectly ordinary days. I would spin, and gather sassafras, or sew, or beat the soldiers' shirts and put my mind onto those things.

The summer passed with no alarms. Each day, no alarms. And so to the next.

I forced myself to adopt the attitude that the Spanish were not here now and the colony not yet abandoned. Beyond that, I would force myself to deal only with what I must in each day. Thinking of the future simply frightened me too much.

True enough, that. We had sufficient evil in any given day, enough for every surviving Virginia soul.

Meanwhile, with our new home soon to be in Bermuda Nether Hundred, Annie and I would not be able to visit Pocahontas much unless our husbands could obtain room on a shallop so that we might sail back upriver to the parsonage. But this seemed unlikely. So we seized the opportunity a week before the move to shuttle over for one more visit.

By now, we knew the Reverend Whitaker would let us see Pocahontas. She lived less as a captive and more as a congregant these days, for she had begun to understand the story of the man Jesus. She seemed to like the way Jesus went from town to town helping people. A son of *Ahone?* She could believe that. Weren't we all the children of *Ahone,* what the English called *God*? Jesus seemed to Pocahontas to be a *quiyoughcosough* and a great one. The English claimed Jesus was more than a pastor, more than a *quiyoughcosough.* He was God in the skin of man, a part of the Holy Three, Pastor Whitaker had explained.

Pocahontas was considering having the good reverend baptize her. Aside from her own father, whom the Spanish had baptized a Catholic, the princess would be the first Indian in Virginia to become a Christian. We had come with goals of achieving baptisms of whole tribes. But the Indians preferred their god, be it god or devil, no one knew for sure.

"Why hasn't her father sent the rest of the arms and men, do you suppose?" Annie whispered as we approached the parson's door.

I shrugged. "Will says Powhatan cannot use the arms or even the swords, but that he enjoys looking at them, viewing them as a victory of sorts over the English. And Will believes, too, that the English captives are all but useless to us but are quite useful to Chief Powhatan."

Annie laughed. "Well, some o' the more shiftless ones might just as well stay with the Indians. We don't need 'em!" Then, growing serious, she added, "But for the fact that Dale holds Pocahontas here against her will."

In July, three months after her capture, the Indians had delivered seven captive Englishmen each carrying a broken matchlock, to Dale's post at Henricus.

The chief had sent a message through the natives who escorted the English prisoners home. Powhatan would be glad, he said, to give us five hundred bushels of corn when we should come to his river and deliver his daughter. The corn, he added, was in repayment for the many more weapons, all of which, regretfully, had been either lost or stolen from him. Upon that bargain, the English and the natives should be forever friends, the message from Powhatan concluded.

Dale had been furious.

"Think us fools? Every time a man dies through Indian arrow or toma-hawk, some Indian runs off with his matchlock, his rapier, and his knife! Powhatan returns just *seven* men and *seven* weapons?" What of the swords, the many other pieces and tools—not to mention the other captives?

Dale had sent a response through the native interpreter.

Your daughter is very well, and we do treat her kindly. We shall continue to treat her with respect no matter how you deal with us. But we cannot believe that the rest of our arms were either lost or stolen from you. Therefore, until you return them all, we will by no means deliver your daughter.

Are we at peace or at war? You choose.

Since then, two months had passed. Two months of silence from the great *werowance*. So, we supposed Powhatan didn't much like Dale's message.

Dale might have been more arduous, more eager to launch an attack and force the issue, but for the fact that Pocahontas was grasping scripture well. Her English, too, was improving aiding the scripture learning. There would be time to retrieve those weapons, but for now, Dale was attempting to retrieve a soul. Dale was as much a militant Christian as he was a militant enforcer.

While Annie and I would soon be unable to visit, Pocahontas had other visitors. John Rolfe still came to see her regularly. We had occasionally met him coming up to the parson's door as we were leaving.

In John's first year of tobacco planting, he'd discovered he must not be curing it properly. "I'm not doing something right," Rolfe had mused many times. He knew that he had so much to learn. The natives hung their tobacco out to dry. He felt certain that the natives' superior growing methods com-bined with his own sweeter tobacco from Trinidad could be just the right mix. *A tobacco to rival the Spanish, grown in Virginia.*

Initially he had befriended Pocahontas over asking her about tobacco. The Indian women tended the tobacco and all the fields, so Pocahontas had much insight, encouraging and advising him as he had hoped. The two had begun speaking a pottage of English and Indian words. Pocahontas would give her ideas on ways of improving his tobacco, and add, "When comes *Cohattayough, vunamun chamay maangwipacus.* Come *Taquitock, chamay apooke.*" *Chamay apooke.* Very much tobacco. And John would smile, knowing she was saying he could expect bigger tobacco leaves next summer and that she was predict-ing a more plentiful tobacco harvest overall.

And he grew to like her. She was bright, and she was kind. What reason had she, a prisoner, to help him? And yet she did.

As for Pocahontas, she was learning the Bible, she was considering becoming a Christian, and she was adapting to life at the parsonage.

Sort of.

Her sister Matachanna had come also for a visit, giving the princess someone who understood why a bodice felt uncomfortable and why boots were just not practical in the woods. She also brought news from her people.

That news was devastating. Pocahontas listened to the words in her native language. No mistaking them as she might English.

"When the soldiers took you away, they also killed Kocoum. I am sorry, sister."

John had been approaching the door when he heard the wail, a mournful cry.

"And my son?" the Indian woman asked bitterly. "My son? Did they kill him, too?"

Matachanna shook her head. "My sister, he is alive and healthy."

"He has no mother as long as I am here."

"He has not you for a mother, but your other sisters and I, we care for him." Matachanna's eyes lit in loving warmth to her young sister. "We raise him up to be fine and strong, much as we did you."

Pocahontas's eyes brimmed, as she said, "When my mother died, I had you."

Matachanna nodded. "The elder Pocahontas, the first Pocahontas. She died giving you life. And you were Matoaka not long. We could not help but call you Pocahontas, as you looked like an arrow flown from her bow!"

This image brought a rueful smile to the younger woman's face. "Well, if she has flown me, she has flown me here! And why has our father not paid my ransom?" Her vivid eyes flashed, eyes that mirrored joy, sorrow, or anger with equal passion. "They tell me my father sends the broken guns, but not the good ones. He returns neither the axes nor swords." Her eyes welled with tears. "I am beginning to think he does not want me! That he values his old pieces more than me."

"I believe our father and the English *werowance* play games," Matachanna said. "Consider our father's choice. If he gives too much, he risks losing his power to the white man. If he gives too little, he risks losing...you."

Pocahontas, her voice filled with grief, said, "As a child, I was friends with the English, and they have betrayed me. I love my aunt and uncle, and they betrayed me as well. And I loved my father, and yet he has not redeemed me." Her eyes welled with tears. "I fear I do not understand, Matachanna, who it is who loves me and who does not. Who values me for me and not for what I can offer them? I feel, sister, as if I am caught between night and day. As if I belong nowhere."

Matachanna hugged her sister and said. "It is possible they tell you not the truth. Stay strong, sister, and let us see if the English and our people can agree soon. Meanwhile, I am here with you. I will stay as long as I might."

Pocahontas smiled gratefully. But she understood the path given her by *Okeus*, who watched from the air, was not an easy one. It seemed to fork in front of her, and she knew not what the future held.

O You Young and Elder Daughters
Early December 1613 ~ Henricus, and on the *Treasurer*

Come, my tan-faced children,
Follow well in order, get your weapons ready;
Have you your pistols? Have you your sharp edged axes?
Pioneers! O pioneers....

O you young and elder daughters! O you mothers and
you wives!
Never must you be divided, in our ranks you move united,
Pioneers! O Pioneers!
—Walt Whitman

Darkness had begun falling early, and we could see our breath most days of the past week. Winter once again beat a grey path to our door. However, the river view this winter would not be from James Town or from Henricus, but from our new home in Bermuda Nether Hundred.

Will had chosen our lot already. Laborers and carpenters were constructing homes as rapidly as they could. The men had completed building on schedule so that we might move and settle in before any snows. That way, come the spring when the fields were opening up and ready to plant, we would be ready.

I knew without seeing it that our new home would be a hastily built wooden structure as poorly constructed as the others. No foundation, just earthfast posts.

Each time we prayed for better housing. Each time we received the same as before.

We'd had to wait for the *Treasurer* to finish ousting the French from North Virginia in Canada. But that ship was home now, and Argall had sailed her up to Henricus to begin the colony's migration fourteen miles back downriver.

The business with the French was troublesome, I mused as I packed. Argall, Dale, and Gates had sworn to uphold the boundaries the English king had granted us. What concern of theirs if those boundaries conflicted with the boundaries the French king had granted *his* people?

Argall had been ruthless, had destroyed the Jesuit mission and French colony there, bringing home prisoners. The admiral had shown cunning in finding and hiding the Jesuits' papers and in ransacking the priests' possessions. He had brought the prisoners back to James Town, consulted with Gates and Dale, and then returned to North Virginia.

The Jesuits had said that their allegiance was to their order and their mission, not to France, and they offered to guide Argall to the *true* French colony. With the Jesuits' assistance in finding the other settlement, Argall had destroyed it as well. Argall had been the fox, the French settlements the henhouses. The admiral had taken much of what he could, loaded the *Treasurer* well. Of this booty, which might have served our own colony well, we had seen nothing except some of the men's clothing. But Argall was the richer for it. We women had discussed it and felt sure of that fact.

Argall had sent some of the French prisoners in a ship bound for France. These released men would tell of the English defiance of their trading post, which Argall reckoned to be a good thing. Let the other European kings know that the English defended their claims. The rest of the Jesuit priests were sitting in the gaol at James Town.

Sir Thomas Dale, I heard, terrified these priests. The marshal could scarcely lay eyes on them without fury bubbling within him. Dale threatened the priests that he ought to get out his ropes, send them to his gallows. Dale hated all Jesuits, viewing them as an inherent enemy of Protestants. The marshal was old enough to recall the St. Bartholomew's Day Massacre instigated by Jesuits against the Protestants in France. These captured Jesuits truly were fortunate Dale had not executed them.

The Dutch, meanwhile, had agreed to defer to the king of England, to recognize that their settlement on Manhattas Island was on English soil. Not French, not Spanish, not Dutch. English.

Now our little gaol at James Town held Spanish, French, and Indian prisoners.

"We have but two pieces of ordnance mounted riverside," I'd heard Will tell Sam. "We're making foreign enemies and unprepared to protect against them should they retaliate." *Vulnerable.* Will wanted me upriver because distance was our only protection, and a weak one at that, as our tally of enemies across the seas grew.

Will said that the Nether Hundred was more beautiful, fertile land than even Henricus. This was small recompense, truly. It was hard to appreciate outer beauty when the inner hunger was so great, the endless working so wearying.

The *Herball* I placed on the bottom of the trunk, wrapping my physick jars in our ragged clothing. The scallop shells I packed carefully as well.

Waiting for us in the new settlement were some fifty or sixty homes, spaced about a half mile apart, around the verge of the river and running along the two-mile-long pale. Altogether, we had eight miles of land enclosed by either palisade or river.

Will said we were three doors down from John Rolfe with George and Tempie's home the most central since Dale had made George Yeardley deputy marshal. Dale, it seemed, had taken a liking to the young man who, like himself, had come from common roots. And years spent in the Low Countries had schooled both men in the art of war. If George found Dale overbearing, he at least appreciated the marshal's goals and was fair in their execution.

As for Will, his Commander had him stationed still at James Town, living in the barracks with Ensign Powell and Lieutenant Sharpe, as well as an Indian friend named Chacrow.

Dale wanted to encourage most of the old settlers to sign on to the Bermuda Hundred Corporation, so he allowed the soldiers to rotate so that they would have time to plant and harvest their corn. It would have been easier if Will lived with us at the Nether Hundred. I envied Tempie this, having George there. But Will was under the command of Lieutenant Sharpe, and James Town was their post.

Now the *Treasurer* prepared to make runs from Henricus to Bermuda Hundred, moving the settlers and their goods. While a few would stay at Henricus and continue farming, most liked the idea of toiling for three years with absolute freedom promised after that time.

By 1617, we shall at last be free! I counted the years. I would then be thirty-seven.

Thomasine had caught my sleeve the previous autumn after Dale had announced his plan for Bermuda Hundred. We'd both been hoeing when she suddenly stopped, a risk, but we were momentarily away from unwelcome eyes. She leaned on her hoe, one foot resting on the other, her chin on the hoe's handle. "Did you ever go to a big city like London when you were a girl?" she asked.

"No, my mother and I rarely left Melcombe. My father traveled far, but not us."

"Well, I did. I went to London with my father. And we had a great way to walk. My father said to me, 'Thomasine, just three more blocks.'"

I nodded, wondering why she told me this.

"And I'd say, 'Yes, sir,' and keep walking. And then at three blocks, he'd say, 'Just two more.' 'Yes, sir.' That was me. Still believin'. And then come two blocks, he'd say, 'Four more.' My father told me once that he did that because if he'd told me how many blocks it truly was, my spirit would have failed."

She looked toward the clouds. "Three more years, Dale says. Three more blocks, my father said. You see what I mean?"

I did. It was an apt question. Our freedom still withheld, we'd put in more years already than we'd expected. Promises broken. In three years, could we count on the governor in charge to keep his word?

At last, it was time to board the *Treasurer* for Bermuda Hundred.

When I saw the plank before me and the sails of the great ship fluttering in the December wind, the scene carried me for a moment to the day in June, also with high wind, when I had taken that step to come here. I felt a core of fear within. Never could I forget the bobbing of the ship in a hurricane. A terrifying journey with a terrifying aftermath.

This voyage was only downriver. I took a deep, deep breath, and helped Tommy aboard.

Pray God, this move be with Your blessings.

The girls followed behind me. Our goods were stowed in the hold, and we settled ourselves in to the 'tween deck.

This move was to be a better one, the best of the three we'd had since leaving England. Yet seeing our few possessions loaded aboard, I felt fear as we again moved into the unknown.

We move the Indians. Then we move in. Always, everyone, moving.

The ship rocked beneath us as the mariners laded it.

"What does our new house looks like?" Janey asked eagerly, and that simple question made me feel so much better. I smiled at the enthusiasm of children. They never do see the past or the future, just the moment. *Which is not a bad way to be.*

"Four chambers, Father says," Janey continued. "A *great* loft for us to sleep, Tommy!"

Tommy giggled although he was probably not too sure what this all meant. But Sister said something wonderful was happening, and he respected that.

Janey took his hand. "Let's go explore this deck." She looked at me. "May we?"

"Aye, but bother no one. Hear?"

"Yes, ma'am."

Meanwhile, Cecily was pensive, quiet. I never seemed to know what was inside her mind although I tried.

At last, as the winds picked up, the ship glided through the water and the chatter of families filled the space. Cecily made her way to sit beside me on a trunk.

She seemed to be working up to something. I took her hand and waited to see what she had to say.

"'Tis time, isn't it, mother. For I am fourteen this spring." It wasn't a question, and suddenly my heart fell. The Virginia Way had begun, and I knew immediately what was upon her mind.

I nodded solemnly. She knew it was time for her to begin another journey, one that would lead her ultimately to motherhood. A long pilgrimage, indeed.

She went on. "I know Tom Bailey plans to ask Father about us marrying in a few months once spring comes and we're all settled at the Nether Hundred. I wonder, what do you say?"

I put my fingers to my eyes but could not stop the vision of what was to be.

Then I looked at her for a moment, the face so much of her father, the grit of someone much older. Every English person in Virginia—man, woman, and child—quickly acquired a toughness that made us different than what I recalled the English in England having. I saw it with every new immigrant.

And, now, my daughter was preparing to marry a full nine, ten, or twelve years earlier than she might have in England.

Part of the toughness. Part of the necessity. Part of being a pioneer.

I felt teary and wondered if such an early marriage were the right thing. Yet, this was the way it happened here with us, as with the natives before us. Virginia had been a wild place before we arrived. It was a wild place now. A woman, not more than a girl, never knew how long she had to live. She wanted to marry, start her family young. Helpers, born into the family. Some of whom would surely die themselves.

"What do *you* say?" I asked her instead of replying. "Do you like Tom?" Loving him might come in time if she liked him, I thought.

She shrugged, and I saw that she still looked very young. "I like him well enough. He's from Aylesbury, in Buckinghamshire, you know."

"He spoke with you, then?"

"No, not directly, but I have heard it said. And I know he's appraising me. I hear from several of the girls who came also from Aylesbury."

The Buckinghamshire group had come in 1612. Tom was in his late twenties and, like so many others, had signed on to the Bermuda venture. He seemed not overly fond of drink, nor prone to profanity, as near as I could tell. Believed in the Holy Word. Had never been pilloried or whipped for missing church or blaspheming the marshal or for any other reason. He seemed a hard worker as well. Truly, could we expect more?

"Your father wants a good match for you. You're nearly of age." *By Virginia standards,* I thought, but did not say it.

Cecily looked neither happy nor upset. She simply looked resigned.

"Father will say aye, then?"

"I believe he will. And if you know of any reason not to wed him, you must speak up, lovey."

She shrugged. "I don't," was all she said.

A Live Pawn for Thy People
March 22, 1614 ~ Bermuda Hundred

*A live pawn for thy people? Then I hope
'T will be a long time ere they make matters up,
So that we still may keep thee hostage here.*
—John Hunter-Duvar

"It's time." Will was packing his rapier, his knife, his matchlock, and matches. He anticipated a battle, a big one.

"Will she be hurt? Will *you* be safe?"

"We will protect her and will treat her kindly, as always. But if you ask if she will be near the center of battle that answer is *aye*. And as for me…" He shrugged. "It's my task, my duty."

"What a mess this is," I murmured.

And 'twas true. Powhatan had responded no further, liking not, we reckoned, the answer that Dale had given. Dale knew Powhatan had more swords and weapons, tools and men within his towns. The old king had wanted us to believe there were not. However, we were receiving little in the way of shipping and supplies from England. We needed that which was ours.

Dale was angry and planned to force Chief Powhatan to relinquish the stolen goods or to fight for them. The marshal was taking one hundred fifty well-armed men to the heart of the king's territory up the Pamunkey River.

One hundred fifty sounded like a large company. But at that place, we were well aware that the Indian king could call up a thousand braves with three or four days' notice, so our men might easily be outnumbered seven to one. We had superior weapons, but they knew the area well. And Dale would be too far from James Town and the Nether Hundred to call for any support. The *Treasurer* and a few smaller ships would have to sail down the James River to the bay, then well up the Pamunkey's River to Matchut, the king's chief residence. Among the soldiers would be Will, Sam, John Rolfe, George Yeardley—nearly the entire fighting force we possessed. Princess Pocahontas would come along as well. Dale hoped seeing her might force the chief's hand.

Yet, Dale was backing Powhatan into a corner. The chief had already said he didn't have our men or weaponry, a desperate wager on Powhatan's part. How could he now say he did have them? And some of the English had spotted a few of the prisoners alive when Powhatan had called them dead.

Sir Thomas Dale had challenged Powhatan's bluff. Now if Dale didn't take action, he would look weak. And if Powhatan admitted to a lie, he, too, would appear weak. There appeared no way to avert the oncoming violence and to allow both military leaders to save face. Compounding this, neither Powhatan nor Dale liked to lose.

Caught in the middle was the young woman, whom we now considered a friend. She had been attending church, had become part of the community, and we all liked her well. She had seemed to accept her surroundings and situation as best she could. She was outspoken, but not arrogant. Her English was continuing to improve. A quick study, the delighted Reverend Whitaker said.

But there remained one other circumstance, an extra card in the game which many of us in the settlement knew, but which Sir Thomas Dale did not.

Pocahontas had fallen in love with the kindly widower who had so often visited her, and he with her.

John Rolfe was now going to attempt to force his love's father to barter her for weapons, which thing John hoped desperately the chief would not do.

The Sonnes of Levi
March 22-25, 1614 ~ on the James and the Pamunkey's Rivers

Nor was I ignorant of the heavie displeasure which almightie God conceived against the sonnes of Levie and Israel for marrying strange wives...
—John Rolfe's letter to Sir Thomas Dale, asking permission to marry Pocahontas

Had I not found a generall desire in the best sort to returne for England: letter upon letter, request upon request from their friends to returne...
—Sir Thomas Dale, 1614, explaining why he cannot leave Virginia and fulfill his duty to the Netherlands

The *Treasurer* departed Bermuda Hundred with a smaller ship trailing behind. Together, the two ships slid through the James River some thirty-five miles downriver to James Town where they dropped anchor for the night.

While in James Town, the soldiers heard the news that Governor Sir Thomas Gates had just set sail for England on his way to fulfill his military obligations to the Dutch.

George, Sam, and Will had all fought with the governor across many a battlefield, so it was with some sadness they learned that he had gone. But Gates's parting words, they heard, were that he would return in a few years.

Will for one certainly hoped so. He eyed the steely Sir Thomas Dale. The man had no compassion, but did possess high religious conviction. On the one hand, Dale kept brutal order. On the other, perhaps the settlement needed Dale's unrelenting discipline. *If we were not living beneath it, we might appreciate it more,* Will thought.

Sir Thomas Dale was not leaving, that much was clear. His three years' leave from the Netherlands had expired, but Dale had sent home a letter with Gates, asking the Company to secure him more time. Dale knew that if he, too, left Virginia, there were no other commanders the people would obey. The *Elizabeth* had arrived in February filled with letters addressed to the Virginia Leaders. Letter upon letter, request upon request from those in England begging Dale to send their friends home. Meanwhile, those in the colony begged to be set free to sail away from Virginia, never to return. Dale was having none of it. Virginia would succeed, and it needed colonists to do so.

On the second day, the ships collected more soldiers and a third ship from James Town, then continued on to Kecoughtan and gathered more soldiers there. At sunrise the following morning, the time had come to leave English settlements behind for good.

Will was onboard the *Treasurer* along with Sir Thomas Dale, John Rolfe, Sam Jordan, and Pocahontas. Will was glad to see some of his fellow soldiers he hadn't seen in a while. One of the last onboard was Hugh Deale, who had been at the Kings Arms that fateful day when Will, Sam, Hugh and John Dewbourne had decided to throw their fortunes with the Virginia venture.

By God, 1609 felt like a lifetime ago.

"Deale, what say, fellow?" Will asked.

Hugh smiled. "I say, we're headin' to Pamunkey, and I'm none too happy about it."

Hugh caught the eye of our friend Walter and stuck out his hand. "You're that Walter Bowles, aren't you? I appreciate you buryin' my wife during the Starving Time. I heard about it from Mistresses Peirce and Yeardley."

Walter ducked his eyes. "It won't nothin'."

"Nah," Hugh said, his eyes misty. "It was something. It surely was."

"Where's our fourth?" Sam asked Hugh, referring to Dewbourne.

Hugh gave Sam a steely look.

"Arrow," was all he said. He put a finger to his temple. "There."

The two men flinched.

"He suffered not," Hugh added.

Will supposed that for three of the original four to survive this long they had done mightily well. The image of an Indian arrowhead piercing his friend's scalp.... Will couldn't think about it, wouldn't picture it.

Down in the 'tween deck, the soldiers had little view, but that didn't matter much. Kecoughtan was the end of land.

This is the last stop before the bay, the last before we enter the Pamunkey's river, the last where we go fully into Indian territory bristling for a fight.

As the ships made their way into the Chesapeake's bay, all knew that the Eastern Shore passed off to their right far across the wide water. Will considered for a moment how very isolated the saltworkers out there would be and felt relieved that he only had to go fight Powhatan's braves.

Realizing how foolish this sounded, even to himself, Will rethought it. "Maybe we should enlist for the saltworks, Jordan," Will said to Sam. After all, Esmy Shichans, the famous laughing king of the Accomac tribe, had been friendly since the colony's founding seven years ago. This despite the tribe's nominal allegiance to Powhatan.

"I'll sign up for the salt!" Sam, his red brows lifted, whispered back to Will, breaking the mood that had hung over them since word of Dewbourne's death.

"Ha! You think what I do. The laughing king would be easy to manage compared to what awaits us *there*." Will pointed toward the left bow where he envisioned the Pamunkey's River to be.

Sam let out a deep sigh. "I hope I make it home," he muttered.

Will laughed. "We've nearly eight score of our best men. Don't be afraid, old man."

"No, Will. I mean *home*. Home to Frances. It's been nearly five years. The Company forbids us to leave even for a visit. I haven't sent for my wife because, well, with Laws of Blood in effect why would I do that to her? So, I wait for the Company to lift the laws, for prosperity to bowl us backward."

Will held his hat in his hands and looked down self-consciously. "Don't expect anything to bowl you soon, friend."

Then, the two men looked at one another. The question hung in the air. Two men, two wives. Which had been the best decision? Will had brought his wife Sam had left his in England. Maybe, the correct answer lay in a third choice: keeping everyone at home.

Just then, John Rolfe pushed through the soldiers and dropped to the floor near Will and Sam. The bench was full. The men noticed the pensive look on their friend's face, Will clapped Rolf's shoulder.

"Make room, make room," Sam called out, pushing those near him down a bit.

"There ain't no room!" someone called irritably from the other end.

"Well, squeeze it in, soldier!" came Sam's reply.

With Sam pushing his way a little left, and Will pushing his way a little right, John was able to sit on the bench between them. He mumbled thanks, then simply hung his head.

"We think the saltworks might not be a bad deal at that. What do you say, John?" Sam tried to lift spirits, his own and his friend's.

John didn't answer, so Sam continued, "What's troubling you, man? Tell old Sam, and see if he can't help." Sam elbowed John, surprised that the pensive man didn't even seem to hear him.

Sam turned to Will and shrugged.

Will pointed to the upper deck and mouthed the word *Pocahontas.*

"Ah. Should have reckoned that."

"John?" Will stared at his friend intently until at last John turned to him. "Does anyone know? Have you told Marshal Dale?"

John shook his head. "The Bible says we're not to marry strange wives from the country we're in. Recall you the Lord's wrath to the sons of Levi and Israel for doing so? Yet, Pocahontas has agreed and wants to become a Christian. She says she loves me, and I love her. I'm torn yet I cannot forget this lovely woman. And I've tried, believe me. Many nights have I lain awake."

Having lost both his wife and daughter, John was terribly lonely, Will knew.

Silence from the three men for a moment. All about, the soldiers traded jibes and wondered what sort of greeting they would meet in the Indian towns. Some even slept, their heads leaning back against the ribs of the ship.

"If the marshal knows of your love, we might avoid much bloodshed. This leaves open a way for negotiation never before considered," Will said.

John nodded then reached into his doublet. "Here," was all he said, handing a paper to Will.

Will unfolded it while Sam leaned over to read it as well.

"Honorable Sir, and most worthy Governor," the letter began. Will scanned it, the pain and torment of his friend apparent to him for the first time. John talked about the mighty war going on within him, about his concerns that his motives were impure, that he knew he should not marry a heathen. And then, John added, one day when he thought he had been successful in putting the princess away from his mind came a thought unbidden.

Why dost thou not endeavor to make her a Christian? This, the prompting of John's inner voice, the Holy Spirit, Will reckoned as John did. The Holy Spirit chastising, asking why John would give up the woman he loved when she might readily agree to baptism? Wasn't he, John, put here to spread the Gospel? Weren't we all?

Will heaved a sigh. "Burdensome weight, my friend?"

"Aye. I love her, Will. But the good Lord only knows what Dale shall say about this...." Fear edged into his voice. John had put his case forth in the letter as best he knew how. But Dale was unpredictable, the gallows being, always and still, his favorite answer to most questions.

Will handed the letter back to John. "You're asking permission. Dale hates it when someone disobeys him. Be contrite and humble if he denies the marriage, and ask no more. But asking once is not a crime."

"If she's a woman worth fighting for, then fight for her." Sam's voice was firm. Will knew Sam was still thinking of Frances.

"You've got Master Hamor here on ship," Will said, knowing John would take his meaning. All correspondence must go through the company secretary Ralph Hamor. "So you haven't missed your chance. Not yet. But if she goes so far as into the hands of her father, and he returns all trade goods, why, then you have nothing."

John nodded.

"Or if the blood of her brethren and yours is spilt on the banks of the Pamunkey's River..." Sam added.

The ship eased up the Pamunkey's River. The fleet was now fully into Indian territory in a river but two miles wide, narrower than the James. Dale ordered his men into complete silence. Now, the silence from the woods rang back at them. Stillness, utter and complete.

But in the same manner that one could feel eyes penetrating from behind, all the ship felt watched.

The ships quietly edged past the town of Chiskiac—or Cheesecake, as we sometimes called it. Chief Ottahotin's people never stirred. No sound, no movement from the shore. Just past Chiskiac, the ships anchored for the night with guard posted.

The next morning, again, silence greeted them. The ships hauled anchor and prepared for the next leg of the journey, further into the land of their enemies.

The Feather'd Arrows Fly
March 25, 1614 ~ on the Pamunkey's River

The flames now launch'd, the feather'd arrows fly,
And clouds of missive arms obscure the sky.
—Vergil

For thine arrows stick fast in me,
And thy hand presseth me sore.
—Psalm 38:2

The river rustled along, and only forest sounds greeted the little fleet at morning time. The stillness was eerie.

Will's superior, Ensign Powell, had called him up top to perform a watch. Will now sat near the stern, his musket propped and ready. And he knew, for certain, eyes were on him. His skin crawled beneath his armor.

Dale was scanning the riverbanks. Nearby, young Harry Spelman stood ready to interpret Indian words to English. Harry's years of living with the Tanks Powhatan and Patawomecks had served the colony well. Argall had rescued him, finally, and Harry had sailed for England only to return once more. Dale was pleased to have him. Most everyone knew some of the tongue, but few were as good as Harry and Tom Savage.

Two or three hours further upriver, Nat Causey signaled Sir Thomas Dale. Nat, Thomasine's husband, was also one of Smith's old soldiers. Causey pointed to a peninsula extending into Purtan Bay on the north bank of the river, saying, "Sir! Werowocomoco, Powhatan's former home, is right over yonder." There lay Werowocomoco and nearby towns Cantaunkack, Capahowasick, Wighsakan, Mattacock, and Poruptanck.

The men might have thought the towns were empty except they knew they were not. Yet, they saw no movement at the river and passed Werowocomoco without incident as the ships continued their course.

Another few hours upriver, the fleet approached the branching of the Pamunkey's River into two smaller rivers, the Youghtanund's River and the Mattaponi's River. Suddenly cries echoed from the riverbank. But the natives had hidden themselves, so the soldiers could hear but not see the criers.

"*Casacunnakack, peya quagh acquintan uttasantasough? Utteke!*"

Will jerked his head to the sound and saw that several dozen braves had come into view and were now running alongside the ship. Each man hurled taunting, questioning words full of bravado. The ship sailed mid-river; the braves could not strike with arrows, so instead they struck with words.

"*Uttapitchewane!*"

"*Mushower!*"

Will understood some of the language. He heard, "The ships go home!" *They hope to intimidate us so that we will go no further,* he thought.

Still the shouts continued.

"*Cuttahamunourcar* Rat-kiffe! *Amuwoir.* Rat-kiffe *wapewh ohshaangumiemuns yowhse!*"

"What do they say?" Dale asked Harry impatiently as the taunts continued.

"They are mocking us, telling us to leave their river, but say if we choose to fight, they are ready! They also say, 'We made a grave for Ratcliffe. We cut him with shells near here.' They can do the same to us, they say."

For some time this continued, the Indians running alongside the ship. Harry translated each new threat and sometimes called retorts if Dale so ordered.

"Thank them," Dale snapped, "for reminding us of the injustice done Captain Ratcliffe." To Spelman, he added, "That man's not worth remembering but to his dishonor, a foolish soldier taking chances. But tell them, for that reminder, we *shall* avenge Ratcliffe's death!"

Spelman had just shouted this message to the natives when the braves suddenly, as one, took cover. Had the message rattled them? No, for at once Will realized the river was now at its narrowest, and the Indians let loose volleys of arrows from their hiding.

Will's armor protected him as some of the arrows landed on the ship or pierced its side. Others flew a little short so that the sounds were of arrows, splashing water, of the *thunk* of arrow splitting wood or rattling off armor.

Nat Causey fell backwards as an arrow pierced and dangled from his unprotected skull.

"Chirurgeon!" someone yelled. "Carry him down!" Now the deck had red splatters of Nat's blood.

Dale's fury unleashed. "Close in on shore. Drop anchor!" he bellowed. "Time to fight, and time to burn!"

The ship came as near to shore as it dared based on the fathom soundings.

From there, the men scrambled into longboats and rowed to land, arrows still flying amongst them. Will and John were in the first boats to land. Other men rowed the boats back to ship and fetched more soldiers.

Pocahontas stayed aboard ship with some of the men, spared the ignominy of watching her people's town ravaged.

As for the braves, the sight of more than a hundred soldiers coming to shore in scattered boatloads must have unnerved them. All boasting fell away as the English soldiers approached.

Will was with Dale and Spelman, as was Will's superior Ensign Powell.

"They're getting a little anxious," Spelman said, as the oars cut through the water. He pointed upriver, "You see, up there on the high ground where the river forks, is their holiest of temples, Uttamussak. We're not close to it yet, and they don't want us to be. That's the source of the bravado, I'll wager. And up the left branch of the river in the Youghtanund territory is Powhatan's chief town."

As the boats came aground, the soldiers clambered out.

Spelman added, "They're trying to keep us from going further."

Dale grumbled. "Too late for that. We shall find the nearest town and plunder, pillage, burn!"

Trundling in Dust and Thunder
March 25, 1614 ~ Mamanassy on the Pamunkey's River

Trundling in dust and thunder
They rumbled up and down,
Laden with princely plunder,
Loot of the tragic Town.
—John G. Neihardt

That town was Mamanassy.

The thundering, clanking, roaring sound of that many soldiers was nearly deafening in the otherwise quiet woods.

The braves began firing, their arrows all but useless hitting the metal clothing. The English had truly only to protect their eyes. Six braves fell and the rest fled, realizing the hopelessness of their situation, Will reckoned.

As the soldiers rushed the town, they found it nearly empty save several elderly souls carried out on gurneys and a few women moving more slowly because of babies strapped to their backs. Several women had small children by the hands. One woman looked back with an expression of petrified fear. A little girl, her deep brown eyes wide, opened her mouth in a silent scream as she saw the silver men and heard their loud guns. These faces etched into Will's mind.

Will looked about and counted about forty homes. And he knew he had to burn them. Burn as ordered.

The soldiers carried out baskets of corn, skins, stone weapons, shells, pipes, and a few English tools they found scattered about in *yi-hakens*.

"Look at this!" Dale cried, holding an iron axe aloft. He slammed the tool to the ground in anger. "Stolen!"

Will knew his leader felt completely justified, but Will himself had never relished the thought of leaving women and children homeless. He carried out a big basket of corn and sat it on the ground. Another soldier picked it up and carried it from the town toward the ships.

Whoosh. How quickly the matting went up in flames after the drought they'd had. Will heard the other homes crackling and burning. His throat closed from the acrid smoke.

He turned his head and saw John Rolfe nearby, a torch in his hand as he lit someone's home.

John threw the torch, stood back, and watched the flames climb. Then Rolfe turned away, shoulders slumped and head bowed.

Will understood. Into the flames and ashes went his friend's chance of marrying Pocahontas.

A Soldier Who Has Lived It
March 25, 1614 ~ Mamanassy, and on
the Youghtanund's River

I hate war as only a soldier who has lived it can, only as one who has seen its brutality, its futility, its stupidity.
—Dwight D. Eisenhower

I have seen children starving. I have seen the agony of mothers and wives. I hate war.
—Franklin Delano Roosevelt

The soldiers quartered overnight near the river, stretching out on the still-cold March ground.

Smoke curled over the treetops, a reminder of the day's destruction. The troops had avenged Ratcliffe's death, and now Mamanassy was little more than ashes.

Dale sent someone back to the ship to check on Causey. The messenger returned with news that the chirurgeon had poured vinegar over Nat's wound and had been able to yank out the arrow, it not being too deeply in Nat's skull. Causey should live, the chirurgeon said, although the injured man would sleep fitfully this night.

Will heard the news with relief. Nat was a decent fellow and truly useful since he'd been upriver exploring with Captain Smith a few years back. Those who had been up these waters had a knowledge the rest did not.

During the night, several of the Englishmen escaped to an Indian town believing life would be better there. Powhatan had previously returned these men to the fort, and now they had made good their threat to leave at their first opportunity. Dale's anger upon learning these men had again escaped caused him to roar. The man's temper stayed near to boiling at all times, so different from calm Sir Thomas Gates.

At sunrise the men reboarded the ships. They would sail up the left river, the Youghtanund's River.

Will was tired, sore, and achy and now found his chest hurt.

He wasn't the only one. In the 'tween deck all about him, the sounds of coughing soldiers echoed off the ship's walls.

Will found himself sitting next to John Rolfe once more while Sam was up top taking a shift at guard duty.

John said nothing, and neither did Will. What was there to say? The burning of Mamanassy meant the end of any hopes for a peaceful outcome. The English would probably sack Matchut, the home of Pocahontas's father. War with the natives would be eternal now.

"Have you seen her?" Will asked at last. He knew Pocahontas was in one of the ship's small cabins.

John's expression was bleak. "No," he said at last. "No. I don't think I could even face her after burning her people's homes." He met Will's eyes. "Did you see those children leaving? That one young girl could have been Pocahontas herself at that age. The little ones were terrified. The corn that was to see them through the winter is right down yonder in our hold." Then he turned his gaze to the roof of the 'tween deck and finally said, "I hate war."

Will agreed. 'Twas an odd thing, to be a soldier and to hate war. Some men, like Dale, seemed to thrive on the power and anxiety that went with a good battle. Others, like Will, Sam and John, just wanted to settle in to their farms, to protect their own property without having to destroy the property of others. The Lowlands were one thing, English and Dutch resistance to Spanish aggressors. No children were directly involved, just the Dutch children the English hoped to protect. Frankly, the thought of those small Indian boys and girls fleeing his torch made Will sick.

Yet the truth was evident. This last skirmish proved that the English and natives could never attain peace. Will sighed and thought, *Resign yourself to many years of ducking Indian arrows and lighting fires, old man.*

Hearts and Power to Take Revenge
March 25-26, 1614 ~ on the Youghtanund's River

Though we came to them in peaceable manner, and would
have beene glad to have received our demaunds with love and
peace, yet we had hearts and power to take revenge, and punish
where wrongs should be offered, which having now don, though
not so severely as we might, we rested content there with and are
ready to imbrace peace with them if they pleased...
—Ralph Hamor, writing of Sir Thomas Dale's reply to
the braves on the shore, 1614

Will laid his head back against the ribs of the ship and shut his eyes. Whether he fell asleep or not, he did not know, but presently Indian shouts startled him. His heart raced, and he instinctively reached for his sword.

Then he remembered he was on ship, out of range of Indian arrows.

He expected his superior to call him topside, and he was right.

Immediately, Ensign Powell stuck his head down the scuttle. "Peirce! Cap'n West needs you here! Rolfe, Sparks—upper deck!"

The fleet had just entered the River of the Youghtanunds. When Will got himself up the scuttle, he saw a dozen braves shouting at them once more from shore. Rolfe was right behind him.

What were the natives saying? Will could just make out a few phrases.

"*Cutchow matowran mussaran?*" came a shout from a more decorated brave. *A captain,* Will thought. Then the brave called once more, this time louder and with more insistence. "*Cutchow matowran mussaran?*"

Voices below in the 'tween deck were quiet now. All the soldiers seemed to want to hear.

John inclined his head and squinted. "They demand to know why we burnt the town," John whispered to Will.

Will nodded. Much as he had thought. Will had picked up Indian phrases from his friend Chacrow.

Dale listened to Harry Spelman's translation. Then Dale said, "We only ask what is rightfully ours. Tell them we came peaceably and would've been glad had they met our demands with love and peace. Yet we do have hearts and power to take revenge and to punish where they offer wrongs. Having done that, and not as severely as we might have, we are now content and ready to embrace peace with them if they please."

Spelman turned Dale's English into Powhatan.

Another brave stepped forward and shouted his response. Dale waited impatiently. "Well, well, what do they say?"

"They say, sir, that they believe some straggling Indians were taunting us. They say they certainly did not abet the Indians responsible and assure us they will punish them."

Dale snorted. He obviously didn't believe that. "They try to smooth things over. Well, we shall play along. We are satisfied with the retribution we have taken. Let's move on to other matters."

The Indian captain shouted once more. Spelman turned to Dale. "He says, 'Why did you come? What do you want?'"

"Tell them we came in peace. We brought the chief's daughter Pocahontas and will hand her over conditionally. Powhatan must first provide all the arms, tools, and swords he's stolen and send back the Englishmen who ran away. Finally, we require a ship full of corn, for the wrong he has done unto us and for putting us to the trouble of coming out here to fetch everything!" Dale said. "Tell them if they will do this, we will be friends. If not, we shall enact revenge." Dale paused. "We shall have peace and satisfaction. If not, *burn all!*"

More shouts from the shore. "They wish time to send for their King, sir."

"And where might Chief Powhatan be?" Dale demanded.

Spelman yelled to the brave, *"Tawnor nehiegh Powhatan?"* Where dwells Powhatan?

"Mache, nehiegh yowrowgh, Matchut!" came the shouted reply.

"I believe that is true, sir," Spelman said to Sir Thomas Dale. "They say he dwells a great distance away at Matchut."

"And where is this *Matchut*, precisely?" Dale asked impatiently.

Harry pointed. "Far up this river. I believe I know exactly where it is. I'd say about forty miles from the mouth of the Youghtanund's River."

"Werowocomoco to Orapax to Matchut? The wily chief stays on the move to avoid us!"

"Indeed, sir."

The ship kept moving with warriors running alongside. To Matchut, then. Will reckoned they had traveled about ten miles from the mouth of the Youghtanund. Thirty more miles upriver meant they would be deep in the heart of Indian country.

One hundred fifty soldiers to Powhatan's thousand braves. They would just have to hope the Indian king didn't have time to gather all his warriors at Matchut.

Minutes Wheeled Like Stars

March 27, 1614 ~ the Youghtanund's River, and at Cattachipitico

She took my strength by minutes,
She took my life by hours,
She drained me like a fevered moon
That saps the spinning world.
The days went by like shadows,
The minutes wheeled like stars.
She took pity from my heart,
And made it into smiles.
—Edgar Lee Masters

By the next morning, they were nearing Cattachipitico as they snaked through the Youghtanund's River. Harry Spelman was pointing out towns as they passed: Righkahauc, Shamapint, Parokonosko, Matunsk with Askecocac on the opposite shore, then Manaskunt.

Along the way, the men had seen much of the wildlife Virginia had to offer. A rattlesnake as thick as a man's arm, yards in length had just gone by the ship. Will couldn't help but wonder, *How vast is Virginia? How far, how deep?* Woods and rivers everywhere, birds and fauna of all sorts.

Argall had visited the mountains further west the Indians had told us about, but the Indians said there were deserts out west, too.

"I wonder if those wild cattle Argall saw live around here as well?" Will mumbled to Sam.

But Sam had no time to respond. Around a bend, another Indian settlement came into view. *Cattachipitico!*

Cattachipitico was closer to the river with Matchut somewhere distant across the fields and forests.

Pocahontas had come from her cabin and was peering over the ship's side, looking, Will thought, exceedingly pensive.

"You trade me, Master Hamor?" Will heard her ask the secretary.

He nodded. "If your brethren be willing, aye. That is the plan."

Curious braves and their wives turned in the direction of the ship. The women quickly rushed into hiding, but the warriors stood tall. The Indians knew, no doubt, that these ships were coming upriver into their territory.

One brave, perhaps a lesser *werowance,* called to the ship, asking why the English were here and what they wanted. Again, Harry explained to the natives, although Will suspected the town knew precisely why the ships had come. The natives sent messages by a variety of means, not all of which the English understood, and distance was little obstacle.

The brave asked for time to send word to his *werowance* Wahunsonacock, Chief Powhatan. Dale granted that.

The English came ashore and with them, Pocahontas. Will saw a look pass between John and the Indian girl and gathered that John had asked Ralph Hamor to gave his letter to the governor. Will then saw Hamor hand Dale the folded paper.

A bold move on Rolfe's part, Will thought. If Dale disagreed, believing marriage between a Christian and a heathen sinful, Rolfe could face whipping or worse. Yet, John had suggested that Pocahontas would consider baptism. A marriage between two Christians should be acceptable. But would Dale see it that way?

As Dale read, his features scowled. It didn't look good. Will turned away and put his eyes onto the native princess.

By now, many of her people were calling to Pocahontas, but the princess lifted her head away, looking to the trees. She spoke not.

At last, two well-decorated braves, one taller than the other but both strong, approached Dale. The taller brave pointed to Pocahontas, and Will heard a stream of words. He thought he caught the Indian word "*nucka-andgum.*"

Sister? Were these Pocahontas's own brothers? Will watched curiously as Harry translated. Yes, Pocahontas was their sister, and they would like to see her. The English had treated Pocahontas badly they had heard.

Pocahontas stepped forward and greeted her brothers warmly. She spoke to them in her own language, something Will could not catch.

Harry inclined in. To Dale, Harry said, "She confirms her well treatment, which the young men say they can see with their own eyes. She says now that she is angry with her father. Does he not love her? What does he value more, old pieces or her?"

Harry caught his breath and said to Dale. "Sir. My word, sir."

"Well, what is it?" Dale grumbled.

"She says that she wants to marry Rolfe!"

Dale lifted his eyebrows. If this were so, a marriage between an established

English soldier and the Powhatan princess could do what endless warfare and ransoming could not: promote peace in the colony.

Dale beckoned to Rolfe. "You may go yourself to the great chief to ask his permission. If he consents, and the girl agrees to baptism, then I shall not stop you."

From where he stood, Will could see Rolfe's look of astonishment. He'd bet the man's heart was beating out of his chest.

A soldier named Sparkes accompanied Rolfe as he set off, and Pocahontas's brothers stayed behind as security that the Indians would not attack the two Englishmen.

The next day, Rolfe returned crestfallen. He had not been able to see the chief; Powhatan's guards would not admit him into the old chief's presence.

Planting time was upon us. Dale told the natives that he would give them until harvest to return the English prisoners and stolen guns and tools. Dale was being, Will thought, unusually lenient. The marshal, it seemed, held hope that Powhatan might yet agree to the marriage.

John Rolfe and Pocahontas had no such hope. Being turned away was as good as a denial in their eyes.

Chamay Wingapo
March 28 to April 3, 1614 ~ Bermuda Hundred

Chamay wingapo. Netab. Eweenetu.
(A great welcome, Friend. We are brothers. Peace.)
—Powhatan greeting

Days later, the soldiers returned to Bermuda Hundred. Pocahontas was with them. The English had left not knowing the answer to the marriage proposal and with nothing resolved. Pocahontas returned to the parsonage.

Nearly a week passed.

Then, two canoes edged to land at the Nether Hundred. These tree trunks, their insides burned out to form a small boat, held four Indians with faces of stone. One with a turkey-feather mantle and a large talon hanging from his left ear, extra ornamentation, indicating he might have been a captain or king of some type.

From my herb garden, I saw the natives pulling the canoes ashore and dropping their paddles inside. The braves stared up at the settlement. The leader gestured and pointed, and one of the braves nodded.

They mean to come in here! I thought. The children were working alongside me, their hands coated with mud and red clay. Even Tommy's face was covered.

"Mama, Indians!" cried Cecily, looking at me for assurance that all was well. I couldn't be certain. We had no palisado wall for protection here along the river, only the other one protecting land. Still, a soldier at the guardhouse would meet the Indians.

I scurried the children inside, shut the door, and dropped the big wooden bolt.

Why are the braves here? I wondered.

As the Indians strode toward the guardhouse, the guards stiffened. One never knew what was afoot in this ongoing war.

But one brave called out *"Chamay wingapo!" Hello, Friend!* This greeting signified the visit as peaceful. Yet the two soldiers, squinting to get a better look, braced with one hand on their matchlocks. Then a familiar voice called out a greeting as well.

"Hello, you know me! I'm Tom Savage. I bring news." Now that he was closer, the guards could see that Tom had a great smile on his face. Tom was deeply tanned, wearing native clothes, and but for his sandy-brown hair was easily mistaken for an Indian himself.

"What have you?" asked the soldier. He eyed the other three braves.

"We will need to see Marshal Dale straight away. For this is Opachisco, uncle of Pocahontas," he said, gesturing to the older man.

The tallest, most decorated brave nodded in greeting. He wore a long, fringed buckskin mantle with necklaces of shell, copper, and pearl that indicated his high standing within the Powhatan Nation.

Tom held his hand out toward the other braves. "And here are two of Pocahontas's brothers. Powhatan assents. He sends them all to witness the wedding!"

The guard stepped back for a moment, stunned. "Powhatan's agreein' to it, then? The weddin', I mean?"

Opachisco was nodding, not understanding all the words, yet knowing what the two Englishmen must be discussing. And he studied the settlement with curiosity, one eye on the men, one roving the fields, the activity, the houses. Very strange. He brought his full attention back to the matter at hand, speaking a few simple words, opening his arms in symbolic friendship, wanting to send promises himself, and hoping the guard would now take his meaning. *"Chamay wingapo. Netab. Eweenetu."* Opachisco met the guard's eyes and then gazed expectantly at Tom, waiting for him to translate.

The guard cast Tom a curious look. "He sayin' hello?"

Tom's face was lit. "More than that! He says, 'A great welcome, friend! We are brothers. Peace.'"

These Stars of Earth
April 3, 1614 ~ Bermuda Hundred

These stars of earth, these golden flowers.
—Henry Wadsworth Longfellow

The villagers are flocking in—a wedding festival—that's all.
God save you, Sir.
—William Wordsworth

It had taken our fleet four days to return down the Pamunkey's River, cross the bay, and back up the James. However, the Indians had made it in much shorter time. Opachisco, Tom Savage, and the two brothers had crossed landward from Powhatan's chief residence, a more direct route. Their canoes they kept hidden in certain places along the rivers.

I saw a crowd of women gathering near the center of the settlement on the River Road. I left the butter churn behind, called to Cecily who was spinning, and hurried out to see. Janey raced behind us, one hand tugging Tommy, who was moving his chubby legs ever as fast as he could. One word I could make out above the din: *Pocahontas.*

"Powhatan gives his consent!"

"The great chief says, 'Aye.' Her uncle is here even now."

"Did you see them in their canoes? Could you tell one was ol' Tom Savage? He's turnin' Indian, sure as I'm born."

"She'll marry Rolfe, all right."

"The parson will have to baptize her first."

"Do you reckon Master Rolfe has heard?"

"Good news travels fast, as they say." This last comment was mine, and I said it happily. John to marry Pocahontas! Did she know? Probably not, for she was at Reverend Whitaker's across the river. "Where's Annie?" I continued, looking around and finding her not there. "Has she heard?"

Margery Fairfax, holding baby Ellen, swung about.

"Can't say," Margery shrugged. "But we haven't seen her."

I was about to send Cecily to Annie's house to fetch her when Annie rounded a corner, her face beaming delight.

"Annie, the wedding! What do you hear?" Margery called. The crowd quieted upon realizing that Annie might have some insight they did not.

"I hear what you do. She's going to marry. Praise be. Dale says, 'Aye,' Powhatan says, 'Aye.' They all agree for once." She laughed. "A true miracle, eh?"

Then her look turned serious. "They'll be wanting to do the ceremony right away. The old uncle won't stay long. How can we prepare in but a few days?"

A murmur went through the women. Why, weddings were a festivity for the whole community. And this one promised to bring more than the blessings of husband and wife. It might bring the union of Indian and English, an end to the violence, peace to the river country. It was as if the Indians and the English themselves married. *Peace!* Was it possible? *Aye,* I thought, *God can bring peace, and He can use that beautiful young woman to do it.* Dale's religious fervor, Whitaker's belief in conversion, the love between John and Pocahontas, and the felling blow Powhatan's fatigue with constant warring, arrows battling armor.

"We lack..." began Emily Wayne. "We have nothing to make the occasion festive." Her eyes filled with despair and hopelessness. Her words brought the throng crashing back to earth. Indeed, she was right.

"We have no fine linens of any kind. No spare cloth. No cloth at all," said Thomasine Causey. We looked about at one another as if someone might know what to do.

When was the last time we'd had anything to celebrate? Oh, we'd had weddings, but never could we muster the spirit to throw a proper wedding. Everyone too tired, too hungry, too ragged, too poor.

"The dress she wears is probably as good as any we could make or have on hand." Nods from the crowd.

"Favors and ribbons?"

Annie looked down at her own bodice and pulled at a tattered brown ribbon. What color it had once been was anyone's guess. She gave it a yank and held it up. "Aye, let's make the best of what we have, for what choice have we?" And thus began the hunt for ribbons to make favors of some type.

"We don't even have enough food. A wedding cake is beyond reason," Margery said, an edge to her voice.

True, that. We had just settled in the Nether Hundred, our first harvest barely a wet seed in the ground. In fact, we were still hungry much of the time.

"Who here has a recipe for *fish* cake?" Thomasine asked wryly. Some tittered, and some groaned.

Sir Thomas Dale had been studying fishing and believed that spring and fall were the seasons to bring in the greatest catches. Everyone had been talking about the great seine he'd thrown to the water, hauling up over five thousand fish as big as cod. We did indeed have salted fish.

"I'm thinkin' fish don't cake well." Betty Dunthorne put in with a sarcastic tilt of her brow.

The cake would have to be simple cornbread. A later time of year would have brought us some wild mulberries and huckleberries, at least.

More women were coming. From various homes strode Tempie, Isabella Pace, Judith Perry, Mary Woodlief, and Joan Flinton, exquisite curiosity on their faces.

"Pocahontas is to be a bride!" Annie burst out.

"But we lack anything to make a festive occasion," Rose added.

Isabella spoke up. "Not everything do we lack. We'll need rosemary and lavender. We know the Mistresses Peirce and Wright have bountiful herbs. And most of us tend physick gardens and can pitch in."

"Oh, aye. Rosemary for the tussy-mussies, for nosegays, for the church," Sarah added. The herb of faithfulness and remembrance. Would any wedding or funeral be complete without it?

"But as to flowers...?" This was Tempie, and for a moment, silence fell upon the group.

She was right, of course. Unlike in England, we had no grand knot gardens. Perhaps, however, we had something better.

Now it was my turn to speak. We rarely sent the children too far afield. But it seemed safe with Pocahontas's own relatives in the town and peace cresting the horizon. I realized with a start that it had *never* seemed safe before. "We'll send the children out to the fields and marshes to find wildflowers, the day before."

"She'll not have roses, but she'll have the fairy spuds, dainty pink and white. They'll be up," said Sarah.

"I know the ones you mean, Virginia's spring beauties. And the violets are already in bloom," I put in.

"And forget not the bluebells of Virginia," cried Emily.

I took a deep breath. How I loved these flowers, so similar to our English bluebells with cheery faces pink and blue. Some called them fairy thimbles, and my mother used to tell me the little blue bells rang to call fairies together.

We realized we knew of many Virginia wildflowers now in bloom: fairy spuds, jack-in-the-pulpits, star chickweed, green and golds, bloodroot, and gentle white saxifrage.

"Let's put sprigs of yellow sassafras flowers around the church to sweeten the air," Tempie said.

Annie was growing excited. "Oh, the colors! What have we? Violet, blue, pink, gold, and white. Who says we in Virginia don't know how to throw a festive day. No cloth, no cake, but we have Virginia wildflowers aplenty." The flowers somehow made everything right again. It would have to be all right. Humble, but spirited. For a town so direly in need of something to lift it.

At that instant, John Rolfe emerged from the Big House, where he had apparently met his future uncle and brothers-in-law. A cheer erupted, and the women flocked to him, anxious for word.

"Well," he said dryly, "I don't suppose you ladies have heard any news to set your tongues afire?" And a grin spread across his face as well.

Thou Art Our Sister
April 4, 1614 ~ Bermuda Hundred

And they blessed Rebekah, and said unto her, Thou art our sister, be thou the mother of thousands of millions, and let thy seed possess the gate of those which hate them.
—Genesis 24:60

Joan can call by name her cows
And deck her windows with green boughs;
She can wreaths and tutties make
And trim with plums a bridal cake.
—Thomas Campion, 1613

Friday morning, our preparations were underway. Typically, the pastor would have read the banns for three Sundays, announcing the wedding and allowing folks time to raise objections to the marriage. However, no one wanted to risk Opachisco changing his mind. Reverend Whitaker waived the banns, and the baptism and wedding were to be Saturday during the ten o'clock service. We had only this one full day to prepare. But at least Sir Thomas Dale had given the women a break from their tasks to decorate the church and to prepare the flowers.

I was mixing and beating the batter of the smaller wedding cakes, the bridal cakes, that each of the guests would enjoy. Beside me, Cecily cracked eggs while Janey added milk and stirred. Bits of cornmeal splattered Janey's apron and face. She looked up at me and laughed, a happy child once more. Gone the frail and sickly soul of four springs ago. In her place a growing girl who seemed mostly to have forgotten her Starving Time although she had ever since appreciated any meal set before her. Her healthfulness contented me.

So much work to do!

Early morning, the children had gone afield, collecting all the wildflowers and herbs they could find. The women had divided themselves up, making cakes and favors, sewing, and preparing flowers and herbs for the tussy-mussy that Pocahontas's bridesmaid Annie would carry. At our house, we set about creating two dozen favors and bridal cakes.

Our ribbons may have been tattered, but we had washed them to make them clean. And our flowers may have been humble, but we had gathered them with fervor. How little we'd had to celebrate since the settlement's birth seven years ago. We would make the most of this. The women's spirit of friendship and unity had never been stronger as if Pocahontas had brought us together as she had brought together two groups of warring men.

Tempie came in, a basket under her arm and her cap tied neatly about her head.

"Mornin', ladies!" she called cheerfully, and Janey raced to give her auntie a hug, but Tempie laughingly held up her hands. "Wait, wait. I need an apron! You are the yellow cornmeal girl! And how fare the corncakes?" she asked me.

I shrugged. We were all used to bridal cakes made of corn instead of wheat, our Virginia wedding cakes.

A few minutes later came Margery, carrying little Ellen. Giles had toddled along with her. Ellen held something that resembled a biscuit. Crumbs covered the child's chin and lips.

"Tasty, Ellie?" Tempie asked her. Tempie had such a glow about her. The limitations of the wedding seemed not to bother her in the least.

The baby smiled back at her. It sometimes amused me, sometimes saddened me, how unaware the babies and children were that we yet lived in poverty, for they knew nothing better.

To Margery, I said, "How did your cakes turn out? These corncakes 'twill be small, but I daren't use *that* wheat." I looked into a tin on the floor with spider webs decorating the wheat like bridal streamers. "Wildflowers and corncakes." We had gone to lengths to make it joyful to honor Pocahontas, but would it be lovely for her, as she deserved?

Margery stepped over the threshold and handed the baby to Tempie. Margery then patted my back warmly. "Joan, do remember wildflowers and corncakes are familiar to our Indian bride. We can't give her a full English wedding, and I reckon she wouldn't want one. But the important parts are there: the word of our Lord, a bridegroom who loves her, and the most cheery time afterward *we* can make, given what we have."

Margery was a kind, quiet soul. I liked her very much, and her words humbled me, for of course, she was right. "Aye. A Virginia wedding for our *true* Virginia bride," I said.

"She has chosen Rebecca as her baptismal name, and that is so prophetic, isn't it?" Tempie said, baby Ellen on her hip.

I was thoughtful. "*Two nations are in your womb, and two peoples born of you shall be divided; the one shall be stronger than the other, the elder shall serve the younger,"* I said, quoting the scripture. "That's what God said to Rebecca. And any children she bears shall be children of two peoples." Pocahontas's birth name, Matoaka, meant *a flower between two streams.* How interesting that her baptismal name carried such power. I felt sure the Reverend Whitaker had guided her to it deliberately.

I continued to feel that her conversion to Christianity carried with it more than we could see or feel. In fact, I had begun to recognize that my instincts often showed themselves in reality later. I often pondered whether I might be a witch, but then I always reckoned that if I were a witch I would surely know it. Instead I chose to believe that God just spoke to me a little more loudly and a little differently than he did to others. Nevertheless, I didn't share my thoughts on the subject too often. I was not interested in drawing attention to such odd ways or being punished as a witch, perhaps.

"She has already borne a son of one nation. If she has another son, it will be very like the Bible story," Margery said.

"Very." I didn't know quite how to feel about the whole thing. I remembered how I had first seen Pocahontas, bathed in light and shadow at the parsonage. We had forced her here. Our soldiers had killed her first husband, Kocoum. She and John seemed content and in love, but did the outcome justify the means of bringing her here? *Light and shadow,* I thought. That was exactly how it felt. The dark within the light, the light within the dark.

But little time to consider that. Bridal cakes and favors remained unfinished.

Just then, Annie came to the door, beaming, and from behind her back she pulled out a bottle of sack. "Well, ladies, Master Ralph Hamor has brought forth a half bottle of sack, which he was saving for a special occasion. He has donated it to the cause!"

A cheer went up from us all. *We were going to have sack-possets!* Maybe only a sip...but at least a small reminder of what we might have had, had we been in England.

"And not only that—Sir Thomas Dale himself has given us another quarter bottle of muscadine wine. Why, the man was positively *festive.*" She widened her eyes as if in disbelief that she had spoken the words *Dale* and *festive* in one thought. Then she cried as if a chant, "Cream and eggs, cinnamon and nutmeg and sack! Who'll help me make it?" Those who had been hoarding cinnamon and nutmeg they'd bartered from ships had parted with some as if it were gold dust.

Cecily and Janey asked to go with Annie, and I cheerfully agreed. So few things to bring joy. A wedding in England would never be without its posset. Did any appreciate it, truly? Here, we did. We surely did.

After the others had left, each to her own work, Tempie pulled an apron from a hook and asked if I might tie it on. Typically, my aprons fit Tempie loosely, for she was so slight. But this time I pulled and yanked the ribbons with barely enough to make a bow.

"A sack-posset! It does feel like a special day, doesn't it?" Tempie said, looking over her shoulder at me, her face lit with a smile. "We'll only have a sip or small dram apiece, but that's better than naught…"

I stopped, mid-twirl of my bow.

"Temperance!"

"What? Aren't you delighted, too? And every time you call me 'Temperance,' I think Indians are roaming the fort. Oh!" She caught herself. "They are. Opachisco and the brothers are here!" She laughed, but I could not be distracted.

"Mistress, a word. You're plumpening up!"

She smiled, her cheeks reddening. "And what of it, Mistress Peirce? Think you not that I don't enjoy venison, corn pone, and mulberry tarts as much as you?"

I rolled my eyes. "Venison we have from time to time, corn pone I'll believe, and 'mulberry tarts' we have, less the tarts. *In* season, not at present."

"Ah, too much corn pone then, topped in butter. And the smoked fish George's men caught, great big fish they were. Did you know that George brought home bear meat? At first I thought, 'Well, we have gone native now,' but truly, Joan, it was actually quite good. George is so often bringing home forest game these days. We had raccoon the other night. It does taste like lamb, and squirrel meat—"

She rambled on, but I was having none of it.

"You're plumpening up," I said again. "Particularly 'round the belly." I raised my eyebrows. "How much 'bear' exactly did you eat?"

Her face shone, and her eyes twinkled. "Well," she said with an exaggerated sigh. "'Tis what happens, you know."

She turned toward me, and I threw my arms about her. "When? Does George know?"

"He will. Soon enough." A look of apprehension painted itself across her smile.

I understood. Never did a woman face childbirth that fear and joy didn't mix themselves together, much as we tumbled the corn batter. I would be mother to her child if anything should happen to her in childbirth, this I knew, and with that thought fear bolted through my heart.

Morn, Crowned With Her Bridal Wreath
April 5, 1614 ~ Bermuda Hundred

Night waned and wasted, and the fading stars
Died out like lamps that long survived a feast,
And the moon, pale with watching, sank to rest
Behind the cloud-piled ramparts of the main.
Young, blooming Morn, crowned with her bridal wreath,
Bent o'er her mirror clear, the faithful sea...
—George Gordon McCrae

There had been weddings at James Town and Henricus with Annie's being the first back in 1608. Since then, many a widower and widow had wed, and many a young girl coming of age had walked the aisle of the church at one settlement or the other.

Yet the wedding of Pocahontas to John Rolfe was a stunning moment, and one none of us who witnessed it would soon forget.

Before we knew it, we were sitting in the little church at Bermuda Hundred where settlers waited to see the first ever marriage of an Englishman to an Indian. Pocahontas was also the first Indian we had baptized to Christianity and one of the first to speak nearly fluent English.

I sat in the second pew with the children. Tempie and George were to my left.

At the front of the church sat Sir Thomas Dale and Jack Laydon. Around me, I saw most of the women at Bermuda Hundred. Soldiers and fishmongers, carpenters and laborers, all looked toward the chancel with curiosity. No one, it seemed, wanted to miss this event.

The day was unusually warm and bright, the sun casting golden shadows through the windows. Wildflowers colored the front of the church with merriness we all felt. The flowers gave a cheerfulness to the church it had never seen. We did keep flowers in the church to keep it passing sweet, but never this many! Others must have thought so, too, as many folks with something like hope in their eyes stared at the magnificent blossoms. The sprigs and sprays may have been but wildflowers, but Virginia was a festive mother and knew how to adorn her woods.

Lovely, I said under my breath. Then leaning to Tempie, I whispered, "I do believe we covered a whole rainbow of Virginia flowers."

She nodded with glistening eyes.

Bountiful flowers and hope and cheer, yet something more. Something more holy upon which I could not place a name. Perhaps the warmth enveloped me because we loved both John and Pocahontas. Perhaps 'twas simply spring, the joy of surviving another winter.

Or perhaps something greater at work, something nameless but wondrous all the same.

The Reverend Whitaker smoothed his black robes, cleared his throat, and began the baptism. Typically a child's baptism would include a passage from the Gospel of John. But in this case the good Reverend read from Mark, for this was the rare ceremony for an adult who had never had opportunity to be baptized.

"*The wind bloweth where it listeth, and thou hearest the sound thereof, but canst not tell whence it cometh, and whither it goeth: so is every one that is born of the Spirit.*"

"I love that," Tempie whispered to me.

Finally after many formalities, Alexander Whitaker pronounced, "The candidate for Holy Baptism will now be presented."

Sir Thomas Dale, her sponsor, said, "I present Rebecca to receive the Sacrament of Baptism."

Reverend Whitaker looked kindly at the beautiful Indian Princess. "Do you desire to be baptized?"

Rebecca Pocahontas said in a clear voice, "I do."

After blessing the water and other prayers, the pastor sprinkled font water on Pocahontas and said, "I baptize you in the name of the Father, and of the Son, and of the Holy Spirit. *Amen.*"

It was done! And on to the wedding.

From the front pew came the bridal party, arranging themselves about the bride. Next to Pocahontas stood Annie as bridesmaid. The princess's two brothers in buckskin breeches, feathers and claws swinging from their ears, flanked the bride on either side. Ralph Hamor stood as best man, wearing his nicest jerkin. Pocahontas's sister Matachanna not being present was the bride's only sadness, I heard. It seems Opachisco had come unsure of the welcome he would receive. He had not wished to bring a woman to the settlement under those circumstances.

Opachisco, Powhatan's brother, would give his niece away, for Powhatan had sworn never to set foot in our settlement. Opachisco, tall and dignified, squinted and studied the congregation.

He must have thought he would never see a day such as this! I thought. *But then, neither did we.*

"You could have been there as a bridesmaid, too," Tempie whispered back to me.

I shook my head. "No, dear. Not I. The true friendship is between Annie and Pocahontas." I glanced over at my friend and then reached for her hand and squeezed. "You and I are heart friends, and so are they."

Reverend Whitaker cleared his throat. "Dearly beloved friends, we are gathered together here in the sight of God, and in the face of His congregation, to join together this man and this woman in holy matrimony, which is an honorable state, instituted of God in Paradise in the time of man's innocency, signifying unto us the mystical union that is betwixt Christ and his Church: which holy state Christ adorned and beautified with his presence and first miracle that he wrought in Cana of Galilee..."

Nothing extraordinary about these nuptials. Everything extraordinary about these nuptials.

The Reverend Whitaker went on until finally he came to the words that brought a hush to the crowd assembled:

"Wilt thou have this woman to thy wedded wife, to live together after God's ordinance in the holy estate of matrimony? Wilt thou love her, comfort her, honor, and keep her, in sickness, and in health? And forsaking all other, keep thee only to her, so long as you both shall live?"

John whispered, "I will."

The Reverend Whitaker turned to Pocahontas.

"Wilt thou have this man to thy wedded husband, to live together after God's ordinance in the holy estate of matrimony? Wilt thou obey him and serve him, love, honor, and keep him, in sickness and in health? And forsaking all other, keep thee only to him so long as ye both shall live?"

Pocahontas looked deeply at her betrothed and, a trace of smile upon her face, replied, "I will."

In an authoritative voice, Reverend Whitaker asked, "Who giveth this woman to be married unto this man?" Whitaker nodded to Opachisco.

Stately Opachisco stood at the front, his black hair almost four feet long, sleek with walnut oil, knotted on the left, shaved on the right. Opachisco had decorated the knot at the crown with deer's hair dyed red to signify that to him, too, the occasion was special. He took the hand of his niece and gave it to the preacher, who in turn gave her to John.

John's voice wavered slightly. "I, John Rolfe, take thee Rebecca, to my wedded wife, to have and to hold from this day forward, for better, for worse, for richer, for poorer, in sickness, and in health, to love and to cherish, till death us depart; according to God's holy ordinance, and thereto I plight my troth."

Then, Pocahontas began, "I, Rebecca, take thee John to my wedded husband..."

I squeezed Tempie's hand in excitement, and my heart leapt with joy. Had it only been a year ago that Pocahontas had sat forlornly staring out the window, unable even to acknowledge Annie's presence? I tried not to think of Kocoum and her little son.

Now a whole new life awaited Pocahontas.

The women had brought the foods they'd managed to prepare to the Big House. Salted fish and corncakes. The sack-posset wasn't plentiful but enough for each guest to have a little.

The bride beamed, a rosy, healthy look to her. She wore a blue bodice with lace trimming. John, handsome in his best doublet and jerkin, breeches and stockings, only one hole that I saw, looked every bit a man in love.

I pulled Tempie beside me and whispered, "I can't believe it. I just can't believe it!"

She laughed. "I know! An Indian princess and an Englishman wed, and we as witnesses to say it's so."

"No, not that. I can't believe *you're* going to have a baby!"

And then she blushed, murmuring, "Ssh! Keep it to yourself, please. Ears are all about."

Master Bailey, from Aylesbury in Buckinghamshire, called to Will during the reception.

"Hm, what is that, do you suppose?" Tempie asked, seeing Will and Bailey lost in conversation off to themselves.

"Oh, business, I suppose." Tempie was having a baby! Babies, weddings... Then, at once, my heart fell as realization struck me.

"Tempie, it's business, sure. Matrimonial business! Master Bailey is asking Will for Cecily's hand."

These Have I Loved
April 1614 to May 1615 ~ Bermuda Hundred

And to keep loyalties young, I'll write those names
Golden for ever, eagles, crying flames,
And set them as a banner, that men may know,
To dare the generations, burn, and blow
Out on the wind of Time, shining and streaming....
These have I loved...
—Rupert Brooke

Record it for the grandson of your son—
A city is not builded in a day:
Our little town cannot complete her soul
Till countless generations pass away.
—Nicholas Vachel Lindsay

And so it was. Will agreed to the wedding, and I supposed I did, too. Reverend Whitaker proclaimed the wedding banns for the next three Sundays. Just a month after Pocahontas's wedding, Cecily at the age of fourteen wed Master Bailey in the church at Bermuda Hundred. She moved with him to his home in the western portion of the hundred. My time with her, so brief, was now over.

Shortly after the wedding, Will left with Sir Thomas Dale to conclude a peace treaty with the Chickahominies. These fiercely independent Indians had never fallen to Powhatan's kingdom. But since Powhatan and the English were at peace, the Chickahominies knew when prudency dictated signing a treaty themselves. What could one tribe, however bold, do against the Powhatan and English nations combined?

Peace fell like a blanket upon the river peoples of Virginia, upon warweary white and red alike. But could peace last? No one knew.

The men with precious *Trinidado* tobacco seeds returned from the Chickahominies and immediately sowed their tobacco. Only John had planted *Trinidado* the first year, but last year and this, John had shared his seeds with others.

When at last the tobacco sprouted, men like Will applied what they had learned from the Indians and from their own experience with tobacco plants. Even Dale himself was making trials at tobacco planting.

Harvest season came, and the tobacco was much improved. Will said he felt sure that each year they could make the tobacco better than the year before. I wasn't quite certain he believed it, but I appreciated his hopefulness. Autumn evenings he sat savoring his own tobacco, a very self-satisfied expression on his face even if the weed still could not compare with what the Spanish grew.

Will had taken some of the silkworms, too, and made trials of feeding the worms mulberry leaves. The worms didn't seem nearly as pleased with the leaves as Will was with his tobacco, though. A silk industry we might have, if only the worms could survive the ocean voyage and thrive once here.

Will, Sam, George, John, and Tom Bailey were each farming their own three acres. Tempie, Cecily, and I helped our husbands in the fields. Janey helped, too, while Sam toiled alone.

While we all had little time to work our land, we still did manage to produce enough corn, our staple food. After harvest, we ground it into meal and rationed it to make it last the year. Turnips and squash, carrots and Indian beans, cabbages and pumpions, peas and parsnips, all these and more prospered in the soil at Bermuda Hundred.

If drought came, we carried water from the river and soaked the earth as best we could; blights and harsh weather we had little control over. We planted after last frost and continued planting throughout the season, finally sowing winter roots and pumpions in the middle of summer.

All this we did during the times we were not working for Sir Thomas Dale. We worked the fields early before the sun, in the short break during midday, and after evening meal.

What we did for ourselves was a good thing, as we sometimes went a year without seeing a ship. During 1615, the *Francis* did come in, as did a Dutch ship called the *Flying Hart,* which agreed to take some of our tobacco in trade for needed goods like vinegar and sugar.

When the *Treasurer* returned later, it brought few provisions for us. The Virginia Company, it seemed, cared little what we had. And they had all but stopped sending new settlers. During all of 1613, 1614, and 1615, no more than fifty new colonists arrived. The Company was nearly bankrupt, and no one believed that Virginia could succeed. Except Sir Thomas Dale, who never, never gave up.

Even so, no one allowed us, who had been in Virginia for years, to go home. We could not even visit England. The Company knew well that if ever we left, we should not return. Nor did anyone give us the vast land grants promised us: fifty or a hundred acres for each man, woman, and child above age ten.

Nearly two thousand colonists had come to Virginia in the years before the number sailing here dried up. We were the three hundred still living, about sixty-five of us women and children, straggling survivors of the long, lean years. The future stretched before us like the endless forests, mysterious and unknown. Our only hope, freedom at the end of three years laboring for Dale in Bermuda Hundred.

We had little choice but to carry on, day to day. We toiled as slaves while trying to keep ourselves fed, waiting and hoping for the time we could choose our own labors and whether we wished to stay or go.

New colonists were still arriving however these came not on ships but were Virginia-born.

Mistress Mary Woodlief began to show first. She gave birth to a son, John Junior, about the time we learned that Annie was expecting again.

Annie was due a few months after Tempie. Annie started to show about the same time Pocahontas became with child. Tempie was now twenty-four, Annie was twenty, and Pocahontas was eighteen. Cecily at fifteen was also expecting our first grandchild.

There could be little doubt that peace with the natives had brought us a measure of hope, even while we remained poor and forgotten and under harsh laws. But no matter. Babies do not know this, and so they come, bringing their peculiar message that God, at least, had not given up on us.

And then the babies began arriving. Safe deliveries all, thanks to the skill of Mistress Wright. Elizabeth Yeardley was born first with little Alice Laydon following, and then Thomas Rolfe, named for his godfather, Sir Thomas Dale. And finally, Cecily's own birthing time came.

Cecily chose Tempie, Annie, Pocahontas, Thomasine, Margery Fairfax, and me as her god-siblings with Tempie and Pocahontas bringing their own babies to the birthing chamber. Mistress Wright delivered the healthy baby girl into the world. Cecily named her Temperance Bailey after the baby's god-mother Tempie. After that, we had Tempie and Little Temp.

Holding my granddaughter for the first time, I looked into her face and remembered Cecily's own birth. That had been only fifteen springs before but felt like two or three lifetimes. After Cecily's father had died, I had married Will. Then Cecily's little brother had died in England, just before Janey's birth. And then the long years here. Everything in my world had changed since Cecily's father Tom had told me I was getting "a mite heavier." If only he and I had known all that was to be. Yet seeing Cecily's contented and happy face made me happy, too. Pray God her life and the life of her little daughter would prosper here, that the future might hold more than the present.

This tiny red-faced squalling baby knew none of that. She had her mother's hair and her father's nose. Maybe. I rocked her and hummed, "*Sleep my baby and do not cry, and I shall sing thee a lullaby.*"

Tempie said, "Joan, we've begun the next generation. We have birthed native English-Virginians—your Tommy, my Elizabeth, and your little granddaughter. Wee Thomas Rolfe carries the blood of all his Indian folk and all his English ones." Her voice hushed. "We are creating something new here. I feel it." She glanced around the room as if she could see it, too.

All I felt was that Little Temp wanted to suckle with her mama. I handed the baby to my daughter and said to Tempie, "Something new, and something old. For things never truly change, do they? The things that matter, friends and family and babies coming into the world. Yet, these children born here are never going to feel too much at home in England. They will always have known the woods and the rivers and the rhythmic hearty sounds Indian words make when a brave calls from a clearing. We will never be exactly like they are, will we?"

Pocahontas, her dark face lit from the fire, turned to me and said, "If we truly have peace all the years of our lives, then we have made something graceful and bold, like an eagle bird."

I put my arms around Pocahontas's shoulders, my cheek against hers, and saw the rosiness on the face of her tiny baby. Little Thomas, more than anything, symbolized that peace. *See that the blood of two peoples flows harmoniously through him*, I thought.

These babies had no cares. They only had mothers who loved them in a world no bigger than their cradles.

"That is so, my friend. May all these babies grow up in peace and, some-day, in plenty."

The Cruel Moon
Early April 1616 ~ Bermuda Hundred

During this time, the Lady Rebecca, alias Pocahontas, daughter to Powhatan, by the diligent care of Master John Rolfe her husband and his friends, was taught to speake such English as might well bee understood, well instructed in Christianitie, and was become very formall and civill after our English manner; shee had also by him a childe which she loved most dearely...
—Captain John Smith

The cruel Moon hangs out of reach
Up above the shadowy beech.
—Robert Graves

Will, newly made ensign, had just returned from small fights with the Warraskoyak and Chiskiac. Occasional hostilities reminded us that we were mostly but not completely, at peace.

The day had been a long one as I worked my garden that evening. I was on my knees, hands in the soil. We worked every hour of the day, still spending most of our time on assigned work orders from Dale. When we completed our shifts for Dale, we scrambled frantically to our work: our own gardens, cleaning, and cooking. I was tired all of the time, it seemed. Even the garden gave me but little pleasure.

I looked up to see Pocahontas walking over.

Before I could greet her, Pocahontas called, "Joan! I have news. I am going to England!"

I pulled up onto my knees and brushed the dirt from my hands. When I studied my Indian friend's face, I found it a mixture of fear and excitement. Her coif and dress were in the English style, but her rich brown eyes deeper than any Englishwoman's could ever be. She was beautiful, exotic—and she was going to England where every woman in the colony wanted to return. My heart went to stone.

She came into the garden. "My husband, my son, and I will go with Marshal Dale to the land of your people," she continued, seeming not to notice my frozen expression.

Why would Dale be taking the Rolfes? In a moment, I understood.

The deadline the Company had given us to prove our success had come at last. Dale would return to his post in the Low Countries, his leave overdue. John would talk with the Company about our striving for tobacco to compete with what the Spanish produced.

As for other commodities, we had little. The hemp and flax did grow well, and we had the native hemp, called silk grass, though from it little yarn we produced. We had not much to spare to send to England. A few Dutchmen, Italians, and Poles were making trials of glass-making, but the workers were unhappy, the results unpromising. Silkworms, a gift of the king himself, had been with us for one year, but most of the worms had died on the passage over. Gold, silver—none. Planks we had sent home as well as sassafras. Tobacco and our settlements, and our peace with the natives, were all we had to show the Company after seven years' servitude.

Pocahontas and little Thomas would be the living proof of our treaty. The Peace of Pocahontas, as we called it.

Still, little had changed. We were in rags. The Company sent few provisions over as its debt mounted. Yet here we struggled to stay alive, to keep our fields growing and victuals in our mouths, to survive the contagions that came and went. And for all that, the marshal whipped young girls and censored our letters home. The Company instructions flogged us onward—harder, more, ever harder.

I nodded but did not meet her eyes.

I wished her not to see the fear, frustration, and longing for home that I felt. Only a letter from the king or from a noble, someone of influence speaking on our behalf, would allow us to go home. We were here, trapped, and required to do the impossible.

I tried to force my voice. "Oh, how wonderful for you, Pocahontas." I still could not look up. Instead, I focused my attention on brushing the dirt off my petticoat. My ragged, ragged petticoat.

Since I did not rise, Pocahontas dropped beside me and touched my shoulder, asking gently, "Is all well? Something hurts your heart, Joan?" Her English had become so much better yet still had its Indian wording.

I shook my head as tears dropped onto my lap.

"No. My heart...it...it does not hurt." *Liar!* I could not brush the tears to hide them because my hands were so dirty. Instead, I took a deep breath, looked over at her, and tried to make my eyes bright. "England!" was all I could say. "Home to England..."

Pray You, Love, Remember
April 17, 1616 ~ Bermuda Hundred

There's rosemary, that's for remembrance; pray you, love, remember.
—William Shakespeare

I expect to pass through life but once. If therefore, there be any kindness I can show, or any good thing I can do to any fellow being, let me do it now, and not defer or neglect it, as I shall not pass this way again.
—William Penn

Others were not as subtle as I tried to be. I overheard Rose, a woman I didn't know well, nattering quietly to her friend that she understood not why *Pocahontas* should be able to go to England while *we* were not even free to write letters home. Why did the governor clearly favor an Indian over us? And on and on.

So we did not look forward to the day Captain Argall loaded Pocahontas, John, and little Thomas aboard the *Treasurer.* For one thing, it rubbed salt in an old, old wound. We felt she was getting special privileges, privileges we ourselves had earned. Try as we might, we simply could not be happy for her.

Tempie and I, at least, tried to put up a good front.

"If I were able to go home, I should want my friends to wish me well," Tempie said as she spun with her wheel next to mine. Annie was the only one we knew who had been happy for Pocahontas rather than feeling sorry for herself.

"I should want the same. But it *is* hard, isn't it?" The humming of the wheel as it spun above my foot soothed me somewhat. I sighed. "This linen thread shall never make a bodice for me!"

"Aye." Tempie's wheel went round.

"The good news is Dale is leaving. And your George shall be deputy governor while the marshal is away until Lord La Warr arrives again."

She nodded. "George isn't a cruel man as Dale is. The Company requires my husband to uphold martial law, but he need not whip young women expecting babies!" She gave her strick an extra hard pull.

"No, indeed. Pocahontas seemed a little apprehensive, didn't she?" I pumped the treadle in steady rhythm.

"She did. They *all* did."

What a sight! A dozen of her countrymen—braves, squaws, and children—were all traveling along to England. What a procession that was. To Pocahontas's great relief and happiness, her sister Matachanna came, as did Matachanna's husband, the *quiyoughcosough* Tomocomo.

"And then to pick up that Spaniard Molina and the English traitor Lembri at James Town..." The spies would sail to England as well.

In the end, watching the stern of the ship glide slowly downriver had brought me terrible grief. Of course Pocahontas should go! She was an Indian princess. She had given us peace.

The *Treasurer* had taken with it all the meager commodities we could gather. The four additional years the Company had given us had expired, so we sent tobacco and sassafras, pitch, potashes, sturgeon and caviar. And Pocahontas. These would have to be enough.

A bang startled us, and Elizabeth began to cry. "Ah, she hit her head." Tempie ceased treadling, stood, and scooped her little one up. She began swaying with the child in her arms then kissed the red mark and said, "It will mend before you marry."

Elizabeth's fall reminded me once more of Pocahontas and her little son, so close in age to Elizabeth. "I hope her youngster Thomas fares all right." I stopped to work the flax a bit.

"And she herself. I hope Pocahontas can withstand the journey. Rose was an ugly old gossip about it, didn't you think?" Tempie placed Elizabeth back upon the floor.

"Hm. I did. When she returns—Pocahontas, I mean—I'll do my best to be happy for her. I hope she brings us lovely stories of her time in England. And maybe seeing her, the Company will renew its support. Somehow." At the moment, we were caught in limbo.

John, we knew, hoped to be back in Virginia before next spring's planting—the Rolfes would only be gone a year from Virginia.

Well, if I hadn't been gracious upon her departure, I vowed to do better upon her return. I would make it up to her. After all, she had been fair with us when we'd held her captive. She had helped John's tobacco—our best and only real commodity. And she had caused a peace which kept my husband safe. Her presence in England might very well inspire more support for our cause. God knew we needed that.

I recalled her gentle touch. *Something hurts your heart, Joan?* she had asked.

Aye. What hurt my heart now was remembering my own envy, the sail gone down the river, and nothing I could do about it until she came home.

The Dropping Tears of Rain
March 19, 1617 ~ Bermuda Hundred,
and in Kent, England

The winds with hymns of praise are loud,
Or low with sobs of pain,—
The thunder-organ of the cloud,
The dropping tears of rain.
—John Greenleaf Whittier

Others you must try to save, as brands plucked from the
flames...
—Jude 1:23

The moon rose high and nearly full over the curls of the James where the river snaked through the land between Henricus and Coxendale. Silent and cold, the edge of spring brought the hope that the Lady Rebecca, our own Pocahontas, would soon return. Or so thought the Reverend Whitaker as his eyes adjusted to the moonlight. A circle of clouds ringed the moon, giving it almost a rainbow haze.

Lovely, he thought, before his mind returned to the Rolfes.

"John will want to plant," mused the parson, looking upon his own glebe land. He was excited for the couple's return. Rebecca—Whitaker preferred her Biblical name—had pledged to help him shine the light on her brethren, to tell them about this Jesus in whom she had come to believe.

New life and new crops and... He knew the townsfolk were poor and ragged. He understood that some had mutinied. But Alexander Whitaker felt a better day coming. The stockholders of Bermuda Hundred, he being one, had just after all received the promised land from Governor Yeardley.

Promised Land. Aye, wasn't it truly a Promised Land here? Canaan, just as the Bible predicted.

Somewhere across the river and in Henricus, an ensemble of frogs sang loudly, plaintively, as dawn broke the sky.

God's music, songs of the animals, the water, and the trees.

No one understood the woodlands and rivers better than Pocahontas and her people. Whitaker had come to have a great respect for the native beliefs, their knowledge of how to survive. They were smart, shrewd. He had seen that firsthand by the quickness with which Pocahontas grasped the Bible and its teachings.

Spring fast approached. "Tomorrow we set our first seed," he mumbled to himself. "Tobacco and corn, cabbage and peas."

But that was tomorrow.

Soon, when the Rolfes returned, the reverend and Rebecca would have much work in front of them. They would till the fields of a different sort, he thought. *God's fields. The work is much, and the laborers are few.*

Whitaker had heard, but did not know for certain, that there might be acrimony between the two strongest Indian leaders. He understood that King Powhatan had fled southward, afraid his brother Opechancanough would join with the English against him. Powhatan was growing older, his days on earth numbered. The preacher would like to see Pocahontas visit her father once she returned home. He hoped all fighting was past between the Indians and the English. He hoped, too, that the Peace of Pocahontas would be everlasting.

As for Whitaker himself, well, his friends had scoffed at his coming here, had teased him about it, had pleaded against it. And at last, when they understood he felt the Lord's calling, had relented.

The pastor glanced into the deep woods and imagined the natives, just waking to begin their day: the fires, the women making pots, the men chipping away at arrowheads. It was for them, most of all, that he had extended his leave from three years to six years and beyond. He touched the Bible and Book of Common Prayer in his hands. *Tools to work the fields,* he thought. He had no plans to depart Virginia.

Now, this beauteous March morn, Alexander Whitaker had never felt so close to God—upon the verge of His river, surrounded by the great forests and fields.

From the door dashed his young servant boy Jacob.

"Good lad!" said the reverend amiably. He liked Jacob, a Christian youth neither saucy nor profane. Jacob walked with the preacher down to the riverside where their little rowboat rested on shore.

Jacob slid the boat into the water and held his hand to help the reverend in.

Whitaker laughed, a happy sound. "Fie, boy, I'm not thirty yet!"

Jacob laughed, too. "Aye, sir. I only mean to help."

The reverend patted his shoulder. "I know you do, lad. You're a good boy, and I but jest."

The boy, looking relieved, used a paddle to push off. The trip downriver to Bermuda Hundred was a short one. Oh, Whitaker could have lived *at* the Nether Hundred and not kept his house in the glebe land. But he enjoyed the solitude and felt it his duty to steward the land, to oversee the tobacco on behalf of the church. In fact, the reverend not only stewarded the church lands but its waters as well, for he loved to fish.

Clouds had whipped up. As the sun began to rise, it was clear to both reverend and boy that a March storm brewed, for now they could see the rich black-blue of the threatening sky. A sudden boom of thunder caused Jacob to jump.

"A tempest, sir!" cried the boy, dipping his paddle as fast as he could. "Oughtn't we to turn back?" His eyes showed fear as they met those of his pastor.

The minister looked up, concerned. A low menacing rumble rolled across the sky. The clouds had blown in quickly. He tucked his Book of Common Prayer and Bible beneath a sack, hoping to keep them dry. He shook his head. "No time, son. We've services this morning, and none but I can perform the catechism."

"Aye." The boy didn't appear any more at ease, but he did as the preacher instructed him.

When the storm came upon them, it entered with a fearsome howl of wind that rocked the boat and tossed the flowing river. The rain began pelting them, hard as little pebbles. The quiet river was awash with whitecaps suddenly. It was still barely dawn.

Now, too late, the pastor wished mightily that they had indeed turned back. But they were almost to the Nether Hundred.

Each now did what he did best: the boy rowed, and the preacher prayed.

The Lord is my shepherd, I shall not want.
He maketh me to rest in green pasture,
And leadeth me by the still waters.

But these waters were anything but still. In a moment, the little boat rocked hard, flipping the prayer book and Bible into the water.

"My books!" the pastor yelled. The precious books were sinking into the murky depths of the James River. Whitaker lunged, reached for them. Too late!

He leaned again, further this time, tipping the boat harder as he tried desperately to get his hand upon a piece of leather.

"Sir!" screamed the boy. "Careful, sir!" The river was brisk, the rain a steady pounding. The boat slickened with water.

And in the span of two heartbeats, the pastor himself toppled into the water amid the downpour. Jacob grabbed the boat and hung on with one hand, reaching for his master with the other.

But like his books, the Reverend Alexander Whitaker, too, sank beneath the churning water.

* * *

A world, an ocean, away in England, the March day was rainy as well.

And there, on a Virginia-bound sailing ship easing its way down the Thames River, a twenty-year-old woman doubled in pain as her husband grasped her hand and pleaded with her. *Please, please do not die.* Nearby, their young son's sickly cries pierced the air.

Distraught, the man lifted his eyes to the rafters of the ship, heavenward, and repeated a fervent prayer.

The Lord is my shepherd, I shall not want.

Please do not let them die. Please.

A verse from Jude flashed into his mind, and he added, *Oh, Lord, snatch them as brands from the flames!*

Her Feet Were Silence On the River
May 1617 ~ Bermuda Hundred

In peace from the wild heart of clamour,
A flower in moonlight, she was there,
Was rippling down white ways of glamour
Quietly laid on wave and air.

Her passing left no leaf a-quiver.
Pale flowers wreathed her white, white brows.
Her feet were silence on the river;
And "Hush!" she said, between the boughs.
—Rupert Brooke

A ship had finally arrived, its sails beating against a May wind keeping its progress upriver slow. In all of the year before only the *Susan* had come in October, bringing us some few supplies. It did seem more and more, as if the Company had abandoned us here. So while we were always excited when we spied a ship in the river, we were more excited than usual this time.

Annie was at my doorstep before I knew it.

"I don't recognize this ship. It's not the *Treasurer*, but do you think this one brings Pocahontas and little Thomas home?" The time of year now was May, planting time, as John had hoped. Aye, I reckoned it could well be the Rolfes' ship.

I dried my hands upon my apron and came to look out. I rubbed my fingers, the flax having made them raw. Then I looked backward at the amount spun. Was it enough?

Well, no matter. I could slip away for a mite. Annie was so eager, even clapping her hands in joy. "I want to see her, Joan! I want to hear what she thought of London and meeting the queen and…and…the masque!"

I smiled and bobbed my head, even as my own heart felt a flutter of jealousy. I pushed the feeling away. *It was right that Pocahontas should go. She is a Princess after all. And the marriage had brought peace.* I felt sorry about my green-faced envy. Yet I still seemed powerless to do anything about it.

Annie had no such misgivings. As much as she herself wished to go home, she was still happy for her friend. Happy, as I should have been. No, I had pledged to make it right with Pocahontas, and now finally might be my opportunity.

We knew the plan was to bring Pocahontas to England's king and queen, the Indian princess a diplomat for the Powhatan royal family. The Virginia Company wished to demonstrate that natives could become Christians, and here in Lady Rebecca Rolfe the Company had its proof.

What had she done? Seen?

I called to Tommy, who hoed out in the garden. "Tommy, go and find Auntie Tempie! She will want to know this."

The little boy nodded and laid aside his hoe. "Yes, ma'am," he said. I watched his ragged little backside dash away.

Drums called the soldiers from their barracks, and the men formed into martial order. Will's friend Chacrow was visiting and he too, fell into formation leading the right file. Governor Yeardley came out looking pleased that his men were giving the new governor such a hale welcome.

Gradually, the crowd of townsfolk began to grow. Ships' arrivals were important days. Letters? News? So much of life in England we desired to know. Tempie came out, great with child once more, her gait having a slight waddle. Tommy held the hand of little Elizabeth. The girl toddled along, a tattered, dirty, once-white linen shift on her. She had her thumb in her mouth.

Tempie stooped as if considering picking her up.

"Don't you dare!" I called. She paused and smiled at me, stood straight, and allowed Tommy to continue bringing Elizabeth.

Janey, whom we now called Jane, had come outside now. She ran to her brother, and *she* lifted little Elizabeth. The child touched Jane's lips with her fingers as if wondering how they worked.

Cecily lived on the far edge of Bermuda Hundred, but she would wish to know. "Tommy, do you reckon you might also run to your sister's and fetch her? Tell her a ship has docked. We're hopeful the Rolfes may be home!"

He sighed. "Yes, ma'am." And off he bolted.

"He's a good boy," Annie murmured, watching him run.

"He is," I said. "Obedient and wanting to be a soldier like his father." I sighed. Men and soldiering! Generation upon generation. "'Tis my destiny, I suppose."

Minutes passed, and the ship drew closer and closer.

Finally, the ship edged to shore, and a mariner tied her off to a tree. Another seaman began climbing the mast to tend the sails while the fellow with the rope leaned over near us.

"Do you bring us news, sir?" called Thomasine Causey.

"What news?" shouted another woman.

A mariner cried, "News ye seek, aye? The king and queen be well, no wars."

"No, no," cried Annie, in a rare fit of impatience. "What of the Rolfes? Who's aboard?"

He raised his voice as the wind picked up, rippling the sails and making it hard to hear him. He appraised the crowd solemnly.

I glanced around and realized once more how very motley we must appear to those on ship.

"Aye," he called. "We have Master Rolfe and the natives onboard. Admiral Argall has returned as governor!" Dale, as we had expected, was not aboard. He had returned to fulfill his agreement with the Dutch after delaying his return two years.

Annie placed her hand upon her heart and turned to me, her attention completely on the Rolfes. "She's home! She's home," she said with a satisfied tone. "Pocahontas is home now. She'll have missed Virginia, you know."

"Argall to be Governor?" Tempie said. "That means the end of George's run. He'll be relieved." The governorship had taken a toll on George with its many pressures, its impossible-to-solve problems. At Christmas, the Chickahominies had broken their pact to bring us corn, and George had led a battle against them. Will and Sam again dodging arrows across a field of Indians, yet the fight had been an easy victory for us. The Chickahominies were not part of the Powhatan nation, and so the peace with them was more unstable. But we had begun to realize the natives did not truly want to be at peace with us, did not want us on their land.

As for Argall, George had been in our eyes the best governor we'd had. We did not pretend to be unprejudiced. When the three years of the Bermuda Hundred agreement ended in January, George had happily given us all our freedom. I knew that George needed the rest from an overtaxing position.

Still, Argall? Governor? What of the Baron De La Warr? What kind of Governor would Argall be, I wondered. Our fate depended on that singular position—the governor.

Suddenly, down the bridge came Governor Sam Argall. I could see Argall's face from where I stood. Did he look smug? I found something about the man bothered me. Perhaps it was the way he'd tricked Pocahontas to use her as a bargaining piece.

"Milling, milling, who told you to mill about?" he yelled at the crowd, waving his hand. "Have ye no work? Or are ye being lazy now that the marshal is not here to enforce the laws?"

I recognized a subtle insult to George's leadership that heightened my sense of unease.

"Please, sir," Annie spoke up. "We wish to see the Rolfes."

The other women nodded and murmured their assent.

Argall made a face. "I see. Well, back, back. 'Tis been a sickly voyage, and many are now ill. We'll need to find homes for them."

I sighed. *We will be boarding the sick. The unseasoned. Again.*

"Sickly, sir?" Annie wrung her apron nervously.

The passengers, pale and wan, were beginning to disembark. I guessed there were about one hundred new settlers aboard, twice the amount that had come in the last four years. *Pocahontas's mission must have been a success!* I watched the newcomers experience the same earth-moving sensation that I myself had felt when I first touched Virginia soil. All new faces. But where were the Rolfes? And the natives?

John Rolfe came into view from the upper deck. He studied those on land and then looked away. No wave or friendly gesture.

"Annie, where is Pocahontas?" I leaned and whispered in her ear.

She shook her head, a fearful expression upon her face. "Don't know. She's probably just down below, getting her little boy ready to come up. That's all."

I nodded. An anxious feeling came to the pit of my stomach. Aye, that was all.

John made his way down the bridge behind others who scanned the river, the woods, the houses. *That was us,* I thought, *just eight years ago. Wondering where we were and what this New World was like.* Now we knew all too well.

Some stumbled, and some held on to others who were stronger. A few of the natives appeared on deck. They were gaunt with sunken eyes. Truly, a hard voyage they must have had.

Several soldiers shuffled us backward. "Give 'em space."

Finally, John's feet touched solid ground. He looked down as if to verify this, then away to the forest and upward to the sky. He did not look our way nor meet our eyes.

And I knew. With a sickening certainty, I knew. *Pocahontas and Thomas. They are not coming home.*

A Virginia Lady Borne
May 27, 1617 ~ Bermuda Hundred

March 21—Rebecca Wroth wyffe of Thomas Wroth gent. A viginia lady borne was buried in the Chauncell.
—Parish Register, St. George's Church, Gravesend

"She was well during the visit." John shuffled his victuals around on his plate, focusing on his fish as if it were the most fascinating thing he had ever seen.

A few days before, John had arrived in James Cittie with Governor Argall. George had then asked several of the women including me to prepare a venison meal for Argall to celebrate his safe return and to welcome him as new governor. Tempie was by this time so great with child that she was unable to be on her feet long.

George was rightfully pleased with his accomplishments, in spite of receiving so little help from the Company. The granary in Bermuda Hundred was filled with corn the farmers had paid in rent. In fact, all the settlements had stored corn, conquering hunger at least for now.

Days past, we had gone begging to the Indians for corn. But now the Indians frequently came to our settlements seeking corn and trading furs.

After a few days more went by, Will and I invited John to our home along with Sam, the Laydons, the Yeardleys, Cecily, and Cecily's husband Tom. Meetings with Argall still occupied George, so Tempie came alone. John had been busy, too, since he retained his position as secretary to the governor, which Dale had given him a few years back. At last, John had the opportunity to tell his story in less formal circumstances.

A grim air hung over the supper. We had so many questions for John, for as yet we knew little of how our friend had died.

"You say she was well before leaving London? Then what happened, John?"

Annie leaned forward on a bench, her eyes red and rimmed.

John hunched, his shoulders rounded, his hands wrapped around the dram in front of him. He stared into it as he nodded. Then he lifted his head and spoke.

The Virginia Company had treated the Rolfes as well as the nearly bankrupt company could afford. The couple had stayed at an old inn, The Belle Sauvage, already so called and not named for the lovely Powhatan Princess.

John went on. "Pocahontas conducted herself so elegantly. How proud of her I was! Oh, we knew people whispered behind our backs, that we were a curiosity. Some stared. The Virginia Company gave us four pounds weekly allowance. I was too poor to dress her appropriately to see the king and queen, so the Company money certainly helped."

Baron De La Warr and his wife had introduced the Rolfes at court and escorted the couple to the king's Twelfth Night masque at Whitehall Palace.

"What a treat for us! The showmanship of Ben Jonson's *Christmas His Masque*, the Earls Buckingham and Montgomery dancing with the queen."

Pocahontas had met both king and queen. Seeing the thin, effeminate King James compared to her father, the tall and domineering Powhatan, Pocahontas had whispered to her husband. "This cannot be a king. Where is the true one?"

This humorous recollection broke the pallor around the table. Even John smiled at the memory. "She said, 'This little man rules so much and so many? Why do they listen to him?' She was unimpressed," John added. "I must say, His Majesty would look pitiably small were he to stand next to King Powhatan."

The Rolfes had also attended a performance at the Globe Theatre. "And, by the by, the great Shakespeare is dead, my friends. Passed just before our arrival," Rolfe declared. This brought a pang as I remembered how Will and I had seen *As You Like It* during our courting.

"Our country mourns Mr. Shakespeare heavily, I presume?" Will put in.

"Just so. And don't we feel the privileged ones that the master based a play on our shipwrecking?" Rolfe said. "*The Tempest,* indeed!"

Sam shook his head. "The *monstrous* tempest. Forget the play, gentlemen. Give me solid land!"

The conversation turned back to Pocahontas, and John went on. "We spent the last months at Brentford. 'Twas there that Captain Smith paid us a visit." Chief Powhatan had adopted Smith as a son in the early years of the colony, so Pocahontas remembered him well. "But Pocahontas had thought him dead. Well, when Smith left Virginia, he was talking out of his head, so they say."

Tempie, the Laydons, and I nodded, for we had seen the soldiers load the injured Smith onto the ship.

"Powhatan had asked about Smith and someone told him the captain had died." He shrugged. "Perhaps this was deliberate so that Powhatan would respect the new governor's authority. Perhaps it was a misunderstanding. However, only when we arrived in Plymouth did Pocahontas learn that Captain Smith still lived. She was not surprised. Her father had told Tomocomo to learn Smith's fate, saying that the English do lie much."

Time approached for the Rolfe's departure, and Smith had still not come to see the princess who had done so much for him while he had been in Virginia.

"When at last Smith did visit us at Brentford, he apologized, saying he'd been occupied with preparations for sailing to New England. But he added that he'd written to the queen to tell her that Pocahontas was the nonpareil of Virginia. This excused nothing in Pocahontas's eyes. Smith's lack of reciprocal kindness while she was in a strange land hurt her greatly." John's face looked pained. Clearly, this incident still upset him.

"Betrayed again," Annie mumbled.

Thank God that neither John Rolfe nor Reverend Whitaker had forsaken Pocahontas. She had borne so many other injustices.

John continued. "Pocahontas turned away, hiding her face and would speak to no one for two or three hours. Finally, she reminded Smith of the courtesies she had done him, saying, 'You did promise Powhatan what was yours should be his, and he the like to you.' Smith had been a stranger in a strange land, and so the captain had deferentially called Powhatan *Father.* Now Pocahontas rightfully expected the same treatment. But Smith refused, saying this was inappropriate since she was a princess."

Now, John smiled, his love for his wife evident. "Well, Pocahontas would have none of that! She set her jaw, saying, 'You were not afraid to go into my father's land and cause everyone but me to fear you! Then you shall not be afraid of this. I tell you, I shall call you *Father*, and you shall call me *Child*, and so I will be forever and ever your countryman.'"

Our bold Pocahontas was not afraid to stand up to an English captain, no not at all.

"Pocahontas truly desired to stay longer. The sheer size of the cities intrigued her."

Annie's eyes met mine. I knew we both were thinking the same thing. Pocahontas had told us that Powhatan was the fabled Don Luis, the Indian whom the Spanish had adopted nearly fifty years before. Pocahontas had undoubtedly heard stories of European cities. But she had sworn us to secrecy, a vow we would not break, concerning Powhatan's identity. I wondered if John knew? If he did, he gave no indication.

John swirled the sack around in his dram and gazed into it again, his eyes so distant I might swear he could actually see old Brentford.

"What a warm, wet winter we had! Did you all have winter here?" John asked idly. Several of us nodded.

"Well, we did not. But 'twas shaping up to be a beautiful spring. My wife said to me, 'Can we not stay longer? I should like to see the English country-side come *cattapeuk,* the time of flowers, spring.'"

John shook his head at the memory. "'No, my dear,' I told her. 'The Virginia Company gives us orders, orders we must abide.' And that was that. Yet," he added, "some of her brethren decided to stay behind at the home of Sir Thomas Smythe upon his invitation."

What a strange picture this made: the grand manse, the Indians as houseguests.

"On the tenth of March, the Virginia Company gave us a stipend. 'Go and do missions work for the Indian children,' the Company told us. We didn't know exactly how to do that. Perhaps we would bring some of the Indian children to our home to teach them about the Bible." He shrugged. "Perhaps we would go to the Indian towns and gather those who might listen to the word of God. My wife was firm in her beliefs."

He smiled at the memory before continuing. "Soon came time to depart. We left the inn at four in the morning, walking to Billingsgate to catch a tilt boat for Gravesend."

"Ah, good!" I said. The open barges were cold and damp, but the tilt boats gave some covering under their canvas tilts. The deck beneath the tilt, strewn with straw, would have allowed Pocahontas and her son a place to rest. The tilt boats served as ferries to Gravesend, Kent, where the docked ships could begin their ocean journeys.

John frowned. "Aye, good matter, indeed. The warm rain stayed with us the whole four hours down the Thames to Gravesend." I reckoned that meant they were drenched from the drizzle. Not good for one's health, no.

"Once docked at Gravesend, we went to the Christopher Inn where we had a chamber. There to rest and to await Captain Argall, who himself had business with the Virginia Company after ours." Surely the Company had wished to give the new Governor last-minute orders.

"Argall and his associates received a twenty-four hundred acre land grant," John added. "That was the cause of the delay. Anyway, come the twentieth of March, Argall left the Company to catch a tilt boat to join us. He arrived, the wind high, and so we boarded the *George* with others awaiting passage to Virginia. Soon after, my wife felt cramping in her stomach, mild at first. Shortly thereafter, my son, too, began crying and doubling over."

"Bloody flux!" Annie gasped.

John nodded. "It began while we were having dinner with Captain Argall in his chamber. Pocahontas could not finish her meal, but rushed to our chamber to lie down. My son lay with his mother. Matachanna tended to her, Tomocomo prayed over her. I, too, prayed. We prayed our English and native prayers. God forgive me, I did not care whose God saved her! Just let her live…" His voice dropped off.

"Yet within hours, she had begun to convulse and was near death. She was a small thing and looked even smaller in the end. The wind had taken us barely away from Gravesend. The dark, heavy clouds made it appear as if all the light had gone from heaven. The captain turned the ship about, and we rowed her ashore. 'I must be with my sister,' Matachanna said, and so she and her husband came in the boat as well. The rain beat steadily." John drew a deep breath and released it slowly.

"Where to go? Back to the Christopher Inn? There was a cottage near the dock. A waterman and his family saw us carry my wife's nearly lifeless body to shore. The kindly old woman said, 'Bring her here, lad. She's the Indian Princess ain't she? I would be right honored to have her in my home. I might even have me a remedy or two before a doctor can see her.'"

Annie had tears in her eyes. "Kindness o' strangers, aye? Such a blessing."

"And, indeed, the old woman did her best. My wife had but hours to live. The woman's son went 'round to fetch a doctor and a pastor. They both arrived as one. 'Twas little the doctor could do by then although the pastor prayed with her. Pocahontas was not awake, and I think heard him not. But we did pray over her, and that, too, a blessing." Tomocomo and Matachanna too had said their own prayers for their sister.

Everyone at the table nodded. The familiar scene. Illness and death, the woes of the world…

"We had met the Reverend Frankwell during our stay at Gravesend. We had attended his service, and afterward he spent some time in conversation with my wife. He was most impressed with her Christian visage, as all were. Her faith, her passion and charity of heart, her love for her son."

A remarkable young woman, barely twenty, she had made such a dramatic impression on all. Those in Virginia as well as those in England, both royalty and commoners.

"Pastor Frankwell said to me, 'She shall rest with the pastors and families of our church in a place of honor. We shall bury her in the chancel.'"

"Ooh." Annie sucked in her breath.

"So wonderful, John," Tempie said.

"And she had a Christian burial at St. George's Church, with those on the *George* and many townspeople in attendance."

A stab went through me. I had been jealous, had not even offered a proper farewell. I was no better than the ungrateful Captain Smith had been. I hung my head, and my cheeks burned with shame I hoped others thought was grief.

A quiet solemnity seemed its own presence, hovering in the balmy May night, whispering through the chamber. 'Twas as if *she*, Pocahontas herself, were even with us. But that could ne'er be.

Could it?

"And Thomas?" Annie whispered. "What happened to the boy?"

John said that afterward, Argall and many on the ship encouraged him to leave little Thomas behind. The child had still been struggling with flux, albeit a milder case.

"We reboarded so to continue our journey to Plymouth. The waters were calm, yet Thomas struggled for his life and that in a peaceful river? How might he fare in open sea? But I had made up my mind. I would get him home somehow. It boded ill, you know. How many sick?" John looked pained at the memory.

"For days, those on ship pleaded with me, 'Leave him, Master Rolfe.' We made our way into the Narrow Sea and then landed at Plymouth. Hamor... Hamor was there. He had gone ahead, and we were to pick him up along with others boarding there."

The great port at Plymouth Hoe was oft the last place English feet touched English soil and also the first place most ships docked upon arrival.

"And?" Annie was impatient. "Where is Thomas, John? What happened?"

John tapped his pipe on the table. "Argall thought Thomas should not survive the voyage. He was probably right. Stukeley offered to keep him for me until my brother could come to take Tommy back to London. You know of Sir Lewis Stukeley? He's now the vice admiral of Devon."

Aye. We knew of him.

"We had stayed with Stukeley at his castle in Affeton upon our first arrival in Plymouth. Pocahontas charmed him, I must say." He smiled, but his gaze was far away. "Well, you know, she had that way."

"She did," Tempie said softly.

"The boy loved Affeton. Well, who wouldn't? The warrens, the pond. Such a grand place. Thomas ran after the geese, saying 'Papa, goo, goo!' *Goose.* I asked Hamor what he thought I should do. Hamor said, 'If he were my son, I'd leave him back. The sea journey will be hard on us all, but especially so on a small, sick boy.'" John trusted Ralph, I knew.

"At last Argall put it to me thus: leave him, and keep him. Bring him, and lose him. *Leave him,*' Argall told me. The man minces no words. I knew not what to do. But Argall has seen far more voyages than I had. I reckoned he knew who might survive and who might not. He assured me that my son was too weak and would never make it back to Virginia. Sir Lewis promised to let my brother Henry know that he had Thomas."

John grimaced, and I believed I knew his thoughts. His daughter Bermuda had died, buried in the Bermudas. His first wife Sarah had not survived the seasoning from England to Virginia. Now his second wife had not survived her seasoning, Virginia to England. And he had left his son, hoping that this part of Pocahontas *should not die*. His baby buried in Bermuda. His English bride buried in Virginia; his Virginia bride buried in England. For John, his loved ones were in the soil across three lands and his living son separated from him by an ocean.

"Thomas reached for me. He called, 'Papa!' I told him I would return. 'I'll be back, but I'm bound away on a ship.' His little eyes so trusting, dark brown like his mother's. 'Go and see the geese, then,' I told him. Thomas smiled and went with Dame Frances, Stukeley's wife. And I left quickly before I could rethink the matter."

"The children, they do get separated from the parents in this Virginia business, don't they?" I murmured, remembering my anguish at leaving little Cecily behind.

John nodded, and I saw great suffering behind his eyes.

"You *will* see him again, John. You will," Annie said.

"Pray God," said John, and then once more silence fell upon the table.

By now, the meal was over, and the men brought out their pipes. As John lit his and took a deep pull, he still focused on the table in front of him, his head bent. "And to think all the while on the ship coming over, I thought I'd talk to the Reverend Whitaker and draw strength from his spiritual vision, his wisdom." He shook his head then lifted his eyes. "I can't believe that good man drowned. When was it you say? Late March?"

We began reckoning.

I spoke up. "Why, John, I believe 'twas the nineteenth of March. A Sunday. When...?" I was almost afraid to ask "When...?" My voice trailed off. "When did she...?"

He paused. "The twentieth of March, a Monday. And buried on Tuesday."

The light was low, and Cecily rose, lighting the candles from the fire in the fireplace. The shadows flickered, dancing across the walls. I took in the dark and rosy faces, so dear to me, around the table.

Silence filled the chamber as the same thought dawned on all at once.

Joined by God in spiritual life and in final death. The two had died nearly the same day.

Greate Is My Loss
May 27, 1617 ~ Bermuda Hundred

And although greate is my loss, and much my sorrow to be deprived of so greate a comfort, and hopes I hadd to effect my zealous intencions and desyres as well in others, as in her whose soule (I doubt not) resteth in eternall happynes: yet such temperance have I learned in prosperity, and patience in adversitie, that I will as joyfully receive evill, as good at the hand of God: and assuredly trust that Hee, who hath preserved my childe, even as a brand snatched out of the fier, hath further blessings in store for me, and will give me strength and courrage to undertake any religious and charitable ymploymt, yourself and the Honorable Company shall command me, and which in duty I am bound to doe.
—John Rolfe, writing from Jamestown, June 8, 1617

"Two destinies entwined," Tempie said at last.

I touched John's arm. "Do you feel some better, knowing for certain now 'twas the will of God?"

"Joan, I do not understand the will of the Lord, nor feign to, but this I know: I will as soon accept pain as blessings from God's hands."

"For where the hand of God leads me, the hand of God saves me," I murmured. My father's favorite saying.

The Virginia Company had commissioned the Rolfes to create an Indian school for furthering missionary work to the natives.

"And what now?" John shrugged. "I know not what to do, nor how to proceed. Without Pocahontas… I fear the life went out of that venture. She had inspired so many, English and Indian alike."

So much promise, hewn too short. I felt heartsick to consider what might have—should have—been.

John's mind seemed turbulent. Each way it shifted, it ran into a wall of doubts. "I know not how I may be censured for leaving my son behind."

Guilt, fear, and uncertainty. A treacherous trio, to be sure.

I reached over and patted his back.

He began shaking his head as if he could shake the thoughts from it, then he grasped his forehead with his hand and squeezed.

But try as he might, the thoughts must have stayed, for he then looked to Will, Sam, Tom, and Jack Laydon, each in turn, seeming to seek reassurance.

"Did I do the right thing, Will? Why did I take her there? Why did I allow Dale to convince me… Why did I ever give favor to the idea? What was I thinking? *This* is her home. She might have lived a long and full life, to be an ancient old woman like her aunts." He ran his fingers nervously through his hair.

Will gave a laugh filled with rue, and I turned to him in surprise. This was unlike my serious, pensive William. "Why, indeed, John? Why, indeed? Do you see the nature of the beast we have created here? You cannot take your wife to your English home, for fear of losing her. The Company will not even allow us to send our wives or ourselves home. 'Tis a blasted hopeless situation sometimes, I fear."

Will cast his eyes around to the other men. There was Sam, the sole survivor of his three friends who, with Will on a long-ago night, had vowed to become Virginia Adventurers. John Dewbourne had felt the arrow plunge into his scalp, and more recently, Hugh had died in an ambush while out hunting. Neither had received any of the promises the Virginia Company had made to them. "Sounded good on paper, did it not, Sam?

And then an unexpected thing happened. The color seemed to drain from Sam Jordan's face. He slapped his dram hard against the table, so differently from the toast the men had shared the night they pledged all they had to Virginia.

"Are you accusing me, Will?" An expression both angry and hurt flashed through his eyes. Yes, he knew. *He* had been the one to suggest this. *He* had been the one to make the case. Eight years ago, Virginia had seemed like Canaan, the Promised Land of the Bible. Literally, the very land promised to the Israelites. The years of toil had worn down even the best of natures such as Sam's.

Now, Virginia seemed more like Egypt where we worked as slaves and tried to make bricks without straw. Little good that we could see had come from all our risks and hard work. We had our three acres at Bermuda Hundred. Three acres for eight years' work.

Sam stood as if to go, but Will made a motion to him. "Sam, brother, no, I am not accusing you. We made this decision together. For better, for worse."

"Not unlike marriage!" Tempie quipped. "We all married Virginia."

Her light comment almost broke the tension in the chamber. Almost, but not quite.

Will touched Sam's sleeve. "Don't go," he said quietly. "We made the best decision we could with the information we had. It may turn out all right in the end."

Sam stared at Will for a long moment then dropped his head. "My wife has died as well," he said.

Sam's face was cold. All conversation stopped, all eyes turned to Sam Jordan.

"Frances died while I was away these years. I intended to send for her once we were no longer under the Laws of Blood. But her sister writes, *She is gone.*"

Now the question hung in the air. All had suffered. Frances had not endured hurricane or starving as I had. She had not felt the brutality of Dale's Virginia or the fear of Spanish invasion. During the hurricane, Will had thought he might lose his wife and his daughter, had felt responsible for placing us in that danger. That Sam had kept Frances safe at home had seemed to Will then the wise and right decision.

It had seemed that way to me, too, many times.

Will's eyes filled with tears. So rarely did that ever happen. He and his friend exchanged a long look. They had fought together in the Lowlands and in the Virginia wilderness. They had made a life-changing decision to come here and to risk their own lives, the lives of their families, and all their fortunes. They had laid everything down as if it were but a wager on a card game. Now the man was coming around, collecting the bets.

Fish, fowl, fruits, nuts, berries—everyone who's been there says you've never seen such…such abundance. Will's voice, quoting Sam from a lifetime ago, came to me.

Frances had kept baby Cecily so that I could see *As You Like It* with Will the night he proposed. "Frances was a lovely woman," I murmured to Sam. "At least, she did not…" What? Suffer? How would that make Will feel? No, no winners sat about the table at this game.

"Frances must have felt I didn't want her here. And of course, I did not. But not for the reasons she must have believed. The chance to make it right, to explain in person, forever gone."

"Loved ones across the ocean. So hard to convey…what it's like here," Tempie said quietly. I knew she was thinking of her mother, the unhealed rift between them.

"Looming larger than the Spanish, the natives, hunger, disease, or Laws of Blood. Our greatest enemy is leagues of ocean," I said. *How I wanted to go home!* All sat in silence for a few moments, no one knowing what to say.

Then, as if remembering something, John's eyes lit. "Say, gentlemen, speaking of ocean travel, one bit of news. The Company *has* made one major concession. You may go home if you choose."

Home? Just like that?

"Home," Tempie murmured. "Going home." I saw that her eyes drooped. She rose unsteadily with a hand on her middle. "Pardon me all, but home is, for me tonight, right down yonder street to my house. A body grows tired when the baby is soon to come. That is exciting news, though, John."

Sam also excused himself, but not before I had given him a promise to pray for his wife and children.

After Tempie and John left, John continued sharing word from overseas with us.

"The laws remain in effect, I suppose? What other news from the Company?" Tom Bailey swirled the contents of his dram, the last of a jug of sack. Even for this special occasion, how few spirits we had.

John said evenly, "Aye. The Laws of Blood are still with us. The Company did not repeal them." A frustrated groan and sigh went up from the table. John raised his hand as if to quiet those gathered. "Captain Argall assures me he will administer the laws fairly."

I'll wager the French in North Virginia didn't find Argall's treatment too fair! And what of his stealing away Pocahontas? I thought, but daren't speak ill of the governor. Such would be a crime. I certainly anticipated the day Lord La Warr returned as governor and captain general.

This I could ask. "And my Lord La Warr? He still desires to come back and take the governorship in person?"

John nodded. "He does indeed. Plans are underway for his departure, even now."

"Well." Will lifted his dram and took a sip. "Argall's a good man. He showed his mettle with the French, he has brought us untold amounts of corn from the Indians when we needed it worst, and forget not, 'twas he who brought you your wife!" He turned to John.

Annie, who had been quiet, spoke up. "He captured her! He tricked her and caused her aunt and uncle to betray her. She was happy with you, John. That I know. But she was happy in her other life too with Kocoum and her little son."

Now it was John's turn to shrug. "Once she was here and Kocoum killed, the deed was done. Dale cast the dice. He gave Powhatan the chance to bargain for her. The sly old Chief chose not to—"

"She ain't a horse to be traded!" Annie interrupted, frustrated.

Again, John made the placating motions with his hands. "Annie, I know. I know. I loved her. I truly did. And I...I know...she loved me as well."

Annie nodded. "She did."

"What else are we missing, being so far away?" Will asked.

"Well, one thing. When I left my...my son with Stukeley..." John's voice faltered then found its strength again. "Stukeley told me he was expecting his cousin, Sir Walter Ralegh, to arrive in Plymouth just after our ship departed. Ralegh has been off to Orinoco in search of the fabled gilded king called El Dorado."

This king El Dorado was reputed to have so much gold that he dusted himself in it. His name had spread throughout Europe. He was the Golden King of the legendary Manoa, a village deep in the Amazon lying somewhere along the Orinoco River.

Tom threw his arm back over his chair and said, "Ah, Manoa! Where even the pots and ladles are made of gold."

Jack Laydon interlocked his fingers and leaned forward. "Think he'll find it this time, John? What's the word on the streets of London?"

John raised his eyebrows. "Well, Ralegh has made some robust promises to the king."

"So it's gold or his head?" Will put in. We all knew of the king's overly friendly stance with Spain, something most Englishmen found offensive at best. What self-respecting Englishman tried to curry favor with the Spanish? If the Spanish ambassador Gondomar bent King James's ear concerning Ralegh's voyage... Well, Ralegh had better fill his hold with golden treasure, or Will might be right.

Gold or his head.

"He wouldn't truly chop off the head of a hero such as Ralegh?" I asked, pouring the last of the sack into the men's drams.

"No, no, I don't think so," Will said, musing.

Yet, news of this sort always set us on edge. Spain's reactions to Englishmen scavenging their territory meant they might look harder at Virginia, which the Spanish, of course, also considered their own.

Aye, Spain was a threat that seemed to renew itself continually. Our peace with the natives had become uncertain with Pocahontas's death. But the largest threat, we would soon learn, would come from within the walls of our own settlement.

His name was Governor Samuel Argall.

This Web of Strangeness
Early to Mid-June 1617 ~ Bermuda Hundred

Here in this web of strangeness caught
And prey to troubled thought...
—Jessie B. Rittenhouse

Within a week of our dinner with John, George Yeardley came around delivering the gossip invitations. And in one week more, Mistress Wright delivered Tempie's little son, who entered the world with a healthy, hearty battle cry.

The baby, we all said, had his father's eyes. But Tempie claimed his nose and chin were Flowerdieu, certainly. The problem, as Tempie saw it, was with none of those, but rather with his name: Argall.

George had insisted that their son should be Argall's namesake and godson since the baby had been born right on the heels of Argall becoming Governor. Tempie had relented, but did not like the idea.

"I do not feel comfortable about the whole thing. I...I do not know why." She gazed at the red wrinkled face in her arms. "Argall. Argall Yeardley. I don't know."

"Don't know about the name or the godfather?" I asked her. She was feeding the week-old baby while I changed the bed linen.

Tempie's face took on an uncharacteristically somber appearance. "Both," she said at last.

"Aye." So we quietly shared our doubts about the governor. Were these feelings born of instinct? Or distaste for Argall's capture of Pocahontas, peace or no peace? I could not deny that I feared far less for Will's safety these days. The Peace of Pocahontas had that effect, certainly. The men fought skirmishes here and there, but not major battles. Still, Tempie felt much better about her own choice of godmother Annie Laydon.

George, however, seemed to have no reservations about Argall as either governor or godfather. Tempie's husband looked most pleased to have Governor Argall stand with him at the baby's christening as Argall pledged his help in the boy's spiritual upbringing. Tempie, still in her confinement, was not there to see George beaming down at his son while Sam Argall himself looked vaguely uncomfortable.

Yet George had little time but to kiss the baby at his baptism before Argall's changes would take the new father away from Bermuda Hundred.

In fact, these changes left my own stomach churning as Will, too, prepared to depart. For Governor Argall had ordered that we return the heart of the settlement to James Town.

James Town! We had all but abandoned the first town except as a military fort upon the move to Henricus six years before. And most settlers had joined the Bermuda Hundred corporation. Here in Bermuda Hundred these stockholders had their land and homes just as Sir Thomas Dale had planned.

All government officials must be at James Town, Argall had decreed. All counselors, all the Governor's Guard, including Will. James Town, now to be called James Cittie, would be the new capital. Argall was attempting to rename it to show the town's renewed importance. To him, at least.

George Yeardley, as second leading man in the colony, would have to uproot to James Town, as would we since Will was part of the Governor's Gaurd. My main comfort was that Tempie and I would still be together. And that we would reunite with Maria Bucke, who had been at James Town all this time.

About the time Pocahontas married, Maria had given birth to a son she named Gershom. Maria had drawn his name from Exodus. *"And she bare a son, whose name he called Gershom: for he said, I have been a stranger in a strange land."* Strangers and pilgrims, aye, that we all were.

And then last year had come little Benomi. Benomi, it was apparent, would never be able to read or write. He would always have the mind of a child. And so in Hebrew *Benomi* meant *Son of my Sorrow.* Each of the names of Maria's children indicated the bitterness, loneliness, and sadness she had felt when they were born. We were glad to be with her again to offer our support to her.

However, Tempie and I had memories of James Town—James *Cittie*— that made us fearful. Besides that, many of our other friends and family would remain at Bermuda Hundred. Cecily and Tom would stay behind. John Rolfe had land next to the Baileys where he would remain for at least part of the year. His duties as secretary would bring him to James Cittie some, too. Annie and Jack Laydon had no reason to leave Bermuda, either.

As for Sam Jordan, he was ready to give up soldiering for tobacco farming and a try at silkworms. Therefore, Sam would stay at Bermuda Hundred as well. After so many years of looking down the barrel of a musket, Sam decided he'd had enough. Sam was mourning the loss of his wife, wondering if he should bring his children over, and trying to move on.

Give up soldiering? Not Will. He would still farm his tobacco and corn, of course, but he was an ensign who hoped soon to be a lieutenant.

Now, over at James Cittie, the men had much work to do. The soldiers and craftsmen must rebuild the sagging, nearly abandoned town.

The night before Will was to leave for James Cittie, I could not sleep. I nudged my husband.

"Will, if James Town was not safe or healthful before, why would it be so now?" I was not at all happy about the move and the separation from loved ones.

Will yawned. "I don't know, Joan. The move doesn't make sense to me, either. The Virginia Company, that I am aware, has not sanctioned such an action. I cannot refute what you say about James Cittie's suitability. But Argall is the governor and admiral. He insists, and we obey."

"But why when the crops are in?" Dale had been so conscientious about making moves only after harvest. *Dear God, am I now defending Sir Thomas Dale?*

Will sighed. "Why, indeed, Joan? Argall says he simply prefers James Cittie to Bermuda Hundred without giving his reasons. He wants to get us there as soon as possible."

The larger question was what personal stake did Argall have in James Cittie? And why the urgency? He must have some reason for moving the government away from Dale's treasured upriver settlements. After all, the threat of foreign attack remained strong.

While Argall moved the government back to James Cittie, he himself went even closer to the ocean. He made his home at Kecoughtan at the mouth of the James River and the bay.

The orders to move were not the only ones Argall forced us to obey. The new Governor had made it clear: any lightening of martial law under George Yeardley had been a mistake in his opinion. The Laws of Blood would return in full force, and the council would have little say in the law's discharge. Argall would mete punishment as he, and only he, saw fit.

The consequences became all too clear with the fate of Master Hudson, once provost marshal general. In Sir Thomas Dale's time, a court had convicted Hudson of diverse crimes. Yet Sir Thomas Dale had pardoned the man, feeling he had intrinsic value to the colony and deserved a second chance. Now, Argall had called Hudson an ungrateful viper for several more errors and had banished the man to exile. Hudson could live with the Indians if he were fortunate. Another proclamation informed us that, should Hudson ever return, Argall would put him to death, no questions to be asked. Hudson was fortunate that his hide was intact. We felt sure he knew that.

Disturbing news from the governor's house seemed to keep coming. Now, we learned of Argall's *edicts*, as he called them. One of these decreed that he forbade all trading with the natives. This meant only Argall himself might profit from Indian trade.

Other edicts proclaimed we were not to converse with mariners on ships. But what if Harrison returned? And how would we obtain our news from supply ships? Apparently, the good governor feared we might give the sailors information they would take back to England. What news did Argall fear we'd share? This meant, too, that we could no longer use our growing proceeds from tobacco to trade with any sailors.

Argall also announced he would put to death anyone who taught an Indian how to shoot a matchlock. Will's friend Chacrow, who knew how to shoot, felt unsafe and stayed away. Will had been one of those who had taught Chacrow to shoot, back in Sir Thomas Dale's day. Dale himself had not minded. During that time, other Indian friends learned to shoot as well.

Argall continued issuing edicts such as strict attendance at church and no waste of ammunition. The punishment for many of these edicts varied from lying neck and heels tied together, to three years' slavery to Virginia, to death.

The Bermuda Hundred settlers, whom George had freed as promised at the end of three years, would now go back to general slavery. The uproar around the colony was so serious and mutinous that Argall reluctantly and finally agreed to give the Bermuda Hundred settlers their freedom once more. Yet Argall's abuse of power was setting dangerous precedents.

In all, these proclamations presented a confining and frightening addition to Dale's laws, laws that George had significantly relaxed during his term of governorship.

Our husbands had left for James Cittie, but Tempie was still in her lying-in period.

I rocked little Argall, just two weeks old, as his innocent, wee eyes gazed curiously around. Tempie's other gossips prepared her chamber.

"Sweet babe," I murmured, kissing the child's forehead.

And while the chair squeaked against the wooden floor and the other women fussed over Tempie, I found my mind wandering.

I wondered about the baby's namesake and godfather. What would these next months hold? Could it...would it be possible for Argall to be even a more horrific force than Sir Thomas Dale himself had been? Dale's aims had been admirable if his techniques cruel.

But no one knew the goals of Captain Argall. Yet it was easy enough to suspect that enriching himself and perhaps enriching his sponsors in England was one.

Pray God, Lord De La Warr would arrive shortly and wrest control from Samuel Argall before this man Argall might do some serious damage.

Under the Graves
Late July 1617 ~ James Cittie

Behold, the hand of the Lord is upon thy cattle which is in the field, upon the horses, upon the asses, upon the camels, upon the oxen, and upon the sheep: there shall be a very grievous murrain.
—Exodus 9:3

Over the mountains
And over the waves,
Under the fountains
And under the graves...
—Anonymous, 17th century

As summer bore down with its blast of iron-forge heat, a contagion came upon us in our new homes at James Cittie. Tempie kept little Argall as safe and close to her as she might, fearing for him and for Elizabeth, now two. I fretted about Little Temp, also two, and wondered how Cecily and Tom fared upriver. I also kept careful watch on Tommy, five, and Jane, twelve. We could only hope that all the young ones were well seasoned enough to endure the sickness.

Perhaps the sun blazed too hard on those off ship, as the seasoning claimed a larger number of newcomers than usual. About a hundred settlers had come in the *George* with Argall, and many were ill or dying. Even some of the ancient planters succumbed, but the great mortality spared my household, the household of my daughter, and those of my closest friends.

With the blistering still heat and sickness came drought. The corn yellowed on its stalks, looking as pale and withered beneath the burning sun as we ourselves felt. We watched our corn die.

The tobacco, whose quality was finally becoming good enough to trade, dried up as well.

Peace with the natives mostly continued even as they themselves fell very ill, losing more than we did to the strange summer contagion. And the

Indians, too, watched their fields dry up. Soon, the tribes would be unable to pay their corn tribute to Governor Argall or any of their debts, causing tensions.

To add to the food worries in both English and Indian towns, a plague struck the deer, leaving a great many where they fell in the woods. The townsfolk whispered that the hand of God had smote again, for all remembered the murrains of the Bible.

When Captain Bargrave's pinnace sailed upriver in late June, it brought most interesting news from England.

"Hey, ho!" cried a sailor. "What do you know? In London, many thieves going to the gallows December last. The king said, 'Pardon some, and send them to Virginia.' So the Virginia Company sent a man to the hangings to choose the three strongest. 'You may live and go instead to Virginia,' said he. Standing at the hangman's noose, two of the condemned men accepted the offer. But not the third. He said, 'Let them go to Virginia! And they will remember me. Hangman, shorten your work!'"

So began the summer of 1617. Besides the cruel hand of the new Governor, all were dying: old planters, newcomers, Indians, deer, tobacco, and corn. And at that, threat of winter famine now hung in the air. Argall rationed stored corn once more, everything cut to half of what it had been.

Perhaps the condemned man had been right.

Governor Argall had assigned the Morton family to live with us, and so I prepared to make my home an inn once more. The family had come in on the *George* and had been living with two men in Kecoughtan, both of whom had died. So now, the Mortons had become my responsibility.

Mistress Morton tried to be helpful, but I could not find it in my heart to be gracious to her. How weary I was of sharing with those I knew not—even as we had little for ourselves. With Mistress Morton were her husband Jacob and her young son Isaac.

Would they survive the seasoning, I wondered? This, a particularly harsh summer.

Besides sharing with and tending to them, I was skeptical of becoming overly friendly with Mistress Morton.

I cannot befriend you, see. For I doubt you shall survive.

Mistress Morton was an amiable sort, and I put her to work helping me with things that needed doing like the mending, collecting eggs, tending the garden behind our home. I still had my daily work that the governor assigned away from home, as well. The governor had overlooked assigning the Mortons chores just yet, so the family could certainly help with what we had at home.

"Ah, I reckon I'm going to like it here," the mistress said with a refreshing cheerfulness. "My husband needed the work, him being a sturgeon dresser and what. A hard journey, but anything what's worth anything is going to be hard, that's what I told him. He's a dour one. I'm sorry about that. He didn't truly want to make the voyage, but willin' to if the opportunity be there. It'll be fine. That's what I told him. 'Never you worry for God's a-with us.'"

She seemed hearty enough. Perhaps, I thought, perhaps...

But no. A few weeks passed, and one morning she had not gotten from bed at the sun's rising. I went to see and found her flushed with fever.

And soon enough, little Isaac fell and Master Morton, too. All ill, lying in a row, bed and floor, moaning and hot and doubly uncomfortable with summer's fire burning all about them.

'Twas the husband that fell most ill with burning ague. *Ah, the seasoning strikes.* How many times had we seen it? Master Morton had not had any time to ply his trade.

Tommy, having no assigned duties from Argall, fetched water for the ill family. Here was a small boy, playing nurse to another small boy. It didn't seem right to me, but the Laws of Blood ordered Jane and me to work, and the Company forced me to bring sick newcomers to my home. What were any of us to do?

Tommy wet rags to put upon the family's heads to cool them. When Jane and I came home after church, we took over for a while. I had little barberry, for I had treated so many seasoning agues. Yet Mistress Morton had touched me with her enthusiasm for a dreary venture. Sassafras I did have. That was always good for the ague. But was there anything else I could do?

I went to Mistress Wright and begged advice.

She gave me a skeptical look. "I don't give my healing talisman out readily, you know."

"I know. I'll keep it safe. I promise. I have a sick and dying family...."

"Everyone's dyin', Mistress Peirce. Don't make you no different."

"Please, mistress." My eyes felt heavy with desperation. *Why was I trying to save this family?*

She sighed and from around her neck pulled off a necklace with a rusty-colored stone about the size of my thumb.

"Agate," she said. "To cure the ague and many other ills. Use it thus: lay the stone upon the forehead of the infirm. While pressing the agate with thy thumb into the forehead, chant, *Crux sancta sit mihi lux* thrice. 'Let the Holy Cross be my light.' The agate shall pull the ague out and absorb it into itself."

"*Crux sancta sit mihi lux*," I repeated, hoping I could remember. "*Crux sancta sit mihi lux.*"

"In this way is Satan repelled while the ague is drawn into the amulet," she continued, a bent finger before her face. "Take it, then. But return it to me before the sun drops below the trees, hear?" she said sternly, narrowing an eye. "I oughtn't to let it go from my body at all, you know. I take a great risk, but the greatest evils befall a body betwixt the setting and rising sun when the dead travel. If I have my agate back by then, all shall be well in my household."

"Aye, aye," I said, feeling humbled. "I thank you, Mistress Wright."

"Go! The sun drops even now."

I rushed back home to do as Mistress Wright instructed.

"What have you?" Mistress Morton asked me, her voice weak.

"Agate to remove the ague."

She took my hand. "You have given me a home. Tended me in my illness. Now you strive to save my family and me. Why?"

I considered that because I didn't know. The whole family were just more bellies needing food, food we may not soon have. Yet I couldn't bring myself to wish the worst on her.

At last I said, "You are me. You came with dreams of a better life, and now those dreams are broken, and the image you see is in a shattered looking glass. Jagged. Nothing fits. I...I am praying for your family." *Because I know you are all going to die,* I thought but did not say. *Everything* was dying, after all. What chance did this unseasoned woman have?

In the end, nothing could save the family, not agate, sassafras or prayer, as father and son both died. But Mistress Morton clung to life.

Jane went to let the soldiers know so that they could remove the bodies from the house. I turned away when they carried little Isaac through the door.

I was sorry to see Mistress Morton linger longest, as watching the others go was painful for her. "They're gone, ain't they? My husband, my son? Gone. Gone," she murmured, her fever at times breaking. "It'll be all right, Jacob. That's what I told him. It still will. We'll get us a little home and some land. You'll see..."

I squeezed her hand. "Mistress Morton. Irene. *The Lord is my shepherd,*" I prayed at her bedside. "Other pastures, a home ye'll have. Maybe here, or maybe in the Shepherd's fields."

Her yellowed eyes opened, but in the room was the specter of death. "That's what I told him. It'll be all right, come what may."

After she had died, I kept their clothes and possessions, giving Jacob's tools to Will. This was our pay for giving shelter and aiding the new arrivals. If they could not survive the seasoning, we rummaged for sorely needed items.

I sorted through the trunk, packed so carefully and so hopefully. I picked up her Bible, opening it to the first pages. There I found the date of her marriage, her mother's and father's deaths and her son's birthdate written inside. Also the date of a young infant girl named Hannah who had not survived a week.

I studied Irene's neat penmanship as she had written, *"Isaac Morton, borne ye 30ᵗʰ day of Marche 1612."* Born almost the same day as Tom.

I shut the Bible and laid it back inside the chest.

Then for some reason I did not fully understand, I began to cry. I wept into my hands, thinking that far too many dreams had died here in Virginia. Far too many had lost their lives, and for what?

Each day, each season, each year, family, friends, and strangers alike walked a path peppered with thorns.

Then I spoke to the still form of the woman for whom the soldiers had not yet come. "God's still a-with you," I whispered, echoing her own words. "It'll be all right. I'm sorry, Mistress Morton. Truly, I am."

And I was.

A Journey of Revenge
August 1617 to April 1618 ~ James Cittie, and at King Phillip's Palace, Madrid

Before you embark on a journey of revenge, dig two graves.
—Confucius

Will had recently received his desired promotion when Lieutenant William Powell received his promotion to captain. All the promoting had begun when Argall raised his favorite, Captain Nathaniel Powell, to sergeant major general. The two Powells were not kinsmen. As a soldier, Nathaniel had seniority in Virginia; he'd come in with the first ships in 1607.

The summer heat turned to cool fall nights. Before long, another winter was behind us, and spring had come. Food was short but we had averted famine. Will stayed anxious much of the time. As a new lieutenant, he had more responsibility than ever to protect the fort at James Cittie. We had not seen the Spanish, but we had not forgotten them.

Little did we know that in a palace in Madrid, a small, shiny nugget threatened to bring us to our knees.

* * *

Don Diego de Molina had spent five years as a prisoner at James Town. Finally, Governor Dale had brought the Spaniard back to England. The governor had hanged the English traitor Lembri from a yardarm just as the ship came in sight of England. Watching his compatriot swing lifelessly from high atop the ship had only fueled Molina's bubbling fury.

Leaving England soon after, Molina was at last about to return to his home country. He carried little with him except much, much hatred.

And that bright autumn morning of 1616, as Molina had glared back at Lands End, the last glimpse of the Cornish shore, he had only one thought upon his mind.

Venganza.

Revenge.

Two years had since passed. Molina had waited patiently, but his time, his opportunity, had now come.

The Duke of Lerma, the Spanish king's close friend and confidante, had the power and authority to secure Molina an audience with King Philip, an audience Molina desired more than life itself. For the years in the Virginia gaol had made him bitter, and he would not—could not—live unless he took *venganza* on the pathetic settlements spread along the James River.

How to do that? Molina had turned the idea of Virginia over in his mind.

Finally, a plan. He would, of course, require the king's blessing, but with the Duke of Lerma's support, how could Molina fail? And Molina had been friends with the duke for many years.

The duke had agreed to help, and at last the day of Molina's meeting with the king arrived.

I have come a long way from the dingy, rat-infested prison in Virginia, he thought. *And when I return to the Chesapeake Bay, the English shall always remember the name Don Diego de Molina!*

Now Molina approached the king's throne room at His Majesty's Palace, the Royal *Alcázar* in Madrid. The eloquent and still angry, Molina waited for his king to beckon him forward.

"Sire." Molina's head bowed deeply as he rested upon one knee. He waited for the king's acknowledgement.

The Duke stood to the king's right, stooping to whisper in His Majesty's ear. The king nodded, saying, "*Usted puede levantarse.*" *You may rise.*

"What is it you wish?" the king asked.

"I wish to thank you, sire, for the favor you have shown me in ensuring my release from the English hovels they call 'James Town.' Others with me were not so fortunate. You are aware that their Governor Dale hanged the man Francisco Lembri upon our first sight of the English shore? For they had learned his identity. Clark, the pilot, recognized him. And the English were determined to see revenge on Lembri, who had turned traitor and guided our vessels through the Narrow Sea in '88."

The king nodded and leaned closer. He was aware of Lembri's help with the ill-fated Armada attack. "A great loss, this Lembri who understood English waters so well. To secure your release we of course had to liberate the English pilot Clark. But you, sir, are worth more than five English pilots. Unless we wish to attack the plantation in Virginia. Then we should need a suitable guide. But…" He coiled his fingers and nonchalantly examined his nails. "We are assured that the English manage their colony poorly, as they manage so many other things poorly. Count Gondomar continues to tickle the ear of the English king. We have Little King James very much where we want him." He laughed mirthlessly. "They say that no one in England believes the Virginia colony will survive. The Indians slaughter them, disease and famine destroy them."

King Philip pounded his fist on the throne's arm suddenly, passionately. "King James does not understand the carefulness with which we tend our Spanish plantations. That we work hard to ensure their prosperity. The English king expects the riches to be free flowing. It is not so easy, Don Diego, is it?"

Molina drew a sharp breath. If indeed Philip's daughter, the *infant* Maria, had married King James's son as Gondomar had tried to arrange, Molina's next proposition would be pointless, even foolhardy. Such an alliance between Spanish and English might have meant long-term peace between the two countries. The marriage had not happened, and hence, Molina had an opening.

"Sire, I bring news of Virginia, and I can attest to the misery of the little colony. As Your Majesty is aware, I have seen firsthand, having been a prisoner there five years." He tried to keep his voice even. He did not wish to betray his pure hatred of the English lest his king suspect his judgment tainted or that he had ulterior motives.

Motives that he certainly possessed.

"And beyond news, sire, I bring Your Majesty something else." Now Molina reached into the pocket hanging on his belt and cautiously retrieved a piece of ore. He held it outward toward the king, and King Philip squinted to see.

"Well, well, what have you?" Philip asked impatiently.

"Silver, sire. Silver from the Virginia plantation. For the English have attempted to keep from my king the true mines of gold and silver in Virginia."

The king's brows lifted in surprise, and the Duke of Lerma leaned forward with a smirk.

"They speak of mines, but produce nothing!" the duke said to His Highness. "Yet see here, we have proof that such fruitful mines in Virginia do exist. And *we* have first claim to Virginia and any riches therein!"

Molina let the silver flash in his opened palm. "Your Majesty would not have the English procuring precious ores such as this? Ores rightly belonging to the Spanish." He looked from the king to the duke, knowing that the duke had already agreed to support his proposition.

"Give it to me!" Philip cried, snatching it from Molina. The king studied it, turning it over in his hands seeing that the piece was indeed silver.

Molina made bold to press his point. "Sire, I ask your royal permission to send me with six ships that I may attack Virginia. For she is indeed a weak plantation. Her soldiers think they are the best in Europe, bragging of their experience in the Low Countries. But I have seen these soldiers for what they are—ill-trained cowards who *know not* how to build a fort nor man it. Six ships, sire, are all I shall need to destroy this colony and collect the silver!"

The don bowed his head again respectfully. "Trust me, sire."

The silver glinted in the king's hand, almost beckoning him to action. Philip turned to Molina and said coldly, "You shall act as if alone. We shall aver that we were unaware of such action." To the duke, he added, "See that this man has the ships he desires. Let them attack!"

A Dark Conspiracy
Late April 1618 ~ Ponta Delgada on the Isle of São Miguel in the Azores

When the Night doth meet the Noon
In a dark conspiracy...
—John Keats

The *Neptune* and her sister ship the *Treasurer,* met one another at São Miguel in the Azores. Both ships were en route to Virginia.

At these islands, Lord De La Warr asked Captain Elfrith of the *Treasurer* to come aboard the *Neptune.* La Warr's ship was overcrowded, and the baron wished to place some of his people aboard the *Treasurer.*

Elfrith hesitated. The baron pressed for numbers, forcing Elfrith to admit that indeed his ship had per ton far fewer passengers than the *Neptune.* Elfrith agreed to bring the dozen people aboard his ship as the baron requested.

La Warr had not noticed Captain Elfrith's reluctance. Otherwise, the baron might have had early warning that the *Treasurer* carried much more than passengers. The *Treasurer's* owners, Governor Argall and Lord Rich, had outfitted the *Treasurer* for a different sort of voyage. The honest baron knew nothing about the *Treasurer's* true mission, and Rich's allies intended to keep it that way.

Elfrith asked, "Might I have your approval, my Lord, to travel ahead toward Virginia? Since we're taking the northern route via Canada, we shall rest there and await you." With good fortune, Elfrith added, he might catch enough fish to bring back to James Cittie.

La Warr agreed. He was greatly relieved about transferring some passengers to the *Treasurer.* The more crowded a ship, the sicklier all aboard were likely to be. The baron had placed the last of his money into building this ship and recruiting the settlers aboard. Lord La Warr knew that his support was the tiny thread that kept the Virginia Company from giving up on Virginia. This present expedition must succeed.

La Warr's visit with the Portuguese Governor of Saint Michael's Island had several goals. The first was to signal friendship and respect since the English ships were passing through Portuguese waters. Spain ruled Portugal, after all. It was imperative that these islands allowed all ships safe passage to Virginia and not hinder their voyages. Perhaps other English ships could stop to water in the Azores after the baron himself opened the way.

The second goal was more personal to La Warr. He hoped this rest mid-ocean would promote good health for both his passengers and himself. The baron understood that if something were to happen to him, his wife would become impoverished. He had promised her they would be together again once more whether he returned to England or she came to Virginia. This was a promise he would keep on his oath.

Besides resting, the baron also sought oranges and lemons, which grew abundantly in the Azores. During his first stay in Virginia, the baron had suffered terribly with scurvy among many other illnesses. He could do little to stave off gout, ague, and flux, but fresh juice on the voyage would go a long way toward preventing and curing the dread and painful disease.

Now, with the *Treasurer* having set off for North Virginia, De La Warr took in the rolling countryside—mountains and lagoons, bountiful sugar, olive oil, pomegranates, oranges, woad for cloth dying, and cheeses from the cattle grazing on the hills above Saint Michael.

A shame such a place, these islands, belonged to the Portuguese under the Spanish flag.

The Portuguese certainly had found these islands first.

Two hundred years before, Prince Henry the Navigator had used his exploring skill to search for the mythical Prester John, leader of a Christian country somewhere. Asia? Africa? No one knew where this mysterious land lay, the land of mirrors showing all the Christian world, located right next to the earthly entrance to heaven! In attempting to find Prester John, King Henry had discovered these nine islands. The Portuguese called this archipelago the Azores, *land of the hawks.*

And no wonder. For even as he stood upon the winding streets of the island's capital city, Punta Delgada, the baron saw several of the great birds circling aloft on the Atlantic winds.

Peregrines, he said to himself.

For many years, tensions from war with Spain and Portugal had made it impossible for the English to use these islands as a port of call. But King James's overly close relationship with the Spanish ambassador had at least opened these islands to English usage once more.

Situated in a lonely ocean, the Azores formed the westernmost border of Europe, a way station for the seafarer en route to Africa or the New World. The islands were nearly but not quite, halfway across the ocean between England and Newfoundland.

Land in the middle of the ocean! God's blessing for the tired seafarer. A perfect location to relade supplies and refresh for the rest of the journey.

Rest, in La Warr's mind, was a good thing. Having required nearly seven years—*seven!*—to recover from his last stay in Virginia, the baron was taking no chances with his health. After a brief stay in the Azores, he would rest again in Newfoundland and then go on to James Town. By breaking the voyage into three parts, Lord La Warr hoped that he would enter Virginia well and strong. Virginia needed him, and his wife needed him.

The baron did not dare allow all the nearly two hundred adventurers to disembark lest they overwhelm the island and embarrass him by untoward behaviors. Instead, the baron chose thirty to come ashore with him, including his servant Affonso from Lisbon who would act as translator. Captain Beamonte, ship's master, and Captain Brewster, the commanding officer, would remain aboard to manage the passengers. The baron also asked his Persian servant, John Martyn, to stay on ship to protect his belongings. Martyn's services were a gift from his wife's brothers, both deeply involved in Persian diplomacy.

The Azorean people were a hardy lot, De La Warr noted. As well they needed to be. In years past, corsairs—English, Algerian and Spanish—had attacked the islands. And when the king of Spain had overtaken the Portuguese Empire, the Azoreans had defended their island longest of all.

The isolation forced the Azoreans to be good stewards of crops they grew, fish they caught, and livestock they possessed.

In that, these Portuguese reminded him somewhat of his own pioneers, the planters in Virginia he would soon be leading once more. For, while his settlers dealt with native attacks, the Azoreans faced very different foes: volcanoes erupting, earthquake shocks, landslides destroying whole towns.

Thinking of Virginia swelled the baron's heart with pride, as well it should have.

Many of England's noble families professed great love and belief in the young colony. Some spoke eloquently of what it meant to keep a foothold in the New World before the Spanish, and now the French and Dutch, usurped all its vast promise. Others, like the baron, believed very much that the New World should be a Christian enterprise, a mission field for the natives. The Indian princess Pocahontas had truly renewed the baron's missionary zeal as well as his hopes for the colony's success.

Virginia should be a land that permitted the Separatists to worship, which was illegal in England. The baron had hoped that the group of religious dissenters now actively planning to come to the New World might finalize their plans in time to come with him. For he felt instinctively that the deep Protestant devotion of these men would be a good thing on Virginia shores.

Other nobility had opened their burses. This much was true.

The powerful Lord Rich had a great interest in Virginia, but Lord La Warr knew that Rich would never dream of coming to the New World himself. Baron De La Warr was amongst the highest ranking of the nobility to support Virginia and the only one bold enough to venture there, to trudge through the muddy streets of James Town and to travel upriver to the Indian towns therewith.

The baron had gone to Virginia the first time at the age of thirty-three, eight years before, only to find the relics of the Starving Time. He had then learned that Sir Thomas Gates and all his party of one hundred fifty had survived the hurricane at sea. The bitter news mixed with the sweet.

Virginia, it seemed, was gentle on no one's heart.

Besides simply going to Virginia, Lord La Warr had given the outrageous sum of five hundred pounds forty shares, more than anyone else of nearly one thousand investors, more even than whole companies had invested.

His financial stake went well past that, as he ventured additional funds toward the actual settling of the colony, money toward specific expenses as they had arisen. The rippling sails of the *Neptune* behind him represented one such expense.

He had sworn to the Company that even if they gave up on Virginia, he himself would not but would continue funding it *alone*.

Lord De La Warr had put the largest part of his inherited fortune toward this Christian colonization he so much believed in, and even more than that, he had now gone deeply in debt to do so. He knew, in fact, that if the colony did not soon produce profit, and if he should not survive while here, his wife and seven children would be left bereft of funds.

Impoverished.

A pang went through the baron, but he allowed himself no such thoughts on this balmy day in late April with the rugged beauty of the grey volcanic peaks stretching before him.

Instead, he silently praised God for the truce which allowed him, an Englishman, to set foot on this Spanish-held Portuguese island—his last and best prayer that the voyage should not weaken him unduly.

God was good.

There being no Protestant churches on this utterly Catholic island, Lord De La Warr had taken prayer on ship before coming ashore. The old church dedicated to St. Sebastian was lovely, but the baron knew that it was inappropriate for him to worship inside, and he dare not risk offending his host, the governor of Saint Michael's Island, Dom Manuel Luis Baltazar da Câmara, Second Earl of Vila Franca.

In fact, strange pairing that they were, the Protestant English baron was finding the Catholic Portuguese earl to be delightful company.

Behind Him Lay the Gray Azores
Late April, 1618 ~ Ponta Delgada on the Isle of São Miguel in the Azores

Behind him lay the gray Azores,
Behind the Gates of Hercules;
Before him not the ghost of shores,
Before him only shoreless seas.
The good mate said: "Now must we pray,
For lo! the very stars are gone.
Brave Admiral, speak, what shall I say?"
"Why, say, 'Sail on! sail on! and on!'"
—Joaquin Miller

Dom Manuel told the baron through De La Warr's interpreter Affonso that he had planned a feast in honor of the Englishman's arrival. Did the baron have a preference as to which day? For Dom Manuel wished to give the baron ample time to rest.

Affonso relayed the message. Lord De La Warr in turn asked his host if Friday might be acceptable. The baron was reckoning on a few days to rest before the feast and a few days to rest after, and then to sail for Newfoundland before the heat became too oppressive.

The earl looked gravely concerned and addressed Affonso. He spoke earnestly and seemed to be, the baron thought, pleading a case.

At last, Affonso turned to his master. "My Lord, he wishes that it may not be on Friday. Any day except Friday or Sunday, the Lord's day. But certainly never on a Friday."

Puzzled, the baron was about to ask why when Affonso continued. "You see, my Lord, he says that he wonders that you do not know about laughing on Friday? He hopes this to be a most festive event. He himself plans to laugh much, but laughing on a Friday brings ill luck and he would not have any brought upon you or upon himself."

The earl spoke once more to Affonso, and Affonso turned to Lord La

Warr. "Of course, the governor says, if you are to see a spider spinning its web, this brings good luck. It is possible one may undo the other. However, the earl prefers to take no chances with wicked fate." And then Affonso added a message of his own, "They are very superstitious here, my Lord."

When at last the feast day came, the Azoreans had done their utmost to make the baron feel welcome, and, he felt honored at the splendid hospitality.

The earl, Dom Manuel, had presented not one but several hogs to be slaughtered at the table, a treat to have fresh meat upon an ocean voyage! And La Warr was impressed at the generosity since pork, or any animal meat, was such a precious commodity. Other platters contained stews, breads and fruits.

The candles placed at intervals down the long oak table flickered.

The baron allowed himself not to feel uncomfortable when those at the table crossed themselves and said a Catholic prayer. Instead, La Warr recognized that the one God might someday put an end to the after-effects of the bloody Reformation which had been causing wars for a hundred years. He did not himself believe in these rituals, but he sensed the sincerity of the earl with his swarthy dark eyes and hair, such a contrast to the baron's grey eyes, red hair, and fair skin. The two men looked nothing alike, and their beliefs were utterly different. If they could be friendly, there was hope for the world, the baron thought.

The baron recognized, too, that Dom Manuel did have other motives; that is, the Portuguese earl coveted English friendship. The earl was aware of the great power the baron held over all those ships sailing to or from Virginia. As more English trafficking crossed near the Azores, Dom Manuel had reckoned that friends of his Spanish king were friends of his. And perhaps those friends would not attack his island ever again.

"Este dia, nós partimos o pão junto com os irmãos. Porque todos os homens, certamente, são irmãos nos olhos do senhor. Nos não são, meu amigo?" The earl was smiling, directing a dish laden with fresh bread to the baron.

Affonso leaned to his lord and whispered, "He says, 'This day, we break bread together as brothers. For all men are indeed brothers in the eyes of the Lord. Is it not so, my friend?'"

Lord La Warr felt warmth come over him at this unexpected graciousness. "Tell him, 'Indeed, I thank him for his kindness.'"

Affonso faithfully repeated, *"Certamente. Eu agradeço-lhe por sua bondade."*

The Portuguese earl beamed and raised his hands in delight. *"Em São Miguel, mais do que todas as outras ilhas Açorianas, nós somos mais hospitaleiros!"*

Affonso nodded and translated. "He says 'On São Miguel, more than any other Azorean isle, we understand true hospitality!'"

The festive meal went on and on until at last two servants brought out the cakes and puddings. 'Twas then that Dom Manuel clapped and called, *"E, agora, música!"* And, now, music!

From the corner of the room stepped a man holding an unusual lute. The man sang as he strummed a lively tune.

"He is playing Portuguese folk ballads, my Lord. And the lute is called a *viola Açoriana,* an Azorean viola," whispered the attentive Affonso.

The evening was proving to be most entertaining. As for the next day, Dom Manuel had promised Lord De La Warr a treat. For, as the fates had decreed, the baron had come to São Miguel at branding time. Tomorrow would be bullfighting with cape and sword.

Now the earl's wife, Dona Leonor de Vilhena, leaned toward Lord De La Warr and raised her eyebrows and nodded to him a clear gesture asking his approval. She gestured toward the bull branding and, forming her words carefully in English, said, "Do you like, my Lord?"

The serious lord, the Third Baron De La Warr, did something he rarely did.

He laughed aloud. Ah, the joy of it! The viola and the pork, the octopus stew, the earl's obvious doting on his own diplomatic moment. And peace between Spain and England that made the Azores a second home in the midst of the long ocean voyage.

"Aye, my lady, I like very much!"

Yet as La Warr departed the feast, he tripped on an uneven stone. His shoe slipped into a crevice, causing him to fall off balance and twisting his ankle as well. He paused to rub the bruise he knew was forming. As he did so, the Portuguese earl pointed to the baron's shoe with an alarmed exclamation.

Even Affonso looked uneasy as he said, "My Lord, your host gives his apologies. He says you must beware, for you have injured your foot. The foot is the symbol of the journey, which means bad fortune is coming your way very soon."

Happened a Most Fearefull Tempest
May 11, 1618 ~ James Cittie

Some [demons] are also in the thick black clouds, which cause hail, lightning and thunder, and poison the air, the pastures and grounds.
—Martin Luther

On the eleventh of May [1618], about ten of the clocke in the night, happened a most fearefull tempest, but it continued not past halfe an houre, which powred downe hailestones eight or nine inches about, that none durst goe out of their doors, and though it tore the barke and leaves of the trees, yet wee finde not they hurt either man or beast; it fell onely about James Towne, for but a mile to the East and twentie to the West, there was no haile at all."
—John Rolfe, June 1618

We had endured the extreme droughts last summer such that the previous fall and winter had been lean, as expected. Last summer's sickness had kept many workers from the field as well. We had not starved, but all were gaunt.

Still, a new spring brought hope of a better crop. One more year behind us.

Virginia could be a violent mother, pouring forth riches of the earth and sky one moment, withholding needed rain and then shattering us with raging temper the next.

The Indian king Powhatan had been in his grave less than a month when wicked skies poured forth frozen fury. Some said the old chief took his revenge at last, and others called it a fearsome omen of things to come. But what things? *God, what evil to befall now?* Some said that demons themselves attacked Virginia.

Whatever its cause, the mighty storm awakened Will and me with a jolt.

The screeching, howling winds flung hailstones the size of small pumpions against the house onto the roof and barn.

Will grabbed for a nightshirt and leapt from bed.

I, too, jumped out of bed and bolted as quickly as I might up the ladder to Tommy and Jane's loft.

If anything, the storm raged loudest in the rafters. The crashes and bangs were almost rhythmic. Here something fell. There something flew. The storm's own rattling and booming provided the background commotion.

In between, we caught the sound of the horse stomping and whinnying in his stall, the cattle lowing. The animals were terrified.

The house shook. Would it stand? I reached the plank flooring and crawled towards my little son's bed.

The bark roof was just over my head, so close I could touch it. I reached for the roof instinctively as if I might stop it from collapsing. *The Indians do build them like this, and they understand this wild Virginia weather.*

I crept over to Tommy's bed and found him, covers pulled upon his head. Jane had bent over him, trying to calm him.

Will was yelling. What was he saying?

"Aye?"

He could not hear me, or I him, over the din of icy stones pelting the whole fort. I crawled back to the ladder and stuck my head down. This time I could understand him.

Will's voice boomed from below. "Thomas, tend your mother and sister. I am going to check on the livestock!"

Where was safest? The roof might give way, so I called to the children, "Come, come!"

We heard the door rip from Will's hand and slam against the wall. He had flung the door open, but he was going nowhere for he saw now that the hail was so huge, a falling piece might split his skull. What manner of evil was this?

Tommy, Jane, and I inched down the ladder to the great room. Once there, I saw that the boy wanted to look brave for his father, yet he had both arms wrapped around my waist and cowered at each peal of thunder.

Will stood in the doorway for a moment, mute, lightning splaying so that we saw night and day in alternating scenes.

Noise assaulted the house: the screaming wind and hail, the banging of shutters, the hammering of stones against the ground and roof, limbs snapping and dropping, even bark ripping off the trees. Once or twice, whinnying of a terrified horse rose above the din.

Will watched in something akin to horror, ignoring the door flapping against the wall, as the enormity of the storm and its consequences dawned upon him. Finally, he grabbed the door and put all his weight against it to push it shut, then he let the latch fall across it.

The livestock were on their own.

There was a time back in Melcombe where I'd wondered if we would have locks on our doors at James Town, and now I knew. But locks could not keep starvation and sickness from our door, they could not keep Indians out, and they could scarcely keep the ferocious weather at bay.

Fall and winter had been lean due to last summer's drought and the death of so many plagued deer. Governor Argall had sent to Bermuda for relief corn to prevent famine. We had counted on this spring and summer to make up for last year's losses.

Now, with Lieutenant Powell promoted to captain of the Governor's Guard, Will stood second to him as lieutenant. The repercussions of the storm would fall heavily to these two.

Will walked to where I and the children stood. He wrapped his arms around us, and his heartsick expression said much.

To the storm outside, Will only murmured, "My crop. Our crops. Corn and tobacco, our food and trade. Gone again, I know it." To me, he said, "Pray God, this storm is not striking with equal violence all over Virginia. Or we be famished again come fall."

The Screech Owl's Cry
May 28, 1618 ~ James Cittie

Poor old pilgrim Misery,
Beneath the silent moon he sate,
A-listening to the screech owl's cry,
And the cold wind's goblin prate…
—Thomas Lovell Beddoes

Seal up your lips, and give no words but mum:
The business asketh silent secrecy.
—William Shakespeare

The first cry sounded almost like a woman or child calling out, but what was she saying? George Yeardley, who had been tossing in bed in the late spring heat, sat up. It had been a restless night anyway.

The voice came again, and this time George realized it was not a woman at all but a screech owl somewhere near his window.

An owl! George reckoned one more ill omen fit well with the sudden, strange hailstorm and the news he had for Tempie, who lay sleeping peacefully beside him.

Haunting, ghostly, an almost warble-like trill sounding into the window through which moonlight also danced.

Virginia nights were already becoming uncomfortably hot, but this was not the reason George had slept poorly and found himself in a sweat. No, it was neither owl nor heat that woke him so much as the nightmare of all that fell upon his shoulders.

He got up and stood near the open window, willing a breeze to come through it. He could not actually see the moon, but its light bathed the commons in soft color, a soothing grey light. The owl warbled again, and George stood listening. Just listening.

What troubles are you bringing me? he wondered of the bird somewhere in the darkness.

How long he stared at the neighbors' houses and the night sky, George could not say. At last, the owl quieted, but George's mind never did.

Tempie rolled over, reaching to put her arm around her husband, and found him gone. She stirred and saw his shadowy figure outlined in the window. Moonlight made his face and hair appear silvery. She watched him reach up and grasp his head in his hands.

"George? What is it?" she whispered, fearing to wake the children. "Are you ill?"

He turned slowly and sat upon the edge of the bed. "You should be asleep," he said at last.

"As should you. But you are not. Something's weighing on you. What is it?"

George drew a deep breath and tried to sound nonchalant. "An owl near the window woke me."

She felt a shiver run through her. An owl! *Good Lord, what next?* What sort of evil did it foretell? She listened but heard nothing. She suspected that an owl which had already flown off would not cause George to be still at the window. "Aye, an owl. Dreadful, witchy bird! But surely, something else is keeping you up. What is it?"

It may as well be now as later, he thought. He drew a deep breath. Where to begin?

"Well, you'll have to know soon enough. This situation with Argall has a number of the counselors worried. This man was once was my friend!" He raised his voice in frustration, then sighed again. Indeed, and the Yeardleys' son, little Argall, would forever carry the legacy of Sir Samuel Argall, both in name and as his godfather.

Tempie sat up, too, and patted her husband's back. "And what are you to do? Argall is the governor now officially. You were but the deputy governor whom Dale appointed when he left. If you should complain of Argall's conduct, some might think you jealous of him receiving your position." She said these words as kindly as possible, fearing to offend her husband.

"That has occurred to me," he said dully. "And yet no one is better suited than I—having once held the governor's office myself."

Tempie felt her heart go upward to her throat. "Better suited than you to...what?"

He reached over, putting his hand upon her leg. "Better suited than I to accompany Argall's letter to England. He must not know the reasons we are truly going to the Company offices. He must believe we are still allies. Otherwise, this man shall lay waste to the colony with his looting of Virginia Company property, his self-serving *edicts*, and his piracy! Now it becomes clear. He makes his home in Kecoughtan by the shore to be near the booty he expects. The Virginia Company is bound to be alarmed at his latest letter. So we shall go, pretending to take care of our own business. We have good enough reason: the Weyanoke land."

Tempie understood. A few months ago while George was still governor, Opechancanough had granted George several thousand acres at Tanks Weyanoke. George had begun to use this property as the base of a tobacco and farming operation, had a mind, even, to place a windmill there. But the land was not truly his until the Company ratified it. George could certainly have handled this through letters to and from the Company. Still, Weyanoke seemed a plausible explanation to give to Argall.

George continued, "The truth, of course, is that we shall go to alert the Company to our genuine concerns. We are not all *pirates!*"

The one word that had struck Tempie's ears was *we*. "We? Are we all going? The children and I as well? To England?" She began to breathe rapidly, not knowing if she were excited about the possibility of seeing her home again or terrified at the prospect of the sea voyage. The hurricane had left a deep scar, a fear of sea travel, upon her. She realized that she would love nothing better than to visit England again after nine years. *Nine years!* But the thought of sailing again filled her with fear. Her belly seemed to have never been the same since she had eaten those red berries during the Starving Time, so she would doubly struggle with seasickness. The children might fall ill amid the cramped quarters and the poor victuals. And they would endure the ever-present threat of Spanish or pirate attack…

Now her mind, too, raced as quickly as her husband's. "What are you saying? That you want us all to go?"

"I am saying I want you and the children with me in case the Virginia Company decides I should not return. I do not know the consequences of this action. I expect to return. Oh, I do. But there exists the possibility the Company will take forceful measures. If this be so, and they make me aware of it as they surely shall do, then we may sell our lands and remain in England. We do not know how the Company shall react when it learns that most of its few assets are…gone."

He choked out the last word. Stolen. Sold off. *How had this happened? Who would have guessed that Governor Argall would think he had license to take what rightly belonged to the Company and appropriate it as his own?*

The Company might take desperate action? Then of course she must go, Tempie realized. For if she remained and Argall learned of his friend's treachery, might he find a way to punish her? And the children? These things her husband had no doubt already considered, but had chosen not to mention.

"When?" was all she could say.

He gazed at her seriously. "Very soon. If the wind is up, we hope to leave by the end of June."

"June?" Tempie was shocked. First he had told her that not only was he leaving for England, but that they all must go. Now he was saying they would have only a month to prepare? For a voyage of this magnitude? And then realizing the conditions, she said, "George, why so soon? And in the heat? Can we not wait until fall?"

He shook his head. "No, absolutely not. The situation is dire, Tempie. The stakes are high, and someone must warn the Company in person. The council agrees. I am the one to do it. I am the highest-ranking Company official here. I wish De La Warr would get himself back to Virginia! But we can wait no longer. The situation just keeps growing worse. Those so-called *edicts*..."

The edicts made it clear that Argall was clamping down so that all profit of the colony—little that it was!—would belong to Argall and to his benefactor, Lord Rich, son of the Third Baron Rich.

Tempie felt confused. "Can...can the crew be ready that soon?" Every ship's crew needed some land time, time to recover from the voyage before setting sail again.

George smoothed his beard as if pondering the question. "Well, six weeks is a minimum to rest up. Aye," he said at last. "If things here were not so desperate, we would never attempt a summer voyage, as you well know. And we would not force the crew to, either." An ill crew could be downright dangerous at sea. All remembered the *Unity*, which had sailed ashore with none well but the master and one boy. Fortunately, another ship had been able to lend her some hands. But the *George* would be alone in the ocean. She needed twelve able-bodied mariners aboard. If George were pushing everyone this way, he clearly felt desperate.

The heat was a concern. The sweating they did now as they sat upon the bed with no breeze to cool them was nothing compared with the late June, mid-July, August heat on the ocean. The sun would beat mercilessly upon the ship, broiling those in the 'tween deck. This, Tempie realized, was nearly the time they had sailed across the first time.

The heat, the calenture, the seasickness, the children...

"George," she said weakly. "No, please." She was becoming ill just thinking of it. If they must go, the autumn would be so much better.

He took her hand. "Argall's piracy unchecked could bring Spanish warships here any time. We'll be fine; the children will be fine. Frankly, Tempie, we have no other choice. I am sorry to say it." He looked down. How many times did Company men put their wives in the way of danger? *Far too many.*

He went on. "Between Argall's looting of Company property, his harsh enforcement of martial law, the hailstorm—*good Lord!*—destroying a portion of our crops all around James Town Island. Then the *George* arrives. Five months at sea? Who has heard the like? Five months, and all her provisions spoiled when we so desperately need them. No, Tempie," he said. "We must depart quickly. The *George* has to rush back for supplies, and we shall also have to make haste to prepare." He squeezed her hand once more. "*Ours* is an important mission!"

"*Ours?*" She smiled and said, "Well, thank thee for the credit, but the mission is *yours*."

"We have to get word back to England immediately. They must hear from me, speaking for the entire council, what it is their governor does. And…" He drew a deep breath. "This will no doubt draw the wrath of Sir Robert Rich."

Tempie nodded even though she knew her husband could scarcely see her in the darkness with just a touch of moonlight upon the bed. Lord Rich was a powerful man with an agenda. And Sir Samuel Argall was a friend, ally, and cousin of Lord Rich. All suspected the earl secretly paid Argall to turn Virginia events in his favor.

Now the heat of the chamber was no match for the chill that went through Tempie. She was beginning to understand all this might mean—the political battles ahead. And what would Argall do when he realized he'd been betrayed?

"Argall will hate you," she whispered.

Her husband murmured quietly, "Aye. And so he will. But 'tis no more than my feelings toward him at the moment."

"George!" Tempie cried in alarm. "That is not the Christian way. We are bound to forgive."

"You just said Argall would hate me. Isn't he to forgive as well?" George had a cynical tone in his voice. "You know the answer. Argall is an arrogant man, greedy and desirous of fame and wealth. A bachelor. He doesn't even *have* a family to support. His riches are his and his alone. He will hate me, and no forgiveness shall there ever be. Unless, of course, it betters his purse. Argall is not a forgiving man."

"And so he is not," his wife replied quietly. She did not like the way this was going at all. A thought occurred to her.

"May I tell Joan?" she asked.

Still holding his wife's hand, George patted it with his other hand. "You may tell her we are leaving for England to tend our affairs overseas. You *may not* tell her why we truly are going. I trust you with this confidence. Even to your closest friend, you must not share this information. Besides," he added, "it will be best she *not* know. For any such information that leaks back from England will bring questions. She might tell Will. If you value your friend's family, you will hear and obey this. I tell you because I cannot *not* tell you. You would know by my manner, as you already have, that something was amiss."

"So what do I do?" she whispered.

"You have but a few weeks to prepare. You will pack the children, let your friends know that business takes us home to England, and never make anyone aware that more than that is going on. I will tell Argall I've business in England and offer to escort his letter to the Company. I will not betray that I have a story to tell the Company. Else he wouldn't allow me to leave anyway. *Martial law* and all that." His anger spilled out on the last phrase. How sick everyone was of martial law! And how much had Argall twisted it to his own uses. The only reprieve the colony had from the Laws of Blood was when he, Yeardley, had been Governor.

"I will make a forceful case to the Company once and for all that they repeal these heinous laws and that newer, just laws replace them. *We deserve Englishmen's rights.* If we are fortunate," he added, "and Lord La Warr has recovered his health, he may be ready to sail if he has not already. I shall certainly urge his speedy departure if he's still in England. We need his kind and generous guidance now more than ever. He has the power and authority to override the tyrant Argall. And his title supersedes Sir Robert Rich's." *At least until Lord Rich inherits his father's barony.*

Lord De La Warr had seemed harsh in his judgments upon us in his first days. But compared to the ferocity with which Sir Thomas Dale meted punishments and the greed of Argall that threatened to topple Virginia's few assets, Lord De La Warr was clearly the most just and able to rule as governor. No one doubted that now.

Tempie was nodding. All of what her husband said she understood even if she still did not want to go.

"That is the plan, then," George finished. "You must begin at once the domestic preparations while I ensure that I have arrangements for the tobacco and corn harvest and management of our property while we're away." He placed a finger upon his wife's lips and noticed she was trembling a bit.

"And give no words but mum, my darling. None but mum."

The Stars Know a Secret
May 29, 1618 ~ James Cittie

The stars know a secret
They do not tell;
And morn brings a message
Hidden well.
—Edward Rowland Sill

I had awakened feeling joyful. Some days were like that. The wildflowers were blooming, and the birds had returned after months of silence. Their songs made me happy. One never realized how quiet the woods had been until they were no longer so. The trees themselves were alive, and on this balmy day nothing could destroy my peace.

I had been up before the dawn and beaten a few linens. A fresh, bright home to match the brightness of the day and even the brightness of my good humor.

The dawn had broken in luminous colors. The mornings in May were the best, bright and mild. I had also gathered a basket of eggs, enjoying that the weather was no longer biting cold as I searched the nests. Despite the heat, the strange hail, and the dry season, I still felt any summer must be better than the last. Mistress Morton's dying words came back to me. *It'll be all right, come what may.* But I pushed the memory of her away. I did not want to think of death this morning. We would have a better season this year. Aye, it had to be. The hail had been hard on our crops. But at least the storm had only struck around James Cittie—another omen that maybe Chief Powhatan had sent it from his grave. Thoughts of death again. *No!*

Instead, as I collected the eggs that morning, I hummed an old ballad my mother used to sing.

> *By a bank as I lay*
> *Musing on a thing that was*
> *Past and gone, Heigh-ho!*

In the merry month of May,
Oh! Somewhat before the day
Methought I heard at the last.
Oh, the gentle nightingale,
The lady and the mistress of all music,
She sits down ever in the dale;
Singing with her notes small,
And quavering them wonderfully thick.
Oh, for joy my spirits were quick...

Tempie, too, had wandered over with her own egg basket. This was a favorite thing of us to do, visit after gathering eggs. This gave us a brief moment before preparing breakfast for our families and the six o'clock drumbeat. I was eager today, for I had something to show her.

"Tempie, don't you love May? The trees are so green again. Another winter behind us! Did you see that some of the herbs are coming up?" Every winter continued to be a challenge for those of us who were Starving Time survivors. We seemed to all feel the fear creeping upon us even as August was rounding the bend toward September and Virginia still warm most of the day. Even chilly mornings worked on us, for they always foretold the bitter to come.

Now with another winter behind us, and the plants rising from the earth, I felt my heart lighter once more. *Another winter past!* I felt almost like a girl again.

"And you won't believe it." I was still carrying on, for I had good news. "The *George* brought a letter from home from Will's cousin Tom Peirce. And one from Tom's wife Alice as well. They are coming, Tempie! Will has been working on Tom for some time. 'I believe the worst is over, Tom. You should get yourself here. Tobacco prices are rising!'" I tried to deepen my voice to sound like Will and laughed at the effort. "Alice is Ensign Spencer's sister, so the Peirces have double reason to come. They're bringing their daughter Elizabeth, too. She's nine years years old. Isn't that exciting?"

I had been rambling so quickly I had failed to notice Tempie's downcast eyes. She tried to smile. "Oh, that's just wonderful to hear, Joan."

Tempie was still staring into her basket of eggs, staring as if she had never seen eggs before.

"Anything new in there?" I asked with a chuckle. Nothing could spoil my mood this day, not even the tallow I would face later.

When she looked up again, tears rimmed her eyes and her voice shook. She tried to force brightness. "I won't be here to meet Tom Peirce's family, lovey. In fact, you'll have to enjoy the rest of the year without me, I fear. Perhaps the next, too." She reached a hand up to her mouth, and the tears began spilling.

I was confused and reached over to comfort her. "What's wrong, Tempie? And…and I don't take your meaning."

She began to cry in earnest now, caught herself and realized she might drop the eggs and so sat the basket at her feet. She tried to compose herself, sighed, and said, "Joan. George tells me 'tis time, time to return…to England." And she began crying anew.

"England?" My words came out as a whimper. "You're…you're leaving us?"

She nodded and wiped her tears away. "Aye, Joan, I love you. You know I do."

"I love you, too," I said, my words sounding like a croak.

"I…I do not want to go. Oh, I would *love* to see home and my mother again, make no mistake! If I could *think* myself there…" She laughed despite herself. "And *think* my way home again. But eight more weeks at sea." She began to shake at the thought.

"Sit down, sit down." We dropped upon the bench in front of the house, side by side. We had been, I thought, side by side through so many things. Now this?

"And George heard an owl's call late last night as he made his decision. So pray, Joan. Please pray for my family."

I took her hand. *An owl!* "I will pray," I whispered. "In the church and at the hearth until you return. But why must you go?"

"Joan, you knew it had to come sooner or later. George's business investments are…growing." Her voice faltered. "He…he needs to see to them in London." She tried to steady her voice. "'Tis truly *for the best.*" She emphasized the words. "Wait and see! Before long, Will shall tell you the same thing, that 'tis time to return. Maybe you'll even sail back to London while we're still there.…" Her voice had a forced brightness. "I am not afraid, truly I'm not."

I gazed at her for a long moment. Every line, every crease in her face said, *Fear.*

"Liar."

She laughed and pressed her cheek against mine. "Aye. I'm lyin'. You know I am. In matter of fact, I am *terrified.*"

And who to blame her? The sea voyage itself was risky enough, but we were hurricane survivors. We had seen a mighty tempest that few Europeans besides ourselves had ever experienced and lived to tell about.

I knew the thought of sailing caused me to quake. Yet my desire to return home had been strong since before Tommy was born. And he was now six.

Besides perilous voyage, there remained the possibility of her growing ill or weakened so that illness in England might take her. *Take her.* 'Twas then that the words hit me full force. *She might never return. Dear God, Death is shadowing me this morning.*

"When...when are you leaving? The fall, then?" I was trying to be practical, yet all the while my heart was breaking.

She shook her head and whispered, "Four weeks."

"Four weeks!"

"Aye." Her voice faltered. "George says there's no time to waste. He'll carry a letter from Argall to the Company."

"I should like to write a word or two to the Company myself," I said indignantly. "Tell George to let them know how matters *truly* stand here."

"Shh. Not so loud, lovey. Martial law. And you know that George is...is friends with Governor Argall. He must be true to that friendship." Her eyes had a peculiar look in them, and I sensed she wasn't telling me all.

"And...?"

"And *what?*" Her voice rose like a five-year-old caught nabbing cakes.

"There's more. I know you, Tempie. I know your voice. I know your eyes. You're hiding something from me. *What is it?*"

She shook her head quickly and leaned to my ear, whispering, "Joan, if you love me, if you value our friendship, I beg you, do not press. I am asking you, pledged on our bond, to take what I have told you at its face value and *do not press.* And do not share your concerns with *anyone. Please.*" Her eyes were both firm and pleading.

We hugged, and I said to her quietly. "Aye, my friend. I love you, and what you have said, I will believe and ask no more."

"Thank you," she whispered.

"When...when will you return? Or—" Suddenly I was afraid of the answer. "Will you return?" I found that I was also whispering although I didn't know why. Now my own voice sounded like a small child.

"I don't know." Her voice grew resolved. "George assures me that if...I mean, when we return, it will be as soon as possible. He dares not stay away from his business here too long."

But I had caught the slip. I turned her toward me and faced her square on. "You said *if.* Is there a chance you won't be back?"

Her eyes filled with tears once more as she said, "Lovey, in this world there are always chances. Let us choose to believe that this will not be a forever farewell."

My throat felt tight suddenly. I whispered, "Aye, that is what we will choose to believe." She hugged me again and then whispered, "And pray for us the whole while, will you?"

Again, she reminded me of a small child. What was she hiding?

"Aye, you know I will every day at dawn. I promise. If all I can do for you is to take you at your word, then this I *shall* do. You need not worry, for I know *nothing,* I and will not guess."

She nodded, sitting in silence for a moment.

Then, "I am afraid," she said simply.

"I know. God will be with ye."

I looked upward over her shoulder. *Won't you, God? You wouldn't let any-thing happen to her? I couldn't survive this place without her. I might make it with her gone for a year, perhaps. But not forever. Dear God, please don't let this be, as Tempie said, a forever farewell.*

And then I wondered. What did she know? Who was she protecting? Herself? George? Sam Argall? Or me?

CONNIE LAPALLO

Never a Ship Sails Out of the Bay
June 25, 1618 ~ James Cittie

Farewell, my sister, fare thee well.
The elements be kind to thee, and make
Thy spirits all of comfort: fare thee well.
—William Shakespeare

Never a ship sails out of the bay
But carries my heart as a stowaway.
—Roselle Mercier Montgomery

The day I'd dreaded had arrived.

The *George* sat imposingly at the shore, its plank groaning beneath the weight of those climbing aboard. Its cheerily painted brightwork glinting in the sun, its sails beating with wind that would carry it away, far away. *Don't go, Tempie.*

We had just a short while before drum call began again, beckoning all back to work for the two o'clock shift. During this break, the Yeardleys' friends from James Cittie had come to send the family off. Bermuda Hundred friends such as Annie and Cecily had no way to get here and probably didn't even know Tempie was leaving. Everything had happened so fast.

While men shook George's hand and slapped his back, Tempie stood apart from her husband. She was near the threshold, bidding goodbye to each friend. Jane held baby Argall for Tempie, and three-year-old Elizabeth seemed unsure what to make of the commotion.

Maria was there with her little flock of children. Little Mara had empty, lost eyes. I reached to touch the child's head. *That is how I feel, too,* I wanted to say. Gershom clung to his mother's petticoat while the baby, Benomi, Maria held to her chest. Benomi, *son of her sadness…*

Maria reached and embraced Tempie with one arm. The pastor's wife seemed genuinely happy for Tempie. Maria was a woman of rare courage.

Adversity had not bowed her although she had let her children's names belie the fear she sometimes felt. I was glad I would still have her here. Yet no one could replace my Tempie.

Tempie hugged each of her friends in turn. I stood back, wanting the moment not to come.

But in the end, all such moments do come no matter how much one wishes them away.

Sorrow and fear threatened to overwhelm me. My heart actually hurt. I could feel the aching pain in my chest.

"I'll return before you know it, Joan! You'll see." Tempie's tone said she did not believe a word of it.

So many things I still wished to tell her. Memories we had shared, times and days we'd endured together. How much we'd left unsaid through the years! Now, in this moment, they were too many and too much. Had we said enough along the way? Did she know that I could never have made it this far without her love, her kindness, her humor?

The ballad I'd sung so happily to myself just a few weeks before now haunted me with its words.

> *Musing on a thing that was*
> *Past and gone, Heigh-ho!*
> *In the merry month of May,*
> *Oh! Somewhat before the day*
> *Methought I heard at the last.*
> *Oh, the gentle nightingale...*

Tempie reached to hug me farewell, and I found all the things I had wanted to say vanished from my mind. Words failed me completely. I tried to speak but could not, and each time I began to say what was in my heart, the words could not get past my throat before it closed up in grief.

I had thought we would walk the path together. I had not considered our journeys might diverge. Now, I faced the lone and desolate dusty James Cittie road. And her path went deep into a forest—so deep that I could not see its end. I only knew it was not here. She would not be here.

"We'll be together again, Joan. I'm coming back. I am. You'll see." Tempie's own voice trailed off. "You'll see."

And I knew that these were just words, hollow and without meaning. For the truth was, she had no way of knowing if she would survive the voyage there, if she would decide to return, and if she could then survive yet another crossing home.

Home to Virginia. How strange that sounded when one was speaking of England! This was a wretched land at times to be sure, but it was indeed our home.

Now, with bitterness welling within me, I realized how true that was. If Virginia collapsed, we should all return to our own counties in England. We had become like second families here, and we women were fiercely devoted to one another. We had taken the new ones in like lambs in a fold. Oh, sometimes we resented the newcomers for what they cost us in care. The dearest remained those that had seen the most with us. In this we counted the oldest of the old planters. For nine or ten years was a lifetime in the New World.

I had prepared satchels of herbs to soothe the belly on the rolling ocean and ones for calenture and sorrow. I had scrawled notes with each bundle. Ginger, agrimony, wormwood, mint, and balm against the seasickness of the belly, sassafras for the calenture. The notes proved fortunate, for giving directions that morning I could not do.

I wanted to say, "Your stomach is weak! And has been since those red berries. So put you the agrimony and ginger in your beer."

I wanted to say, "You are the best friend I ever had."

I wanted to say, "I will never forget you. You will always be inside my heart no matter how many leagues of ocean or fathoms of sea separate us."

And I wanted to say, "Please come back. I cannot bear it here long without you."

But in the end, all I could murmur was, "Go with God."

And, whatever thoughts might roam her head, all she could do in response was nod.

And then the ship was gone. It had become smaller and smaller and fainter, too. The quiet echoed within me, a great emptiness. And I found myself staring down the river, whispering under my breath a song that would never seem happy to me again.

> *Musing on a thing that was*
> *Past and gone, Heigh-ho!*

I kicked along the stones at the riverbed, an odd shell here or there. And my mind wandered as the old tune beat round and round my head. I found myself thinking, *It's just you and me now, Maggie.*

> *Methought I heard at the last.*
> *Oh, the gentle nightingale…*

As the *George* glided down the James River toward open sea, those of us left behind at James Cittie had no idea that two other fleets of ships were bearing down upon us: English ships carrying deadly bloody flux—and a Spanish fleet bent on revenge.

We're Out to Seek the Gold Tonight

July 7, 1618 ~ on a Spanish Man o' War
on the Atlantic between Spain and Virginia

The moon is up, the stars are bright.
the wind is fresh and free!
We're out to seek the gold tonight
across the silver sea!
The world is growing grey and old:
break out the sails again!
We're out to see a Realm of Gold
beyond the Spanish Main.
—Alfred Noyes

The Spanish flag flew proudly over the six warships departing Cadiz, Spain, for Virginia.

Don Diego de Molina stood at the helm. At last, he thought, he would return to Virginia as general of his fleet.

He had not forgotten the smug *Almirante* Newport, the one-armed Englishman, trying to force a confession from Molina back in '11. *Newport did not realize the influence I had with the king of Spain himself,* Molina thought. Or perhaps Newport did suspect it, and that was precisely the admiral's fear.

No matter. For holding Don Diego as a common prisoner all those long years, the English would pay.

Molina envisioned the face of the present governor, Argall. He imagined Argall's astonishment as he learned a Spanish fleet had entered the Virginia bay. A bay soon, perhaps, to return to its rightful Spanish name, *la Bahia de Santa Maria*, the Bay of Saint Mary.

Molina had little fear of the small English colony. His plan was simple. He would first overpower the fort at Point Comfort. Although the English watch would see the distinctive silhouette of Spanish caravels, they had little ordnance or ships to stop him.

Molina had seen the forts there. He knew their weak construction, their guns—or lack thereof. No Spaniard ever built a pathetic fort like that. As well, he knew that the English were half-starved, impoverished, and angry at their forced labor.

Once overrunning Point Comfort and Kecoughtan, Molina would move his fleet upriver to James Town. The don would bring the haughty settlements to their knees. He would make them rue ever taking him prisoner, and he would bring honor to his king, his country, and himself.

La venganza es dulce.

Revenge is sweet.

A storm raged over the Atlantic as the six warships moved closer to their destination, Virginia. The wind whipped and battered the sails of the flagship, and the sky darkened threateningly.

Meanwhile, on the flagship itself, another storm was making.

"The crew grows mutinous," the ship's master informed Molina one month into the voyage and nigh halfway to Virginia. "They fear we may be sailing to our deaths, *mi general.*"

Molina spat. "They know not the sickly, hungry colony I have seen. We will overpower them and seize the silver mines for ourselves. Then the English 'Virginia' will become, as it rightfully is, North Florida!"

At that instant, three of the crew approached Molina, cursing him, demanding answers. How many English were there? How many ships? What precisely was the attack plan? How did Molina know that the forts were not now well armed? And was Molina certain they would indeed find silver?

Molina would not answer questions such as these. He cursed in return and reached for his scabbard.

Too late. The larger of the men had drawn his knife first.

With Ships the Sea Was Sprinkled

July 7, 1618 ~ on the *George*,
on the Atlantic between Virginia and London

The ocean's surfy, slow, deep, mellow voice, full of mystery and awe, moaning over the dead it holds in its bosom, or lulling them to unbroken slumbers in the chambers of its vasty depths.
—Thomas Chandler Haliburton

With Ships the sea was sprinkled far and nigh,
Like stars in heaven...
—William Wordsworth

The storm had died down considerably, as squalls were wont to do. Just a few remaining winds. The sky dropped to a soothing purple.

The churning sea now quieted to a low rumble as if speaking. What it said, Tempie did not know. Softly upward from the hold drifted the ever-present scent of tobacco, which could occasionally mask the smell of seasickness. With the twenty thousand pounds of tobacco lay bundles of sassafras roots, all rolling and shifting as the ocean rocked the ship. Great chests held the precious, but censored, words of the colonists, sheathed in letters, bound for England.

Tempie could just hear the murmuring of talk in the main chamber of the 'tween deck.

How many more weeks to England? St. Swithin's Day, the fifteenth of July, would soon be upon them. Whatever weather befell that day would mark the next forty days, so legend said.

What was that story? St. Swithin had been a bishop in his earthly days. The old legend said that he wished to be buried outdoors where folks and animals would tread on him and the rains cover his body. For nine years, his remains had lain outdoors just as he wished. But when the monks tried to move his body to a grand cathedral, a heavy rainstorm blew through the countryside. The saint had been disturbed, legend said. Tempie found an old rhyme running through her mind.

St. Swithin's day if thou dost rain
For forty days it will remain
St. Swithin's day if thou be fair
For forty days 'twill rain nae mair.

Odd how little time the settlers in Virginia had to think about such things as holy days and old tales. But here on ship she had time. Too much time.

Just ten days after St. Swithin's would be St. James Day, the anniversary of the great hurricane which had struck her fleet nine years ago, the last time she'd been on ship.

Nine years. The good Swithin had lain in the countryside nine years, and she had endured Virginia and its wild world for nine years. Strange, that.

She pushed memories of St. James and the hurricane to the outside of her head. She must. For she could not relive the long days and nights thrown around the dark of the *Falcon's* 'tween deck in a raging tempest, the likes of which neither she nor any living soul in England had ever seen before. She squeezed her eyes shut. No, she would keep her thoughts on old St. Swithin.

Keep your mind on blessings, she told herself.

Blessings. Joan had been on the *Blessing* in the hurricane. The hurricane! No matter what she did, the thoughts crept in. She would keep them at bay by a force of will, she decided.

How wonderful it would be to see her mother again. Somehow, trying to mend the breach, the two had begun writing letters. And now, her mother was growing old. Tempie longed to see her mother to ensure that all was right between them.

Oftentimes, Virginia settlers said that the hardest part of living an ocean away was not being able to offer final goodbye to loved ones. They prayed in the James Cittie church and hoped the wispy words carried through the ethers to the place where loved ones were, far aloft from the burial chapel in England.

It had been that way when Tempie's sister Marie died. A stab went through Tempie anew at her sister's loss although it had been five years since she had learned of it. To think her mother had survived and Marie had not.

So a journey to her mother's home in St. Michael at Thorn in Norwich, Norfolk, was in order. *At last, at last, I shall see you again, mother!*

Meanwhile, George had been corresponding with Tempie's nephew, Marie's son Edmund. George hoped to hire him on as his tobacco agent. Edmund would travel to Holland or England, as the case may be, to broker the tobacco.

Then, too, George was eager to see his own brother Ralph again. The Yeardleys would lodge at Ralph's home in Cheapside for most of the visit with a journey to Norfolk, of course.

Somewhere in the just fallen darkness of the nearby 'tween deck, George sat, battling for his opponent's queen on a chessboard. A few men played cards while others moved the little pegs of Nine Men's Morris about the game board. A flickering lantern provided all the light necessary.

Someone piped a song. Its notes eased themselves beneath the closed door of Tempie's little cabin where the children were sleeping soundly. One more day passing. A ship's cabin for her, George, and the children to share! Such luxury compared to the days onboard the *Falcon,* crowded with so many men, women and children, all sharing straw mattresses while people picked over everyone to move about.

No, thank you.

Of course, most passengers on this journey still did sleep on mattresses in the middle deck. Tempie was grateful to have a separate chamber. And, fortunately for all, on this voyage filled mainly with sassafras and tobacco, the crowding of so many souls in a small area was minimal.

Yet, when the *George* returned, it was likely to be otherwise, depending on how many new people Sir Thomas Smythe could sell on starting a new life in Virginia.

So, as sea voyages went, this was a quiet one. Tempie had suffered seasickness, but the herbs had helped. And she had enjoyed getting to know Susanna Lothrop, Reverend Whitaker's sister. Susanna was returning to England, disappointed that the parson had left little in the way of earthly possessions. She and her other brother Jabez had come to settle the reverend's estate and found little but a few books of Latin and Greek, a book of theology, and a string of shell beads Pocahontas had given him at her marriage. The beads meant a great deal to the pastor, his servant Martha had said. It was fitting, Tempie thought, that the good man's Bible and prayer book had gone beneath the waves with him.

"What else have we?" Susanna had cried. Her bitterness was, in fact, understandable. She had traveled all this way to settle his estate only to find she may as well have remained at home.

Susanna had taken opportunity on ship to air her feelings. "My brother sacrificed his life to this cause, and for what? *One* converted Indian woman? He could have won the souls of hundreds had he stayed in his thriving Yorkshire parish. But no one could tell him. No one could make him stay home. 'God calls me forth,' he said. I shall never forget it. Yet, with all his education, his connections, he…" Susanna's voice was morose.

"He made a marvelous difference," Tempie had interrupted. "One soul, aye. But that soul was Pocahontas, whose marriage to Master Rolfe has encouraged the Company to try to save Virginia and has caused us five years of peace. Susanna, you cannot imagine the number of lives, both English and Indian, that have been saved. And their son Thomas is a beautiful boy. His living self is proof that one day English and Indians may yet live together in peace. Thomas is a covenant, a promise of that fact." Tempie had not known where the forcefulness of her words came from, but she allowed them to spill out. The reverend's sincerity had been impressive, his drowning a tragedy. But his life, Tempie was convinced, had not been for naught.

Tempie had then grasped Susanna's hand, saying with all the sincerity she possessed, "If you had but met Pocahontas—Rebecca—you would know that your brother's was a worthwhile endeavor. My friend Joan said that the two of them, your brother and Pocahontas, shared one common trait: deep, soulful eyes. You must believe a divine purpose yet exists in the meeting of these two. I do," Tempie finished with conviction.

The conversations with Susanna were not always so dramatic. Hours and days on ship were long, and Susanna one of the few women to talk with. Together the two wiled away time. Susanna spoke of home, which she missed. "Did you e'er hear tell of our stepbrother and stepsister? Our new mother had two children from her first marriage to Dr. Fenner, a son named More Fruit Fenner and a daughter called Faint Not Fenner. How glad we were that our own mother had named us!" She smiled. "Although Alexander was always too gentle to laugh with the rest of us."

Still, Susanna said, their own mother had died when Alex was only four. Their new mother had been good to him and to all her new children. And then their father, Dr. Whitaker, had died when Alexander was ten years old and their stepmother was with child. Little Jabez had been born after their father's death. "She named him Jabez because she said she bore him with sorrow," Susanna said. "Now, Brother Jabez wishes to stay in Virginia." Her tone was mournful. "To lose two brothers to such a place. Sorrow, indeed!"

Tempie patted Susanna's arm. "Susanna, perhaps Jabez shall prosper there. And Parson Whitaker died doing work in which he believed. You think his life amounted to naught because it ended so soon. But his belief in the natives and in Pocahontas, his kindness to her, and his desire to see her a Christian have had great consequences for us. These have brought us peace with the Indians, which we never had before then. And who knows? Perhaps greater things than we know shall come from his sacrifices."

Susanna nodded, even as she was dabbing away tears of grief. Yet Tempie could tell that Susanna remained unconvinced. In Susanna's eyes, her brother's mission had been a failure. One native soul saved. One.

Through Susanna, Tempie had learned much about the young drowned pastor. "We were very, very poor after our father died," Susanna had said. "And yet Alexander went to Eton at thirteen on a scholarship for the poor and needy. Our brother Samuel managed to go as well." And both boys had eventually graduated as Cambridge scholars. Susanna's pride in her brothers was obvious, her loss at Alexander's death immense.

Tempie recounted the loss of her own sister Marie, adding, "I suppose it doesn't matter which side of an ocean you be. When a brother or sister dies young and far away, how harsh to be unable to mourn proper their passing." And so she had become quite close to Susanna on the voyage.

But this night, although she enjoyed Susanna's company, Tempie had chosen to be alone in her little cabin.

Truly, she should snuff the pewter candlestick and go to sleep. Yet, she could not resist scrawling these few thoughts into a daybook she had brought. For if she had no one else to talk to, she had this.

What a lonely feeling, to be caught somewhere on an ocean, partway between Europe and the New World, Africa off ahead in the distance. I can almost imagine the Dark Continent, the tribal songs of eventide. And If I could but see them, I know whales and porpoises swim below the keel of the ship, lonely beneath the deep as I am above.

She wrote, enjoying the soft curls of the letters on paper. Just as Maggie had, Tempie, too, loved to write. Oh, she was not as eloquent as her friend had been. Maggie had loved the sound of poetry, especially if she could sing the words. But for Tempie, words on paper still gave comfort, especially when she was alone.

Thoughts of the sea made her curious. Was Lord La Warr, her distant cousin, perhaps sailing right this moment toward Virginia? She hoped so. That could make all George's trepidations for naught. The colony would be in sound hands when La Warr arrived.

What other ships were out this night? How many might there be on the whole Atlantic? This she would never know, of course. But she always wondered, and not without a little apprehension. For while some ships sailed harmlessly to fish in Newfoundland or to trade with Africans on the West Coast, some meant harm to other ships or to her home in Virginia.

* * *

Many, many leagues to the southeast, far beyond the range of Tempie's hearing, the sound of Molina's body splashing into the ocean gave a few angry Spaniards a good deal of satisfaction. The dying look of the startled Molina had been hard to decipher. Pain, fear, anger—and bitter, bitter disappointment.

The Last Great Englishman
July 7-10, 1618 ~ on the *Neptune*
off the coast of Cape LaHave, Canada

Lead out the pageant: sad and slow,
As fits an universal woe,
Let the long, long procession go,
And let the sorrowing crowd about it grow,
And let the mournful martial music blow;
The last great Englishman is low.
—Alfred, Lord Tennyson

The cramps came on as suddenly and as violently as the storm the *Neptune* had encountered off the Canadian coast, the far north corner of Virginia. Contrary winds had battled the *Neptune* every league since she'd departed the Azores. The ship's master estimated that with a stop to refresh at Cape LaHave in Canada, the entire voyage would take the outrageous length of four months.

Now, a summer storm promised to make the winds the ship battled even more dramatic and powerful. The *Neptune,* it seemed, would never reach land.

In his cabin, Lord De La Warr drew up his legs as wave after wave of fiery spasms rocked his body, just as the storm rocked the *Neptune* and its consort, the *Treasurer.* La Warr had felt unwell since leaving the Azores. Now that illness had taken a worse turn.

The baron's servant Martyn appeared, and La Warr grabbed the man's jerkin. "Bring me Affonso!"

A few moments later, as night descended around the storm, a pallid and shaken Affonso appeared at his lord's chamber. He bowed his head low. "Aye, sir?"

"Poison, Affonso! Were you in on it with your Portuguese brethren?" De La Warr's voice was raspy, his throat dry.

"No, no, sir!" cried the stricken Affonso, understanding that his life depended on his Master believing him. *"Meu Senhor!"* he said, lapsing into his native Portuguese. "My Lord, it cannot be that I have been a traitor to you. For I, my Lord—I, too, have received the terrible sickness!"

One by one, almost every soul who had stepped ashore at São Miguel fell ill of the bloody flux. Moans and cries, drowned by the storm, wafted from the ship.

The beautiful island of Saint Michael, Archangel of Heaven, had turned into a malicious angel of death.

Winds continued to buffet the ship, heaving it in the wrong direction, holding the ships back from reaching the Canadian coast. Of one hundred eighty onboard, some thirty were desperately ill and fighting for life. Their suffering increased as the winds relentlessly pummeled the ship.

The rumor of poison spread around the ship like a kitchen fire. *Poison? Poison!* Would Portugal and Spain risk war with England over this? Perhaps this was to sabotage the English colony. Were the affable Dom Manuel and his wife capable of such treachery? Would His Lordship survive?

The first to fall ill had been those who had gone ashore to dine with St. Michael's governor. 'Twas clear, whatever the cause might be, something—or someone—at St. Michael's had been the culprit. But the likelihood of this being a poisoning dropped as others on ship also became victims. Still, many clung to the Portuguese poisoning conspiracy, which would later throw vast turmoil into Virginia Company meetings.

One by one, those who had the dread disease fell.

The calenture, seasickness, ague—these were harsh enough to endure at sea. But the horrible bloody flux was a nightmare to contend with in close quarters and sharing chamber pots.

One, two, three bodies in the ocean. Ten, eleven, twelve.

Lord De La Warr told Martyn the Persian to fetch Captain Brewster.

Edward Brewster was an old soldier of Virginia. He had served beneath Lord La Warr in the Lowlands many years before. At the baron's request, he had come with La Warr to Virginia that summer of 1610. And it had been he, Brewster, who had rowed the longboat upriver from Point Comfort to deliver the news to the settlers abandoning the colony. His Lordship had arrived! 'Twas a glorious day but for the news of the Starving Time. Glorious because the baron's arrival had saved Virginia, as all had turned back to resettle James Town.

Lord De La Warr, his health restored, had sent a letter to Brewster while both men were still in England. He was letting his old captain know that he was returning to the colony and wanted Brewster to be his first in command.

Edward Brewster had not hesitated. "Certainly, my Lord." And he had received his commission aboard ship.

Now Captain Brewster entered the still, deathlike chambers of his commander, the governor and captain general. Brewster saw with fright the ghastly pallor of the baron, who looked not so much as a lord but as a common man. A common man who was most certainly dying.

Brewster was not a squeamish man. He had gotten in trouble in Virginia for telling George Percy, that son of an earl, what he thought of him. He'd even brazenly confronted Sir Thomas Dale. Governor Gates had sent Brewster home, saying that the man might fare better with a rest from Virginia.

Yet as Brewster looked into the fading eyes of the man he had served so long and so well, he felt the weight of what he knew was coming.

"Captain Brewster—Edward, sit, please."

"Yes, my Lord."

"I do not think I shall make it, Edward."

"Sir, you shall! You are a baron with the fierce, fighting blood of nobility. I…"

De La Warr cut him off. "No time for false assurances, my friend."

Captain Brewster dropped his head. "How may I serve you, my Lord?"

"Just this: I hereby put you in command of all my men, my tenants, and my goods. My business at hand, both upon ship and once in Virginia. We shall hope that most of these several hundred souls make it to Virginia even if I do not. We shall hope Virginia—" His voice broke. "We shall hope Virginia can survive. My investment is tremendous. It must support my wife while also repaying the Marquess of Buckingham and others who invested with me. The cattle and goats I had sent ahead, my servants, my land, all in your hands now. Make sure something—anything—remains for my wife. I would die believing I have not impoverished her."

Later that evening, Lord De La Warr himself closed his eyes within sight of the North Virginia coast at Cape LaHave where Argall had destroyed the French settlement.

Captain Brewster announced, "If we can but land, our Lord La Warr shall have the proper Christian burial he so deserves and would desire. However far north it may be, his body shall still rest in his beloved Virginia." *Lord La Warr. Gone!*

"I shall attend to the burial of my lord and master, captain," Martyn said to Brewster, but Brewster would have none of it.

"You may be the man of the chamber, but I am commander of his affairs. *I* shall see to it!"

The ships landed at the cape, and the baron's men prepared to lay the devoted Governor for Life in the soil of North Virginia. A carpenter named Wilcocks joined two trees to form a wooden cross while a joiner constructed a coffin. A stonecutter from Essex worked for six days to carve La Warr's name and title into a flat rock, adding beneath it, *Governor for Life and Captain General of Virginia.* These monuments would be in place before the ship departed.

Over one hundred surviving passengers, those who were able, stood in a circle around the gabled coffin Wilcocks had quickly built. Some twenty to thirty more were ill aboard ship, unable to attend.

All knew not one would be present there were it not for the baron's devotion to the cause. And somehow, all wondered exactly what they had gotten themselves into.

It was a question every soul in Virginia had asked himself at least once.

"I think he should have liked to lie at rest in Virginia rather than at sea," said a cousin of La Warr's wife to no one in particular.

An attorney named Will Farrar, standing with one hand clasping the other in front of him, head bowed, glanced upward at the man on his left and nodded agreement. Farrar felt somehow light-headed as an unnatural wave of pain swept him. He closed his eyes against the thought of what lay ahead.

Among the throng of mourners also that day were one Richard Peirce and his wife, the former Bettie Phippen. The unnatural rumblings in Bettie's insides made her know that she would soon stretch out in agony moments after saying, "Amen."

Richard was Will's cousin, Bettie my niece. They stood on the shores of Newfoundland, already facing death. We had encouraged them to come.

The baron would have turned forty-one that day. The solemnized ceremony complete, the crew and passengers buried La Warr alongside Affonso, who had protested his innocence 'til the last.

A Most Pestilant Disease
August 14, 1618 ~ James Cittie

> *The people which arived were soe poorely victualled that had they not been distributed amongst the old Planters they must for want have perished; with them was brought a most pestilent disease (called the Bloody flux) which infected all most all the whole Collonye. That disease, nothstanding all our former afflictions, was never knowne before amongst us.*
> —Brief Declaration of the Ancient Planters, c. 1624, in reference to the *Neptune*

Lord De La Warr is dead. No one could believe it. No one knew what it meant. But the lovely ship *Neptune* at last came into the James River, and the baron's death was the first news we on James Town Island received.

All who had hoped that our Lord La Warr would put an end to Argall's greedy practices were sorely disappointed. I realized once more how noble Lord De La Warr seemed next to Dale's cruelty and Argall's corruption.

We learned quickly what had happened. The *Neptune* had stopped at the Azores, they said, and the fine feast had turned ugly when the baron and all who ate with the Portuguese governor had grown very ill.

The first thought—*poison!*—had been dispelled after others who had not eaten there had also begun to fall. Since then, thirty passengers had died.

Amongst those who were ill but whose bodies seemed to rally was Bettie Phippen Peirce. Bettie was my brother Tom's daughter, married to Will's cousin, Richard Peirce. Bettie had acted as older sister to Cecily while Cecily lived with the family. Now, I would act as mother to Bettie while she lived in Virginia.

There was little doubt where the Peirces would stay as they acclimated and until they were settled, and that was our house.

That meant, of course, that we were bringing the bloody flux directly into our own home. But we had been the ones who had urged them to come, and if the voyage would cost Bettie her life, then it would be me tending her.

Richard, still well but weak from traveling, walked alongside his wife as Will and the Reverend Bucke carried the ill young woman across our threshold.

"Oh, God," she murmured, and the Reverend Bucke kindly placed a hand upon her head in comfort.

"That is a good place to start," he said.

She glanced up at him and said, "Pray for me, pastor." He nodded. He undoubtedly knew, as we all did, that many in homes, in ditches, and under tents would need his prayers this night. If the flux had spread upon ship, it would also likely spread here.

We had suffered many illnesses, but no mass contagion of bloody flux. Until now. The Azorean gift, we called it. I looked down into Bettie's grey and swollen face, her half-open and bloodshot eyes, and said, "No worries, lovey. We'll do the best we can for you."

"Praise God, Will, for the Frenchman," an exhausted Richard mumbled.

"Frenchman, Richard?"

"Aye." Will's cousin drew in a deep breath. "We had laid the poor baron and others to rest in Canada and then stayed a while to refresh." He paused. "I don't mind telling you that after so many weeks at sea, such difficult winds, and so many yet falling ill, Virginia seemed a long, long way off."

The sick and dying had lain sprawled both within the ship and onshore in the warm, summer sun. The groans of twisted men, women, and children had filled the air. Some died and their fellows buried them there. Friends carried others, on stretched linens held aloft, back to the ship. Some died onboard, some disembarked here in Virginia, Richard explained. "Yet, a godsend. There come a Frenchman to the bay, a French ship with such bounty of fish and furs and fruit, which we asked to buy. The Frenchman obliged, preparing us a feast when we were unable to procure these items ourselves. Well, Will, it was a miracle. A plain miracle. It saved our minds and our souls as well. And on we went."

I, listening to the conversation, found it strange that after Argall's treatment of the French, one of their ships should treat ours so well. *Perhaps they simply hoped for no trouble with the* Neptune *and* Treasurer, I thought.

"If Brewster had his way, we'd have attacked that Frenchman, too," Richard murmured as he drifted off to sleep. The captain of the *Neptune* had said no, that without orders doing so would be illegal.

"Friendship is a sight better than war," I said to no one in particular as I carried linens out to the line to beat.

Meanwhile, Richard and Bettie Peirce weren't the only ones with us. When the ship had docked and the passengers wearily touched land once more, a full sixteen weeks had passed since they left England. One soul staggered down the bridge, and I reckoned she didn't know where she was. Her eyes seemed confused.

Once down the bridge, she wandered over to a pine tree and used it to keep herself from falling. She looked up, and then away at the river. And then she fell to the ground.

Will carried her back to our house, and we learned her name was Lydia Quarles. Her husband, Master Quarles, a brickmaker, had died on ship.

Lydia had striking, curly red hair, made more dramatic by her pallor. Her freckles stood out as if not even belonging on her face.

Most of the old settled families had taken in at least one or two of the vagabond *Neptune* colonists.

Argall had taken hold of all Lord La Warr's supplies and goods and left these newcomers to shift for themselves. Argall had used some of the better sort, mostly carpenters and craftsmen, and put them to work on his own personal projects. One man was even building Argall's house!

I tended the two women, but as it were, Richard took but mildly ill and was able to care for himself. He would have been able to help with his wife. But now that he was mostly recovered, Governor Argall pulled Richard away and put him, too, to the building of his house.

I seethed with disgust, with anger.

"He'll take the one once we've recovered him, but he won't tend the sick, now will he? He'll expect *me* to nurse Mistress Quarles back to health!" I whispered fiercely to Will. I glanced over my shoulder at the limp form. No, she could not hear me. A pang of guilt shot through me. I hated to speak badly of the ill. Yet I spoke truth: this I knew.

Will agreed with a resigned look. "Indeed," he said with a sigh.

Argall provided the newcomers nothing but corn. No clothing and no lodging. Richard returned at night and slept with us.

"I am grateful, cousin," he said to Will. "For many are a-sleeping in the church this damp night."

And so it went.

Meanwhile, the cramping and ague took hold of Mistress Quarles harshest so that after three days, she fully collapsed. After six, she had no idea where she was and began calling for her husband.

I kept a cool, damp piece of linen on her forehead and tried to reassure her.

"Lovey, Ben cannot come to you just now." I feared reminding her, in her state, that he was dead.

She opened her eyes wide in confused alarm. "What mean you? Tell Ben the cows need milkin', and he'll have to be the one to do it. He's a lazy rascal, you see." She laughed slightly. "Milk them. Tell him… What was your name again, mistress?"

"I am Mistress Peirce. Joan." I sighed. I had told her my name at least thrice that day. But each time 'twas a new experience for her.

"You'll get to the market fair and buy me some pretty silk, won't you?" She looked at me earnestly, and I took her hand. Illness could not dim the bright hopeful blue of her eyes, however sunken they may be. I nodded grimly.

"Silk, you'll have."

But as she grew weaker and the cramping worsened, I expected she would never touch silk again in this life. Perhaps, I mused, the angels wore silk gowns.

Mistress Quarles at last fell into a long sleep, her breathing growing more ragged until finally she was gone. She'd had only the barest idea that the ship had docked, that she was in Virginia, the land o' plenty.

Plenty o' troubles, I thought as I set fire to her linens and watched her bedding go up in flames.

Where They Want for Themselves
August 28, 1618 ~ James Cittie

And to thinke the old planters can releeve [the new arrivals]
were two much simplicity; for who here in England is so chari-
table to feed two or three strangers, have they never so much; much
lesses in Virginia, where they want for themselves.
　　—Captain John Smith, testifying about conditions in
　　　Virginia

As a few weeks went by, Richard recovered and Bettie improved. Will helped Richard build his family a home during the hours Richard wasn't building Argall's house. Soon the Peirces moved out.

There was no more Mistress Quarles for which to care. But soon Tommy doubled over. He could not even make it up the ladder to his chamber, and so we tried to make him comfortable on the floor. Will, too, had the flux mildly. Fortunately for him, his duties kept him often away from the town where the flux was harshest.

The work for the healthy doubled. We had to take care of our households and Argall's duties, as well as housing and tending the sick and sharing our food with our houseguests.

The crops were faring poorly this year. The summer had brought searing heat, hail, and drought. Two poor crop years in a row meant the granary was near empty. We tried vainly to feed those with flux and ourselves as well. Worse, the ship brought news that we should expect great multitudes soon, and these would come bringing few provisions. Governor Argall was alarmed and wrote to England immediately what great misery would ensue if the Company sent more settlers without food. Now, we could only hope that those in England would receive the letter and heed Argall's words.

When Mistress Quarles had died, I'd been relieved—grateful, even—as I usually felt when those off ships could not survive the seasoning. I could not help it. That was how I felt, and I realized it was an honest emotion, born of hardship and suffering and of bearing the illness of strangers, unasked for, undesired.

This stranger had increased the chances that our own family would become ill, and now Tommy had the dreaded disease.

I cleaned up behind the sick little boy, and I felt rage boiling within me. It was not compassionate to feel that way, this I knew. Yet those were my feelings and no denying them. *Thank God, Mistress Quarles has passed,* I found myself thinking, while trying desperately to push such a thought from of my mind.

No, truly. Thank God. I cannot care for one more stranger in this house. It is enough to care for the children, for my husband, and for myself. A few relatives need a home. I would expect that. Friends need help. We are there for them. We work hard for what little we have! But caring for strangers—sick, dying, and without so much as a pint of meal to see them through. We must share our little corn and watch our homes fill with the contagion that might be the death of us. It is too much.

How bitter my thoughts this August morning.

God will punish you for such wicked notions, I thought. I prayed immediately for forgiveness. *A contrite heart, oh, Lord, you will not ignore!* But it might be too late. The thought was there. Even after praying, I remained glad to have one less ill stranger to tend.

While I tried to ask God to forgive me, I realized that I was still very, very angry.

When my own insides began to cramp unnaturally, I was not at all surprised. Here was the punishment I had feared.

Now Jane began to care for me, for she herself had it not. Yet.

I had given birth to four babies, but never had I felt pain and spasms such as these. Sweat made my hair wet, and I tried to relieve myself outside away from the house.

It was not always possible to do so and Jane had a horrible mess to clean up.

We had tried to prepare herbs, but they began to run low. Sage would quell the expelling of blood, but of sage I had little. The herbs had dried up with the corn.

Reverend Bucke was giving Christian burials as best he could. He would pray over the departed. Sometimes the dead lay in a row at the front of the church if it had been a bad dying day. The vagabonds cleared out; we moved the dead in.

When the pastor himself took ill, Reverend Wickham tried to help. His eyes were dim, but he had the funeral liturgy mostly memorized. Maria Bucke had picked up flux as well, and young Mara did her best to help her mother. Mara was still a small, frail girl with wide eyes that seemed not fully sure of what was going on about her. Despite this, her love for her mother was obvious.

As for me, I wondered how Cecily and Tom Bailey were upriver. And what of little Temperance? Was Sam Jordan ill up at Bermuda Hundred? Or how about Annie, also upriver? And how were Jack and their girls? We understood that the bloody flux had spread through the settlement so that almost everyone had it at least mildly. Most recovered, some did not. It depended much, it seemed, on how sturdy a body was before the illness struck. The newcomers fared poorest of all, as they usually did. A long, rough journey, a new climate, and summer heat with which to contend. Was it any wonder?

For one thing I was most glad: Tempie, with her already weak stomach, was still in England.

Godspeed, Tempie, I thought. *I miss you. You know I do. But I thank God you're on a ship, maybe even in London by now, and miles from this place!*

The Heart of London Beating Warm
August 28, 1618 ~ London

A rumor broke through the thin smoke,
Enwreathing abbey, tower, and palace,
The parks, the squares, the thoroughfares
The million-peopled lanes and alleys,
An ever-muttering prisoned storm,
The heart of London beating warm.
—John Davidson

"Now the fair's a filling!
O, for a tune to startle
The birds o' the booths here billing,
Yearly with old Saint Bartle!"
—Ben Jonson

By late August, the *George* had completed its passage up the Narrow Sea and into the Thames.

The Yeardleys disembarked at Gravesend. While there, Tempie's mind flew to Pocahontas, for the princess had died here. Next, a tilt boat to Billingsgate, and there, waiting for them, was London.

Tempie found London striking. *How could it be so big? Had it always been so? So many people, hundreds of thousands. And so much noise. A lifetime, an ocean away from humble homes with towering Virginia pines, oaks, pokahichary, and walnut trees all about.*

And in London, no birds except scavenging pigeons.

It was a peculiar first thought but in Virginia every spring and summer, birdsong filled the air, from so many different colors and styles of birds, Tempie could not describe them all. Now in London she could see the muddy streets with houses, taverns, and shops sprawling in every direction and crowded close together as if all the buildings were angling for a glimpse of the Thames, London's highway. London Bridge spanned over the Thames, massive, both river and bridge. Weaving, winding, cobbled, filth-strewn streets with Hackney carriages barreling down them. Fishmongers and fishwives, tavern keepers and buckled-over old men all jostling one another away from the hurtling wheels.

Tempie scooped little Argall up in her arms. His toddling would never do here! George had Elizabeth on his back. The children had wide eyes, especially Elizabeth, who had some idea that this was a place very foreign from her world of muddy paths and deep forests.

Tempie tried to sidestep the mess horses had left behind, but in so doing found elbows coming at her. Obviously, she was walking too slowly for a crowd moving against her, headed toward the docks. Still minding the pressing crowd and the dirty streets, Tempie flinched and nearly tripped over two yapping, snarling dogs lost in their own canine argument.

"I have a baby!" she cried, but her small voice could not reach above that din. The crowd pushed Tempie toward the dogs, and she wondered what she would do if she fell atop them. *Fall over Argall like a tent so that the dogs bite me and not him* flashed through her mind. At what speed could a mother form a plan to protect her child!

At the last moment, a milkmaid with several ducks distracted the dogs, sending the pair on a joint mission of duck chasing. Now the dogs were the milkmaid's problem.

Thank God for the ducks, Tempie thought, heaving an agitated sigh. She could not even bring herself to feel sorry for the milkmaid, who was now amid the chaos of quacking and flapping, shouting, "Yaw! Git!" at the dogs.

A hand with a firm grip grabbed Tempie's arm and pulled her to the side. *George,* she thought with relief. The crowd had separated them and that, it was abundantly clear, was dangerous.

George's protective arm about her was reassuring, but the crowd and the noise did not abate.

Traders yelled to be heard above the din.

"Ribs of beef and many a pie!"

"Pepper and saffron!"

"Pewter pots!"

And suddenly London felt overwhelmingly large to Tempie, something she had not expected. Her clothes were ragged, 'twas true. She had thought she'd be self-conscious about that. But the crowd was agitated and noisy. No one noticed a thing.

A sudden memory jolted her. The sounds of the birds had been one of the first things she had noticed when she disembarked and first set their feet on Virginia soil. The liveliness of squirrels as big as coneys, terns and eagles, and every manner of crawling, flying creature it seemed. Now, here it was nine years later, and she had become so accustomed to the sound that she missed the birds singing.

So she found herself exuberant to see a familiar city and stunned by the immensity of it all at once. Virginia's vastness rolled away into its endless forests and wide rivers.

London, she thought. *London!* And the word both thrilled and terrified her.

She would await the day eagerly when her family began their journey to the English county of Norfolk, but for now they would be at Ralph Yeardley's apothecary shop here in Cheapside.

"The Bartholomew Fair is going on over yonder at Smithfield. We can catch a day of it, perhaps," said George, raising his voice above the noise and glancing at his wife. He gave her a hint of a smile. "Didn't I recall someone harping about *roast pork* over and again after the Starving Time?"

She laughed. "The great fair!" She exclaimed, gasping as she added, "A pig, roasted whole and piping hot, all one can eat!" Pork was a longstanding tradition of the fair, and her mouth suddenly began to water at a delicacy that so many in London took for granted.

How long had it been since she'd seen a fair, a *true* fair! Any fair? And this one was the grandest of them all. Folks would come from all over England for it. How she would enjoy introducing her children to England, the world she had grown up in, the world they may never call home.

"Aye, indeed, let's!" she yelled back. She reckoned there must be some ten days or so of the fair remaining. The lord mayor of London always opened the fair on St. Bartholomew's Eve, the twenty-third of August. The fair continued for a fortnight at the Church of St. Bartholomew, built by that very Saint himself.

Her heart lifted at the thought of the fair. Goods and cloth of every imaginable sort, puppets and waxworks, wrestling and archery, rope-dancers and conjurers, tumbling and plays.

Meanwhile, all about, the hawkers would be crying in their best sing-song voices.

"What do you lack? What's it you buy?"

"Rattles, drums, halberds, horses, babies o' the best? Fiddles o' the finest?"

"Buy any gingerbread, gilt gingerbread?"

"Hey, now the fair's a-filling!"

Drums would thump, and the fiddlers would play merrily. Ballads would echo across the grounds in sheer jubilation. *Bartholomew Fair!*

Suddenly she remembered the old proverb:

> *St. Bartholomew*
> *Brings the cold dew.*

Well, she didn't give one whit about the cold dew. She was back in London at long last, and *she was going to have roast pork!* She squeezed her husband's hand. She had not truly wanted to make this voyage, but now suddenly she was glad she had come.

For a moment, she wondered about her friends in Virginia....

I hope they are well. Won't it be exciting to tell them about Bartholomew Fair?

As for George, he had many things on his mind other than the bustling city or the twittering of Virginia birds. Even the fair he had mentioned mainly for the benefit of his wife. For George had on his person Sam Argall's letter to the Virginia Company. And if George didn't miss his guess, the governor's words were going to enrage the Company.

It was what the Company would do next that he didn't know.

A Fearful, Nightmare Dream
September 1, 1618 ~ Sir Thomas Smythe's home on Philpot Lane, London

Or was the whole a fearful, nightmare dream?
—Charles Heavysege

"It's been a nightmare."

With these words, George Yeardley opened his meeting with the Virginia Company. George felt faint even now. The weight he bore on his shoulders pressed upon him, more than equal to the weight he'd lost on ship.

Everything—his life, his livelihood, his experience—all had hinged on Virginia becoming a success. Now, Argall's ineptitude threatened to bring it down. All of it.

There was much to discuss.

"What part nightmare, Yeardley? The natives? Sickness?" Sir Thomas Smythe had an alarmed expression. He understood that *nightmare* in Virginia could be a phantom of many sorts.

Now, George found an acid taste in his mouth. Perhaps, he reasoned, he was becoming ill. Yet he knew if that were so, 'twas only part of the sickness he felt within.

He had welcomed Argall as a brother, had believed the outcome of the admiral's encounter with the French had shown his skill at sea and at warfare.

George appreciated good soldiering, however he found it.

Too, the capture of Pocahontas, while upsetting the women, had certainly been a boon to the Company. Argall had managed to bribe old Japazaws and his wife, and Dale had used Pocahontas to bargain with the natives, first for return of stolen weapons, then for peace.

George had admired Argall enough to name his own son after him.

Now, it fell on George to betray the man who had betrayed his Company with thievery and greed of the most dishonorable sort.

Which brought George back to the question at hand. "No, my good sirs," George said. "We are at relative peace with the natives. Our truce with Chief

Powhatan endures, despite the death of both the great chief and his daughter Pocahontas. Opechancanough affirms the treaty. The Chickahominies have given us some little troubles around Christmas, but nothing a company of men and weapons couldn't handle. As to sickness, while we did have an unusual amount of illness last summer, that is not the nightmare of which I speak."

The council members' deep concern seemed etched on every line of their faces. Never, never did the news from Virginia return to them with even a glimmer of promise. Now they braced for the latest tragedy or folly which involved their friends, their land, and their investments, their hope dim of ever receiving returns.

"Go on, Yeardley," Smythe said, stroking his beard as if trying to calm himself.

"No, sirs. The trouble, I am afraid to say, lay within. Within our own ranks. Within...*us*. The trouble—and I beg pardon, seeking not offend any around this table."

Smythe waved his hand. "We need truth, and if it offend any, so be it."

George wished that assurance could relax him. But it could not.

"The trouble, gentlemen, is with our governor himself. Samuel Argall raids Company lands and livestock. He keeps all from trading with the natives but himself. He has issued unjust 'edicts,' as he calls them. He forbids anyone to speak with an arriving mariner. He keeps the *Treasurer* locked tight at all times. Only a few trusted souls may enter that ship, and we all suspect something hidden there. He listens to no one but himself." George Yeardley drew a deep breath. "He is arrogant—that itself is no crime—but he has absconded with Company property and put it to work for himself. *Our* Company lands and stocks he claims as his own."

Cries of outrage went up from the table.

"Good God, Yeardley!"

"No, indeed, I shan't believe it!"

"Can this be true? Samuel Argall robbing us?"

George realized the delicate position he was in, for any could presume George simply jealous about giving over his governorship to Argall—even if such jealousy did not exist. George Yeardley, frankly, had been thrilled to hand the government over to Argall.

"Believe it," George Yeardley said evenly while his heart pounded under taint of betrayal of his old friend. George stood at the head of the table making his speech and wanted more than anything to sit. He felt light-headed, weak. But he did not wish to look so—*ever*.

"Thank the Merciful Savior that Lord La Warr shall be there soon to seize control from someone who would presume to steal from his own Company, his own friends!" Just the words of Sir Edwin Sandys, son of the Archbishop of York, had a calming effect upon the room. Aye, Lord La Warr would be there soon enough—should already be there—to take *Governor* Argall in hand.

George sighed. "Indeed. And that was most the reason I came—to ensure that his lordship was en route. And I am certainly pleased to hear that he is. Yet I know not how much damage Argall may inflict in the meantime."

This was a troublesome question, but all were confident of Lord La Warr's abilities and leadership.

George spoke again. "You will want to see this, gentlemen. A letter from our governor."

George handed a sheath of folded papers to Sir Thomas Smythe, who broke Argall's wax seal. Smythe skimmed the letter then slammed the papers onto the table such that it startled those present.

"Is this the man we nominated governor? Such incredible arrogance, gentlemen! Truly, he thinks highly of himself or meanly of us that he should address us with such...such...disdain, such impudence! Gentlemen, truly I tell you, he chastises *us* as though we were but his servants!" Smythe didn't sputter often, but he was sputtering now.

Argall had upbraided the council for not showing *him* enough respect and confirmed that he sold the Company's cattle as instructed.

"Who in God's earth has instructed him to sell our livestock?" The elderly Lord Carew, master-general of the ordnance and royal favorite, had gone scarlet.

"Now, now." Sir Robert Rich spoke up. "'Twas I who recommended Argall to you. His abilities are strong, his valor proven. Perhaps this is indeed a misunderstanding." Rich raised his eyebrows in a gesture that appeared skeptical. "Perhaps our friend, the good George Yeardley, *believes* he knows what the governor is doing. Perhaps he does not adjudge fairly." Rich's tone had a bite to it, almost a threat. Lord Rich's father was not only the powerful Third Baron Rich but the king had just made him the First Earl of Warwick as well. The man glaring at George would soon be both a baron *and* an earl.

George understood Rich's need to discredit him. Rich was Argall's patron. The influential Rich had supported colonization as enthusiastically as had his father before him. But the Riches had a reputation for piracy, viewing it as a justifiable means of becoming wealthy, supporting England by tearing down Spain. The Riches were unabashed Puritans, all Catholics their enemies.

Yet King James was close to the Spanish ambassador Gondomar and was friendly—some said overly friendly—with Spain. Feeling that the English king himself would not look after English interests, the Riches took matters into their own hands. Argall was an experienced naval captain, Virginia Company admiral, and Rich's cousin. What better partner for Rich to have?

Sam Argall, master navigator and fisherman, gave Rich a mighty ally in the Spanish hotbed waters of the Caribbean.

Suddenly, George felt dizzy as the full implications dawned on him. He reached back to steady himself on his chairback and said faintly, "Gentlemen, truly, I must sit. The long voyage has taken its toll on me, I fear." *And so has the complete helplessness of honorable men against the dishonorable in the chess game called the New World.*

Sir Edwin Sandys gave George a sympathetic nod then turned to call angrily down the table at Rich. "See here!" Sandys stood and pointed at Rich. "Captain Yeardley has a fine reputation with the Company. Dare you not besmirch his name, sir!" Sandys was in parliament. He knew how to face confrontations.

Lord Rich, too, bolted to his feet. Before Rich could give an angry retort, Smythe banged his gavel and shouted, "Silence, silence, gentlemen! We shall never settle this if we fight amongst ourselves. We have a fantastical issue to resolve. Let us do so peacefully."

Sandys and Rich took their seats, but both glared across the table at one another.

"Now, what more have you to tell us, Captain Yeardley?" Smythe asked, a weary sound to his voice. "We must get the facts."

George nodded at Smythe and Sandys gratefully. "Thank you, sirs. Argall knows *not* that I bring this information to you. I...I did not let on. I did not think he would allow me to leave." George reddened. Why did he feel like a schoolboy tattling on a friend?

"Good, good. We might catch him unawares. Write, write!" Smythe demanded of the secretary. "We must compose a new letter to Argall *at once.* The *William and Thomas* is to sail any time with Blackwell's group."

George looked askance at Smythe, and Smythe explained. "Puritans, Yeardley, headed for Virginia. A very crowded ship, I understand. Obviously, our previously written letter of encouragement to Argall shall not suffice."

Now Mr. Fotherby, the Company Secretary, reached within a sheath of papers for a letter addressed to Samuel Argall, Governor. Fotherby crumpled it furiously.

"And we shall compose a new letter to Lord La Warr as well," Smythe said. "We shall order him to arrest Argall immediately and to send him home for questioning and punishment."

Thank God that the colony would by now be in the capable hands of De La Warr, the men murmured—little knowing the baron's body rested peacefully beneath an elm in Newfoundland.

Not a Star Shining
September 8-9, 1618 ~ James Cittie

Tears—not a star shining—all dark and desolate...
—Walt Whitman

Giles Fairfax and young Tom had explored the woods of Bermuda Hundred and James Town Island together. The two leggy six-year-olds had chased deer when they could find them and learned where the huckleberries and maypops grew in the hardwoods.

Margery had named Giles after her father Giles Browne, she said. Sometimes I would see Giles holding his little sister Ellen's hand while Margery carried her youngest, Anthony.

As for Tommy, he supposed Giles was just about the best friend a boy could have, and they both dreamed of being soldiers. Will had taught Tommy all about the matchlock and ordnance. Giles's father Master Fairfax was a brickmaker, but, as all men in Virginia did, Fairfax knew a thing or two about matchlocks himself.

I told Tommy that he would be leaving for London soon. He was nearing seven. The learning we had provided here would help some although we weren't much of a petty school, 'twas true. For grammar school, he would need to go to England, so we were waiting for some opportunity to send him. Will insisted, after all. Yet secretly, I didn't want Tommy to leave any more than he wanted to go. He was my adoring little boy. Perhaps the youngest always are? He took care of me, and he was my little man while Will was off at Kecoughtan or other settlements.

Tommy himself protested mightily against London.

"I'll not leave you. Who'd take care of you while Father's away?" He wrapped his little arms around me and said as forcefully as a small boy might, "You need me here."

To some extent, it was true. I did need him. He was a great help around the fields and with the livestock. I remembered how he had even helped me tend families from arriving ships. He rarely complained about any task given him, for he was a child of hardship. And Jane would marry soon. She was now fourteen, so Tommy was all I'd have left at home shortly. With Will gone so much, I both needed and loved Tommy's company.

Yet, Will had delivered his verdict about Tommy's studies, and so I could not let Tommy know how I truly felt about him leaving.

"And how will I learn to be a soldier if I am not here? There are no Indians in England. And I could never leave Giles!" He tried to pout. It didn't work.

I lifted his chin with my hand. "You are too old to make such a face. And when you return, Giles will be here. You two will always be friends," I assured him.

But inside I wondered. Could I truly let him go? Even if it were best for him?

Tommy reckoned he should enjoy his friend as long as he could, for as early as next spring, Tommy would depart on a ship to England.

After church on Saturday, Giles ran over, holes in his breeches, a grin on his freckly face. "Where's Tommy, Mistress Peirce? We're aiming to explore the upland woods tomorrow after church, and we'll hunt Indians!"

I laughed. Tommy had recovered from the flux, praise God, and he would probably have the strength to play. I suspected the sunshine would do him good, so I agreed. "Aye, hunting Indians you'll be? Suppose you catch some?"

Giles looked earnest. "Oh, I don't expect we'll actually catch them," he said seriously as if I thought he truly might.

I supposed Giles had overheard his elders talking about the sudden troubles this week with the Chickahominies. Not all the Chickahominies, just a handful.

It had all begun a few weeks back when Dick Killingbeck left Kecoughtan after asking permission from Governor Argall to go see his wife at Bermuda Hundred. Argall had agreed, but Killingbeck, an old planter from one of the first ships, had gone instead on a trading mission with the Chickahominies. Argall had forbidden all such missions, saying the law permitted only the governor such trade.

Killingbeck and his four men had met with the natives, bragging on all the goods they had. And somehow, the braves had decided they could simply take what they wanted rather than trade for it. After stealing the goods, the Chickahominies had fled into the forest.

The Chickahominies were a warlike tribe, and though giving tribute since the days of Pocahontas's marriage, they were yet not happy about it. Even Powhatan had been unable to get this tribe fully coerced into his kingdom.

All the town was still talking about the thievery. I reckoned that was why Indians were on Giles's mind this day.

"You'll be a fine Indian fighter one day, Giles. But we've been mostly at peace for four years now. I hope we never need your services, sir." I feigned seriousness. But I couldn't resist tousling the boy's red hair, something I suspected Giles was used to.

He smiled. "If you do, I'll be a-ready."

"Well, you can find Tommy out back, tending the goats. And how is your mama?" I added before he dashed off.

"Oh, mama is right good, Mistress Peirce!" he called over his shoulder. "She was churning butter when I left. Ellen was trying to help her tend Anthony. He's just little, you know. I told her I had to see Tommy on Indian business, and she said that would be all right." He touched his hat as if trying to be gentlemanly, and then, in a great rush to catch up to Tommy, he turned and scurried for the back of the house.

I watched the two boys run through the fields, and I reflected that it hadn't been that long since they both had been born. I wondered if Margery had plans to send Giles to study back home? I reminded myself I must ask her at church in the morning. Perhaps we could arrange for the boys to sail together. Wouldn't Tommy love that?

I didn't see Margery or the children at church though and speculated she might be ailing. But Giles had not said so. He'd said she was fine. *I'll just wander over to say hello afterwards and make sure she is all right,* I thought, as Reverend Bucke began with opening prayers. *And Argall shall punish her for her absence.* As a first offense, she would lose a week's provisions and rations. No exceptions, no excuses.

We had gotten as far as the Lord's Prayer when suddenly a woman screamed from the back of the church. All heads swung about.

It was Margery. Her coif was askew on her head, her dress muddied, her cheeks crimson from running the mile or so from her home near the Neck o' Land. Sweat poured from her face.

She gasped for breath, saying, "Mercy, help, oh, mercy!"

She then dropped to her knees as if she would collapse. Master Fairfax was up from his pew and at his wife's side in an instant, kneeling by her. I turned to look back at Reverend Bucke, who had a confused look upon his face.

Margery grasped her husband's hands and said, "The children! The children. Chickahominies. The children. Go!" She was shaking her head as if trying to shake the thoughts out of them.

Every man in the church leapt to his feet. No one asked permission to leave. They bolted for the door as one.

The women and children gathered around Margery, helping her to a pew.

Margery sobbed, and Maria Bucke put her arms around the woman kindly.

Margery, stricken, cried, "My babies, Maria! My...babies..."

She looked up at each of us, gathered around. "The Chickahominies got my babies," she said, tears streaming down her face.

She spilled out her story. Margery had left two older boys with her children and come to prayer alone. She'd gotten part of the way to the church only to hear a scream as the natives had approached her home. Seeing her, the Chickahominies had given chase, but she was far enough away from them that she had turned to run with all her might to the church.

My mouth gaped open, and I grabbed for Tommy. His eyes were wide, and he turned his head upward to me. "Giles is all right. He's an Indian fighter!" He said it with all the faith a little boy could muster.

No, Giles was not all right, and neither were little Ellen and Anthony, nor the older boys who had been at the house that morning.

Before, I had been unsure about sending Tommy away to England, even though I knew it was best for his studies. I had hated the idea of having so little part in his rearing.

But after seeing little Giles's gabled coffin laid into the church grounds next to the smaller ones of Ellen and Anthony, my heart changed. It broke for Margery, for sweet Giles and his little brother and sister. And while my heart still ached at the thought of sending Tommy away, I knew that Margery would *never* have her children back. Tommy's schooling was only for a short time, a few years, I told myself. I took a long look at my son, who wanted so much to be a soldier and Indian fighter.

The warrior blood. 'Tis always the same, generation to generation.

Let him go to England where he could receive proper schooling beyond what I could do. He would face many challenges without his father and me across the Atlantic, but murderous Chickahominies while he was alone at home would not be one.

A Basket of Earth
Mid-September, 1618 ~ Kecoughtan

*Opechankanough sent to Captaine Argall, to assure him the
peace should never be broken by him, desiring that [Argall] would
not revenge the injurie of those fugitives upon the innocent people
of that towne, which towne he should have, and sent him a basket
of earth, as possession given of it, and promised, so soone as possibly
they could catch these robbers, to send him their heads for satisfaction, but he never performed it.*
—John Smith's Generall Historie

"A basket of earth? By God, don't tell Margery."
Margery had received a day's reprieve from work to bury her children,
but that was all. The settlement under martial law was a prison, and never
more so than with Argall at the helm. Argall cared only for himself and his
riches, that much we understood more as time passed.

Isabella Pace and I were working at making tallow. The deaths of the children had been only two weeks before, and all the settlement was still grieving
the loss. Margery herself had spoken little since the incident. She hung her
head and worked.

Now, as the smoky, smelly tallow wafted upward, Isabella and I looked
over our shoulders with an uneasiness we'd not felt for a while. The whole
town was talking about the killings and the peace offering—a basket of earth.

The braves had come only a mile from James Cittie and struck with terrifying surprise and swiftness. The children hadn't stood a chance. The thought
of these small ones...their fear.... *Stop!* I could not think of it, could not stand
to imagine their horror.

Opechancanough had sent a basket of earth from the murder site, avow-
ing to Governor Argall that treachery such as this would not happen again.
Isabella remarked idly, "I heard the Indian messenger called the killers
'renegades,' said they weren't welcome back in the native towns. Not ever.
Opechancanough said he would take their heads off if he could catch them."

I pushed the coif back from my brow as sweat ran down my face in tiny rivers. Tallow. I had come to hate it. September was still far too warm in Virginia to stand over the hot mess, but here we were. Our names had come up on the dreaded tallow-making list.

"Do you believe Opechancanough speaks the truth?" I asked her. I wasn't sure I did. Will was concerned about the new chief. Powhatan had been a little more predictable. Pocahontas's father had said at the end of his life that he was through with fighting, that too many men on both sides had died. We even heard that Powhatan had moved further south in his final few years fearing that Opechancanough would band with the English against him.

No one, it seemed, not even his own brother, knew exactly where Opechancanough stood although the new chief pledged unending peace. Powhatan had been dead just five months before the murders of the Fairfax children occurred. Was it a sign of things to come? I stirred the hot tallow as hard as I could, trying not to think too much. While the Chickahominies were not truly a part of the Powhatan kingdom, Opechancanough had answered for them, so they were not wholly removed either.

"I don't know, I don't know, Joan." Isabella was musing, her cheeks rosy and wet from the heat, her coif soaked in sweat.

The basket of earth had come from the place where the murders occurred. This was to show that those sites were now a gift to the English, Opechancanough had said.

Then the messenger had enquired about our guns. "Your *pacussac-ans* are sick, are they not? We notice you do not use them."

Argall, we heard, had realized the Indians were fishing for information. Argall had asked the Company for more gunpowder, it had never come, and now the natives had taken note. The natives did not understand our matchlocks. We knew that a few years back some Indians had stolen gunpowder and planted it, hoping to grow their own. In their minds, guns could be sick, and gunpowder was a crop. This mystery we wished to preserve at all costs. Thousands of braves still vastly outnumbered us in this wilderness.

"We have a peace pact. We do not need guns, do we?" Argall had declared with bravado.

Argall had set himself up as the only one to trade with the natives, which made no one happy on either side.

"The governor assured Opechancanough that we will not seek revenge, Isabella." I hated to think of Margery hearing *that*. The memories of Gates and Dale had been long. For every action against our settlement, a swift penalty. By not showing the natives such behavior came with a price, was Argall selling us all for silver? "It seems we have our own Judas. As long as the trade goods keep flowing to Argall himself, the Indians may do what they please. That's Argall's message to the Indian king, which is not only greedy, but dangerous."

A Cry that Shiver'd

October 15, 1618 ~ Sir Thomas Smythe's home on Philpot Lane, London

A cry that shiver'd to the tingling stars,
And, as it were one voice, an agony
Of lamentation, like a wind that shrills
All night in a waste land, where no one comes,
Or hath come, since the making of the world.
—Alfred, Lord Tennyson

The Bible talked about weeping, wailing, and gnashing of teeth, and that was all but the reaction going on in the Virginia Company offices at Sir Thomas Smythe's home on Philpot Lane.

First the Company had learned that Argall's treachery and greed had pushed the Company even closer to the brink of bankruptcy through Argall's personal use of Company land and stock. An investment of eighty thousand pounds, lost.

The *Diana*, just returned from Virginia, came bearing news that the *Treasurer* seemed outfitted as a warship. The Company now understood that Argall's and Rich's piracy schemes might bring the wrath of both Spanish and English kings upon their heads. Antagonizing the Spanish further could lead to a Virginia massacre or to outright war.

The ship shared other devastating news. Bloody flux was taking a terrible death toll upon Virginia. And, most sorrowful loss of all, this dreadful disease had cost the life of the Honorable Lord La Warr. To the men sitting around the great table, this good man had been their friend, their hope, and the most generous contributor to their cause.

Baron La Warr had pledged to bring his whole wealth into the colonization efforts of Virginia. He loved the land there. He believed in it. His going there had been the greatest hope of saving the Company's few remaining assets from Argall.

And now La Warr was dead.

If a giant, collective heart could give up the ghost, then that was the effect in the offices that day. Troubles had come at them as an army in a legion. The men were weary, the Company out of money.

Some swore it was over. They'd contribute no more, cut their losses and walk away.

Others said that they would never now collect on old subscriptions. Who would throw money to a defeated cause? Money on which no returns would ever come.

And some said there was no man fit enough to be governor and captain-general of such a place as Virginia now that Lord La Warr had died.

Sir Edwin Sandys, a hopeful zealot, had other ideas, however. He for one refused to abandon the vision of Virginia just when new ideas of managing government and allowing men there the freedom to live under English—not martial—law had come to the forefront.

Just when the Virginia Council had birthed a thought to allow the colony to govern itself on day-to-day matters, giving to it a representative body, a General Assembly.

And just when the time seemed ripe to introduce new commodities for the betterment and welfare of all Englishmen, not just those living in Virginia. Commodities that would help erase Virginia's dependence on the smoky weed, tobacco.

No, Sir Edwin Sandys was not prepared to give up on the colony yet. He presented a plan to Sir Thomas Smythe. Sandys had a new choice for governor, a young man with experience in Virginia, who had proven hearty enough to endure its challenges and who was a soldier truly bred in the art of war in the battlefields of the Low Countries. This soldier might not have nobility, but he was an honest, hard-working man. Dale had liked and trusted him, after all. This was perhaps the highest endorsement any Virginia leader could receive. Besides, the Company might be able to procure some honor upon the man, raise him up just a little. Why, look at Dale himself! Or Gates. These men had proven themselves in many battles but had no real titles outside of hard work, courage, honor, and knighthood.

Sandys presented his thoughts to Smythe, who nodded, afraid to hope. The plan just might work. If they could get the lotteries generating more funds to keep the venture going, they could perhaps soon see profits. Tobacco brought some income to the men in Virginia, but the Company must find other commodities as well. If the Company sent large amounts of settlers to the colony, those settlers could get right to work on other commodities like silk, wine, and ores. The Virginia Company could not seem to earn enough, unlike Smythe's other great companies exploring East India and Turkey. Aye, Smythe agreed to the idea, too. And Smythe liked the proposition for governor. This man might just be the one for the formidable task at hand.

George Yeardley would make a fine governor and captain-general.

The Last Council of Mercy
October 15, 1618 ~ James Cittie

I am the last
Council of mercy in their hearts where they
Mete justice from a thousand starry thrones.
—A.E. Russell

Back in Virginia, trouble was brewing between two men with tempers like firebrands.

The first time I had seen Captain Brewster since his return to James Cittie, I was surprised. His voyage on the *Neptune* had been a difficult one and had even left the captain lame. He had broken his leg at sea. How, I did not know. The withering of his leg had left his body crippled but not his spirit. He had a crude crutch tucked beneath his arm. I was ashamed when I heard some laughing. One man, perhaps the victim of Brewster's tongue in an earlier time, called out, "He broke his leg. Would that he had broken his neck instead!" Another said, "Aye, then we'd have been troubled with him no more. As long as that man's about, there shall always be sedition and mutiny."

Captain Brewster had come by our home sometime after that, dragging his bad leg, seeking Will. Brewster was attempting to find homes for De La Warr's servants, and he wondered if Will would pay the passage of a laborer named Jack Cartwright. Will had been able to sell some of his tobacco on the last ships and so he agreed, setting Cartwright to work. Argall was providing nothing to De La Warr's people. Brewster was farming them out as he could.

Brewster had always had a bitter way about him, and this had not changed. He had once years ago even struck George Percy as Percy headed a company of soldiers about to battle the Paspahegh. It was dangerous for the natives to see a subordinate strike a leader.

If anything, Brewster had grown more bitter, it seemed, with his treatment under the regime of Governor Argall. Brewster explained to Argall that the dying La Warr had entrusted him with his estate.

"That was at sea, Brewster! You're in Virginia now, and I am ultimately in charge of all that you see including the goods of the baron. Sorry as I am about his death."

Argall didn't look sorry. He seemed, rather, to relish the control he had managed to keep longer than expected.

Brewster asked for food for his settlers, but Argall declined. "There's victuals about. Let them labor and earn it!" Argall had put the men to work for their food, but gave them not lodging.

Captain Brewster had reached the end of his patience. Lord La Warr's affairs were in a shambles.

First, Brewster had learned that ten men La Warr had sent in 1617 to prepare for his coming had not built housing, had not prepared crops. Instead, Argall had confiscated a man named Carpenter, whom De La Warr had placed in charge, to do the governor's own work. Three of the ten were dead, the other six loitering about the country and half-starved, including Carpenter's wife.

His Lordship had sent six cows and fourteen goats, expecting his men to husband them. Argall had taken the cows. Captain West, Lord La Warr's brother, the goats. But the livestock had not, as Brewster could determine, been put to work on the lordship's behalf.

The same day, Brewster had confronted Argall. Brewster demanded fair treatment for the baron's goods and men. "What, sir, shall I tell the baron's wife? How shall I say that his entire investment is seemingly lost, lost, lost!" The only one making money off his lordship's investment was Argall himself. The governor enriched himself at the expense of the good baron, who had left his wife deeply in debt to support this venture.

"Throw Brewster in close prison!" Argall ordered one of his men. The soldier dragged Brewster to the gaol with instruction that Brewster talk to no one but his gaoler. And anyone caught talking to Brewster would face pain of death.

Lying on the ground where Brewster had stood was his ragged crutch.

The settlement rumbled with the news. Martial law was still intact, but the penalty of death was only for those who threatened the governor. Argall would punish talking with execution? And Brewster himself had not threatened the governor. He had only asked for that rightfully in his charge.

Argall's decision was swift: he would put Brewster to death.

Now Reverend Bucke, Reverend Wickham, John Rolfe, and others of the martial court stood up and pleaded Brewster's case. "Do *not* put him to death, sir! We plead for his life. Spare him," cried an impassioned Reverend Bucke.

Brewster himself showed great remorse. Weeping, Brewster said, "Sir, if you will be but pleased to spare me my life and to send me into England or employ me in any place in Virginia for the colony, you will find that I will lead a new life and become a new man. I never knew *God* until this day, sir!"

Argall's eyes were cold. He cared little whether Brewster lived or died, and Brewster's plea moved him not at all. But the governor understood, too, that if he lost the support of these men, he would have a tough time of it.

"Release him!" Argall said. "Put him on a ship for England. He is never to come to this colony again, never to speak ill of the colony or of any of its leaders including me."

The situation was clear. Argall was a tyrant. Could anyone save the colony before Argall inflicted damage of a broader nature?

They Can Fool the Devil
Late October, 1618 ~ Kecoughtan

Upon the ocean seas, a warlike Portuguese
In sport did us displease while we sailed...

We steered from sound to sound, and many ships we found
And all of them we burned, as we sailed, as we sailed.
—Old Ballad about Captain Kidd

People have discovered that they can fool the devil; but they
can't fool the neighbors.
—Edgar Watson Howe

The *Neptune* had just left Virginia for England with Captain Brewster aboard. Brewster was prepared to give the Virginia Company an earful about his treatment and about Argall stealing Lord La Warr's goods. Argall had ordered him not to speak ill? He cared not.

Governor Argall was pleased. *Good, La Warr's* Neptune *was gone. Its sister ship, Argall's* Treasurer *had work to do.*

Argall and Rich had outfitted the *Treasurer* as a man-o'-war. A few had seen the inside of the ship, and they were surprised. If she were truly a fishing ship, where the fishing tackle? Where the nets and hooks? No, there were none of these, as any who had climbed aboard the *Treasurer* from the *Neptune*, when both ships had moored at the Azores, could tell you. They knew. They'd seen her forbidden and dangerous trappings.

Fishing, aye! Fishing for Spanish goods, an illegal and dangerous mission. Dangerous not only for the *Treasurer* and her men, but also for us in the colony. The Spanish, if they sought retribution, would avenge against all for the sins of one.

Here in Virginia, it was difficult to get a good look at the ship, for Argall's men were guarding her tightly by night and by day.

The truth had become all too clear. The *Treasurer's* Captain Elfrith was a notorious pirate. Lord Rich and his father had hired Elfrith in times past to prey on Spanish shipping.

Now we understood this Elfrith was the same captain who had brought a Spanish ship filled with looted grain to Bermuda five years before. The settlers had needed the food supplies, true. But as with all such ill-gotten gain, the ship had also brought an unexpected consequence: black rats. Rats that swam from place to place across the Bermuda islands. Some colonists even pulled in fish with rats in their bellies. The rats had bred, nesting in almost every tree and roof, burrowing in the ground. The black pests had eaten crops in the ground as well as stored corn and wheat. Even with traps, cats, and hunting dogs, years had gone by before the rats were under control.

Argall ordered some of the baron's men and others aboard the *Treasurer*. Whether these men were interested in becoming pirates mattered little to the governor.

And when the *Treasurer* loosed from her moorings in the waters at Kecoughtan, easterly winds pushing her toward the bay, she had a clear, published mission. The Virginia ship would be going to the West Indies to trade for goats and salt.

However, never was a goat that needed a gun put to it on his rope. And surely, Argall expected the salt to put up a handsome fight by the looks of intimidating ordnance aboard the *Treasurer*.

We asked ourselves, what consequence could *we* expect from Elfrith's piracy? Rats? Or something worse?

I had little time to consider what this meant before I received a note from Cecily in Bermuda Hundred, brought to me by a shallop traveling between the two towns.

I read the note quickly, and my heart raced. *Tom is very sick with flux, Little Temp and I are yet well, but I feel I may have it oncoming. Please send Jane to help.*

Strength to Meet Sorrow
Late October to early November 1618 ~ James Cittie, and Bermuda Hundred

With strength to meet sorrow, and faith to endure.
—Frances Sargent Osgood

I knew Cecily didn't want to take me away from my own house and duties, but I decided to go myself, leaving the household in Jane's charge. A pinnace was heading upriver, and I begged passage, promising to pay in tobacco. I knew Will would agree, and the captain did too.

Would Argall miss me from my task list? I thought I should chance it. Argall's men had assigned Judith Perry to work with me at spinning, and she swore she'd cover for me so that Argall would never know. That meant she risked flogging herself, but we women were determined to stand with one another.

Hours later, at the Bermuda Hundred bridge, I saw that in the year and a half since I had last been there, the settlement had grown. The homes were filled with more livestock and settlers milling about.

A woman with a long and unhappy expression saw me climbing off the pinnace. She stopped me, trying to strike up a conversation. It struck me that I no longer knew every face in the colony.

I didn't wish to brush her away but said, "I'm sorry, mistress. I'm in a hurry. I have to get to the Baileys' house."

She took the pipe from between her teeth and pointed it. "Thataway, mistress. Road bends over to the west and off behind the church. But I'm sure you know that. The flux been right bad righ'chere. What's going on at the 'big town'? We've had two runs o' the fluxes."

"Fluxes there, too. I come because Cecily Bailey is my daughter, and her family is ill with it," I said over my shoulder as I set off down the road.

I walked past other houses, trying to avoid questions. I understood well the danger Cecily and her family were in. I tried not to think of it, but shifted my satchel of herbs this way and that, crossing the old creek path.

At last I saw her home and a face in the window I recognized. Cecily was alive! "Praise God, Cecily," I said as she dropped into my arms. I searched her pale face. "And the family?"

She swallowed hard and said, "Tom has died. Reverend Wickham hast buried him." And then she began to sob.

So did I. "I am sorry I was not here sooner, I…I came as fast as I could." She nodded. "I know."

As we stood in the doorway wrapped in each other's arms, a small girl came to stare at us curiously. Little Temp! Black curls and pixie eyes like her Grandpa Tom Reynolds, lost so long ago in the war. I loosed from Cecily and knelt before the small girl. "Do you know your grandma, child?" I asked her.

Rather than answer, she turned to her mother and said, "Mama, my belly hurts."

I spent the next weeks nursing the little girl and then her mama. I had learned something of what worked and what did not because of my other flux patients. Tommy and I had the flux rather mildly, but not so Cecily and Little Temp. They were suffering badly. I fought fear as I tried to nurse them back to health. If only I had Mistress Wright's agate. But I knew she would never have let me bring it upriver and keep it so long. There were, after all, spirits walking after the sun set.

Cecily and Little Temp ate the broth of stewed chickens, but little else.

I kept the fire warm and them near it. And I prayed. Every day, all day, I prayed as I worked, taking care of them and working the remaining harvest as best I could. John Rolfe was back at James Cittie, but perhaps Sam Jordan would help us with the tobacco.

Thoughts troubled me as I worked. Had I been wicked? I'd been grateful for those who died, knowing it was simpler for me than feeding and caring for strangers. Dear God.

I worked early and late doing the things Tom might have done, the things Cecily was not able to do. I kept firewood in the house and the fire stoked. I walked the chamber pots outside and emptied them an appropriate distance from the house. I wrung the necks of chickens to make pottage for my two girls, the eighteen-year-old and the three-year-old. I swept and scrubbed. Bloody flux left its marks on a house.

Cecily and Little Temp suffered, getting no better and no worse. I didn't know what to think, so I just kept fighting it, fighting the flux as if it were Argall, as if it were the Chickahominies who killed Giles, as if it were the sickness, poverty, and hopelessness we all felt.

Just fighting.

One night, I tossed beneath the blanket. Guilt, shame, and a deep weariness weighed on me. I had wished people dead. What if Cecily had been in a strange place and someone had cared for her as I did Lydia Quarles? Hoping it would all end soon? When had I become such a person?

As I drifted into a restless sleep, Lydia Quarles's pallid, confused face kept coming into my mind. I tried to push it away. I saw images of so many who had died in my care—my mother and my little son John, Elizabeth Mayhew and old Grace, Maggie, Annie's tiny baby, the Mortons, and Lydia. All the faces jumbled together, and I tossed and turned on the straw mattress, feeling very helpless and ridden with guilt. Maybe I hadn't done enough. Maybe I had done the wrong things…. Shame burned my cheeks. Sometimes, I reckoned, it was harder to be the one left behind.

Then a strange thing happened.

For the first time in a long while, I had dreams filled with color. I saw my father waving from the bow of the *Seawynd*. The ship sparkled as if new while the water and sky were a rich azure. The ship must have been moored in Virginia, for white blossoms fell from a large dog tree, blanketing the ground like snow.

I climbed aboard and found to my surprise all those who had died recently, even Giles and his little brother and sister. Giles pulled my sleeve and said, "Did you bring Tommy?"

Everyone seemed to be talking at once. I lowered my head when Mistress Quarles came to me. Her eyes were clear, and she had a big man by the arm. "This is my Ben," she cried happily. And she pointed to her bodice, all of blue silk. "He remembered!"

Did she not hold me responsible for her death? "I'm sorry…" I tried to say.

She cocked her head. "For what, dearie?" she said and then blended into the crowd.

Mistress Morton came forward, wanting me to meet her little daughter Hannah, who had died before the family left England. Hannah ran forward holding her brother Isaac's hand. *There are too many children here! They shouldn't be on this ship. They should be on land playing.*

"But we're playing here, Mistress Peirce," Giles said as if reading my thoughts. He grinned a freckly grin, and I wrapped my arms around him.

"I am going to tell your mother I saw you here," I whispered into his ear.

"Oh, thanks. Tell her I'm just fine, and tell Tommy, too!"

I looked around. Where was Maggie? Everyone else seemed to be here. Before I had time to consider it, my father pushed over to me, throwing his arms around me in an embrace I could still feel the next day. And then he swung me around in a happy, loving spin.

As he put me down, I said, "Father, are you the captain? How did you find all these people?"

He shrugged. "They were at the bridge. I help out this way." It seemed the most natural thing in the world. I nodded.

"But where is Maggie?" Maybe it had just been too many years. She's just taken another ship, I thought as if that made perfect sense.

My father gave me a puzzled look. "Why, she had work to do. Didn't you hear?"

"Oh." Disappointment washed over me. Then a sober realization struck as reality and dream blended. "Father, Cecily and Little Temp are very sick."

He smiled, and his face did not look tired or worn. He stared away over the bright water as if mulling things over. He turned back to me and said slowly, "I believe they're going to be all right, Joanie. Aye, they'll be all right. Don't worry, Joanie. No ship is coming for them, not now."

The next morning, I opened my eyes as the sun burst over the river. The sky turned bright colors, and I marveled over the previous night. The dream of my father had been so real that I felt as if he'd just left from a visit.

Over the next few days, both Cecily and Little Temp grew steadily stronger until at last the danger had past.

We had made it through. They had made it through. I squeezed Cecily's hand. "Who needs agate when one has God?" I said to her.

She looked at me curiously and then said, "I give up. Who?" And we laughed, the first laughter in days.

I sat with Little Temp on my lap, and for a moment—just a moment—I could forget where we were and what we had endured. The little girl's smile and innocence lifted me and made me feel light. Now I understood joy.

"Tell me a story, grandma."

"Well," I began. "Once when your great-grandfather Phippen was a-sailing 'cross the Narrow Sea, way back in England a long time ago, he saw a ship he knew to be Algerian pirates…"

The pilgrim badge weighted my neck. The legacy from my father, so long ago. My ancient grandfather had brought it home from a pilgrimage to Compostela, and my father had left it to me. My father's brothers had called the old badge worthless, but it had great value to my father and me. Many times, I myself had felt like a pilgrim traversing a faraway land. *Father, could you have known where I would be? Aye, I think maybe you could. Somehow. And do you watch over your grandchildren and me even now?*

The fire roared upward, as if someone had pitched more kindling into it. *Aye, indeed, he is here.*

Direful Change
November 18, 1618 ~ the Kingdom of Ndongo, Africa, and in a Powhatan Indian Town, and in James Cittie

Eight things there be a comet brings,
When it on high doth horrid range:
Wind, Famine, Plague, and Death to Kings,
War, Earthquakes, Floods, and Direful Change.
—Johann Jacob Grasser and Johann George Grossen, 1618, created to warn German schoolchildren

The fourth and last comet, *appearing this year* [1618], *was that which* all the earth *looked upon with* astonishment.
—Increase Mather

Somewhere in Africa in the land the Portuguese called São Paulo de Loanda, a lone young woman stood in the night air, looking upward with great fear.

The star with a shimmering long, red tail sped across the Angolan skies.

Santa Maria, Mãe de Deus, she murmured, using the words the Portuguese priest had taught her village to pray to Christ's mother. Then in her native Angolan tongue, she added to the moon above, *I do not think this a good thing.*

* * *

Three *quiyoughcosoughs* studied the night sky above their town on the Powhatan River in Virginia. The hair-star shot through the sky like an arrow from *Ahone's* bow.

At the same time, within the Indians' longhouses, their *yi-hakans*, braves and children, old men and women alike all doubled in pain while their insides cramped and gave forth blood.

Blood like the blood-red hair trailing this star.

One of the priests pointed upward, murmured a prayer, and all three bowed their heads and echoed it.

It was clear to them that *Okeus,* the god of justice, had sent this plague upon them.

But why?

* * *

At James Town, through separate windows and out separate doors, Governor Samuel Argall and the rest of the colony stood awestruck as the great comet sped across the Virginia skies.

A comet foretold as nothing else could the death of a king or birth of a new government. Or could it mean famine, plague, or flood—any number of disasters or great change.

"Is King James in danger, do you reckon?" Jane asked me. She had heard people talking about how a comet predicted King Harold's loss to William the Conqueror.

The comet silently moved across the night sky, its silence deafening, all that it left unsaid the more terrifying.

"And Edward the Confessor. Wasn't there a comet before he died, too?"

I shook my head. "I do not know what it means. For us, it could be… well…" I turned my gaze in the direction of the Big House. "I don't know," I said quickly. But her question left me wondering. If we saw the comet *here,* did it predict death to our king, the only likely way he might lose the throne, or would the comet signify something about our own Virginia government? Could a comet portend death to the English king if English subjects watched it fly over Virginia?

These were questions I knew not the answer to. With a sigh, I thought, *How I wish my father were still alive, that I might ask his opinion.*

My mind darted across the ocean to London, and I wondered if Tempie could see the blazing star as well. Thousands of miles apart across a huge and mighty ocean, we had not seen one another in almost five months. I missed her so. All that we had in common at this moment were the night skies. We could see the same moon and the same stars, and perhaps, even, the same blazing comet.

God, please bring Tempie home to Virginia safely and, um, God save the king! I added as an afterthought. *God save King James and Queen Anne as well. But mostly, God save Tempie!* I smiled at my own irreverence.

Yet, that comet was worrisome.

I wondered as I studied it. Were Englishmen in England seeing it, too?

The Moone to Bloode
November 18, 1618 ~ Cheapside, London

Yee men of Brittayne wherefore gaze yee so,
Upon an angry starre? When as yee knowe
The Sun must turne to darke, the Moone to bloode,
And then t'will bee to late to turne to good.
—King James, assuring his subjects that no man knew the
meaning of the comet, 1618

Nov. 18— *A comet under the extreme part of Libra was*
visible to me. False rumor of the Queen's death.
—William Camden's London diary, 1618

"Yon flies the angry star!" cried a boy beneath the window of Ralph
Yeardley's home on Great Wood Street in Cheapside where Tempie,
George, and the young children were staying during their sojourn.

Ralph went to the window in concern as he heard more yells. Vagrant
boys, he guessed. One pitched a stone at Ralph's shop sign, apparently. Those
in the room suddenly heard a bang and the sign creaking on its chains.

Ralph pushed open the window. "Get on, you!" he yelled at them. "Go
on!" Sounds of running and laughing until the night quieted once more.

Tempie couldn't resist a smile. "They've hit your artichoke, Ralph."

"Hm?" Ralph looked over at her, his brows still furrowed in concern until
he understood her humor. His apothecary shop was located at the Sign of the
Artichoke, so a painted artichoke graced the shop. Ralph and his family lived
on the upper floors, and the fresh aroma of herbs drifted tantalizing upward
at all times.

"Blasted boys," he mumbled. "Afraid they'll throw a rock through my
glass and break my jars. Happened a few weeks ago and left distilled waters,
simples, and compositions all over the floor. The rock broke my most beautiful jar, the *fructus cardamomi,* and of course, I lost all the cardamom fruit
in it. I mean to get me a mastiff to tie up down there. But this lot, ah, I

reckon they're just watchin' the sky like everyone else," Ralph said. The hinge groaned as he pulled the window shut once more.

George Yeardley drew a deep breath, something of a sigh, and he met the eyes of his brother and wife.

"I suppose you're right about that. They're just watching the angry star as we are. Night after night the comet returns as if it's mocking us."

Many had taken to calling this comet "angry," with the comet tail blood red dangling fearsomely in its wake. "The star with long, blazing red hair. What do you suppose it means?" Tempie whispered.

George shook his head. "No one knows. Galileo says one thing. Brahe something else. Lilly a third thing. Lilly says its shape, like a sword, portends war in the Palatine. But others are sure it signifies..." He stopped short.

"Signifies? King James?" Tempie asked. Both men nodded at the same time, but no one wanted to say the actual words: *the king's death.*

Ralph Yeardley spoke up. "Everybody through my shop door the past two weeks whispering the same thing: *the queen herself is already dead!* That the king hides the news, and 'twas the comet foretold it.

"The queen is ill with dropsy. She is *not* dead." George Yeardley's tone carried contempt. "Have we not enough turmoil without contriving it?" He stepped to Ralph's tobacco box. "May I, brother?"

Ralph nodded. "Of course."

George laughed. "I need the smoke to clear my brain."

But all the idle talk was to be expected, for no more momentous sign existed for any government, new or old, than a blazing star in the heavens. And here the Virginia Company was with *this* star mocking them just as the Company this day made George Yeardley its governor! Was the comet predicting the demise of the Virginia Company?

George had not sought the office of governor and captain general, had not wanted it, but Sandys and Smythe had argued, even pleaded, that he take it. "With Gates and Dale committed to the Dutch military, the baron's death, and the great need for a soldier experienced in Virginia, you are our best choice," Sandys had said. *Our only choice,* he might have added.

Dale's previous endorsement had carried much weight. Dale had liked Yeardley enough to make him commander of his lead settlement, Bermuda Hundred, and had left Yeardley in charge at Dale's 1616 departure.

George accepted with reservations, but he did accept. If he had said no, he was unsure what the council might have done. Disbanding the colony was not out of the question. In fact, that thought had certainly crossed the men's minds.

George's first task: arresting Governor Samuel Argall. Overturning

Argall's administration and his hold on the young colony, ridding Virginia of her pirates, smoothing the waters with Spain and all the Spanish colonies.

It had been less than three weeks since the king had beheaded Sir Walter Ralegh to punish him for not finding El Dorado and for raiding the Spanish territories. Ralegh had already suffered a great loss this year because his son had died when Ralegh's expedition seized the town of St. Thomas.

"Strike, man, strike!" Ralegh had called out his last words to the executioner. The king had now proven he would behead one of England's great heroes to appease the Spanish. The Virginia Company needed to take seriously Argall's affront to the Spanish, that much was certain.

The Company also would ask the king to sign a new charter with more power going into the hands of the adventurers and planters. The company signed the instructions to George Yeardley this day, the eighteenth of November, as the comet soared more boldly than ever across London. Many of the recommendations had come from George Yeardley himself.

George's foremost task after Argall's arrest, was to repeal Dale's bloody martial laws. A deed about six years too late in George's own estimation. The Company had written hope for just government and fair treatment of the planters directly into the new charter.

Beyond that, the planters themselves for the first time would have a voice in their own affairs: a General Assembly with two men elected to represent all other landholders, no matter the size of their acreage.

For, who knew better than a planter in the Eastern Shore what laws best befitted the Eastern Shore? Who understood better than a planter in Paspahegh country, near James Cittie, what to enact where *he* lived? Who better than those setting up the college, far upriver, what needs they had? Not the council at James Cittie although they had final say as to reasonableness. And *certainly not* the Virginia Council here in London. So far removed were they, they had little understanding of the challenges, the poverty, the danger, the very wildness of frontier Virginia.

No, the planters themselves. They were the ones who not only knew best, but had earned such a right.

The best news of all, the news that would send the colonists cheering, was that all the old planters—those who were in Virginia before Dale had left in May 1616—would receive special privileges. The Company deemed these "ancient planters." *Based on enduring the worst Virginia had to offer,* Yeardley prayed. *Could it ever be worse than what had come before?*

To the ancient planters, special privileges and extra land. Land in their own names, one hundred acres for each man, woman, and child who was over age ten upon sailing. Those arriving since 1616 would receive fifty acres each. *Land.* How wonderful to bring news such as this.

For good reason was this momentous document called *the Great Charter.*

George's tasks were formidable: rebuilding the plantation, encouraging morale amongst disheartened settlers, initiating the General Assembly, and revoking martial law.

Lord Rich had hoped this change might mean a bit longer to run his piracy operation from Virginia, an act he considered one of supreme patriotism. One he flaunted, despite it now being illegal. *If our king weren't so unreasonably close to the Spanish king.* Ah, well, measures were measures.

Yet, Sandys's choice of removing Rich's cousin Sam Argall as governor indicated that the Rich faction might have to yank its allegiance from Sandys. Which it was in the process of doing.

The Virginia government had never looked so hopeful and so fragmented at the same time.

George Yeardley suspected his old commanding officer, Sir Thomas Gates, would not now ever return to Virginia. Not since Gates's old friend Smythe was losing favor with the Virginia Company. Too many were questioning Smythe's policies, blaming him for failures not solely his fault. *And Gates living in a rented property of Sir Thomas Smythe's over in Kent,* Yeardley thought. No, Gates was never coming back, despite promises Gates had made to the Company the previous year before the vast fight between the factions. Loyalty would force Gates to side with Smythe. Yeardley sighed with genuine regret. *Too bad.* Except that opened the door for Yeardley himself to be a leader.

And George Yeardley had felt long ago that the answer lay in strong, sound, *reasonable* government, not through Dale's Laws of Blood, nor through the self-serving government of Argall. No, in 1616, Yeardley had possessed ideas of good governance, and all too little time to pursue them before Argall had arrived to take over. At that time, Argall had criticized the Yeardley administration.

Now, Argall himself would receive a supreme surprise.

Arrest.

"Shall we count the charges against Argall, Ralph?" George asked, as he lifted the lid of the tobacco box. "Embezzlement, extortion, troublemaking, theft, maladministration of the colony, and probably, by the time I return, piracy."

Ralph shook his head and whistled. "Unbearable," he mumbled.

Tempie looked at both men uneasily. She was making it a point to stay within the room. She wanted to hear all they said. She was unable to fathom that her little son carried such a name. *Argall.*

George used the bowl end of the pipe to collect a small amount of tobacco. Then he pulled a piece of flint and steel from the box and dashed the flint against the steel. A spark. "Ah!" He lit the tobacco and drew a deep pull from the pipe.

Virginia's new governor sat in silence for a moment, the only sound the air he blew into the room as Ralph and Tempie watched. He dropped into a chair near the fire, and his brother walked over and sat down as well.

"I can't believe we've lost Lord La Warr, Ralph."

Ralph, too, was a member of the Virginia Company. The baron's passing had been a shock to all. Did nothing ever go the Company's way?

"Without the support of one in so high a position…" Ralph's voice trailed off.

"Argall corrupt, La Warr dead, Rich furious, Smythe in jeopardy, Gates refusing to help out of loyalty to Smythe, the king angry at Sandys…and a blazing comet warning us, to boot!"

Tempie walked to the chair behind her husband and put her hands on his shoulders. All the weight of Virginia's success or failure seemed to now fall squarely on the shoulders where her hands rested, and it scared her.

George Yeardley set the pipe onto a table, then rubbed and warmed his hands in front of his brother's fire. He reached a hand up to pat Tempie's.

"One other matter. I understand that the Company has made an offer to your cousin Pory to be secretary," he said to his wife.

Tempie and John Pory were first cousins, but she hadn't seen the man since she was a child. She knew his reputation, however. He was both well-read and a fluent writer, a natural choice to be secretary. Having a family member gave Tempie a modicum of peace.

"Good. You'll need sure help." Tempie was concerned about the tasks ahead for her husband. The ship's journey, coupled with worry, had already been hard on him.

"One thing is for certain, my dear." George's tone was serious. "We cannot return to Virginia bringing new government until this dreadful omen is past and out of the skies. 'Twould be foolhardy to travel beneath it. Despite Virginia needing us to remove Argall *immediately.*"

She nodded solemnly. She understood and had expected as much. How long had the comet been flying over? Some had seen it for as long as a month. Surely it had to leave soon, she thought. "Howe'er long it take."

But tomorrow, George set off on another journey which was to be the journey of a lifetime. Not traveling so far in distance but in stature. He wished to be happy about it. But he wasn't at all sure he wanted all that this entailed.

If such a thing, being governor and captain general, led a man to ill health, what was it worth?

"While you go to visit your mother, I'll leave at dawn for Newmarket."

Tempie nodded. This she knew. She knew also that her husband would return to London a changed man. How could he not? Didn't meeting the king change one?

Tempie barely knew which frightened her more—the comet, or facing her mother after almost ten years apart.

A Bag~Pudding the King Did Make
November 19-21, 1618 ~ Traveling from London
to Newmarket, Kent

A bag-pudding the king did make,
And stuffed it well with plums;
And in it put great lumps of fat,
As big as my two thumbs.

The king and queen did eat thereof,
And noblemen beside;
And what they could not eat that night,
The queen next morning fried.
—English Nursery Rhyme

The high road between Cheapside and Hoddesdon was rutted, mucky, and in places nearly impassable. George Yeardley spurred his brother's bay, Bushrod. As a soldier with much training on the battlefields of the Low Countries, George rode confidently although he missed having his own horse.

Riding ahead, George's livery Laurence urged his own horse forward. Now George drove Bushrod at a brisk canter to keep pace with Laurence, for the overcast skies were a concern. The November rain seemed to be holding off, or so the men hoped, but the air was damp and the clouds dreary. A bad rain could muddy out the road through the Lea Valley, causing a delay in George's travel.

It would take George and Laurence a full day's ride, some twenty miles, to reach the market town of Hoddesdon. There George hoped to lodge at the White Swan or the Golden Lion. From Hoddesdon, early morning if the weather held, George would go another day's ride to Royston. After a night's stay at the Black Bull, the final leg of his journey would be to Newmarket Palace.

Newmarket Palace.

The very thought of it thrilled him. He had not allowed himself to become unseemly proud, but he wanted to be. He desperately did.

In just a few days, I, George Yeardley, son of a merchant-tailor, have an audience with the king. Who would have thought that soldiering in poor Virginia would lead to this?

Tempie, traveling to her mother's home this day, was very, very proud of him, he knew. And when he returned to Tempie, he would be Sir George, Knight, and she Dame Temperance, Lady Yeardley. *God knows,* he thought of his wife, *no one deserves it more.*

Once on High Street in Newmarket, the king's new palace rose up before George Yeardley.

"Suppose he had to build it, hey?" said Laurence, as he drew up beside his master's horse. "The king do love the heaths, like any good Scotsman!"

George Yeardley had to agree. King James had come to rule England from Scotland upon the death of Queen Bess and had scarcely set foot in the country before he discovered East Anglia's heathlands. The king had fallen in love with the little town of Newmarket, and the town had never been the same.

Almost immediately, James had begun spending large amounts of time in the rural village so filled with heaths reminiscent of his boyhood. Newmarket was the king's place of greyhounds and hare hunting, hawking and tilting— all the pastimes in which James delighted, both as participant and as viewer.

After renting out inns for a few years, James had built a palace that took over the sites of the ancient inns. Now, sitting upon an acre at High Street and Sun Lane, the king's palace was, George thought, quite striking.

When the king came to Newmarket, so did the court. And George's suspicion that he might be catching the king in a jubilant mood was correct. For just the day before, young Prince Charles had celebrated his eighteenth birthday here at Newmarket.

With any luck, George reckoned, the festivities for the Prince of Wales might overshadow the rumors of the king's or queen's predicted demise as the glaring comet continued to race headlong through the skies over England.

In fact, the court and the king himself were all in a fine mood. The king had let it be known that he took no more notice of the blazing star than of the morning star.

Perhaps no one quite *believed* that the king believed that, as it flew in the face of all logic as well as incredible evidence of times when comets had marked death or profound changes in countries. But the king said it, and all about him said to his face, "Aye, sire! So true."

The evening before, the king, prince, and court had celebrated in high rural style at the nearby farmhouse of a man named Gamige. When George rode into New Market, all were still talking about the event.

Henry Wriothesley, the Earl of Southampton, an enthusiastic Virginia Company supporter and friend of Sandys, met George and regaled the governor with tales of the sumptuous feast the previous evening.

Since the number of lords and marquises in town had been few, the king had even asked knights and squires to join the planning, Sandys said. All had thrown ideas into it and decided that each would bring his own meats. And such it had been, each trying to best the others. Some had brought curious items, some extravagant, and some huge.

The king himself brought a great chine of beef and the Marquis of Hamilton four pigs encircled with sausages. Sandys told George that he had brought two turkeys, six partridges, and a whole tray of buttered eggs. Sir George Goring, known for his great good humor, had borne away the bell with his own invention: four huge fat pigs, piping hot, bitted and harnessed with ropes of sausages all tied to a monstrous bag pudding.

"A shame that the queen weren't here for her son's birthday, but she's ill back at Hampton Court." The earl dropped his voice somewhat. The queen had been sick of any number of illnesses since the comet appeared. No one thought it a good omen.

Yet, Sandys assured him, the king was still aglow following the feast.

"You've a fine day to be knighted, Yeardley," said the earl. George was humbled. He had never envisioned himself respected in the presence of earls and kings, but the earl viewed Virginia as serious, important business.

The king didn't like the Earl of Southampton, but Sandys's involvement with the Virginia Company, his title, and his role in Parliament forced a certain grudging respect. Sandys had put it to good use. It was he who had secured the knighthood for George.

"I had opportunity at the banquet to speak with His Majesty about you myself. His Highness is eager to learn more about the customs of the natives and what that land is like. I told him, sir, that *you* were the man with whom to speak. 'Tis only you men so versed in the New World who have the true answers. One cannot buy knowledge born of experience."

And George Yeardley understood at once that this was what made him truly valuable. Virginia was such that only those who had lived it could understand it.

The nobility ruled England, this much was true. But who of the nobility had actually ventured themselves to Virginia? Only a bold few. One noble, Lord La Warr. One brother of a noble, George Percy. And a handful of knights. No, the common man was settling Virginia—which might, in fact, make such men uncommon. Of nearly twenty-five hundred who had come to Virginia these past eleven years, only four hundred yet survived. But those who were still fighting for the cause were proving their mettle.

"I am honored, my Lord."

I, With Many a Fear

November 22, 1618 ~ St. Michael at Thorn, Norfolk, and Newmarket Palace, Kent

Bright Star! with laughter on her banners, drest
In thy fresh beauty. There! that dusky spot
Beneath thee, that is England; there she lies.
Blessings be on you both! one hope, one lot,
One life, one glory!—I, with many a fear
For my dear Country, many heartfelt sighs,
Among men who do not love her, linger here.
—William Wordsworth

Tempie knelt before her mother, holding the older woman's hand. Mistress Garrett lifted her other hand to her daughter's cheek.

"Sakes, child, you're but a wisp of the girl who went to Virginia. Age is supposed to fill thee out, not waste thee away!"

Tempie smiled self-consciously. She knew that after a decade in Virginia, she looked two decades older. "'Twas a long nine years, mother. Very long." Tempie's voice drifted away. She was unsure how much her mother knew. "But I'm home now."

"Home to stay?"

"No, mama. Not to stay."

"Oh. Why can't you stay? Won't that George Yeardley agree to it?" Tempie caught a tinge of anger.

"Our home is in Virginia now, mama. We've received a grant of two thousand acres from Opechancanough, the Indian king. The Company has validated the grant, so it's ours."

"Opee-what? You're dependent on *savages* to give you land? *You are a Flowerdieu.* You are not some ragged street woman to live in a hut in Virginia!"

Tempie sighed. This was going as she had expected. "In Virginia, I'm fairly ragged, mother. We all are." Might as well put the truth out there. "But one day, we'll have more. George has in mind to build a windmill, to farm the land. *The land is good,* mama. Fresh and green and wide. Wide as an ocean, deep as an ocean. Virginia will be a jewel in the king's crown one day."

"Jewel, fie."

"I do have news. The Company appointed George the governor and captain general, mother, because Lord La Warr has died. Why, the king is knighting George, perhaps today. My husband is at Newmarket this very moment!" At least, Tempie hoped so. That highwaymen had not waylaid him en route. No, she would not think that.

Mistress Garrett looked unimpressed. Tempie knew the expression. A knight who took her daughter away to Virginia was not chivalrous in her mother's mind. And that was that.

And then Mistress Garrett began to weep. "I have lost one daughter, pray God, let me not lose two!"

Tempie started to cry, too. Where was home, anyway? She was no longer sure.

A few moments of silence ensued, both women feeling their respective pain.

Then, "Tempie."

Tempie lifted her eyes as her mother spoke.

"You endured a hurricane?"

"Yes."

"And starvation?"

"Yes." Tempie, self-conscious, dropped her head.

"Two ocean voyages?"

Tempie nodded.

"Childbirth, with ague and flux like the Angel of Death, all about? Gave shelter to the poor, the sick and dying, too, I reckon?"

"I did. All of these and more, mother." What use to hide?

Silence again, as Mistress Garrett considered this.

Tempie lifted her eyes again and saw that her mother's face had softened. Mistress Garrett caressed her daughter's hollowed cheek. At last, the older woman said, "Then you are indeed a Stanley-Flowerdieu. Temperance, my sweet daughter, go in peace with God's grace and blessing. I will not have us part on sour terms as before. I *must* bless what I cannot change." Then the old woman pointed a finger at Tempie defiantly. "Child, show them how a Flowerdieu conquers the wilderness!"

Meanwhile, sixty or seventy miles away at Newmarket, Tempie's husband was feeling the touch of a father's hand. That is, the king's sword upon George's shoulder.

There, George Yeardley, new governor of Virginia, found himself in the presence of his king, a king still in high spirits from a son who had lived to attain his eighteenth year.

"Tell us thy name?"

"George Yeardley, Your Majesty."

"I see. For how many years hast thou been in Virginia?"

"Sire, I arrived nine and a half years ago. I was on the *Sea Venture,* ship-wrecked in the Bermudas. I have served there under Sir Thomas Gates, Lord La Warr, and Sir Thomas Dale. Later, upon Sir Thomas Dale's departure, I served as deputy governor." He tried to keep his voice confident, but it had a slight croak, despite his best efforts.

Am I truly having an audience with the king? Has the king taken a moment from all his duties to ask me *about my experiences in Virginia?*

"It is well. We wish thee to tell us about Virginia. It sounds a marvelous land. We are most interested in the religion of the natives. What think you of it? The princess Pocahontas, Rebecca, graced our presence, and our councilors did spend much time in discourse with the Indian priest, Tomocomo. We wonder what it may be you know of their religious habits, what you have learned in your time there."

George cleared his throat and warmed to a topic he, too, cared much about. "Sire, the natives do believe in the resurrection of the body, that when this life is finished, they go to certain fair, pleasant fields. The soul takes its solace there until the end of the world when it shall return to the body once more. Then body and soul live together in bliss for all time."

"Ah." King James cocked his head. "I reckon, then, that the Gospel must have been at some time known to those people and now is lost. Only this fragment remains."

The conversation continued much longer than George had expected. The king's curiosity about his colony seemed boundless, and well, George was an old-timer in the colony. He was proud of the land, Virginia, and all that the hapless souls there had accomplished despite everything against them.

George felt some odd yearning to return, and he had much, much to do when he did get his boots back in Virginia. Tempie had gone to visit her mother, and once the Company had made all its arrangements, the ship could depart within a few months. Hopefully, the comet would be gone by then.

At last, George Yeardley bared his shoulder to receive the touch of the king's sword, dropping to his knees in front of King James. George's head bowed low before his monarch while his heart raced with the thrill of this moment. The responsibility with which the Virginia Company and king graced him weighted his shoulders symbolically, as the king's own sword soon would.

The king reached out and with his sword touched the naked shoulder of the Virginia governor. And then the king spoke words of the old French, words that had dubbed knights for hundreds of years, hearkening back to the old Norman days when their French ancestors had come to the land of the Angles and Saxons and conquered it.

"*Sois, chevalier, au nom de Dieu!*" *Rise, knight, in the name of God!*

Sir George Yeardley stood and lifted his head until his eyes met those of James, King of England, Scotland, Ireland, Defender of the Faith....

"*Avancez, bon chevalier,* Sir George Yeardley." *Advance, good knight.*

The day had been momentous, certainly. However, George and Tempie were then unaware that others—even some they considered allies—were also making plans for Virginia, plans to which George Yeardley was but an obstacle.

Enemy Sly and Serpentine
Late December 1618 ~ Lord Rich's home, London

O enemy sly and serpentine...
—Robert Burns

Lord Rich was obviously enjoying the scene set before him. The candles flickered, the fireplace roared, and a servant delivered a finely engraved decanter of Rich's finest claret. Not that the man in front of him would care how fine it was.

Tippler, he thought with a hint of disdain.

No matter. Lord Rich had his guest's attention as well as his friendship, and he had an offer to make.

"More claret, sir?" A servant bent low, and the earl's guest held up his glass for the servant to fill.

"Indeed. Why, thank you."

The servant offered more to Lord Rich, who blocked his glass with his hand and shook his head. "But you may leave the claret," Rich added.

The servant nodded. Lord Rich waited for his man to depart the room. He wanted no prying ears to hear what he was about to propose.

When Rich heard the door click firmly, he decided to lay his plans onto the table.

He set his glass down and studied the man before him. The gentleman was fifteen years Rich's senior, a Cambridge scholar and author, geographer and protégé of the great Hakluyt himself as well as a former member of parliament. Someone who happily accepted hospitality from his friends across Europe and even into Constantinople and, thus, a world traveler if not something of a cadger. A hopeless gossip, a faithful correspondent, an excellent writer, and a drinker.

But for the drinking, the man might actually achieve greatness, Rich thought. Yet, this man was reliable enough for the purpose Rich had in mind.

Rich stood, took hold of his most elegant mahogany and gold walking stick, and began pacing the room.

Tap, tap, tap. The stick made an authoritative sound on the oak floors as Rich walked.

At last, Lord Rich said, "We have been friends many years."

The man before him took another sip of claret and nodded. "Indeed, my Lord. I am honored by your friendship, sir."

"As am I." *Tap, tap, tap.* "And I have a proposition for you, my friend. Employment, or 'an assignment,' if you will."

The guest looked up in surprise. "In the stead of my present employ for the Virginia Company?"

Lord Rich smiled. "In *addition to* your present employ, for I shall retain your services as well. I daresay a few extra pounds would be welcome?"

A smile spread across the guest's face. "Indeed, my Lord! Thank you, sir!"

"More claret?"

"Aye, if you don't mind."

"Help yourself."

As his guest poured, Lord Rich continued walking. "I need someone abroad to watch my interests." He suddenly raised his voice, startling his friend, who still had the bottle in his hand. "I will *not* have my cousin Sam Argall arrested and ignominiously brought to trial either here or in a Virginia court!"

"And rightly so, my Lord." A sly grin spread across the other's face. "You would wish me to keep you informed of goings-on in Virginia? I shall be there and in a position to do so."

Tap, tap, tap. Rich walked to a chair and dropped onto the plush red velvet, propping the walking stick beside him. "Aye, my friend. That is *precisely* what I wish you to do. And rest assured, I will pay you handsomely for your services: for the news you provide and for the tasks I ask of you on behalf of my personal affairs."

His guest dipped his head obligingly. "Ah, the pleasure is mine, my Lord." The older gentleman began pouring himself more claret, but his host reached over and stopped him. Lord Rich wanted his guest's full attention.

"The king takes a dim view of piracy. I have no need to tell you that."

The guest nodded. "A Spanish lover, that one."

"Indeed. His Majesty is a Catholic lover, a Spanish lover, and his actions are an affront to every good and faithful believer of the Protestant church. And, most especially, to Puritans like myself." Lord Rich was an ardent Puritan. His own religious view went far, far past Catholicism to the other side. The health of Rich's father, the Third Baron Rich and First Earl of Warwick, was failing. Both father and son were, perhaps, the fiercest Puritans in any position of power in England; the king's actions were particularly galling to them. Stealing from the Spanish weakened Rich's Catholic enemy, Spain. It was patriotic! If the king didn't see it that way, the earls would just have to stay below His Majesty's sights.

Quietly looting Spanish ships and treasures was a venture for God *and* for profit. Lord Rich had learned well from his Puritan father, whose reputation for such was notorious.

Lord Rich intended to keep his father's good name and wealth-producing ventures going upon his father's death. Lord Rich had already inherited his father's despisal of all things Catholic and Spanish. He, like his father, would become the highest-placed and most powerful Puritan in England. He took a sip of his own claret. *A most satisfying place to be.*

To safeguard his Virginia ventures, Rich needed to protect his strongest ally in Virginia, Samuel Argall. Argall and Rich desired the same things. They wished the Virginia Company to abandon their venture in Virginia. At which time, Rich was confident, he alone could run a piracy operation based out of both Virginia and Bermuda. He expected he could keep the Indians happy as well.

Rich released his guest's hand. "Go on, pour yourself another, and so shall I. We two will celebrate and toast to our arrangement. For I have more to ask of you." Rich knew he needed the help of the man in front of him.

The guest cocked his head with interest. More assignments meant more money. "Yes, my Lord?"

"Most immediately, I want you to delay that ship the *George.* Sir George Yeardley's ship." The sarcasm pitched in Rich's voice as he acknowledged the knighthood bestowed on the new Governor. "You, sir, are just the one to, shall we say, have an eleventh hour crisis which prevents the *George* from sailing?"

The guest raised his eyebrows as understanding dawned on him.

Glasses refilled, and Lord Rich said, "I am sending my own ship out, post haste, a sleek pinnace called the *Elinor.* With a few delaying tactics from you, the little *Elinor* shall best the grand *George...*"

His guest laughed. "*George* the ship *and* George the governor!"

Lord Rich nodded approvingly. "Precisely, sir. I will not have my man Argall arrested like some London street thief. Argall has done well. He has managed my affairs properly, as near as I can tell from so great a distance. He is doing the task every good Protestant Englishman *should* be doing, and that is raiding the Spanish fleet! Our curse is a king too infatuated with Spain, too hopeful of marrying his son to the Spanish princess. The laws against piracy are a travesty to our country. Are we in agreement as to your role?"

His guest murmured assent. "Absolutely, my Lord."

"You do not mind, uh, duplicity despite family ties?"

John Pory lifted his glass. "Not a widow's mite, my Lord. Oh, not a mite."

Pioneering Don't Pay

January 19, 1619 ~ on the *George* at Plymouth, England

Pioneering don't pay.
—Andrew Carnegie

George Yeardley was uncharacteristically tense.

"Your cousin Pory's 'delays' have held us up unduly," he said, agitated. The ship had docked at Plymouth to gather new passengers, but much later than planned.

Tempie shook her head. "Don't fault me because he's my kinsman. The Earl of Warwick nominated him, and the Virginia Council voted him in." She gave him a nudge. "I had nothing to do with it."

Which was true. Having made his acquaintance anew, Tempie wasn't sure she liked Cousin Pory that much. She glanced over at Pory trying to find quarters to make himself comfortable for the next three months or so. The ship's Master, William Ewens, and George himself, had hoped to depart Gravesend several weeks earlier than they had. Every day's delay, with Virginia's summer growing closer, would take a toll on new arrivals. Besides, the situation in Virginia with Argall in charge was surely growing more desperate.

Pory had begged off. First, his trunk had arrived late. He'd had difficulty ensuring that his affairs were in order. Lastly, when finally the ship had hoped to leave, Pory had fallen ill and needed "just a week more" of recovery time.

With a hundred settlers waiting to depart, time was indeed money. George did not want to lose any of the interest he'd managed to secure. *If they say they want to go to Virginia, get them on a ship, immediately!* That was how the Virginia Company operated. Settlers at dock were settlers who might hear more about the things truly going on at James Cittie. More than that, though, was the expense of feeding and maintaining the *George's* crew.

At last, Pory was ready, if not greatly enthusiastic.

Tempie had heard Cousin Pory refer several times to adventuring his carcass to such a dangerous place. Well, indeed. *I'm a woman, and I've adventured my* carcass *twice.*

But John Pory was a bit eccentric. He'd managed to pack a trunkful of books and sworn that wouldn't be enough. He bragged to the crew how much he had enjoyed Paris and Venice and Constantinople. She'd heard him say he was curious to see the New World, yes, but didn't know how he would keep himself entertained.

Ha! thought Tempie, overhearing. *Fortunate you'll be to stay alive! We don't get none too bored in Virginia.* If it wasn't the Indians, it was the Spanish, the French, illnesses, famine, droughts, and mutinies. Virginia, it was certain, offered its own kind of adventure—if *entertainment* wasn't quite the word.

No, Tempie wasn't sure about her cousin. She wasn't sure about him at all. His holding up the ship's departure seemed just a bit too...planned. Perhaps it was her imagination. Just a woman's wiles and instincts. Perhaps she was just anxious about another ocean crossing.

However, one thing that eased her mind somewhat was the presence of chirurgeon John Woodson onboard. *For a dollop of red berries in the Starving Time, I'll pay the rest of my life.* Her stomach had plagued her on the voyage over although the herbs had certainly helped. Tempie expected as much, maybe worse, on the journey home. She had met the chirurgeon and his wife Sarah as they were boarding. She found she liked them very much.

Also coming along was Tempie's own nephew, Edmund Rossingham, son of her sister Marie.

George himself was in bad humor, no way to start a long sea voyage. He was concerned about doing the unthinkable when he arrived in Virginia: arresting a Virginia governor. Tempie knew that George hoped for the element of surprise.

Beyond that, George had a new government to install. His assignments were ambitious, and he, of a mild temperament compared to many at James Cittie, was anxious.

Some onboard already had fevers. A few women were expecting with two who would likely deliver onboard ship. Three babes in arms and at least a dozen children, not to mention the vagabond children rounded up on the London streets. Wee and starving.

Just this month, the king had asked the Company to take some of these burdens, these orphans, off his hands. The king's men had rounded up the children, sent them to the prison at Bridewell, and now, a portion of the first group was onboard. A nuisance, the king had called these young ones. Running wild, hiding beneath stalls, foraging for victuals. Some were even petty thieves.

As servants in Virginia, the children stood their best chance at a home and a new life. They'd have to work and work hard. Most of all, they'd have to survive the seasoning. Tempie felt a chill suddenly, and it wasn't January seeping through the ship's ribs. She understood that many of these who now looked about vacantly would not see the next winter in Virginia. She surveyed the children's faces, some as old as sixteen, others just eight. One little girl wore little but rags. Her large blue eyes showed the fear the children must have all felt. Tempie knew she could not think about it, she would have to push the thought away. *They do have a chance, a slim one, but what chance at Bridewell? Little the first, none the second. After all,* Tempie reasoned, *I am bringing my own children back to live there.*

When the ship arrived in Virginia, Tempie knew, settlers would come asking to pay the fare of these little ones—the healthier ones, at least. Those children would become servants for a period of seven years. After that, who knew? Perhaps a better life did await.

As for her own little ones, a question remained. How would the seasoning affect her children, born in Virginia? And would seasoning strike George and Tempie at their second arrival? Or did one's body adapt?

She noticed that both children were asleep, curled on a mattress. She pulled a dingy blanket over them and bent to kiss their heads. *Sleep well, my children.*

George's senior position had given the Yeardleys the unbelievable luxury of a small cabin on the ship both crossings. Tempie knew she was more fortunate than the poor, expectant mothers in the main part of the 'tween deck, especially if sickness struck the ship.

For a moment, Tempie's heart swelled with pride for her husband. George had come to Virginia with his most valuable possession his sword, and now he was a wealthy landowner and a knight, and she, Dame Temperance, Lady Yeardley. The Yeardleys had returned to England to warn the Company that La Warr should come immediately. Little had they known this journey would end with George as governor of a volatile situation.

She had brought along her daybook and planned to continue her journal if the rocking of the ship didn't make such impossible. She had herbs along to calm her stomach and chamomile for nerves. Ralph had graciously refilled the satchels she had brought over.

A woman nearby began hacking, a deep chesty cough.

Pray God. Another sea voyage. No hurricanes, please! No Spanish pirates, no calenture or plagues. No endless seasickness. Just get us home safely to Virginia.

What, she wondered, did this voyage hold?

And what would her friends think when they learned she had a title now?

George Yeardley, pondering the events at the Virginia Company, could little know that in just eleven days, fire would destroy Sir Thomas Smythe's primary London residence at Deptford. The loss of this magnificent home would give Smythe an emotional setback that would permanently damage his health. And the battle between Smythe and Rich had heated even further when Smythe's son had married Rich's sister without Sir Thomas Smythe's permission. The collapse of the Virginia Company had begun.

What Sir George did know was that a battle faced him in James Cittie. What mischief might Sam Argall be getting into with Lord De La Warr gone and he, Yeardley, not yet there to stop him? George wasn't sure what worried him most—Argall's piracy or the man's looting of Company stock.

Back in Virginia, as fate would have it, the piracy was proving much more dangerous.

Songs of Pilgrims Unreturning
Late February 1619 ~ James Cittie

And one remembers...
Ah! the beat
Of weary unreturning feet,
And songs of pilgrims unreturning!...
The fires we left are always burning...
—Rupert Brooke

Will eagerly awaited the arrival of his cousin Tom Peirce, a Puritan. Lately we, too, had become more sympathetic to Puritan ideals. Maybe with the wildness about us, the laying aside of Anglican beliefs was natural. We wished to have a more personal relationship with our Bible. One could certainly not rely on preachers, a number of whom had died along the way.

"Cousin Tom hoped to come with Blackwell's group." Will was rapping his fingers impatiently on the table. "But he should have been here long before this. His June letter said the ship would sail no later than September, and here 'tis, nearly *March*." His unspoken question hung in the still frigid air of late February.

I pumped my foot rhythmically. Spin, spin, spin. I nodded in concern. Tom would be coming with his wife Alice and their two children. Gabriel was about eleven and Little Elizabeth a few years younger.

Will was not the only one anxiously awaiting Tom and Alice Peirce. Master Spencer was as well, for Alice Peirce was his sister.

Tom's letter sat on a corner of the table. Will pulled it to him and studied it as if it might give clues to the whereabouts of his cousin.

"Perhaps the ship was simply late leaving Gravesend or Plymouth," I said, wetting my fingers as the strands of hemp twisted round and round. "Maybe some difficulty obtaining supplies or funds?"

"Perhaps." But Will's brow furrowed, and I could see the helpless expression in his eyes.

I left my bench and stood behind him, placing my hands upon his shoulders. I leaned to his ear and whispered, "If anything should happen to them, it will not be..."

"Nothing shall happen to them, Joan!" Will yelled, pulling away and slamming his hand upon the table. I cowered backward.

Then he shoved the papers away such that they flew into the air and then scattered to the floor. "Nothing shall happen to them," he muttered, throwing his chair back and walking out the door with a slam.

I stood in the silence, the papers all over the floor and Will gone. *Will had been a gentle man when I married him, gentle as any soldier might be. But the long years in Virginia had exacted great toll upon us, upon all of us.*

I knelt, picking up the papers one by one. I could see Tom's neat writing as I skimmed the letter.

Reverend Blackwell...retrieving letters from the Virginia Company... shall settle our accounts before I depart...left my last will and testament with my brother Edward in London...purchased sack, cheese, vinegar and conserve of roses, barberry, and sloes...

I paused to look up. Conserves! How helpful these would be. Rose petals beaten with sugar were a marvelous physick, cooling the stomach, heart, and bowels. The beaten roses could also hinder vapors and the spitting of blood. And barberry conserves aided ailments of the belly and fevers. Conserved sloes would heal a burning throat come winter. I felt a growing excitement. I had done without conserves for so many years. I continued skimming the letter.

...the sugar, almonds, and marmalade, as you asked....taking the barge from London to Gravesend....Gabriel and Elizabeth cannot cease talking of seeing Indians....Alice so glad Joan is there and that we may stay with you until seasoned....much obliged for such kindness...wonderful to see you again, Cousin. I look forward to seeing our cousin Richard Peirce as well. I cannot wait. God be with you and with us on our journey. Regards to my brother Spencer, my cousins Peirce, and to your wife and children.

Now my excitement quickly turned to fear. My heart ached to think of the family lost at sea. And how might that have happened? Spanish attack or shipwreck?

No, I will not think of it.

I set the pages in a stack on the table and went to the rocker, all desire to spin lost.

Sometimes, I found the rhythms of little things helped me abide the sorrows and uncertainty. The spinning of the wheel, the rocking of the chair. These things comforted me although I knew not why.

The rocker creaked on the plank flooring in the otherwise silent chamber. I stared at the fire and tried not to think at all.

As for Will, I could not be angry with him, for I understood the helplessness, the self-blame. And then I finished the thought I had begun earlier.

Will, if something should happen to them, it will not be your fault.

Three for a Wedding
March 12, 1619 ~ James Cittie

One for sorrow,
Two for mirth,
Three for a wedding,
Four for a birth,
Five for rich,
Six for poor,
Seven for a witch,
I can tell you no more.
—Traditional English rhyme for counting magpies

Will remained distressed about his cousin's absence. Suddenly, something we perhaps should have expected, but had not, occurred.

About two weeks before Easter, I was hanging clothes upon the line when I saw some black birds. One on the gate, one on the tree, and one swinging from a cattail in a marish patch. We called them red-winged blackbirds although the birds' wings were scarlet at the top with a yellow band below and black beneath that. They resembled the blackbirds both here and at home and also our English black and white magpies.

Conk-reeeeeeeee. The bird on the gate sang loudly as if to get my attention.

"I see you there, Mr. Red-wing. Where's your wife? Don't know if you mean to be a bad omen or a good," I mumbled to the birds. "Or maybe you just mean to rest!" I smiled at my own humor. *Do blackbirds with red wings carry a prophecy as do a magpie?* This I could not answer, for we had no red-winged blackbirds where I had come from or in all of England that I knew of.

The same day, John Rolfe dropped by for a visit. His duties as recorder and secretary general for the colony had kept him at James Cittie. His hope, however, was to get back to his land in Bermuda Hundred, situated next to Cecily's property, and to work the tobacco.

John's *Trinidado* tobacco was growing better and stronger every year so that we could almost compete with the Spanish weed. This improvement was in great part due to Pocahontas's help and to the help of her kinsmen who had often come to visit the Rolfes at Bermuda Hundred. Finally, something we could produce and sell back to England to give us money. The tobacco required much labor to turn into something useful, but we felt it worth the effort. The factors worked in London, brokering the tobacco across European countries.

John rapped on the door, and I invited him in.

"G'day, Joan. Is Will around?" He seemed nervous. Why might that be? Of course, being the penman for Governor Argall and his tricks might have anyone's nerves jangled, I reckoned.

"Come in. He'll be home soon. May I fetch you a dram of mulberry beer?"

"Thank you, I will." He smiled, wiping the sweat from his brow with the back of his hand. He removed his hat and used it to fan himself.

"The summer heat is coming on us sooner than usual this year, aye?" he said.

"Aye," I answered idly as I retrieved the beer from beneath a shelf.

Jane came in after working the yard garden, and her face lit at seeing John. His lit too, I noticed.

"Good day, Master Rolfe."

He stood and bowed slightly with his hat held over his chest.

I stopped pouring into the dram, and my heart began to pound. "Marriage!" I shouted, for in a moment I understood. *Three for a wedding. The old red-wings had been right.*

John flushed as if caught. Jane, too.

Forgetting the beverage, I dropped into in the rocker.

"Fourteen. *Fourteen!* I shall never get used to it!" I exclaimed at last. "Like your sister, you shall be a mother at fifteen," I said to Jane.

Jane came over and knelt by the rocker. "I do wish to marry Master Rolfe, mother. He has not pressed me. He is a..." She paused as if not wanting to speak of John in front of him. But she gathered her courage and continued. "He is a kind and gentle man. He's clever and hardworking, too. He'll make a good husband, and I'll be a good wife."

I heaved a sigh from my deep inside. "Fourteen."

John put in, "As soon as my time as recorder is up, I plan to move back to my land at Bermuda Hundred. Then Jane and her sister shall be neighbors..."

To Jane I whispered, "Does your father know?"

She shook her head. "But Master Rolfe did speak with me privately."

Will and John were fast friends. Will would consent, of this I was certain.

The Deep Wide Sea of Misery
Mid-March 1619 ~ James Cittie

Many a green isle needs must be
In the deep wide sea of misery,
Or the mariner, worn and wan,
Never thus could voyage on
Day and night, and night and day,
Drifting on his dreary way...
—Percy Bysshe Shelley

So few ships had come the past several years. When at last the *William and Thomas* arrived, we prayed this ship carried our cousins, and indeed, it did.

I scarcely saw Tom Peirce, for he went with Will to Master Spencer's house to discuss matters. Planting season was upon us, and not a moment to waste.

Meanwhile, Jane and I went to visit Alice and her children right away rather than attending church after completing our assigned morning work. Missing church could cause us serious trouble with our erratic Governor, but Maria promised to beseech Reverend Bucke not to report us. If my friends were not always there to help me, I had no idea how I would have survived.

We found the rest of the Peirce family at their new home which Will and Master Spencer had built them. The men had chosen to believe the best, that the family would arrive soon.

The first thing I noticed was that I saw only a daughter, Elizabeth. There was no sign of Gabriel.

Alice was sitting at the table, weeping. A child, who must have been Elizabeth, was trying to comfort her mother. "Mama, don't be sad. Mama, don't cry. Please, mama."

I rushed over to Alice and wrapped my arms around her, saying, "Alice, I am Joan, Will's wife. And we are so glad you've arrived at last!"

Alice stopped sobbing for a moment and gazed up at me. "Gabriel didn't make it. Ah, such a stinking voyage we had. Oh, Lord, it could not have been any worse."

Alice was a small but sturdy woman, and that, I suspected, had served her well. For the voyage of the *William and Thomas* had been appalling.

I sat on the bench beside her holding her hand. I had so many questions, I scarcely knew where to start. But I'd already heard that one hundred eighty settlers boarded this ship and only *thirty* had come off of it alive. Overcrowded conditions and the appearance of the flux meant that illness had raged through the ship. Five of every six settlers had died onboard. This family was fortunate that only Gabriel had died, I realized.

"Didn't ye...didn't ye depart in September?" I asked at last. "What happened?"

"Oh, we embarked in September, 'tis so, that. We thought we might have been here by Michaelmas, if winds were good. But late September, then October, came and went. And November passed. Then December went into January, January into February. The seas were cold, the winds bitter and contrary. The flux struck some, and others took with the cough." She paused. "Some had both."

I felt ice running through my veins as I tried to imagine such a voyage.

"We were at sea six months!"

Six months?

"But...but that's impossible. I've heard of a voyage no longer than seventeen weeks, that of the *Neptune* which came in last summer. And the *Nepune* made stops at the Azores and Canada."

"Our pilot got lost, couldn't find the bay. Up and down the coast we went, I suppose."

What kind of pilot couldn't find the mouth of a bay as large as the Bay of the Chesapeakes?

"Gabriel, he got the flux and the cough. I knew there wasn't any hope for him, Joan." Her voice croaked. She didn't need to tell me the rest, for I understood. They had pitched his lifeless body over the side.

"How old...?"

"He was eleven and growing to be such a fine young man." She put a rag to her eyes and dabbed away the tears. It would take a long time to recover from the horror of this. I squeezed Alice's hand then turned my attention to the child.

"And you, Elizabeth, you took not ill?"

"Well, a little, ma'am," she said. "But not like Gabriel. He just kept getting worse and worse..." Her little voice trailed off. I tried to imagine what it must have been like for this young girl to see so many around her sick and dying. I put my arms around her and held her tightly. "You're safe now,"

I said. *At least, I hope so.*

"Cousin Alice, change into something you've packed, and let Mother and me burn the clothes you have on," Jane volunteered.

She was right. The clothes carried the illness on them, perhaps. They most certainly had stains from the sickness surrounding the family. Clothing was scarce, but sickly clothing we needed not.

"Alice, Jane and I are going to prepare meals for you and your family and give ye a chance to rest," I said.

Jane nodded and suddenly I realized we would have to prepare for Jane's wedding and tend to these survivors, all at once. And our chores and work schedule under martial law continued unabated as well.

Good thing, I thought. *Good thing I'm a hearty soul, or I should not bear the illness and surprises cast on me all at once.*

Flying From Far Away
April 3 to April 14, 1619 ~ James Cittie

And a pinnace, like a fluttered bird, came flying from far away...
—Alfred, Lord Tennyson

Yett endeed as it is ffallen out, Capt Argall being gon with his Ritches...
—Sir George Yeardley writing to Sir Edwin Sandys, April 1619

A sleek, quick little pinnace glided into the moonlit waters of Kecoughtan where Governor Argall made his home. The ship's master, a man named Lowndes, stopped at Point Comfort and reported to Captain Tucker as required. Lowndes posed a question to the captain and hoped it sounded innocent enough.

"Where might I find Governor Argall? At James Town?"

"You're alone?" A pinnace unescorted across the ocean was an unusual thing.

"Aye. We had no troubles. Now, where might I find Governor Argall?" the master persisted.

"Not at James Town, but here at Kecoughtan. You have goods for trading?" Captain Tucker asked hopefully. A pinnace had little room for cargo, but perhaps she had a few things stored away.

The *Elinor's* master took off his cap and scratched his beard.

"A few minor goods. We're so small, you understand, that we can't store much in the hold but what we need for crossin' the ocean." He shrugged. "We do have salad oil, sack, and nails."

"Well, that's something. You bring settlers, then?"

"No, not that either," said Lowndes, becoming uncomfortable.

"Then what's a wee vessel like yourself even botherin' to make the voyage for if you're not here to do some heavy trading and haven't brought settlers?" Captain Tucker was suspicious suddenly. "May I check your papers, master?"

The ship's master nodded. "You may indeed. I have nothing to hide. I am mainly here to see the governor."

Captain Tucker pulled open the sheath and recognized the handwriting and seal of Lord Rich. "He's the owner of the pinnace, I take it?" the captain asked.

"Aye." The ship's owner, Rich, was a powerful man. Lowndes knew that he would have no further trouble.

He was correct.

"You'll be wanting to bunk here overnight, I presume, sir?" Tucker asked.

"No, you presume wrong. I can make it to Kecoughtan tonight? How far is it, exactly?"

"Just a mile to the mainland. But you're sure you want to move upriver in the dark?"

Lowndes nodded. "It's urgent that I speak with the governor as soon as possible."

This was highly irregular, but there was no reason the master *had* to stay the night. "As you wish. It's your hide traveling upriver by night, not mine. I suppose it's a little safer than it once was. Ever since Pocahontas married Master Rolfe, we've had little trouble with the Indians."

The ship's master nodded. "Another thing for which the colony can be grateful to Governor Argall."

Captain Tucker thought he might choke. But he decided to speak no ill of his governor. After all, martial law made such things risky. Indeed, Captain Brewster had almost lost his life at the governor's ill pleasure.

In less than an hour, the *Elinor* had departed Point Comfort and soon had come upon a settlement that must be Kecoughtan. The hour being eight o'clock, most settlers were in their beds. The ship's master knocked upon a few doors, roused one man, and that man pointed him to the larger home of Governor Argall.

Argall's manservant Story answered the door, and his first response was irritation. "The governor won't see some scrubby ship's captain at this hour! Sleep on ship, and come to him in the morning."

The captain put up his hand in protest. "My good man, fetch the governor. I have orders from none other than Sir Robert Rich, the future Baron Rich and Earl of Warwick, himself. And I am to deliver my message *now*."

Confused, but daring not to disobey the urgency in the captain's voice, Story called to the governor, who emerged from his chamber. Having already prepared for bed, Argall had on only his long shirt.

"What the devil?" said Argall irritably. He looked as if he would pillory this stranger's ears come daylight.

"We should talk, sir. *Now*, if you please. Upon orders of Lord Rich." He glanced at the manservant, who was eyeing the scene curiously. "In private, if we may."

Argall brought Lowndes into a smaller chamber and shut the door. "You see," Lowndes told Argall after receiving a dram of sack, "we left from Plymouth. *They* left from London."

The experienced Captain Argall understood immediately. "Ah ha. Saved you a week's travel up the Narrow Sea, did it?"

The master's look was sly. "Indeed. And with good Master Pory's help abetting us, delaying Governor Sir George Yeardley, and our own quickness. It were little trouble to arrive before the lumbering *George*."

But they still must escape Virginia before the *George* arrived, the ship's master explained. "She is even now closing in on the Bermudas."

Lowndes now delivered the news he had dreaded. With a swallow he said, "They are stripping you of your governorship in disgrace, sir."

Argall looked at him in shock. "How dare they after all I've done for Virginia! Conquered the French, captured Pocahontas. I alone have kept peace, up and down the coast. And have they a better man? A baron or an earl to stand in for me?" Argall didn't truly care to be governor. He preferred being on the ocean. But he also didn't like being cast out in disgrace.

Lowndes gave a sarcastic grin. "No. Sir Edwin Sandys has put forth his man George Yeardley. *Sir* George Yeardley. He is governor and captain general of Virginia following Lord La Warr."

Argall raised his eyebrows, and his face whitened, evident even in lantern light. "The devil, you say? That's outrageous! Yeardley knows nothing of how to run a colony, evidenced by the chaos he left previously. And they've even knighted the man? Has Smythe gone mad?" Argall was perhaps a bit jaundiced in his opinion of who would be a better governor.

But the ship's master agreed with him. "Sir Robert Rich is furious. You are his cousin and friend. And he'll not have the likes of George Yeardley arresting you, governor."

Argall looked stunned. *To be arrested as a criminal, and by the likes of that tailor's son George Yeardley?*

"And it appears Yeardley returned to England but to betray you to the Virginia Company. Prepare yourself for flight, sir."

In less than a week, an incredibly short period of rest after an ocean crossing, the little *Elinor* was gone back out to sea.

Upon her she took former Governor Samuel Argall, whisked to safety from the impending arrest. Argall had appointed Captain Nathaniel Powell as acting governor.

As the *Elinor* made for open sea, Argall only wished he could see the anguish in Yeardley, his former friend, upon realizing he'd failed.

Rumors began flying between settlements almost immediately.

We learned that the disgraced Argall had fled, which was particularly shameful because the holy season of Easter was still upon us.

Another rumble came from Kecoughtan saying Rich had spirited Argall away before George Yeardley could put the scoundrel in cuffs. If this were true, I thought I now understood Tempie's secrecy at her leaving. I had wondered who she'd been protecting. My friend had been shielding Will and me from Argall's wrath should the governor have questioned either of us about George Yeardley.

Some said that Sir Robert Rich himself would come to govern the colony, but others swore no such thing would happen. It became hard to know what to believe, so all we could truly do was wait.

I watched the river more closely than ever. If these rumors were true, Tempie must be coming home soon. I scarcely dared hope.

I had little time to consider what this all meant, as Reverend Bucke had duly read the banns. Jane and John were to be married on April 14 at James Cittie.

Sam Jordan came from Bermuda Hundred a few days ahead of time along with Cecily and Little Tempie.

"How'd you get away, old man?" Will asked him.

Sam's grin was sly. "Business at the capital city. And it certainly is business, the business of seeing my cousin's daughter wed!" We laughed, but the truth was that we were still very much prisoners of martial law.

"With Argall gone, maybe you won't get a whipping, Master Jordan." Jane said, smiling at Sam. Jane, I noticed, looked radiant.

My granddaughter had grown since I'd seen her. How wonderful to have her with us! I picked her up and kissed her.

Sam pulled me aside. "May I speak with you?" He cleared his throat. "Joan, do you remember when I came to see you after Cecily's father had died in the war? I told you then little Cecily came from a good bloodline. We all do."

This was so. Sam was my mother's first cousin while Will and my father were second cousins. Even Cecily's father and I had been distant cousins. We were all of one blood, truly.

"I remember. You and Will brought me tulips from Holland, giddy like boys over them." I smiled at the memory. "You two were so good to me. And then Will became the father to Cecily that she never had."

Sam's eyes were on Cecily. "Cecily has grown to be a fine young woman, but Virginia is no place to be alone. Especially for a mother. And I, too, am alone."

Suddenly, I understood. "Sam, you wish to marry Cecily? Is that what you're asking?"

He nodded. "This is indeed what I desire," he said softly. "She feels likewise, but we've agreed to abide by your wishes. And, of course, I'll ask Will's permission. In any event, I've pledged to help her get the crops sown on her land."

"Sam," I said warmly, "you've been a delightful friend and a wonderful cousin. I'm sure Will would agree."

"I promise to be as good a father to Little Tempie as Will was to Cecily."

A few moments later, Sam went to speak with Will, and then Will beamed. *He's delighted that Sam might be the father of his future grandchildren,* I thought.

I whispered to Jane. "Would you mind if your sister married with you at the church, if Reverend Bucke might waive the banns?"

Jane's eyes sparkled. "No, mother, not at all. I feel blessed we're all still living and together to celebrate a wedding!" *True words, those.*

And that was how it happened. Both girls had what we came to think of as our Virginia Wedding. The spring wildflowers were in bloom. The decorations and corncakes were humble, but both my girls were as happy as I'd seen them in a long while. So I supposed the old proverb rang true. *One wedding brings another.*

Now, my only sadness was that Jane would also be moving to Bermuda Hundred to the three acres that John tilled there. However, the girls would be neighbors, as John had promised.

My other heartache was that I did not know if the rumors of the Yeardleys returning were accurate.

That would change within a few days.

My Dream of You
April 16-18, 1619 ~ James Cittie

I ask but one thing of you, only one,
That always you will be my dream of you;
That never shall I wake to find untrue
All this I have believed and rested on,
Forever vanished, like a vision gone...
—Amy Lowell

Two days after the wedding, word again spread from Point Comfort up to James Cittie. The *George* had returned! George Yeardley was aboard, and he was to be the new governor. Yeardley's delay had been costly since Argall had escaped.

The girls, Sam, and John had already sailed for Bermuda Hundred. I felt a momentary disappointment that they would not be able to see Tempie, and that Tempie would miss seeing her little namesake. But as usual in Virginia, everything happened too quickly to think much about it.

Maria Bucke brought the news to me first. I threw my arms up with a thrilled shout. I had missed Tempie so much. Well, at least George had returned—'twas a good sign that Tempie might also be aboard. Had she decided to come home? What if she hadn't? How was her health?

Pray God the ship brought no contagion. The colony was still recovering from bloody flux.

I had prayed every day for my friend and her health, as I'd promised Tempie I would. Now I grabbed Maria's hands and went about in a little jig. She gave a cheerful laugh and joined in, for she had missed Tempie as well.

"Oh, and you'll never be able to guess. The king has knighted George!"

I stopped mid-dance. "What's that you say?"

Maria chuckled. "I said, he's *Sir* George Yeardley now, and Tempie is Dame Temperance, Lady Yeardley. Isn't that exciting?"

"Oh. Oh, it is."

Maria angled her head at me, for my words seemed not to match my face, I reckoned.

Tempie was now the governor's wife. George had an audience with the king himself, and Tempie had become Dame Temperance. With those words, I understood in a moment that things could never be the same between us. In our day, we had been equals, one helping the other. As the Bible said, one falling down, his friend helping him up. We were in no way equals now. And never could be again.

Suddenly, all my joy at Tempie's arrival eroded into fear and loss, like an axman dropping a tree in a single cut.

"You don't look all that thrilled for her, Joan." There was something of accusation in Maria's tone. But how could she understand? Tempie and I had been friends of the heart, and to have something like a change in status come between us would be the greatest loss.

I tried to cover my feelings. I forced a brightening and said, "Oh, no, truly, I am delighted." I searched for sincere words which I hoped would sound the ring of truth. "No one deserves a knighting more than George Yeardley. He is a kind man, a good leader. He will not sully Virginia's good name nor plunder her stock." I felt my conviction growing. *Yes, focus on George.* "'Tis a hopeful day for us in Virginia that the king has bestowed him a knighthood."

Maria smiled, seemingly reassured. "Dame Temperance. Who'd have thought?"

Again, my heart fell. "Aye, who'd have thought? Well, I suppose it's time for me to finish my churning."

"And time for me to return to mending shirts." Then she added, "I know you can't wait to see Tempie, you two being so close through the years and all. And the children will have grown so!"

As I shut the door behind Maria, I wondered at it all. And how would I hide my feelings from Tempie—I corrected myself—*Dame Temperance?*

My Husband Was a Valiant Knight
April 20, 1619 ~ James Cittie

My father was as brave a lord
As ever Europe did afford,
My mother was a lady bright,
My husband was a valiant knight...
—English Ballad

When at last the *George* made its way upriver slowly, my heart leapt and fell at once. Up, down.

At last, Tempie emerged from the 'tween deck, and I caught a glimpse. She looked tired, disheveled, and hungry. My heart ached for her friendship despite my misgivings. I was, after all, still her closest friend. I hoped.

As she made her way down the bridge, I saw her face more closely. She had a ghastly pallor, deep circles, and gauntness in her cheeks. She lifted her eyes and saw me, and her face shone. For this she seemed to exert all her remaining strength.

Maria and I rushed to her and then caught ourselves. We dropped our heads in a respectful bow, and I said politely, "Welcome home, my dame."

Maria added, "My Lady Yeardley, welcome."

Tempie looked hurt. "'My Lady Yeardley, welcome?' After nearly a year away? That is the best you can do? Joan, I'm surprised at you!"

I looked up, stung. "Begging your pardon, my lady, but 'twould be improper not to give you the respect you deserve as the wife of a knight. We...we *are* proud of you." *How to separate real pride from real fear?*

"No!" she said firmly, obviously stung herself. "What would be improper is to give an old friend a cold greeting."

I felt, in those words as if she could see right through my fearful heart.

She then puckered her face in a grimace and shook her head. "Joan, Maria." She gestured to the fort, the tattered houses, the chickens running through the streets, the ragged smiths hammering their iron. "Think where we are. We are in James Cittie, not London. We friends are all the same station here, knighthood or no. I am not, nor ever will be, 'Dame Temperance' to you. To servants, aye. To newcomers, aye, as well. Respect for an office is an important thing. But to you, I'm just Tempie." She laughed. "I ceased being Lady Yeardley at the Plymouth Hoe!"

We gave a leap of joy then as both Maria and I hugged her tightly. "My friend, my friend, we all missed you so much and were so afeared for you!"

She sighed deeply. "Well, it was a long, sore voyage. We lost fourteen including several orphans and two babes born and died at sea." She shook her head. "A pity. The mothers, both of them, beside themselves with grief. No proper midwife."

How heart-rending to think of little babes thrown overboard. Of course, at sea there was no other choice.

"George brings many changes. Many, indeed. But the happiest news is the end of martial law!"

"Hallelujah!" Maria cried.

"Much news, ladies. Much news. But that can wait. First, get me to my new home, the governor's house, and let me sleep for a day or two in a true bedstead which doesn't rock!" she said.

"After we feed you well," I added.

The ceremony to read George Yeardley's orders as governor and captain general for a period of three years would ensue.

Drums rolled and banged as George asked a crier to make a public proclamation. "If the said Samuel Argall does owe any debts to any persons in our land, or if Argall has wrongfully taken anything from any man, come complain to Sir George Yeardley and he will give them satisfaction."

For most of us in the colony, George being governor and captain general in itself gave us satisfaction and hope. We were pleased at his good faith in trying to make losses right.

The Steps of Freedom
July 30 – August 4, 1619 ~ James Cittie

Oh, we are weary pilgrims; to this wilderness we bring
A Church without a bishop, a State without a King.
—Author unkown, *Puritan's Mistake*

Slow are the steps of freedom, but her feet turn never backward.
—James Russell Lowell

Captain Bargrave believed....that there was not any man in
the world that carried a more malitious heart to the Government
of a Monarchie than Sir Edwin Sandys did....[Sandys] tell-
ing Capt. Bargrave that his intent was to erect a free state in
Virginia...
—Sir Nathaniel Rich, criticizing Sir Edwin Sandys for
promoting popular government in Virginia, 1623

The pewter pitchers stood lined up on a plank near the church.
The church doors were open, allowing the dream that a breeze might come. But alas, no movement of wind, just the utter stillness of Virginia in July.

Tempie fanned herself. Actually, we all did as we listened to the proceedings inside.

The month before, Sir George had sent warrants to each of the eleven settlements requesting that the men assemble and elect two representatives each. Every free man and tenant had the right to vote. And toward the last of July, shallops and canoes and small sails had filled the riverfront, all elected men coming to take their seats at the General Assembly.

The summer had been another hot one, and hundreds more settlers were dying. The Company's fine hopes for an ironworks had come to a halt, at least temporarily, with the death of Captain Blewitt, who was the artisan in charge of building them. Death exacted a great toll so that one never knew whether to fear summer sickness or winter famine more.

Most of these assembled representatives were well. But not all. George Yeardley, John Pory, and Master Shelley were ill among others.

Sir George had asked almost every household in James Cittie to lodge a representative. We were able to have Sam Jordan—a boon for Will, as he saw little of his old *chamay* or *chum,* an Indian word we had picked up.

Maria looked exhausted. Caring for three children and being the pastor's wife had taken its toll on her, I reckoned. Yet, undaunted, she was here to help.

All day for the next week or two—we knew not how long—we should be gathering water from the well for filling the men's flagons. George Yeardley had asked us—Tempie, Maria, and me—to do this chore, as we were some of the most senior women in the colony. 'Twas a small task, but Sir George wanted us to slip in and fill flagons without interrupting. He added that we should be prepared to serve in other ways if necessary. The heat looked to be unbearable, and so we would alternate with Jane, Alice Peirce, and Isabella Pace.

Sir George was at the front of the church in his usual chair. At either hand of the governor sat the General Council—Reverend Samuel Maycock, John Rolfe, Captain Nathaniel Powell, Captain Francis West, and the Reverend Wickham. John Pory was also a member of the council, but as secretary and speaker, his chair faced the governor. Mr. Twine, the clerk, positioned himself beside Pory. Tom Peirce, as sergeant-at-arms, stood at the bar.

In the choir sat the settlements' representatives, including Sam Jordan, who was here to represent Charles Cittie. Captain William Powell and Ensign Spence represented James Cittie, which left Will commander of the Fort in the interim. There were eleven settlements in all: James Cittie, Charles Cittie, Henricus, Kecoughtan, Martin's Brandon, Flowerdew Hundred, and four others. George had named his property *Flowerdew* in honor of Tempie's family.

We have certainly grown westward! I thought, and then felt as if I had done this before, been here before. I understood what it was. I recalled the time eight years ago when I had sat in this church prior to Argall's expanding it and seen a Westward growth. *More to come,* I murmured, not even sure why I said it. Perhaps it was true. Perhaps we had created a viable colony at last.

John Pory, as speaker, invited Reverend Bucke to the front.

Reverend Bucke walked to the pulpit and cleared his throat.

"Gentlemen, let us bow our heads and pray," he commanded, and all obeyed. We outside bowed our heads as well.

"For so much as men's affairs do little prosper where God's service is neglected, we pray that it may please God to guide and sanctify all our proceedings to His own glory and to the good of this plantation."

"Amen!"

Governor Yeardley then said, "Let us remind ourselves to be respectful of the Lord and His lieutenant, our most gracious and dread sovereign, His Majesty, King James."

"Hear, hear!" cried a few as Speaker Pory entreated the burgesses to retire from the choir and into the body of the church.

Next, the speaker called each man in order and by name, and one by one, each came forward to take the Oath of Supremacy.

"I, Captain William Powell, do truly and sincerely acknowledge, *et cetera*, that our Sovereign Lord, King James, is lawful and rightful king, *et cetera*, and that the pope neither of himself nor by any authority of church or See of Rome, or by any other means with any other, has any power to depose the king, *et cetera*, or to authorize any foreign prince to invade him, *et cetera*...."

"I, Ensign William Spence..."

"I, Samuel Jordan..."

And on it went, but not without a few issues. Should Captain Ward be present? The Virginia Company hadn't given him authority to be in the colony. Yet Ward had brought in many fish, a great help. The representatives voted that he could stay provided the Company gave him permission by next year's meeting.

"Well, what of Captain Martin, then? Should *his* representatives from Martin's Brandon be here today?" George's voice sounded almost gruff. "May I remind ye, his patent states that he is exempt from all laws we make!"

A murmur went through the church. Tempie, Maria, and I leaned in.

"Well then that makes Martin's men—pardon, sirs!—no more than spies," one of the representatives declared, irritation obvious in his voice. No one cared too much for Captain Martin.

"Hear, hear!"

"Call Martin in and ask him whether he will agree to abide by our laws. If he won't, he shall have no part in making them," George ordered.

"The feud between my husband and Captain Martin continues," Tempie whispered. Martin had taken George to court as soon as the new governor had arrived back to Virginia. It seems Captain Martin had left corn under the Reverend Whitaker's care. Martin had gone to England and returned to find Whitaker dead and the corn eaten. Whitaker's servants said they had needed these base provisions to survive. Martin wasn't having it and blamed the governor in charge, which at that time had been Yeardley.

"Fie on Martin! He has sullied his own name, ever since he left his men behind for the Nansemonds to murder during the Starving Time. Remember?" I whispered in return. "We called him coward then, a name he cannot escape."

Yet Tempie was concerned. George's illness had lingered, but he was here in spite of it. "I do not care for the pressures of his position as governor," she grumbled quietly to me.

"But he serves well. The best and most just governor we have yet had. We need a man such as George to keep rascals like Martin in proper place," Maria put in.

Tempie seemed to relax a little. "George says the assembly had to meet in July this year, the soonest he could pull the burgesses together. But next year he shall hold the assembly in March so the heat shall not be a factor."

Perspiration poured from our three faces. I said, "Aye. Fine idea, that!"

As men raised their flagons, we quietly went to them with our pitchers. We poured until our pitchers were dry, refilling from the bucket. As the bucket emptied, we took turns hurrying to the well. Again and again we poured.

The men wiped sweat from their brow and mopped their faces with kerchiefs. Their faces were rosy red.

"How can they pay attention as hot as they are?" Maria whispered to Tempie and me. I shrugged. We were hot as well. It was all I could do to remember when it was my turn to fill the flagons.

"Think Cousin Pory likes his water?" Tempie said with a smirk. The tippler had to forego his claret and sack. Little enough of that to be had here. Wines came over in shipments, quickly gone. The beer we made from sassafras, mulberries, pumpion, and corn tasted strange. Water might have been unhealthful, but it was the best we had.

Pory had taken control as speaker, his time in the House of Commons giving him knowledge and understanding of such proceedings that Sir George lacked. Even I could tell that Pory disliked George. His manner toward the governor was condescending, as Pory seemed to talk down his nose at George. Yet, here, in a little parliament, John Pory was in his element, and he seemed for the moment to have put aside his differences with the governor.

Now a Mr. Davis from Paspahegh raised a new complaint about Martin.

"See?" I whispered. "Constant troubles surround the man!"

Pory put Davis under oath, and then Davis explained.

It seems Captain Martin had given his man, an ensign, a small ship to trade for corn in the bay. But the voyage had been difficult, and the men had no success in gaining corn. As the shallop was returning home, it met with a canoe coming out of a creek where the shallop could not go. The ensign had attempted to entice the Indians to trade their corn. The Indians refused, so the English had taken their arms aboard the canoe, forcing the Indians to sell and measuring the corn with a basket in the shallop. Before leaving, the ensign had thrown the natives some copper beads and other trucking stuff.

"I heard this from the ensign myself, sirs," Davis finished.

"I am aware of it, Davis. Opechancanough's messengers have complained to me, saying the Indians involved seek justice," George Yeardley said wearily.

"Such outrages as Martin's man committed might well breed danger and loss of life to others trading in the colony afterward," I heard one burgess say emphatically.

Hums of agreement. The men created an order to Captain Martin that he and the gang who had been on the shallop answer this accusation thoroughly. The order further required that Martin seek the governor's permission and leave security with him before each trading mission, assurance against such an outrage occurring again. All other men in the colony did so; Martin would too.

"This is why such a body is a good thing," Maria said idly. "England cannot answer everything, the day-to-day challenges we have. The good Lord knows how many such things I've heard from my husband."

"They do not understand us in London, either. What we endure, what life is like on the frontier," Tempie added.

And these thoughts lifted my heart. Perhaps we truly were moving toward a civilized society. Perhaps by redressing wrongs we committed against the natives, peace would remain. Perhaps my grandchildren should not grow up in such a dangerous world.

Perhaps.

The lawmaking continued.

"I propose no trading of dogs to the Indians!" Murmurs of assent. The Indians might indeed turn our mighty mastiffs and greyhounds against us.

But some challengers were evident. This first General Assembly of the people met five of six days with a break on the sabbath. And during that break, Mr. Shelley, the burgess from Smythe's Hundred, died. The summer sultriness had been too much for him.

By the sixth day the meeting was called adjourned 'til next March. The men could not go on under such oppressive heat. Our governor's health was failing, and most of the men were suffering from the heat, filled flagons or no. And the realistic thought was how many more burgesses would die? For we could not keep all the assembly alive even through a week.

However, the mood in the colony was hopeful despite the heat and Mr. Shelley's death.

George Yeardley was the most just governor we old planters had yet seen. Martial law was at last dead under the Great Charter, and we had been able to choose our own burgesses to create laws that affected our settlements, a far cry from a lord in England choosing these laws for us. Investing in the colony in England was much different from living here amidst all Virginia's challenges.

Aye, things looked promising.

Captain Ward took the *Sampson* up to Monhegan Island in North Virginia to fish. He brought but little fish home for lack of salt, but it still helped ease our need for victuals.

Abraham Piercy, the cape merchant, sent the *George* up to Newfoundland as well to trade and to buy fish to relieve the colony. The captain discovered he could arrive at the fishermen's bank in fourteen days and return in less than three weeks, even with bare winds. The *George* brought so many fish home in such short time that it proved the voyage could truly be a savior for the Colony when crop harvests were lean.

The next ship to arrive was the *Trial,* bringing healthy cattle, mares, and horses. This last finally removed the fear of famine.

It seemed for once that the worst might be over. We had survived Argall's treachery and colony-wide bloody flux. A lean supply of corn the last two summers had made way for fish and cattle this year, and thus far the corn and tobacco had fared well, too. Our one concern remained the hundreds of new settlers overrunning us. How would we house them? And would the food hold out for us all?

However, the summer would not be over before more unwelcome surprises arrived.

Never Was a Cargo More Adrift
Late August 1619 ~ James Cittie

[The Treasurer] had gone to rob the king of Spain's subjects by seeking pillage in the West Indies and this was done by direction from my Lord of Warwick.
—Sir George Yeardley

The transports move stealthily to sea—
The sea so prone to take strange freightage eagerly—
But this sad freightage even the sea disowns
And lifts its storms and frowns in darker mood
And never was a cargo more adrift...
There are no ports, no country's flag, no waiting hands
In any land on earth for it.
—Kathryn White Ryan

The burgesses had barely returned each to their own settlements when word came up the river from Point Comfort.

A Dutch man-o'-war, the *White Lion,* had docked. The ship's commander was a Cornishman named John Colyn Jope, a Puritan, along with his pilot, one Captain Marmaduke. Other English corsairs called Jope the Flying Dutchman because he sailed from Dutch ports and had a reputation for sending a pinnace out and stripping a ship before the other pirates could reach it.

Jope carried with him a Dutch letter of marque. With this document, Jope could legally seize Spanish cargo on the open sea, he said. However legal it may have been, the Spanish cared not. Piracy was piracy to them. Jope and Marmaduke sought victuals in exchange for trading the contents of the ship—some twenty negroes, stolen from the Spanish.

Jope pleaded his case, and Governor Yeardley reluctantly agreed. Up to this point, we'd had Indians as well as a few French, Spanish, Italians, Dutch, Dutchmen, Helvetians, Persians, and Poles in Virginia, but never Africans. The men and women would become indentured servants to those willing to repay the Virginia Company for the funds used to trade for them.

However, more was to come.

Less than a week later, in the middle of the night, Will received the governor's order. "Come, now!" and Will, in his sleeping shirt, obeyed. He jumped to his feet and quickly dressed.

"Will? Why the urgency?" I asked sleepily.

"God knows," he said as he dashed out the door, weapons in hand.

Tempie came to my house the next morning. Her face was grim, the toll on the governor apparent in her expression.

She sat herself down at my table and asked for a dram of something. I gave her mulberry beer, which had an unusual, but not a bad, flavor.

"So? Where's Will, and what's happening?" I asked her.

She put her hand on my arm. "George asked me to inform you. Hear this, Joan. It's Argall again...."

"Argall!" I screeched. *Was he back? What terrors this time?*

"No, no." Tempie interrupted me. "But our old governor has caused us new problems. Problems my husband, of course, must address."

I leaned in, concerned, and let her finish.

Tempie continued, "Where hast the *Treasurer* been all these months? She disappeared to get us goats and cheese. But where did she truly go? Well, soon we shall find out. A messenger arrived in the night saying the *Treasurer* had returned at last. She is down by the bay at Kecoughtan.

The *Treasurer's* captain, that pirate Elfrith, sent word to the governor little knowing that the governor is now George and not Argall! That Argall has fled in disgrace." Her voice sounded contemptuous. "So George has sent Will, John Rolfe, and Captain Ewens in a shallop to escort the *Treasurer* back to James Cittie. For the Virginia Company has given George severe instructions to seize the ship and arrest the captain." John was back in James Cittie, I knew. Which was fortunate, as George trusted him.

"But why Will? Why not Captain Powell?"

"Because Powell was too close to Argall. George trusts him not. Not fully, anyway."

Captain Ewens was a sea captain. He would well be able to guide the *Treasurer* back to us.

"Rich has employed this Captain Elfrith before, Joan. Elfrith is an infamous pirate."

Our eyes met. Rich and Argall were playing a dangerous game with the Spanish.

We would have no news until the men returned, which occurred three days later.

By the time Will, John, and Captain Ewens had arrived at Kecoughtan, the *Treasurer* had fled. Captain Elfrith had learned that his friend Argall was no longer governor and that Yeardley was to arrest him.

The *Treasurer* had left bad feelings in its wake. Captain Tucker of Kecoughtan had sent a messenger to Yeardley while delaying Elfrith. Tucker had told Elfrith that he would not trade victuals for stolen slaves, no matter the cost or need. The people of Kecoughtan had given Elfrith and the men onboard a cold welcome.

Elfrith had guessed, and rightly, that the governor might arrest him for piracy and for endangering the colony's welfare.

Will came home, sagging with defeat that they had not been able to constrain Elfrith and bring him back to James Cittie.

"Tucker scared Elfrith off, all right. And for this I cannot fault Captain Tucker. For he is well aware of the danger Elfrith and his 'mission' may have placed us in once more."

"You may starve, you corsair!" Tucker had screamed at Elfrith.

Elfrith had left, but not before imparting these words to Captain Tucker. "Well, mind ye. Ye'd best get some ordnance at Point Comfort, or this colony shall be quite undone ere long, I have heard tell from some Spaniards down in the West Indies that the Spanish shall be here come spring."

My stomach dropped as if it had a heavy stone in it, for I had been a military wife long enough to understand the implications.

We had no place of strength to retreat to, few ships we could depend upon. We possessed soldiers, but not enough. We had no earthmen or engineers to build us true forts to fight off the Spanish. Our ordnance was few, and the carriages which held them decrepit. We stored not enough ammunition or powder, shot or lead. Our men could fight two whole days, perhaps, with what they had. And for that, not one true gunner in all of the colony.

Now the colony lay, like a baby bird in a nest, wondering if the Spanish cat should attack it. This would be a long autumn and winter. The heart of the colony, so jubilant at having its own General Assembly, went right out of it on that one bit of news from Captain Elfrith.

And what happened to the *Treasurer* and its African captives we would not learn until later, either. But we would see them again.

A Day of Thanksgiving
December 4, 1619 ~ James Cittie

Wee ordaine that the day of our ships arrival at the place as-signed for plantacon in the land of Virginia shall be yearly and perpetually kept holy as a day of thanksgiving to Almighty God.
—First instruction in the Berkeley Plantation's charter, 1618

As fall moved toward winter, we waited, reckoning each day a good one when we heard no news of attack in the bay. But then, we reminded ourselves, Elfrith had said *the spring.*

The Company sent us ships one after the other. Never had so many settlers inundated us. Some had signed on with the Company directly. Many more were for the particular plantations, groups of investors pooling their money to bring colonists over, hoping to make a profit where the nearly bankrupt Virginia Company had failed.

The Virginia Company was thrilled to have these particular plantations. Allowing these investors to run their own plantation within the larger colony of Virginia took much burden off the Company itself. To encourage them, the Company gave them large grants of land, and each of these plantations gave itself a name.

One of these plantations that held interest for Tempie and me was Berkeley Hundred. While in England, the Berkeley sponsors had encouraged George to become their fifth investor. George had initially accepted. But later upon reflection he had withdrawn his acceptance. Given his duties as governor, George felt he should not become involved in another venture. "Lest the interests of one cause me to make poor decisions for the other," he had said, and Tempie agreed.

More importantly, we learned that Mary Woodlief's husband would be in charge of the venture. Mary had stayed behind when Captain Woodlief had returned to England to straighten out his business. We had seen little of Mary since she had stayed in Bermuda Hundred when our husband's military and government business had brought us back to James Cittie.

The ship *Margaret* arrived, the thirty-five colonists lusty and healthy. "Praise God!" Tempie whispered. She fully expected to be putting up some of the passengers for a few days until the *Margaret* continued upriver to the site chosen for it. I expected to have visitors as well. Each time a ship's passengers came in sickly, we all risked illness housing them.

"No bloody flux! No plague." I crossed my fingers to counter any bad luck I might have just brought us by saying that aloud. Tempie crossed hers, too.

As it turned out, Governor Yeardley asked Will and me to house Captain Woodlief for a few days while he housed George Thorpe. Sir George had thought the captain might be more comfortable in a home where he already knew the settlers. The Powells housed the well-respected Ferdinando Yate, who had kept the ship's diary, while the other settlers were scattered about the town as usual.

The captain said that their ship had first touched at Kecoughtan, as he had friends there.

Captain Woodlief had many questions, one of the first being how his family fared. "Do you know, Mistress Peirce, how my Mary and John and little Ann might be?" His eyes held a glint of fear, as did all those who returned from England when asking about their loved ones.

"No, captain, I'm afraid I don't." I dished him some pumpion and corn pone. "I haven't seen Mary since I went to Bermuda Hundred when my daughter Cecily's family was ill."

After dinner, Captain Woodlief sat with Will, each man smoking a pipeful of Virginia tobacco. Will asked after England; Captain Woodlief asked about affairs in Virginia.

Woodlief had plans for his own hundred, which the Virginia Company had approved. "Two hundred men, Lieutenant Peirce! That's what we promised to plant here at the new plantation to be named for Sir Thomas Wainman. And then, too, I'm in charge of the town of Berkeley Hundred of which these thirty and odd men on ship are a part. Berkeley is a well organized effort," Woodlief said.

Will agreed although we understood that Captain Francis West, Lord La Warr's brother, was filing complaints against George Yeardley stating the plans for Berkeley Hundred infringed upon his family grant at Westover. George had assured West that Berkeley was situated further toward Shirley Hundred. George undoubtedly had an enemy in West as he had an ally in Woodlief.

"We had hoped to have Governor Sir George Yeardley onboard as a

Berkeley investor, but he declines."

Will nodded. "The man's hands are full. So many ships, so many settlers, do they send us at all times." Will chuckled. "No offense, captain."

Woodlief laughed, too. "None taken."

"Some come in healthy like yourselves. Some come in with many dead or a-dying, and we must bring them into our homes, nurse them upon our own already stretched resources." Will rubbed his eyes as if the very memory tired him. "This can be a challenging proposition, sir. Being an old settler yourself, I'm sure you recognize your good fortune in all the ship being well upon arrival. For three hundred settlers have died just this single year. Most of them, as always, newcomers."

Woodlief agreed, saying, "The gentlemen sponsors, as our first instruction, have ordered me to initiate a holy day of thanksgiving each year to commemorate the date of our own safe arrival on the land to be called Berkeley Hundred."

"Well, then, Captain Woodlief," I said, though I was not part of the conversation, "I pray Mary and the children shall take part in that with you, each and every year."

To myself, I thought, *I have seen too many hopes shattered here in Virginia to believe it may be true.*

A Prosperous and a Good Land
Mid-December 1619 ~ James Cittie

A prosperous and a good land,
'T will take you fifty miles to ride
O'er grass, and corn, and woodland.
—Charles Mackay

"I know the land I shall ask for. Without a doubt unless someone else requests the same." Will was musing over George Yeardley's announcement that land dividends were forthcoming for the ancient planters, we who had been here since before the departure of Sir Thomas Dale three years prior.

"Where?" I sat beside him at the table and placed a hand upon his arm.

He paused and turned toward me. "You have been a rock for me, Joan. Through all that this venture has offered, for what we have endured."

I shrugged. "Did I have a choice?"

"Well." He pulled on his pipe then blew the smoky air slowly. "You could have given up. You could have made life miserable for both of us. And who would have blamed you? I brought you here with promise of a better life. Now, full ten years and more, we have had little enough of that."

"Perhaps the best lay ahead?" I said. This was the thought I always brought to mind. I could not bear to think that we could have more years like those behind us.

In fact, we had just received word that Jane and John were expecting their first child. Will said John was more contented than he'd seen him in a long while. We had one grandchild and, come summer and God willing, would soon have another. And Tempie and George were expecting another child about that time, too.

"Indeed, it would seem so. Perhaps. Now, this land—" In front of him lay a slate, and on it, I saw he had drawn a crude map of Virginia. He used the pipe to point to one little piece of land. "This. Mulberry Island."

"Ah, the beautiful little island jutting out, the place where we turned back when Lord De La Warr arrived!" Someone back in the colony's first year had christened the island after the hundreds of mulberry trees visible from the rivers as the ships passed.

"Mulberry Island has many advantages for us, Joan. Militarily, it is one of the best locations on the river. The water on three sides offers natural defense from foreign invaders. The land is fertile and plush. And we shall work toward spinning silk."

I understood immediately. The little silkworms loved to eat mulberry leaves. What better location to experiment with silk than on an island filled with mulberry trees? The worms had not fared well in the first shipment, but no one was giving up on them. King James himself was making trials of silkworms and mulberries at his Westminster Palace. The king sincerely hoped that silk would replace tobacco and smoking, habits he abhorred.

"See here." Will drew a line from James Cittie to Mulberry Island and from Mulberry Island to land across the water. Then, from across the water back to James Cittie. "A triangle. Easy to travel between any two points. And Rolfe has his land across the water, the land given to him by Powhatan as a wedding gift." The land there had no name. We called it simply "Across the Water." The men fully expected that one day James Cittie would encompass both sides of the river much as London straddled the Thames.

"Ewens has his land across the water as well. That will be the next place I hope to plant."

"What about Sam and Cecily? Tom Bailey has earned land, though he is not here to claim it." *How sad*, I thought.

"The last I spoke with Sam, he wants to stay up in the Charles Hundred area." Bermuda Hundred was officially "Charles Hundred" now although most of us continued to call it by the old name. Will continued, "Sam chose the site where the River of the Appomattocks branches off from the James River. The resulting point is also a prime defensible location. His advantage is being far from incoming Spanish. His disadvantage, being far from the port at James Cittie. Charles Hundred has its port, of course, but…" I understood. Many ships traveled no further than James Cittie.

Will continued. "Sam and Cecily will procure Tom Bailey's acreage and—this is marvelous, Joan—the land shall go into the name of little Temperance Bailey! She'll surely be one of the youngest landholders in Virginia." Little Temp, at four years old, would own several hundred acres. "The Bailey land will be by a creek near Sam's land if Sam has his choice. Sam will husband all of their property until Little Temp is married or of age."

Cecily had stayed behind in England so that she might turn ten and become a landholder in her own right. Now, not only had she earned land for herself, but her little girl had also inherited land. My heart filled with joy at the fulfillment of long-awaited promises.

"And the Yeardleys?" I asked.

"Of Yeardley's wishes, I have not heard. But a likely choice is adjacent to Tanks Weyanoke, his gift from the Indians."

"Maria told me that she and her husband would choose a parcel on the Neck-o-Land near James Island and his Parish."

"A nice location not far from the church," Will replied.

Then he sat for a moment, tapping his pipe idly. He bit his lip.

We'd been married too long for me to not recognize the pensiveness. What was on his mind?

"Something troubles you, Will?"

He turned his eyes toward mine, and I knew instinctively that I should not like what he was about to say.

"Do you think we shall not get the land at Mulberry Island?" I asked.

"Oh, no. I believe we have a fair chance. And I have come to have a good deal of respect for Spencer, Alice's brother. He shall join Cousin Tom, Rolfe, and me in managing our lands in the Maine and at Mulberry Island."

"Well, that's a good thing. A corporation of the four of you." Tight bonds. Will, his cousin Tom, Tom's brother-in-law, and our son-in-law John. Trustworthy, one and all. A strong alliance made for prosperity.

Will sighed as if he could put off the inevitable no longer. "You know 'tis past time for Tommy to go to school."

My heart fell. I knew. My resolve upon the death of little Giles had wavered although I knew sending Tommy to England was the right thing to do.

"I know."

"And we have another issue. The problem, as I see it, is we shall not have enough workers for the land at Mulberry Island—or wherever it may be we receive our patent. Tobacco requires the labors of so many men. If I use the proceeds from the tobacco to pay the passage of others, I receive fifty acres for each man or woman *and* someone to ensure that the crops are hearty. Here's a splendid opportunity indeed! All our hard work, Joan. All our trials and suffering—they have not been for naught. No, not all." He squeezed my hand.

I drew a deep breath. If what he said could actually succeed, we might find ourselves wealthy landowners in but a few growing seasons if the tobacco price stayed high, didn't become a victim of glut. If the weather held. No more hailstorms! If the Indians and settlers could avoid war.

"Many *ifs*, Will. Yet much hope as well."

"Barring a great upheaval again, I believe that the risks we've endured here shall pay handsomely, are beginning to pay even now."

"But where will you get these servants? And what has this to do with Tommy?"

He looked down and away. "The servants? From England. From Somerset, from Dorset, from Cousin Tom's home in Shropshire, my other cousins' home in Kent. From London, a great source to find those seeking opportunity. In time, when the servants have worked off their indentures, they, too, shall have land. And have the opportunity to bring yet others over. Virginia, from sea to sea, Joan! Sea to sea. I believe it shall happen, in time."

"Aye." Suddenly, though, I understood what Will was trying to say. "William Peirce, we are going to England *with* Tommy! Going to England like Tempie and Pocahontas." At last. Losing Tommy would not be so bad if I could return to see my brothers, my home, the bay I had loved so dearly.

"Joan." His voice interrupted my thoughts. "Not you, dear. Only Tommy and I."

How Quick the Soul's Alarm
Mid-December 1619 ~ James Cittie

How quick the soul's alarm!
—Frederic W. H. Myers

"What? Why? How could you say that, even suggest that?" I felt the tears coming and turned away from him. "Don't you love me? How could you *leave* me? How could you let me stay behind in this…this…place… I have longed to leave for so many years?"

He tried to wrap his arms around me, but I shook him off and pushed him away. "No!"

"Joan, sea travel is dangerous. You understand that well enough. You have been through the hurricane. Roaming pirates, dangerous storms. I am not so eager as you to leave my business and, well, *my home,* behind. Nor to leave you," he said softly. "And John, Tom, and Will Spencer will see to the business of the land, but you know I prefer to watch over these things myself. We have at last a respectable home here in James Cittie. Someone needs to see to it, make sure that our possessions are intact—"

"Possessions?"

"Aye," he said firmly. "Possessions. I will be bringing home many servants, I hope. But we have more to consider here. What if something should happen to Jane during her delivery? Who if not you will be there to ensure proper care? Or if Cecily and Sam should fall ill, what of Little Temp?" His voice caught. "Sickness, ever present. You are good with physick, Joan. Who can we trust better than you? We want our grandchildren to survive, to live to behold the legacy we *will* leave. No, I do not think it in our best interest for you to go. Joan, I would not go myself if I didn't have to do it, would not send Tommy if it weren't imperative. I will see Tommy situated in a good school, either with your brothers, my cousins, or in London." There was finality to his words.

"So that's it, then. You've made up your mind. When will the two of you leave?" My voice sounded far away, detached.

"On the *George,* which I reckon to sail in January. The cold weather will make for a healthier voyage. I can go for little charge as an officer on the Company ship. Roger Smith will, I believe, go as well. And Ewens shall master the ship. We could not be in finer hands. We'll still be here for Christmas…"

"Bah! Christmas." Then I dropped my head and said nothing. Again, someone I loved would be an ocean away from me. Again, I would be alone. "What if…what if…you never…what if you never…?" I could not finish, but he understood. Tempie, George, and John had returned. Pocahontas and her son Thomas had not.

"What if I never return? Joan, I'm a tough old soldier. I've been through battles against the Spanish *tercios,* the most formidable soldier Spain has to offer. I've fought the sea with buckets of water slung overboard. I've lived as a castaway on an island for a year. And I have looked at an arrow aiming for my eye—before my musket put it down. I promised you I would return when Jane was born. I promised you I would keep our family together in Virginia. And, here I am once more, promising you that for this one sacrifice, the rest of our lives can be better, the heritage of our children stronger. Do you believe me?"

I said nothing again, feeling the swirling pain of fear, of anger, of hurt and resignation.

"Next voyage, you shall go," he said with emphasis. "Next voyage. Upon my word."

The silence rang like bells, like wedding bells and funeral bells. Like all the years of bells and drums calling us to church and to work. But this time, the drumming and ringing was in my head, a clapper banging against a great iron bell, again and again. The drummer pounded madly. *No!* I wanted to scream at the bells and drums to cease, to return me to the moment we had discussed the land, *our* land. To take away the endless chance and risk that Virginia brought, the path turning and tumbling away out of sight. The rocks. The rocky path to Compostela.

My hands clasping my forehead could not stop the pealing, banging, throttling, the realization that I would have to face the next year and a half alone. For that was how long these voyages typically took, several months at sea, a year to recover from the journey, then, the voyage home.

Will let me sit in what he perceived as silence while my head rang with drums and bells, bells, bells.

After a moment or two, he murmured, "Joan?"

I took a deep breath and gathered my courage.

"Take the shell," I whispered. "My scallop shell. And you had better keep it unbroken and return it to me!" I said suddenly with some emotion rising which I understood not. "Bring your half back to me. My pilgrim shell, for I shall *never* forgive you if you don't."

He nodded. "Of course." His voice was also a whisper. "I will bring the shell whole and with it, my love, I will bring you whatever you desire from London."

"*You* are all I desire to have come to me from London. Only you."

"As you wish. You shall have it," he said in a croak. "I swear an oath on it. I swear."

Lord De La Warr had sworn his wife an oath as well. But oaths were drowned easily by seas, by calenture, by Spanish chain-shot boring the hull of a ship. An oath didn't mean much to me.

Stars Hung Under a Sea
December 31, 1619 to January 6, 1620 ~ James Cittie

It is moonlight. Alone in the silence
I ascend my stairs once more,
While waves, remote in a pale blue starlight,
Crash on a white sand shore.
It is moonlight. The garden is silent.
I stand in my room alone.
Across my wall, from the far-off moon,
A rain of fire is thrown...
There are houses hanging above the stars,
And stars hung under a sea:
And a wind from the long blue vault of time
Waves my curtain for me...
—Conrad Aiken

All the Ancient Planters being set free have chosen places for
their dividends according to the Commission. Which given all
great content, for now knowing their own lands, they strive and
are prepared to build houses and to clear their grounds ready to
plant, which given the [planters] greate encouragement, and the
greatest hope to make the Colony florish that ever yet happened to
them.
—John Rolfe, January 1620

On December 31, George Yeardley presented Will with a patent to six hundred acres at Mulberry Island. Will's length of time in Virginia and his rank and service as lieutenant put him near the front of the list. And on January 6, just one week later, my husband and son waved goodbye to all of us.

Sam, John, and Will all owned their own shallops now, bought by trading tobacco to a shipwright. Cecily and Sam had sailed downriver for Will's farewell, bringing, of course, Little Temp. The Jordans could come, and they needed ask permission of no one, not governor or sea captain. The freedom was becoming very real to us all now.

Also gathered that day were the Rolfes, Tom and Alice Peirce, and Richard and Bettie Peirce. The Buckes were there, as was Tempie.

And in a strange memory twisting 'round my skull, I remembered the *Deliverance,* a scrappy ship forged in the Bermudas, bringing Will and Sam, George and John home to us. We—I—had stood in this very place. That day, Tempie and Jane had lain dying of starvation in the little cabin. I, in my hunger-stupor, had collapsed upon seeing what I believed were long-dead phantoms upon a peculiar ship. And I had glimpsed my father, who had been long dead, there with them.

I had been a seaman's daughter and a soldier's wife. I had watched so many leaving, so many ships sailing, that perhaps, one day, it should not bother me so much.

Today was not that day.

I wept, and Jane and Cecily held me, as they wept, too.

Tommy, wanting so much to be a man, tried not to cry. But seven-year-olds are not quite men, try as they might to be. When a tear slipped out, he wiped it quickly. And then he gave up the ruse and ran to me, his arms around my waist, his eyes shining.

"I'm coming back, mama. You'll see! And then I'm going to be a soldier." Tommy was slight, slighter certainly than Will. My son had come into a world where food had rarely been plentiful. I could not imagine him in battle. But I was certain, no mother could ever envision her son in a war.

I put my hands on both his cheeks, feeling their softness. When I saw him next, his cheeks could be rugged, even with a scrap of beard, perhaps. *Virginia giveth, and Virginia taketh away.*

Here we were, a family splintered again. Will's parting look was one of regret, perhaps. Uncertainty, maybe. Love, surely.

On the bridge, Will turned around, one hand reaching into his sack. Triumphantly, he pulled something out. I squinted through tear-swollen eyes.

A scallop shell.

It was traveling back to England.

I Have Come a Long Way
Late February 1620 ~ James Cittie

Nihumili kutali, lunikomi lugendu.
(I have come a long way; the journey has exhausted me.)
—Tanzanian Proverb

The little moon my cargo is.
—Richard Le Gallienne

One month passed slowly. Will and Tommy were, I reckoned, somewhere in the middle of the Atlantic while I was left here alone. Well, not completely alone—but Jane and Cecily had their own families, and what had I?

My heart wrung with distress. Yet I tried to stay busy as if by sweeping I could sweep away my fears. And now I remembered how my mother had swept so thoroughly while awaiting my father's returns. Perhaps it had been the same with her. Yet, if she were afraid for him, she had never let on. She'd just swept and swept and swept.

A knock at the door brought George Yeardley.

"Sir George? Is anything...wrong?" *Of course, he has no information about Will.*

"No, no, Joan. Nothing at all is wrong. Well, 'tis more that I have a favor to ask of you."

A favor? What could the governor of Virginia wish of me?

"We have word of a ship's arrival at Point Comfort. She is making her way here, even now. The *Treasurer,* to be precise. There are, uh, passengers."

I felt confused. "Passengers? I don't take your meaning." If I were to have houseguests, well, so be it. But the governor had never made a special visit to ask it.

"Africans, Joan. We are going to have to find them homes. Upon the *Treasurer* are nine Africans, the remainder of the Spanish slaves Captain Elfrith collected from the *São João Bautista.* Elfrith has traded all he could to the Bermuda governor, who took some of the Africans willingly. Now the captain knows not what to do with the rest of the negroes. Our *former* governor has left us with quite a hornet's nest of problems."

George's disdain was palpable. "The *Treasurer* had escaped to Bermuda. She's a leaky old vessel. I am surprised she made it that far, *most* surprised she made it back here again. Well, Governor Butler in Bermuda has taken two thirds of the... shall we call them hostages? Argall has escaped, leaving us with the problems of his creation. Joan, I am asking you to bring a negro woman into your home. We are giving the women to homes with women. Men to homes with men. You are an old planter, well familiar with the ways of James Cittie. We are asking the ancient planters for help."

I dropped into the rocker. "What in the world shall I do with a woman who cannot even speak English?"

"Teach her?"

"Good lord, governor, sir!"

Only a few hours later, before I had a chance even to take in what George had asked of me, I heard a knock. And when I opened the door, I saw Tempie. Beside her stood one very frightened-looking African girl. I reckoned her to be about sixteen. She was thin as a wisp, wearing what I suspected was the same dress she'd worn since her first days of captivity.

"Joan, we believe the Portuguese baptized her as *Angela,* but her language seems to not pronounce the final letter. That is why she gives her own name as *Angel* or *Angelo.* Thank you for helping us. We have just seven for which to find homes. Two of the women will stay at my house, and a few of the men will work as servants for George."

I nodded. I was, indeed, speechless.

"Angelo," Tempie said slowly, "This is Mistress Peirce."

I was still trying to understand the task. Did Angelo speak any English at all? Would she be underfoot? Would we get along? Would she be belligerent? Frightened? How would this work?

"Come in, the both of you, please," I finally managed to say.

Tempie stepped over the threshold, and Angelo, after seeming to determine that is what she should do, did the same.

Angelo's head hung. She stole a glance upward at me as if not wanting me to know that she, too, was sizing me up.

"It is a very bad situation, Joan," Tempie said somberly. "We have given the Spanish reason to attack us now. The Portuguese had captured the slaves for the Spanish islands. Our king has made treaty with Spain, whose dominion includes Portugal, and even the Dutch sponsor of the *White Lion* has revoked his consent for privateering. Yet, what have we? A ship of men and women with no place to go."

"Well, what if the Spanish come? Won't our having someone stolen from their ships condemn us?"

"If they come, Joan, we are already condemned." Tempie's eyes showed that she understood the seriousness of the situation and wondered if I did. "George is trying to locate someplace along the river for a fort, but we simply don't have the tools to build and the munitions to...to protect us."

"I...I don't know, Tempie."

"Joan, if not you, then who? We're having a hard time of it, finding four others with experience as we have. We're mostly keeping the hostages nearby at James Cittie."

"Does she speak any English?" I whispered.

"Near as we can tell, very little. She apparently learned a few words on ship and while she was in Bermuda."

"Was she with a family in Bermuda?"

Tempie shook her head. "No. Governor Kendall suspected the *Treasurer* had taken these negroes at sea from a Spanish ship, so he put them in a long-house at St. George's Town. When Lord Rich's ally, Nathaniel Butler, became governor, he selected some of these captives to be his servants and sold others. The rest he sent back to Virginia. Now no one here knows what to do with these captives. As for Angelo, I...I chose her for you myself because I felt sorry for her. I knew you would be kind to her."

I could see why Tempie felt such compassion. The sadness of Angelo's face spoke more than she would be able to say, at least yet.

I reached out and touched the stranger's arm. She flinched and then relaxed as if she decided I meant no harm. For the moment.

I did not even know how to begin. We had other indentured servants, but they had agreed to be servants. We paid their passage; they worked for a time and then were free of their indenture and received their land. Of course, these had all been English, and we had understood one another. Will had worked them in the fields. I'd scarcely seen them. Even the Dutch, Poles, and Italians who came over had made a choice. This situation was completely different.

"Hungry?" I said to her. She glanced up, and I glimpsed her eyes, which were rich and dark. *Hungry* must have been a word she knew. She nodded.

I had pottage in the kettle and motioned her to the table. She walked to it, but continued to hang her head in what appeared to be fear and defeat. She looked uneasy and did not sit.

"Outside of her native language, we believe she speaks Portuguese best," Tempie said. Soldiers such as George and Sam spoke some Spanish from their time in the Low Countries, so with their help, we might be able to communicate a little.

"Tonight, a meeting in the Big House about the *Treasurer*. The old work-horse of a ship is falling apart, and 'tis a wonder she was able to leave Bermuda. I suspect they'll scrap her."

That seemed a fitting end to the ship that had terrified the French, captured Pocahontas, and stolen African slaves. "Would that we could have scrapped *Argall*," I said.

Tempie laughed, but not a laugh of amusement. "Indeed. But the question remains of what will become of Elfrith and the men onboard." Then she hugged me and said, "I have to leave you now, Joan. Goodbye, Angelo."

Angelo looked up. What this poor woman must have been through!

As Tempie walked out, I saw that Angelo was glancing covertly around the house. She must have little idea of where she was, or who I was, or what would happen next. For a moment, she reminded me of Pocahontas. But even Pocahontas could speak some of the language and was yet in her own country although a captive at our settlement.

I gestured to the bench in what I hoped was a reassuring manner. She sat, but seemed afraid she might do the wrong thing and offend me. Her arms she kept near her body, her shoulders hunched protectively. *She is trying to make herself as small as possible, as if she could become so small, she would disappear,* I thought.

Argall's attempts to enrich himself by piracy had stirred trouble beyond all imagining, and we might pay for it for years to come. I felt angry that he had put us in this position. However, lest Angelo think I directed the anger at her, I did not betray it as it flashed through me.

Instead, I filled a bowl with warm pork pottage and placed it before her along with a spoon.

"Pottage," I said, attempting to smile encouragingly.

She studied it, and I could see she had not eaten in a while.

"For you." I pointed toward her. "Hungry?" I rubbed my stomach in what I hoped was a worldwide gesture. What had I agreed to? And without even Will's help?

"*Jesus?*" she asked suddenly. "*Jesus Cristo?*"

"Jesus Christ?" I did not know the Portuguese word for Jesus, but could that be what she was saying? Was she asking if I were a Christian?

I nodded. "*Si. Jesus Cristo,* uh, lives here." I gestured about the house. "And here." I placed my hand on my heart.

"Ah," she said quietly. "*Jesus.*" She placed her hand onto her heart as well.

To my utter surprise, we had found one common belief. Perhaps we could build on that.

The Tears of the Orphan
Late February 1620 ~ James Cittie

Kud mbelawa a hada a hwad.
(The tears of the orphan run inside.)
—Cameroonian proverb

Love ye therefore the stranger: for ye were strangers in the land of Egypt.
—Deuteronomy 10:19

"She's a Christian, Tempie!" I said to her when she came by later to check on us.

Angelo had gone to the room that would be hers. Even though she didn't speak the language, I felt it impolite to speak of her in her presence.

Tempie shrugged. "The people in her village have been Christians for over a hundred years. *Católicos.* Catholics. Our way of worshiping will seem a bit strange to her."

"A bit? So…what happened to her? The Portuguese aren't supposed to capture Christians." There was an understanding—a law, in fact—that one Christian could not enslave another.

"I do not know the full story although I have heard parts of it from George. We gather that she's from the Portuguese colony called Angola in the Kingdom of Ndongo."

Angelo peered cautiously from the doorway at us. I gestured for her to come out. Apparently the word *Ndongo* had caught her attention.

"*Jesus,*" I said, pronouncing it as she did and with my hand on my heart once more for emphasis.

She gave me something that was almost a smile and she looked relieved, I thought.

"*Jesus,*" she agreed. It was as though the one shared word gave us each reassurance. And we needed reassurance because I had no idea how this was going to work.

"*Sim. Mucu Ndongo,*" she said hesitantly, in what I guessed was a mixture of Portuguese and her Angolan language. She patted her chest as she spoke, sounding each syllable as though that might help us understand her words.

I am from Ndongo, I thought.

Tempie said, "A fierce tribe banded together with an unethical Portuguese governor. The Portuguese king had ordered the governor not to attack Christian towns and villages. The attacking tribe was called..." Tempie stopped as though realizing that to say its name would strike fear anew in Angelo.

Instead, Tempie spelled the tribe's name: *Imbangala.* "They are *not* Christians, nor do they even respect the African gods. The other tribes say the, uh, *that* tribe worships evil itself. Everyone fears them. This tribe travels and pillages, neither planting nor tending livestock, but relying instead on the work of other tribes. This hated band leaves an area destitute, so George said, even killing all the life-giving palm trees just to drink the fermented sap."

"But why would they not tap the palm? So that others could benefit from the same tree. Even themselves later."

Tempie's eyes shone with understanding. She and George had clearly discussed this. "Ah, but Joan. That is the idea. They aren't coming back. And why should anyone behind them have use of the tree? They capture, kill, and even....well, they are cannibals."

I gasped in horror, casting a sideways glance at the African woman standing nearby. What had she endured? I was only beginning to get an idea of the terror.

Along the way, I learned, the Imbangala had captured the innocent. The Portuguese governor had exploited this. So the Imbangala brought the still-surviving men, women, and children as slaves to Luanda, the capital of the Portuguese colony in Angola. There, the Portuguese instructed the prisoners in the Catholic faith and baptized them all, even though some, like Angelo, had already been Christians. The Portuguese then loaded the negroes onto a ship called the *São João Bautista,* sailing toward the Spanish holdings to sell them as slaves.

"Christians are not supposed to enslave other Christians!" I said indignantly.

Tempie agreed. "Yes, that is against their doctrine. I don't know how they justify it." She continued, "George said that near Mexico in the Bay of Campeche the Portuguese ship ran into the *White Lion* and the *Treasurer.* Argall had instructed his ship to take whatever Spanish goods they could get. What does his man happen upon but a ship filled with Africans. So the *Treasurer* has returned, bringing them here and causing untold diplomatic difficulties to us all."

"Is there no way to get Angelo to her homeland? No way at all?" I knew the answer, but felt I had to try.

"No," Tempie said. "Unfortunately not. As George put it to me, 'We are not going to sail to Portuguese Angola and release them! Even if we did—if we could—what would we do? Sail to Luanda and loudly remind the Portuguese that we (thank you, Argall!) pirated one of their ships? But that now we have changed our minds and are returning the slaves? And even if we *could* do that, do you think the Portuguese would then release Angelo? No, the Portuguese would put her back on the next ship to Mexico where she would be a slave, certain death.' For us, she will be as an indentured servant."

Tempie grimaced. "You can tell I asked these same questions, Joan. I am no happier than you are. However, George pointed out that, *even if* we could get her to Luanda and somehow beyond the Portuguese settlement, *the evil ones have destroyed her village and her people.* No one will know where the scattered folks seeking refuge have gone. And wouldn't that tribe like to see *us* coming? No. And we are not going to execute these Africans. So we are left with servants. Servants who need a home and place of indenture."

I understood. "She will stay with me, or she will stay with someone else in Virginia, but she cannot go home."

"Home," Angelo said suddenly. She had heard, and apparently understood, that word.

I looked at Angelo, who I knew would never see her home again. She had high cheekbones and skin a rich brown, darker than the natives. Her eyes were dark, curious, and fearful. *She must yearn for her own home,* I thought. Had she been married in Africa? Had she left children behind? Again, Pocahontas flashed through my mind, and, inexplicably, the Paspahegh queen, whose last moments I had witnessed so many years before. The image of an African baby, crying for his mother, came to me suddenly, and I felt great sadness.

I could only imagine how devastating it would be to see one's village destroyed, being plucked from one's family and captured by the ferocious, frightening warriors and given to the relentless Portuguese. Then, to be re-captured at cannon and musket-point by English ships, brought to Virginia, turned away, held in Bermuda, and then brought back here. Like it or not, I now grasped that she had come through a long line of circumstances that had brought her to me.

How, oh how, would we make this work?

"*Mucu Ndongo. Angola.* Home." She spoke quietly. For I sensed she understood as I did that she would never see her home again.

A Stone From Home
Late February 1620 ~ James Cittie

Umwáansi aguciira icoobo, Imáana ikaguciira icaanzo.
(When an enemy digs a grave for you, God gives you a
hidden door.)
—Burundian proverb

Azru n-tmazirt yuf mraw n-wasif.
(A stone from home is worth ten from the riverbed.)
—North African proverb

Angelo and I spent some time together as I showed her how we washed laundry, how we made repairs on clothes or spun hemp, where to draw water, and how we ground and stored our corn. Many of these things, I came to understand, she, too, had done at home, albeit with slightly different tools.

Slowly, we were able to communicate through a few words. She seemed willing to learn although I sensed still a fear within her that I might beat her, or worse, for any wrong thing she might do.

On the fourth day, Tempie came by, saying, "I have some good news, Joan. No worries! The Buckes say they'll take her."

"Take Angelo?"

"Aye. We knew you weren't comfortable with her presence; that she may, perhaps, be more a burden than a help, especially without Will here."

"I appreciate that, Tempie," I said. "And it's nice of the reverend and Maria to offer. But Maria is great with child again. She'll not have the strength. No, I'm grateful that you asked after her, but...again, no."

She seemed surprised. "No? Why? What has changed in your mind? Is it that she is more helpful than we thought?"

I shook my head. "No, for she has much to learn about the way we do things, although I 'spect she could teach us a few ways of her own peoples. No, that is not the reason. George said she was ripped from her village, which was destroyed? Taken in possession by the Im...that evil tribe? Then handed from there to the Portuguese. Paraded by them as a piece of inventory. Rebaptized. Loaded onto a ship. Sick with many others. Then, part of a noisy, smoky sea battle that must have terrified her until the *White Lion's* crew forced her onto their ship. And then from there to the *Treasurer?* Brought to James Town, rejected, and sent from there to Bermuda. Held in a dank longhouse as a prisoner for six months, carried back to James Town, and finally, given to us."

Tempie looked at me curiously. "Aye. That is the size of it. Why ask you?"

"Because each time someone has stolen her or handed her off, she has endured a new round of terror. Each time she has not known where she was going or to whom. Or why someone was moving her." I glanced at Angelo, now patting dry and putting away trenchers and spoons. Yet she never looked fully relaxed—there was a tension to her carriage.

She seemed surprised. "If you're certain."

"I'm certain. Let her stay with me. Here am I—my daughters have married, my son has years of schooling before he can return. Will won't be back for perhaps eighteen months or more, and I'm alone in the house. Without martial law, we no longer have duties from the governor, so I could spend some time working with her. God knows, I have swept this floor enough! Of course, she'll need to learn to worship in our church. This is where the reverend can help by teaching her." There were, of course, no Catholic churches in Virginia. Nor did we want any.

A light shone in Tempie's eyes. "I see where you are going with this. If we look upon our Christian Africans as ours to help through the transition to becoming a settler of Virginia, then we are, perhaps, doing some little missionary work."

"Some little, yes. A better place for her would be her own land with her family, but George has aptly pointed out that this is not possible. She is, after all, already a Christian, so are we not helping a sister in Christ through a most tragic personal experience? Traders brought her from hand to hand across the ocean until she reached us. Might we be a sound port? And not a frightening one?"

"I'm glad I know you, Mistress Peirce," Tempie said.

"If you can take two African women, I can at least take one. Tomorrow, I'll begin teaching her as many words as possible. The more she learns, the stronger she will be. And I pray she will, in time, lose her fear." *And accept,* I thought, *that this is her new home. And there is no going back.*

As Virginia had forced us all to accept.

The Bells of Stepney

May 9 to June 7, 1620 ~ James Cittie,
and Sir Thomas Smythe's home on Philpot Lane, London

When will you pay me?
Say the bells of Old Bailey
When I grow rich
Say the bells of Shoreditch
When will that be?
Say the bells of Stepney
I'm sure I don't know
Says the great bell at Bow.
—English Nursery Rhyme

Yf you shall thinke ffitt to send any men before Christmas I
pray send at least 6 moneths victuall with them….I pray thinke it
not strange I should wryght thus to send victualls with your people
for you may be pleased well to conceave that yf such nombers of
people come upon me unexpected, and that at an unhealthfull
season and to late to sett Corne I cannott then be able to feed them
owt of others labors…
—Governor Sir George Yeardley to the Virginia Company,
June 7, 1620

P*lease.*
George Yeardley sat late into the night, writing the letter that had been troubling him for so long.

I understand your good intentions, but please hear what I am saying.

You send far too many people with no victuals to feed them and at unhealthy seasons. You ask us to make commodities when all we can do is feed the people whom you send.

Meanwhile, in the courts of the Virginia Company in London, many whom Sir George had called friend were petitioning against him. The cries rang out.

"We need noble blood!"

"To move Virginia's leadership from a baron to a tailor's son is *not* fitting."

"Beyond fitting, it can never succeed."

"Lord La Warr has been the governor and captain general since 1609. With his loss, you bestow the enterprise to George Yeardley—*Sir* George Yeardley?"

The message of the petition, presented with arguments, was clear. The settlers would follow a nobleman, an earl or baron. Even Gates and Dale had only led under Lord La Warr, never on their own authority. The settlers would not—could not—let a common man lead them.

The petition went around, and Captain Argall had signed. That was to be expected. Argall was in England as the Company tried him for piracy. Lord Rich, now the Earl of Warwick, was working to muddy the arguments against his friend.

But other signers, could Sir George have then seen them, would have surprised him. Captain Francis West; Doctor Lawrence Bohun, physician general of the colony and La Warr's own doctor; Captain Daniel Tucker, Starving Time survivor; Captain Roger Smith, a man who would one day play an interesting role in our lives. And leading the signers, the cruelest blow to George Yeardley, was his own former commander, Sir Thomas Gates. Gates may have liked and respected Yeardley, but even he believed only a nobleman could be a strong governor and captain general.

As George Yeardley attempted to handle the impossible with divided support at home in England, his problems mounted. For one thing, settlers were pouring off ships.

During April and May alone, the Company and particular plantations had sent seven hundred fifty souls to Virginia, all disembarking and registering with Governor Yeardley at James Cittie.

The *Trial* with forty passengers; the *Falcon* with thirty-six aboard; the *Jonathan* and the *Merchant of London* bringing four hundred settlers; the *Swan of Barnstable* with seventy-one colonists; the *Duty* had fifty-one aboard; and the *Francis Bona Ventura* carrying one hundred fifty three.

It was true that the *Trial* and the *Falcon* had also brought cattle and mares that we sorely needed. But the other ships had 'tween decks crammed with passengers. They were coming in an unhealthful time of the year despite John Pory and George Yeardley's warnings to the Company.

For in Virginia, it was a known fact: arrive in the warm weather, lie beneath a cold grave. Somehow, the Company did not understand the truth of that statement. Yet we had told them. Letters home stated it. Numbers of those dying proved it. George Yeardley had argued it to them himself in London last year.

Yet Sir Edwin Sandys's zeal to prove that Virginia could succeed was, in a twisted result, causing the deaths of many.

We watched the haggard waifs pour off the ships, and we knew. The vast majority would not live to see the winter. The ague would take them, sure.

Tempie said that George's concern was something deeper. "The Company is assigning land far afield, scattering plantations a hundred miles up and down the James River, putting miles between each one. With no central settlement, George says we make ourselves easy prey for the natives. Even as the natives become more threatened by loss of land."

"But, Tempie. We're at peace. We've no need to worry about that! Many a thing we've to worry about, but the peace is established."

"The peace *was* established before the deaths of both Pocahontas and Powhatan. Opechancanough—well, who knows? The old chief says, 'The sun will fall before I break my treaty,' 'I value our good friendship above all else,' and such...such platitudes. But no one knows what's in his heart, not truly."

She was right. The incident with the Chickahominies remained an open wound both in the attack itself and in Argall's failure to avenge it.

Tempie went on. "We've known the Indians to be treacherous. How do we defend scattered settlements? We can't, says George. Those plantations are alone in the wilderness. The problem is we then lose our strength in numbers."

Meanwhile the settlers came, needing homes for a day, a week. A month. Again and again, our flustered friend and governor required those of us, especially in the port of James Cittie, to open our small homes to strangers, to feed them, to nurse them as they fell ill.

"We do not have adequate housing for so many!" George Yeardley had written to the treasurer and council in England.

And poor George was in a difficult way, for Sir Edwin Sandys needed to defend and protect him against many a foul word in London. Many continued to say that Sir George was not nobility, had been improperly knighted, and was not fit to hold such office.

"George is ill," Tempie told me. She was deeply concerned about the strain his untenable position put upon him. The Company would blame George if large numbers of newcomers died, as would surely happen due to the time of year and inadequate food and shelter. The men signing the petition would say, "See here! It is just as we said it would be. George Yeardley is an unfit leader."

Now, George must convince Sir Edwin of the scope of the problem. Sending so many over without adequate food or housing in the dying season and after planting meant we were all struggling to keep from going hungry again, that new settlers slept wherever they could. The old settlers were rightfully resentful, and most newcomers would die before spring. And then the Company would likely blame George's leadership for the many deaths. He also continued to be deeply worried about how vulnerable the new little settlements were, strewn up and down the river.

George needed Sir Edwin to understand that an inundation of settlers caused food and housing shortages. George did not wish to berate his friend and sponsor, but he also needed to let Sir Edwin know that *this was not working*. Any settler, any soldier, any member of the Virginia General Assembly—even any child here—could report exactly that.

George housed new arrivals with the old planters as he knew full well that putting them on the ground under tents would add to their already fragile health.

The soldiers came around time and again. "Mistress, got a woman, her boy and a baby. Can you give 'em shelter, two nights is all. Two nights and they's off to Smythe's Hundred."

When the ships kept arriving, some groaned, and some held their heads. Some cursed, and some swore they wouldn't bring strangers into their homes ever again.

We saw the throngs disembarking, and we knew. First, we'd shelter them. Then, we'd feed them. Finally, we'd nurse them. Then into the ground they would go.

Sometimes, the ships even arrived two a day. Such was the case with the *Jonathan* and the *London Merchant*. On these ships came ninety women, mostly in their twenties. The Virginia Company arranged to pay their passage. If one of these women and a settler wished to marry, the husband must repay the Company for his wife's passage. If the young woman didn't marry upon arrival, she became an indentured servant, working off her passage for the next seven or so years.

Meanwhile, the *Duty* brought in poor and homeless boys aged about eight to sixteen, culled from the streets of London. These boys had apprenticeships and employ of various sorts for seven years or so until they, too, worked off their passage.

"Where'd you get that lad you got workin' for you?" someone would ask, and the other would reply, "Oh, he's a *Duty* boy."

My assigned family from the *Jonathan* were the Everetts. Ambrose and his wife Jane had brought along two children—Ambrose Junior, who was twenty and Esther, fifteen. While I didn't appreciate the intrusion any more than I ever did, I had to admit I liked the Everetts. The mistress and her daughter were hardworking and polite.

The mother was not well coming off ship, and the father, too, soon took ill. Ambrose Junior found a man to pay his passage, someone he'd known in London, and went to work for him as an indentured servant over in Paspahegh's.

And so the nursing begins.

Ester stayed remarkably well and continued to help me tend to her parents. Angelo also helped as much as she understood what I needed.

"Oh, mistress, I doesn't wish to be a bother. Let me make me own bed, please. Let me beat the sheets when I'm done sleeping," Esther would say.

I was impressed; I'd had many an older woman not offer to help.

"Why did your family come, Esther?" I asked her, as she and Angelo and I swept and tidied the house.

"My father, he'd been working at the shipyard. That's where 'e saw the broadside in Stepney. That's where I'm from. Do you know Stepney, ma'am?"

I nodded, suppressing a smile. Her accent had already given her away as a Cockney, someone born within the sound of the bells of St. Mary-le-Bow, so they say.

"Well, 'e saw the broadside, talking about Virginia and what a great land it be. He said 'e reckoned we all might go, just take ourselves there and make a new start. My mother, she was a-feared of it. She didn't want to go. My brother was a-willin'. I didn't have much say, ma'am. Neither did mum, truly. So as soon as the two be well, we'll be going to find us someone to pay our passage. That's how we come, you know. We're going to have to work it off. But we Everetts, we don't mind hard work, now do we? My mother—" She cast a glance at the woman, whose ague seemed to be creeping higher. "She's a fighter."

Esther rushed to take the wet rag lying on her mother's head and dunk it in the bucket anew, hoping the cooler rag might lessen her mother's fever.

And none of you have hardly a mite's chance of surviving the season, I thought sadly. This young woman was the same age as my Jane.

"What about 'er, Ma'am? Does she speak English?" Esther was eyeing Angelo, who was eyeing Esther in return.

"She speaks a little English, more Portuguese, and of course, her own African language. She's from Angola in Africa."

At the word *Angola,* Angelo looked to me and smiled. "Angola," she said in a rich voice. "I am Angola."

Now I studied the two ailing newcomers, lying on bedsteads lined against the wall. *My home looks like a hospital.* How many had died in here? The

Everetts were too ill to leave the house. This had happened many a-time before.

Soon, the agues and the seasoning took both parents, and we learned that Ambrose, Junior, too, had died. This left Esther wondering what would become of her. She had stayed well, remarkably.

I knew what I was going to do. I would ask Will to pay the passage on Esther, and she would stay with us as another servant. Will had said we needed servants, didn't he? He was scouring the English countryside for them. As for Esther, she had a better chance of surviving if she were here with me rather than marrying some poor laborer who might work her to death.

Virginia certainly did make for strange bedfellows, that much was certain.

"Oh, Lord," I said aloud. "What a crew we are going to be. Esther the Cockney, Angelo the Angolan, and me!"

In June, the Swan of Barnstaple brought me a letter from Will. I took it down to Back River, the same where I had felt so defeated before Tommy was born. Count your blessings, Tempie had said.

Now I sat alone and read. My dearest Joan, the letter began. He was well and so was Tommy! Traveling in the winter is so much easier than in the summer heat, he added. Now if only we could open the Company's eyes to that!

Tommy was healthy and eager to learn about England, the home he had never known. Will had enrolled him in school in Melcombe under my brother Tom's watch. Tom had heard we'd cared for Bettie and Richard upon their coming in, for which Tom was most grateful, Will said.

As soon as I can, my loving and patient wife, I am coming home to you. Home to Virginia.

It was so then. Will didn't feel any more at home in England than Tempie, George, or John had. I held the letter against my bodice. I didn't know whether to laugh or cry. I thought of my little house, still with its same look of poverty. There was no denying it. How strange to call a little house like that home.

Will had added a note in the sheaf which I found after reading the rest. As I read, the tears flowed. Tears it would be, then. "I have pledged to myself that if these servants and tobacco bring us prosperity, I will build you a house. It will be grand by Virginia standards. You'll see. I won't forget my promise. You'll have the finest house in Virginia. Because you have been patient and have never given up. Well, not completely." I heard his wry humor, and through my tears, I laughed.

God bless that man, that old soldier. "You will, too. Build me that house, Will Peirce," I said to the paper and the river.

Your Humble Graves
Mid-June to Late October 1620 ~ James Cittie

Sleep sweetly in your humble graves,
Sleep, martyrs of a fallen cause;
Though yet no marble column craves
The pilgrim here to pause.
—Henry Timrod

As the year 1620 grew older, Jane and Tempie were not the only one who was now expecting, as Margery Fairfax and Maria were also with child.

John sent a shallop to carry me upriver just before Jane's birthing time in the middle of June. How much had changed that I could be gone for a month without fear of flogging! Under Tempie's supervision, Angelo and Esther looked after the house and tended our chickens and goats. To have not known freedom in ten years. How we appreciated it!

I arrived at Charles Hundred, finding Jane in good spirits. When her time came, another woman would act as Jane's midwife since Mistress Wright remained at James Cittie. Mistress Hill had come to Virginia with her husband the year before, but her husband had not survived the seasoning. Now with two children to support alone, Mistress Hill received tobacco by acting as midwife upriver. She possessed her own sets of charms, prayers, and magic, which must have worked as both Jane and her new baby Elizabeth fared well.

Relieved that Jane and her baby were so healthy, I was eager to be present at Margery's delivery just over a month later.

Margery Fairfax had never quite recovered from the deaths of her children at the hands of the Indians, yet she had welcomed the birth of another child with great happiness. I had not seen her smile since before the day in 1617 when she had fallen onto the floor of the church, weeping that her children were dead.

Now, new life brought new hope, and we women who had known her so long celebrated with her. God would not bring any more cruelty to her, of this we were sure.

Yet, fate proved us wrong when Margery passed away during childbirth. None of Mistress Wright's charms or prayers could save the dying woman.

The baby, a girl, had died, too.

Reverend Bucke solemnized the graves of mother and daughter in the churchyard at James Cittie. Maria Bucke stood with us, head bowed, her belly great with child, holding Gershom's hand. Maria's daughter Mara grasped the hand of Benomi. Even Benomi seemed to sense the seriousness of the day. And then we all went back to our homes, feeling such loss we could not describe. With so many other fears, must we confront childbirth fears as well? *The terror of childbirth, a specter standing over the bed of mother and child.*

Making it all worse, the cries of "witch!" resumed when Mistress Wright passed. We heard the whispers. "Mistress Wright hath cursed the Fairfax family. She cursed them long before when the Indians killed the children."

One woman said she had lived near Mistress Wright in Yorkshire. "Everyone in her home of Hull knew the woman practiced black magic."

Mistress Wright, with her sharp tongue, didn't help her own cause much. Some of the women said the midwife had even *admitted* to practicing the black arts.

Now, Tempie and I both had broken hearts. First the death of Margery and her young daughter, then the accusations against Mistress Wright, who had delivered our children safely. We would speak no ill against her.

Tempie said, "One day, the court shall try Mistress Wright on witchcraft. I hope George is governor at that time. Maybe we can save her life."

Tempie and I were determined to move on. It hurt too much not to, so we tried to lay aside our sadness and our fear. I said, "If we do not, how will we ever be able to face your laboring, or Maria's to come?"

Several months later, Tempie sent her gossips notices to come to her bedside. Mistress Wright worked hard on Tempie's behalf as if having lost one mother this summer, she refused to lose another.

When all was over, Tempie had a son with a thicket of black hair. I had prayed for Margery and prayed for Tempie. God had, at least, heard my prayers for Tempie and her son little Francis, for both remained well.

Maria's laboring time came some months later, as the nights took on the chill of winter to come.

Tempie and I came to Maria's bedside with hope as Maria prepared to birth her fourth child. Annie and Thomasine were still in Charles Hundred, so Maria selected as her other gossips Isabella Pace, Judith Perry, and Maria's own step-daughters, Elizabeth and Bridget.

Elizabeth and Bridget Bucke had at last arrived in Virginia. Bridget had married Anne Laydon's brother John Burrows. Thus did our web of families become even more entangled, as some had been kinsmen prior to arriving, some became kinsmen while here, and some became family just by surviving together in Virginia. Maria was like that. She had become like a sister to Tempie and me.

I held Maria's hand, and she squeezed hard. Her brown eyes shone with pain, with fear, and with courage. Mistress Wright pushed us aside as she prepared the childbirth hymns. *"O infans, sive vivus, sive mortus, exi foras, quia Christus te vocat ad lucem,"* she cried. We repeated the prayer thrice, as we always did.

At last, Maria's little son came squalling into the world.

"What shall you call him, mother?" Bridget asked, holding her new baby brother.

Maria smiled, contented. "Why, we shall call him Peleg." And then she quoted Genesis, *"And unto Eber were born two sons: the name of one was Peleg; for in his days was the earth divided!"*

The divided earth, our land, had given us all more faith in the future than anything that had yet happened in our Virginia world.

Relief washed over me. Maria had survived the birthing and so had little Peleg. The name Maria chose this time reflected the hope she felt that the worst truly was behind us.

But for Maria, it was not to be. For a week later, before she had left her confinement, our friend became feverish and weak. Within a fortnight more, she had slipped away from us quietly into the night.

The Reverend Bucke's sermons were always mournful, but never more so than when he buried his wife Maria near Margery Fairfax and Margery's baby girl.

Yes, the land was divided. But what had being here cost us? What would it cost us still?

Brightly Shone the Moon That Night
December 29, 1620 ~ James Cittie,
and at Menmend on the Pamunkey's River

Good King Wenceslas looked out, on the Feast of Stephen,
When the snow lay round about, deep and crisp and even;
Brightly shone the moon that night, tho' the frost was cruel,
When a poor man came in sight, gath'ring winter fuel....

"Sire, the night is darker now, and the wind blows stronger;
Fails my heart, I know not how; I can go no longer."
"Mark my footsteps, my good page. Tread thou in them boldly.
Thou shalt find the winter's rage freeze thy blood less coldly."
—John Mason Neale

So wishinge you all and your people here in Virginia ye
happines of a newe Yeare, I rest
Yours verie ready to doe you service.
—Sir George Yeardley, January 10, 1620

Our glasses were raised in toast that December evening of 1620. Oh, the New Year would not officially ring in until March 25, but traditionally we all welcomed it during the Twelve Days of Christmas, today being the fifth day.

I glanced around the chamber at those closest to me: Tempie, but a ghost of her had been left when the Starving Time ended. Jane, too, had survived the Starving Time thin as a shadow.

John Rolfe held his glass in toast to Jane, his wife, and to the babe. Jane, sitting in a hand-hewn rocker in the corner raised her face and smiled. She was aglow with new motherhood as she rocked little Elizabeth, whom she called Bessie. At last Jane had a real baby named Bessie to love after so many years of hugging the little rag doll she had brought from England. The doll had patiently listened to Jane's fears of the Indians, her belly burning from lack of food. At six months, the little girl had John's eyes, Jane's mouth, and her own head of curly hair. Little Bessie had never seen her half brother, Pocahontas's son Thomas, but John hoped this would happen soon.

Reverend Bucke and his family had moved, which began when William Fairfax, Margery's husband, declared he could no longer live in the home where first his children and now his wife and baby daughter had died. Reverend Bucke said he could not stay in his home, either. This way too, the reverend reckoned he'd be closer to his land. So Master Fairfax moved further out, and the Reverend Bucke bought Fairfax's house.

We ached for Maria although her son Peleg was thriving, as Tempie nursed him along with her own son. Maria would have been so pleased. And Peleg's name would always remind us of the time when the earth became divided, when Virginia was hewn into parcels of field and wood with our names on them.

John and Jane had received land at Paspahegh and Mulberry Island with Will. John also had land across the water, a wedding gift from Powhatan which the Company had ratified.

John, his glass still lifted, said, "Alexander Pope said it best, did he not? *Hope springs eternal in the human breast. Man never is, but always to be blest!*"

We all joined in the toast to Jane and to Bessie, for long lives and prosperity. *May the worst be behind us,* I thought, my eyes on the children who represented the future of Virginia.

Sam Jordan in turn held his glass up, offering a toast to his bride Cecily. Little Tempie had grasped Bessie's blanket and was pulling it downward, trying to glimpse her baby cousin. At four, Tempie was the living ashes of her father, Tom Bailey, Tom's footprint left behind him in the New World while he rested in the soil at Charles Hundred.

Yet as I looked at Little Tempie, something in the child's face reminded me of my long-ago lost husband, Tom Reynolds, too. *See, my husband-soldier, you are not truly gone.*

I wondered how fared Will and our Tommy. I told myself Tommy was healthy and happy in England, for I could not allow myself to believe anything else. *He will enjoy a true school and learn well,* I hoped.

Richard and Bettie Peirce were living out at the Neck o' Land, just off of James Town Island. They were not here tonight, but seemed to be well recovered from the flux. Mercy had come to their aid when they survived their terrible voyage.

I wondered how Cousins Tom, Alice, and young Elizabeth were doing this evening. There were many Elizabeths in the Peirce family, a tribute to a long-dead, great-great-grandmother, I supposed. *The spirit of the generations, moving through,* I thought with some satisfaction. At eleven, Elizabeth had just a few more years before she, too, would marry. *So young.* But we were adapting to the idea.

As for Annie Laydon, she was still living out in Charles Hundred. I rarely saw her these days, but occasionally word came to me that Annie was well. She had birthed her third daughter, Katherine, not long after we had left Bermuda Hundred. The whipping had caused Annie to lose her little son, but not her hope or her spirit. She was, and would always be, my Annie.

My friend Tempie had come alone. George, she said, was spending late nights with the rest of the council, examining witnesses and gathering evidence proving the malpractice of Sam Argall. This, she said, was happening on both sides of the ocean. "They cease at midnight, then George comes home weary with the weight of the colony's struggles," she had told me. Which weight, she feared, was taking its due toll.

George was but thirty-two years old, yet his time as governor had aged him to a remarkable degree. The settlers kept coming and coming. The crops, as ever, could not keep abreast of those who needed corn. George had tried to explain this issue to the Company, whose only thought was that the new settlers would help create commodities to sell. The Company could not understand the pressure and anger we felt here. How hard it was to keep corn stored when we continually had to feed it to many mouths who had not helped to grow it.

As for old Argall, his ship the *Treasurer* lay capsized and sunken in a creek off the James River. It seemed a fitting end since the ship had caused us so much misery. Argall himself had arrived in England amidst much controversy. Some called him a thief, a few said he was a hero. He was, however, no hero to us.

John Rolfe said, "I'd like to offer another toast as well. "My good sirs and ladies, to Sir Thomas Dale, lost in the Indies. Never to return to Virginia."

Sir Thomas Dale? Perished? The man had an immortal quality as if death might be afraid to come forward and lead him home. For a moment, I envisioned a skeletal figure, clad in a black hooded cloak, carrying a scythe. No, Sir Thomas Dale would fight the Grim Reaper. And Dale would, undoubtedly, win.

This was news I had not yet heard. We lifted our glasses in toast to the departed, if not with a full heart then at least with a full glass. Dale had turned the colony around, but had dealt many cruelties in the process. 'Twas hard to toast such a man. He gave land and took life. Annie's lost baby seemed, somehow, symbolic of those who had died needlessly under such a man's reign. Tempie rolled her eyes at me, and I knew she felt the same.

"Let's toast the 'never to return to Virginia' part," Tempie whispered wickedly to me.

Sam spoke. "What happened to Dale, John?"

"Well, as I understand it, Dale was Admiral of the largest and best appointed fleet that ever did depart England for India. Dale's fleet went to Engano Island seeking the fate of the last English ship there, arriving only to find a heap of English skulls. Dale took revenge and reboarded."

We could not imagine Dale *not* taking revenge.

He continued, "But Dale's men had brought on ship with them the flux. And that, my friends, is what at last took down the mighty Dale."

A collective sigh, perhaps of grief or disbelief, went through the room.

After the bottoms turned upward, Sam took a turn. He held his glass of sack highest, and in a loud voice announced, "Let us lift the mood this Christmas. I say, to the Virginia Adventurers. Were but Will here to drink it!" He was, no doubt, recalling the night in the Kings Arm Pub with John Dewbourne and Hugh Deale, Maggie's husband.

Maggie! Our dear friend, missing this night.

Cecily and Sam opened in a Christmas carol, and as we all sang, I felt my heart drop at the memory of the loss of Maggie. I could remember a time when my heart actually crumbled with her death during that winter of our starvation, 1610.

> *God rest ye merry, gentlemen*
> *Let nothing ye dismay,*
> *For Jesus Christ our Savior*
> *Was born on Christmas Day...*

I raised my voice only to hear it falter. Indeed, I felt the merriness seep from me.

Maggie should be here with us as well.

But the past was the past and no changing it. Maggie had left a legacy to Tempie and me, and we knew we would never forget her.

At times like these when we were all close, I wondered at the Hand that knew our goings out and our comings in. How had we survived? Truly, what hand plotted such a strategy?

> *To save us all from Satan's power*
> *When we were gone astray...*

Gone astray. I touched the old pilgrim's badge around my neck. Still there, still solid and heavy from its lead, still recognizable as a scallop shell. My great-grandfather had taken the pilgrimage to Compostela, and the badge had brought me here. Whether that meant I had gone astray or not remained for me to see. I had taken a pilgrimage of my own—a pilgrimage that was in no way done yet.

> *From God our heavenly Father*
> *A blessed angel came,*
> *And unto certain shepherds*
> *Brought tidings of the same...*

I always thought Grace Fleetwood was something of an angel, never knowing exactly why.

Maggie was our angel, too, of course. She was a real, flesh-and-blood angel, all too human when illness took its toll. A true angel now, fussing with St. Peter. I envisioned her grabbing another soul by the arm. *Listen, we got to get us an ally here. Someone who knows what's going on up top...*

A sad smile born of wry amusement and old grief left me not knowing whether to laugh or to cry. When tears glistened in my eyes, I thought I understood which it would be.

Love never dies, Maggie. I will always love you. I will always remember you, my whole life. Howe'er long it be. I dropped my head.

At that moment, one voice rose above the others, sweet and clear. Like a nightingale.

I looked up, startled. I saw Tempie, too, react. No one else seemed to notice anything, as they poured out their hearts by moonlight and candlelight. But there it was. The voice I knew so well.

> *'Fear not,' then said the angel,*
> *'Let nothing you affright,*
> *This day is born a Savior*
> *Of virtue, power, and might;*
> *So frequently to vanquish all*
> *The friends of Satan quite.'*
> *O tidings of comfort and joy,*
> *For Jesus Christ our Savior was born on Christmas day.*

It couldn't be! I glanced at Tempie. She had stopped singing, a confused look crossing her face. She looked around as though expecting to see a...*ghost.* Goose prickles raised on my arms.

Not a ghost, but...an angel. Just as the carol says.

Maggie? Tempie and I stared wordlessly at one another. It was so, then. Maggie was never truly gone from us.

Tempie reached around, giving me a hug, and whispered in my ear. "You hear her, too! I know you do."

I would have spoken if the lump in my throat had allowed me. Instead, I just nodded, letting my cheek bounce up and down against her ear, now wet from my tears.

> *And left their flocks a-feeding*
> *In tempest, storm, and wind…*

The hurricane!

I remembered the night of Maggie's death, how I had said I wished I could hear her voice again. Tempie had reassured me with, "One day we will." She had meant heaven, of course, but could it be…

> *O tidings of comfort and joy,*
> *Comfort and joy.*

Comfort, yes. And as the word *joy* drifted off into the night and away, my heart leapt. I knew then as never before that true friends never leave us. They are with us always, even unto death.

As the silver moonlight sifted through the windows, the firelight and candles took on a brighter, warmer glow.

The group completed its carol, but oh, how I wanted it to continue, for another verse, another song, an entire day. Let me hear that blessed voice lingering across James Town once more.

Suddenly Jane asked, "Do you remember, mother, how Maggie used to sing to us that cold, hungry winter?"

Her question caused me to wonder: had she felt Maggie's presence, too?

My tone was cautious. "Oh, it's been so many years, and you were so little. I'm surprised you remember. What brings this to your mind?" I was curious about such things and did not let on why I was asking.

Jane shrugged. "I don't know. Perhaps singing *always* makes me think of Maggie, how she brought us joy in such a bleak time. It's one of my few good memories of that first winter." Then, quickly, as though she feared she may have hurt our feelings, she added, "Not that you and Auntie didn't do your best to bring cheer to the house."

Tempie smiled playfully, holding up her hand in protest. "No, no. You have just assured me that all those evenings spent rolling acorns across the floor with you were for naught."

Jane smiled, too, and hugged Tempie. "I can assure you, they were not for naught, Auntie."

I put my arms around them both. How blessed we were.

But as though needing a parting word with Maggie, I found myself thinking, *Come again soon, sweet friend. And one day, Maggie, you and I and Tempie shall meet again, not in a humble cottage, but in the mansions God has prepared for us. And where I know you already are.* An image flashed into my mind of Maggie, her hands wet and brown from the acorns she was grinding, a piece of hair straggling into her eyes, a wide smile upon her smudged face. How I missed her. *I will see you then. And you shall sing your nightingale song, and I shall sing my sparrow's song.*

I could almost hear Maggie's response, the same she had given me many years before on ship. *And God shall love the both of us for lifting our voices, whate'er our gift may be.*

Tempie took my hand and squeezed it. She seemed to know my thoughts as always. I saw that her eyes sparkled with tears in the rosy glow of the candles, which made me realize that even sadness can bring a light to one's eyes.

"Fear not, then," said the angel…. But surely, we had endured the worst Virginia had to offer. "Fear not." Suppose Maggie were giving a warning? Oh, surely not. I shook off the thought, physically shaking my head and squeezing my eyes shut.

But the thought persisted. *A warning?*

* * *

A full moon rose, casting silver across the plantations, over the river, and onto the fields east and west, and far beyond to the *yi-hakans* of the Indian towns. Within those *yi-hakans* sat native families, discussing in hushed tones the troublesome English.

White moonlight covered the rounded roof of one great longhouse in Menmend, the seat of the great chief Opechancanough. Inside this longhouse, a gathering of lesser chiefs representing a thousand bowmen mumbled about the loss of their lands. About stolen fields, hunting grounds and town sites where the English had made their own towns with wooden palisades to keep *them* out. What, they respectfully wondered, did their *werowance* Opechancanough plan to do about it?

In response, Opechancanough stood and raised his voice, shouting a war cry to his chiefs. A promise, a threat. Firelight glinted from his deep brown eyes, and those eyes shone with the anger of fourteen winters of warfare and uneasy peace.

You will tell your bowmen this.

"*Tsantassas, numma husque?*" *Strangers, white men, will you go home?* Opechancanough made an *away* motion with his hands, crying, "*Uppoushun!*"

He pointed as though across the great wide water. *The ships go home!*

The chiefs cheered agreement, as Opechancanough grabbed a knife and slashed at his own his wrist. He raised both arms upward triumphantly, one still grasping the knife as the other dripped blood downward.

"*Vnekishemū tassantassas! Poshenaan, numpenamun Tassantassas nehpaangunnū!*" *Or we will cut the white men! They shall flee or we will see their blood!*

He paused and looked around the circle of his chiefs, a woman on either side of him. His eyes narrowed. "*Nepunche Tassantassas.*"

The white men shall be dead.

A wolf's cry—distant, lonely—seemed to punctuate and give life to his words.

And somewhere near our homes at James Cittie, the single haunting howl of a wolf echoed across the moonlit water. Soon a chorus of wolves joined the lone crier. We paused in our Christmas toast to listen—causing me to shiver and reminding us once again that Virginia, still, was a very wild place.

* * *

Author's Note:
What's Fact, What's Fiction?

In this book, as in the first book, *Dark Enough to See the Stars in a Jamestown Sky*, historical and genealogical accuracy was my primary aim. I tried to understand the adventurers as *people* first by tracing their family trees and migration patterns. The records are scant, but by mixing, matching, and cross-referencing, I drew certain conclusions in a "connect-the-dots" kind of way. Using old records, letters, and genealogies, I attempted to learn as much as possible about the background, tastes, and personalities of those who actually lived.

I have not played fast and loose with the facts. These people were real and, despite their flaws, they remain the earliest heroes and heroines of our country. The more I read, the more astounded I became by the raw courage of these men, women, and children. I was careful, therefore, not to malign any real people or create aberrant story lines except where the records indicated such events might likely have happened. It would be unfair and, worse, disrespectful to create wild story lines unless there were some basis in fact. In my opinion, deviating too far from known facts is unfair to those no longer alive to defend themselves.

In matters of religious convictions, I incorporated the predominant beliefs of those who settled Virginia—that is, Anglican. Virginia was officially under the Church of England although there were some who leaned toward other Protestant theologies such as Calvinism (John Rolfe, for example). A few held beliefs that were more Puritan. In fact, the Reverend Meese was known to be "too Puritan" for the tastes of most colonists in Virginia during his tenure of the Starving Time. However, church was important to the Virginia colonists. The charters as well as the *Lawes Divine Morall and Martiall* mandated church attendance fourteen times weekly at an Anglican service. The charters and the king strictly forbid Catholicism in Virginia.

I tried to let the facts speak for themselves, making what I considered reasonable assumptions where facts were missing.

Real History, Real Politics, Real Timelines

The political leaders—both English and native—their personalities, biographies, and actions are based on fact. The history, timeline, and events are also factual, as are the genealogies inasmuch as we knew them. The Spanish scare, the kidnapping of Pocahontas, Argall's piracy, and the backdrop of events all happened. All of the governors, treasurers, and captains were real, and the actions I wrote about, for the most part, I based on eyewitness accounts.

The Native American words used in this book are also authentic—at least, as authentic as they can be considering they come to us from Englishmen of the time who copied down the sounds they heard. The Powhatans had no written language, so sadly and ironically, most of what we know of the language is filtered through the English. William Strachey and John Smith kept vocabulary lists that are our best resources today. Thomas Savage and Henry Spelman were fluent speakers, but if they penned such documents, they have not surfaced.

Other Real People: The Cast of Characters

Real people include Joan, Will, and Jane Peirce; Cecily Bailey and her husband (first name unknown); the Yeardleys; Samuel Jordan; John (Jack) and Anne Laydon and their children; Reverend and Maria Bucke and their children (Mara, Benomi, Gershom, and Peleg); and William and Margery Fairfax. While the Fairfax children's names are unknown and therefore created, I did find the name of Margery's father, Giles Browne. Therefore, I chose the name Giles for her son. Mistress Flowerdieu did remarry Captain Garrett. Marie Flowerdieu Rossingham was indeed Temperance Yeardley's sister, and Marie's son Edmund did come to Virginia in 1619 to act as a factor for George Yeardley. Susanna Lothrop, Reverend Whitaker's sister, did come to settle his estate, departing on the *George* in 1618.

Who Was Fictitious?

Maggie Deale, Walter Bowles (the soldier), Master Harrison (sailor), John Dewbourne and Hugh Deale (friends of Will and Sam) and Dobbs the blacksmith were fictitious although they represent the many unnamed mariners and planters whose stories we will never know. Some, like Walter, may have survived the Starving Time, but unless they lived fifteen years more until the 1625 muster or are mentioned in other records, their names are lost. Their contributions remain significant, however, and unfortunately we will probably never know the names of most.

When choosing surnames for the fictitious characters, I often draw from signatures on the Third Charter or from other documented early Virginia settlers.

Jamestown Personalities

ARGALL, Sir Samuel (1580–1626) — History is mixed in its assessment of Argall. He pioneered the more direct route to Virginia and also well understood its fishing grounds. His kidnapping of Pocahontas, by enlisting her aunt and uncle to trade her for a large copper kettle, seems harsh. Yet Pocahontas's rejection by her father Powhatan, her embracing of the colonists' ways, and her marriage to tobacco pioneer John Rolfe led to the long-term success of the colony. None of this would have happened without Argall. During his governorship, his handling of Company property and his piracy exploits using the *Treasurer* in 1619 were also controversial.

DALE, Sir Thomas (1561-1620) — Apparently of lowborn status, Dale yet rose to heights in military circles prior to Jamestown that in those days (where privilege was everything) shows he must have had remarkable military ability. His strict, even harsh, enforcement of the *Lawes Divine Morall and Martiall* was a positive turning point for the colony.

GATES, Sir Thomas (1561–1621) — Gates traveled with Sir Francis Drake when Drake attacked Spanish settlements in the Caribbean, and he was also present at the rescue of the first Roanoke Island settlers in 1586. A veteran of the wars with the Spanish and in the Lowlands, Gates was a strong leader and a good organizer. He was the first signer of the 1606 charter. His take-charge manner on Bermuda and at Jamestown demonstrates a phenomenal leader, particularly when coupled with compassion unusual for a seventeenth century military man. Gates planned to return to Virginia, but seemed to change his mind when his friend Sir Thomas Smythe was ousted as Virginia Company treasurer.

MARTIN, John (d.c. 1632) — Martin was a commander under Sir Francis Drake and one of the seven original councilors in April 1607. He returned to England and then sailed back to Virginia in August 1609, finding himself at odds with Capt. John Smith. In 1616, Martin received one of the first permanent land grants, a vast tract of 4,500 acres on the south side of the James River. Here he founded Martin's Brandon Plantation, which held a special, controversial charter putting it outside of the Virginia Company's authority. Martin died in Virginia around 1632.

NEWPORT, Christopher (1565?–1617) — Newport's reputation as an expert mariner and privateer flowered when he brought in the *Madre de Dios,* the largest-ever Spanish prize in 1592. With one arm lost to battle, Newport yet led the preliminary expedition to Jamestown in 1607. He also commanded the first three supply expeditions during 1608 and 1609. Newport was among those shipwrecked in Bermuda from 1609 to 1610 as part of the Third Supply. In 1611, he made his final voyage to Virginia when he commanded Sir Thomas Dale's three ships. The Virginia Company granted his widow lands, and his three sons subsequently lived in Virginia.

PERCY, George (1580–1632) — George Percy was the eighth and youngest son of the Eighth Earl of Northumberland. He came to Virginia with the first colonizing expedition in 1607 and stayed until 1612. He served as president of the colony during the Starving Time and once again for a few months when Lord De La Warr had to leave due to illness in 1611.

PORY, John (1572-1636) — A highly educated world traveler, author, and protégé of geographer Richard Hakluyt, John Pory was an influential writer of his time. Despite a reputation as a tippler, Pory accomplished much. He associated with many important figures, including John Donne and John Milton, and Shakespeare may have drawn from Pory's translation of Leo Africanus for Othello. John Pory and Temperance Yeardley were first cousins (she was his "cousin-german," as Pory put it), and Pory came to Virginia as George Yeardley's secretary. Yet Pory maintained a secret association with Sir Robert Rich, who was working against Yeardley. Pory kept meticulous records of Virginia's first General Assembly and traveled to New England as well. Always with an affinity for sharing news, Pory returned to England in the early 1620's and began the first newspaper.

RICH, Sir Robert (1587–1658) — Sir Robert Rich, the Second Earl of Warwick, was the most powerful English Puritan of his time and a member of the House of Lords. Rich viewed piracy, then illegal, as a legitimate way to cripple the Catholic Spanish fleets. Rich supported colonization, but seemingly more as means of attacking Spanish ships from Virginia and Bermuda. Both the East India and Virginia Companies struggled with diplomatic issues Rich had caused them. The colonists in Virginia and Bermuda didn't appreciate Rich's antagonism of the Spanish, fearing he would bring Spanish attack upon them. Disenchanted with Virginia, Rich then turned his attentions to New England. He helped procure the 1628 patent for the Massachusetts Bay Colony, becoming its second president. In 1635, he founded the settlement of Saybrook in Connecticut. Rich commanded the parliament's navy during the Civil War, fighting against King Charles, but ultimately opposing Charles's execution.

ROLFE, John (1585–1622) — John Rolfe was on the ill-fated *Sea Venture*, which shipwrecked on Bermuda. His first child was born and died on the island, and his first wife Sarah died sometime after their 1610 arrival at Jamestown. A pious, industrious man, Rolfe's innovations in bringing Caribbean tobacco to Virginia to replace the bitter tobacco of the Powhatan peoples turned the Virginia economy around and gave it its first mass-marketable commodity. His love for and marriage to the Indian princess Pocahontas—a wrenching decision based on his Calvinist beliefs about marriage to "heathens"—demonstrates a man who nonetheless acted on his conscience. By uniting the colonists and the natives, the Rolfes' marriage brought "the Peace of Pocahontas" to the settlement until her death in 1617. Rolfe later married "Janey," Jane Peirce, the young daughter of Joan and William Peirce. Jane bore him a daughter, Elizabeth, in 1620. Rolfe died soon after the 1622 massacre.

SANDYS, Sir Edwin (1561–1629) — "Choose the devil if you will, but not Sir Edwin Sandys!" With these words, King James decried the election of Sandys to a second term as Virginia Company treasurer. Sir Edwin Sandys believed in colonization, religious tolerance, and, according to Captain Bargrave, possessed a malicious heart toward monarchy. Sandys's political nonconformity in parliament put him at odds with his king, who also had authority over the Virginia Company. In April 1619, Sandys won election as treasurer amidst much bickering since the Company had splintered three ways. Sandys's new policies initially revitalized the colony. Hoping to diversify commodities and lessen dependence on tobacco, Sandys sent thousands of colonists to Virginia. This resulted in overcrowding and shortages of food and housing. However, Sandys's intentions were sincere, his belief in Virginia's potential genuine.

SMYTHE, Sir Thomas (1558–1625) — An English entrepreneur, Smythe held the Virginia Company's highest office from 1606 until 1619 and was pivotal in deciding to continue the Virginia Company despite its lack of profits. Smythe financed many trade ventures besides the Virginia Company including the East India Company, the Levant Company (for trade with Turkey), and the Muscovy Company (for trade with Russia). He held other prestigious positions including commissioner to the Royal Navy and special ambassador to the tsar of Russia. In his will, Smythe founded the "The Sir Thomas Smythe's Charity," still in existence, which provides financial and pastoral support to needy persons, usually disabled or elderly, of West Kent.

SOMERS, Admiral Sir George (1554–1610) — Somers became a knight in 1603 and a founder of the London Company. A naval hero and admiral of the Third Supply expedition, he was known as a "lamb on land and a lion at sea." His bravery during the hurricane shows the lion emerging. He claimed Bermuda for England and died there from "a surfeit of pork" in the fall of 1610. He was attempting to bring hogs back to Virginia to aid the colony's food supply. His nephew buried Somers's heart in Bermuda but returned his pickled body to England.

WEST, Thomas, Lord De La Warr (1577–1618) — A strong leader, member of nobility, and pious man, De La Warr suffered health issues which prevented him from accomplishing all he would have liked in Virginia. Still, his firm hand following the Starving Time and strict enforcement of the code of martial law enacted by Gates initiated the turnaround in Jamestown's fortunes. He died on his second voyage to Virginia, which had longstanding implications in that he was not able to shut down Argall's piracy scheme promptly. De La Warr's reputation, name, and financial contributions were a key factor in Virginia keeping its foothold in the New World.

YEARDLEY, Sir George (c. 1577–1627) — As Gates's right-hand man in battle at the Lowlands, Yeardley learned with the best. He was Captain of the governor's guard and later deputy governor during 1616 to 1617. Yeardley was governor again—this time as governor and captain general—during 1619 when adventurers patented their first land and the Virginia General Assembly met for the first time. His actions show him an ardent supporter of self-government and free enterprise. He became the wealthiest man in Virginia in his time, building the first windmill in the colony at Flowerdew Hundred. The Knight's Tomb at Jamestown Church is likely to be his grave.

Tradesmen to Virginia in 1611

The Council of Virginia listed the artisans and craftsmen they sought in a letter to the Earl of Sandwich, 20 February 1611:

The Trades-men to be sent into Virginia under the Comaunde of Sir Thomas Gates

Phisisions	Husbandmen. 30
Appothecaries	Iron Finers. 2
Chirurgions	Gardiners. 10
Millwrights for Iron Mills. . . . 2	Iron Founders. 2
Fishermen. 20	Saylers. 20
Iron Miners. 4	Hamermen, for Iron. 2

Watermen.........10
Edge tole makers for Iron Work...2
Sparemakers...........2
Colliers for charcoale.......2
Laborers............10
Woodcutters.......2
Brickmakers.........4
Shipwrights.......2
Bricklayers...........6
Ship Carpenters.......20
Lymeburners.......2
Calkers.......10
Sawiers.......15
Edge tole makers.......2
Smithes.......4
Coopers.......6
Masons...........2
Baskett Makers.......2
Bakers...........2
Cutlers.......2
Brewers.......2
Armorers.......2
Swine herdes.......2
Tanners.........2
Spinners of Pack threade...2
Last-makers....... 2
Cordage makers.......2
Shoemakers.......2
Bellowes Makers.......2
Taylors.......2

Millers.......2
Clapboardmen.......10
Mat makers.......2
Potters of Earth.......4
Gunpowder makers.......2
Net makers.......6
Saltpeter men.......2
House Carpenters.......10
Salt makers.......2
Uphoulsters of feathers
Braziers in Mettle men.......2
Hempe planters
Distillers of Aqua Vite.......2
Hempe dressers
Sadlers..........1
Turners
Collier-makers.......2
Millwrights for Water mills
Furriers.......2
Fowlers
Stockmakers for peeces.....2
Pike makers.......2
Wheele and Plowrightes....6
Leather dressers
Gun makers.......2
Minerell men
Tyle-makers.......2

Source: Alexander Brown's
The Genesis of the United States, 1890.

Did the Indians Really Use Magic Against the Settlers?

Yes. Reverend Alexander Whitaker and Captain George Percy each reported two incidents, both occurring in 1611.

To the early colonists, witchcraft was a very real and powerful phenomenon. In one letter, Alexander Whitaker compared the native priests to being "like our English witches."

Rain Dance Ritual

One incident Percy and Whitaker each described was a dance the Nansemond Indians performed. The purpose of the dance, the English soldiers learned, was to cause rain to fall within about five miles to extinguish the men's matches and to wet and spoil their powder.

Rain did indeed fall although not enough to accomplish the natives' purpose. Percy notes that neither "the dievell whome they adore nor all their Sorceries" could stop the English from cutting down the Nansemond corn, burning their houses, and bringing prisoners back to the fort. Yet the English were impressed and amazed that rain did fall immediately following the dance.

Hallucinations

Both George Percy and Reverend Alexander Whitaker described hallucinations amongst the English in 1611 with Whitaker indicating the Indians had promised such beforehand.

About a week before Sir Thomas Dale's departure for the falls of the river, a messenger from Powhatan arrived bearing a strange message. Powhatan forbade Dale from going upriver and demanded two Indian prisoners. Should Dale not meet these demands, Powhatan "threatened to destroy us after a strange manner," according to Whitaker. The messenger promised that in six or seven days Powhatan would cause the English to be unable to speak and then kill them. Dale was "very merry" about this message, obviously finding the threat amusing.

Percy says that once upriver, "one thinge amongst the reste was very remarkable." While at prayers in this Indian house, "a fantasy possesed" the soldiers. I think we are to infer from this that Sir Thomas Dale, being in the house, must also have been seized with the hallucination.

Whitaker says, "a strainge noise was heard comeing out of the Corne towards the trenches of our men, like an Indian *hup hup!* and *Oho Oho!*, some say that they saw one like an Indian leape over the fire and runne into the corne with the same noyse." The men could speak nothing but "Oho, oho"—speechless, just as Powhatan had promised.

Believing that their fellow Englishmen were all Indians, the soldiers took "the wronge endes of their armes" (Whitaker) and "did fall pell mell one upon an other beating one an other Downe and breaking one of an others heades." (Percy). Percy says the fantasy ended before the soldiers could inflict serious harm. It does sound as if the men could have killed one another, hearkening back to Powhatan's promise to kill them.

Mysterious Escapes

Whitaker tells us that many mysterious things happened when dealing with the natives. For example, Indians "being bound with stronge lyne and kept with great watch have escaped from us," without the English knowing or being able to prevent it. "All which things make me thinke that theire bee great witches amonge them and they are verry familliar with the Devill."

Was Anne Laydon Really Whipped?

Anne Laydon did receive a whipping that caused her to miscarry. We don't know exactly when the whipping occurred except "in the time of Sir Thomas Dale's government." This would be between the years 1611 and 1616 when Anne would have been between about seventeen and twenty-two years old. The court testimony is the only surviving mention of this incident.

A Court held ye xxiii th of May 1625

….And further [Mrs. *Perry*] sayeth that in the time of Sir *Thomas Dale's* Government *Ann Leydon* and *Jane Wright* and other women were appoynted to make shirtes for the Colony servants and had six nelde [needle] full of threed allowed for making of a shirte, which if they did not performe, They had noe allowance of Dyett, and because theire threed [was] naught and would not serve, they tooke owt a ravell of the lower parte of the shirte to make an end of the worke, and others that had threed of theire owne made it upp with that, Soe the shirts of those which had raveled owt parte proved shorter then the rest, for which fact the said *Ann Leydon* and *Jane Wright* were whipt, And *Ann Leydon* beinge then with childe (the same night therof miscarried).
– *Minutes of the Council and General Court,* H.R. McIlwaine, Ed., 1979, p. 62.

Did Anne lose a boy or a girl?

No one living today knows, but we do know that the Laydons had four surviving girls listed in the January 1625 census. The children's ages are not in the muster, but we can determine three of the girls' birth years from other sources.

Virginia Laydon. . . . . . . born December 1609
Alice Laydon. . . . . . . born between 1610 and 1617

Katherin Laydon. . . . . . born circa 1617
Margerett Laydon. . . . . . . born circa 1624

We cannot know exactly when Anne's whipping took place or whether Alice would have been older or younger than the child Anne lost due to the whipping.

What Happened to Henricus and Bermuda Hundred?

Henricus

After its early importance as a place of safety, Henricus quickly fell into disrepair when Bermuda Hundred became Virginia's leading settlement in late 1613.

In the mid-1620's, Henricus became known as Farrar's Island. Attorney William Farrar with his bride Cecily Bailey Jordan received the island as a land grant. (Cecily is the same young girl in this story.)

The original settlement was on the north side of the James River, which in 1634 became the Parish of Henrico. However, Dutch Gap Canal changed the landscape and river flow, clipping off the piece of land so that Henricus is now in Chesterfield County on the south side of the river.

Henricus is the place where Alexander Whitaker taught Pocahontas Christianity in his church. Whitaker's little church of 1611 became the first church in Henrico Parish, which survived and thrived. One notable early church in the parish is St. John's Church in Richmond where Patrick Henry gave his famous Liberty or Death speech prior to the revolution.

Today, Chesterfield County, Virginia, commemorates Henricus in its Henricus Historical Park, located near the old settlement off Route 10 in Chester. (For more information, see www.Henricus.org.)

Bermuda Hundred

Bermuda Hundred, with its promise of freedom after three years' labor, gave the colonists of 1613 more hope than perhaps any event before it. Sir Thomas Dale had first forced the native Appomattocks off the land and then offered any settler who joined a share in Bermuda Hundred Corporation and absolute freedom by 1617. Bermuda Hundred became the first incorporated town in what would one day be the United States.

Most settlers did sign on, and Bermuda Hundred became the leading settlement in the spring of 1614. Even when Governor Samuel Argall moved the government back to Jamestown (then called James City) in 1617, most of Bermuda Hundred's landholders continued on there. The 1619 instructions to the Berkeley Hundred settlers mentioned the "Bermuday granary."

In honor of the prince, the Company changed the name to Charles Hundred, and this settlement encompassed both sides of the James River. However, over time the name Bermuda Hundred endured, although the name Charles remained in Charles Hundred, north of the river, which became Charles City County.

By 1691, Bermuda Hundred had become an important port in Virginia.

During the Revolution, Benedict Arnold looted goods from Richmond and dropped them at Bermuda Hundred. In 1780, Bermuda Hundred lost to Richmond as the new capital of Virginia.

As the eighteenth century wore on, smaller farms grew to larger plantations, and the face of Bermuda Hundred changed. The wife of one of these plantation owners was Mary Randolph.

In 1824, Mrs. Randolph published *The Virginia Housewife,* the first cookbook to exclusively feature American dishes. Included are recipes such as "Hare or Rabbit Soup," "Gumbo—a West India dish," "Fried calf's feet," and "Oyster catsup." This cookbook is a classic that includes, for example, the earliest published American recipe for fried chicken. *The Virginia Housewife,* reprinted at least nineteen times by the Civil War, is still in print.

In 1820, a freed slave named Archibald Batte moved to prominence in Bermuda Hundred. Batte, who became a slave owner himself, prospered as Bermuda Hundred postmaster and storekeeper.

A site once strategic may always be strategic. Many of Virginia's early fort sites played important roles in the Civil War in Virginia. Such was the case when Major General Benjamin Butler, aiming to take Richmond, made his headquarters at Bermuda Hundred in 1864.

The Civil War effectively ended plantations. A new railroad and steamship wharf gave Bermuda Hundred one last breath until these, too, lost their importance. Bermuda Hundred became a sleepy little sixteen-acre village of a dozen homes and outbuildings, an early twentieth century schoolhouse, a cemetery, and a church.

Bermuda Hundred is in the National Register of Historic Places.

To visit Bermuda Hundred today, travel from Route 10 in Chester down Bermuda Hundred Road past the Honeywell Plant. The village sits there on the water as old Bermuda Hundred always has. There's little to mark the past except for a monument placed by the Daughters of the American Revolution:

BERMUDA HUNDRED
ESTABLISHED 1613
BY SIR THOMAS DALE.
FIRST INCORPORATED VIRGINIA TOWN 1614
HOME OF JOHN ROLFE,
COLONY RECORDER WHO MARRIED POCAHONTAS.
REV. ALEXANDER WHITAKER
MINISTERED HERE.
EARLY PORT OF RICHMOND
ERECTED 1938
BY
BERMUDA HUNDRED CHAPTER D.A.R.

Dutch Gap, 1611
Sir Thomas Dale Creates the First Canal in the U.S.

Where and when did the name Dutch Gap originate?

Some old stories say the name originated because Dutch laborers dug the gap. Others say that Union General Benjamin Butler's nickname was "Dutch," and so, since the canal was Butler's idea, the canal carried his name. After the Civil War, a Yankee touring the southern battlefields speculated on where Dutch Gap got its name. In 1866, John Townsend Trowbridge told these stories of the name's origin:

> It is said that a Dutch company was once formed for digging a ship-canal at that place. But a better story is told of a Dutchman who made a bet with a Virginian, that he could beat him in a skiff-race between Richmond and City Point. The Virginian was ahead when they reached the Gap; what then was his astonishment, on arriving at City Point, to find the Dutchman there before him. The latter had saved the roundabout seven miles by dragging his canoe across the peninsula and launching it on the other side.

The Real Origin of "Dutch Gap"

I hate to disappoint Mr. Trowbridge, but the origin of "Dutch Gap" is far more sophisticated than a misguided Virginian's attempt to race a Dutchman. Instead, the name hearkens back to the military prowess of Virginia's earliest leaders.

In 1611, Sir Thomas Dale, using military strategy he had learned in the Netherlands, ordered his men to dig a canal across the peninsula then called Henricus (later Farrar's Island). The gap converted the peninsula to an island providing his new settlement the safety of water on all sides.

In 1614, Ralph Hamor, wrote:

> *[Henricus] stands upon a neck of very high land, 3 parts thereof environed with the main River, and cut over between the two Rivers, with a strong pale, which maketh the neck of land an island.*

The colonists called the cut-through "Dutch Gap," "Dale's Ditch," or "Dale's Dutch Ditch." (The early settlers, who came of age during the Elizabethan era, loved using alliteration and sometimes puns in their naming.)

Today, the National Oceanic and Atmospheric Association (NOAA) says, "Dutch Gap, the first canal dug in the United States, was cut through in 1611."

The Digging of "Dutch Gap Canal"

The Union army called their project "Dutch Gap Canal," not recognizing that the "gap" in its name already signified a canal or cut through.

In August 1864, General Benjamin F. Butler decided that a canal could best cut off the seven additional miles snaking around Farrar's Island. (I believe it may have surprised him to know that a Virginian had accomplished this 250 years before, but on with the story.)

This area could *not* have been named for General Butler. First, I can find no evidence that Butler's nickname was "Dutch." Secondly, General Butler wrote to his wife Sarah about Dutch Gap being on a map, proving Dutch Gap was already on the maps at that time and not named for General Butler himself.

> *I also moved out from Dutch Gap, you will see it on the map, and carried some of the enemy's works.*
> – General Benjamin Butler to his wife Sarah, August 17, 1864

After the Civil War, in 1873, Dutch Gap was completed.

In the late 19th century, engineers also cut channels through Hatcher Neck, Jones Neck (formerly Rochdale Hundred) and Presquile (off Turkey Island). Today, all four of these oxbows of the James River still meander from Richmond, but the cutoffs allow a direct course to the sea as well.

Where Did Argall find Bison?

In 1613, Captain Samuel Argall reported discovering "Cattle as big as Kine [oxen]." This is the first known English sighting of bison, but where did it happen?

Argall had sailed from Point Comfort upriver to the headwaters of the Pembroke River. The Pembroke is now the Rappahannock, and its headwaters are at today's Chester Gap, Virginia, in the Blue Ridge Mountains. (Chester Gap is in Rappahannock County and is about six and a half miles from Front Royal.) Argall said that he marched "into the Countrie," so the bison were near or at Chester Gap, depending on how far he marched.

Since the Rappahannock is only navigable by ship as far as Fredericksburg, Virginia, Argall apparently used a shallop to make the rest of the voyage.

Fredericksburg is 62 miles from the Chesapeake Bay. To reach Chester Gap, Argall would have sailed another 122 miles upriver, a total of 184 miles. To verify that Argall did indeed mean he reached the Chester Gap area, we can note that he said he traveled 65 leagues, which is equal to 195 miles—very close to 184 miles.

> The 19. of March: and returned myselfe with the ship into Pembrook [today's Rappahannock] River, and so discovered to the head of it, which is about 65. leagues into the land, and navigable for any ship. And then marching into the Countrie, I found great store of Cattle [bison] as big as Kine, of which, the Indians that were my guides, killed a couple which wee found to be very good and wholesome meate, and are very easie to be killed in regard they are heavy, slow, and not so wild as other beasts of the wildernesse.
> –Captain Samuel Argall, writing to Master Nicholas Hawes, June 1613

Pocahontas's Story

Calculating Pocahontas's Age

The Disney movie *Pocahontas* has gone a long way towards promoting Pocahontas as a young adult when John Smith arrived in 1607, but she was indisputably a child.

The Simon Van de Passe portrait, created in January or February 1617, is the only known portrait made of Pocahontas in her lifetime. This portrait states that Pocahontas was "in the 21st year of her age" (meaning she had passed her twentieth birthday). This would give her a birth date of 1596. Therefore, she would have been about eleven years old when the settlers landed in 1607.

In 1612, Pocahontas was about sixteen years old. At that time, William Strachey wrote that Pocahontas had married a "private captaine called Kocoum some two yeares since." Therefore, she was old enough to be married by about 1610 when she would have been about fourteen.

Were Pocahontas and Anne Laydon Really Friends?

I created the friendship between Pocahontas and Anne Laydon, but their brief early friendship is certainly possible.

Anne Laydon arrived in October 1608 as a maid with Mistress Forrest. These were the only two Englishwomen to arrive until that time. In August 1609, the next group of about ninety women would land as part of the Third Supply.

Mistress Forrest doesn't appear in the records any more, so it's impossible to know when she died. However, the woman's skeleton (labeled JR156) found during excavations at Jamestown *may* be Mistress Forrest.

Pocahontas continued to visit the fort until February 1609 when Powhatan moved his chief residence much further away to Orapax. For a period of time—early October 1608 to February 1609—Pocahontas and Anne could have been at the fort at the same time. If Mistress Forrest had died upon arrival, Anne and Pocahontas would have been the only girls in the fort.

Pocahontas, was 1596, would have been about twelve during this time while Anne, born circa 1594, was about fourteen. It's possible, maybe even likely, that Anne Laydon's curiosity about the native princess would have brought her out to see Pocahontas. Pocahontas was friendly with young settlers, even cartwheeling with the boys.

Anne survived long-term through some incredible circumstances. I like to think that Pocahontas may have taught her some things about Virginia that helped her.

Pocahontas's Last Words?

Occasionally in books or articles, writers say that Pocahontas's last words were "All must die. 'Tis enough that the child liveth." However, no one knows Pocahontas's last words. If anyone wrote them down, that document is not extant.

The misconception of her dying words came about from a document John Rolfe wrote following his wife's death.

> *The Indyans very loving, and willing to parte with their childeren. My wives death is much lamented; my childe much desyred, when it is of better strength to endure so hard a passage, whose life much greatly extinguisheth the sorrow of her loss, saying all must die, but tis enough that her childe liveth.*
> —John Rolfe, June 1617

In June 1617, Rolfe wrote to Sir Edwin Sandys that he expected to be able to carry on the missionary work he and Pocahontas had planned to do, adding that the Indians were "willing to parte with their children."

Rolfe continued that the natives lamented Pocahontas's death and desired to see young Thomas Rolfe when he was strong enough to travel back to Virginia. Thomas's survival, Rolfe says, helped assuage the natives' grief at the loss of Pocahontas. It was the Powhatans, not Pocahontas, who said, "All must die, but tis enough that her childe liveth."

Does Pocahontas Have Any Descendants?

John Rolfe left young Thomas behind in England in 1617. Thomas suffered from the same illness that his mother, Pocahontas, had just died from, and Rolfe feared the boy would not survive the voyage. It appears John never saw his son again, for John himself died just five years later.

By the time he was about nineteen in 1634, Thomas had come to Virginia. His stepmother's father, William Peirce, paid Thomas's passage. Thomas married in Virginia and had an only child, Jane Rolfe, born about 1655.

In 1675, Jane married Colonel Robert Bolling. (Many sources prove this.

See John Frederick Dorman, *Adventurers of Purse and Person, Fourth Edition,* 2007, p. 27.)

Jane Rolfe Bolling had one son, John Bolling. Therefore, Pocahontas and John Rolfe had one son, one granddaughter, and one great-grandson.

But the story doesn't end there.

John Bolling had six children—Jane, John, Elizabeth, Mary, Martha, and Anne Bolling. The 1994 edition of *Pocahontas and Her Descendants* (authors Brown, Myers, and Chappel) lists thirty thousand names.

After first wife Jane Rolfe died, Robert Bolling married Ann Stith. Thousands of others today descend through this line.

Descendants of Jane Rolfe Bolling call themselves "Red Bollings," while descendants of Ann Stith Bolling are "White Bollings." I am a White Bolling. Being descended from Colonel Robert's second wife, we White Bollings cannot claim descent from Pocahontas although we call all Red Bollings (Pocahontas descendants) our cousins.

Some in the United Kingdom believe they are Pocahontas descendents from a first marriage of Thomas Rolfe. A marriage record does exist for a Thomas Rolfe and Elizabeth Washington, dated 13 September 1632 at Saint James, Clerkenwell, London. However, if this Thomas were Pocahontas's son, he would have been only about seventeen years old—a very young age for male marriage in England at that time. (The average age men married was twenty-seven or twenty-eight.)

The story goes that Thomas married Elizabeth in London and had a daughter Anne. After Elizabeth's death, Thomas left Anne behind with a cousin and sailed for Virginia. Anne then married in England and left descendants.

The problem is that this Thomas Rolfe is not the same man as Pocahontas's son. William Thorndale disproves it definitively in "Two Rolfe Negatives," *The Virginia Genealogist*, Vol. 34, #3 (July-September 1990), p. 209-213.

Therefore, the only proven descendants of John Rolfe and Pocahontas are the Red Bollings.

However, both William Strachey and Mattaponi oral history say that Pocahontas was married about 1610 to Kocoum, a Powhatan warrior. Mattaponi oral tradition says that Pocahontas and Kocoum had a son prior to Pocahontas's kidnapping in 1613. If indeed Pocahontas and Kocoum had a son, then Pocahontas may also have descendants through her husband Kocoum.

Pocahontas's death record in the burial register at St. George's Church in Gravesend, Kent, reads:

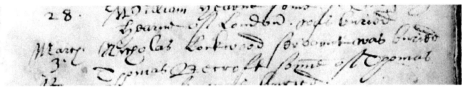

This image came from the parish register of *Gravesend St. George* with kind permission of the Medway Council in Kent, UK.

> *Rebecca Wroth, wyffe of Thomas Wroth, gent., a virginia Lady borne, was buried in ye Chauncell.*

The record is under the date of 21 March 1616, Old Style (meaning that today it would be 1617).

When was Temperance Bailey born?

I'm including this section for the many descendants of Temperance Bailey since in this book I introduce a different birth year for her than the one generally accepted.

In the early years of Virginia, girls typically married at fourteen and had their first children around fifteen. This was a world where young girls (along with widows) were the primary source of new wives. Most women who arrived on ship were already married.

The January 1625 muster gives Temperance Bailey's age as seven, and all sources I've encountered state that Temperance must, therefore, have been born in 1617.

Yet the muster is sometimes in error. Examples of incorrect data in the muster include the ages of Temperance Yeardley's children, arrival dates of some settlers as 1606 (the earliest settlers arrived in 1607), and incorrect arrival years for some ships.

The muster appears to be in error in Temperance Bailey's case. By 1632, young Temperance had married, been widowed, and then married second husband Richard Cocke. The proof of these events comes from a court record dated 5 June 1632 referring to Richard Cocke "having married the relicte [widow] of the sayd Brown." The court document also mentions "the children of the sayd Brown." The marriage of Temperance Bailey to Richard Cocke is proven, and a later John Brown (d. 1677) had a daughter Temperance. A birth year of 1617 would mean that Temperance would have married at around twelve and borne her children at around thirteen and fourteen in order to have remarried at fifteen. Even by Jamestown standards, this is young nearly to the point of being impossible.

My observation is that, during this time in Virginia, young girls married at fourteen and not sooner. This early age was already something very different from that to which the colonists were accustomed. In England at this time, the average age for a woman's first marriage was twenty-five or twenty-six—nearly twice the age that women married in Virginia. (See *Birth, Marriage & Death: Ritual, Religion, and the Life-Cycle in Tudor and Stuart England,* David Cressy, 1997.) The colonists seemed to be emulating the Native Americans, who also married at about fourteen.

However, if Temperance Bailey were born around 1615, she could have been a wife in 1629 (age fourteen), a mother in 1630 (at fifteen) and possibly again in 1631, then widowed and remarried by seventeen—much as her mother before her.

A birth date of 1615 also places Temperance's mother Cecily at a reasonable age to be a Virginia wife and mother. The muster gives Cecily's age as twenty-four (which we have no reason to suspect), so Cecily's birth year would have been about 1600. She would have married at about age fourteen and given birth to Temperance at about fifteen. My belief is that 1615 is a more reasonable birthdate for Temperance than 1617, both from the standpoint of custom and practicality, and that's why I have used it in this book.

Uncovering Virginia's First Women and Children

The Colony's Population in May 1613
According to a Spanish Spy

On May 28, 1613, Spanish prisoner Don Diego de Molina described Virginia's military situation to his king by letter sewed into the sole of a shoe:

> *At the entrance [to the bay] there is a fort, or to say more correctly a [flaco de tablas?] ten hands high, with 25 soldiers and 4 iron guns. Half a league from here there is another one, but smaller, with 15 soldiers, without artillery. There is still another smaller one, all of which are inland, half a league off, against the Indians; this has 15 soldiers more. Twenty leagues higher up is*

this Colony with 150 persons and 6 guns. Still higher up, twenty leagues off, is another strongly situated settlement, to which all of them will be taken, when the occasion arrives, because there they place their hope. Here there are a hundred persons more and among them as among the people here there are women, boys and field labourers, so that there remain not quite two hundred effective men and they are badly disciplined.
—Don Diego De Molina, May 1613

The Facts: Molina's Account of the Colony as of May 28, 1613

First Fort (Point Comfort). . . . . . . 25 soldiers
Second Fort (Fort Henry). . . . . 15 soldiers
Third Fort (Fort Charles). . . . . 15 soldiers
Jamestown. 150 settlers
Henricus. . . . . 100 settlers
Total excluding Women, Boys, or Field Laborers 200 "Effective Men"

This means that 145 men are at Jamestown and Henricus:
$(200 - 25 - 15 - 15 = 145)$.

These 145 men are apportioned among 250 total settlers at these two settlements, meaning that the populations at Jamestown and Henricus = 58% "effective" men (145/250).

If we assume an equal proportion of effective men at Jamestown and Henricus, then:
58% x 150 = 87 men at Jamestown.
58% x 100 = 58 men at Henricus.

Total men =
55   at Point Comfort and at Forts Henry and Charles
87   at Jamestown
58   at Henricus
200 men

From this we can calculate the number of women, boys, and field laborers as follows.

The Interpretation: Estimated Populations in Virginia, May 1613

Settlement or Fort	"Effective Men"	Women, Boys & Field Laborers	Total Population
Point Comfort	25	0	25
Fort Henry	15	0	15
Fort Charles	15	0	15
Jamestown	87	63	150
Henricus	58	42	100
Total	200	105	305

We can't know how many women and children were part of the 105 women, boys, and field laborers in May 1613. However, in May 1616, John Rolfe counted 65 women and children. Few settlers arrived between May 1613 and May 1616, so we can know that probably no fewer than 65 women were included in the 1613 list.

Who Were the 65 Women and Children in 1616?

I have been able to identify up to 50 of the 65 women and children in John Rolfe's 1616 Census.

These 65 women and children that John Rolfe counted in May 1616 would be those who would later be called ancient planters. Hundreds more women and children either immigrated to Virginia or were born there by 1616, but did not live to be counted in this census.

A footnote in the chart indicates some uncertainty.

Women and Children in Virginia Still Living in May 1616

		Ship	Appearance in Virginia
1	Pocahontas (Rebecca) Rolfe	Born here	c. 1595
2 [1]	Mistress Forrest	*Mary & Margaret*	1608
3	Anne Burruss Laydon	*Mary & Margaret*	1608
4	Thomasine Causey	*Lyon*	1609
5	Temperance Flowerdieu Yeardley	*Faulcon*	1609
6	Joan Peirce	*Blessing*	1609
7	Jane Peirce	*Blessing*	1609
8	Virginia Laydon	Born here	1609
9	Joan Wright	*(Ship Unknown)*	by 1610

10	Maria Thorowgood Bucke	*Deliverance*	1610
11	Elizabeth Joones (Jones)	*Patience*	1610
12 [2]	Mrs. Horton	*Sea Venture*	1610
13 [2]	Elizabeth Persons Powell	*Sea Venture*	1610
14 [2]	Mrs. Eason	*Sea Venture*	1610
15 [2]	Bermuda (infant son) Eason	*Sea Venture*	1610
16 [3]	Mrs. Woodlief (Woodliffe)	*Sea Venture*	1610
17	Joane Salford	*(Ship Unknown)*	by 1611
18	Sara Salford	*(Ship Unknown)*	by 1611
19	Mara Bucke	Born here	1611
20	Elizabeth Dunthorne	*Tryall*	1611
21	Margery Browne Fairfax	*(Ship Unknown)*	1611
22	Sisley Bailey Jordan Farrar	*Swan*	1611
23	Amelie Ackland Waine	*Swan*	1611
24	Joan Flinton	*Elzabeth*	1612
25	Rachel Davis	*(Ship Unknown)*	by 1613
26	Susan Usher? Collins	*Treasurer*	1613
27	Gercian Bucke	Born here	c. 1613
28	Thomas Rolfe	Born here	c. 1615
29 [3]	Elizabeth Yeardley	Born here	c. 1615
30 [3]	Temperance Bailey (Bayley)	Born here	c. 1615
31	John Woodlief, Jr.	Born here	c. 1615
32	Mary Bailey	*(Ship Unknown)*	by 1616
33	Martha Key (Keie)	*(Ship Unknown)*	by 1616
34	Isabella Smith Pace	*(Ship Unknown)*	By 1616
35	Mary Beheathland Flint	*(Ship Unknown)*	By 1616
36	Mary Bouldin(g)	*(Ship Unknown)*	By 1616
37	Elizabeth Lupo	*George*	1616
38 [3]	Benomi Bucke	Born here	c. 1616
39 [3]	Ann Woodlief (Woodliffe)	Born here	c. 1616
40 [3]	Ann Usher	Born here	c. 1616
41 [3]	Katherine Laydon	Born here	by 1617?
42 [3]	Joan Wright's child	Born here	Unknown
43 [3]	Joan Wright's child	Born here	Unknown
44 [3]	George Pace, Jr.	(Arrived w/parents or born here)	Unknown
45 [3]	Thomas Peirce	(Arrived w/parents or alone or born here)	Unknown
46 [3]	Elizabeth Smalley	Here in 1617	Unknown
47 [4]	(Child) Fairfax	Killed in 1617	Unknown
48	(Child) Fairfax	Killed in 1617	Unknown
49	(Child) Fairfax	Killed in 1617	Unknown
50	(Youth) Fairfax	Killed in 1617	Unknown

[1] The woman's grave, labeled JR156 and found in 1997 within Jamestown's fort, may be that of Mistress Forrest.
[2] May not have been still living.
[3] May not have arrived or been born yet.
[4] A marriage record exists for Willm Fearfax and Margery Browne on 19 October 1606 in Claypoole, Lincoln, England, so presumably the Fairfax children came with their parents or were born here.

Populations During the Middle Years

By...	May 1610	Jun 1610	Mar 1611	May 1613	May 1616	Apr 1618	Mar 1620
Cumulative # Arrived	675	925	938	1,711	1,766	2,364	3,696
Estimated Cumulative # Perished	(615)	(575)	(738)	(1,406)	(1,415)	(1,964)	(2,775)
# Still Surviving	**60**	**350**	**200**	**305**	**351**	**400**	**921**
% dead	91%	62%	79%	82%	80%	83%	75%

Survivors Comprised of:

Able Men				200	286	200	670
Women							119
Boys				105	65	200	39
Young Children							57
Indians						4	
African Men	0	0	0	0	0	0	15
African Women	0	0	0	0	0	0	17

Despite thousands of immigrants, the Virginia population had difficulty swelling beyond a few hundred souls until 1619 or 1620. The old settlers seemed to be hardened to Virginia and once acclimated, survived much better than did the new arrivals.

The chart above also indicates the very few settlers—just 55—to arrive between May 1613 and May 1616. The members of the Virginia Company lost very much hope when young Henry, Prince of Wales, died in November 1612. The colony lingered on with little to show in the way of commodities except tobacco trials.

The Company proposed the idea of "particular plantations," plantations that particular groups of investors would run as subgroups of the Virginia

Company. Settlers sent to particular plantations helped the numbers of colonists to grow significantly. The organizers of particular plantations were confident that they could do a better job than the Virginia Company as a whole. Berkeley Hundred was one such particular plantation.

Between May 1616 and April 1618, nearly 600 settlers arrived, but the net population only increased by 46 persons. An epidemic of flux in 1618 took a toll on all settlers, old and new.

When Sir Edwin Sandys became treasurer of the Virginia Company, he proposed that sending many settlers (despite the Company's near-bankruptcy) would provide the means of sending money back to the demoralized stockholders. The unfortunate result of this policy was overcrowding, inadequate food, and lack of shelter for these new arrivals.

However, by March 1620, the numbers in Virginia had more than doubled from two years before.

> *At the latter arrival of the ship called the George in Virginia, which was in April, 1618, the number of men, women and children was about 400, of which about 200 was most as was able to set hand to husbandry, and but one plough was going in all the country, which was the fruit of full twelve years labor, and above one hundred thousand marks expenses* [about 67,000 pounds], *disbursed out of the public treasury over and above the sum of between 8,000 and 9,000 pounds debt into which the Company was brought, and besides the great expenses of particular adventurers. The colony being thus weak, and the treasury utterly exhaust, it pleased divers lords, knights, gentlemen and citizens (grieved to see this great action fall to nothing) to take the matter anew in hand, and at their private charges (joining themselves into societies) to set up divers particular plantations...*
> —Virginia Company Records, 20 May 1620

Did Molina Plan an Attack on Virginia?

Yes. Two mentions of Molina's planned attack occur in the records. The first comes from the Court Minutes of the East India Company, 12 June 1618:

> *Letter read from Henry Bacon, lately returned from Sir Walter Raleigh's voyage, stating that Don Diego de Mollena, who*

was prisoner in Virginia, incites the King of Spain to send forces to suppress Virginia, by the hopes of a silver mine there, from which he shows a piece to justify the truth thereof.

—*Calendar of State Papers,* Court Minutes of the East India Company, Court Minutes Book, Vol. 4, p. 177.

In 1625, George Percy wrote that Molina, following his return to Spain, did get as far as bringing "six tall ships" to attack and uproot Virginia. However, a mutiny grew, leading to Molina's stabbing death. "Their course was altered, and their former determination ceased." We only know that this attack occurred between Molina's return to England in 1616 and Percy's writing in 1625, probably around 1618 or 1619.

> *Don Diego stayed nott longe in England. Butt was sentt hoame where he was made Generall of six tall shippes in All lyke-liehoode and as we weare after certenely informed sett outt of purpose to Supplantt us. Butt haveinge bene att Sea about A monthe A mutenie did growe amongste them in so mutche thatt one of diegoes company stabbed him to deathe Whereupon their Course was alltered and their former determinacyon ceased.*
> —George Percy, 1625

The Yeardleys' Trip to England

It is unclear whether George Yeardley departed for England in 1617 or in 1618. There's also no evidence indicating whether or not his wife Temperance went with him to England. However, historian Alexander Brown felt that Yeardley sailed on the *George* in 1618.

The nobles and the foods they brought to celebrate the birthday of King James's son were real, as was Gamige's farmhouse.

Philip Mainwaring reported this about Yeardley's conversation with the king:

> *This morning the King knighted the new Governor of Virginia, Sr Edward [George] Yardly, who, upon long discourse wth the Kinge, doth prove very understandinge. Amongst many other things, he tould the King that the people of that country [the natives] do beleeve the resurrection of the body; and that when the body dyes, the soule goes into certaine faire pleasant fields, there to solace it self untill the end of the world, and then the soule is*

to retourne to the body againe, and they shall live both together happily and parpetually. Heareupon the King inferred that the Gosple must have been heretofore knowne in that countrie, though it be lost, and this fragment only remaynes.
— Philip Mainwaring to the Earl of Arundell, November 1618

Dysentary, Piracy, and Slaves: One Meal May Have Changed History

Dysentery

In 1618, Lord De La Warr died along with thirty others on his ship the *Neptune*. The cause of death: bloody flux. What exactly is bloody flux? It is bloody diarrhea or dysentery which may be caused by amoeba, bacteria, or salmonella. However, since the 1618 outbreak became an epidemic, the likely culprit is the bacterium *Shigella dysenteriae*. *S. dysenteriae* causes fever and stomach cramps along with dysentery.

The death rate from this type of infection can go as high as fifteen percent. The number of passengers on the *Neptune* was purported to be between 150 and 220 with 200 being likely. Thirty deaths out of 200 people would be exactly fifteen percent.

S. dysenteriae has toxins which cause it to be the most potent and severe dysentery. The disease spreads through food and water (particularly in developing countries), from person to person, and sometimes through houseflies.

It is unknown whether or not De La Warr contracted his illness while visiting the Azores, but it does seem likely. For one thing, the settlers said of the *Neptune* "with them was brought a most pestilent disease (called the Bloody flux) which infected all most all the whole Collonye. That disease, notwithstanding all our former afflictions, was never knowne before amongst us." (Although there were individual cases of bloody flux reported as far back as 1607, these dysenteries appear to have been the non-epidemic sort.)

The infected *Neptune* newcomers arrived at the colony and spread the disease amongst all the settlements.

If indeed the baron's visit to São Miguel led to his illness, the ironies are great. First, the baron deliberately stopped to *improve* his health. It is my belief that the baron stopped in São Miguel for oranges and lemons, a known cure for scurvy. Lord De La Warr had suffered badly from scurvy during his previous days at Jamestown.

He probably also hoped to rest from the weariness of a sea voyage to better his chances of survival and keeping his health strong.

Second, the baron undoubtedly desired to improve diplomatic relations with the Azores, Portuguese islands under the Spanish flag. The Azorean leader, Dom Manuel Luis Baltazar da Câmara, Second Earl of Villa Franca—whose little island had suffered many attacks—probably hoped for the same.

Yet, because the baron fell ill shortly after leaving the island, the leaders on ship suspected foul play. They believed the sumptuous feast to be a ruse, a way to poison Lord De La Warr.

The baron died during the summer of 1618, but the Portuguese Earl died in 1619, perhaps weakened by the illness if he too contracted it.

Piracy

Imagine if the feast caused Baron De La Warr's illness. One meal. Lord De La Warr's death before reaching Virginia was a severe blow to Virginia Company morale in England and in Virginia. Many thought the baron's death would effectively end the colony. However, perhaps the most serious consequence of his death was leaving Argall free to run his piracy operation for eight more months. De La Warr would have arrived in August 1618. In January 1619, Argall sent out the ill-fated *Treasurer* on a piracy mission while claiming the ship would trade for goats and salt in the West Indies. What the *Treasurer* actually did, with a Dutch consort ship, was to capture a Spanish ship filled with slaves.

Imagine if this had never happened...

The English were a culture with few slaves although the Portuguese and Spanish were slave owners. Sometimes Jamestown critics attempt to link the labor-intensive tobacco boom with bringing slaves into the colony. But this is not the way it initially happened.

The Earl of Warwick, a devoted Puritan, had two primary goals: to cripple the Catholic Spanish and to enrich himself. The type of booty was not particularly important to him. The Spanish ship *São João Bautista* was unfortunate enough to cross the paths of the two well armed men-of-war.

Angelo's story

Was Angelo a Real Person?

Yes. Angelo was a real person, and she did live with the Peirces. Many of the captive Africans appear in the muster without names. The Peirces, however, gave Angelo's name as well as her ship, the *Treasurer*. Ages weren't in the Peirces' muster, so we don't know how old Angelo was. We can assume she was probably young and initially healthy since the Portuguese felt she was able to labor in the mines. Angelo also managed to survive a long ordeal and for at least five years at Jamestown.

Angelo and her fellow captives come from the Kingdom of Ndongo under their king, Mbandi Ngola Kiluanji in West Central Africa (today's Angola). Angelo would have spoken Kimbundu. Her home was probably Kabasa, the capital city of the Kingdom of Ndongo with a population of twenty to thirty thousand, which the Imbangala violently attacked in 1618 and 1619.

Was Angelo Really a Christian?

Yes, the peoples of Ndongo were "ancient Christians of the land" according to one account of the period. Angelo's baptismal name was undoubtedly Angela, but her name appears as "Angelo" in two different lists of settlers from 1624 and 1625. Since we have no other record to indicate anyone called her "Angela," I've used Angelo in this book. I believe the Peirces called Angela by the name as she pronounced it. It's also possible that Angelo gave her own name to those taking the musters.

How Much of Her Story is True?

Thanks to research by Engel Sluiter, John Thornton, and Linda Heywood, we know far more about the circumstances of Angelo's capture than we otherwise would have.

The Imbangala were a brutal, cruel cannibalistic tribe who pillaged other tribes. The worst possible circumstance for the Ndongan people occurred when the Imbangala became mercenaries of the Portuguese governor. Governor Luís Mendes de Vasconcellos gave the Imbangala guns that enabled them to overwhelm the weapons of the Ngolans and to capture or kill them.

Thornton says that from 1618 to 1621, fifty thousand Africans became captives. In 1619 alone, thirty-six ships carried these away captives to become slaves at the Portuguese and Spanish plantations of South America.

Angelo departed from on what she would have called a *malungu,* a Portuguese ship called the *São João Bautista* along with about one hundred others.

She might have ended up in South America but for the piracy of Virginia governor Samuel Argall under his patron the Earl of Warwick. The Virginia ship *Treasurer,* carrying a marque from the Duke of Savoy, traveled in consort with the *White Lion*, an English ship carrying a Dutch marque. These marques gave both ships permission to raid enemy ships. The two happened upon booty that consisted of people

The *White Lion* arrived in Virginia first, expecting to find Argall still in charge. The captain quickly recognized that the present governor, Yeardley, was hostile. He pleaded that he had no food and nothing to trade but the captured Africans. The colonists reluctantly traded, not quite believing the story.

Soon after the *White Lion's* departure, the *Treasurer* arrived in Virginia. Captain Elfrith fled when he realized his ally Argall was no longer governor and that he would likely be arrested. Adding to Elfrith's troubles, Savoy was no longer at war with Spain, and so his marque was invalid.

The *Treasurer* then sailed to Bermuda where it initially received a cold welcome. This greeting turned warm upon the arrival of the new governor, an ally of Warwick. The *Treasurer's* twenty-nine surviving captives were housed in a longhouse in Bermuda. About six months later, the *Treasurer* brought about nine Africans back to Virginia, including Angela. Angelo's odyssey was a long one involving many months of fear and captivity on the *São João Bautista* and on the *Treasurer* and then in Bermuda.

The Virginia census, once thought to be 1619 but since proven to be 1620, lists thirty-two Africans. These would be the "twenty and odd" who arrived from the *White Lion* and the nine from the *Treasurer.*

Dangerous Cargo

Sometimes, historians allude to the fact that tobacco was labor intensive and that for the English in Virginia slavery was the natural choice. This is not so at all. Unlike the Portuguese and Spanish, the English did not have a culture of slavery. Laws treating Africans as chattel and slaves do not appear in Virginia until the 1650's.

During the early period beginning in 1619, these captives apparently had the same status as white indentured servants, meaning they would be free in seven to ten years.' (Anthony Johnson was one such captive from this episode who became a landowner and slave owner, and who named his farm "Angola.")

It's important to recognize that no one in Virginia was happy about these stolen African citizens. The English king, James, had forged a close relationship with the Spanish, and those in Virginia feared what their own king might do. Jamestown's colonists were also well aware that this piracy might well be the trigger to provoke a Spanish attack upon them. They did need servants, but this was not initially the way they would have obtained them.

Lord De La Warr's Story

Where is Lord De La Warr Buried?

Where did Lord De La Warr die, and where was he buried? Upon the surface, the reports seem to conflict.

Thomas Hopkins said De La Warr died in the *Neptune* and added that Captain Brewster (who claimed to be in command upon De La Warr's death), wished to capture several ships at De La Have, Canada. This would indicate that, by the time the ship reached Canada, De La Warr had died on ship since Brewster was then in command.

John Smith wrote that, following the baron's death, "At last they stood in for the coast of New-England, where they met a small Frenchman, rich of Bevers and other Furres. Though wee had here but small knowledge of the coast nor countrie, yet they tooke such an abundance of Fish and Fowle, and so well refreshed themselves there with wood and water, as by the helpe of God thereby, having beene at Sea sixteene weekes, got to Virginia, who without this reliefe had beene in great danger to perish."

(It is not surprising that John Smith stated that the baron died in New England. He himself had named the coast "New England" and was undoubtedly promoting the use of that name.)

John Martin (Martyn), the Persian, stated that he was in the *Neptune* with La Warr and that De La Warr "dyeing by the waye, [Martin] went still on the voyadge to Virginia in the shippe, and the body of the said Lo: Delawarre was carried thether and buried there."

John Salmon reiterated this point, saying of the *Neptune,* "which shippe the said Lord de la Warre went but dyed in the shippe before they came at Virginia."

Lady De La Warr and a man named Baker said that the baron died in Virginia.

John Pory wrote that the baron "died in Canada." (John Pory was in James City, Virginia at that time.) Sibella Counstable says that the *Treasurer* (accompanying the *Neptune*) "put into Canada."

So we have testimony that De La Warr died at sea, in Virginia, in Canada, and on the New England coast.

Buried at Jamestown? Delaware Bay?

Modern interpretations sometimes state that the baron lies buried near Delaware Bay and that this is how the bay received its name. However, the area around Delaware Bay received its name much earlier than 1618. William Strachey wrote that on 6 September 1610, Samuel Argall "in the latitude of thirty-nine, *discovered another goodly bay,* into which fell many tayles of faire and large rivers, and which might make promise of some westerly passage; the Cape whereof, in thirty-eight and a half, he called Cape La Warr."

Other historians say that, since the baron was buried in Virginia, he must be buried at Jamestown. But the evidence suggests that, while firsthand accounts do indeed say that De La Warr was buried in Virginia, the area is not Jamestown. It's not even the area we typically think of as Virginia.

Buried at LaHave, Nova Scotia

By most accounts, the baron died on June 7, 1618 (A few say July 8.) Whichever the case may be, De La Warr died during the heat of summer. The ship finally arrived at James City on August 14, 1618. It would have been imprudent to carry the baron's body back to James City, being at least five, probably nine, weeks since La Warr's death. When the deponents state that De La Warr was buried in Virginia, they must have meant Canada, Northern Virginia—then part of the region of New England.

In 1606, King James granted the land between 34° to 41° north latitude to the Virginia Company of London (London Company), and land between 38° and 45° north latitude to the Virginia Company of Plymouth.

The London Company's tract called Southern Virginia stretched from present-day Cape Fear, South Carolina, to Long Island, New York. The Plymouth Company claimed Northern Virginia—from present-day Washington, D.C., to Nova Scotia, Canada.

At the time of De La Warr's death in 1618, the upper boundary of North Virginia remained at 45° north latitude. Since LaHave, Newfoundland, Canada, sits in 44° north latitude, the English claimed LaHave as being in Northern Virginia.

The settlers of Southern Virginia at Jamestown had felt so strongly about protecting their king's grant of both North and South Virginia that in 1613 Captain Samuel Argall sailed to LaHave to oust the French settlers. The French claimed this as their tract, but the English claimed it as theirs.

So assembling the pieces, it seems that Lord De La Warr died off the coast of Canada near LaHave (called then "De La Have"), and the colonists brought his body ashore to bury him. The English would have called this Canada (considered part of Virginia), New England (the region) or Virginia, so all accounts do concur.

When French ships (called "Frenchmen") appeared, Brewster, already in charge, wished to fight. But the *Neptune's* captain declined, saying that Brewster had no commission to do so. Rather than fighting, the French ships supplied the sea-weary colonists with foods that allowed them to continue their long journey to South Virginia.

Also, there are no reports of a burial ceremony at James City for the baron, as there surely would have been both ceremony and first-hand reporting of such a momentous loss at Jamestown. All those deposed to testify about De La Warr's death had some connection with the actual voyage.

What Happened to Lady De La Warr After Her Husband Died?

Cecily, Lady De La Warr, had a prolonged legal battle with former Governor Samuel Argall because her husband's assets had been ill-stewarded. This legal battle was unfortunate for Lady De La Warr, although the records from the High Court of Admiralty provide a wealth of information about De La Warr's last days and Argall's actions upon the *Neptune's* arrival in Virginia.

Lady De La Warr inherited land from her husband's investments, but her funds were exhausted since they were all invested in Virginia.

King James, in an unusually generous gesture, granted Cecily, Lady De La Warr, 500 pounds ($121,361) per year to honor her husband for his sacrifices. Lord De La Warr's patronage of the cause of Virginia was critical to Virginia's survival. Besides his financial contributions and his willingness to come to Virginia himself, his nobility added legitimacy to the venture.

Cecily Shirley West, Baroness De La Warr, survived nearly half a century after her husband's death, dying in 1662 and living to see her husband's dream come to fruition.

Today, Lady De La Warr is not completely forgotten in Virginia.

Shirley Plantation, established in 1613, still carries Lady De La Warr's maiden name, Shirley. This plantation, granted to Lord De La Warr and his wife in 1613, fell into the hands of Edward Hill I in 1638. Eleven generations of Hill-Carters have owned the home, and it is the oldest family business in the United States. (To visit Shirley, see www.ShirleyPlantation.com.)

After the death of Thomas West, Third Baron De La Warr, the baron's brother Francis West claimed Westover Plantation on behalf of the West family. Westover Plantation is still in existence as well. (See www.jamesriver-plantations.org/Westover.html)

Captain Argall gave the name La Warr to the cape of the "goodly bay." So today, Delaware Bay, Delaware River, and the State of Delaware commemorate Lord De La Warr.

"Eighty Thousand Pounds—Lost."

How great was the loss?

The Virginia Company struggled throughout its existence. By the time the Company learned of Lord De La Warr's death in 1618, matters looked particularly bleak. The Company had invested twelve years' work, time, and money in the colony and had little to show for the eighty thousand pounds shareholders had contributed.

How great was that loss? Today, those eighty thousand pounds would be roughly equal to $11.7 million, a tremendous failure. It's easy to understand the hair pulling that was going on in 1618 and why the Virginia Company kept considering abandoning the project.

By the time King James revoked the Company's charter in 1624, the Company had spent about two hundred thousand pounds—$28.1 million in 2009 dollars.

How Much Had Each Shareholder Invested?

In 1609, investors like the Peirces paid 12 pounds 10 shillings for each share. How much would that be today? Each pound today would have a purchasing power of about $215, so both those who came to Virginia (planters) and those who invested in England (adventurers) paid roughly the equivalent of $2,685 per share in 2009 dollars.

> 12 pence = 1 shilling
> 20 shillings = 1 pound
> 1 pound then ≈ $215.00 today

In 1610, the Virginia Company asked for three more subscriptions at the initial price of 12 pounds 10 shillings for a total contribution of 37 pounds 10 shillings. These three subscriptions totaled about $8,055 in 2009 dollars.

If you consider the planters in Virginia had invested thousands of dollars in the Virginia Company and yet, in their own words, the Company still treated them like "slaves," you can understand their frustration. On one hand, Dale needed to run a taut operation to get the settlement back on track following so many disasters. On the other, the poor conditions and food, the rampant illness, and the rigid work schedule meant that all were disheartened. Besides this, ten or more years went by before the colonists saw any dividend—in this case, land but not monetary profit.

When Prince Henry died in 1612, heart and hope in the enterprise failed. Yet despite dwindling numbers of supply ships, the Company still would not allow colonists to return home to England.

Therefore, when Governor Yeardley at last received instructions in 1618 to free the colonists and to give them land, the settlers celebrated. Still, many more struggles were ahead for them, their fear of the Spanish remained, and their shores swelled with ill newcomers who needed more food and shelter than they possessed.

How Much Did the Lottery Winner Receive?

There is a lotterie in hand for the furthering of the Virginia viage [voyage].
—John Chamberlain, 1612

Desperate for funds, the Virginia Company instituted a lottery in 1612. The cost of a ticket was two shillings, six pence—about $29 today. Altogether, the prizes totaled £5,000 ($1,144,530 in today's dollars). The top prize was "fayre plate," fine silver place settings, valued at £1,000, or $229,220 in today's dollars. Thomas Sharplisse, a tailor, received this prize.

In addition, the Company gave a silver spoon valued at ten shillings ($73) to those who contributed three pounds ($686) to the Company.

In general, lottery ticket sales were a disappointment although a number of companies, churches, and individuals bought tickets.

Our Virginia plantation's motion is so slow at this instant I can perceive no pulses to beat to purpose. The city adventurers look no further than 10 percent, and all others engaged grow weary of so often contributions…which is the cause the great lottery lies as

if there were no life in the foundation.
—Samuel Calvert, December 1613

How Much Did the Virginia Company Pay the Rolfes?

While John and Rebecca (Pocahontas) Rolfe were residing in England, the Virginia Company gave them a four pound per week allowance. In today's dollars, this would be about $853 per week.

Source for 2009 dollars from 17th century pounds: *www.measuringworth. com*. My calculated Retail Price Index (RPI) comes from the calculator in "Purchasing Power of British Pounds from 1264 to Present" in 2009 dollars. The website's stated mission is to "make available to the public the high quality and most reliable historical data on important economic aggregates." The RPI is perhaps the best indicator of what the purchasing power of a pound in Jacobean England would be in today's U.S. dollars.

A Declaration for the certaine time of dravving the great ſtanding Lottery

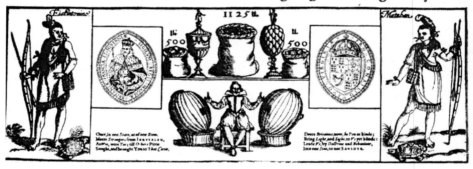

"A Declaration for the certaine time of drawing the great standing Lottery"
Virginia Company Broadside Heading London, 1615

Virginia Firsts

The Virginia Company and the settlers of Virginia accomplished a number of "firsts" in the land that would one day be the United States. Creating the first canal in 1611 was but the beginning.

Other accomplishments include the first glass factory, iron works, windmill, brick house, free school, church, State House, incorporated town, sericulture (farming of silkworms), corn whiskey, and wine production. The early Virginia settlers were also the first to sow apples, peaches, figs, wheat, and hemp. Virginia had the first jury trials and courts of justice. Yet no accomplishment exceeds that of the first General Assembly of 1619.

America's First Representative Body:
The Virginia General Assembly, 1619

On 18 November 1618, the Virginia Company gave the colonists the right to elect representatives from each settlement. This assembly had the right to enact laws so long as these laws followed the laws of England and the Company approved them.

The first General Assembly took place from July 30 to August 4, 1619, and consisted of Governor Sir George Yeardley, six councilors, and twenty burgesses—two from each of the ten settlements. (Two additional burgesses from Captain John Martin's plantation were dismissed because Martin's charter gave him special privileges to make his own laws.)

The Virginia General Assembly, begun in 1619, is the oldest continuously operating legislative body in the Western Hemisphere, as well as the model for the U.S. Senate, which was created during the Great Compromise of 1787.

> *The most convenient place we could find to sit in was the quire of the church where Sir George Yeardley, the governor, being set down in his accustomed place, those of the Council of Estate sat next him on both hands, except only the Secretary then appointed Speaker, who sat right before him, John Twine, clerk of the General assembly, being placed next the Speaker, and Thomas Pierce, the Sergeant, standing at the bar, to be ready for any service the assembly should command him.*
>
> *But forasmuch as men's affairs do little prosper where God's service is neglected, all the Burgesses took their places in the quire*

till a prayer was said by Mr. Bucke, the minister, that it would please God to guide and sanctify all our proceedings to his own glory and the good of this plantation.

Prayer being ended, to the intent that as we had begun at God Almighty, so we might proceed with awful and due respect towards the lieutenant, our most gracious and dread Sovereign, all the Burgesses were entreated to retire themselves into the body of the church, which being done, before they were fully admitted, they were called in order and by name, and so every man (none staggering at it) took the oath of supremacy, and then entered the assembly.

— John Pory, 1619

Those at the First General Assembly
Thursday, July 30 to Wednesday, August 4, 1619

John Pory's Minutes of Attendence:

Sir George Yeardley:
  Knight, Governor and Captaine
  General of Virginia

Members of the Council:
  Mr. Samuel Macock
  Mr. John Rolfe
  Mr. John Pory (Secretary &
    Speaker)
  Captain Nathaniel Powell
  Captain Francis West
  Reverend William Wickham
  John Twine, Clerk of the
    General assembly;
  Thomas Pierse, Sergeant of
    Arms.

Plantations and Representatives:
For James Citty:
  Capt. William Powell
  Ensigne William Spense

For Charles Citty:
  Samuel Sharpe
  Samuel Jordan

For the Citty of Henricus:
  Thomas Dowse
  John Polentine

For Kiccowtan:
  Capt. Wm. Tucker
  William Capp

For Martin-Brandon, Capt. John
  Martin's Plantation:
  Mr. Thomas Davis
  Mr. Robert Stacy

For Smythe's Hundred:
  Capt. Thomas Graves
  Mr. Walter Shelley

For Martins hundred:
  Mr. John Boys
  John Jackson

For Argals Guifte:
  Mr. [Thomas] Pawlett
  Mr. [Edward] Gourgainy

For Flowerdieu Hundred
  Ensigne [Edmund] Rossingham
  Mr. [John] Jefferson

For Capt. Lawnes's Plantation
  Captain Christopher Lawne
  Ensigne Washer

For Capt. Warde's Plantation:
  Capt. Warde
  Lieut. Gibbes

Tobacco: The Smoky Weed Saves the Colony

> There is an herb called uppowoc…but the Spaniards generally call it tobacco…its use not only preserves the body, but if there are any obstructions it breaks them up. By this means the natives keep in excellent health, without many of the grievous diseases which often afflict us in England.
> —Thomas Hariot, 1588

Early Prediction of Tobacco Success ~ 1607

Ralph Hamor credited John Rolfe with getting Virginia's tobacco crop going. It's worth noting, however, that tobacco was one of the crops Captain Christopher Newport early thought could be a success. On 21 June 1607, Newport predicted what future tobacco profits could be: "Tobacco after a yeare or two 5,000£ a year." By 1617, the income from tobacco was £4,710 pounds, very close to Newport's prediction.

Of course, Newport believed—as did everyone else—that many commodities would comprise the Virginia profits. Newport mentioned clapboard and wainscot, sassafras, "terra sigillata" (a type of clay used for medicinal purposes), rich dyes, furs, pitch, rosin and turpentine, maple gum, apothecary drugs, oils, wines, soap ashes, wood ashes, extract from mineral earth, iron, copper, and good fishing for mussels. "To conclude," Newport wrote, "I know not what can be expected from a comon Wealth that either this land affords not or may soone yeeld."

Native Tobacco – "Weake, and of a Byting Taste"

> *Here is great store of tobacco, which the salvages call apooke: howbeit it is not of the best kynd, it is but poor and weake, and of a byting taste; it grows not fully a yard above ground, bearing a little yellow flower like to henbane; the leaves are short and thick, somewhat round at the upper end; whereas the best tobacco of Trynidado and the Oronoque, is large, sharpe, and growing two or three yardes from the ground, bearing a flower of the breadth of our bellflowers in England; the salvages here dry the leaves of this apooke over the fier, and sometymes in the sun, and crumble yt into poudre, stalks, leaves, and all, taking the same in pipes of earth, which very ingeniously they can make."*
> – William Strachey, 1612

Year	Pounds of Tobacco
1614.	170
1616.	2,300
1617.	18,839
1618.	49,528

These figures come from the Sackville Papers. Lord Sackville was recording tobacco poundage from Virginia for the sake of customs.

John Rolfe Obtains Tobacco from Trinidad

No one knows how John Rolfe procured his first tobacco from Trinidad, but at the time such trade was illegal. The Spanish, attempting to keep a tight hold on their tobacco, had threatened death to anyone who sold tobacco seeds.

Trinidad was under Spanish control, but Spain failed to keep a watchful eye on the island. Therefore, the Trinidadians traded their sweet Orinoco tobacco directly, and illegally, with the English and Dutch. The king of Spain put an end to this thriving trade in 1612.

John Rolfe received his tobacco seeds in 1611 or early 1612, planted them in 1612, and sent a small shipment back to England in 1613.

By 1614, the colonists felt the commodities with greatest potential were silkgrass, silkworms, and tobacco. Tobacco, of course, prevailed.

> *The valuable commoditie of Tobacco of such esteeme in England (if there were nothing else) which every man may plant,*

and with the least part of his labour, tend and care will returne him both cloathes and other necessaries. For the goodnesse whereof, answerable to west-Indie Trinidado or Cracus (admit there hath no such bin returned) let no man doubt....I may not forget the gentleman, worthie of much commendations, which first tooke the pains to make triall thereof, his name Mr John Rolfe, Anno Domini 1612, partly for the love he hath a long time borne unto it, and partly to raise commodity to the adventurers...

Onely of the hopefull, and merchantable commodities of to-bacco, silke grasse, and silke worms: I dare thus much affirme, and first of Tobacco, whose goodnesse mine own experience and triall induces me to be such, that no country under the Sunne, may, or doth affoord more pleasant, sweet, and strong Tobacco, then I have tasted there, even of mine owne planting, which, how-ever being then the first yeer of our triall thereof, wee had not the knowledge to cure, and make up, yet are there some now resident there, out of the last yeers well observed experience, which both know, and I doubt not, will make, and returne such Tobacco this yeere, that even England shall acknowledge the goodnesse thereof.
—Ralph Hamor, 1614

Ralph Hamor's statement in 1614 that the colonists would soon produce such fine tobacco "that even England shall acknowledge the goodnesse there-of" makes it sound as though those in England criticized the early crops.

When Dale sailed with Pocahontas and John Rolfe in 1616, the ship car-ried the 1615 crop of tobacco, a larger shipment than previously sent. From that time on, tobacco shipments continued to increase.

Around 1618, a settler named Thomas Lambert further improved tobacco when he discovered a way to hang the tobacco leaves to dry rather than drying it on the ground as the natives had.

Soon the colonists were using tobacco as currency.

Rolfe's tobacco sold for thirty-six pence (three shillings) per pound in 1616, one-third the price the Spanish then fetched for their tobacco. Still, the Virginia colonists recognized it for the start it was.

All our riches for the present doe consiste in Tobacco, wherein one man by his owne labour hath in one yeare raised to himselfe to the value of £200 sterling; and another by the meanes of six servants hath cleared at one crop a thousand pound English.
—John Pory, 30 September 1619

Signatures of the Virginia Players

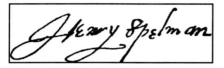
Captain Henry Spelman

Sir Edwin Sandys

Sit Ferdinando Wainman

Sir Thomas Dale

Captain Daniel Tucker

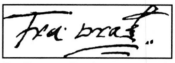
Sir Francis Drake

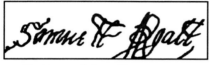
Sir Samuel Argall

John Pory

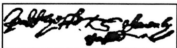
Captain John Ratcliffe

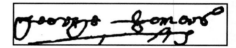
Sir George Somers

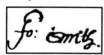
Captain John Smith

Sir Robert Rich, 2nd Earl of Warwic

George Percy

Sir Thomas West, 3rd Baron De La Wa

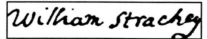
William Strachey

Sir Thomas Gates

Sir Thomas Smythe

Native American tribes in Virginia fall primarily into three linguistic groups: Algonquin, Siouxan, and Iroquoian.

The tribes of eastern Virginia were for the most part Algonquin. In the central portion of the state, the tribes were mostly Siouxan. Iroquoian tribes tended to be located more in the southern and western parts of the state.

Algonquin Tribes: The Powhatan Confederacy

There were about 35 Algonquin tribes surrounding Jamestown. These tribes, living in approximately 160 scattered villages throughout eastern Virginia, were all part of the confederacy of the great leader, or *mamanatowic*, whom the English called Powhatan but whose given name was Wahunsonacock. Powhatan himself was a member of the powerful Pamunkey tribe, which had recently conquered most of these tribes. Tribes paid tributes of corn to Powhatan while keeping their own *werowances*, or lesser chiefs. Powhatan referred to his empire as *Tsenacomoco*. John Smith estimated there were 3,000 bowmen. Perhaps the total native population was about 8,000 in these tribes.

Here are the tribes mentioned most frequently in primary documents of the era:

Virginia Tribes

AlgonquinTribes

Accomac. . . . . Eastern Shore
Appomattock. . . . . On the Appomattox River
Arrohattoc. . . . . Henrico County
Chesapeake. . . . . Princess Anne County
Chickahominy. . . . . On Chickahominy River
Chiskiac (Kiskiack). . . . . On York River
Kecoughtan. . . . . Elizabeth City County
Mattaponi. . . . . On Mattaponi River
Moraughtacund. . . . . On the Rappahannock River
Nansemond Isle of Wight. . . . . Nansemond, Norfolk Co.
Pamunkey. . . . . King William County
Paspahegh. . . . . Charles City & James City Counties
Patawomeck (Potomac). . . . . Stafford and King George Counties
Powhatan. . . . . Henrico County

Warraskoyak. . . . . Isle of Wight County
Weyanoke (Weanoc). . . . . Charles City County
Werowocomoco. . . . . Gloucester County
Wicocomoco. . . . . Northumberland County
Youghtanund. . . . . on Pamunkey River

Iroquoian Tribes
Meherrin. . . . . On the Meherrin River
Nottoway or Mangoac. . . . . On the Nottoway River

Siouxan Tribes
Manahoac. . . . . Primarily on the Rappahannock River, but also through much of Northern Virginia
Monacans. . . . . On the James River from the Falls to the Blue Ridge

English Glossary

Ague
Fever with chills, shivering and sweating, as seen in malaria.

Archipelago
A chain or cluster of islands.

Astrolabe
Mariners' instrument that determined latitude by measuring the sun or a known star.

Banns
In the Anglican church, the proclamation of an upcoming wedding, usually announced for three Sundays before a couple wed. These allowed parishioners to bring forth objections.

Blockhouse
A strong fort where the second story overhangs the first and which contains gun ports.

Bloodletting
Withdrawing blood in order to cure illness or disease.

Bodice
"Pair of bodies," or tightly fitted garment for the upper body.

Bodkin
A dagger with a slender blade.

Breeches
In this period, men's breeches were knee-length.

Bridge
During this period, a bridge may refer to a wharf or dock. Jamestown's bridge was a dock.

Brightwork
Polished metal on a ship.

Broadcloth
Fabric made from wool.

Broadside
Sheets of paper, distributed or posted, used to spread news or to publish an idea or an opportunity. Newspapers didn't exist during this period, so broadsides served a similar purpose.

Burse
> A purse.

Cadger
> Someone who traveled from place to place peddling wares.

Calenture
> At this time, a delirious fever believed to be related to the heat like sunstroke.

Catechism
> Instruction in the Anglican beliefs.

Caudle
> A type of fermented drink, such as brandy.

Censer
> A vessel for burning incense in a church.

Chain-Shot
> Two half-balls joined by a chain. These were formerly used in naval warfare.

Chirurgeon
> A surgeon. *Chirurgeon* is the original spelling and pronunciation, which became corrupted to *surgeon*.

Churching
> A Christian ritual that blessed new mothers and gave thanks for their survival.

Coif
> Women's headwear consisting of a piece of linen coming across the forehead and down the side of the head, then gathered and tied at the back of the neck like a close-fitting cap.

Coneys
> The original word for European rabbits.

Conserve of Roses
> A Jacobean medicinal recipe of beaten rose petals and sugar, believed to cure many things.

Corps de Garde
> Literally, a "body of guard"—a company of soldiers on guard, or a watch-post occupied by soldiers on guard.

Corsairs
> Pirates.

Cross Staff
> A mariners' instrument used to determine latitude through the Pole Star; used to determine the angles between two objects.

Doublet
> A man's close fitting buttoned jacket. Jerkins were sometimes worn over doublets.

Dram
> A small drink of an alcoholic beverage.

Dutchmen
> Dutchmen in Jamestown were not Dutch but German. The English referred to them as *Dutchmen* because the Germans called their language *Deutsch*.

Earthfast
> Supported by the earth, as the posts of the houses dug into the ground.

Fathom Soundings
> Fathoms, or depth of water, were estimated using a

sounding line, a piece of rope with ties to mark the depth in fathoms. Fathom soundings were readings of how deep the water was.

Favors (Bridal)
The bridesmaids would create little flower bouquets for wedding guests.

Fens
A type of wetland. England has many fens.

Fie
Exclamation of disapproval.

Fire Ships
A desperate battle technique where wooden ships filled with flammables are set afire. The crew steer them toward enemy ships hoping to set them ablaze and then jump overboard.

Flagon
A pitcher used for drinking.

Flux
Dysentery. (Also called "bloody flux.")

Frenchman
The settlers referred to the French ship itself as "the Frenchman."

Gaol
Jail.

Glebe
A plot of land, belonging to an English parish church, intended to yield a profit for the church.

The Hague
The seat of government for the Dutch Republic.

Halberd
A long, two-handed pole weapon with a blade similar to an axe.

Heaths
Open, uncultivated land containing low shrubs and heather, especially in Great Britain. Also called a moor.

Helvetians
The Swiss. John Smith also referred to them as "Switzers."

Hogsheads
A large cask, often of liquid, what we might call a barrel.

Jerkin
A man's close-fitting jacket, often worn over a doublet.

Kirtle
A long, fitted garment reaching to the feet.

Letter of Marque
A document from one country allowing a private citizen to seize goods of another.

Linen-fold
A simple style of relief carving in oaken walls to make them look like linen.

Longboat
A boat rowed by eight or ten oarsmen, two on each row.

Lying In
A woman's month-long confinement during and following childbirth.

Man-o'-war
A warship; a powerful sailing ship outfitted with multiple ordnance (cannon).

Manhattas

Today's island of Manhattan. Also at the time called Manna-hata from the Lenape language.

Marish

Of a marsh. During this period, *marish* was used much as we would use the word *marshy*.

Masque

A dramatic entertainment where players usually wear masks and represent mythological or allegorical figures.

Mastiff

A very large and ancient English dog breed, used for protection. which can weigh two hundred fifty pounds or more.

Matchlock

Type of musket with a slow-burning match struck by a lock, thus freeing up both hands.

Matins

Anglican morning prayers.

Maypop

The edible fruit of the passion flower. The natives called it *maracacok,* which became *maycocks* and maypop.

Michaelmas

The feast of St. Michael the Archangel, falling on September 29.

Morion

A kind of open helmet somewhat resembling a hat.

Morris Dance

The English ritual folk dance where the dancers step and jump rhythmically to music.

Murrain

A disease among livestock which resembles a plague.

Muscadine

A type of grape used in making fine and port wines.

Muskcat

The settlers, never having seen a skunk, sometimes referred to it as a *muskcat.* Later, the English adopted a version of the Algonquian word for the animal, *skunk.*

Narrow Sea

An old term for the English Channel. The plural "Narrow Seas" usually referred to the English Channel and the Straits of Dover.

Naturals

The English sometimes referred to the natives as "Naturals," the ones who were in Virginia naturally.

Nine Men's Morris

A strategy game where each player begins with nine pieces.

Nosegay

A bouquet to make the nose happy, covering any smells.

Ordnance

Cannon.

Pale

Another word for palisade, the wooden structure sur rounding a town.

Palisado

 The settlers sometimes used this Spanish word for a palisade, a fort made of wooden planks standing upright in the ground.

Pamunkey River

 Today's York River.

Pembroke River

 Today's Rappahannock River.

Petticoat

 A skirt.

Physick

 A collection of remedies made from such things as plants, herbs, roots. Also called *physicks*.

Pieces

 Guns.

Pike

 A pole weapon. A long, thrusting spear.

Pitch

 A sticky, water-repellent by-product made by distilling trees, particularly pine used as a caulk or sealant in shipbuilding.

Planters

 Settlers who "planted" (settled) the plantation of Virginia.

Pokahichary Nuts

 The English did not have these nuts in England, so they adopted the native word, which later was shortened to *hickory*.

Pone

 The settlers were used to making bread with wheat, but in the New World corn was more adaptable and plentiful. In making cornbread as the natives did, the settlers adopted the native word for bread, *pone*.

Posset

 A hot drink of milk curdled with wine or ale, often spiced.

Potash

 A fertilizer made by burning hardwood and then boiling the ashes, leaving a potassium salt.

Pottage

 Soup or stew, cooked in a pot.

Pumpion

 During this period, the settlers called the native melon *pumpion,* which later became *pumpkin.*

Quadrant

 Navigational tool for determining latitude based on the North Star.

Rapier

 A thin sword with a cup-like hilt to protect the hand, used to thrust.

Royal *Alcázar*

 A royal palace in Madrid, previously a 9th century Muslim fortress.

Sack

 A type of fortified sweet wine, such as sherry. These were very inexpensive in the 17th century.

Sack-Posset

 A custard made with cream, eggs, spices, and sack (sweet wine).

Score

A group of twenty.

Seine

A fishing net with floaters on the upper edge and sinkers on the lower so that it hangs vertically in the water.

Separatists

Those who believed reforming the Church of England was hopeless and the only solution was to separate from it.

Shallop

A light boat used for shallow waters and powered by oars or sails.

South Sea

During this period, the English referred to the Pacific Ocean as "the South Sea."

Spindle

A round stick or shaft used to form and twist thread.

Stricks

Bundles of broken flax or hemp which are ready to spin.

Tercios

Elite infantry forces of the Spanish military during the 16th and 17th centuries, combining firepower with pikes.

Tiercel

A male falcon. Sometimes also called a *tassel*.

Trencher

A wooden board or plate on which food is served.

Trinidado

During this period, the English sometimes called tobacco from Trinidad *Trinidado* to distinguish it from that grown elsewhere.

Truck

To trade.

Tussy-mussies

Nosegays or bridesmaid's bouquets.

Tutties

Tussy-mussies, nosegays, or bridesmaids' bouquets.

Upsitting

The time during a woman's month-long lying in (following childbirth) where she is allowed to sit up and her linen is changed.

Whorl

A disk of stone or pottery that acts as a flywheel on a spindle, causing the spindle to spin thread more quickly.

Will with the Wisp

An early term for *will-o'-the-wisp*, coming from the name *Will* added to *wisp*—a bundle of hay used as a torch. Will-o'-the-wisps are phantom lights in marshes that seem to recede if one approaches them.

Woad

A flowering plant valued for its ability to produce indigo, a blue dye.

Yardarm

Either side of the horizontal pole attached high on the ship's mast.

Youghtanund's River

Today's Pamunkey River.

Glossary of Powhatan Words and Phrases

The Powhatan Indians of Virginia spoke an Eastern Algonquin dialect. Their language is, regrettably, extinct today. However, several lists of words and phrases remain. The best of these is William Strachey's *Historie of Travaile into Virginia Britannia*. John Smith also includes a vocabulary of words and phrases in *Works, 1608-1631*. The English spellings of native words vary considerably across documents.

The Powhatan tribe of Virginia contributed more words to English than any other tribe in the United States.

Ahone
  The benevolent creator.

Amuwoir
  To take heed of.

Apooke
  Tobacco. (The English word *tobacco* derives from this.)

Arrahaquotuwh
  Clouds.

Casacunnakack, peya quagh acquintan uttasantasough
  "In how many days will there come hither any more English ships?"

Chamay
  Friend. (Also spelled *chama* or *chammay*.) The English word "chum" derives from this.

Cohattayough
  Summer.

Commotoouh
  Steal.

Cutchow matowran
  To burn.

Cuttahamunourcar
  To make a grave.

Eweenetu
  Peace.

Husque
  By and by, quickly.

Kameyhan
  Rain.

Maangwipacus
  Leaves.

Mache, nehiegh yowrowgh, Matchut
  Now he dwells a great distance away at Matchut.

Mawchick Chamay
  "Very much friends," the best of friends.

Mushower
  "The ships go home."

Mussaran
  A town.

Nehpaangunn
  Blood.

Nepunche
  To be dead.

Netab
  "We are brothers" or "I am your friend." The principal word of kindness.

Nuckaandgum
A sister.

Numma
Will you go home?

Numpenamun
Let me see it.

Ohshaangumiemuns
Shells.

Okeus
The god of justice.

Pacussac-ans
Guns.

Poshenaan
To flee anything.

Puccoon
The English called this plant bloodroot. The natives used it to paint their faces and bodies red.

Quiyoughcosough
Priest. (The English spelled this various ways, including *quiockosite* and *quiyoughquisock*.) The word seems to be derived from the name of the native god *Okee* (also written *Quioccos*).

Rahsawans
String.

Taquitock
The time of harvest and when leaves fall.

Tawnor nehiegh Powhatan?
"Where dwells Powhatan?"

Tomahawk
Also spelled *tamahaac,* meaning "what is used in cutting" or "he cuts." The English compared these to hatchets.

Tsantassas
White men, the English

Unekishemū
Blood.

Uppoushun
"The ships go home."

Uttapitchewane
You lie.

Utteke
"Get you gone."

Vunamun
See.

Wapewh
A hurt or cut.

Werowance
Chief.

Wingapo
Greetings; welcome.

Wow
Exclamation of surprise. This word became part of the English language.

Yowhse
"Hard by" (Nearby).

18 Generation Descendency Chart
From William Phippen to the Lapallo Children

William PHIPPEN
1551-1596
Of Melcombe Regis,
England
m. Jane JORDAINE

Joan PHIPPEN
1580-1650
Born in Melcombe Regis
Arrived in Jamestown, 1609
m. Thomas REYNOLDS

Cecily REYNOLDS
b. 1600, Melcombe Regis,
Arrived in Jamestown, 1611
Jordan's Journey Plantation
m. Thomas BAILEY

William COCKE
1674-1717
of Henrico, Virginia
m. Sarah PERRIN

Thomas COCKE
1639-1697
of Malvern Hills Plantation
m. Margaret POWELL

Temperance BAILEY
1617-1651, Henrico, Virginia
m. Richard COCKE of
Bremo Plantation

Sarah COCKE
1696-1750
Henrico, Virginia
m. William COX

John COX
1710-1793
Prince Edward, Virginia
Furnished supplies to the
Continental Army
m. Lucretia WYNNE

Thomas COX
c. 1743-c. 1794
of Bluestone Creek,
Mecklenburg, Virginia
m. Obedience

Hester A. NASH
1836-1911
Mecklenburg, Virgina
m. William R. RICKMAN

Mary COX
b. 1814
of Halifax, Virginia
m. William P. NASH

Archer COX
of Halifax, Virginia
m. Polly HATCHELL
in 1802

Mary Elizabeth RICKMAN
1872-1931
Mecklenburg, Virginia
m. Charles H. BURGESS

William Garner BURGESS
1897-1972
Mecklenburg, Virginia
m. Annie Etha TUCKER

Hazel Lee BURGESS
b. 1918
in Richmond, Virginia
m. Peyton Rudolph
CHRISTIAN

Sarah A. LAPALLO, b. 1990
Michael C. LAPALLO, b. 1991
Kerry A. LAPALLO, b. 1994
Adam C. LAPALLO, b. 1996
Born in Richmond, Virginia

Connie Maria MAIDA
b. 1962
in Richmond, Virginia
m. Christopher LAPALLO

Marie A. CHRISTIAN
b. 1942
in Richmond, Virginia
m. Michael MAIDA

Preliminary source: Cockes and Cousins, Virginia Webb Cocke, 1974

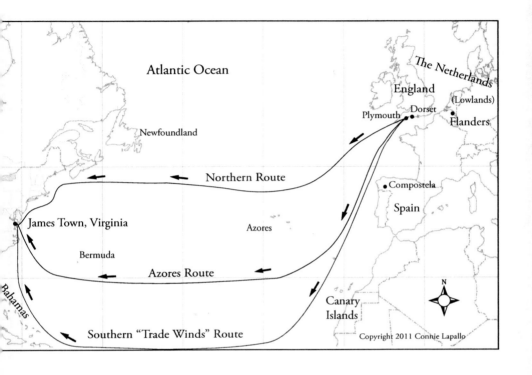

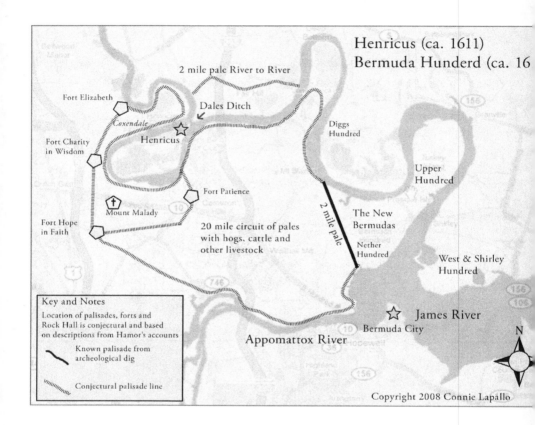

Henricus (ca. 1611)
Bermuda Hunderd (ca. 16

2 mile pale River to River

Fort Elizabeth

Dales Ditch

Coxendale

Henricus

Diggs
Hundred

Fort Charity
in Wisdom

Upper
Hundred

2 mile pale

Fort Patience

Mount Malady

The New
Bermudas

Fort Hope
in Faith

20 mile circuit of pales
with hogs, cattle and
other livestock

Nether
Hundred

West & Shirley
Hundred

James River

Appomattox River

Bermuda City

N

Key and Notes

Location of palisades, forts and
Rock Hall is conjectural and based
on descriptions from Hamor's accounts

Known palisade from
archeological dig

Conjectural palisade line

Copyright 2008 Connie Lapallo

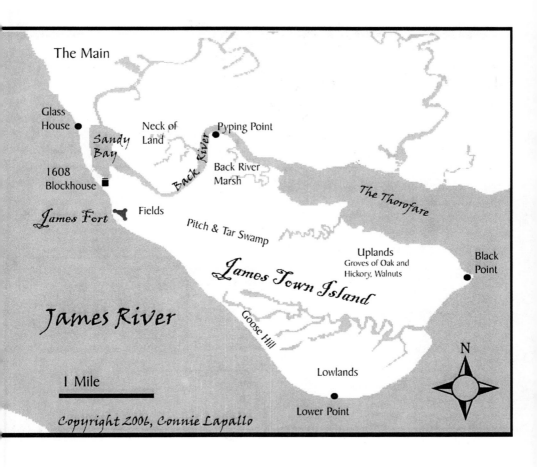

Fitzpen – Thickpenny – Phippen Family Tree

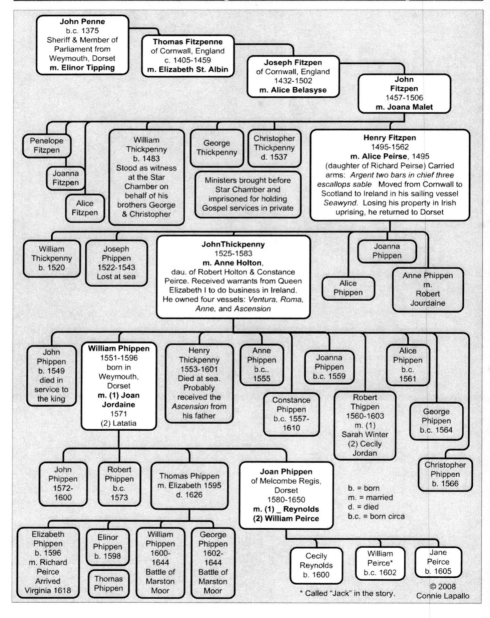

John Penne
b.c. 1375
Sheriff & Member of Parliament from Weymouth, Dorset
m. Elinor Tipping

Thomas Fitzpenne
of Cornwall, England
c. 1405-1459
m. Elizabeth St. Albin

Joseph Fitzpen
of Cornwall, England
1432-1502
m. Alice Belasyse

John Fitzpen
1457-1506
m. Joana Malet

Penelope Fitzpen

Joanna Fitzpen

Alice Fitzpen

William Thickpenny
b. 1483
Stood as witness at the Star Chamber on behalf of his brothers George & Christopher

George Thickpenny

Christopher Thickpenny
d. 1537

Ministers brought before Star Chamber and imprisoned for holding Gospel services in private

Henry Fitzpen
1495-1562
m. Alice Peirse, 1495
(daughter of Richard Peirse) Carried arms: *Argent two bars in chief three escallops sable* Moved from Cornwall to Scotland to Ireland in his sailing vessel *Seawynd*. Losing his property in Irish uprising, he returned to Dorset

William Thickpenny b. 1520

Joseph Phippen 1522-1543 Lost at sea

JohnThickpenny
1525-1583
m. Anne Holton,
dau. of Robert Holton & Constance Peirce. Received warrants from Queen Elizabeth I to do business in Ireland. He owned four vessels: *Ventura, Roma, Anne,* and *Ascension*

Joanna Phippen

Alice Phippen

Anne Phippen m. Robert Jourdaine

John Phippen b. 1549 died in service to the king

William Phippen
1551-1596
born in Weymouth, Dorset
m. (1) Joan Jordaine
1571
(2) Latatia

Henry Thickpenny 1553-1601 Died at sea. Probably received the *Ascension* from his father

Anne Phippen b.c. 1555

Constance Phippen b.c. 1557-1610

Joanna Phippen b.c. 1559

Robert Thigpen 1560-1603 m. (1) Sarah Winter (2) Cecily Jordan

Alice Phippen b.c. 1561

George Phippen b.c. 1564

Christopher Phippen b. 1566

John Phippen 1572-1600

Robert Phippen b.c. 1573

Thomas Phippen m. Elizabeth 1595 d. 1626

Joan Phippen
of Melcombe Regis, Dorset
1580-1650
m. (1) _ Reynolds
(2) William Peirce

b. = born
m. = married
d. = died
b.c. = born circa

Elizabeth Phippen b. 1596 m. Richard Peirce Arrived Virginia 1618

Elinor Phippen b. 1598

Thomas Phippen

William Phippen 1600-1644 Battle of Marston Moor

George Phippen 1602-1644 Battle of Marston Moor

Cecily Reynolds b. 1600

William Peirce* b.c. 1602

Jane Peirce b. 1605

* Called "Jack" in the story.

© 2008
Connie Lapallo

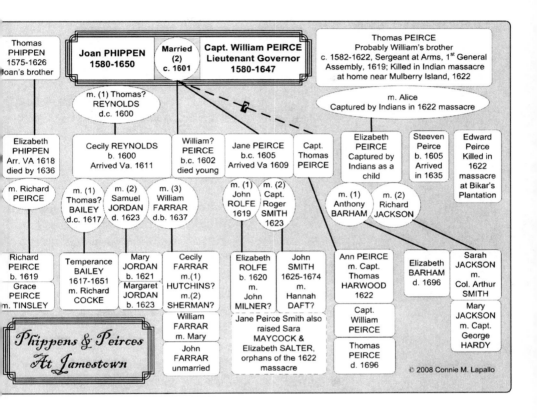

Thomas
PHIPPEN
1575-1626
Joan's brother

Joan PHIPPEN
1580-1650

Married
(2)
c. 1601

Capt. William PEIRCE
Lieutenant Governor
1580-1647

Thomas PEIRCE
Probably William's brother
c. 1582-1622, Sergeant at Arms, 1st General
Assembly, 1619; Killed in Indian massacre
at home near Mulberry Island, 1622

m. (1) Thomas?
REYNOLDS
d.c. 1600

m. Alice
Captured by Indians in 1622 massacre

Elizabeth
PHIPPEN
Arr. VA 1618
died by 1636

Cecily REYNOLDS
b. 1600
Arrived Va. 1611

William?
PEIRCE
b.c. 1602
died young

Jane PEIRCE
b.c. 1605
Arrived Va 1609

Capt.
Thomas
PEIRCE

Elizabeth
PEIRCE
Captured by
Indians as a
child

Steeven
Peirce
b. 1605
Arrived
in 1635

Edward
Peirce
Killed in
1622
massacre
at Bikar's
Plantation

m. Richard
PEIRCE

m. (1)
Thomas?
BAILEY
d.c. 1617

m. (2)
Samuel
JORDAN
d. 1623

m. (3)
William
FARRAR
d.b. 1637

m. (1)
John
ROLFE
1619

m. (2)
Capt.
Roger
SMITH
1623

m. (1)
Anthony
BARHAM

m. (2)
Richard
JACKSON

Richard
PEIRCE
b. 1619
Grace
PEIRCE
m. TINSLEY

Temperance
BAILEY
1617-1651
m. Richard
COCKE

Mary
JORDAN
b. 1621
Margaret
JORDAN
b. 1623

Cecily
FARRAR
m.(1)
HUTCHINS?
m.(2)
SHERMAN?

Elizabeth
ROLFE
b. 1620
m.
John
MILNER?

John
SMITH
1625-1674
m.
Hannah
DAFT?

Ann PEIRCE
m. Capt.
Thomas
HARWOOD
1622

Elizabeth
BARHAM
d. 1696

Sarah
JACKSON
m.
Col. Arthur
SMITH

William
FARRAR
m. Mary
John
FARRAR
unmarried

Jane Peirce Smith also
raised Sara
MAYCOCK &
Elizabeth SALTER,
orphans of the 1622
massacre

Capt.
William
PEIRCE
Thomas
PEIRCE
d. 1696

Mary
JACKSON
m. Capt.
George
HARDY

Phippens & Peirces
At Jamestown

© 2008 Connie M. Lapallo

Connie Lapallo

grew up surrounded by history in Mechanicsville, Virginia, not far from where her ancestors first arrived at Jamestown. She first wrote professionally at sixteen as a reporter for the *Richmond News Leader.*

Lapallo has given hundreds of presentations on the Jamestown women and children who appear in her novels Dark Enough to See the Stars in a Jamestown Sky and When the Moon Has No More Silver. She is presently working on the third novel in her Jamestown trilogy as well as a biography of Sir Thomas Gates.

She has homeschooled her four children since 1997 and still lives in Mechanicsville.

www.ConnieLapallo.com